Praise for Thomas McGuane's

CLOUDBURSTS

"[An] outstanding career-capping volume.... Brief, stormy, and refreshing, McGuane's stories erupt like the namesake of this marvelous collection." —*Publishers Weekly* (starred review)

"A masterful addition to the form."
—*Minneapolis Star Tribune*

"A career-spanning collection of short stories from McGuane, who's observed America's outskirts with equal measures of pathos and humor." —*Kirkus Reviews* (starred review)

"Sharply observed.... McGuane belongs on the social observer shelf with other short story masters including Ann Beattie, John Cheever, and Roald Dahl.... Simply a masterpiece."
—*New York Journal of Books*

"More than a few [stories] are what you might call, what you should call, masterpieces.... A great writer."
—*Washington Independent Review of Books*

Thomas McGuane

CLOUDBURSTS

Thomas McGuane lives on a ranch in McLeod, Montana. He is the author of ten novels, three works of nonfiction, and three previous collections of stories, *To Skin a Cat, Gallatin Canyon,* and *Crow Fair.*

Also by Thomas McGuane

CLOUDBURSTS

CLOUDBURSTS

Collected
and
New
Stories

Thomas McGuane

Vintage Books
A Division of Penguin Random House LLC
New York

FIRST VINTAGE BOOKS EDITION, FEBRUARY 2019

Several stories first appeared in the following publications: *Esquire*: "Viking
Burial"; *McSweeney's*: "Little Bighorn" and "River Camp"; *The New Yorker*: "The
Casserole," "Cowboy," "The Driver," "Gallatin Canyon," "The Good Samaritan,"
"The House on Sand Creek," "Hubcaps," "Ice," "Motherlode," "Old Friends,"
"Papaya," "A Prairie Girl," "Riddle," "Stars," "Tango," "Vicious Circle," and
"Weight Watchers." Many of the stories were previously published or collected
in the following collections: *To Skin a Cat* (Dutton, 1986): "Dogs," "Flight,"
"Like a Leaf," "A Man in Louisiana," "The Millionaire," "Partners," "The Road
Atlas," "A Skirmish," "Sportsmen," and "Two Hours to Kill"; *Gallatin Canyon*
(Alfred A. Knopf, 2006): "Aliens," "Cowboy," "Gallatin Canyon," "Ice," "Miracle
Boy," "North Country," "Old Friends," "The Refugee," "Vicious Circle," and
"Zombie"; *Crow Fair* (Alfred A. Knopf, 2015): "Canyon Ferry," "The Casserole,"
"Crow Fair," "The Good Samaritan," "Grandma and Me," "The House on Sand
Creek," "Hubcaps," "Lake Story," "A Long View to the West," "On a Dirt Road,"
"Motherlode," "An Old Man Who Liked to Fish," "Prairie Girl," "Shaman,"
"Stars," and "Weight Watchers."

The Library of Congress has cataloged the Knopf edition as follows:
Name: McGuane, Thomas, author.
Title: Cloudbursts : collected and new stories / Thomas McGuane.
Description: New York : Alfred A. Knopf, 2018.
Identifiers: LCCN 2017039288
Subjects: | BISAC: FICTION / Short Stories (single author). | FICTION /
Literary. | FICTION / Humorous.
Classification: LCC PS3563.A3114 A6 2018 | DDC 813/.54—dc23
LC record available at https://lccn.loc.gov/2017039288

Vintage Books Trade Paperback ISBN: 978-0-345-80592-8
eBook ISBN: 978-0-385-35022-8

Book design by Betty Lew

www.vintagebooks.com

Printed in the United States of America
10 9 8 7 6 5 4 3 2 1

For Laurie, my light

The world was still changing, preparing people for one thing and giving them another.

—*Peter Taylor,* "The Old Forest"

Contents

CLOUDBURSTS

SPORTSMEN

We kept the perch we caught in a stone pool in front of the living-room window. An elm shaded the pool, and when the heavy drapes of the living room were drawn so that my mother could see the sheet music on the piano, the window reflected the barred shapes of the lake perch in the pool.

We caught them from the rocks on the edge of the lake, rocks that were submerged when the wakes of passing freighters hit the shore. From a distance, the freighters pushed a big swell in front of them without themselves seeming to move on the great flatness of the lake. My friend that year was a boy named Jimmy Meade, and he was learning to identify the vessel stacks of the freighters. We liked the Bob-Lo Line, Cleveland Cliffs, and Wyandotte Transportation with the red Indian tall on the sides of the stack. We looked for whalebacks and tankers and the laden ore ships and listened to the moaning signals from the horns as they carried over the water. The wakes of those freighters moved slowly toward the land along the unmoving surface of water. The wakes were the biggest feature out there, bigger than Canada behind them, which lay low and thin like the horizon itself.

Jimmy Meade and I were thirteen then. He had moved up from lower Ohio the previous winter, and I was fascinated by his almost-southern accent. His father had an old pickup truck in a town that drove mostly sedans, and they had a big loose-limbed hound that seemed to stand for a distant, unpopulated place.

Hoods were beginning to appear in the school, beginning to grow drastic haircuts, wear Flagg Flyer shoes, and sing Gene Vincent songs. They hung inside their cars from the wind vanes and stared at the girls I had grown up with in an aspect of violence I had not known. They wolf whistled. They laughed with their mouths wide open and their eyes glittering, and when they got into fights they used their feet. They spent their weekends at the drag races in Flat Rock or following their idol Iggy Katona around the dirt tracks. Jimmy and I loved the water, but when the hoods came near it all they saw were the rubbers. We were downright afraid of the hoods, of how they acted, of the steel taps on their shoes, of the way they saw things, making us feel we would be crazy to ever cross them. We were sportsmen.

But then, we were lost in our plans. We planned to refurbish a Civil War rifle Jimmy's father owned. We were going to make an iceboat, a duck blind, and a fishing shanty. We were going to dig up an Indian mound, sell the artifacts, and buy a racing hydroplane that would throw a rooster tail five times its own length. But above all, we wanted to be duck hunters.

That August we were diving off the pilings near the entrance to the Thoroughfare Canal. We had talked about salvaging boats from the Black Friday storm of 1916 when the Bob-Lo steamer passed. The wash came in and sucked the water down around the pilings. Jimmy dove from the tallest one, arcing down the length of the creosoted spar into the green, clear water. And then he didn't come up. Not to begin with. When he did, the first thing that surfaced was the curve of his back, white and Ohio-looking in its oval of lake water. It was a back that was never to widen with muscle or stoop with worry because Jimmy had just then broken his neck. I remember getting him out on the gravel shore. He was wide awake and his eyes poured tears. His body shuddered continuously, and I recall his fingers fluttered on the stones with a kind of purpose. I had never heard sounds like that from his mouth in the thousands of hours we talked. I learned from a neighbor that my screams brought help and, similarly, I can't imagine what I would sound like screaming. Perhaps no one can.

That was the month that my father decided I was a worthless boy who blamed his troubles on outside events. He had quite a long theory about all of this, and hanging around on the lake or in the flat woods hunting rabbits with our .22s substantiated that theory, I forget how. He found me a job over in Burr Oak cleaning die-cast aluminum molds with acid and a wire brush. That was the first time I had been around the countrypeople who work in small factories across the nation. Once you get the gist of their ways, you can get along anyplace you go because they are everywhere and they are good people.

When I tried to call Jimmy Meade from Burr Oak, his father said that he was unable to speak on the telephone: he was out of the hospital and would always be paralyzed. In his father's voice with its almost-southern Ohio accents, I could feel myself being made to know that though I had not done this to Jimmy, I was there, and that there was villainy, somehow, in my escape. I really don't think I could have gotten out of the factory job without crossing my own father worse than I then dared. But it's true, I missed the early hospitalization of Jimmy and of course I had missed having that accident happen to me in the first place. I still couldn't picture Jimmy not able to move, being kind of frozen where we left off.

I finished up in August and stayed in Sturgis for a couple of days in a boardinghouse run by an old woman and her sixty-year-old spinster daughter. I was so comfortable with them I found myself sitting in the front hall watching the street for prospective customers. I told them I was just a duck hunter. Like the factory people, they had once had a farm. After that, I went home to see Jimmy.

He lived in a small house on Macomb Street about a half mile from the hardware. There was a layout duckboat in the yard and quite a few cars parked around, hot rods mostly. What could have explained this attendance? Was it popularity? A strange feeling shot through me.

I went in the screen door on the side of the house, propped ajar with a brick. There were eight or ten people inside, boys and girls our own age. My first feeling, that I had come back from a factory job in another town with tales to tell, vanished and I was suddenly afraid of the people in the room, faster, tougher kids than Jimmy and I had known. There were open beer bottles on the tables, and the radio played WJR and the hit parade.

Jimmy was in the corner where the light came through the screens from two directions. He was in a wheelchair, and his arms and legs had been neatly folded within the sides of the contraption. He had a ducktail haircut, and a girl held a beer to his lips, then replaced it with a Camel in a fake pearl-and-ebony cigarette holder. His weight had halved and there were copper-colored shadows under his eyes. He looked like a modernized Station of the Cross.

When he began to talk, his Ohio accent was gone. How did that happen? Insurance was going to buy him a flathead Ford. "I'm going to chop and channel it," he said, "kick the frame, french the headlights, bullnose the hood, and lead the trunk." He stopped and twisted his face off to draw on the cigarette. "There's this hillbilly in Taylor Township who can roll and pleat the interior."

I didn't get the feeling he was particularly glad to see me. But what I did was just sit there and tough it out until the room got tense and people just began to pick up and go. That took no time at all: the boys crumpled beer cans in their fists conclusively. The girls smiled with their mouths open and snapped their eyes. Everyone knew something was fishy. They hadn't seen me around since the accident, and the question was, What was I doing there now?

"I seen a bunch of ducks moving," Jimmy said.

"I did, too."

"Seen them from the house." Jimmy sucked on his cigarette. "Remember how old Minnow Milton used to shoot out of his boathouse when there was ducks?" Minnow Milton had lived in a floating house that had a trap attached to it from which he sold shiners for bait. The floating house was at the foot of Jimmy's road.

"Well, Minnow's no longer with us. And the old boat is just setting there doing nothing."

The next morning before daybreak, Jimmy and I were in Minnow Milton's living room with the lake slapping underneath and the sash thrown up. There were still old photographs of the Milton family on the walls. Minnow was a bachelor and no one had come for them. I had my father's twelve-gauge pump propped on the windowsill and I could see the blocks, the old Mason decoys, all canvasbacks, that I had set out beneath the window, thirty of them bobbing, wooden beaks to the wind, like steamboats viewed from a mile up. I really couldn't see Jimmy. I had wheeled him in terror down the gangplank and into the dark. I set the blocks in the dark, and when I lit his cigarette, he stared down the length of the holder, intently, so I couldn't tell what he was thinking. I said, "What fun is there if you can't shoot?"

"Shoot," he said.

"I'm gonna shoot. I was just asking."

"You ain't got no ducks anyways."

That was true. But it didn't last. A cold wind came with daylight. A slight snow spit across the whitecaps. I saw a flight of mallards rocket over and disappear behind us. Then they reappeared and did the same thing again, right across the roof over our heads. When they came the third time, they set their wings and reached their feet through hundreds of feet of cold air toward the decoys. I killed two and let the wind blow them up against the floating house. Jimmy grinned crazily. I built a fire in Minnow Milton's old stove and cooked those ducks on a stick. I had to feed Jimmy off the point of my Barlow knife, but we ate two big ducks for breakfast and lunch at once. I stood the pump gun in the corner.

Tall columns of snow advanced toward us across the lake, and among them, right in among them, were ducks, some of everything, including the big canvasbacks that stirred us like old music. Buffleheads raced along the surface.

"Fork me that there duck meat," said Jimmy Meade in his Ohio voice.

We stared down from our house window as our decoys filled with ducks. The weather got so bad the ducks swam among the decoys without caring. After half a day we didn't know which was real and which was not. I wrapped Jimmy's blanket up under his chin.

"I hope those ducks keep on coming," he said. And they did. We were in a vast raft of ducks. We didn't leave until the earth had turned clean around and it was dark again.

THE MILLIONAIRE

It was merely a house beside a lake which had been rented, winterized to extend the period of time it could be let, though it was hard to see who would want its view after summer was over, a view of places just like it, divided by water. It was furnished with the kinds of things owners wish renters to have within the limits of their anxiety about damage, impersonal things. Strangely, the owners stored their golfing trophies here, old trophies, and the miniature golfers on them, their bronze coats flaking, belonged to another age. One foot tipped too far; their swings were still British and lacked the freedom of motion American trophy makers later learned to suggest. Something of the reflected stillness of the lake was felt in the living room and the wraparound porch, where the outdoor furniture seemed out of place and the indoor furniture had inadvertently weathered.

Betty was a handsome blonde in her middle forties wearing a green linen Chanel suit. She walked into the house, stooping with two suitcases and managing to clutch the house keys with their large paper tag. Iris, her fifteen-year-old daughter, in the late stages of pregnancy, awkwardly looked for something to do. Betty set the luggage down and stared about with a Mona Lisa smile. She shot a glance at Iris, who was heading for the radio. Iris stopped.

"I guess the landlord saw us coming," said Betty. Iris made an assenting murmur in her throat; it was clear she was yet to develop any real attitude toward this place. "Though blaming him for scenting misfortune seems a bit academic at this stage of the proceedings."

"Mom, where's the thermostat at? I'm getting goose bumps."

"Find it, Iris. It will be on the wall." Iris turned and looked off the porch toward the lake. Betty kept talking. "When we went to stay on the water in my youth—when we went to Horseneck Beach, for example—the water made a nice smell for us. It seemed to welcome us . . . the smell of the ocean. But this lake! Well, it has no odor."

"It's smooth out there. Nice for waterskiing."

"In your condition?" Betty walked to the phone and picked it up. "A dial tone. Good . . . So, anyway, let's batten down the hatches. Pick yourself a little delivery room. I'm in shock! I have traipsed a hundred miles from my home for a summer surrounded by strangers and their weekend haciendas. If only I'd been clever enough to bring something familiar, my Sanibel shells, anything."

"I'm familiar," said Iris with a pout.

"Not entirely, you're not."

Iris sat down to rest, knowing she shouldn't place her hands on her stomach complacently. She had come to view its swelling as something strange, and the acceptability of that view comforted her.

THE PORCH AND THE ROOM HAD FALLEN INTO SHADOW, AND the end-table lamps made a yellow glow. Betty stared past her drink while Iris, in her bathrobe, combed out her wet hair. When Claude, who was Betty's husband and Iris's father, came in the house, still dressed for business and somehow out of place in this summer cottage, he first peeked through the partially opened front door with either dread or uncertainty. But when he did come in, he did so as the house's proprietor.

"Hello, Mother."

Betty didn't yield too quickly, so Claude tried Iris. "How is our royal project?" he asked.

"Hi, Daddy."

Claude clasped his hands before him and turned to Betty. "Dja stock up? Scotch?"

"We have that," said Betty. "We also have some terrifying concoctions belonging to the owner. Mai-tai mix. Spañada wine."

"Sid'll be down. Save it for Sid."

Betty asked, "Did you stop off?"

"Nope," said Claude. "This is my first. Cheers."

"Cheers," said Betty. "No, Iris, no record."

"Sid wanted to meet me for one quick one, but I said, Do you realize what kind of miles I got in front of me?"

"I think I'll watch sunset from the porch," said Iris unnoticed. She went through the sliding door to the porch, where she felt day fade before the electric lights of the house. If she tried, she could make out what her parents were saying to each other, but she didn't try.

Claude said, "Can she hear us?"

"Who's supposed to bring my stuff up from home?"

"I'm seeing to it. I didn't want to look like we were moving out. The Oakfields were staring from their lawn."

"How come Sid's coming up? Does he have to know?"

"Sid knows all. He's bringing up a low-mileage Caddy Eldo he wants us to try. Burgundy. Vinyl top. The point is, life doesn't have to come to an end. Oh, no."

Betty drifted off. "Could be gorgeous," she said.

"And Judge Anse and his wife will come by. Make sure Iris doesn't back out."

"Remind me to thank them for finding us this priceless bide-a-wee. I could smell the wienie roasts from down the beach. This place is like a ballpark."

"You can always go home, babe, and return when it's all over."

Strangely enough, they toasted this, too, touching glasses. Claude winked. Betty said, "You."

That night when they played gin rummy, Betty was the only one who seemed to have any vitality. Claude leaned a tired, stewed face on one hand and stared at the deck with uncaring eyes. Iris played and kept score. Betty played like a demon; she was in a league of her own. She could shuffle like a professional, making an accordion of the cards between her hands.

"My final pregnancy was ectopic," said Betty with an air of peroration. "Otherwise, Iris, you would have had a little baby brother or sister. The ovum—egg to you—the ovum developed in the cervical canal, not in the uterus where the darn thing was supposed to be. Gin!"

"Great," said Claude. "It's over."

"I see the doctor tomorrow," said Iris. "Right?"

Betty gathered all the cards together in a pile. "Iris, I would hope that it's clear why you cannot—repeat, cannot—fritter around in the discard pile and expect to get anywhere."

BETTY AND IRIS WORKED CLOSELY TOGETHER INSERTING leaves into the dining-room table. As the table expanded, the living room–dining room combination became less of a no-man's-land. Iris and Betty quit shoving and moved around the table, looking at all the comforting empty space on its top. Steaming pots in the kitchenette abetted the festivity.

"Your assignment is to set the table," said Betty. "Ten-four on that?"

"Ten-four."

"I will sit at this end, your father at that end. Dr. Dahlstrom goes right there, and Miss Whozis, his girlfriend, goes there. If she has a poodle, the poodle remains in the car."

"You don't even know her, Mother."

"I said if there is a poodle. Iris, I love dogs!"

"Really? What about Brucie?"

"So here we go with Brucie again. Brucie was a mongrel, I don't miss him at all. He might have been a dear dog if you weren't designated to pick up after him. No, Brucie would have never been put to sleep if he had learned to potty outside."

"My favorite part of this is the smell of the upstairs cedar closet."

"My favorite part of the whole damn thing was when your father learned of your condition and burst into tears. Boo-hoo-hoo. Like Red Skelton."

"I meant the house."

Claude seemed to try to come in from work differently every time. That night he ran in the door carrying his briefcase like a hot cannonball. And his voice was elevated.

"Dr. Delwyn Dahlstrom and his *chiquita* are right behind me," he cried.

"What of it?" said Betty, smoothing her sleeves. "Our society is reduced to Iris, her gynecologist, and his bimbo. What difference does it make if they're early?"

"I want a shower."

"Not if they're five miles back, kiddo. No way, Jose."

"Grab me a pick-me-up. I'm gonna go for it."

Claude rose to the occasion. When the doctor came, he pulled open the front door as if revealing the grand prize on a quiz show. Dr. Delwyn Dahlstrom, a portly, grinning Scandinavian, swung his arm to indicate Melanie, a bug-eyed redhead of twenty-five years with a purse of pinto calf.

"We stopped off," Melanie explained. "See, so if we're late, that's how come, 'n' 'at."

Claude spread his arms for the coats. When he got them, he transferred them to Iris and then hurried around the center island to the bartender's side and began pulling noisy levers on ice trays while the others tried to talk.

Claude said, "I remember Delwyn making bathtub gin in the urinalysis machine. Does that date me?"

"You wouldn't happen to have mai-tai mix?" Melanie inquired.

"And enough Spañada to sink a battleship," said Betty.

"Betty's right," said Melanie. "My taste in drinks is corny. I'm a workin'-class gal."

Dahlstrom's spirits made the dinner a noisy good time for everyone except possibly Iris, who was too young to drink and came to seem almost frozen. And maybe Claude noticed it, even though technically Iris wasn't his department, because he abruptly slumped into his chair and held his head for an odd instant of silence. The others looked at him, and it passed.

"Are you feeling baby move regularly?" Dahlstrom asked Iris.

"Yes," said Iris with a red face.

"And still our young man has not come forward?" the doctor inquired.

"Delwyn," said Claude, "it goes like this: He has not come forward. Iris is fifteen. Iris is going on with her life. If the young man comes forward, Iris's life doesn't go forward. Use your brain, Delwyn. The story is, Iris goes on with her life."

"And Claude handles the private adoption," Betty added. Dahlstrom looked all around himself in search of something; then, his focus sharpening, he suddenly noticed Melanie. "Melanie," he said, "go find yourself a snack."

Betty pulled a contraption out of the closet, something made of metal tubes and cloth. "When I get back to the only home I've known since being dragged from Massachusetts as a young bride, it will be Indian summer. Indian summer! To think! I am very lightly complected. So this is going to make a difference on those long days ahead." With a clattering rush of fabric and aluminum, a red-and-green-and-yellow beach umbrella sprang open. Betty was drunk.

Claude said, "Jesus H. Christ." And the doctor said he didn't get it. Melanie said she knew what it was, it was a beach umbrella, and Betty said she still didn't have the dunes of childhood and that that stupid odorless lake out there didn't have so much as a single Pocahontas or other legendary figure associated with it, unless it was the propane man she had been unable to reach on the phone all day.

"In my mind's eye," said Betty, "I will be able to sit next to the Atlantic."

"Bearing Portuguese immigrants," said Claude.

"I will hear—shut up, Claude—the cry of gulls and the moaning of sea buoys."

"I don't get it," said Dr. Dahlstrom. "I thought she was from some burg near Boston."

Claude detonated a sigh. "Yeah, she is," he said, well within her hearing. "But here's the catch. It had a trolley stop near the water. I'll never hear the end of this if I live to be a hundred."

But Melanie took up for Betty. "I'm like Betty when it comes to mountains. I used to live with my dad in Denver. Even in traffic jams—like going to a Broncos game—you could see right over the top of the cars all the way to . . . all the way to . . . what was it, Pikes Peak?"

The doctor said reverently, "My favorite is La Jolla." The syllables seemed to come from his chest.

"I go on standing for something," said Betty. "Year after year."

"Namely, the eternal sea," said Claude. Quite suddenly, he realized that Iris was at the foot of the stairs. She beheld the adults.

"Good night, everybody!" she cried. "And thank you!" It wasn't until she'd gone up and was safely out of earshot that Dr. Dahlstrom said, "Thanks for what?"

Everyone but Melanie fell into a kind of state; she stared from one distant gaze to another, then shrugged. Finally, the doctor said, "You got around the courts on the adoption?"

"Mmmhm."

"Who's the pigeon?"

"Yup," said Claude. "Who's the pigeon? A judge. Yes, a judge, and his hearty but barren wife of thirty years. I like the guy. A real diamond in the rough. State college. Babson-type portfolio of investments. Getting on in years. Wealth. Half hour a day on the rowing machine. Plus, if he morts out, she has family. Betty and I went over this one good."

"How did you find this fellow?"

The question didn't make Claude comfortable. "Through a thing down at the plant," he said. "We tipped a few. This and that. Said his life had everything but kids. A bulb went off." Claude looked around to find someone to break the silence. He didn't seem to like this silence at all, and no one was coming forward to break it. Just whose side were they on?

"You know," said Claude, "I'm not the biggest guy on the block. Just a Quonset building, a couple of presses. One shift. One time clock. One faithful foreman. I make the calls. I say, *You build it, I'll sell it.* I call on everybody. I call on the competition. We make beautiful music together. And then one of my boys, a Polack, sticks his big mitt in a punch press. It goes up next to the roller and never comes out. I offer my most sincere regrets. I don't say, What's with your mitt in the roller? I'm sad for him, but, no, he wants it all. He wants my business. You can't have it, I say. It's that simple: You can't have it. You can have reasonable compensation, but no more. I want it all, says the Polack. And he has counsel who feels so confident, he has taken it on as a contingency bond. I say, You lean on me, I lean on you. I call on the judge, not as a finagler but as a red-blooded American with his own business. I sell myself to the judge. Meanwhile, the Polack's lawyer is sending me poison-pen letters. Shit. You reach a point where you don't know whether you're part of what makes America great or not."

"Eight hours from now," said Dr. Dahlstrom, "I'll be dropping gallstones in a porcelain pan. I can't deal with this."

"You know what I'm in a mood for?" said Melanie. "A diner. Some ham and eggs. The night shift. Neon."

"That is Melanie," said Dahlstrom. "That is her magic."

"I'm going to let those dishes sit till morning," said Betty, apparently overfaced by the magic of Melanie. Conversation trailed off;

a car started up; things in the foreground seemed impossible to notice. Their four faces hung in the air.

Claude wandered over to the bar and made himself a nightcap. He was already in a cloud. Betty went up the stairs, and Claude slumped in the peculiar apelike repose produced by patent recliner chairs. He was almost dreaming, but it wasn't a dream; it was something he remembered—Iris saying, "Daddy, I know you didn't want this for me, but as long as the baby is healthy, can't we . . . ?"

Among the key effects Betty brought to the lake was Claude's stadium blanket in blue and maize, his school colors. Iris covered him with it, knowing he had to work tomorrow and needed his rest.

PASSING TIME WAS A KIND OF SEDATIVE FOR BETTY AND IRIS. For the moment, they were old friends. When Claude came home at night, he thought they were babbling, and sometimes there was a genuine issue: Iris still wanted the baby; then Betty wanted the baby because of the one she had lost through her ectopic pregnancy; then Betty and Iris thought they could team up and raise the baby. Under the last plan, Claude would have to move out. Even Claude thought so.

They lay out on the lawn with bright tanning reflectors under their chins; they were stretched on lawn chairs; and the heat, the big midwestern heat, was everywhere.

"Sunbathing will make an old bag out of you in a New York minute."

"What do you call this lake?" Iris asked.

"Don't move your head when you talk, Iris! You're blinding me. I don't know, Lake Polliwog or some fool thing. Don't you wonder what's going on at home? I see grass growing knee high. I see four feet of morning papers on the porch; a storm door slams back and forth in the wind. Maybe the fire department broke in looking for bodies and stole my silver. The TV we left on to discourage burglars has become some kind of haunted Magnavox. It's awful what your mind will do to you. We never got around to putting a decal on the picture window, so the birds with broken necks have gone on piling up. Life just rushes at you, and the birds keep dying."

"My feet are swollen. And my fingers, too."

Iris held her hands up in the glare and examined their watery thickness. "I could go for a foreign film right now," she said. "In the picture this girl is pregnant. Out of wedlock in Italy. It's a spa, and Marcello Mastroianni is careless about cigarettes and their effect: on the unborn. The spa carries extremely complicated pastries which resemble pretzels. There's a bilingual midwife, and all the cars are low slung. Sometimes the girl rides in the cars with Mastroianni. Sometimes they pass the evenings playing chess, which they call 'shess.' The girl only knows how to play checkers, which they call 'sheckers.' When she says, 'King me,' they're pleasant about it and give the girl soda water, a ring, a buncha stuff. Finally the baby is born, so pink, so perfect and all. They call a wet nurse from the village, but the baby won't have a thing to do with this stranger. The baby returns to the girl . . . by suction."

"Iris, that's impossible. A baby can't fly through the air by suction."

"Mom, it's a movie."

"What about Marcello Mastroianni? Does he get around by suction, too? When your father was courting me, it was like a real movie. He lived in a boardinghouse. The lady who ran the place raised enormous Belgian hares. And when the lady slept, the Belgian hares guarded the stairs. They had two big teeth in front, and if you didn't go up the stairs in a slow and dignified fashion, one of those huge rabbits would have you by the leg like that!"

"What were you doing up the stairs of Dad's boardinghouse?"

"Not what you think, young lady."

"I'm sure."

Silence; then Betty said, "I'm not going to let this pass."

"So don't."

"I'm terribly afraid that you have confused my morals with your own."

"What a lovely remark," said Iris in a broken voice.

"The truth shall set ye free."

"You big ole bitch."

The two were now sitting up, reflectored heads facing each other like two nodding, miserable sunflowers.

"You won't hear this child calling you what you called me," said Betty. "You won't hear it call you anything."

BETTY HAD ALWAYS ENJOYED HER COCKTAILS, BUT SHE NEVER drank in the daytime. That changed. It didn't make her sentimental or angry or any of the usual things. It just sped her up. She didn't drink that much, but it was enough to get her darting around and creating an atmosphere of emergency.

One unseasonably cold afternoon, Iris sat dog-earing a paperback with the glass porch doors closed and the oven door open to supplement the baseboard electric heating. Betty was coasting past the windows about the time Claude was expected. Suddenly, she froze in place. "Here comes your father followed by Sid Katzendorf in a Cadillac! It's the low-mileage Eldo!"

When Claude came in, he was equally excited. Even Iris felt the desperation in this; there had never before been any conversation about Cadillacs. It was just desperate.

"A beauty," Claude said, "and it's loaded. But let's don't rush. You drive it. Try it in a few spots, the freeway, here in the neighborhood. At first it seems like the *Queen Mary,* but you'll get the hang of it. If you like it, tell Sid to mark it sold. We can swallow the tab. I'll spare you the details. Try the factory air."

When Betty went out the door, things calmed down. Claude had bought Iris a Swiss Army knife, the one that must weigh a pound, and she immediately treasured it. Then they had some orange juice. It almost seemed as if the Cadillac were a decoy.

Iris thought Claude loved her.

"Iris," he said, "you're going to survive all this. You're going to finish school. You're going to go to college. If that Polack and his squashed hand don't take my company away from me, I'll give it all to you. How's that sound?" Claude hugged Iris and said, "Then I'll never lose you." The whole house seemed to go quiet. Iris marked her place and put the book aside. She opened and closed each blade and implement of the knife. He loves me very much, she thought. The evening sun got under the clouds and began to suggest a normal summer evening. The door burst open, and Betty ran in, struggling for composure. When she spoke, her voice was tragic and bore the keening finality of a summing up. She quit talking like Massachusetts.

"We're going along the freeway. I see this other Cadillac, but it's a two-tone. I'm sitting there trying to think which I like better. Obviously, the driver of the other Caddy is having the exact same thought. We get real close and head for the identical off-ramp. Suddenly it looks like we'll collide. I swerve. I crash into a jalopy. The jalopy takes off. Why did the jalopy need to be there in the first place!"

"That's it?" said Claude. "Where's Sid?"

"Sid has gone. He said, 'You own it.'"

"Whatever happened to us, Claude? Whatever happened to our luck?" Iris was free to assume what she had brought upon them.

ABOUT HALFWAY THROUGH THE LAST MONTH OF IRIS'S PREG-nancy, the adoptive parents came by to meet her. Betty did it up as an occasion with fresh flowers on the end tables. Claude checked his watch, shot his cuffs, looked out the window at rapid intervals. Iris had been dressed in high-octane maternity clothes: a conical navy-blue dress with a whimsical, polka-dotted, droopy bow tie.

At the very moment of the Anses' arrival, Claude seemed to panic. He was frozen in the hallway babbling in a low voice. "They can't find the door. They're gonna walk into the lake!" He started to call out in a high, tinny voice, projecting crazy merriness, "Back there! Right where you parked! You missed it! You missed . . . the front door!"

"Iris!" said Betty. "Animate!"

They finally came inside, and the introductions were achieved as the judge looked carefully at everyone, settling finally on Iris, whom he examined at length until she said, "I'm not a horse." But the judge took it well and said this was a happy day in their lives. Judge Anse and his wife, Mona, were a couple in their fifties. Judge Anse seemed unable to leave his judicial air at home and put a considerate pause before each remark, a pause that left one feeling scrutinized. His wife looked very scrutinized. It was easy to think that her desire for a baby was all she had left under scrutiny.

"We had a baby once," said Mrs. Anse without varying the tone of her voice. "We had it such a short time we didn't have time to name him. It appeared in the obituary as Baby Anse, comma, boy. But we had him and he was ours. For a while."

"Are you familiar with ectopic pregnancy?" asked Betty of no one in particular.

"Is it a problem?" said Judge Anse.

"You can say that again."

"Nothing she's got, I hope," said the judge, jerking his thick head toward Iris.

"No, it's something *I* had," said Betty.

Judge Anse said he worked hard and there was no one to leave it all to, and we can't live forever. That seemed to anger him and he used off-color language. He asked the present company to excuse his French. Iris sat blankly in the middle of a discussion of what a difficult age it was for raising children. It was hard to tell whether this was a reference to Iris or to the age in which the baby would live. But it must have been the latter because Claude said conclusively that the country had nowhere to go but up.

Mrs. Anse kept a level gaze throughout this, directed upon Iris. Iris felt this gaze and was ready for anything. When Mrs. Anse smiled and asked her question, Iris was ready. "What was the young fellow like?" she inquired.

"A real gorilla," said Iris.

"Have we mentioned Iris's grades?" Betty asked in panic. "Straight As."

"THE AGENCIES WOULDN'T TALK TO US," SAID MONA ANSE IN a cracking voice. "They told us we were too old."

"Well, not exactly true," said the judge patiently.

"It is for a Caucasian baby. Old. That's all we heard. We heard it from the state, from the Lutherans, from the Catholics. Old. People suggested every crazy thing you can imagine: midgets, pinheads, boat people. I may be old, but I won't be taken advantage of." The judge rested his hand on the back of his wife's. "If you're old, you get a brown one. You have no choice in the matter."

"Let 'em whine," said Claude to the empty middle of the room. "They're getting a bargain."

Later, Iris found out how they met Judge Anse. "Your father is being sued by a man at the plant who lost something in a machine," said Betty, blandly.

"Lost something?" said Iris. "Lost a what?"

"A limb. That's how we got to meet Judge Anse. He's hearing the case."

Iris thought for a moment and said, "Isn't that like selling my baby?"

"Iris, isn't it time you grew up?"

THE NIGHT THE CONTRACTIONS BEGAN, THE WHOLE THING almost fell apart. Iris bolted and was found two hours later hiding in a boathouse clear on the other side of the lake. By the time they got her back to the house, Betty was behind with the buffet. Somehow, everything went back into place, and when Judge and Mrs. Anse and Dr. Dahlstrom arrived, Iris was secured upstairs. Supplies were laid out. Dahlstrom had been playing golf, and Claude had to lend him some carpet slippers to keep him from marking up the floor with his cleats.

"What are you hoping for?" asked Dahlstrom.

"We don't care as long as it's got five of everything," said the judge. Dahlstrom made a Dagwood sandwich. Betty went up and down the stairs at frequent intervals. Claude seemed edgy but remarked that the leading indicators were up.

Dr. Dahlstrom was balancing his sandwich on one palm and building with the other, when Betty came down and said, "Delwyn, now."

"Betty, wait for the pretty part." Betty sat while Dahlstrom ate his sandwich, holding it between bites in front of his admiring gaze like a ship model. When he finished, he said, "And now the good doctor will work his magic. You people pace and wring your hands, whatever blows your hair back." And he went up the stairs.

There was no way to disguise the waiting. Betty mentioned a Big Band Era retrospective on FM but got no response. Everyone was quiet, but Claude seemed to be smoldering. He slumped down inside his suit coat and stared. After a while, he said, "A good deal was had by all." This was not lost on Mrs. Anse.

"To whom do you think you are speaking?" she asked, simultaneously with a moan from the second floor.

"Simmer down, Mona," said Claude. "Simmer down."

"I don't want this ruined."

"Try the salad. Betty used walnut oil."

"This end is well done," said Betty pointing at the roast. "You can see the rare from where you are."

"You'd think I'd feel young tonight. But I don't. I wonder why?" asked the judge.

"Have you tried Grecian Formula Nine?" asked Claude.

"You're a crumb," said the judge. "You're an insufferable crumb."

"And why not?" Claude flared. "I'm about to become a grandfather. How do you think that makes me feel? And Betty, my childhood sweetheart, this whole goddamned thing is going to make a grandmother out of her. You know what this means, Judge? This means we're starting to die. That jackass doctor upstairs is shoving us into history."

"If that's how you feel," the judge said. "That's how we feel."

So, by the time Dr. Dahlstrom arrived at the top of the stairs to announce a successful birth, Claude and the judge were at a stalemate. Claude's moment of vindication lay in his climbing the stairs alone, without looking back, to view the baby lying in its mother's arms. Whatever was going on around her, Iris was too happy and too far away to notice the arrival of Judge Anse and his wife, or to realize that her baby was a millionaire.

A MAN IN LOUISIANA

That winter, Ohio exploration had its meeting at the Grand Hotel in Point Clear, Alabama. Barry Seitz went along as special assistant to Mike Royce, the tough, relatively young president of Ohio Exploration. Barry knew spot checks could happen anytime, and as this was his first job that could go anywhere, he memorized everything. The range of subjects ran from drilling reports in various oil plays in the Southeast to orthodonture opinions concerning Mike Royce's impossibly ugly daughter. It was Royce's thought that the girl's dentist was "getting the teeth straight, all right, but blowing her profile." Barry was to "mentally note" that Mike Royce wanted to get together some three- and four-year-old snapshots of the girl and arrange a conference with the dentist. Barry didn't envy the dentist. The girl had inherited her father's profile and would always be a rich little bulldog.

The winter meeting was going to be shortened and therefore compressed because Mike Royce had just decided that he hated the South. So everyone was on edge, and the orthodontist issue seemed quite inflamed the longer Royce contemplated his daughter's mouth. Barry could see the pressure forming in his boss's face as he stared past the crab boats making their way across the dead-slick bay. Barry arranged to have some pictures same-day delivered, and he was with his boss when he thumbed through the snapshots.

"I thought I could trust that guy," said Royce from a darkening face. "He did this to me."

A number of the things Mike Royce said were irritating to Barry, and when Royce was angry, he said everything in a blur of exposed teeth that made part of Barry think of defending himself. But Barry knew he was on the cusp of failure or success. At thirty, a backward move could be a menace to his whole life; and while he knew he wouldn't be in Royce's employ forever, he wanted to stay long enough to learn oil-lease trading so that he could go out on his own. Once he was free, he could do the rest of the things he wanted: have a family, tropical fish, remote-control model airplanes. The future was an unbroken sheen to Barry, requiring only irreversible solvency. One of Barry's girlfriends had called him yellow. She went out with the morning trash. Having your ducks in a row does not equal yellow. Barry was cautious.

On the last day of their stay in Point Clear, Alabama, Mike Royce rang for Barry. Barry went down to his room and found Royce in a spotted bathrobe, his blunt feet hooked on the rungs of his chair, staring at the photographs of his daughter arranged chronologically. The little girl's square head did seem to change imperceptibly from picture to picture, though Barry could not tell the influence of hormones from the influence of orthodontic wire. From left to right, the child seemed to be losing character. In picture 1 she was clearly a vigorous young carnivore, and by picture 7 she looked insipid, headed nowhere. It seemed a lot to blame on the dentist, who, Mike Royce pointed out, would be on the carpet Monday first thing. Barry wanted what Mike Royce wanted. So Barry wanted those teeth right, but it wasn't like he could jump in there with his pliers.

Now Royce turned his attention to Barry. He did not ask Barry to sit down but seemed to prefer to regard him from his compressed posture in his bathrobe.

"Billy Hebert," he said. "Remember him?" He was spot-checking a mental note.

"Lake Charles," snapped Barry.

"Feature player in that deal down there. Now Billy's main lick, for fun, is to hunt birds." He reached Barry a slip of paper. "That dog is in Mississippi. I want you to get it and take it to Billy in Lake Charles."

"Very well."

"If you remember back, we need to be doing something out of this world for Billy. Big feature like that don't grow on trees."

Barry could see the rows of private piers from Royce's window. A few people had gone out carrying crab traps, towels, radios. They seemed to mock Barry's dog-hauling mission with their prospects. But it was better than hearing about the girl's teeth.

A haze from the paper mills outside Mobile hung on the water. The causeway bore a stream of Florida-bound traffic. Bay shrimpers plied the slick, and playoff games sounded from every window of the resort. He knew cheery types lined up in the lobby for morning papers. They seemed happy enough, looking like a bunch of mental patients. But when riding mowers hummed with purpose on a December day in the Deep South, it seemed cruel and unusual to have to haul a dog from Mississippi to a crooked oil dealer in Louisiana.

THE ROAD TO THE SMALL TOWN IN MISSISSIPPI ON ROYCE'S note wound up from the coastal plain past small cities and shantytowns. Barry ate at a drive-in restaurant next to an old cotton gin and drove up through three plantations that lay along the Tombigbee in what had been open country of farms and plantations. Arms of standing water appeared and disappeared as he soared over leggy trestles heading north. Barry began to be absorbed by his task. Where am I? he thought. He liked the idea of hauling a dog from Mississippi to Louisiana and didn't feel at all demeaned by it, as he had back at the Marriott. He passed a monument where the bighearted Union Army had set General Nathan Bedford Forrest free, and he felt giddily—no matter how many GTOs and pizza trucks he passed—that he was going back in time, toward Champion Hill and Shiloh. Every third house had a fireworks stand selling M-80s and bottle rockets, and every fifth building was a Baptist church. Oh, variety! he thought, comparing this with Ohio.

He reached Blue Wood, Mississippi, shortly after noon and stopped at a filling station for directions to the house of Jimmy F. Tippett, the man who had advertised the dog. Hearing his accent, the proprietor of the filling station, a round-faced man in coveralls, asked Barry where he came from.

"Chillicothe, Ohio."

The man looked at Barry's face for a moment and said, "Boy, you three-fo' mile from yo' house!"

He took a dirt road out past a gas field, past a huge abandoned World War II ammunition factory and rail spur. The town of Blue Wood had the air of an Old West town with its slightly elevated false-front buildings. Half the stores were empty, and the sidewalks had a few blacks as the sole pedestrians. Barry drove slowly past the hardware store, where a solitary white man gripped his counter and stared through the front door waiting for customers. "My God," Barry murmured. He couldn't wait to grab that bird dog and run. The teeth of Mike Royce's daughter were behind him, familiar and secure. The creepy stillness had gotten to him.

Jimmy F. Tippett's house was on the edge of a thousand-acre sorghum field. It was an old house with a metal roof and a narrow dogtrot breezeway. Because of its location, Barry thought it had a faint seaside atmosphere. But above all it spoke of poorness to Barry, and dirty stinking failure; his first thought was, How in the world did this guy lay hands on any dog Mike Royce would buy? Hunching over in the front seat after he'd parked, Barry gave way to temptation and opened Royce's envelope with a thumbnail. Inside was two thousand dollars in crisp hundreds. This, thought Barry, I've got to see. Never run into one for over fifty dollars.

He got out of the car, walking around the back of it so he could use it as a kind of blind while he looked things over. There were great big white clouds in the direction past the house and a few untended pecan trees. There had been a picket fence all around, but it looked like cattle or something had just walked it down into the ground. Here and there a loop of it stood up, and the pickets were weathered of most of their white paint and shaped at their ends like clubs in a deck of cards.

The pattern of shadows on the screen door changed, and Barry interrupted his thought to understand that one of the shadows would surely be Jimmy F. Tippett. So he strode up to the house, gulping impressions, and said, "Mr. Tippett, is that you?" but thinking how easy it was to picture a bullet coming through the screen door.

"Yes, sir," came a voice.

"I'm Barry Seitz. I represent Mr. L. Michael Royce. I'm here about a dog."

The screen door opened. Inside it stood a small man about sixty years of age, in khaki pants and starched white shirt. He had an auto insurance company pen holder in his pocket and a whistle around his neck. His face was entirely covered by fine dark wrinkles. A cigarette hung from the corner of his mouth. He looked Barry over as though he were doing a credit check. "Tippett," he said. "Come in."

Barry walked in. It appeared that Tippett lived entirely in one room. "I can't stay but a minute. I've got to get this dog to Louisiana."

"Have a seat," said Tippett. Barry moved backward and slipped into a chair. Tippett watched him do it. "I'll get the whiskey out," said Tippett. "Help you unwind."

"I'm quite relaxed," said Barry defiantly, but Tippett got down a bottle from a pie safe that held the glasses, too.

"You want water or S'em Up?" asked Tippett.

"Just straight would be fine," Barry said. Tippett served their whiskey and sat down next to his television set. His drink hand moved slightly, a toast. Barry moved his. It was quiet.

"You go to college?" asked Tippett.

"Yes," said Barry, narrowly avoiding the word "Wesleyan." "And you?" he asked. Tippett did not answer, and Barry feared he'd taken it as a contemptuous question. Nevertheless, he decided not to go into anything long about college being a waste of time with a bunch of smarty-pants professors. In fact, Barry had a sudden burst of love for his old college. He felt a small ache looking around the bare room for days of wit and safety before he'd been on unfathomable missions like this one. Dogs, tooth pictures, oil crooks, a secure future. Tippett was humming a tune and looking around the room. I know that tune, thought Barry. It's "Yankee Doodle Dandy." You bastards fired on our flag first. Fort Sumter.

"What's that song you're humming?"

"Oh, a old song."

"Really! I sort of remember it as a favorite of mine."

"That's nice. Yes, sir, that's nice. Some of these songs nowadays, why, I don't like them. They favor shit to me." There was a worn-out shotgun in the corner, boots, a long rope with a snap on it. Barry handed Tippett a thick stack of bills. Tippett pocketed it without looking.

"Let's have a look at this expensive dog," said Barry.

"Expensive? I got about twenty-five cent an ar to work the prick."

Tippett whistled through his teeth, and a pointer came in from the next room on his belly and laid his head on Tippett's knee. "Thar Bandit."

"Fine-looking dog," said Barry. About all Barry knew about Bandit was that he was mostly white.

"He get better lookin' when you turn him a-loose. Fellow need enough country for a dog like Bandit. Use a section and a half of bean field in five minutes." Tippett stared once again at L. Michael Royce's money. "This any good?" he asked, holding it up. Barry just nodded. A long silence followed. Barry felt that a kind of intimacy had formed. This man had something that he and Royce and the man in Louisiana wanted. When he took the dog to the car on a lead, Tippett said, "I was sixty-six in August. I'll never have another dog like that." He didn't pet Bandit before going to the house: he never looked back.

Barry started down the road with Bandit on the seat beside him. As he went back through Blue Wood, the huge clouds he had noticed driving to Tippett's seemed to enlarge with the massive angular light of evening, and the empty buildings of the town looked bombed out and derelict. A man was selling barbecue from an outdoor smoker. Barry stopped and ate some pork and slaw while he looked at the four-way roads trailing off into big fields. He thought, I'd like to give that dog a whirl. The man rolled down the lid on the smoker.

"Like anything to drink?"

"S'em Up," said Barry. He had decided he would run Bandit.

Barry drove alongside the vast soybean field with its tangle of stalks and curled leaves and long strips of combined ground. There were hedgerows of small hardwoods wound about with Osage orange and kudzu. Some of the fields had gas wells, and at one county-road corner there was a stack of casing pipe and a yellow backhoe as battered as an army tank. When the road came to an end, the bean fields stretched along a stream course and over low rounded hills as far to the west as Barry could see. This is it, he thought, and stopped.

Bandit stirred and whined when the engine shut off. He sat up and stared through the windshield at the empty space. It made Barry apprehensive to not quite understand what riveted his attention so. I wish I had more information, he thought, a little something more to go by. Nevertheless, he turned Bandit loose and thought for the short time he saw him that Tippett was right, that he got prettier and prettier, in his burning race over the horizon.

Until he was gone. It was as though Mike Royce towered up out of the Mississippi horizon to stare down at Barry in his rental car, clutching the orthodonture photographs and Barry's employment contract.

He got out and started running across the bean field. He ran so fast and uncaringly that the ground seemed to rise and fall beneath him as he crossed the hills. He hit a piece of soft plowed ground, and it sapped his strength so quickly he found himself stopped, his hands gripping his knees. Oh, Bandit, he cried out, come back!

Just before dusk, he came through a grove of oak on the edge of a swamp. A cold mist had started up in fingers toward the trees, and at their very edge stood Bandit on point, head high, sipping the breeze, tail straight as a poker, in a trance of found birds. Barry thought he cried out to Bandit, but he wasn't sure, and he knew he didn't want to frighten him into motion. He walked steadily in Bandit's direction. The dog stood at his work, not acknowledging him. When he was about a hundred feet away, the covey started to flush. He froze as birds roared up like brown bees and swarmed into the swamp. But Bandit stood still and Barry knew he had him. He admired Tippett's training in keeping Bandit so staunch and walked to the dog in an agony of relief. Good Bandit, he said, and patted his head, Bandit's signal to go on hunting: he shot into the swamp.

The brambles along the watery edge practically tore his clothes off. His hands felt sticky from bloody scratches. By turns he saw himself strangling Royce, Tippett, and the man in Louisiana. He wondered if Royce would ever see him as a can-do guy again. From Cub Scouts on he had had this burden of reliability, and as he felt the invisible dog tearing it away, he began to wonder why he was running so fast.

He reached higher ground and a grove of hickories with a Confederate cemetery, forty or fifty unknown soldiers. He sat down to rest among the small stones, gasping for air. What he first took to be the sound of chimes emerging distantly from the ground turned out to be his own ringing ears. It occurred to him that some of the doomed soldiers around him had gone to their deaths with less hysteria and terror than he had brought to the chase for this dog. Maybe it wasn't just the dog, he thought, and grew calm. Maybe it was that little bitch, her crooked teeth and her brute of a father.

It was dark and Barry gave himself up to it. A symphonic array of odors came from the ground with the cooling night, and he imagined the Confederate bones turning into hickory trees over the centuries. Shade, shelter from the wind, wood for ax handles, charcoal for barbecue. Bones.

But, he thought, standing, that dog isn't dead yet; and he resumed his walk. He regained open country somehow and walked in a gradual curve that he thought would return him to his car. Maybe his feet remembered the hills, but he wasn't sure and he didn't care. His eyes recorded the increasing density of night until he could no longer see the ground under him. The moon rose and lit the far contours of things, but close up the world was in eclipse. He came to a pond. Only its surface could be seen like a sheet of silver hanging in midair. As he studied it, trying to figure out how to go around, the shapes of horses materialized on its surface. He knew they must be walking on the bank, but the bank itself was invisible, and the only knowledge of horses he had was the progress of their reflection in the still water. When the horses passed, he walked toward the water until he saw his own shape. He watched it disappear and knew he'd gone on around.

Back in the bean field, Barry felt a mild wave of hysteria pass over him once more, one in which he imagined writing a memo to Royce about having been knee-deep in soybean futures, much to report, et cetera, et cetera; by the way, couldn't seem to lay hands on Louisiana man's dog, et cetera, et cetera. Hope dog-face girl's teeth didn't all fall out. More later, yrs, B. After which, he felt glumly merry and irresponsible.

When he got to his car, it occurred to him that this had all happened a couple of miles from Tippett's house. No great distance for a hyena like Bandit. So he drove over there, to find the house unlighted and silent. He walked to the door. A bark broke out and was muffled. Barry knocked. The door opened and Tippett said, "I thought you went to Louisiana." Barry followed Tippett into the empty room. Tippett had a loose T-shirt on, and his pants were held by the top button only. Barry looked all around and saw nothing.

"He come back?"

"You lose that dog?" Something tapped across the floor in the next room. He doesn't want to go to Louisiana, he thought, and he surely doesn't want to go with me. A wave of peace came over him.

"Yeah, I did," said Barry. The old man studied him closely, studied his face and every little thing he did with his hands. Barry quit surveying the old man's possessions and wondering what time it was somewhere else. "What do you suppose would make a trained dog just go off and leave like that?" Barry asked. He was playing along: he knew the dog was here.

The old man made a sound in his throat, almost clearing it to speak something which must not be misunderstood. "Son," he said, "one day you'll understand that anything that'll eat shit and fuck its own mother is liable to do anything." Barry thought of the men down in the Confederate graveyard. He considered the teeth of Mike Royce's daughter and his own "future." Above all, he thought of how a dog could run so far that, like too many things, it never came back.

LIKE A LEAF

I'M UNDERNEATH MY SMALL HOUSE IN THORNE. THE REAL-estate people call it a "starter" home, however late in life you buy one. It's a modest house that gives you the feeling that either you're going places or that this won't do. This starter home is different; this one is it. It's perfect for a jerkwater town like Thorne.

From under here, I can hear the neighbors talking. He is a suc-cessful man named Deke Crowley. His wife is away, and he is having an affair with the lady across the street, a sweet and exciting lady I've not met yet. Frequently he says to her, "I am going to impact on you, baby." Today, they are at one of their many turning points.

"I think I'm coming unglued," she says. "Can't we go someplace nice for a change?"

She has a beautiful voice, and underneath the house I remember she is pretty. What am I doing here? I'm distributing bottle caps of arsenic for the rats that come up from the river and dispute the cats over trifles. I represent civilization in a small but real way, and when I hear him say "Maui," I know he's deceiving her and she'll never get there. He's going to use her up right here where she's at.

Deke Crowley laughs with wild relief. Once I saw him at the municipal pool, watching young girls. He was wearing trunks and allergy-warning dog tags. What a guy! To me he was like a crude foreigner or a gaucho.

Anyway, I came down here because of the rats. Read your his-tory: they carry Black Plague. Mrs. Crowley was on a Vegas excur-sion with the Thorne Symphony Club. When I get back inside, the flies are causing a broad dumb movement on the windows. We never had flies like this on the ranch. We had songbirds, apple blossoms, and no flies. My wife was alive then and saw to that. We didn't impact, we loved each other. She had an aneurism let go while carding wool. She just nodded her pretty face and headed out. I sat there like a stupe.

They came for her and I just knocked around the place trying to get it. I headed for town and started seeing the doctor. Things came together: I was able to locate a place to live in, catch the Series, and set up housekeeping. Plus, the Gulch, everyone agrees, is Thorne's nicest neighborhood. A traffic violator is taken right aside and lined out quick. It's a neighborhood where folks teach the dog to bring the paper to the porch, so a guy can sit back in his rocker and find out who's making hamburger of the world. I was one of this area's better cattlemen, and town life doesn't come easy. Where I once had coyotes and bears, I now have rats. Where I once had the old-time marriages of my neighbors, I now have Impact Man poking a real sweet gal who never gets taken someplace nice.

My eating became hit or miss. All I cared about was the World Series after a broken season. I was high and dry, and when you're like that, you need someone or something to take you away. Death makes you different like the colored are different. I felt I was under the spell of what had happened to me. Then someone threw a bottle onto the field in the third or fourth game of the Series and almost hit the Yankee left fielder, Dave Winfield. I felt completely poisoned. I felt like a rat with a mouthful of bottle caps. All my sense of fairness was settled on Winfield, who is colored, like I felt having been in the company of death. Then Winfield couldn't hit the ball anyway, and just when Reggie Jackson got his hitting back, what happens? He drops an easy pop fly.

What were my wife and I discussing when she died? Jerry Lewis in *The Nutty Professor*. It seems so small. Sometimes when I think how small our topic was, I feel the weight of my hair tearing at my face. I bought a youth bed to reduce the size of the unoccupied area. The doctor says because of the shaking, I get quite a little bit less rest per hour than the normal guy. Rapid eye movement, and so on.

Truthfully speaking, part of me has always wanted to live in town. You hear the big milling at the switching yard and, on stormy nights, the transcontinental trucks reroute off the interstate, and it's busy and kind of like a last-minute party at somebody's house. The big outfits are parked all over with their engines running, and the heat shivers at the end of the stacks. The old people seem brave trying to get around on the ice: one fall and they're through, but they keep chunking, going on forward with a whole heck of a lot of grit. That fact gives me a boost.

And I love to window-shop. I go from window to window alongside people I don't know. There's never anything I want in there, but I feel good because I am excited when somebody picks out a daffy pair of shoes or a hat you wouldn't put on your dog. My wife couldn't understand this. Nature was a shrine to her. I wanted to see people more than she did. Sit around with just anybody and make smart remarks. Sometimes I'd pack the two of us into the hills. My wife would be in heaven. I'd want to buy a disguise and slip off to town and stare through the windows. That's the thing about heaven. It comes in all sizes and shapes.

Anyone in my position feels left behind. It's normal. But you got to keep picking them up and throwing them; you have got to play the combinations or quit. What I'd like is a person, a person I could enjoy until she's blue in the face. This, I believe. When the time comes, stand back from your television set.

I don't know why Doc keeps an office in the kind of place he does, which is merely the downstairs of a not-so-good house. I go to him because he is never busy. He claims this saves him the cost of a receptionist.

Doc and I agree on one thing: it's all in your head. The only exception would be aspirin. Because we believe it's all in your head, we believe in immortality. Immortality is important to me because, without it, I don't get to see my wife again. Or, on the lighter side, my dogs and horses. That's all you need to know about the hereafter. The rest is for the professors, the eggheads who don't have to make the payroll. We agree about my fling with the person. I hope to use Doc's stethoscope to hear the speeding of the person's heart. All this has a sporting side, like hunting coyotes. When Doc and I grow old and the end is in sight, we're going to become addicted to opium. If we get our timing wrong, we'll cure ourselves with aspirin. We plan to see all the shiny cities, then adios. We speak of cavalry firefights, Indian medicine, baseball, and pussy.

Doc doesn't come out from behind the desk. He squints, knowing I could lie, then listens. "My house in town is going to work fine. The attic has a swing-down ladder and you look from a round window up there into the backyards. You can hear the radios and see people. Sometimes couples have little shoving matches over odd things, starting the charcoal or the way the dog's been acting. I wrote some of them down in a railroad seniority book to tell you. They seem to dry up quick."

"Take a trip."

"I can't."

"Then pack for one and don't go."

"I can do that." "Stay out of the wind. It makes people nervous, and this is a windy town. Do what you have to do. You can always find a phone booth, but get out of that wind when it picks up. And anytime you feel like falling silent, do it. Above all, don't brood about women."

"Doc," I say, "I've got a funny feeling about where I'm headed."

By hauling an end table out to the porch, despite that the weather is not quite up to it, and putting a chair behind it, I make a fine place for my microwave fettuccine Alfredo. I can also watch our world with curiosity and terror. If necessary, I can speak when spoken to, by sipping my ice water to keep the chalk from my mouth.

A car pulls up in front of Crowleys'; Mrs. Crowley gets out with a small Samsonite and goes to the house. That saves me from calling a lot of travel agents. The world belongs to me.

I begin to eat the fettuccine Alfredo, slow, spacing each mouthful. After eating about four inches of it, I see the lady from across the street, the person, on the irregular sidewalk, gently patting each bursting tree trunk as she comes. Since I am now practically a mute, I watch for visible things I can predict. And all I look for is her quick glance at Deke Crowley's house and then a turn through her chain-link gate. I love that she is pretty and carries nothing, like the Chinese ladies Doc tells me about who achieve great beauty by teetering around on feet that have been bound. I feel I am listening to the sound of a big cornfield in springtime. My heart is an urgent thud. To my astonishment, she swings up her walk without a look. Her wantonness overpowers me. Impossible! Does she not know the wife is home from Vegas?

I look up and down the street before lobbing the fettuccine Alfredo to a mutt. He eats in jerking movements and stares at me like I'm going to take it back. Which I'm quite capable of doing, but won't. I have a taste in my mouth like the one you get in those frantic close-ins hunting coyotes. Sometimes when I told my wife I felt this way, she was touched. She said I had absolutely no secret life. The sad thing is, I probably don't. But that look when the dogs are onto a coyote, you never forget it.

I begin sleeping in the attic. I am alone and not at full strength, so this way I feel safer. I don't have to answer door or phone. I can see around the neighborhood better, and I have the basic timing of everybody's day down pat. For example, the lady goes to work on time but comes home at a different hour every day. Does this suggest that she is a carefree person to whom time means nothing or who is, perhaps, opposed to time's effects and therefore defiant about regularity? I don't know.

Before I realize it, I am window-shopping again. Each day there is more in the air, more excitement among the shoppers, who seem to spill off the windows into the doors of the stores. The sun is out and I stand before the things my wife would never buy, not risqué things but things that wouldn't stand up. She seems very far away now. But when people come to my store window, I sense a warmth that is like friendship. Anytime I feel uncomfortable in front of a particular store, I move to sporting goods, where it is clear that I am okay, and besides, Doc is fixing me. My docile staring comes from the last word in tedium: guns and ammo, compound bows, fishing rods.

When I say that I am okay, I mean that I am happy in the company of most people. What is wrong with me comes from my wife having unexpectedly died and from my having read the works of Ralph Waldo Emerson when my doctor and I were boning up on immortality. But I am watching the street, and something will turn up. In the concise movements of the person I'm most interested in, and in the irregularity of her returns, which she certainly despises, I sense a glow directed toward me, the kind of light in a desolate place that guides a traveler still yearning for a destination.

SO OKAY, SHE WALKS HOME. SHE IS VERY NEARLY ON TIME. She walks so fast her pumps clatter on our broken Thorne side-walk. She swings her shoulder bag like a cheerful weapon and arcs into the street automatically to avoid carelessly placed sprinklers. She touches a safety match to a long filter brand, as she surveys her little yard, and goes in. She works, I understand, at the county assessor's office, and I certainly imagine she does a fine job for those folks. With her bounce, her cigarettes, and her iffy hours, she makes just the kind of woman my wife had no use for. Hey! It takes all kinds. Human life is thus filled with variety, and if I have a regret in my own so far, it is that I have not been close to that variety: that is, right up against where it throbs but at this exasperating remove.

I need a break and go for a daylight drive. I take the river road through the foothills north of Thorne—a peerless jaunt—to our prison. It is an elegant old dungeon that has housed many famous western outlaws in its day. The ground it rests on was never farmed, having gone from buffalo pasture to lockup many years ago. Now it has razor wire surrounding it and a real up-to-date tower like out east.

One man stands in blue light behind its high windows. When you see him from the county road, you think, That certainly must be the loneliest man in the world. But actually, it's not true. His name is Al Costello, and he's a good friend of mine. He's the head of a large Catholic household, and the tower is all the peace he gets. The lonely guy is the warden, an out-of-stater, a professional imprisoned by card files: a man no one likes. He looks like Rock Hudson, and he can't get a date.

Sometimes I stop in to see Al. I go up into the tower and we look down into the yard at the goons and make specific comments about the human situation. Sometimes we knock back a beer or two. Sometimes I take a shot at one of his favorite ball clubs, and sometimes he lights into mine. It's just human fellowship in kind of a funny spot.

But today I keep on cruising, out among the jackrabbits and sagebrush, high above the running irrigation, all the way around the little burg, then back into town. I stop in front of the doughnut shop, waiting for the sun to travel the street and open the shop and herald its blazing magic up commercially zoned Thorne. Waiting in front is a sick-looking young man muttering to himself at a high relentless pitch of the kind we associate with Muslim fundamentalism. At eight sharp the door opens, and the Muslim and I shoot in for the counter. He seems to have lost something by coming inside, and I am riveted upon his loss. By absolute happenstance, we both order glazed. Then I add an order of jelly-filled, which I deliver, still hot, to the lady's doorstep.

I'M GOING TO STOP READING THIS NEWSPAPER. IN ONE WEEK, the following has been reported: A Thorne man shot himself fatally in a bar, demonstrating the safety of his pistol. Another man, listening to the rail, had his head run over by every car of a train that took half an hour to go by. Incidents like these make it hard for me to clearly see the spirit winging its way to heaven. And though I would like to stop reading the paper, I really know I won't. It would set a bad example for the people on the porches who have trained Spot to fetch.

"Did you get the doughnuts?" I called out that evening.

I know they've been talking when I see Deke Crowley give me the fishy look. I cannot imagine which exact locution she used—probably that I was "bothering" her—but she has very evidently made of me a fly in Deke's soup. There is not a lot he could do, standing next to his warming-up sensible compact, but give me this look and hope that I will invest it with meaning.

I decide to blow things out of proportion. "You two should do something nice together!" I call out. Deke slings his head down and bitterly studies a nail on one hand, then gets in and drives away. "Maui! Ever hear of it? Mountain Travel: they're having a special!"

YOU THINK YOU GOT IT BAD? SAYS HERE A MAN OVER TO Arlee was jump-starting his car in the garage; he had left it in gear, and when he touched the terminals of the battery, the car shot forward and pinned him to a compressor that was running. This man was inflated to four times his normal size and was still alive after God knows how long when they found him. A hopeful Samaritan backed the car away, and the man just blew up on the garage floor and died. As awful as that is, it adds nothing whatsoever to the basic idea. Passing in your sleep or passing as a pain-crazed human balloon on a greasy garage floor produces the same simple result year after year. The major differences lie among those who are left behind. If you're listening, please understand I'm still trying to see why we don't all cross on our own, or why nice people don't just help us on over. Who knows if you're even listening?

"SO," I CRY OUT TO THE PERSON WITH EXAGGERATED INNO-cence, illustrating how I am crazy like a fox. "So, how did you enjoy the doughnuts?"

She stops, looks, thinks. "That was you?"

"That was me."

"Why?" She is walking toward me.

"It was a little something from someone who thinks somebody should take you somewhere nice." My foot is in the door.

"Tomorrow," she says from her beautiful face, "make it cinna-mon Danish." Her eyes dance with cruel merriment. I feel she is of German extraction. She has no trace of an accent, and her attire is domestic in origin. I think, What am I saying? I'm scaring myself. This is a Thorne local with zip for morals hoping to fornicate her way to Hawaii.

I decide to leap forward in the development of things to ascer-tain the point at which it doesn't make sense. We are very much in love, I say to myself. I recoil privately at this thought, knowing I am still okay if not precisely tops. I am neither a detective nor a complete stupe. Like most of the human race, I fall somewhere in between.

"Tell you what," she says with a twinkle. "I come home from work and I freshen up. Then you and me go for a stroll. How far'd you get?"

"Stroll . . ."

"You're a good boy tonight and I let you off lightly." Mercy. My neck prickles. "Deke tells me you still own that ranch. Maybe we can go out there one of these days and work on the fence!" She laughs in my face and heads out. I see her cross the trees at the end of the street. I see the changing flicker of different-colored cars. I see mountains beyond the city. I see her bouncing black hair even after she has gone. I say quietly, I'm lonely; I had no idea you were not to have a long life. But I'm still in love.

I call Doc. I tell him I'm going it alone. I call him a quack. I must have laid one on him because he never said a word.

SHE STOOD ME UP AND IT'S MIDNIGHT. I HAVE NEVER FELT like this. This house doesn't belong to me. It belongs to the person, and I'm lying on her bed viewing the furnishings. It's dark here. I can see her coming up the sidewalk. She will come alongside the house and come in through the kitchen. I am in the back room. I'll say hello.

"Hello."

"Hello." She's quite the opposite of my wife, but it's fatal if she thinks this is healthy. She's in the same tight dress and appears to view this as a clever seduction. "It's you. Who'd have guessed? I'm going to bathe, and if you ask nice you can help."

"I want to see."

"I know that." She laughs and goes through the door undressing. "Just come in. You'll never get your speech right. Do I look drunk? I am a little. I suppose your plan was a neighborhood rape." Loud laugh. She hangs the last of her clothes and studies me. Then she leans against the cupboards.

"Please turn the water on, kind of hot." She is sitting on the side of the tub. I think I am going to fall, but I go to her and rock her in my arms so that she kind of spreads out against the white porcelain.

She looks at me and says, "The nicest thing about you is you're frightened. You're like a boy. I'm going to frighten you as much as you can stand." I undress and we get into the clear water. I look at the half of myself that is underwater; it looks like something at Sea World. Suddenly, I stand up. "I guess I'm not doing so good. I'm not much of a rapist after all." I get out of the tub, a tremendous boob.

"You men oh my God are like peas in a pod. You can hardly tell them apart."

"That Deke has caused you to suffer."

"Oh, crap."

"It's time he took you someplace nice." So I'm on the muscle now and it gets worse when she bugs me about the ranch, acreage et cetera, and seriously impolite questions.

I am drying off about a hundred miles an hour. I go into the next room and pull on my trousers. I don't even see her coming. She pushes me over on the daybed and drags my pants back off. I am so paralyzed all I can do is say, Please no, please no, as she clambers roughly atop me and takes me, almost hurting me with her fury, ending with a sudden dead flop. Every moment or so, she looks at me with her raging victorious eyes.

"You think you're any different? Don't make me laugh." She bounces up and returns to the bathroom while I dress again. There is a razor running and periodic splashes of water. Whether it is because my wife has to sit through this or that I can't bring her back, I don't know, but the whole thing makes me a different guy. In short, I've been debased.

She tows me outside, clattering on the steps in wooden clogs, sending forth a bright perfume to savage my nerves. I see there is only one way my confused hands can regain their grasp: I burst into tears. She pops open a small flowered umbrella and uses it to conceal me from the outside world. It seems very cozy in there. She coos appropriately.

"Are you going to be okay now?" she asks. "Are you?" I see Deke's car coming up the street. The Impact Man, the one who never does anything nice for her. I dry my tears posthaste. We head down the street. We are walking together in the bright evening sky under our umbrella. This foolishness implies an intimacy that must not have gone well with Impact Man, because he arcs into his driveway and has to brake hard to keep from going through his own garage with its barbecue, hammocks, and gap-seamed neglected canoe, things whose hopes of a future seem presently to ride on the tall shapely legs of my companion.

I can't think of something really right for us. The only decent restaurant would seem as though we were on a date, put us face-to-face. We need to keep moving. I feel pretty certain we could pop up and see Al Costello, my Catholic friend in the tower. He always has the coffeepot going. So we get into my flivver and head for the prison. It makes a nice drive in a Tahiti-type sunset, and by the time I graze Staff Parking to the vast space of Visitors, the wonderful blue-white of the glass tower has ignited like the pilot light on a gas stove.

"I want you to meet a friend of mine," I tell the lady. "Works here. Big Catholic family. He's a grandfather in his late thirties. It looks like a lonely job and it's not."

The tower has an elevator. The gate guards know me and we sail in. The door opens in the tower.

"Hey," I say.

"What's cooking?" Al grins vacantly.

"Thought we'd pop up. Say, this is a friend of mine."

"Mighty pleased," Al says. He has the lovely manners of someone battered beyond recognition. She now glues herself to the window and stares at the cons. I think she has made some friendly movements to the guys down in the yard. I glance at Al, and evidently he thinks so, too. We avert our glances, and Al says, "Can I make a spot of coffee?" I feel like a fool.

"I'm fine," she says. "Fine." She is darn well glued to the glass. "Can a person get down there?"

"Oh, a person could," says Al. I notice he is always in slow movement around the tower, always looking, in case some geek goes haywire. "Important thing, I guess, is that no one can come here unless I let them in. They screen this job. The bad apples are soon gone. It takes a family man."

"Are those desperate characters?" she asks, gazing around. I move to the window and look down at the minnowlike movement of the prisoners. This would have held zero interest for my wife.

"A few, I guess. This is your regular backyard prison. No celebrities. We've got the screwballs is about all we've got."

"How's the family, Al." I dart in.

"Andrea Elizabeth had strep, but it didn't pass to nobody in the house. Antibiotics knocked it for a loop."

"For Christ's sake!" says my companion. We turn. He and I think it's us. But it's something in the yard. "Two fairies," she says through her teeth. "Can you beat that?" After which she just stares out the windows while Al and I drink some pretty bouncy coffee with a nondairy creamer that makes shapes in it without ever really mixing. It is more or less to be polite that I drink it at all. I look over, and she has her widespread hands up against the glass like a tree frog. She is grinning very hard, and I know she has made eye contact with someone down in the exercise yard she seems to know. Suddenly, she turns.

"I want to get out of here."

"Okay," I say brightly.

"You go downstairs," she says. "I need to talk to Al."

My heart is coated with ice. I'm mortified. But down the stairs I go and wait in a green-carpeted room at the bottom. There is a door out and a door to the yard. I don't want to sit in the car trying to look like I'm not abetting a jailbreak. I'm going downhill fast.

I must be there twenty minutes when I hear the electronics of the elevator coming at me. The stainless doors open, and a very disheveled Al appears with my friend. There is nothing funny or bawdy in her demeanor. Al swings by me without catching a glance and begins to open the door to the yard with a key. He has a service revolver in one hand as he does so. "Be cool now, Al," says my friend intimately. "Or I talk."

The steel door winks, and she is gone into the prison yard. "We better go back," says Al in a doomed voice. "I'm on duty. God almighty."

"Did I do this?" I say in the elevator.

"You better stay with me. I can't have you leaving alone." He unplugs the coffee mechanically. When I get to the bulletproof glass, I can see the prisoners migrating. There is a little of everything: old guys, stumblebums, Indians, Italians, Irishmen, all heading into the shadow of the tower. "We're just going to have to go with this one. There's no other way." He looks crummy and depleted, but he is going to draw the line. We have to go with it. She will signal the tower, he tells me. So we wait by the glass like a pair of sea captains' wives in their widow's walks. It goes on so long, we forget why we're waiting. We are just doing our job, just two little old Americans.

Then there is a small reverse migration of prisoners, and she, bobby pins in her teeth, checking her hair for bounce, waves up to us in the tower. We wave back in this syncopated motion, which is almost the main thing I remember, me and Al flapping away like a couple of widows.

As we ride down in the elevator again, Al says, "You take over from here." And we commence to laugh. We laugh so hard I think one of us will upchuck. Then we have to stop to get out of the elevator. We cover our mouths and laugh through our noses, tears streaming down our cheeks, while Al tries to get the door open. Our lady friend comes in real stern and we stop. It is as if we'd been caught at something and she is awful sore. She heads out the door and Al gives me the Smith.

In the car, she says with real contempt, "I guess it's your turn." Buddy, was that the wrong thing to say. "I guess it is." I am the quiet one now. She gives me a wary glance.

There is a great pool on the river about a mile below the railroad bridge. It's moving but not enough to erase the stars from its surface, or the trout sailing like birds over its deep pebbly bottom. She's a ghost of the river. It's such a relief.

DOGS

No one imagined how it would turn out for Howie Reed. But it all began when he was beaned at the rodeo picnic when the Jacquas, the Hatfields, and the Larrimores uniformly felt that everyone was so sick and tired of having to clean up the fairgrounds that a game would be fun.

Howie Reed got beaned in the first inning. It was softball and he didn't even fall down. At fifty-one, he was close to the average age of all the players. It was a stately game with no scores.

Right after that he went on a trip. He was gone for about two weeks, and just before returning, he called his friends to tell them he had walked into a door at the bank and blackened his eyes. When he got home, the black eyes were almost gone. But it was clear that he hadn't walked into a glass door. Howie had had his face lifted. It is not possible to really explain the effect on us, his old friends and acquaintances, of his new glossiness: the incisions behind the ears, the Polynesian serenity of his new gaze, left many of our circle in Thorne speechless.

The next time we all got together it was for a trout fry welcoming the new internist to town. In an area of long winters like ours, the entire community grows to hate all its professional people in about five years. A new doctor is taken in with urgent affection. The arrival of Dr. Kaufman, fresh from the Indian Health Service at Wolf Point, was no exception. A horseshoe pitch was improvised; an extension cord was found so that a television set could be left running in the yard for guests following serials. Most of us drank and pitched horseshoes or skipped stones on the beautiful river. Howie fainted.

Dr. Kaufman examined him and then came over to the carport where some of us had gone to avoid the sun. There, Dr. Kaufman assured us that Howie was faking and that we should realize our friend was a mild hysteric; bring him a glass of water, possibly. Even given Dr. Kaufman's diagnosis, it was awfully touching to see our old friend stretched out with his sleek new face aimed at heaven, the river flowing past him like time itself. In my view, it was either that very time, or the beaning, that explained Howie's face-lift and faints. But that didn't lessen my concern for him.

No one noticed exactly when Howie left, but he was gone by the time the party wound down. And if there was any worry over him, it was lost in the uproar of the Kaufmans' discovering that the thirteen-year-old corgi the doctor had owned since his medical-school days was gone. Sylvan Lundstrom, who was everyone's lawyer and Johnny-on-the-spot, called the police, the sheriff, and the radio station, carefully describing a generic corgi from the Kaufmans' American Kennel Club guide to breeds. It would be morning before we could reach the drivers' training group at the school; they were usually most successful in finding lost dogs. Mrs. Kaufman said she wished she knew less about the experimental purposes to which stray dogs were often put.

The dog was not found.

Monday I saw Howie in front of the Bar and Grill at the lunch hour. He was going out; I was going in. Howie is in insurance and busy as all get-out, and a good kind of family man. So the following seemed odd.

"You're on the phone with an old girlfriend," said Howie. "Your wife is at your elbow. Your heart is pounding. Your old girlfriend says, 'Just wanted to call and say I still love ya!' 'You too!' I shout like I'm closing on a huge policy. How much of this the old lady buys, I can't say." Howie shoots off with a little wave. I am not painting Howie as an ugly customer but as a troubled guy who didn't ever talk like this. It used to be you'd bump into him and he'd tell you something homely like the difference between whittling and carving (whittling you're not trying to make something). Now everything seemed so final.

Howie's wife went back to South Dakota in September, for good. To show he wasn't upset, Howie had his car painted JUST MARRIED. He went to a sales conference in Kansas City and forced a landing en route in Bismarck. He had to pay a huge fine for that, which he could certainly afford. But Dr. Kaufman assured his new admirers that forcing a landing was a well-known thing disturbed people do. When Howie finally got to Kansas City, his company made him Salesman of the Year.

By October, Howie seemed completely his old self. The face finally seemed to be his own. His wife stayed away. We had another softball game after the fall rodeo. He was still driving the just married car, and he was wearing a sweatshirt copy of the Shroud of Turin. He was all over the field and drove in four runs.

Dogs kept disappearing. It was making the paper. Dr. Kaufman was not building a practice as rapidly as he wished and he threw a Thanksgiving party, supposedly to introduce Diana, a yellow Labrador he had bought to replace the corgi. He said the corgi had left a hole in his heart that nothing could fill, but he let his pride in the new dog show. We all went to the party, even the other doctors. Howie was so disheveled looking we asked if he was in disguise. "To be the leading adulterer in a small Montana town," he said mysteriously, "is to spend your life dodging bullets. It is the beautiful who suffer." His whiskers pressed through the taut skin of his face. For the moment of our nervousness, in the central-heating itch of fall's first frosts, it was as if the house were equipped with self-locking exits. We were quiet in the drifting cigarette smoke for just a moment, then went back to our carefree ways. Right out of the blue, Howie added, "What the hell, I forgive you all. Everything I know I learned from Horatio Alger."

The dinner was served buffet style, and we ate with our plates in our laps. The Kaufmans' new dog was beautifully trained and took hand signals, retrieving everything from black olives to ladies' pumps with a delicate mouth. When we'd nearly finished eating, Howie said to a young woman, a dental hygienist, in a voice all could hear, "That food was so bad I can't wait for it to become a turd and leave me."

Dr. Kaufman diverted our attention by sending Diana on a blind retrieve into the bedroom. When she returned, Howie asked Kaufman what he had to "shell out for the mutt." And so on, but it got worse. Spotting a pregnant brunette in her thirties, he said, "I see you've been fucking." Mrs. Kaufman tried to distract Howie by describing the problems she had had keeping the grosbeaks from running every other bird out of the feeder.

"You know what?" said Howie.

"What is that?"

"I wish you were better looking," he said to Mrs. Kaufman.

"Get out now," said the doctor.

"Suits me," said Howie, once the mildest of our chums. "I've monkeyed around here long enough. I prefer white people." So Howie left and the party went on. Actually, the relief of Howie's departure contributed to its being such a terrific party. We all told stories that, for a change, weren't deftly to our own credit. I thought once or twice of making a plea for Howie—we'd been friends the longest—but thought better of it. Dr. Kaufman had had to be restrained, once.

When the time came to go, it was discovered that Diana was missing. Mrs. Kaufman cried and Dr. Kaufman said, "I guess it's pretty clear that crazy son of a bitch has my dog."

In order to keep the police out of it, I agreed to go see Howie. At first I tried to get someone else to do it, but when I saw how anxious some of the others were to call in the authorities, I got a move on. He really had been a friend to all of us. But the pack instinct, whatever that is, was on alert. I think I felt a little of it myself, sort of like "Let's kill Howie."

Anyway, I made the feeling go away and drove up to Howie's house, a cedar-and-stone thing of the kind that went through here a while back. Diana met me at the door. Howie turned and wearily let me follow him inside. Various dogs gathered from the hallways and side room and joined us in the living room. Howie made drinks.

"I'm glad it's you," Howie said, handing me my Scotch. "The bubble had to break. Margie gone. Salesman of the Year. Every breed I ever dreamed of." He gestured sadly at our audience: Diana, a black Lab, an Irish setter of vacant charm, a dachshund, a few mixed breeds who seemed to have a sheepdog as a common ancestor, all contented. And the old worn-out corgi.

"We didn't know what you were going through," I said. I didn't know who I meant by "we," except that I thought it was in the air when I left the party that we were pulling together over a common cause. "It started I guess when you got beaned." Howie looked at me for a long time.

"That wasn't it. I admit the beaning was what gave me the idea.

I fell down to gain time to think. I lay there and thought about how happy I was that my marriage was on the rocks. The time had come to be off my rocker whether I felt like it or not. Margie had a guy, but it wasn't enough. Then the company saying the future belonged to me. It was too much. I did the fainting business because I needed a jinx, I was superstitious.

"One thing led to another and I started grabbing dogs. It sounds crazy, but I felt like Balboa when he saw the Pacific. I'd never known anything like it. By the way, getting caught is no disgrace."

I took Diana down to the Kaufmans, and Dr. Kaufman, who is such a young man, made a seemingly prepared speech about how much Diana had cost and how in a practice that was starting slowly, you cannot imagine how slowly, Diana had been a crazy sacrifice both for himself and for Mrs. Kaufman. Among the party guests there was the gloom of drama slipping away, of a return to the everyday.

In another two hours I had restored each dog but one to its rightful owner. The doctor and his wife said they were glad to be shut of the arthritic toothless corgi, hinting it was Howie's punishment to keep it. Howie said it suited him fine.

Anyway, as things go, it just all blew over. And in fact, by spring, when Howie started having some chest pains, probably only from working too hard, he went to Dr. Kaufman, joining our new doctor's rapidly growing list of devoted patients.

A SKIRMISH

The schoolroom was small, and we had the same teacher all day long. You could smell the many coats that hung in the back of the room. The burr-headed boys sat on one side and the girls with their elaborate hair sat on the other. Between the two there was an idle hostility, which did not seem to have anything to do with sex but, rather, a plain and small hatred awaiting transmogrification and secrecy.

Our lunches were all stored on a table in black pails. We lived in such proximity and confinement that we had powerful attitudes about what constituted a proper lunch. Freakish lunches—imaginative preparation, ethnic hints, dainty wrappings—singled out the hapless owner as a pampered twit. I vividly remember how we silently accepted a trick miniature pie that was going the rounds of the grocery stores and could be eaten one-handed. A heartbeat from being singled out, each one of us seemed to arrive the same day with an identical pie.

That year, reproductions of Civil War forage caps, blue or gray with crossed sabers, came into our world. Every boy bought one. Just three boys got the rebel model, because where we lived, the indigenous saint was Abraham Lincoln and he took care of the slaveholders years ago, the men in gray. The three who bought the rebel model were the Emery brothers: Bill, Buck, and Dalton. They had nothing to do with the South. They were what was called commonass hoodlums, who already had a running battle going with the game warden and a flourishing business in stolen hubcaps. But these hats drew the brothers close for the first time, and entirely away from the rest of us. Bill, the youngest, was thin and humorless and the most daring thief. Buck was feebleminded and got his crewcut by the calendar so he always looked the same. He didn't appear to have had the same mother as the other two. Dalton, ready to graduate, charming and crooked, was prison bound. When the Emerys found out about my big Lincoln Logs set, they decided I was the brains behind the Union forces, the men in blue.

When the school bus dropped us off that night, I took the route past the old stone quarry, a place we caught sunfish in summer. A path went around the back of the quarry, so close to the water you could see the shear of stone that dropped into vertical invisibility at the shore. I could see the Emerys drifting along slowly behind me, but I was sure I could make the shortcut to my house before they caught up to me. I was wrong; they made a rush and overwhelmed me at the edge of the sumac.

Buck stood flat on the end of my foot while Dalton and Bill pushed me over backward.

My leg was in a cast for two months. But the torn ligaments didn't really heal until after summer began. My schoolwork suffered because the Emerys stared at me while I studied and asked to sign my cast, forcing me to refuse, making it appear that I was hostile toward them and the one causing all the trouble.

When my cast was cut off, my leg was thin and white.

Across the windblown playground where deer tracks appeared in the muck, Buck Emery watched my crooked walk.

Buck often rode the bus with me, never taking his dark, stupid eyes off my face. His straight stiff hair was even and short. From any angle there was always a spot where you could see straight through to his white scalp, luminous under the hair with a gristly glow.

There was a sentimental attempt to rehabilitate Dalton in his last term at school. He was so clearly going to do badly in life because of his suave and malicious disposition that it seemed appropriate to put him in a position of authority. It was hoped that a day would come when he would not see petty theft or feeling up girls as the be-all and end-all he viewed them as now. The principal appointed him one of the safety-patrol boys and gave him the crossed white shoulder straps that identified the officers. He wore them with his Confederate forage cap and supervised the boarding and exiting of the bus. One day when we stopped at the end of our road, he got off the bus with me and stared fixedly at my blue cap. He asked if I was still loyal to the boys in blue. I said that I was. But I knew he could see I was shaking. He said that if I was interested in my health, I would desert. As scared as I was, I thought of Abraham Lincoln and said, "Never."

"Have it your way."

MY BEDROOM WAS AN UNFINISHED ADDITION OVER THE attached garage. The walls were made of what was called beaverboard. I could step through a window at the far end of the room and into a huge, humid elm, go up and see the tops of the woods around us or climb down into the yard. I had a crystal set in my room and spent long hours wearing the earphones, moving the whisker of wire over the nugget of crystal in its lead enclosure trying to catch the radio signals borne through the air around me. The room had no heat. Instead I had a thin electric blanket whose wires stood through the fabric like varicose veins. The blanket had a white plastic control with a wheel, numbered 1 through 9. In January, 9 just got me through the night; by April I'd be down to 4; then in October I'd start back up the dial again. I think the crystal set and the electric blanket supplied me with the largest general ideas about the world I would acquire in my grammar-school years, vastly bigger than anything discovered in class, where the glacial communion of the three R's was held.

The last time that I used the 5 setting, Buck appeared in my window on a clear night and hung there, arms and legs spread to the corners of the window frame, wearing his cap and staring in at me in my bed. I didn't move throughout the long time he hung there, and I don't recall his climbing down. Instead, he seemed to disappear from the hypnotic center of the very fear I felt. I spent the rest of the night watching the same empty window in which I expected one day see the atomic flash marking the end of the world.

SUDDENLY IT WAS SPRINGTIME. FROGS ROARED IN THE WOODS. Jack-in-the-pulpits sprang from black mucky soil in secret. Pike appeared from the big lake and sought the muddy canal that crossed our woods and swamps. I could see them from the high bank, gulping water into their wolfish jaws and finning indolently beneath the undercut bank.

I started my paper route, learning all over again to put the three-way fold in the daily edition so it could be thrown like a piece of kindling. Among my newest subscribers were the Emerys. "I didn't know they could read," said my father jauntily.

I delivered their paper first. It completely threw my route off. If I rolled my papers before school, I could deliver the Emerys' paper immediately after school was out and while they were still finishing the chores their father required of them. Their father was in "haulage," his term for intermittent employment. Chores in haulage might consist of stacking scrap iron or salvaged copper pipe, and it might mean cutting down a wild honey tree the old man had found in the woods while the boys were in school. The Emerys ran a line of muskrat snares and gigged bullfrogs. They could take a copperhead in their hands with impunity and make it strike through a piece of inner tube stretched across the mouth of a mason jar, spitting its poison inside. My father said that the Emerys had ability, which was his way of accounting for those who, though doomed, were undeserving of remorse.

Some days there were no chores. Bill, Buck, and Dalton would be lined up silently on the lawn. I pitched the paper, sailing it past their expressionless faces. Then I made off on my bike, putting all my weight on first one pedal, then the other.

Summer was making its way right over the top of us. I played baseball after dinner, every one of the players sick on Red Man. I caught turtles. Because I hated books, my mother bribed me to read the Penrod stories and *The Master of Ballantrae*. Later, in the hope that I might be an entertainer, she drove me to play Mr. Interlocutor in the annual minstrel show. Wearing a swallowtail coat, I read in a hysterical voice from cards she had typed, crazy questions to Mr. Bones and others.

When the slow-moving green-to-brown water of the canal got warm enough, we swam in it. We drifted under the fallen trees that stretched over its mirror surface and caught the sunning turtles when they tumbled off. I had five of them, small painted and mud turtles whose cool weight in my hands and striving far-focused eyes thrilled me. The flare of shell, the arrangement of openings for head and legs, their symmetry and gleam of burnished camouflage, were aching to comprehend. I didn't deliver papers that week. It seemed half the town called my father about it. I wouldn't explain myself; I guess I had the feeling that others might be listening. My father looked on in confusion as my paper route was turned over to an Estonian boy down the canal who had recently joined the Confederacy.

I had a path in the sumac that wound through low ground to a bank of cattails where red-winged blackbirds flickered and sang. The maroon seeds had a salty taste, and to be undaunted by their rumored poison was part of the heroism of sojourning in the low ground. This same path crossed stands of milkweed with its pods of pagan silk and drew me close to the paper globes of hornets suspended in shadows. On the path I sometimes found a mother opossum with her infants stuck to her underside like stamps. The sumac path wound around and forked into itself. It seemed never to be the same from day to day. I now spent all my time in either the gravity of school supervision or close watching in my own home. My disappearances into the sumac were the only exception to all the unwelcome order.

I always wore my Federal cap on these junkets and carried a Barlow knife. I had wedged a piece of wood inside the knife that kept the blade point slightly exposed, so that it could be flicked open against the seam of my dungarees.

ON THE NINTH OF JUNE, I PLACED MY UNSATISFACTORY REport card on the kitchen table and headed for the sumac. I wandered down in it until I couldn't feel the heat of the sun but instead felt the cool breath of air from the mudbanks and sinkholes around me. A small hawk used my path for a whirling departure that cleared cobwebs at face level for fifty yards. At the first fork I found a snare that was meant for me. A powerful elm bough had been drawn down with a piece of old rope, the rope wound with vines, and the loop staked to the ground and covered with last year's brittle leaves. I tripped the snare with a stick, and the report of the bough carried through the bottom. I sat down and watched the rope snare turn in the air ten feet above me. In the climbing ground, I could hear the diminishing whisper of shrubs against pant legs. Then it was still.

I WAS TAKEN PRISONER THE FOURTH OF JULY, A DAY THAT will live in infamy. My parents left for a long weekend on a cabin cruiser, which was really how summer always started for us, not flowers or south winds so much as cabin cruisers. The Emerys must have known because they took me right at the foot of our road. Dalton got my Barlow knife, and when we reached the canal, Bill threw my forage cap into the water and shot it full of holes with his .22. I was held in a piano packing crate from Mr. Emery's haulage business.

"If you escape, we'll know where to find you," said Buck, with his way of looking through me. Buck was the one who would, years later, live alone with his father and help keep up the trapline. Dalton was in and out of prison. And Bill was killed in a rocket attack on the Mekong Delta. "If we have to go looking for you," Buck said, "we may finish you off." I know all this was talk, but there was something to Buck that lay outside of all agreements. He had shoved girls at school and disrupted the most official fire drills. No one used the drinking fountain without the fear that Buck Emery might push their teeth down on the chromium water jet.

"Just write a statement saying Abraham Lincoln was a coward and you go free," said Bill excitedly.

"But your knife is gone," said Dalton, "never to be seen again."

They left me with a pencil and a lined tablet in case I wanted to make a confession. I was given matches, a saucepan, a jug of water, and a box of Quaker Oats.

I saw the sun cross the sky and go into the swamp. The sound of frogs came up; not just the unpunctuated singing of the common green frogs but the abdominal bass of bullfrogs. The whip-poor-wills lasted an hour or two, and the screech owls came out. A cold spring moon mounted high above the piano crate, and I fell asleep as its white light poured through the slats.

When I woke up I was chilled deep down. It was just first light and Buck was staring in at me. "Do any writing?"

"No, and I won't."

"It's your funeral," he said in his thudding way. He bent his face to better see me. Then he was gone.

I dumped the oats into the saucepan and let them soak while I pulled down rough handfuls of splinters from the crate for a cooking fire. I had to have this to do. I was frantic inside the small box, getting close to battering myself against its insides. The morning light glittered on the links of chain holding the crate shut, and the frogs were silent in the cold. My hand shook when I lit the matches, not so much because I was chilled, or that I could not repudiate Lincoln, but because the box had seemed to shrink to an intolerable size and my heart was trying to pound its way out of my chest. When the fire was going, I threw the gruel that was meant for my breakfast out of the box onto the ground. It dripped slow and cold from the chain while the tongue of fire reached out from the splinters. I tore more wood loose and threw it atop the fire, forcing the flames to the side of the box and wishing it were the battlements of Vicksburg with the slavers inside watching their kingdom fall.

The smoke rolled over me and I grew faint. I remember thinking as I hovered between terror and opportunity that the sparks were like a shower of meteors on a winter night. I was quite certain I was burning up for glory.

The next thing I was in the Emery parlor, a plain room with antlers on the wall and a great painting of a waterfall so huge that the little tourists at its base seemed to cower at its majesty. I reeked of woodsmoke. The stairs to the second floor went up at a steep angle like a ladder. The carpet runner was just nailed to the risers. There were a lot of chairs, no two alike. Bill, Buck, and Dalton were in three of these chairs, and their father was standing over close to me where I was stretched out on the lumpy divan. Mr. Emery was little and hard and he had already cut a switch. He may very well have used it before I woke up, because the three looked like the most ordinary schoolboys you could picture. I was even scared of their old man.

I tried to tell from the way we walked as we went outside what he thought of me, but all I knew was that he was thinking, as we used to say, "in his mind." I caught a look of the boys watching. "They're not like you, are they," said Mr. Emery, almost to himself.

"No," I said, barely touching the word.

"They have to go and show off. I'm out of work, and the boys act like they wasn't all there."

I looked at the house. It seemed locked up like a dungeon. "You'll always have something you can do," said Mr. Emery. He had a way of holding a cigarette between his thumb and forefinger and curling it in toward the palm of his hand. "My boys will go where they're kicked. Anyway, why don't you get out of here where I don't have to look at you. I won't tell nobody you tried to burn us out."

"Thank you," I said.

TWO HOURS TO KILL

It was about a mile by car to the corrals and kennels. The trees were as tall as the pines in the North, maybe taller. But there was Spanish moss on them and on the cables that held up the telephone poles going along the road and turning up toward the house. Off to the north there were strips of lespedeza and partridge peas and some knocked-down field corn with crows flocking in it, tilting wedges of black in the autumn light. The weather that fall afternoon was still and warm, though the sun had the muted feeling of late in the year.

John Ray was waiting at the side of the corrals, a walking horse tied to an oak limb where he stood. He had called Hank at the dealership and given him the news of his mother. Hank had asked John Ray to get him a horse.

"I know you're shocked at me," Hank said, "but they can't get anyone out here for two hours, and I'm just not going to go up to that house. And there's nothing anyone can do now."

John Ray always looked starchy in his khaki working clothes, but he twisted around in them in a self-deprecatory way, as if to say that it was all one to him. There was a big bell on the side of the tack shed, and Hank asked him to ring it when the ambulance came.

"What did you find when you went up there?" Hank asked quietly.

"It wasn't no answer."

"So you just let yourself in?"

John Ray worked the bill of his cap in his fingers. "Yes, sir."

"Seem to go quietly?"

"I believe so, yes."

"In bed?"

"No, off in the side room there."

Hank looked over at the kennels. Pointers were jumping up and down the chain-link sides of it and barking. "Get Tess and Night for me, John, and I'll saddle up."

Hank went into the tack shed and pulled down an old worn trooper saddle with rings on it to tie canteens and check cords. There was a waterproof tied to it that hung down behind the stirrups like a shroud; dust had collected in the folds. Hank saddled the horse and put on its bridle. It was a great big dignified-looking shooting horse with a roached mane and a long homely head like you saw in old cavalry pictures, a smooth-mouthed bay that had been branded by four or five owners. Hank thought that when the courts were done with the estate, when his sisters came down from Cincinnati and his brother from Anchorage, this horse might collect some more brands.

So John Ray brought Tess and Night on a forked check cord. The two lunged and stretched out on their hind legs as John Ray helped Hank tie the end of the check cord behind the saddle. The two dogs then jumped out in front of the horse at the end of the rope while Hank mounted and started down the road behind them. The dogs dug in and seemed to strive to tow the horse, who sauntered along, absorbing the jerks as he had done with hundreds of other broke and unbroke bird dogs in the course of acquiring the four or five brands on his hip.

Hank went about a half mile off the end of the road. There was an overgrown sorghum field that practically abutted a stand of longleaf pine, and beyond that it was all broken-up little fields, some clear-cut; and where it had grown brushy, the hedgerows were laced up shut with vines and brambles of kudzu and wild honeysuckle. It was still too green and early. Hank normally waited until it had frozen and the frost-killed foliage had dried in the cold, because the dogs couldn't smell as well when it lay on the ground and rotted.

Hank got down off the horse, which stood empty-saddled, and held the straining dogs. He walked down the check cord and whoaed the two dogs, vaulting at the end of the rope toward the quail fields beyond. "Whoa, Tess," he said. "Whoa up now, Night." The dogs stood on all fours staring ahead and, except for the trembling that shook them, did not move when Hank unsnapped their shackles. He made them stand while he coiled the check cord carefully and walked back to the horse and tied the coil to the back of the saddle. They continued to stand while he remounted and sat for a long moment looking down at the waiting dogs and finally said, in a long-drawn-out utterance, "All night, now."

The dogs shot off on separate but somehow communicating angles, tails popping, heads high, as they ran through a small field of partridge peas and wire grass and shoemaker berries. They used up this field and cracked through a tall hedge, obliging Hank to canter along after them, losing them at the hedge and picking them up again in the next field, his shotgun slapping up under his left knee and coming out the far side with a strand of honeysuckle trailing from the trigger guard.

A big runoff ditch came up in the red soil, a place Hank normally rode out around, but he took it at a canter today and vaulted over it, seeing the big dark channel fly under him as he sailed into the rough growth. Hank thought about that ditch and wondered if he would jump it coming back. I'll jump it at great speed, he concluded.

When he came into the next field, the dogs were on point, Tess forward and Night behind at an angle, honoring. When Hank reined the bay past the low sun, the light flared red at the edge of the horse's nostrils. He stopped and got down, pulling the double-barreled gun from its scabbard, breaking and loading it while he kept one eye on the dogs. Night cat-walked a couple of steps, and Hank made a low sound of disapproval in his throat, and the dog stopped. Hank walked past the dogs, watching straight ahead for the covey rise. He presumed the birds were on the little elevation of ground under the old pines.

No birds, but the dogs were still on point, and Hank pulled off his hat to run his hand across his forehead. He didn't understand it. He went back and stood next to Tess and tried to figure out what she was pointing. Both dogs were quick to honor any shape that might be another dog on point. He got down on one knee and saw the gravestones. Tess and Night were absorbed in distant knowledge backing the grave markers just as they would back a shopping bag blown in off the highway. Hank shouted at them and gestured harshly with the gun. "Get out!" he shouted, and the dogs cowered off and watched him. He got back on the horse and pointed out ahead. The dogs resumed, a little slow at first.

Hank felt the blood recede from his face. There had been a community of tenant farmers here raising shade tobacco. The town was gone, the tobacco was gone, the church burned. Except for the graves, the people were altogether gone. Maybe they have heirs, he thought angrily, maybe they have rich sons of bitches living in Boca Raton who'd never fuss if I threw those headstones away.

There was a clear little swamp a mile or so farther on. It was circled by trees, and lily pads floated with their entirely green stems clearly visible for many feet underneath them. Quail had come out to feed, and the dogs pinned them down forty yards south of it. Hank got off his horse once again, prepared his gun, and walked the birds up. When the quail roared off, he dropped two of them. The rest of the covey made a whirling crescent into the trees. He tried to watch them down, at the same time calling Tess and Night in to retrieve—"Dead birds! Dead, Night; dead, Tess"—and, as they worked close, coursing over the ground the birds had fallen on, "Dayyyid" and "Dead!" when Tess picked one up and a triumphant "Dead!" when Night found the other and the two dogs brought them to hand.

He was sure he had watched the covey down fairly well when the bell began to ring, carrying pure as light turned to sound in the still trees. He stopped and gave it a listen. The music resumed, and he felt its pressure, a pressure as irritating as a command to begin dancing. He climbed on the horse and reined him toward the down covey.

Then the bell came again, this time without any of the music, like a probe or like the light that went on in his office, in the roar of the air conditioner that meant "Customer." I don't want this customer, he thought. He rode toward the swamp and felt a wave of courage that quickly receded. He wheeled the horse and yelled, "Tess, Night! Come here to me!" It's nearly dark, he thought, too dark to see that ditch. The dogs shot past, and in a moment he could not see them. He broke the horse into a rack until he saw the brush irrigated by the runoff. He pricked the horse lightly to set him up, released him, and felt as if he were going straight to heaven. The horse went down into the ditch, and Hank was knocked cold by impact as the horse scrambled without him, scared backward forty feet, and then turning to run home, dragging the broken reins.

He woke up in the ambulance. The driver was straight ahead of him, a black silhouette. The paramedic was next to him, a woman with a braid pinned up under a cap. Beside Hank was another figure, entirely covered.

"Don't drop me off first," he said.

"I'm sorry," the woman said, "but it is important that we drop you off first."

"I don't want to be dropped off first," said Hank.

"You we drop first," the woman said in a voice that had turned ugly.

City lights licked across the two in front. They arose, penetrated the windshield, and passed. Hank tried to anticipate them, and once when the ambulance was flooded at a stoplight, he looked over.

They wheeled him inside. He was in a room that sounded like a lavatory. People walked around him. When a doctor put a needle in his arm, he explained, "I really didn't want them to drop me off first." And then it came, a miracle of boredom.

PARTNERS

When Dean Robinson finally made partner at his law firm, his life changed. Edward Hooper, one of the older partners, did everything he could to make the transition easier. Between conferences and dinners with clients, the days of free-associating in his office seemed over for Dean. "You're certainly making this painless," Dean told him one hot afternoon when a suffocating breeze moved from the high plains through the city. Dean had felt he ought to say something.

"An older lawyer did the same for me," said Edward.

"I hope I can thank you in some way," said Dean, concealing his boredom.

"I thanked mine," said Edward, "by being the first to identify his senility and showing him the door." Dean perked up at this.

Edward Hooper's caution and scholarly style were not Dean's. Yet Dean found himself studying him, noting the three-piece suits, the circular tortoiseshell glasses, and the bulge of chest under the vest. It fascinated Dean that Edward's one escape from his work was not golf, not sailing or tennis, but the most vigorous kind of duck hunting, reclined in a layout boat with a hundred decoys, a shotgun in his arms, and the spray turning to sleet around him. At Christmas, Edward gave the secretaries duck he smoked himself, inedible gifts they threw out every year.

Friday evening, Edward caught Dean in the elevator. Edward wore a blue suit with a dark blue silver-striped tie, and instead of a briefcase he carried an old-fashioned brown accordion file with a string tie. He had a way of shooting his cuff to see his watch that seemed like a thrown punch. One side of the elevator was glass, affording a view of the edge of the city and the prairie beyond. Dean could imagine the aboriginal hunters out there and, in fact, he could almost picture Edward among them, avuncular, restrained, and armed with an atlatl. Grooved concrete shot past as they descended in the glass elevator. The door opened on a foyer almost a story and a half high with immense trees growing out of holes in the lobby floor. By this arrangement, award-winning architects had made the humans passing through denizens rather than occupants.

"Here's the deal," said Edward, turning in the foyer to genially stop Dean's progress. He had a way of fingering the edge of Dean's coat as he thought. "One of my clients wants me for dinner tomorrow night. Terry Turpin. He's not much fun, and I'd like you to walk through this with me. He's the biggest client we've got." Edward looked up from Dean's lapels to meet his eyes with his usual expression, which hovered between seriousness and mischief. For some reason, Dean felt something passing from Edward to himself.

"I see you massaging this fellow's great big ego," Edward went on, "forming a bond. It's shit work, but it's unique to our trade."

"I'll be there," said Dean, thinking of his ticket to elevated parking. It occurred to him that being the only unmarried partner was part of his selection, part of his utility as a partner. But being singled out by the canny and dignified Edward Hooper was a pleasure in itself. Actually, it didn't make sense.

DEAN LEFT HIS CAR IN TOWN ON SATURDAY NIGHT AND RODE out to the Turpins' with Edward. The house was of recent construction, standing down in a cottonwood grove where the original ranch house must have been; the lawn was carefully mowed and clipped around the old horse corral and plank loading chute. There was a deep groove in the even grass where thousands of cattle had gone to slaughter in simpler times. Dean and Edward stepped up to the door, Edward giving Dean a little thrust of the elbow as though to say *Here goes* and knocked. He had a lofty way of treating important moments as gags.

There came the barking of deep-throated dogs, and the door parted, then opened, fully revealing Gay Nell Turpin. She flung her arms around Dean, then held him away from her. She was an old girlfriend, actually his favorite one, and this hearty greeting concealed some lurid history, an old trick of well-situated women.

"I can't believe it!"

"Neither can I," said Dean, feeling the absurdity of his subdued reply. He hadn't seen her in a decade, and she was making him nervous. Gay Nell took him by the arm as though she needed it for support. "I haven't seen this man since spring break in nineteen-what." Terry Turpin appeared at the end of the front hall and blocked off most of its light. He took in his wife, clinging to Dean's arm. "A little wine," he said, "perhaps a couple of candles?"

Dean thrust out his free hand. "Dean Robinson," he said. "How do you do?"

"I'm getting there, pardner," said Terry Turpin, looking at the hand and then taking it. Terry still seemed like the football star he had been. Gay Nell had always had a football player, and this was certainly the big one. Dean had been a football player too, a disconsolate benchwarmer. Terry's face was undisguised by its contemporary cherubic haircut, his thighs by his vast slacks. He smiled at Edward without shaking his hand and turned to lead them into the living room. Dean, behind him, marveled at the expanse of his back. But the face was most astonishing: handsome, it was nevertheless the face of a Visigoth with tiny incongruous ears.

A television glowed silently in the living room, running national news, and when the sports came on, Terry took a remote channel changer from his pocket, flipped on the volume, got the scores, and turned it down again. Terry didn't pour them drinks, but he went to the bottles and named off the brands. Then he went to the half-size refrigerator, pulled open the door, and said, "Ice."

"You've really made this place your own," Edward said, gazing around. Is that a compliment? Dean wondered. Probably just amiable pandering, something he needed to learn.

"It is our own," said Terry.

Edward turned to Dean, but without full eye contact. "Terry has an air charter service that fills a gap."

"A gap?" said Terry. "The Northern Rockies?" Terry's excitement over this point gave Dean a chance to look at Gay Nell, still as pretty as when they had dated, holing up here and there. She had a long chestnut braid down the middle of her back and bright, black eyes that missed nothing. At one time, she had seemed to be astonished at everything she heard, a fizzy vitality that brought attention to herself. That astonishment had been modulated to the point that it was now a mystery whether she was hearing any of this at all, the bursts of enthusiasm less frequent, the absent gaze the more characteristic. Dean felt he interested her less now that flannel was a larger part of his day.

They moved like a drill team to the dining room. Next to the table was a vast window with a white grid overlay to suggest multiple panes. A pond had been dug out and landscaped, and the perfection of its grassy banks and evenly spaced, languorous willows depressed Dean. A silent woman in an apron began to serve the meal. Dean was in a swoon to find his old crush on Gay Nell still intact, though he missed the commode-hugging party girl she'd once been.

"Well," said Gay Nell, raising her glass. "How good to see everyone so healthy and so prosperous!" They all raised their glasses. The burgundy made red shadows on the tablecloth. Dean had his throbbing hand on Gay Nell's leg. Edward stared at him and he removed it. "And how thrilled we are to have you at our table tonight." Dean knew his Gay Nell; it took little to get her lubricating.

"You seem quiet," said Terry to Dean. I wonder if he noticed, Dean thought, looking back at the slab face with its small ears and the corded neck set about with alpaca. Gay Nell seemed serene, practically sleepy.

"Dean has learned restraint since rising to partnership. It's very becoming." No one patronized like an elder statesman better than Edward.

"Partner!" said Gay Nell. Only a pretty woman could chance a screech like this one. Dean jumped and Terry swung his big bovine face in the direction of his wife who all but cowered as she spun one of her several rings.

"They've got me on a trial basis. I could be sent down anytime."

"Oh, no, no, no," said Edward. "It's quite final. That's the charm."

"We haven't got titles in my racket," said Terry. "Just the balance sheet and a five-year plan."

Dean listened, nodding mechanically, and asked himself how Terry even got anyone to ride in his airplanes. He thought there would be a polite way to ask the question, but feared hearing all too clearly how America was beating a path to his hangar. And he sensed something else: that Terry could be bridling at the idea that a smooth transition was under way here, from Edward, the firm's certified gray eminence, to a rising star whose performance might be limited by an on-the-job-training atmosphere. Even Dean couldn't guess how much of this might be true. He dropped the thought because it led nowhere, and it was difficult to think of anything more than Gay Nell's leg, the yellow dress with its wet handprint.

Dinner seemed to go on and on, a less attractive form of nourishment, thought Dean, than an IV bottle. The work at hand was the airing of Terry's dream of "tying up the big open." When Dean raised his eyebrows slightly at this notion and looked across at Gay Nell, he realized she watched his lips, the very ones that had just said "big open," with rapture. It was a smoke screen for the leg operation and drew them closer in complicity. As she rippled her thigh he reexamined his theory that women were wild animals who preyed on little furry mammals such as men.

Nevertheless, this dinner, where something was meant to happen, reminded Dean of his poor preparation for a life of enterprise. He had managed to reach maturity still thinking that you sat down to dinner only in order to get something to eat. Any kind of ceremony, it turned out, ruined his appetite. Like a child panicked by broccoli, he stole a glance at his unfinished meal.

Edward drove Dean back to his car in silence. It was late enough that the streets were quiet. Then, as if to emphasize his silence, Edward turned on the radio. When they got to Dean's car, Edward said, "You didn't do well, Dean." Edward's face looked very serious. "And you had your hand on the leg of the client's wife. Good night."

Dean was in shock. After he had let himself into his apartment, he asked himself if he were crazy—he could think about nothing but Gay Nell and what he had viewed with pride as his courage that night—and decided that, well, maybe he was. He danced alone to Bob Marley's "Rebel Music," the weight of the partnership in direct conflict with the Jamaican beat.

ON MONDAY, AWKWARDNESS BETWEEN DEAN AND EDWARD could be felt throughout the office. It was equally certain to Dean that it was Edward's intention that this be so. They stopped outside the firm's library for the usual lighthearted word, and Edward gave him, he thought, rather a look. "How was your weekend?"

"It was all right," said Dean. "It was fine. Watched football. Took some dry cleaning. Uneventful."

"I see."

"Everything improved once the part with your client was behind me."

"Terry is a good client," said Edward boring into Dean with his stare.

The chill expanded from Edward to other key lawyers in three days, and the feeling that he was welcome was gone. Dean had plenty of work to do and his first thought was to do that, do it well in a blaze of productivity. Instead he called Gay Nell with the door of his office wide open. "I still love you," he said.

"Is that so," she inquired. "Strangest call of the year." When he hung up the phone, he felt ruin rising around him. He called Edward's office. "Edward, don't go around to your cronies and teach them to gaze at me like an undisciplined schoolboy. I don't enjoy it. Even though I'm a partner in the firm, it's taken all the strength I possess to stay interested in this inane profession in the first place." Edward breathed on the other end in astonishment. Dean hung up, pressing the phone into the cradle and holding it down with both hands. He began to stroll the office, speaking out loud. "Is there some sort of decertification procedure for new partners?"

Edward rang up on the interoffice line. "Terry in touch this a.m. Might go away."

"Good riddance. Less shit work for you."

In just moments, Edward was in the doorway, his face moving toward him. It was hypnotic. Was Edward on his feet? Was Dean's own chair gliding? Edward's face came forward, and as it became a mask, one that made a final and mythic ceremony of disappointment, an emotion too small to have ever held the attention of an important tribe. "You evil puke," said the mask. "We'll find a way to cut off your balls." This was the Edward Hooper that Dean had always heard about.

———

BUT SOMETHING QUITE DIFFERENT BEGAN TO HAPPEN. WORD got out that Dean had stood up to his client. In his despair, he had called Terry and told him to piss up a rope. Evan Crow, an estate planner, seized Dean's hand silently one afternoon. And when Dean suggested the whole thing didn't sit very well with Edward Hooper, Evan got out his actuarial tables and, massaging the bridge of his nose, pointed out that Edward wouldn't live long enough to make his opinion matter. Other lawyers in the firm stopped by, leaned into his office doorway clutching papers, and winked or left brief encouraging words that could be reinterpreted in a pinch. "Giving my all for love," Dean reflected, "seems merely to have advanced my career."

Finally, he bumped into Hooper once again. "Edward," said Dean, "I don't know if you realize how low the water supplies are in the Prairie Provinces. But in case you don't know or don't want to, let me tell you that the old potholes that made such a lovely nursery for waterfowl are very much dried up. Wheat farmers are draining the wetlands in the old duck factory."

"I don't get it. What's the punch line?"

"Do as you wish," Dean drawled. "But I think that it is very much in your best interests if you never shoot another duck."

Early one morning, before the coffee was made, before the messages from the day before were distributed through the offices and the informal chats had died out in the corridors, Dean's phone rang. It was Edward Hooper. Dean hadn't talked to him in months.

"Can you come down?"

Dean had just put the jacket of his suit over the back of his chair. He started to put it back on but, on second thought, ambled out the door toward Edward's office in his shirtsleeves, tie tugged to one side. He gave the closed door a single rap. One hand in his pocket, he eased the door open. Edward was at his desk. Under a wall of antique duck decoys sat Terry Turpin, elbows on the arms of a Windsor chair, fingers laced so that he could brace his front teeth on the balls of his thumbs. He seemed thoughtful. He tipped his face up and smiled with a vast owlish raising of his brows as if to say, *Where's the end to all this surprise?*

"Terry," said Edward measuredly, "asked to see you."

"My size has gotten to where I need to see everybody," Terry said, illustrating the idea of size with vast upturned mitts.

"I'd heard you were clear up to Alberta," said Dean.

"And the desert the other way."

"How's Gay Nell?"

"She's off to the coast for a cooking seminar. And we bought us a little getaway in Arizona."

"All that cactus." Dean sighed, hinting most gently that going to Arizona might not be the brightest idea in the world.

"Let's come to order," Edward broke in. "I think Terry is looking for a little perspective on his air freight and charter service."

"No, Edward," said Terry patiently. "On everything."

"I meant that," said Edward.

"Ed, try to stay one jump ahead of me, okay?"

"Okay," said Edward, looking into the papers in his lap.

Sometimes, Dean thought, silence can have such purity. It was so quiet in the room, like the silence of a house in winter when the furnace quits. Edward got to his feet slowly. He's going to leave this building, thought Dean.

Edward shaped and adjusted the papers in his hand. He looked at them and squared up their corners. He set them on the desk. He gave Terry a small, almost-Oriental smile. "Goodbye," he said, "you deserve each other." He sauntered out, his gait peculiarly loosened.

"Well, he looked happy," said Terry with a pained expression. "What do you suppose he meant by that? Am I following this?"

THE ROAD ATLAS

Across the way, a woman was posting the special in the window of the hotel. It was hot all along the street, and the sky was hazy from the evaporation of irrigated fields. Bill Berryhill came out of his brothers' office and looked for his car. He was wondering why he could not get through a common business discussion with them without talk of level playing fields, a smoking gun, a hand that would not tremble, who was on board, and what was on line. When he got up from the table and said he had other things to do, Walter, the eldest brother, took the cold cigar from his lips and dangled it reflectively.

"Billy," he said, "this is a family. Without your interest we're clear to the axle. What are we going to do?"

Bill enjoyed the iridescence of this sort of thing and never meant to bring it to a stop. Walter was being a little bit dull, though, looking at Bill's eyes for his answer.

"I'm not a team player," said Bill. "It's sad, isn't it?"

The middle brother, John, wearing a bow tie and blazer, busied himself with papers, jerked his chin with a laugh.

"Where does that leave us?" John asked, clearly expecting no sane reply.

"You'll just have to thumb it in soft," said Bill.

He found his car next to the hardware store, a pink parking ticket fluttering under the windshield wiper. Beneath the other wiper blade, old tickets curled and weathered. The car, a Cadillac of a certain age, had a tall antenna on its roof. Inside, a big radio was bolted to the dash with galvanized brackets. Bill Berryhill relied on this for his cattle and commodity reports. A border collie slept on the backseat, among receipts, mineral blocks, and rolls of barbed wire. He had a saddle in the trunk.

I seem to lose my energy in those meetings, Bill thought. He fished a Milk-Bone out of the glove box, and the border collie got to her feet. "Here, Elaine," he said and reached it back. She snapped it away from him and he started the car. A glow of irrigation steam hung over everything. A breeze, an August breeze, would make it more comfortable but less beautiful. A woman ambled by, loosening the armholes of her wash dress. Bill angled the vent window at himself and drove through town, dialing at the big radio. He swept through the band before finding Omaha; he slumped down and took in the numbers.

He drove way out north of Thorne and up through the sage flats to his trailer house, trying to hit the Maxwell House can with his snoose. The trailer sat on a flat of land under a bright white rim of rock. It seemed to belong there. Bill had improved a spring above the house with a collection box. A chain-link kennel and a horse corral had shelters with a steel feeder for hay. He had his cutting horse in there and a using horse. The cutting horse was called Red Dust Number Seven, and the using horse was called Louie Louie. There was a window box with some dope plants and a neat row of mountain ash around the front of the trailer. On the rimrock above the trailer sat the satellite dish, and it provided great reception for Bill's favorite shows: Wimbledon, the World Series, the Kentucky Derby, the America's Cup, prizefights, and elections. He went inside shooing flies as he went.

He turned on CNN for the news loop and called Ellen on the phone and asked her for lunch. He started a small sandwich assembly line. "As against apathy," he told himself, "I have the change of seasons, the flowing waters, and the possible divestiture of my brothers." Bill had wanted a sensible mix of conservative investments he wouldn't have to think about. But John and Walter had gotten them into an RV distributor, a cow herd, a gasohol plant, and a grain elevator. Bill wasn't interested in these going concerns, and he felt guilty about shirking all the fellow feeling. If only he could interest himself in keeping up with the Joneses, he could head off the troubling clouds.

From the window over the sink, he could see two irrigators cross the hillside carrying rolled-up dams on their shoulders; the ends of the fabric blew in the drying wind. One man had a shovel, and a small red-heeler dog bounced behind them.

Maybe Ellen and I can make something out of all this, he thought.

Bill made the sandwiches. News briefs from the theater-sized screen threw parti-colored shadows around the trailer walls. Quarterlies piled by the recliner chair were wedged inside each other to mark the places Bill had left off. Ellen knocked on the door and came in. Bill was putting the lunch on the table. When she closed the door, the aluminum walls shook. "How are you?"

"I'm great," she said. She was a strong-featured brunette in her late twenties. Her hands were coarsened by outside work, but it made her more attractive, a widow. She came for lunch fairly often and sat right down and began eating. They each liked ice water, and Bill put a chiming pitcher of it on the table. He gazed around at the condiments. She reached him the Tabasco from behind the ice-water pitcher. They ate in relaxed silence. This is really nice, thought Bill. "I'm not getting anywhere with my brothers and it's my fault," he said. "Goddamn it, this is Big Sky Country, this is the American West. It shouldn't be a problem."

"It's a problem if you're so defeated by it."

Bill wished they could make love after lunch. All energy would pass to his abdominal nerves. But it was out of the question. Volition would fill the air. And it seemed he didn't want that. Bill and Ellen had a lot in common, not as much as Bill would wish, but many things: a love of reading, wryness, superfluous lives on land that had gone up in value while losing its utility. It could seem to him that her bereavement was her real location. She sustained in her actual home the air of a life lived elsewhere, just as Bill's education had removed him. More than that, they faced lives that could be behind them. Bill thought that while it terrified him, it might well have consoled Ellen to know that the struggle for love and wholeness did not have to be gone through again. He even thought it was mean-spirited to view her beauty and merit as things wasted because they were not offered up to use. Still, all such considerations produced cloudiness and an irresolute foreground.

"I met a girl at that little gift shop who wanted to meet you. Tina. Said she could come out. I'm sure she'll sleep with you."

"I'll have to look into it," Bill said wanly. His brothers weren't like this. They'd show merriment for Tina. They'd want to get them a little and not think it over. Bill reached across and took Ellen's hand. It was strong. It weighed something. He wished she wouldn't smile when she looked at him. She wasn't pornographic. Sometimes when he went volitionless, her eyes glittered as though a little victory were at hand. What victory? Watching someone pull himself out of a hole?

A small cloudburst hit the trailer, the kind you can see all the way around in the mountains. Bill got up to look out. It hit so suddenly that the drops of water threw dust in the air. His two horses swiveled into the wind, their tails blown up along their flanks. Then it stopped and Bill opened the door to let the air, fragrant with cedar, fill the trailer. He sat down and refilled their ice water.

"Let's do something this year before it's too late," Bill said.

"For example?"

"I'd like to go to Monticello," said Bill. But suddenly he could not understand why it had to be impossible for him and Ellen to be happy in an ordinary way. Then it subsided. Monticello went in one ear and out the other.

"Why don't we make a real trip," he said. "We'll take the horses and go to Texas. That'll get us south and sort of east. We'll be almost there."

"The Texans will be funny. We can go to the Alamo."

"If it's all right, I'd like to visit Bunker Hill."

"Then let's leave our horses at home."

"I don't feel like eating," said Bill.

"I really can't appeal to your needs, can I?" said Ellen.

But as the days went by, the trip did acquire some actuality. They bought a road atlas, even though Bill had often said the road atlas had ruined American life. But the road atlas made it clear that their trip was pretty much of a zigzag. Still, they spent frequent evenings in the trailer foreseeing the meaning of their destinations.

JOHN AND WALTER ASKED IF THEY COULD ALL HAVE A DRINK at the hotel. When they got there, Bill was already seated next to the pensioners in the lobby. An old cowboy with a tray bolted to his electric wheelchair shot in and out of the bar delivering drinks. The three sat around a table that gave them some distance from others and moved their whiskey thoughtfully on coasters like Ouija styluses. John produced a sentimental appearance in his bow tie, his hair parted closer to the crown than was currently fashionable. Walter, astonished gull-wing eyebrows and dark jowels, looked the power broker he was with his wide tie and grim suit. They weren't such bad fellows, Bill thought. They have the advantage of the here and now, and Bill was man enough not to blame his slipping gears on them.

"What's the deal on the cows?" Walter asked.

"I'm going to can about thirty head."

"How come?"

"Old, dry."

"Ship all the steer calves?"

"I don't think so," Bill said. "The market's not very good, but it has to get some better. Fifty-five counties in drought relief. A lot of cattle went through early. It'll be back a little by fall. But I want to hold the heifers over and sell them as replacements. I don't see two droughts in a row."

"What'll you do after you ship? You going to feed them yourself?" Walter said with an ironic smile, his mouth left of center.

"No, Walter. I'm going to hire that out," Bill almost shouted.

"Easy, big feller," said Walter. "Be cool."

"Refill?" asked John, holding his arm up. A little circular gesture told the old cowboy to scoot into the atmospheric lighting of the bar. John began to talk with his air of halting introspection. He was very likely to say something specious, but the appearance of its having been tugged from the depths of consideration made him difficult to contradict.

"Walt and I have been kind of forging ahead all year as though we had your proxy."

"So you have," Bill said. He gave a vast sigh.

"We take it that things can't stagnate altogether and the day will come when you'll want to get a grip, but that day is not here now."

"That sort of describes it," Bill said. "And it sort of doesn't. I see the three of us as being fortunate, don't you?"

"What we have long understood," said Walter, "is that you feel a mandate for greater meaning, and we don't oppose that. John and me are just two little old MBAs. We want more of what we've got, and we're too old to change. When we get this thing right, we—or one of us—might run for office."

"But," John cut in, "by way of reassuring you, Bill. We're thriving on all the fronts we have chosen to fight on."

"Oh, yeah? What about the gasohol plant?"

"We dialed it down to an enriched feeder deal. The pig guys are knocking our door down."

"I thought maybe you trapped yourself there. Do you want to buy me out?"

"Not necessarily," said John, indenting the bows of his tie. "No doubt we would disagree about valuation."

As soon as John began to demur, sinking his chin into the softness of his neck, Walter cut across and said, "Let's say that's the case. No one was ever killed by a hypothesis."

"Ten times earnings," Bill said.

John's and Walter's disparaging chuckles were hair-trigger affairs that gave them away better than anything Bill could have made up. Bill saw himself as Jefferson while John and Walter were the twin halves of Hamilton's brain.

"Come on, you crooks, give me a number," said Bill, and his brothers raised their eyes to the plaster ceiling. Just then, Bill felt a gust of power in the room, a brief touch of the thing that held these men's interest, and he did not necessarily despise it any more than he would despise weather. If he ever worked it out with Ellen, he might not want to have mishandled this. "The trouble with this sort of thing," said Bill, "is you never know who the Honest Johns are, do you? I mean, we hang it on profits, and the company suddenly goes into a long-range development plan, and the profits go down."

Walter was hot. "How do you go into long-range development retailing RVs and selling pig feed?"

"You'd find a way," said Bill.

Before things got out of hand, John spoke up. "You've got the performance to date. Our little-bitty deal couldn't stand hostility. We could never move around with that hanging over us."

"Rest assured the cows aren't going into long-range development," said Bill. "I'm holding my end down."

"Don't be a son of a bitch," said Walter. Walter didn't give a damn right now, and you had to listen to him.

"It's clear the both of you view me as a problem."

"No, we don't," John chimed in. "But your search for meaning is a bore."

Bill felt trapped by the characterization. These brutes were sincere. Walter and John got to their feet. This was going nowhere.

BILL HAD HIRED AN ACID CASUALTY TO FEED CATTLE FOR him, an ideal hand who never looked to the right or the left and kept his mind firmly on a job it was very hard for most people to keep their minds on. He called himself Waylon Remington, though Bill was quite sure that was not really his name. All that was left of Waylon's hairdo from the good-time days was a long goatee. He talked to himself.

It had taken Bill a long time to get used to lining Waylon Remington out on a job. He would give Waylon his instructions and get no reaction whatsoever. It was fairly disconcerting until Bill realized that Waylon heard him perfectly well and would act as instructed. But Bill felt very solitary telling him what to do as though making a speech in an empty room.

Today, he explained to Waylon Remington how he wanted his stackyard arranged. "Just get the big hay panels from near the house and wire them up in a square around the stack. Make sure your entryway is on level ground so you can get in and out with the tractor." Bill and Waylon were driving down through the hay meadow as Bill spoke. "And use plenty of steel stakes on those panels around the entry, or the whole shitaree will fall down. Remember you have to drive that tractor all the way around the stack to get ahold of the round bales." Waylon Remington stared at the hood ornament.

"Now," said Bill as they reached the irrigation headgate, "let's get out here." The two got out and went to the flume. It was about half full. The water took off toward the south, split up a couple of times, and fanned onto the field. "Now, Waylon." Bill glanced over at Waylon Remington, just two feet away. His mouth was open, and Bill could hear the breath in his teeth; his lower lip was cracked and dry. "I need for you to be moving those dams just once a day from now on because we're starting to lose our water for the year. Keep moving them twelve steps at a time but one time a day instead of three."

He went down alongside the Parshall flume. "Keep track of these numbers on the gauge. If you see a big change, either up or down, come get me, and we'll read the tables and make another plan. You never know when they'll shut down the center pivots upstream. So, it could change . . . Waylon?"

Bill wanted to get the horses, but he wasn't confident Waylon could keep a horse moving; so he put the truck into four-wheel drive and took him around four or five more projects. Tighten about a mile and a half of fence, adding clips and stays as he went. Fix the chain in the manure spreader. Add hydraulic fluid to the front-end loader and hit all the grease zerks. They drove past the salt blocks set out in old tractor tires, checked fly rubs, tanks, and springs. This didn't require Bill to talk, and it got pretty quiet in the cab. Then Waylon Remington began to hum. He hummed the Jefferson Airplane's "White Rabbit." Bill began to panic. Could he really leave?

BILL PUT FIVE YEARLINGS INTO THE PEN AND WARMED UP RED Dust Number Seven in front of them. The young horse was cinchy and liable to buck the first few minutes. He stopped him and rolled him back a couple of times.

Bill trotted Red in a circle. He had him in a twisted wire snaffle and draw reins, and he kept Red's head just flexed enough that he could see the glint of his eye on the inside of the circle. Red was getting so that if Bill took a deep seat and moved his feet forward in the stirrups he would start down into his stop. Then he'd likely as not run his head up and be piggy about turning. This was where Bill thought he was the roughest. Red kind of straightened up when he had a cow in front of him.

Bill cut a yearling out of the small herd. The steer just stopped and took things in. The steer moved, and Red boiled over, squealing and running off. Bill took a light hold of him, rode him in a big circle, then back to the same place on the steer. This time, Red lowered himself and waited; and when the cow moved, he sat right hard on his hocks, broke off, stopped hard, and came back inside the cow. Now he was working, his ears forward, his eyes bright. This little horse was such a cow horse; he sometimes couldn't stand the pressure he put on himself. The steer then threw a number 9 in his tail and bolted. Red stopped it right in front of the herd. He was low all over, ready to move anywhere. Bill tipped his head and saw the glint: of eye and the bright flare at his nostrils. Bill cut another cow.

This one traveled more and let Bill free Red, moving fast across the pen. Bill was pleased to be reminded that this was a horse you could call on and use. After a minute more, Red was blowing, and Bill put his hand down on his neck to release him.

The colt's head came up as though he were emerging from a dream, and he looked around. Bill wished he never had to be anywhere else.

FIRST, THEY WERE GOING TO DRIVE, THEN A NERVOUSNESS about being gone so long came over them. Bill said, "Why are we going on this trip anyway?"

"I wanted to go to the Alamo, and then you wanted to go to Monticello, I think, and Bunker Hill."

"What happened to that?"

"You said the Texans would be funny and let's skip Texas. And then we were going to go—I don't know, something about Thomas Jefferson."

"That seems inappropriate. We'd spend the whole time explaining to strangers what we were doing."

"Well, we'll just go somewhere else," Ellen said. She was looking long and hard at Bill, who was clearly in some kind of turmoil. He knew that, even while they talked, his brothers were making things happen. Bill didn't seem to want what he and his brothers owned, but he didn't want it taken away.

"I don't know about Monticello," he said. "It's just a big house. The Alamo and Bunker Hill speak for themselves." Bill felt serious failure very close now.

"Listen," she said, "I'm going to take this trip." In her green cotton shirt, she seemed mighty. Bill didn't say anything. "You ought to come, Bill. But I'm beginning to think you won't."

"I'm going to miss you. You think I've just quit, don't you?"

"I don't know whether you have or not," she said. "But something's got to give. What'd you do with the road atlas?"

FLIGHT

During bird season, dogs circle each other in my kitchen, shell vests are piled in the mudroom, all drains are clogged with feathers, and hunters work up hangover remedies at the icebox. As a diurnal man, I gloat at these presences, estimating who will and who will not shoot well.

This year was different in that Dan Ashaway arrived seriously ill. Yet this morning, he was nearly the only clear-eyed man in the kitchen. He helped make the vast breakfast of grouse hash, eggs, juice, and coffee. Bill Upton and his brother, Jerry, who were miserable, loaded dogs and made a penitentially early start. I pushed away some dishes and lit a breakfast cigar. Dan refilled our coffee and sat down. We've hunted birds together for years. I live here, and Dan flies in from Philadelphia. Anyway, this seemed like the moment. "How bad off are you?" I asked.

"I'm not going to get well," said Dan directly, shrugging and dropping his hands to the arms of his chair. That was that. "Let's get started."

We took Dan's dogs at his insistence. They jumped into the aluminum boxes on the back of the truck when he said, "Load": Bonny, a liver-and-white female, and Sally, a small bitch with a banded face. These were—I should say are—two dead-broke pointers who found birds and retrieved without much handling. Dan didn't even own a whistle.

As we drove toward Roundup, the entire pressure of my thoughts was of how remarkable it was to be alive. It seemed a strange and merry realization. The dogs rode so quietly I had occasion to remember when Bonny was a pup and yodeled in her box, drawing stares in all the towns. Since then she had quieted down and grown solid at her job. She and Sally had hunted everywhere from Albany, Georgia, to Wilsall, Montana. Sally was born broke, but Bonny had the better nose.

We drove between two ranges of desertic mountains, low ranges without snow or evergreens. Section fences climbed infrequently and disappeared over the top or into blue sky. There was one little band of cattle trailed by a cowboy and a dog, the only signs of life. Dan was pressing sixteen-gauge shells into the elastic loops of his cartridge belt. He was wearing blue policeman's suspenders and a brown felt hat, a businessman's worn-out Dobbs.

We watched a harrier course the ground under a bluff, sharp-tailed grouse jumping in his wake. The harrier missed a half dozen, wheeled on one wing tip, and nailed a bird in a pop of down and feathers. As we resumed driving, the hawk was hooded over its prey, stripping meat from the breast.

Every time the dirt road climbed to a new vantage point, the country changed. For a long time, a green creek in a tunnel of willows was alongside us; then it went off under a bridge, and we climbed away to the north. When we came out of the low ground, there seemed no end to the country before us: a great wide prairie with contours as unquestionable as the sea. There were buttes pried up from its surface and yawning coulees with streaks of brush where the springs were. We had to abandon logic to stop and leave the truck behind. Dan beamed and said, "Here's the spot for a big nap." The remark startled me. "Have we crossed the stage-coach road?" Dan asked.

"Couple miles back."

"Where did we jump all those sage hens in 1965?"

"Right where the stagecoach road passed the old hotel." Dan had awarded himself a little English sixteen-gauge for graduating from Wharton that year. It was in the gun rack behind our heads now, the bluing gone and its hinge pin shot loose, groove in the stock where he used it to hold down barbed wire when climbing fences.

"It's amazing we found anything," said Dan from afar, "with the kind of run-off dog we had. Rip Tide. You had to preach religion to Rip every hundred yards or he'd leave us. Remember? I can't believe we fed that common bastard." Rip Tide was a dog with no talent, loyalty, or affection, a dog we swore would drive us to racket sports. Dan gave him away in Georgia, and he made a great horse-back dog, just too much for guys on foot.

"He found the sage hens."

"But when we got on the back side of the Little Snowies, remember? He went right through all those sharptails like a train. We should have had deer rifles. A real wonder dog. I wonder where he is. I wonder what he's doing. Nineteen sixty-five. I'll be damned."

The stagecoach road came in around from the east again, and we stopped: two modest ruts heading into the hills. We released the dogs and followed the road around for half an hour. It took us past an old buffalo wallow filled with water. Some teal got up into the wind and wheeled off over the prairie.

About a mile later the dogs went on point. It was hard to say who struck and who backed. Sally cat-walked a little, relocated, and stopped; then Bonny honored her point. So we knew we had moving birds and got up on them fast. The dogs stayed staunch, and the long covey rise went off like something tearing. I killed a going-away, and Dan made a clean left and right. It was nice to be reminded of his strong heads-up shooting. I always crawled all over my gun and lost some quickness, too much waterfowling when I was young. Dan had never been out of the uplands and had speed to show for it.

Bonny and Sally picked up the birds; they came back with eyes crinkled, grouse in their mouths. They dropped the birds, and Dan caught Sally with a finger through her collar. Bonny shot back for the last bird. She was the better marking dog.

We shot another brace in a ravine. The dogs pointed shoulder to shoulder, and the birds towered. We retrieved those, walked up a single, and headed for a hillside spring with a bar of bright buckbrush, where we nooned up with the dogs. The pretty bitches put their noses in the cold water and lifted their heads to smile when they got out of breath drinking. Then they pitched down for a rest. We broke the guns open and set them out of the way. I laid a piece of paper down and arranged some sandwiches and tangy apples from my own tree. We stretched out on one elbow, ate with a free hand, and looked off over the prairie, to me the most beautiful thing in the world. I wish I could see all the grasslands while we still have them. Then I couldn't stand it. "What do you mean you're not going to get better?"

"It's true, old pal. It's quite final. But listen, today I'm not thinking about it."

I was a little sore at myself. We've all got to go, I thought. It's like waiting for an alarm to go off when it's too dark to read the dial. Looking at Dan's great chest straining his policeman's suspenders, it was fairly unimaginable that anything predictable could turn him to dust. I was quite wrong about that.

A solitary antelope buck stopped to look at us from a great distance. Dan put his hat on the barrels of his gun and decoyed the foolish animal to thirty yards before it snorted and ran off. We had sometimes found antelope blinds the Indians had built, usually not far from the eagle traps, clever things made by vital hands. There were old cartridge cases next to the spring, lying in the dirt, .45-70s; maybe a fight, maybe an old rancher hunting antelope with a cavalry rifle. Who knows. A trembling mirage appeared to the south, blue and banded with hills and distance. All around us the prairie creaked with life. I tried to picture the Indians, the soldiers. I kind of could. Were they gone or were they not?

"I don't know if I want to shoot a limit."

"Let's find them first," I said. I would have plenty of time to think about that remark later.

Dan thought and then said, "That's interesting. We'll find them and decide if we want to limit out or let it stand." The pointers got up, stretched their backs, glanced at us, wagged once, and lay down again next to the spring. I had gotten a queer feeling. Dan went quiet. He stared off. After a minute, a smile shot over his face. The dogs had been watching for that, and we were all on our feet and moving.

"This is it," Dan said, to the dogs or to me; I was never sure which. Bonny and Sally cracked off, casting into the wind, Bonny making the bigger race, Sally filling in with meticulous groundwork. I could sense Dan's pleasure in these fast and beautiful bracemates.

"When you hunt these girls," he said, "you've got to step up their rations with hamburger, eggs, bacon drippings—you know, mixed in with that kibble. On real hot days, you put electrolytes in their drinking water. Bonny comes into heat in April and October; Sally, March and September. Sally runs a little fever with her heat and shouldn't be hunted in hot weather for the first week and a half. I always let them stay in the house. I put them in a roading harness by August first to get them in shape. They've both been roaded horseback."

I began to feel dazed and heavy. Maybe life wasn't something you lost at the end of a long fight. But I let myself off and thought, These things can go on and on.

Sally pitched over the top of a coulee. Bonny went in and up the other side. There was a shadow that crossed the deep grass at the head of the draw. Sally locked up on point just at the rim, and Dan waved Bonny in. She came in from the other side, hit the scent, sank into a running slink, and pointed.

Dan smiled at me and said, "Wish me luck." He closed his gun, walked over the rim, and sank from sight. I sat on the ground until I heard the report. After a bit the covey started to get up, eight dusky birds that went off on a climbing course. I whistled my dogs in and started for my truck.

VICIOUS CIRCLE

John Briggs sat on his porch on a dreary hot August day with a glass of ice water sweating in his hand, listening to opera on the radio. The white borders of the screen doors were incandescent with mountain summer. Through them he could see the high windswept ridge above his house, where the bunchgrass could not get a hold, leaving only a seam of shale to overlook the irrigated valley.

Earlier, at the farmers' market at the fairgrounds, he'd strolled among the pleasant displays of food and craft. A bearded youth offered handmade walking sticks; next to him, with a cage full of rabbits, a woman in a Chiapas folk costume sold angora tooth-fairy pillows while tugging strands of angora from a rabbit asleep in her lap. An extraordinary variety of concrete yard animals surrounded a display of bird feeders with expired Montana license plates folded for roofs. A hearty woman with her fists on her hips offered English delphiniums, which, she explained again and again, had never been crossed with Pacific Giants, "not ever!" The Hutterites, in suspenders and straw cowboy hats, had a vast array of vegetables; their long table faced lines of people, five deep, eyes fixed upon the produce. A girl in jeans and a bustier played a harp, almost inaudible over the sounds of the crowd, beside a table selling geodes and specimens of quartz.

Briggs had a large shopping bag into which he placed his purchases: carrots, kohlrabi, baby beets bought from a woman in a Humane Society T-shirt, and Flathead Lake cherries from an old man in an OFFICIAL PARTY SHIRT from Carlos'n Charlie's in Cozumel. A woman with the forearms of a plumber spotted Briggs and stepped from behind a meager display of homegrown lavender to block his path. She gazed at him fixedly and, as he grew uncomfortable, asked, "Is anything coming to you?"

Briggs shook his head tentatively. The woman let out a vehement laugh with a faint whistle in it. A mirthless grin spread ear to ear.

"Is it possible," she asked, "that you don't remember me at all? Two a.m.? January? Roswell, New Mexico? Ring a bell?"

Trying to conceal his discomfort, Briggs said that he was afraid it was possible he didn't remember.

"You glutton!" she roared.

He could see that the onlookers were not on his side. The woman followed him for several yards, a steady, accusing stare as he made his way through lanes of boxed produce. He heard the word "glutton" again, over the otherwise gentle murmur of the market. He also heard her ask the crowd whether people like him ever got enough. She was right; it was outrageous that such a thing could have slipped his mind, whatever it was. He was dismayed to have shared some potent event with this woman and be now unable to even recall it. He tried again, but nothing came. Perhaps it had been long ago—but no, she'd said January. Was he losing his memory?

He stopped to look at the midsummer light bouncing off the hoods of cars lined up alongside the park. Someone touched his elbow, and he turned to a young woman with a blue bandanna tied around her neck. She had on one arm a basket filled with parsnips, heavy August tomatoes, onions shedding golden paper in the hard light. "Don't blame yourself," she said shyly. "She's asked a dozen people the same question, and they couldn't remember either." The woman seemed to redden. He was greatly absorbed by her gray eyes and her fine, clear forehead; it seemed to him the kind of face that only profound innocence could produce.

Her name was Olivia, she said, and she was buying vegetables for herself and her father. Not today, not tomorrow, not until Wednesday could she meet for a drink. In fact, she didn't want to meet for a drink at all, but in the end they could agree on no convenient meeting place other than a bar. He would have to wait.

Olivia was on time. She'd suggested the Stockman Hotel, which had a popular bar and was midway between their homes. Her yellow cotton dress was stylish but out-of-date, maybe a generation out-of-date, and must not have originally belonged to her—an elegant hand-me-down. The bar was busy with ranchers, an insurance man, a woman who drove for UPS, and two palladium miners;

everyone was talking, except for three men from a highway crew who didn't know anyone and stared straight ahead, holding their beers with both hands. An empty booth remained, and Briggs led her there, trying not to appear coercive. Olivia sat quickly, clasping her fingers, elbows on the table, and looked around. She seemed happy. Her shoulder-length hair was parted in the middle and pulled behind small, pretty ears that were unpierced. She had a sensual mouth for a shy girl, though he supposed he ought not to have seen this as a contradiction.

"Do you know something?" she said, almost whispering. "I don't remember your name."

"John Briggs."

"Oh. I see. Just like that."

"What do you mean?"

"I mean . . . it's just two syllables!"

"I know. It's like a dirge or a march, isn't it?" he said.

"John-Briggs-John-Briggs-John-Briggs," she chanted.

"Exactly. In second grade, Jerome Ozolinsch sat next to me, and he had such a hard time learning to spell his own name, I became grateful for mine's brevity. I worried about other things instead. I wished for jet-black hair that would lie flat like Superman's." His own hair was russet brown and sprang out. He wished he'd said "shortness" instead of "brevity." There was something silly about the phrase "grateful for mine's brevity," but it seemed to have gone unnoted.

A barmaid came to their table, in jeans and a T-shirt advertising a whale-watching boat on Prince of Wales Island; the breaching whale in the drawing was bigger than the boat, whose worshipful passengers were lined up like a choir. She knew Olivia, and they exchanged pleasantries. Briggs ordered a St. Pauli Girl, and Olivia ordered a double shot of Jim Beam, with a water back.

Briggs was careful not to react. When their order was in, Olivia studied the time on her watch and then on the wall clock, before adjusting the watch. "Four forty-two," she said.

He guessed she was nearly, but not quite, thirty, at least a decade younger than him. She wore no rings or other insignia and, in general, was remarkably undecorated, though a glance revealed possible eyeliner and just enough lipstick, the absence of which might have been odd—not pretentious, but odd. Her eyes traveled around the bar and landed on him, just as their drinks arrived. "Still hot," she said, and smiled brilliantly.

This felt like a journey to Briggs, though he couldn't have said why.

"Still hot," he concurred, thinking, I need to add something. Hot plus what: Dry? Windy?

"Drought-drought-drought," she said, much as she'd said his name, in modest march time. "We lost our well and had to drill another, two hundred feet at I forget how much a foot, but a lot. Ruined our yard, that man out there with his machine, hammering away."

"I saw on the bank that it's ninety-seven." Jesus Christ, Briggs thought, tell her you saw a zebra!

As she drank, reacting to the bitterness of the whiskey, she looked straight at him. "You know what would be so sweet," she said, "is if you'd get me a paper from the lobby." Smiling in compliance, Briggs got up and went out. At a table in the large bay window, three young Mormons in suits craned to watch the heat-struck pedestrians. One unfurled the sports section of the *Gazette*; another leaned forward, holding his head in his hands. Briggs dropped a quarter into the honor-system jar and took a copy of the paper to Olivia. She had a new drink in front of her.

The bar's manager, Jerry Warren, who was small, ingratiating, and somehow like a frog in a polo shirt, sidled up to the table. Olivia knew him.

"In September," he said, "I'm going to Ireland—"

"Are you Irish?" Briggs interrupted.

"No, to hike the Ring of Kerry, hike all day, booze till two, feel up German girls—"

Briggs glanced at an expressionless Olivia.

"—and visit ring forts or the odd castle. The brochure promises your money back if you don't, like, burst into spontaneous verse by day two, though I expect most of the poetry ends up being directed at your raincoat." He rested his hand on the table, then slowly extended a forefinger. "Next round's on me."

"The trouble is, when you just want to get to know someone," Olivia said, with surprising volubility once Warren was gone, "there's no such thing as neutral ground. Like just now, people come up and assume ... But, well, here's another round." She raised her face in gratitude to the barmaid. "Jerry always tells me his travel plans, no matter how late it gets. He has some crazy jet-lag remedies you ought to hear. By the next morning, I can hardly remember what they were."

"It's five o'clock," the barmaid said. "You're entitled to all of this you want."

When she was gone, Olivia said, "I suppose we did start before five. That woman at the farmers' market, she must've had someone in mind."

"Funny way to figure out who."

"Or she was just, you know, revisiting the experience."

"Anyway, that's how we met!" But this didn't feel right, so Briggs added, "Neighbor."

After thinking about this, she asked, "Have you noticed that out in the country, 'neighbor' is a verb?"

This struck Briggs as a sudden move away from intimacy. Five o'clock had brought a crowd big enough to elbow up to all surfaces—not just the bar but the walls—and the air of day's-end ebullience was infectious to Briggs, who was a loner, and tired of being one, but seemed unable to do anything about it.

"It's kind of aggressive, isn't it?" he said. "Usually about how someone failed to neighbor."

"Yes." She sighed. "And the speaker always makes you think that he neighbors even while he's asleep." She covered Briggs's hands with her own. "How 'bout you?"

"I don't do a lot of neighboring," he said.

Olivia took this in somberly. "I must strike you as desperate," she said. The tone had changed, and her smile was slack.

"You do not."

"Thank you."

She had nearly finished her complimentary double, and Briggs, on his second shell of draft, realized that she'd put away six shots of whiskey, which suddenly seemed to be sinking in; the slow movement of her eyes beneath lowered lids, which he had first taken for flirtatious warmth, now appeared to be the start of some narcosis.

"That Ring of Kerry thing doesn't sound like much fun, does it?" she said into space.

"Oh, I'll bet it's beautiful there."

"But just getting through a wet day to end up in a pub . . . Is that the reward? And where did he get that about German girls?" Only now did she look up at Briggs.

"He was probably trying to entertain us."

Olivia looked surprised. "Oh! Well. Now I'll be grateful. I'm so dense." At that moment, Warren passed their booth. "Hey, Jerry! That was great," she called out.

He stopped.

"What was great, Olivia?"

"About the ring of German girls in raincoats."

Jerry glanced at Briggs before moving on. "If I can just get through this drought," he said as he plunged into the crowd.

"What does he mean?" Olivia asked. "I'm missing connection after connection." She gestured for another round. The barmaid waved back, and Olivia commented, "I really like her, but she's a huge slut. Ready for another?"

"I don't know if I can drink more beer. My teeth are floating."

"Your teeth are—?"

"I'm bursting with beer."

"Maybe you should drink something more concentrated. Beer's mostly water. I wish alcohol came in the same size as an aspirin. You just wear out your digestion trying to cop a buzz. And this stuff"—she pointed—"tastes like kerosene. Your teeth are floating! That's a scream."

Briggs didn't feel comfortable doing more to prevent the arrival of another round, but when she'd finished it, he wished he had.

"Olivia."

"What."

"You okay?"

"Where are we going with this?"

"I thought you were about to faint."

"Oh, how wrong you are."

Briggs caught Jerry Warren's eye and made a writing gesture with his right hand on his left hand. Warren winked his understanding, and Briggs turned back to Olivia. "Let's get outside while we have a little of this day left," he said. He could tell that this was heard from a great distance. He stood up to enforce the suggestion and then thought to extend a hand, which Olivia took as she got to her feet and quickly leaned against him.

"Going to have to do it like this, aren't I?"

"Not a problem. Out we go."

Briggs escorted her through the front door so deftly that their exit was barely noticed. The one woman who stared was told by Olivia "No worries" in an Australian accent. As soon as she stepped outside the heat hit her and she began to topple. Briggs had to take her around the corner to find a quiet spot. "I want to help you here, Olivia. You're having a bit of trouble with your balance."

"How did I let this hap-pen? A little birdie says it's time for me to scoot," she said. With her hands at her shoulders, fingers fluttering outward, she did the birdie.

"How about if you let me drive you home?"

"Bor-ing."

"I'm afraid I require it. Where is your car?"

"A, we identify make and model."

"Can you do that for me? And parking place?"

She looked left and right. "You know, John Briggs, I'm going to flunk that test."

"No problem. We'll go in mine." He helped her into his twenty-year-old sedan. She told him they'd be lucky if the jalopy made it to her house. The car had old-style seat belts, and fastening hers across her lap produced from Olivia a languorous smile. "There!" he said briskly, to undo the smile, then went around to his side, got in, looked over at her amiably, and turned the key.

"Doesn't look like you're going to try to take advantage of me."

"Nope."

"It wouldn't be hard. All aboard!" She imitated a train whistle.

They headed north and, just as they left town, she said, "Hey, there's my car!" But then she was uncertain. It didn't really matter to Briggs, unless she turned out to be right in wondering whether his car would make it. They were halfway to her house before she spoke again. She said, "Ooh, boy, this is a bad idea."

Grassland spread in either direction all the way to the horizon. From the west, a thunderstorm, zigzagged with wires of lightning, was moving swiftly toward them, until the road ahead began to darken with rain.

Briggs drove without trying to talk until they reached Olivia's town. She pointed out various turns and landmarks, letting her hand fall back onto her lap each time. The trees formed a canopy above the street where she said she lived, a street on which either invidious competition or the boundless love of property had prevailed in the form of one perfect lawn after another and hedges that seemed to have been purchased in sections. At length, she said, "This is it, with the red shutters. Who else has red shutters? Nobody. Just us. Has red shutters. Have red shutters."

Briggs made sure the coast was clear for assisting her to the house. Olivia had lost some ground since they set out, and it seemed unlikely that she would be able to walk safely. A man in bicycle shorts went by, leading a Newfoundland; there was a Rollerblader, a very old and slow woman pulling a wagon of groceries, a FedEx man delivering to the house next door, and then it was time to rouse Olivia all over again and go for it. "I'm so sorry," she said as he steadied her beside the car. "I see the jalopy held up better than I thought it would. Shouldn't have said what I said. 'Never ridicule what you don't understand,' my father told me."

Briggs reached for the door, but it opened before he touched it, and a severe-looking older man in a starched white shirt appeared. He had a high, domed forehead and piercing blue eyes. He inspected Briggs and, speaking to him but looking at Olivia, who stood with her head hanging, said, "We're at it again, I see." Briggs helped her into the front hall and passed her arm to the man he guessed was her father, expecting to retreat to his car, but then the man closed the door behind the three of them and said, "Wait here," with what, in other circumstances, might have seemed an intolerably brusque tone. Briggs stood in the hallway as Olivia went off without a word, climbing the stairs with the aid of her father. He could make out the corner of a dining-room table, a section of transom window, dark wainscoting, old family photographs on either side of the stairway.

"So sorry to leave you standing there," the man said when he returned, guiding Briggs forcefully into the house. "I'm Olin Halliday, Olivia's father. Not too proud to eat in the kitchen, are you?"

Briggs obediently followed Halliday through swinging doors. The kitchen met more than the ordinary domestic requirements, with a freestanding chopping block, a commercial-grade stove, and a double-doored freezer. Halliday pointed to a dripping bag suspended over a large mixing bowl. "Making cottage cheese. Not ready yet. I hope you like brisket. I like brisket way too well, and I never seem to get it quite like I want it, though this time I'm close. I try to smoke it long enough to start the neighbors complaining. Then I know I'm on the right track. Like everything else, you have to put in the time."

At last they were seated on stools at the chopping block. Halliday carved the brisket with a broad razor-sharp knife, which he wielded rapidly, each perfect slice just tipping over of its own weight as he started the next. Coleslaw, "my tomatoes," beet greens, corn bread, and iced tea. "Should have beer, but I can't keep it in the house," Halliday said. Then he began to eat with the absorption of a hungry man eating alone. Briggs waited a moment before following suit, the food so good it created an appetite.

"As you have seen," Halliday said, mouth still full, punctuating with his fork, "Olivia cannot drink. Cannot but does, and shouldn't. She is the kind of alcoholic usually described as 'hopeless,' but of course she is not hopeless, and I'm not without hope. Are you?"

"I hardly know Olivia."

"There's a difference between taking responsibility, Mr. Briggs, and blaming yourself for everything. There should be a line between the two. Olivia does not see that line."

With every remark, Halliday scrutinized Briggs, and because of his sky-blue eyes, his gaze may have seemed more penetrating than intended. Just then Olivia called down in a near screech, "Tell him what they did to me!" Halliday and Briggs looked at each other in silence, Briggs alarmed.

He said, "What does she mean by that?"

"It's always something new," Halliday said, looking away. "She has hung on to her job at the hospital. I've helped there; an argument can still be made that she's viable."

"You tell him."

"I'm afraid this could go on. Have you had enough to eat?"

"Yes."

"Don't be worried; this is the best place she could be."

"I hope so."

"I'm her father, Mr. Briggs, and I'm a doctor."

Briggs felt no urgency to respond. After a moment had passed, he asked, "Where is Olivia's mother?"

"Olivia's mother is no longer living. I delivered Olivia, and I adopted her. Olivia's mother was not married."

"Has her mother been dead for a long time?"

Halliday smiled cheerlessly. "She's been dead almost since Olivia was born. She jumped off Carter's Bridge and went all the way to North Dakota before what the fauna of the Great Plains had left of her was found. It was sad, it was unforeseen, and it was certainly not anybody's fault, least of all Olivia's, but Olivia doesn't see it that way."

"What can you do to help someone get over that?"

"Nothing that's worked, as you can see. But now I'm going to try something new and, to tell the truth, I'm optimistic. Olivia is almost pathologically shy, and I'm persuaded that this is connected to the grudge she holds against herself. She is quite dependent upon me, especially financially, which has caused plenty of resentment. That's my only lever, but it's a good one. Anyway, long story short, I am going to require Olivia to join Toastmasters International."

Halliday watched complacently as his new idea sank in. Briggs suspected that he wasn't the first stranger on whom it had been floated. He began to wonder what other miracle cures Halliday might have attempted on the poor girl. "I don't get it."

"You don't have to get it. Olivia has to get it. I'm going to help Olivia ground herself. I want to revise her core values. You don't know the boyfriends she's had. I want her to learn to recognize and avoid losers. But she's got to learn how to boldly share her message. She's got to quit going off on tangents. I think if she looked within and learned the skills of public speaking that she would delight audiences with dynamic presentations by simply unleashing her inner self."

"I've never heard of anything this crazy."

"I take that as a compliment. It doesn't bother me to be ahead of the crowd."

Briggs left immediately, making his exit as rude as possible. As soon as he was under way in his car, he was aware of the smell of Olivia's perfume, which was somehow more conspicuous in her absence. He hardly had a profound connection to her, but he could not get her out of his mind. For the first time his car actually did seem like a jalopy. Halliday had surely taken him for a loser.

I don't have a garage, he could have explained. *Why leave a good car sitting out in the weather?* This was the first of his imaginary dialogues with Olivia. One about drinking left him believing that she was possessed, an idea whose tawdry allure was obvious. He imagined a priestly intervention during which evil spirits were exorcised, and Halliday, with his pop theories, stayed well to the rear. Briggs understood that these daydreams were meant to allay some heartache.

Briggs spent most of September making repairs on his place, getting ready to go back to work. He repainted the shutters, a maddening job because of all the louvers. He set pack-rat traps and pruned the raspberry patch. He alphabetized his library, a recurrent task, since he never put books back where they belonged. He changed the water filter in the basement and removed the ghastly mushrooms that had volunteered there. The lawn seemed to have stopped growing, so he put the mower in the garage. Next to the barn was a stack of old boards that had warped and rotted beyond use; he pulled the truck around in order to haul this trash to a safe place for burning. He was nearly finished when he reached for a heavy sheet of exterior plywood, which he had to raise on its edge to drag it to the truck. As he lifted it, he felt something like the blow of a stick against his leg. He raised the plywood higher and saw the coiled rattlesnake, dropped the plywood, and backed away with a chill. He drew up his pant leg and saw where the fangs had gone in and the slight reddening around the marks. He pulled off his work gloves and decided he'd take the back way to the hospital in his truck. He wondered how bad this was going to be.

It was a half-hour drive, and the serious ache and swelling commenced. He parked close to the emergency entrance, next to two old ambulances, and limped into the waiting room. The nurse, filling out forms, was a long time acknowledging him, and when she did so it was by the mere raising of her head. When he explained what was wrong, she told him to have a seat. They must see a lot of snakebites, Briggs thought. The spot where he'd been bitten was now quite enlarged and had acquired a dusky cast that worried him.

Eventually, the nurse instructed him to fill out a form, which he did with growing awareness of the pain. Then she said, "I'll take you to your room. You'll be spending the night." She turned and Briggs followed her down a brown corridor with the usual antiseptic smell and stainless-steel tables on wheels. She left him in the room. He propped one foot on the toe of the other to alleviate the rhythmic ache and found himself perspiring. He reached for the remote control, turned the TV on, and then turned it off immediately.

A few minutes later, Olivia entered in a nurse's uniform. "Let's get rid of those pants," she said. As Briggs lay in his shorts, Olivia bent close over the wound and studied it in silence. "Right back," she said, and left the room. When she returned a few minutes later, she had a metal tray with a syringe on it. "I don't like this stuff," she said, "but the poison has spread and we've got to use it. It will help with the pain. We're talking pronto." Briggs had planned a conversation designed to crack this mystery, but Olivia was leaning over him, studying his eyes as she pressed the hypodermic into him, and with the enveloping wave he was overcome. "Feels so good," she said quietly. "Doesn't it?" He nodded slowly, infinitely grateful for the bite of the rattlesnake. She held his face in her hands and gazed at him as he went under. "I just know it feels so good."

When he awoke the next morning, he doubted everything he remembered. He checked his leg to see if he'd been bitten by a snake, and thank God he had. He noticed that the pain was gone. He rang the call button next to his bed. A nurse entered, a tall, peevish woman of fifty, carrying a copy of *Field & Stream*. "I'm better, and I'm going home."

"Doctor will decide when you can go."

With Briggs's impatience growing, it was a blessing the doctor came soon. Close to retirement age, he was a well-groomed silver-haired man, exceedingly thin, in polished walking shoes, cuffed serge pants, and a sparkling white smock.

"How do you feel?"

"I feel fine, ready to go home. I suppose the nurse is off today."

"What nurse?"

"The one who treated me last night."

"I treated you last night. You were sound asleep, like you'd passed out. In any case, I couldn't wake you: I went ahead and did what I thought best. I gave you a good slug of antivenin."

"I clearly remember a woman coming in and treating me."

"I hope she was pretty. It was a dream."

"Let me ask you something. Is Dr. Halliday on duty today?"

The doctor looked startled and a little evasive. He said, "Dr. Halliday lost his license to practice a long time ago. Of course, we feel terrible about it. His daughter has stayed with us, and we hope that's some help in a very regrettable situation."

Briggs left the hospital in the same dirty clothes he'd worn to paint and clean his yard. He drove home, parked by the woodpile, and killed the snake with a hoe, then went up to the house to read his mail and check his phone messages. He felt an incongruous sadness about killing the snake, which had tried in vain to get away. The refrigerator was still well stocked, and he started a pot of spicy vegetable soup. He smelled mothballs and remembered the blankets he'd put in storage the day before.

On Wednesday, he took three shirts and a sport jacket to be dry-cleaned. He usually went to Arnold's, where he had an account, but it was closed on Wednesdays, so he drove a few extra miles and carried his things into Bright's. The smell of cleaning fluid was a little stronger in Bright's, and he wondered whether that meant they were more thorough or just harsher on the clothes. To the left of the long counter, a broad woman with her back to him operated the electrical revolving rack. She said, "Be just a sec," and compared a slip with that on several garments going past. She found what she was looking for, a tuxedo, and took it down to hang on a rigid rack next to the cash register before turning to Briggs: it was her, the woman who'd accosted him at the farmers' market. She recognized him first and covered her mouth with her hands. "I wondered if I'd see you again. I so have to apologize to you! I completely and utterly thought you were someone else."

"Don't give it a thought," Briggs said with reserve. He added, "I gather you took a number of other people for someone else."

This puzzled her. "No, just you."

"I was led to think otherwise. Guess it's my turn to apologize."

"Can we call it even Steven?"

He hoped to have a chance to speak to Olivia about this. So, later in the fall, when he received an invitation to her wedding, his first thought was, Of course I'll go.

In the receiving line, Olivia, jubilant and tipsy, hung around the neck of her new husband, a glass of champagne in her hand. The wedding party was clamorous, gathered under the old trees behind the house with the red shutters. The husband was a specimen of tidy manhood, with black, tightly clipped hair, blue eyes, and ears like little seashells; he wore a perfectly tailored dark summer suit and a colorful tie that spelled out the word "Montana"—not the state but Claude, the French couturier. Briggs wondered if he was wrong in thinking the groom wore eyeliner. Olivia touched the champagne glass to the tip of her nose and giggled when Briggs appeared. He knew right away that he wouldn't be able to ask his questions. He pumped the husband's hand and wished them all the luck in the world. He meant it, even though he felt the same queer longing on seeing Olivia. It was her husband's turn to go for a ride.

During the ceremony, rain clouds had grumbled overhead, and now the shower began. The wedding party rushed to the house with hilarity, and Briggs decided this would be a good time for him to leave, but Olivia detained him, resting her outspread fingers on his shirt while the rain fell on them both. She was remarkably heedless in her beautiful wedding gown, and Briggs caught sight of the groom's face in the hall window. "You were so good to me that time and so patient with my father," she said.

"Where is your father?"

"We got him out of here." She was close to him as she spoke. He felt her breath on his face and his heart was racing. "I'm glad I had the chance to"—she smiled—"to give you a lift when you were in the hospital."

The rain redoubled, sweeping down through the canopy of leaves, and they fled to the house, Olivia disappearing into the happy crowd. Briggs didn't know quite what to do with himself. He made his way back to the kitchen where he'd dined with Dr. Halliday. It was empty. He went to the sink and ran the tap until the water was cold, filled a glass, and drank it down. The pandemonium outside elevated for an instant as the kitchen door opened behind him. When he put the glass down and turned around, he was looking into the face of the groom, aggressively close to his own. He stared at Briggs in silence. "I hope you understand that you will never put your nasty hands on her again," he said. "Get over it."

Briggs looked at this handsome well-cared-for man. "It will be hard to give up," Briggs said.

"But you will, won't you?"

"I suppose. It was so intense, the last time, in my car, the airbags deployed. But, yes, you have my word."

The groom reached out his hand, and Briggs took it. The hand was so clammy that Briggs had an instant of sympathy. In the groom's face nothing changed. "Have we got a deal?" the groom asked, and Briggs pretended to agonize over the decision. He let the conflicts play themselves out on his face, then heaved a great sigh.

"We've got a deal," he said, his voice resigned.

As they strolled back to the party together, Briggs decided that spicing things up in this way was absolutely the last favor he would do for Olivia. He watched the groom go to her and whisper in her ear. Olivia looked over at Briggs, smiled at him sadly, he thought, and waved. Hello? Goodbye? He wasn't sure.

The rain had stopped, and something caused the wedding party to gravitate to the stately elm shading the lawn, its leaves just starting to change color. Briggs followed until he was part of the half circle of celebrants facing Olivia, who stood on a small dais, placed there, he supposed, for this purpose. "I'd like to propose a toast!" she called out, in a voice that carried remarkably. He barely heard her words but stared, spellbound, at her wide, confident smile, the steady movement of her head as she took in all the guests, and the hand gestures that would have been clear from the nearby mountains. Her voice rang out expressively, each syllable occupying its own time and space. At the end of her toast, she clasped her hands to her chest and bowed modestly to the admiring applause and, without looking, reached out a regal hand to her new husband.

COWBOY

THE OLD FELLER MADE ME GO INTO THE BIG HOUSE IN MY stocking feet. The old lady's in a big chair next to the window. In fact, the whole room's full of big chairs, but she's only in one of them, though as big as she is she could of filled up several. The old man said, "I found this one in the loose-horse pen at the saleyard."

She says, "What's he supposed to be?"

He says, "Supposed to be a cowboy."

"What's he doin in the loose horses?"

I says, "I was lookin for one that would ride."

"You was in the wrong pen, son," says the old man. "Them's canners. They're goin to France in cardboard boxes."

"Once they get a steel bolt in the head." The big old gal in the chair laughed.

Now I'm sore. "There's five in there broke to death. I rode em with nothin but binder twine."

"It don't make a shit," says the old man. "Ever one of them is goin to France."

The old lady didn't believe me. "How'd you get near them loose horses to ride?"

"I went in there at night."

The old lady says, "You one crazy cowboy go in there in the dark. Them broncs kick your teeth down your throat. I suppose you tried bareback."

"Naw, I drug the saddle I usually ride at the Rose Bowl Parade."

"You got a horse for that?"

"I got Trigger. We unstuffed him."

She turns to the old man. "He's got a mouth on him. This much we know."

"Maybe he can tell us what good he is."

I says, "I'm a cowboy."

"You're a outta-work cowboy."

"It's a dyin way of life."

"She's about like me. She's wondering if this ranch supposed to be some welfare agency for cowboys."

I've had enough. "You're the dumb honyocker drove me out here."

I thought that was the end, but the old lady said, "Don't get huffy. You got the job. You against conversation?"

We get outside and the old sumbitch says, "You drawed lucky there, son. That last deal could of pissed her off."

"It didn't make me no never mind if it did or didn't."

"Anymore, she hasn't been well. Used to she was sweet as pudding."

"I'm sorry for that. We don't have health, we don't have nothin."

She must of been afflicted somethin terrible, because she was ugly mornin, noon, and night for as long as she lasted, pick a fight over nothin, and the old sumbitch bound to got the worst of it. I felt sorry for him, little slack as he ever cut me.

Had a hundred seventy-five sweet-tempered horned Herefords and fifteen sleepy bulls. Shipped the calves all over for hybrid vigor, mostly to the south. Had some go clear to Florida. A Hereford still had its horns was a walkin miracle and the old sumbitch had him a smart little deal goin. I soon learned to give him credit for such things, and the old lady barking commands off the sofa weren't no slouch neither. Anybody else seen their books might say they could be winterin in Phoenix.

They didn't have no bunkhouse, just a Leisure Life mobile home that had lost its wheels about thirty years ago, and they had it positioned by the door of the barn so it'd be convenient for the hired man to stagger out at all hours and fight breech birth and scours and any other disorder sent down by the cow gods. We had some doozies. One heifer had got pregnant and her calf was near as big as she was. Had to reach in and take it out in pieces. When we threw the head out on the ground she turned to it and lowed like it was her baby. Everything a cow does is to make itself into meat as fast as it can so somebody can eat it. It's a terrible life, and a cowboy is its little helper.

The old sumbitch and I got along good. We got through calvin and got to see them pairs and bulls run out onto the new grass.

Nothin like seeing all that meat feel a little temporary joy. Then we bladed out the corrals and watched em dry under the spring sun at long last. Only mishap was the manure spreader threw a rock and knocked me senseless and I drove the rig into an irrigation ditch. The old sumbitch never said a word but chained up and pulled us out with his Ford.

We led his cavvy out of the hills afoot with two buckets of sweet feed. Had a little of everything, including a blue roan I fancied, but he said it was a Hancock and bucked like the National Finals in Las Vegas, kicking out behind and squalling, and was just a man-killer. "Stick to the bays," he said. "The West was won on a bay horse."

He picked out three bays, had a keg of shoes, all ones and aughts, and I shod them best I could, three geldings with nice manners, stood good to shoe. About all you could say about the others was they had four legs each; a couple, all white marked from saddle galls and years of hard work, looked like maybe no more summers after this. They'd been rode many a long mile. We chased em back into the hills, and the three that was shod whinnied and fretted. "Back to work," the old sumbitch tells em.

We shod three cause one was going to pack a ton of fencing supplies—barbwire, smooth wire, steel T-posts and staples, old wore-out Sunflower fence stretchers that could barely grab on to the wire—and we was at it a good little while where the elk had knocked miles of it down or the cedar finally give out and had to be replaced by steel. But that was how I found out the old sumbitch's last good time was in Korea, where the officers would yell, "Come on up here and die!" Said they was comin in waves. Tells me all this while the stretcher pulls that wire squealin though the staples. He was a tough old bastard.

"They killed a pile of us and we killed a pile of them." Squeak!

We hauled the mineral horseback too, in panniers, white salt and iodine salt. He didn't have no use for blocks, so we hauled it in sacks and poured it into the troughs he had on all these bald hilltops where the wind would blow away the flies. Most of his so-called troughs was truck tires nailed onto anything flat—plywood, old doors, and suchlike—but they worked all right. A cow can put her tongue anywhere in a tire and get what she needs, and you can drag one of them flat things with your horse if you need to move em. Most places we salted had old buffalo wallers where them buffalo wallered. They done wallered their last, had to get out of the way for the cow and the man on the bay horse.

I'd been rustlin my own grub in the Leisure Life for a good little while when the old lady said it was time for me to eat with the white folks. This wasn't necessarily a good thing. The old lady's knee replacements had begun to fail, and both me and the old sumbitch was half afraid of her. She cooked good as ever but she was a bomb waitin to go off, standin bowlegged at the stove and talkin ugly about how much she did for us. When she talked, the old sumbitch would move his mouth like he was saying the same words. If the old lady'd caught him at that they'd a been hell to pay.

Both of them was heavy smokers, to where a oxygen bottle was in sight. So they joined a Smoke-Enders deal the Lutherans had, and this required em to put all their butts in a jar and wear the jar around their neck on a string. The old sumbitch liked this okay because he could just tap his ash right under his chin and not get it on the truck seat, but the more that thing filled up and hung around her neck the meaner the old lady got. She had no idea the old sumbitch was cheatin and settin his jar on the woodpile when we was workin outside. She was just honester than him, and in the end she give up smokin and he smoked away, except he wasn't allowed to in the house no more nor buy ready-mades, cause the new tax made them too expensive and she wouldn't let him take it out of the cows, which come first. She said it was just a vice, and if he was half the man she thought he was he'd give it up for a bad deal. "You could have a long and happy old age," she told him, real sarcastic-like.

ONE DAY ME AND THE OLD SUMBITCH IS IN THE HOUSE HAULing soot out of the fireplace on account of they had a chimney fire last winter. Over the mantel is a picture of a beautiful woman in a red dress with her hair piled on top of her head. The old sumbitch tells me that's the old lady before she joined the motorcycle gang.

"Oh?"

"Them motorcycle gangs," he says, "all they do is eat and work on their motorcycles. They taught her to smoke too, but she's shut of that. Probably outlive us all."

"Oh?"

"And if she ever wants to box you, tell her no. She'll knock you on your ass, I guarantee it. Throw you a damn haymaker, son."

I couldn't understand how he could be so casual about the old lady being in a motorcycle gang. When we was smokin in the Leisure Life, I asked him about it. That's when I found out him and the old lady was brother and sister. I guess that explained it. If your sister joins some motorcycle gang, that's her business. He said she even had a tattoo—Hounds from Hell—a dog shootin flames out of his nostrils and riding a Harley.

That picture on the mantel kind of stayed in my mind, and I asked the old sumbitch if his sister'd ever had a boyfriend. Well yes, he said, several, quite a few, quite a damn few. "Our folks run em off. They was only after the land."

By now we was in the barn and he was goin all around the baler, hittin the zerks with his grease gun. "I had a lady friend myself. Do anything. Cook. Gangbusters with a snorty horse and not too damn hard on the eyes. Sis run her off. Said she was just after the land. If she was, I never could see it. Anyway, went on down the road a long time ago."

FALL COME AROUND, AND WHEN WE BROUGHT THE CAVVY down, two of them old-timers who'd worked so hard was lame. One was stifled, the other sweenied, and both had cripplin quarter cracks. I thought they needed to be at the loose-horse sale, but the old sumbitch says, "No mounts of mine is gonna feed no Frenchmen," and that was that. So we made a hole, led the old-timers to the edge, and shot them with a elk rifle. First one didn't know what hit him. Second one heard the shot and saw his buddy fall, and the old sumbitch had to chase him all around to kill him. Then he sent me down the hole to get the halters back. Liftin them big heads was some chore.

I enjoyed eatin in the big house that whole summer until the sister started givin me come-hither looks. They was fairly limited except those days when the old sumbitch was in town after supplies. Then she dialed it up and kind of brushed me every time she went past the table. There was always something special on town days, a pie maybe. I tried to think about the picture on the mantel but it was impossible, even though I knew it might get me out of the Leisure Life once and for all. She was gettin more and more wound up while I was pretendin to enjoy the food, or goin crazy over the pie. But she didn't buy it—called me a queer, and sent me back to the trailer to make my own meals. By callin me a queer, she more or less admitted to what she'd been up to, and I think that embarrassed her, because she covered up by roaring at everyone and everything, including the poor old sumbitch, who had no idea what had gone sideways while he was away. It was two years before she made another pie, and then it was once a year on my birthday. She made me five birthday pies in all, sand cherry, every one of them.

I BROKE THE CATCH COLT, WHICH I DIDN'T KNOW WAS NO colt as he was the biggest snide in the cavvy. He was four, and it was time. I just got around him for a couple days, then saddled him gentle as I could. The offside stirrup scared him and he looked over at it, but that was all it was to saddlin. I must of had a burst of courage, cause next minute I was on him. That was okay, too. I told the old sumbitch to open the corral gate, and we sailed away. The wind blew his tail up under him, and he thought about buckin but rejected the idea, and that was about all they was to breakin Olly, for that was his name. Once I'd rode him two weeks, he was safe for the old sumbitch, and he plumb loved this new horse and complimented me generously for the job I'd did.

We had three hard winters in a row, then lost so many calves to scours we changed our calving grounds. The old sumbitch just come out one day and looked at where he'd calved out for fifty years and said, "The ground's no good. We're movin." So we spent the summer buildin a new corral way off down the creek. When we's finished, he says, "I meant to do this when I got back from overseas, and now it's finished and I'm practically done for too. Whoever gets the place next will be glad his calves don't shit themselves into the next world like mine done."

Neither one of us had a back that was worth a damn, and if we'd had any money we'd of had the surgery. The least we could do was get rid of the square baler and quit heftin them man-killin five-wire bales. We got a round baler and a DewEze machine that let us pick up a bale from the truck without layin a finger on it. We'd smoke in the cab on those cold winter days and roll out a thousand pounds of hay while them old-time horned Herefords followed the truck sayin nice things about me and the old sumbitch while we told stories. That's when I let him find out I'd done some time.

"I figured you musta been in the crowbar hotel."

"How's that?"

"Well, you're a pretty good hand. What's a pretty good hand doin tryin loose horses in the middle of the night at some Podunk saleyard? Folks hang on to a pretty good hand, and nobody was hangin on to you. You want to tell me what you done?"

I'd been with the old sumbitch for three years and out of jail the same amount of time. I wasn't afraid to tell him what I done, for I was starting to trust him, but I sure didn't want him tellin nothin to his sister. I trusted him enough to tell him I did the time, but that was about all I was up to. I told him I rustled some yearlins, and he chuckled like everybody understood that. Unfortunately, it was a lie. I rustled some yearlings, all right, but that's not what I went up for.

The old man paid me in cash, or rather the old lady did, as she handled anything like that. They never paid into workmen's comp, so there was no reason to go to the records. They didn't even have the name right. You tell people around here your name is Shane, and they'll always believe you. The important thing is I was workin my tail off for that old sumbitch, and he knew it. Nothin else mattered, even the fact we'd come to like each other. After all, this was a goddamn ranch.

The old feller had several peculiarities to him, most of which I've forgot. He was one of the few fellers I ever seen who would actually jump up and down on his hat if he got mad enough. You can imagine what his hat looked like. One time he did it cause I let the swather get away from me on a hill and bent it all to hell. Another time a Mormon tried to run down his breeding program to get a better deal on some replacement heifers, and I'll be damned if the old sumbitch didn't throw that hat down and jump on it until the Mormon got back into his Buick and eased on down the road without another word. One time when we was drivin ring shanks into corral poles I hit my thumb and tried jumpin on my hat, but the old sumbitch gave me such a odd look I never tried it again.

THE OLD LADY DIED SITTIN DOWN, WENT IN THERE AND there she was, sittin down, and she was dead. After the first wave of grief, the old sumbitch and me fretted about rigor mortis and not being able to move her in that seated position, which would almost require rollin her. So we stretched her onto the couch and called the mortician, and he called the coroner and for some reason the coroner called the ambulance, which caused the old sumbitch to state, "It don't do you no never mind to tell nobody nothin." Course, he was right.

Once the funeral was behind us, I moved out of the Leisure Life once and for all, partly for comfort and partly cause the old sumbitch falled apart after his sister passed, which I never suspected during the actual event. But once she's gone, he says he's all that's left of his family and he's alone in life, and about then he notices me and tells me to get my stuff out of the Leisure Life and move in with him.

We rode through the cattle pretty near ever day, year-round, and he come to trust me enough to show how his breedin program went, with culls and breedbacks and outcrosses and replacements, and he took me to bull sales and showed me what to expect in a bull and which ones was correct and which was sorry. One day we's looking at a pen of yearlin bulls on this outfit near Luther, and he can't make up his mind and says he wishes his sister was with him and starts snufflin and says she had an eye on her wouldn't quit. So I stepped up and picked three bulls out of that pen and he quit snufflin and said damn if I didn't have an eye on me too. That was the beginnin of our partnership.

One whole year I was the cook, and one whole year he was the cook, and back and forth like that but never at the same time. Whoever was cook would change when the other feller got sick of his recipes, and ever once in a while a new recipe would come in the *AgriNews,* like that corn chowder with the sliced hot dogs. I even tried a pie one time, but it just made him lonesome for days gone by, so we forgot about desserts, which was probably good for our health as most sweets call for gobbin in the white sugar.

The sister had never let him have a dog cause she had a cat, and she thought a dog would get the cat and, as she said, if the dog got the cat she'd get the dog. It wasn't much of a cat, anyhow, but it lasted a long time, outlived the old lady by several moons. After it passed on, we took it out to the burn barrel, and the first thing the old sumbitch said was "We're gettin a dog." It took him that long to realize his sister was gone.

Tony was a border collie we got as a pup from a couple in Miles City that raised them, and they was seven generation of cow dogs just wanted to eat and work stock. You could cup your hands and hold Tony when we got him, but he grew up in one summer and went to work and we taught him down, here, come by, way to me, and hold em, all in one year or less, cause Tony'd just stay on his belly and study you with his eyes until he knew exactly what you wanted. Tony helped us gather, mother up pairs, and separate bulls, and he lived in the house for many a good year and kept us entertained with all his tricks.

Finally, Tony got old and died. We didn't take it so good, especially the old sumbitch, who said he couldn't foresee enough summers for another dog. Plus that was the year he couldn't get on a horse no more and he wasn't about to work no stock dog afoot. There was still plenty to do, and most of it fell to me. After all, this was a goddamn ranch.

The time come to tell him what I done to go to jail, which was rob that little store at Absarokee and shoot the proprietor, though he didn't die. I had no idea why I did such a thing, then or now. I led the crew on the prison ranch for a number of years and turned out many a good hand. They wasn't nearabout to let me loose till there was a replacement good as me who'd stay awhile. So I trained up a murderer from Columbia Falls; could rope, break horses, keep vaccine records, fence, and irrigate. Once the warden seen how good he was, they paroled me out and turned it all over to the new man, who they said was never getting out. Said he was heinous. The old sumbitch could give a shit less when I told him my story. I could of told him all the years before, when he first hired me, for all he cared. He was a big believer in what he saw with his own eyes.

I don't think I ever had the touch with customers the old sumbitch did. They'd come from all over lookin for horned Herefords and talkin hybrid vigor, which I may or may not have believed. They'd ask what we had and I'd point to the corrals and say, "Go look for yourself." Some would insist on seein the old sumbitch and I'd tell them he was in bed, which was nearly the only place you could find him, once he'd begun to fail. Then the state got wind of his condition and took him to town. I went to see him there right regular, but it just upset him. He couldn't figure out who I was and got frustrated because he knew I was somebody he was supposed to know. And then he failed even worse. They said it was just better if I didn't come around.

The neighbors claimed I'd let the weeds grow and was personally responsible for the spread of spurge, Dalmatian toadflax, and knapweed. They got the authorities involved, and it was pretty clear I was the weed they had in mind. If they could get the court to appoint one of their relatives ranch custodian, they'd have all that grass for free till the old sumbitch was in a pine box. The authorities came in all sizes and shapes, but when they got through they let me take one saddle horse, one saddle, the clothes on my back, my hat, and my slicker. I rode that horse clear to the saleyard, where they tried to put him in the loose horses—cause of his age, not cause he was a bronc. I told em I was too set in my ways to start feedin Frenchmen and rode off toward Idaho. There's always an opening for a cowboy, even a old sumbitch like me, if he can halfway make a hand.

ICE

THE DRUM MAJOR LIVED A SHORT DISTANCE FROM OUR house and could sometimes be seen sitting pensively on his porch wearing his shako, a tall cylinder of white fake fur, the strap across his chin, folding the *Free Press* for his paper route. I was reluctant to so much as wave to him, since this was a time when my greatest concern—originating I don't know where—was that I was a hopeless coward. Although we saw each other every day at school, any greeting I sent his way fell on deaf ears, and I had long since given up getting any sort of response at all, a situation said to have begun when he scored 156 on the school-administered IQ test. I had the route for the *News,* so it was unremarkable that we didn't speak.

When one Thanksgiving he single-handedly captured an AWOL sailor and escorted him to the brig at the nearby base, I began to study him in the hope he held the key to escaping my cowardice.

I delivered papers in the evening and, as the year grew late, was often overtaken on my bicycle by darkness and by fear. I flung my rolled papers toward porches and stoops and onto lawns, and I was sometimes pursued by dogs, once taken down in an explosion of snow and bicycle wheels by a wolfish Irish setter. I had a recurrent fantasy of a muscular ostrich pursuing me in the dark and pecking down through my skull into my brain, another of several fears stemming from my single childhood trip to the zoo.

I always delivered my papers as promptly as possible; the drum major delivered his whenever he felt inclined to do so. One afternoon in early October, he unexpectedly chose to address me; he accused me of making him look bad by getting my papers onto people's porches and lawns before his. When I tried to respond, he cut me off and directed me to wait until his papers had been delivered before delivering mine. I complied with his instructions, tossing my papers onto lawns at all hours and dodging any customers who tried to complain.

I went to great lengths to observe the drum major practice on the big windblown and sometimes snowblown football field, where he would strut toward the goalposts trailing a stingy cape, the gray wintry lake just beyond, twirling his baton, the white shako tilted back arrogantly, culminating in the blissful high toss and recapture of the spinning chrome-plated baton, preferably without getting beaned by one of its white rubber ends. At actual game time, when he was leading our cacophonous marching band in disordered frenzy, the entire drama depended on his actually catching the baton, so that what was meant to accent a larger spectacle became the focal point of an otherwise lurching rigmarole. There was something about his haughty gaits and their seeming disconnection from the confused uproar of the band behind him, in its modest and unattractive costumes—threadbare maroon with gold piping, led by a hugely overweight youngster doing a Grambling State–style shimmy while flogging his glockenspiel with a felt-covered hammer—that was more attractive to a modest crowd that sometimes threw horse chestnuts at the drum major.

What lay behind this behavior? I think drum majors were about to be replaced by majorettes and what had once been honorably athletic had become effete and clouded with some unspoken sexual ambiguity, however inappropriate with reference to our own drum major, all of whose pert and blossoming girlfriends seemed to wind up losing their reputations. Nevertheless, the crowd hoped for a humiliating disaster. I, strangely, hoped for his success: I waited for that high toss to produce, as though by the hand of Praxiteles, the most graceful division of space, a split second of immortality for the drum major and for me a lesson in courage. At the same time, another part of me shared the crowd's unspoken wish to see the drum major on all fours with the baton up his behind or wrapped around his neck. As would become habitual for most of us, we wanted either spectacular achievement or mortifying failure, one or the other. Neither of these things, we were discreetly certain, would ever come to us: we'd be allowed the frictionless lives of the meek.

Our school played Flat Rock on the last Saturday of October, when winter was already in the air, the trees shabby with half-shed leaves. I was shivering in the crowd on the rickety exposed bleachers, watching our band wheel onto the field. When the drum major at last tossed the baton in its high glitter, it fell so far behind him that he had to dash into the band to retrieve it. Too late: he was swept aside, forced to stand, hands on hips, until the musicians had passed, his baton on the ground, twisted like a pretzel. I admit that I joined the baying crowd, our community. As he bent to pick up his bit of wreckage, we were beside ourselves. In that uproar I was without fear. I thrilled to the courage of the mob. Still, it wasn't quite the courage I was looking for.

The following week, the drum major seemed even more isolated at school, though as always he seemed to expect this. Mrs. Andrews, the beautiful young wife of our thuggish football coach who had given up her own remarkable athletic skills to teach us history, made a special effort to console him; I remember how gently she bent beside his desk to correct his work while, across the aisle, Stanley Peabody, with his flattop, pegged charcoal pants, and Flagg Flyer blue suede shoes, attempted to see down her blouse. Mrs. Andrews, with shining auburn hair piled atop her head, a single strand of imitation pearls curling down from her throat, was accustomed to being ogled and seemed to know Stanley only by a quick glance at the roster taped to her desk.

I was surprised by the attention she paid the drum major. From then on, I was a great student of any and all interactions between him and Mrs. Andrews, viewed as scarlet with erotic undertones, and abetted by the smirking of the other boys. But their behavior was no more than a salute to Mrs. Andrews's lovely figure. One incident does stand out, when, after long abstaining, Mrs. Andrews first called on the drum major in class. By now, I believed I sensed something quiet and subtle between the two of them.

"What," she asked, looking straight over the top of his head of curly brown hair, "was the principal result of the Crédit Mobilier scandal?" She seemed timid.

Legs stretched in the aisle, crossed at the ankles, fingers laced behind his head, the drum major said, "You tell me." He gazed at her with quiet annoyance that seemed to intimate possession.

We felt an electric silence, and I thrilled to what I viewed as amorous badinage disguised as classwork. Mrs. Andrews's face colored to the roots of her auburn hair. Stanley Peabody peered broadly. His sidekick, Boly Cardwell, a prematurely wizened teen with lank blond hair cascading over his forehead, grabbed his crotch surreptitiously and rolled his eyes in feigned ecstasy.

"Perhaps," she said, "you feel I have asked you the wrong question."

"Could be." The drum major had the affectless James Dean look down pat.

"In that case, why don't you pose a question for the class based on this week's reading?"

He leaned forward, dropped his elbows to his knees, drew his feet back under the chair, and held his head for a moment before he looked up. He said, "Who's buried in Grant's tomb?"

By the end of the day, he was the most important boy in school. People lingered to watch him pass in the hallway and gave him plenty of space at his locker.

Mrs. Andrews added girls' physical education to her teaching load, and from then on she seemed always to have a whistle around her neck. She moved with a new formality even when teaching history. While Stanley Peabody and Boly Cardwell headed a small group that gathered in the bleachers to run wind sprints, the drum major sat apart, focusing on Mrs. Andrews. On coed gym days, her husband, Bud Andrews, was also on the field, coaching the boys, a classic phys-ed instructor in sweats and a severe crew cut that bared the top of his scalp. One cold, dark afternoon when the windows of the gym were silver with reflected light and the air was sour with sweat, Coach Andrews suddenly sprang into the bleachers, lifted the drum major into the air, and shook him like a rag doll. The drum major managed to retain his smile, even as his head was flung about.

Coach Andrews was briefly suspended, and the drum major was assigned a history tutor, though everyone agreed that Mrs. Andrews could hardly be blamed for her husband's freak-out.

I spent my paper-route earnings on small things, an imitation Civil War–era forage cap, a British commando knife, steel taps for my shoes, muskrat traps; I had gotten caught by some magazine coupon swindle whereby I tried to win a baby monkey whose huge eyes dominated the advertisement, but when I fell behind in my payments and began to doubt if the monkey would ever be shipped,

I switched schemes and wound up on an easier payment plan with a flying squirrel that bit me savagely and flew around our basement for two days before escaping through the window. My father said, "Next time you've got ten bucks to spare, don't throw it away on a squirrel." My luck changed when, digging up a jack-in-the-pulpit as a gift for my mother, I discovered an old brass compass, which I attributed to voyageurs, coureurs de bois, Jesuits, Récollets, and their various bands of Potawatomi, Wyandotte, and Huron. Few facts came my way that could not be magnified. That compass was always in my pocket, an obvious talisman, the one thing that stood between me and the dreaded unknown.

As a test, I went back to delivering my papers on time, but the drum major had forgotten all about me. In January, I skated out onto Lake Erie, which that year was frozen nearly to Canada. I stared at its ominous expanse. I left the shore one evening on my hockey skates, a wool cap pulled over my ears and a long scarf wound around my neck and crisscrossed over my chest beneath my blue navy-surplus pea jacket. I meant to learn courage out on the ice, to avoid the specter of cowardice by skating all the way either to Canada or, if the icebreaker had been through, to the Livingstone ship channel. I struggled over the corrugations of the near-shore ice, then ventured onto glassier black ice that rewarded me with long glides between strokes of my hollow-ground blades. Bubbles could be seen and, occasionally, upended white bellies of perch and rock bass, as the sheen of glare ice, wide as my limited horizon, spread east toward Ontario; I dreamed of landing on this foreign shore, from whence the Redcoats once launched sorties against our colonial heroes. I would tell Mrs. Andrews what I had done. Reading schoolbooks had embittered me against the British and the American South, while my uncles handled the job for Germany and Japan. I meant to visit the old British fort at Amherstburg and skate home with tales of imperial ghosts and whatever other secret existences I might discover in places where no human is expected.

Such dreams in the gathering darkness enlivened my skating, and I raced on, stroke after stroke, toward the hiding place of those who once sought to crush our revolution. I would one day see this as the template for many disasters I had much later created for myself, but at the time, risking my life on the same days I worried about paper cuts or infected pimples produced no sense of contradiction. I felt only the allure of the hard, black, and perfect cold-snap ice unblemished by wind during its formation. Impossible to imagine the drum major out here like some animated Q-tip, I gloated, prancing among the crows and ice-killed fish.

Except for those crows, I was alone out there, out of sight of land or, as I then called it, Michigan, though I knew land lay to the west by the pale sunset still faintly visible. That's how I thought of it: I can't see Michigan anymore. I believed that if I let coming darkness turn me back, I would never be any good and the fog of cowardice would forever envelop me.

The ice seemed to rise before me and disappear into the twilight as though they were one and the same; I had to slow down in case the ice came to an end. Lights that had briefly shone on the Michigan shore were gone now, and I had yet to see my first Canadian light or the outlines of the fort I'd imagined. I touched the old compass in my pocket. Then it was dark.

When I stopped to reconnoiter, I felt the cold penetrate, and I adjusted my scarf. It was time to go home, I knew, but I couldn't leave this undone at the first wave of panic. I had to press on into the plain blackness long enough to prove that it was I who elected to return and not those forces determined to make me worthless in my own eyes. Such thoughts produced an oddly inflexible rhythm to my skating, by which I reached my feet through a distance I couldn't judge by sight until I contacted the hard floor of ice.

Now the sound of my blades, which had seemed to fill the air around me, was replaced by another as murmurous as a church congregation heard from afar. I glided toward the sound when suddenly a vast aggravation of noise and turbulence erupted as a storm of ducks took flight in front of me; it was water. I heard the ominous heave of the lake. I turned to skate straight away—or not quite straight, because after some minutes of agitated effort I found myself at water's edge again, water sufficiently fraught that it had broken back the edge of ice, heaving it in layers upon itself. I skated away from that too, and, when once more surrounded by darkness and standing squarely on black ice, I stopped and recognized that I was lost. I was suspended in darkness. A step in any direction and I would drown in freezing water.

The feeling of being completely lost was claustrophobic, like being locked in a windowless room. I had an incongruous sense of airlessness; it came to me that I was going to die.

I lashed out first at my entangling fantasies, the hated Redcoats especially, the pursuing ostrich—and then against death itself. My bowels began to churn, and I squatted on the ice with the pea jacket over my head, pants around my knees; I recited the Lord's Prayer in a quavering voice. And I was answered: a deep rhythmic throb that gathered slowly into a rumble. I stood and gazed into the darkness; as I pulled up and fastened my pants, a light emerged, followed by several others, streaming toward me in a line. At the moment the sound was most intense, a black all-consuming shape arose before me. It was not the god I expected: a lake freighter whose wake caused the ice to groan all around me, bound for Lake Superior. The lights streamed away and it was silent again.

I extracted the compass from my pocket and began bargaining with death. If anyone was looking on, it would be clear that whatever benefits I might be entitled to would have to be channeled through the old instrument, in whose tremulous magnetic needle I had placed all my faith. It took some concentration to hold panic at bay and rotate the battered brass case until I had north pinned down; then, staring down at the ornate w through the cloudy glass held just under my nose, I began to skate as rapidly as I could, moving fast on the cold mirror beneath me, creating my own wind, knowing that if the compass didn't work after its many years in the ground I would skate straight off the ice into a world from which I would not return. Myopic faith kept me stooped over my cupped hands as I pressed on with all I had on and on toward W.

The light of moon and stars was enough to see by if I'd known where I was going; and in a short time I could make out a half-dozen squarish shapes in my path, ice fishermen's shanties. There were several of these little villages in the area, and I tried to figure out which of them this might be. They were all quite similar, small houses placed over a round hole spudded through the ice through which the occupants could angle for perch or hang for hours, iron spear in hand, to await the great pike drawn to their hand-whittled wooden perch decoy. By night, the shacks were all deserted.

But one shanty revealed a flickering light, and to it I attached all my hopes. At its door, I made out voices, and I stopped before knocking. They were voices from my classroom, and I listened as if dreaming to what sounded like a quarrel. First the drum major, cocky and bantering. The other seemed to plead and whimper and was, of course, Mrs. Andrews. And then there were different sounds, less precise than words. I had no business knowing what I knew.

I landed a long way from where I'd put on my skates and was obliged to traverse a considerable distance on my blades, tottering upon pickerel grass, water-rounded glass shards, and pebbles, waving my arms around for balance while thanking everything around me for further days on earth. But in a scrap of tangled beech-woods, these pious thoughts soon crumbled before my lurid new vision. Light from the small houses that lined the narrow road to the shore made of my flailing progress wild shadows in the leafless trees. I heard dogs barking behind closed doors, and one home-owner let his beagle out while watching me from his porch. I tried to manage my movements, but I couldn't walk normally, nor could an observer see that I was wearing skates. The beagle approached to within ten feet and sat down, emitting a single reflexive bark as I passed his lawn. The owner remained on his porch and in silence watched me go by.

I didn't go on the ice again that winter. It seemed there were better things to do. As the days grew longer, I often saw the drum major starting his paper route as I got home from mine. We didn't speak, but my customers got the news on time.

OLD FRIENDS

JOHN BRIGGS WAS MADE AWARE OF THE FACT THAT SOME sort of problem existed for his friend and former schoolmate Erik Faucher by sheer coincidence. A request for news came from the class secretary, Everett Hoyt, who had in the thirty years since they'd graduated from Yale hardly set foot out of New Haven. With ancestors buried at the old Center Church in spitting distance of both the regicide Dixwell and Benedict Arnold's wife, Hoyt was paralyzed by a sense of generational inertia. It was said that if he hadn't gotten into Yale, he would not have gone to college at all but would have remained at home, waiting to bury his parents. Now, in place of any real social life, he edited the newsletter, often accompanying his requests with small indiscretions delivered with a certain giddiness—which he called *Entre News*—concerning marital failure or business malfeasance, and they almost never made it into the alumni letter.

Hoyt phoned John Briggs at his summer home in Montana, on a nondescript piece of prairie inherited from a farmer uncle, and, while pretending to hunt up class news, insinuated that Erik Faucher, having embezzled a fortune from a bank in Boston, had gone into hiding.

"I have heard through private sources that our class scofflaw is now headed your way."

Briggs waited for the giggle to subside. "I certainly hope so," he snapped. "I've missed Erik." But he began to worry that Erik might actually come.

"See what you can do," Hoyt sang.

"I don't understand that remark, Everett."

"Perhaps it will come to you."

"I'll let you know if it does."

Faucher's ex-wife, Carol, called around five in the morning, having declined to account for the time change. "How very nice to hear your voice," said Briggs, producing a cold laugh from Carol. "How are you?"

"I'm calling about Erik. He has not been behaving sensibly at all, some very odd things to say the least."

Briggs absorbed this in silence. He knew if he said anything at all, he'd have to stand up for Faucher, and he wasn't sure he wanted to.

"Carol, you've been divorced a long time," he said finally.

"We have mutual interests. I don't know what sort of plan he has in place. And there's Elizabeth." Elizabeth was their daughter.

"I'm sure he's made a very sensible plan."

"I don't want Elizabeth to wind up sleeping in her car. Or me, for that matter."

"I don't think we should argue." This was in response to her tone.

"Did I say we should? I'm saying, Help. I'm saying, It's about time you did." When Briggs failed to reply, she added, "I know where he's going and who to put on his trail."

Briggs's friendship with Faucher had been long and intermittent. Arbitrarily assigned as roommates at the boarding school they'd attended before Yale, they had become lifelong friends without ever getting over the fact that their discomfort with each other occasionally boiled over into detestation. Sometime earlier they had been sold loyalty much as the far-fetched basics of religion are sold to the credulous. When Briggs was in his twenties and had sunk everything into a perfectly legitimate though very small mining company in Alberta with excellent long-term prospects but ruinously expensive short-term requirements, Erik rescued him from bankruptcy by finding a buyer who bought Briggs out at a price that restored his investment and even gave him a small profit to accompany this dangerous lesson. Erik explained that he'd had to waste a valuable quid pro quo on this and waved his finger in Briggs's face.

When Erik was pulled from the second story of a burning whorehouse on assignment for UNESCO as part of a Boston Congregationalists' outreach to hungry Guatemalans, Briggs made a desperate stand to keep the matter out of the newspapers and saw that nettlesome citations on his dossier were expunged.

Against these decades of loyalty, they seemed to search for an unforgivable trait in each other that would relieve them of this abhorrent, possibly lifelong burden. But now they had years of continuity to contend with, and it was harder and harder to visualize a liberating offense.

"I'M GLAD YOU CALLED," HE SAID TO ERIK WHILE HOLDING A watering can over the potted annuals in his front window. "Everyone else has said you're headed this way."

"Everyone else? Like who?"

"Like Carol, the vulgar shrew you took to your heart."

"Carol? I don't know how she tracks my movements."

"And things are not so well just now?"

"Oh, bad, John. It's not wrong to claim the end is in sight." His voice struck Briggs like a saw.

"I do wish this came at a better time. I'm on a short holiday myself, the theory being rest is indicated—"

"I won't be any trouble."

"Is that so?"

Erik arrived at night while Briggs was preparing his notes for a company stalemate in Delaware for which he was serving as an independent negotiator. It surprised Briggs that Faucher had found him at all, having ventured forth from the Hertz counter at the Billings airport with nothing but a state map. He arrived with a girl he'd picked up on the way. Briggs met her after being violently awakened by Erik's jubilant goosing and her feral screeches. Her name was Marjorie, and Faucher confided that he called her Marge, "short for 'margarine,' the cheap spread." This was not the sort of remark Briggs appreciated and was therefore exactly in the style Faucher had adopted over the years. Around midnight, Faucher reeled downstairs to inquire, with a hitch of his head, "Do you want some of this?"

"Oh, no," John said. "All for you."

Thereafter Marjorie, who seemed an attractive and reasonable girl once she started sobering up, came downstairs to complain that Erik had asked her to brush his teeth for him. John advised her to be patient; Erik would soon see he must brush his own teeth and would then go to sleep. Briggs offered her the rollout on the sun porch, but she returned wearily to Erik, having gone to the front window to cast a longing eye at the rental car. She wore a negligee that just reached her hips and, when she slowly climbed the stairs again, presented a view that was somewhat veterinary in quality. The aroma of gin trailed her. When Briggs went to bed, he thought, Who drinks gin anymore? A full moon made bands of cool light through the blinds. The Segovia he'd put on at minimum volume to help him sleep cycled on, "Recuerdos de la Alhambra," again and again.

He hadn't been asleep long when he was awakened by noises. In the kitchen there were intruders. Briggs heard them, thumping around and opening cupboards and speaking in muffled tones. He wondered for a moment if he had forgotten that he was expecting someone. Once out of bed, he slipped into his closet, where his twelve-gauge resided on parallel coat hooks for just such a time as this. Briggs quietly chambered two shells and lifted the barrels until the lock closed.

In the living room, he knelt behind the big floral wing chair that faced the fireplace and its still-dying embers. From here he could see the intruders as silhouettes, moving around the kitchen, briefly illuminated by the refrigerator light. He lifted the gun and, resting it on the back of the chair, leveled it at the closer figure. Only then did he recognize the man as his nearest neighbor, with whom he shared a water right from the irrigation ditch and a relationship that strained to be pleasant; the other intruder was the man's wife, a snappish, leanly attractive farm woman who was less diplomatic in concealing her distaste for Briggs. Listening to their conversation, Briggs understood that they expected him to be out of town and were raiding his refrigerator for beer. Briggs decided that confronting them would create waves of difficulty for him in the future and that this episode was best forgotten or set aside for use another time. So he put the gun away and crept back to bed. The neighbors departed a short time later with a farewell fling of beer cans into his roses.

Faucher's voice came from the top of the stairs. "Were those people looking for me?"

"No, Erik, go back to sleep. They've gone."

———

MARJORIE WAS THE FIRST UP: SHE HAD A REMEDIAL GEOMETRY class to teach. "Always a challenge after a long night," she explained to John. She wore a pleated blue skirt and a pale-green sweater that buttoned at the throat. Her hair was drawn back from a prettily modeled forehead. She was at the stove, one hand on her hip, the other managing a spatula. "Potatoes O'Brien and eggs. Then I've got to run."

"But you don't have to cook—"

"Oh, I can't have a day with missing pieces." She cast a brilliant smile at him and held it just long enough to suggest he'd missed the boat. Erik wouldn't be getting up for breakfast because, she explained, he had an upset tummy. She held the spatula in the air while she said this, suggesting by a jotting motion that she was only reciting facts as they had been given her. Then she made a tummy-upset face. Marjorie reminded John of teachers he'd had— punctilious, too ready to use physical gestures to explain the obvious, a hint of the scold. They ate together with the unexpected comfort of strangers at a diner. She paid absolute attention to her food, looking up at him intermittently. She raised a forefinger.

"First thing he said to me was 'You're amazing.' I have learned that when they tell you you're amazing, it's over before it starts."

"Just as well. Neither of you was feeling any pain."

"I never have any idea what will happen when I get drunk. But why would you get drunk if you knew what was going to happen?" she said. "You probably get off just watching people make mistakes. That's not a nice trait, Mr. Briggs!"

She smoothed her skirt and checked it for crumbs. "I'm out of here," she said as she stood up. "What's it like?" She went to the window and craned to see the sky. "Not too bad. Okay, bye."

THEIR BOARDING SCHOOL WAS MODELED ON ENGLISH PUBLIC schools and built with iron ore and taconite dollars. In four years, the boys were made to see America through some British fantasy and believe that the true work of the nation fell to pencil-wristed Episcopalians who sang their babies to sleep with Blake's "Jerusalem" or uttered mild orotundities like "great good fortune" and "safe as houses." Their hostility toward each other was such that dormitory reassignment was considered, but they seemed always to find a reason to mend their differences. They kept up a sort of friendship at college, but when Erik moved into a rented place on Whitney Avenue with an Italian girl from Quinnipiac, they lost track again. After college, each had been in the other's wedding, and they had, for a short time, lived in the same New Haven neighborhood while they attempted to launch their careers. Then, as John was less and less in the country and Faucher relocated to Boston, they became part of each other's memories, and certainly not ones either enjoyed revisiting, though they continued to make sentimental phone calls on holidays, euphorically re-creating soccer triumphs on the rare occasions they were actually together. John Briggs didn't know quite why Erik Faucher was visiting him now. Surely this would be a dumb place to hide; he must want something.

When Briggs heard the shower start upstairs, he went outside and smelled the new morning wind coming through the fields. There were a few small white clouds gathering in the east, and a quarter mile off he could see a harrier working its way just over the surface of the hills. From time to time it swung up to pivot on a wing tip and then resumed its search.

The window of the upstairs bathroom opened, and a wisp of steam came out, followed by the head of Erik Faucher. "John! What a morning!" Briggs was swept by a sudden and unexplained fondness. But when Erik began singing in the shower, Briggs found his voice insufferable.

Erik appeared in the yard wearing light cotton pleated pants, a hemp belt, and a long-sleeved blue cotton shirt. Though his hair was uniformly gunmetal gray, he still had the eyebrows that John associated with his French blood. John did not expect much accurate detail about the previous night's bacchanal, as it was clear he held his liquor less well than he used to. It was Erik who'd said that a Yale education consisted of learning to conceal the fact that you were drunk. He raised his vigorous black eyebrows. The wordless greeting made Briggs impatient, and he relinquished the pleasant sense that he could drink better than Erik.

"This is my first day in the American West. Of course I hope to start a successful new life here." Erik claimed to have flown from

Boston, only less convenient than Kazakhstan, now that centralized air routes had made Montana oddly more remote. He didn't seem tired or hungover, and his frame looked well exercised.

"I see Marge made off with the rental car," he said.

Briggs made him some coffee and a piece of toast, which Erik nibbled cautiously while reading the obituaries from a week-old *Billings Gazette*.

"One of these Indians dies, they list every relative in the world. This one has three columns of kinfolks: Falls Down, Bird in Ground, Spotted Bear, Tall Enemy, Pretty on Top. Where does it end? And all their affiliations! The True Cross Evangelical Church, the Whistling Water Clan, the Bad War Deeds Clan. All I ever belonged to was Skull and Bones, and I ain't too proud of that! So please don't list it when I go. I'm no Indian."

Briggs reflected that he could read the paper perfectly well and spare himself the non sequiturs. He eyed the bright prairie sun working across the window behind the sink. He treasured his solitary spells, infrequent as they were, and wasted very few minutes of them. This one, it seemed, was doomed.

"Look at us, John, two lone middle-aged guys."

"Filled with blind hope."

"Not me, John. But I'm expecting Montana will change all that. What a thrill that the bad times are behind me and the real delights are but inches away!"

Briggs wasn't falling for this one. He said, "I hope you're right."

"One of my great regrets," said Erik solemnly, "is that when we were young, married, and almost always drunk, we didn't just take a little time out to fuck each other's beautiful wives."

"That time has come and gone," Briggs said.

"A fellow should smell the roses once in a while. Now those two are servicing others. Perhaps, in intimate moments, they tell those faceless new men how unsatisfactory we were, possibly including baseless allusions to physical shortcomings."

"Very plausible."

Their wives had despised each other. Carol was a classic but now-extinct type of Mount Holyoke girl from Cold Spring Harbor, New York, a legacy whose mission it was to bear forward to new generations the Mount Holyoke worldview. When their daughter,

Elizabeth, was expelled from the college for drug use, Erik's insistence that there were other, possibly more forgiving, institutions had placed him permanently outside the wall that sheltered his wife and child. When, even with certified rehabilitation, Elizabeth failed to be reinstated at Mount Holyoke, she lost interest in college altogether and joined the navy, where she was immediately happy as a machinist's mate. Faucher was bankrupt by then, a result of habitual overextension, and his inability to support Carol in the style to which she had been accustomed led to divorce and Carol's current position as a receptionist at a hearing-aid outlet on Route 90 between Boston and Natick. Very few years had brought them to this, and neither understood how.

Briggs had always been quite uncomfortable with Carol, and he had been greatly relieved when it was no longer necessary for them to speak. His own wife, Irena, was a beauty, a big-eyed russet-haired trilingual girl from Ljubljana whom he'd met at a trade conference in Milan, where she was translating and he was negotiating for a Yugoslav American businessman whose family's property had been nationalized by the Communists. John and Irena were married for only a few years, long enough for her to know and loathe the Fauchers. Briggs wasn't sure what else went wrong, except that Irena hadn't much liked America and had been continually exasperated by Americans' assumption that Briggs had rescued her. With John flying all over the world, she was stuck with the Fauchers. In the end, aroused by the independence of Slovenia, she grew homesick and left, remarking that Carol was a pig and Erik was a goat.

All of this lent Erik's wife-swapping lament its own particular comedy.

Faucher was surveying the hills to the east. "Don't worry about me overstaying my welcome," he said. "I'm quite considerate that way."

"Farthest thing from my mind," Briggs said.

"Do you have an answering machine?"

"Yes, and I've turned it on."

"A walk would be good," Faucher said. "We'll teach those fools to wait for the beep."

"I want you to see the homestead cemetery. It's been fenced for eighty years and still has all the old prairie flowers that are gone everywhere else. I have some forebears there."

They followed a seasonal creek toward the low hills in the west where the late-morning sun illuminated towering white clouds whose tops tipped off in identical angles. The air was so clear that their shadows appeared like birthmarks on the grass hillsides. Faucher seemed happier.

"I was glad to get out of Boston," he said. "It was unbelievably muggy. There was a four-day teachers' demonstration across from my apartment, you know, where they go 'Hey, hey, ho, ho, we don't want to'—whatever. Four days, sweating and listening to those turds chant."

Briggs could see the grove of ash and alders at the cemetery just emerging from the horizon as they hiked. About twice a summer, very old people with California or Washington plates came, mowed the grass, and otherwise tended to the few graves: most homesteaders had starved out before they'd had time to die. These were the witnesses.

As they came over a slight rise, a sheet of standing rainwater was revealed in an old buffalo wallow; a coyote lit out across the water with unbelievable speed, leaving fifteen yards of pluming rooster tails behind him. Erik gazed for a moment, and said, "That was no dog. You could run a hundred of them by me and I'd never say it was a dog. Not me."

At the little graveyard, John said, "All screwed by the government." He was standing in front of his family graves, just like all the others: names, dates, nothing else. No amount of nostalgia would land him in this sad spot. "Cattle haven't been able to get in here since the thirties. The plants are here, the old heritage flowers and grasses. Surely you think that's interesting."

"I'm going to have to take your word for it."

"Erik, look at what's in front of you," Briggs said, more sharply than he intended, but Faucher just stared off, not seeming to hear him.

Needle-and-thread, buffalo, and orchard grass spread like a billowing counterpane around the small headstones, but shining through in the grass were shooting stars, pasqueflowers, prairie smoke, arrowleaf balsam, wild roses, streaks of violet, white, pink, and egg yolk, small clouds of bees, and darting blue butterflies. A huge cottonwood sheltered it all. Off to one side was a vigorous bull thistle that had passed unnoticed by the people in battered sedans; hard old people who didn't talk, taking turns with the scythe. They looked into cellar holes and said, "We grew up here." No sense conveying this to Erik, who mooned into the middle distance by the old fence.

"I could stand a nap," he said.

"Then that's what you shall have. But in the meanwhile, please try to get something out of these beautiful surroundings. It's tiresome just towing you around."

"I was imagining laying my weary bones among these dead. In the words of Chief Joseph, 'From where the sun now stands I will fight no more forever.' Who was in the house last night? I hope they weren't looking for me."

"That was my neighbor and his wife. They stopped by for a beer."

"Well, you know your own society. This would seem very strange in Boston."

FROM THE ALCOVE OFF HIS BEDROOM, WHICH SERVED AS HIS office and which contained a small safe, a desk, a telephone, and a portable computer, he could look through the old glass windows with their bubbles and imperfections and see Erik sitting on the lawn, arms propped behind him, face angled into the sun like a girl in a Coppertone ad. Briggs was negotiating for a tiny community in Delaware that was being blackmailed by a flag manufacturer for tax abatement against purported operating costs, absent which they threatened to close and strand 251 minimum-wage workers. A North Carolina village that had lost its pulp mill wanted the company, and if Briggs worked as hard as he should, one town would die.

He explained this to Faucher as they drove to town for dinner. Faucher made a bye-bye movement with his hand and said *Hasta la vista* to whichever town it was that had to disappear. But it was otherwise a nice ride down the valley, mountains emerging below fair-weather altocumulus clouds, small ranches on either side at the heads of sparkling creeks. A self-propelled swather followed by ravens moved down a field, pivoting nimbly at the end of each row, while in the next meadow, already gleaned, its stubble shining just above the ground, a wheel line sprinkler emitted a low fog on the regrowth. A boy in a straw hat stood at a concrete headgate and, turning a wheel, let a flood of irrigation water race down a dusty ditch.

Town was three churches, a row of bars, a hotel, and a filling station. Each church had a glassed frame standing in front, the Catholic with Mass schedules, the Lutheran with a passage from the Bible, and the Evangelical with a warning. The bars, likewise, had bright signs inviting ranchers, families, sportsmen, and motorcyclists respectively. Different kinds of vehicles were parked in front of each: old sedans in front of the ranchers' bar and pickup trucks in front of the video arcade and next to the hotel some foreign models from Bozeman and Livingston. The clouds were moving fast now because of high-altitude winds, and when Briggs parked and got out of the car, the hotel towering over him looked like the prow of a ship crossing a clear-blue ocean.

Faucher scanned his menu vigorously. "My God, this all looks good and will look even better after a nice cocktail." He was a vampire coming to life at sundown; with each drink pale flames arose beneath his skin.

They ordered from a ruddy-faced girl who seemed excited by every choice they made, especially the Spanish fish soup with which they both commenced. She had a Fritz the Kat tattoo on her upper arm, which Faucher peered at over the top of his menu. John asked for a bottle of Bandol, and when the candles had been lit, he thought the way lay clear for Erik to make himself plain. Erik looked down at the table for a long moment, absentmindedly rearranging his silverware. He sighed and raised his eyes in self-abnegation. "I feel right at home here," said Erik. "Talk about your fresh start!" Briggs remained quiet and didn't take the bait.

The mayor came to the table with the vibrant merry hustle with which he drew all attention to himself. Briggs introduced him to Faucher, smiled patiently, and did not rise but stared at the mayor's fringed vest. Following a local convention, the mayor asked John when he had gotten back.

"I've been back about five times this summer," said John, "from

Tanzania, Berlin, Denver, and Surinam." He was always exasperated at being asked this question.

The mayor held his head in his hands. "Surinam! Never heard of it! Denver, I've heard of! What's in Surinam?"

"Bauxite."

"Baux—"

"Pal," said Faucher, "give it a rest. We're trying to eat." He made a shooing motion and the mayor left; Faucher raised his eyebrows as he asked Briggs, "How can we miss him if he won't go away?"

The last time Briggs had seen him, Faucher had been insuring marine cargo out of a nice office on Old Colony Avenue in Boston and doing rather well, especially in the early going, when Everett Hoyt had tipped him off to opportunities with far-ranging classmates. Now, Faucher said, he was an investment adviser at a tiny merchant bank in Boston, a real boutique bank. He liked meeting his people in St. Louis Square on warm spring days (he had a key) to lay out the year's strategy, clients who were charmed by his arrival on a Raleigh ten-speed. For a long time he had made cavalier decisions about his clients' investments, but now, in harder-to-understand times, they trusted him less and obliged him to chase obscure indices across the moonscape of U.S. and foreign equities. He vowed to deepen his mystery. He kept a hunter-jumper at Beverly and dropped into equestrian talk to baffle the credulous, using terms like *volade* and *piaffe* and *volte* to describe the commonplace trades he made (and commissioned), or comparing a sustained investment strategy to such esoterica as Raimondo d'Inzeo's taking the Irish Bank at Aachen on the great Merano. His own equestrian activities, he admitted, consisted in jumping obstacles that would scarcely weary a poodle, in company with eight- and nine-year-old girls and under the tutelage of roaring Madame Schacter, a tyrant in jodhpurs married to a Harvard statistician. To his clientele, yachts and horses were reassuring entities, things to which one's attention could turn when times were good.

Faucher said, "John, I've got to tell you, nothing makes me happy anymore. I need new work. I want to be more like you, John. I need a gimmick. You get the time-zone watch from Sharper Image, and the rest is a walk in the park. Whereas my job is to reassure people who are afraid to lose what they have because they don't know how they got it in the first place. John, it's not that I mind lying, but I like variety, and I'm not getting it." His face was mottled with emotion Briggs found hard to fathom. "I desperately wish to be a cowboy."

"Of course you do, Erik."

"That family"—Faucher pointed conspicuously toward a nearby table with a rancher, his wife, and their three nearly grown children—"has been here an hour, and they have never spoken to each other once. Don't people here know how to have fun?" The family was listening to this, the father staring into the space just over his plate, his wife grinning at a mustard jar in fear. "We do that when we hate each other," Faucher said.

"I don't think they hate each other, Erik."

"Well, it sure looks like it! I've never seen such depressing people."

Marjorie proceeded from the bar with a colorful tall drink. She was wearing a red tunic with military buttons over a short skirt and buttoned boots, hair pulled tight and tied straight atop her head with a silver ribbon. Briggs was glad to see her; she looked full of life. She said, "May I?"

Briggs got quickly to his feet and drew a chair for Marjorie, steadying her arm as she sat. Faucher looked very glum indeed. He said in an unconvincing monotone, "Sorry I missed you this morning. I understand you cooked a marvelous breakfast."

"It filled us up, didn't it?" she said to Briggs.

"All we could eat and no leftovers," Briggs agreed.

"What'd you do with the rental car?" Faucher barked.

"In front of the bank, keys under the seat."

Faucher lost interest in the car. "Not like I'll need it," he said with a moan.

The ranch family stood without looking at one another, obliging at least two of them to survey the crown molding. The father glared at Erik and dribbled some coins to the table from a huge paw while his waitress scowled from across the room. Karaoke had started at the bar, and a beaming wheat farmer was singing "That's Amore."

"Can I get a menu?" Marjorie asked, craning around the room.

"Has it possibly occurred to you that we're having a private conversation?" Faucher said.

Marjorie stopped all animation for a moment. "Oh, I'm so sorry." She looked crushed as she arose. Briggs tried to smile and opened his hands helplessly. She gave him a little wave, paused uncertainly, picked up her drink, and then turned toward the bar and was gone.

Briggs's face was red. "I'm surprised you have any friends at all!" He was practically shouting.

"I only have one: you."

"Well, don't count on it if you continue in this vein."

"I suppose it made sense for me to make two changes of planes plus a car rental to have you address me with such loftiness," Faucher wailed. "I came to you in need, but your ascent to the frowning classes must make that unclear."

After dinner, they had a glass of brandy. And then Marjorie appeared at the karaoke and managed to raise the volume as she belted out "Another Somebody Done Somebody Wrong Song," followed immediately by a Cher imitation, pursed lips and slumberous eyes. "I Got You Babe"—she directed various frug moves and Vegas gestures in Faucher's direction.

Feeling under attack, Faucher urged Briggs to call for the bill and pay it promptly. "I can't believe how quickly things have gone downhill," he said, as if under mortar fire.

Marjorie followed them out of the bar. She was so angry she moved in jerks. She walked straight over to Briggs and said, "You think you're above all this, don't you?" Then she slapped him across the face, so astonishing him that he neither raised a protective hand nor averted the now-stinging cheek. "You want another one?" she inquired, lips flattened against her teeth.

"I think I'll hold off," Briggs said.

"Ask yourself what Jesus would do," Faucher suggested.

Marjorie whirled on him, and John hurried away toward a boarded-up dry-goods store where he'd parked; Faucher joined him. When they got to the car, they looked back to see Marjorie's friends restraining her by the arms theatrically. A cowboy with a goatee and jet-black Stetson stared ominously as their car passed close to him on the way out of town.

"Don't drive next to them, for Christ's sake!" Faucher said. "The big one is about to come out of the bag!"

Faucher mused as they drove south into the piney hills and grassland.

"People have become addicted to hidden causes. That's why you were the one to get slapped. They've been trained to mistrust anything that's right in front of their eyes. That woman was a turnoff. Everything reminded her of family, like it was a substance. Not the family or my family but just family, like it was liverwurst or toothpaste. You can't imagine the difficulty I had preserving the pathetic taco I was trying to sell as an erection in the face of all that enthusiasm for family. I told her she was amazing, and that seemed to take all the wind out of her sails. Oh, John, my path has been uneven. I've made so many enemies. Some of them intend to track me with dogs."

"Outlast them." Briggs listlessly watched the road for deer.

"I hope I can. Really, I've come here because you never quite give up on me, do you?"

"We're old friends," Briggs droned.

"Perhaps once I'm a cowboy, you'll invest your remarks with greater meaning. Anyway, to continue my saga: I knew the noose was tightening; charges were being prepared. But I had been so nimble over the years at helping my clients improperly state assets for death taxes that they saw the wisdom in dropping all complaints against me."

Erik had moved in with his daughter and harassed her with dietary advice until she drove him to the bus station. Settling for a year in Waltham, he lived on the thinnest stream of remaining Boston comforts that shielded him from free-falling disclosure of his curiosity-filled investment days. He might have stayed, but the only job he could find was teaching speed-reading with a primitive machine that exposed only a single line of text at a time, gradually accelerating down the page; that didn't appeal to him. He went back to Boston to "clean some clocks," but important inhibitions were gone and he crossed the line, running afoul of the law at several points, especially attempted blackmail. Nevertheless, he survived until a client—with whom he had reached a mutually satisfactory settlement exchanging forgiveness for secrecy—died;

and that brought snoopy children into Faucher's world, followed by investigators, and "Net-net, I'm on the run."

JUST BEFORE SUNRISE, BRIGGS HEARD FAUCHER CALLING TO him. He climbed the stairs, pulling on a sweatshirt and his shorts, and entered the guest room. He found Erik kneeling next to the window, curtains pulled back slightly. He gestured for Briggs to join him.

In the yard below, two men stood smoking next to a vehicle with government plates. The smoke could be smelled in Erik's room as he stared hard at them. "They're here for me, John," he said. "I can't believe you've done this. Now I'm going to jail."

"You know perfectly well that I didn't do this," Briggs said. But nothing could prevent him from feeling unreasonably guilty.

"Judas Iscariot. That's how I shall always know you."

They carried Faucher away. Briggs ran alongside in an L.L. Bean bathrobe pouring out offers of help, but Erik waved him off like a man shooing flies.

THE WEATHER BEGAN TO CHANGE, AND THE HIGH WHITE clouds that had remained at their stations for so long moved across the horizon, leaving ghostly streaks in their place. One quiet afternoon, while John looked at the casework that was to follow the demise of the town in Delaware and the new prosperity of the town in North Carolina—mine mitigation in Manitoba, bike paths, a public swimming pool, a library wing in exchange for ground permanently poisoned by cyanide—the phone rang. It was Carol, bringing news that Erik was going to prison. He had been ruinously disagreeable in court, which inflated the sentences to which his crimes had given rise. She aired this as another grievance, as though little good could be extracted from Faucher now. "You were with him, John, why didn't you help him?"

"I didn't know how to help him. We were just spending time together."

"You were just spending time together?"

"I'm afraid that's it. I feel I wasn't very perceptive."

"You have my agreement on that," said Carol. "He left you literally eager for imprisonment. You had a chance to put him back on his feet, and you let him fall."

"Well, I don't know the facts. I—"

"You don't need to know the facts. You need to listen to what I'm telling you."

"Carol, I don't think you understand how tiresome you've become."

"Is that your way of commiserating with me?"

"Yes," Briggs said simply. "Yes, Carol, it is."

AT TIMES, JOHN WORRIED THERE WAS SOMETHING HE SHOULD have done. The whole experience had been like missing a catch on the high trapeze: the acrobat is pulling away from you, falling into the distance. Or perhaps the acrobat is pulling you off your own trapeze. Neither thought was pleasant.

It was inevitable that he would get worked once more for the newsletter. Hoyt wanted to know how Briggs had found Faucher.

"Breathing," Briggs said.

"You've got good air out there," said Hoyt. "I'll give you that."

In November, on his way to the town in North Carolina he had saved from oblivion, he stopped in Boston, rented a car, and drove to the prison at Walpole, but Faucher refused to see him. Sitting in his topcoat in the pale-green meeting room, Briggs rose slowly to acknowledge the uniformed custodian who bore his rejection. He was furious.

But once he was seated on the plane, drink in hand, looking out on the runway at men pushing carts, a forklift wheeling along a train of red lights, a neighboring jet pushing back, he felt a little better. His second drink was delivered reluctantly by a harried stewardess—only because Briggs told her he was on his way to his mother's funeral. At this point, a glow seemed to form around Briggs's seatmate, and Briggs struck up a conversation, ordering drinks for both of them as soon as the plane was airborne. The seatmate, an unfriendly black man who worked for Prudential Insurance, actually was going to a funeral, the funeral of a friend, and this revelation triggered a slightly euphoric summary of Briggs's friendship with Faucher, delivered in remarkable detail, considering that Briggs's companion was trying to read. Briggs concluded his description of his visit to the prison by raising his arms in the air and crying, "Hallelujah!"—a gesture that made him realize, instantly, that he had had enough to drink. The seatmate narrowed his eyes, and when Briggs explained that, at long last, a chapter of his life was over, the man, turning back to his open book, said wearily, "Do you actually believe that?"

NORTH COUNTRY

Austin was the more obviously vigilant as they made their way under the canopy of the ancient climax forest, the overgrowth of low alders and ferns towering over him and Ruth. They both had huge canisters of bear spray they'd bought in New Hazelton, but only Austin had ever had to use it—an experience that gave him no confidence, since the bear stopped only feet away as the can emptied, and seemingly thanks to mature reflection rather than violent arrest. As he shook the nearly weightless can, the bear, on its hind legs, elevated its nose and just chose not to maul him. He told Ruth the spray worked great. "Point and shoot," he said. "Nothing to it."

They followed a game trail paralleling an unnamed creek that emptied a long way to the south into the main stem of the Skeena River, nearly a hundred miles from its debouchment into the North Pacific. It was mostly forest of cedars and hemlocks, silent except for the small dark winter wrens and the many generations of ravens, the young who squawked and the bearded old with their ominous *kraah* and an inclination to follow the intruders.

This was a world Austin knew. Bearing his heavy pack, he moved with the rocking gait of a Sherpa while Ruth, equally fit, found the near-rain-forest conditions almost impossible. She studied Austin's measured stride and tried to emulate his concentration on the space in front of him, his alertness to the least resistance, and the continuous reference to an objective he somehow kept clear in his head.

Both were in their late twenties. Austin kept his auburn hair cropped close and, combined with the rapier sideburns he affected, the look strengthened his somewhat arranged individualism. He had made a sort of sub-rosa living near wild places since his late teens, guiding hikers and heli-skiers around Revelstoke; and he'd helped mining companies search for metallurgical-grade coal in the high country on the Montana–British Columbia border, where from time to time a dope plane flying right on the deck soared down the alpine valleys into the United States. His mother, a Canadian nurse who married an American merchant mariner, had given him half his nationality. He was either a dual citizen or stateless, depending on whom you talked to or, rather, how he felt. When the subjects of religion, nationality, and race came up, he said, "I don't believe in that stuff," and he didn't. What he believed in was money, but he never had enough for his problems—or for Ruth's either.

Ruth came from Burnaby, British Columbia, a tough town whose greatest product was Joe Sakic, the Avalanche center. Her mother left her and her father, a millwright, when Ruth was just a child and Sakic was still playing for Lethbridge. Her father admitted that he didn't know quite what to do with her, and she moved out at fourteen to skateboard, then waitress at Revelstoke, and finally develop her skiing to instructor competency, which provided a seasonal living yet made each year an uncertainty.

Ruth, like Austin, was a heroin user; both would have been more entrenched if their income had been predictable. Their love of the outdoors and great physical enthusiasm sustained the long dry spells; but these always contained some component that led back to using, and that led back to Vancouver, that phenomenal aperture to the drugs of Asia.

Their most reliable connection was a Sikh gallery owner, Sadhu Dhaliwal, who specialized in North Coast art above the table, drugs and protected antiquities under, the most honest junk dealer in Van with a clean business mind under his made-to-measure five-yard muslin turban. Ruth had put Austin onto him: you got a better shot with East Asians who were utterly paranoid about the immigration service and played it straight, at least in the details. There was nothing straight in the big picture, of course, but the big picture always spoiled everything for everybody.

And they were wise; they never went to Vancouver unless, as a kind of enfranchisement, they were prepared to use. To land in that town with empty pockets hoping to improvise your way onto the golden thoroughfare was to risk terrible consequences, and they were far too smart for that. Hence this trip through a primeval forest known with surprising intimacy by Austin. In certain respects, it was a perfect life: you descended from some of the wildest country left on the planet, sunburned and hard muscled after a season of gazing upon creation, straight down into the city of man where bliss came in a blue Pacific wave and the most beautiful hookers lined up around the cruise-ship terminals and chatted about the future.

They were happy to be together and joked affectionately about how they'd met. "Whose futon is this, anyway?" And "You're not my cat!"

Several curious ravens were following, now so preoccupied that they blundered into trees and then croaked in dismay. They really did suggest mischief. Once, when he stayed for a week with the Gitxsan band near Kispiox, Austin heard a story about ravens meeting in the spring to discuss the tricks they'd play that year. He liked his stay with the natives, Christmas lights on the houses year-round. Perhaps they trusted him too much, but that was life. He saw ravens perform a kind of funeral on his lawn at Kamloops, when his cat was afraid to leave the house, the same lawn where they taught their young to fly after they'd been shoved from the nest. Though the neighbors complained about all these noisy birds, he loved them. He went down to Mexico with Ruth on some transaction, and when he got back the ravens were gone. The neighbors had done away with them. He and Ruth were not in such great shape after Mexico, and the raven thing got them so down they ran from it and didn't light until they found another rented house, a trailer this time, in Penticton, where, right after getting his flu shot from the national health service, Austin briefly decided he was an American. They had started drinking, which was a feeble alternative, though it led to the same place. It was time to go up-country again, this time with a plan that took them to this forest just north of the Skeena with his prized information from the natives.

"*Austin.* I have to take a break."

They stopped and shrugged off their packs, which slumped to the ground, but as soon as they stood still the mosquitoes began to find them. Ruth could feel them against her hands as she tried to wave them away. They rose in clouds from beneath the ferns and forced the two to resume hiking. "We're close," said Austin, his voice betraying a slight impatience with Ruth. He had a GPS, which he took from his pocket while he walked, glancing at its small screen before putting it away. "I can't tell; it's in kilometers, but close."

"I don't know how you ever found it in the first place."

"The old-fashioned way, work. Not a lot of people like to crash around in brush the grizzlies think they own. I had general stuff from the First Nations guys, but I still had to work my ass off."

"I hope we don't see bears today."

"Squirt 'em."

"That's pretty cold. I'm frightened."

He wasn't cold, really; he'd already heard the distinctive woof of a bear but declined to worry Ruth about it. He kept his eyes on the lighted swatch of huckleberries near their path and saw the moving furrow in the bushes, but an encounter never came.

He was thinking that if he'd had this GPS with him on the first trip he wouldn't have brought Ruth here at all. They'd be back in Van on the yellow brick road like the time they were so loaded looking at war canoes in the Museum of Anthropology. The security guards kicked them out, and they ended up crashing in broad daylight in Stanley Park after being expelled from the Ted and Mary Greig Rhododendron Garden for falling on the rhododendrons. Ruth was troubled that they'd found themselves among so many homeless and saw it as a sign. Austin was amused by her love of portents, her belief in symbols, and almost wished he could share it. He considered himself too literal minded, though he also felt that if he'd been no more practical than Ruth they'd both be doing shit work around ski resorts the rest of their lives, never really having the merest glimpse of the great beyond.

A couple of times it had gotten away from them. The most humiliating, of course, was when they'd had to move back in with Ruth's dad, the millwright, holed up sick in his basement, but at least they weren't in a program. That had been a close call; yet it seemed after each of their grand voyages they'd moved a little closer to a program. The old guy was off making plywood like the good automaton he was and thought Austin and Ruth just *kept getting the flu.* That's why, when Austin thought about his dual citizenship, he concluded that Canada still had a little innocence left. If you could look at a forest and see plywood, you were still innocent.

Austin found the clearing and waited at its edge, in the manner of a host, for Ruth to catch up.

"Here it is."

The totem pole lay stretched out in ferns and moss, strikingly distinct from the forest around it. Shafts of light entered the canopy and illuminated the clearing in pools of brightness. Austin and Ruth moved along its length, staring at the details of the carving, strangely mixed parts of animals, birds, humans, salmon.

Ruth gave a huge sigh, and Austin said, "What'd I tell you?"

Then he walked to the end of the pole, where a fearsome animal head raised fangs toward the canopy. He took out a cell phone and dialed. After a moment he said, "You want me to start at the top? Okay, it looks like a wolf. Is there a wolf clan? Well, it looks like a wolf. Ruth, what's the next one? Ruth says mosquito turning into a human. If I recall my Gitxsan, that's Fireweed Clan. And she says, yes, Wolf's a clan, too. Then frog with hawk's beak, followed by another mosquito with a frog on its head, then it looks like a beaver dancing with a raven, and last is two bear cubs, one of which is turning into a boy. They're pretty well separated; I know you could cut them up. I mean, the fucking thing is forty feet long. You'll be happy, Sadhu, and if we're good to go on the you-know-what, I'll just give you the coordinates, and Ruth and I will see you in Van." He stopped talking and took the GPS out of his pocket again. "Hold on, Sadhu, it's finding satellites now. All I gotta do is push MAN OVERBOARD, then I can give you the numbers . . ." Austin recited the position, longitude and latitude down to minutes of degrees, and then hung up. He turned to Ruth with a huge grin.

She asked, "Is there a lot?"

"Is there a lot!" He thought, We're going to have to pace ourselves or we'll be dead inside a year. "Yeah, Ruth, there's a lot."

ZOMBIE

ORVAL JONES, A WIDOWER, HAD A BIG GREEN WILLOW TREE he was very proud of. This thing sat out on their lawn like a sky-scraper, and Jones bragged about all the free air-conditioning he got out of it. The neighbors, almost to Harnell Creek, were a Cheyenne family, always working on their cars, whom Jones referred to as "dump bears." After the Indians, the road kept going but in reduced condition until it was just a pair of ruts that turned to impassable gumbo at the first rain shower but finally led to an old ranch graveyard in a grove of straggling hackberry and box elder.

Dulcie Jones came home to introduce her boyfriend to her father, who had trained her in the values of law and order and so understood her difficult and sometimes-perilous work. She was twenty-four, a pretty dishwater blonde with a glum heart-shaped face and a distinctive V separating her upper incisors. She held a cigarette between the ends of the first two fingers of her right hand, the arm extended stiffly as though to keep the cigarette at bay. She wore gold earrings with a baseball hat. Beside her stood Neville Smithwick, sly as a ferret in his pale goatee and sloping hairdo. Dulcie was an escort girl and sometime police informant, though her father was aware of only the latter portion of her résumé as well as her day job at an optometrist's office. All-knowing Neville was her dupe. As a fool, he had made her work easier. Under ordinary circumstances, Dulcie served her customers as they expected. If she should suspect they were impecunious, however, she turned them over to the police, who saw to it their names appeared in the paper with varying results: laughter at the office, families ruined, and so on. In such referrals, she got paid by the fuzz. No tips.

Smithwick's father, Neville Senior, had hired Dulcie to do away with his son's virginity on the pretext of Neville Junior's interviewing her for a job, during which exchange Junior was meant to succumb to her erotic overtures. This scheme Neville Junior absorbed but dimly. Rather than be frustrated by his obtuseness, Dulcie quite sensibly went about her day, with Neville in tow, so that, should the project collapse, she'd at least get a few errands out of the way.

When she introduced Neville to her father, her father said in a not particularly friendly, half-joshing way, "I may have to give Neville a haircut."

"You and what army?" said Neville.

Orval seemed to sober up. He was pushing sixty but still wore pointed underslung cowboy boots that aggravated his arthritic gait. The snap buttons on his polyester western shirt were undone around the melon of his small, protruding stomach, the underside of which was cut into by the large old buckle he'd won snowmobiling. He gave off an intense tobacco smell, and his gaze seemed to bounce off Neville to a row of trees in the distance.

"Well. Come in and set, then. If you get hungry, I'll bet you Dulcie'd cook something up."

"I don't eat anything with a central nervous system."

"You what?"

Mr. Jones twisted the front doorknob and kneed the door over its high spot as they went indoors. Dulcie was pleased to have caught her father early. It was only a matter of time before he would begin asking, "Will this day never end?"

Orval brought Neville a Grain Belt and Neville thanked him politely. "You seem like a well-brought-up feller," said Orval Jones.

"I'm a virgin," said Neville. This remarkable statement was true. But Neville had developed expectations, based on some exceedingly provocative suggestions by Dulcie, which were not so completely lost on him as Dulcie had imagined. From his vast store of secondhand information, he had concluded that he was about to hit pay dirt—3-D adult programming. In fact, she told him he'd need a condom and, in the resulting confusion, stopped at Roundup to help him pick one. But once inside the drugstore, he embarrassed her by asking if they were one-size-fits-all, like a baseball hat, and then balked when the clerk explained he had to buy them as a three pack. Neville told him that the thought made him light-headed.

Orval was on the sofa and seemed defeated by Neville's very existence. Nevertheless, he made a wan attempt at conversation.

His jeans had ridden up over the top of his boots to reveal spindly white legs that seemed to take up little room in the boots, just sticks is all they were. The terrible bags under his eyes gave the impression that he could see beyond the present situation.

"Neville, you say you come from a banking background."

"Foreground."

"Ha-ha. You've got a point. And do you—uh, actually work at the bank too?"

"Hell, no."

"Hell, no. I see. And what do you do?"

"TV."

"TV sales?"

"I watch TV. Ever heard of it?"

"I suppose that should've been my first guess."

"Uh, yeah."

Neville had learned from television that remorseless repartee was the basis of genial relations with the public. He really meant no harm, but not having any friends might have alerted him to the dangers of this approach. The appearance of harmlessness disguised the violence he had inside him and would save him from ever being held accountable for its consequences, when he quite soon gave it such full expression. *He wouldn't hurt a fly.*

NEVILLE SENIOR MANAGED THE SOUTHEAST AND CENTRAL Montana Bank; he was a genuinely upright and conventional individual who worked hard and played golf. His wife had died some years ago, so he had had charge of Neville Junior from early on. In the winter, he went once a month to St. George, Utah, fighting Mormons for tee times, and returned refreshed for work. He was a happy, well-balanced, thoughtful man who had accepted the work ethic he'd been raised with and which caused him to spend too little time with his only child. Their prosperous life was such that there were no duties that his son could be assigned that would instill the father's decent values. And he didn't want him on the golf course with his various hairdos. Walking down North Twenty-Seventh in Billings with his tax attorney, he once passed a youth with pink, blue, and green hair not so different from Neville Junior's. "When I was in the navy," the attorney said, "I had sex with a parrot. Could that be my child?"

Neville Junior worried him. The boy had been raised by a television set, as his father readily admitted. It was bad enough that his language and attitudes came directly from shows he'd seen; he seemed to have found sufficient like-minded companions to keep him from questioning his way of life. What was unsettling was that long after his age would have made it appropriate, Neville Junior had failed to show any interest in girls. As the nice-looking son of a bank president, he should have been cutting a wide swath. Girls liked him and came around to watch TV with him; girls that sent his father's mind meandering in ways inappropriate to his age and state. His frequent attempts to catch his son in flagrante delicto resulted only in an invitation to join the couple innocently watching the late movie. It was not so many years ago that he himself had boogied under the strobes of big cow-town discos where today's dowagers once wriggled in precopulatory abandon.

For a banker, Neville Senior was remarkably free of malice, and his great wish was to overcome the gap of loneliness that lay between him and his heir. It's possible that he imagined that bringing Neville Junior into the randy orbit that seemed to include everyone but Neville Junior would have the effect of giving the two some ordinary common ground upon which they could begin to talk like a couple of guys. Boning up on *TV Guide,* as he had once done, proved futile. Real watchers like Neville Junior had a subtle language not easily penetrated by poseurs. He just stared when his father asked if there was anything good on tonight.

"Neville," said the father, "two things: I wish I'd been a better parent."

"You've been all right. Don't sweat it. What's the second?"

"Sex," barked Senior. "Why aren't you interested in sex?"

"Don't get your panties in a wad, Dad. Virginity is no disgrace. At least it keeps you from weighing sixty pounds and being covered with giant sores."

"It doesn't have to be that way."

"It only has to be that way once, and you can count me out."

"It should be seen as a gift, a gift of love and joy that perpetuates the race."

"Perpetuates the race? Are people still in favor of that?"

"I don't know how you've become so cynical at your age."

"You can't accept that I'm happy, can you?"

"Are you?"

"Considering the cards I've been dealt."

"Have they been such bad cards?"

"You tell me."

"I guess I can't."

"Just because you named me after yourself doesn't mean I have to turn out like you."

"No, I suppose that wouldn't be any good."

"I'm not saying that. Different isn't good or bad. It's different is all it is. Get it?"

"You could change your name. I'd understand."

"I've thought about it. I've never thought of myself as Neville."

"What have you thought of yourself as?"

"Karl."

"With a *C*?"

"With a *K*."

Much later, when Neville Senior had decided that life was not worth living, he would give this Karl-with-a-*K* idea a final thought.

FROM HIS SUITE AT THE NORTHERN HOTEL, AS A SUMMER SUN descended on city streets blue with heat, pressed in upon by angular storefronts and shade-hunting pedestrians, Neville Senior called an escort service. Given that the city police had been recruiting undercover officers lately to nab concupiscent johns, this was risky business, but Neville Senior believed the scrutiny was directed at streetwalkers, and so he felt relatively safe, if a bit frightened. Anyway, when it came to your own flesh and blood, risk was unavoidable. He had cash, plenty of it, and he intended to buy Neville Junior out of his dubious virginity and joyless view of things. More than that, he wanted to buy him the high road to the human race, which in his view was bound together more by fornication than anything else. In his life, courtship was fornication, life was fornication, and grief revealed but one road back to the light of day and that was fornication. The only answer to life's complexity: fornication.

Dulcie arrived straight from her shift at the optometrist, and Neville Senior welcomed her in his most courtly manner. "Came right away," she said. "Two saps in the waiting room with drops in their eyes." She seemed taken aback at first by his nervousness and perhaps foresaw the long hard work sometimes necessary to overcome the anxiety of skittish customers for the sake of the almighty dollar. Bummer.

Dulcie kept her purse beside her; the cell phone inside it required only a single key to be pressed and her mission would be accomplished, either by an arrest or the heading off of an assault. It seemed she would have to buy time to size up the transaction. Some adjustment of plan was required because unexpectedly this geezer had a plan of his own. After a long day at the optometrist's shop, Dulcie was glad to learn that the heavy lifting would come later, but at the very least they had old man Neville for procuring. That it was for his own flesh and blood was hardly extenuating, and one way or another she'd get paid. Anything to get away from dreary folks reading the acuity chart: "P . . . E . . . C . . . F . . . D—I can't read that last line . . ." *Of course you can't, you need glasses!*

He gazed at Dulcie with admiration: at first lustful but, when she noticed, adding avuncular overtones and calling her "dear" so as to assure her he wasn't getting ready to whip it out. She might have been touched if she'd known this modest transaction would later in the year result in his suicide—though it was not easy to say what might get through to Dulcie Jones, barrel racer.

WHILE DULCIE WENT OFF TO SPRUCE UP IN THE BUNKHOUSE, Orval gave Neville a tour of the place, apologizing for the disorder of the kitchen as they passed through. "It takes a heap of living to make a home a heap!" he said merrily. Neville said he bet Orval had a million more where that one came from. When they were out of earshot, Orval said, "You're kind of a smart-ass, aren't you?" He got right in Neville's face.

"If you say so," Neville said, as though trying to help Orval in the best way he knew how. Orval was thinking of slugging him and stared at the spot on Neville's face where he imagined landing the blow. Overcoming the temptation, he asked how Neville had met his daughter, making it clear by his tone that he was sorry it had ever happened. He'd been counting on a cowboy or someone in law enforcement.

"My dad introduced us. She's going to be our new vice president. He wanted me to get to know her on behalf of our business."

"Vice president? Vice president of what?"

"Of our bank, Southeast and Central Montana Bank. Member FDIC."

"What about the optometrist?"

Neville remembered her looking without glasses at the road map that morning.

"I guess she doesn't need him," he said, suddenly wondering if Dulcie was farsighted. He might not feel as safe with her at the wheel. He'd been so relaxed watching his day go by in the rearview mirror, never going rigid against his seat belt as he did whenever he distrusted the driver. He so looked forward to what he expected from Dulcie, and yet he felt the responsibility of considering her as a candidate for vice president of the bank. He realized he didn't quite understand the situation but knew he would do anything in the world for his father, to whom he helplessly longed to reach out. But this was different. The bank had always been kept from him, so that his father's asking him to do something connected with his livelihood suggested a change.

"You want to drive the tractor?" Orval asked. Neville understood he was being humored, but he hadn't expected Orval to go rural on him this quickly.

"I doubt it."

"Well, what would interest you, Neville?"

"You got any archaeological sites?"

Orval went outside, started the tractor, and backed it up to the loaded manure spreader. It was clear he had decided to go about his business, but Neville followed him innocently as he drove out into the pasture and then activated the PTO, showering the youth with turds. Neville saw right through his apologies and walked back to the house, looking for Dulcie. He had a mean-spirited impulse to tell her that her father would not be welcome at the bank. But all that was tempered by the attraction he felt for her, aroused by her various provocations and double entendres. His girlfriends had always acted as if being available was enough. It wasn't; he required much more. Neville enjoyed this sense that Dulcie was after him like a bad dog, and knowing she was just trying to get the vice president's job made it all oddly spicy.

"What happened to you?" she asked, when he caught up to her in the yard.

"I'm not too sure."

"I think it's time we got us a room."

"Amen to that," Neville said, with a look of terror. She was flicking at him with the backs of her fingernails, loosening some of the debris.

Neville leaned well out the window as he drove to wave goodbye. Orval's return wave seemed to say *Good riddance* and confused Neville, who thought they'd hit it off.

Once out of the driveway, Dulcie made the gravel swirl under the tires. They were heading now for the Absarokee cutoff; she told Neville she had a good spot in mind. She held his gaze until he said, "Watch the road."

They wound along well-kept hay meadows, tractors in the field spitting out bales, swathers moving into the dark green alfalfa and laying it over in a pale-green band close behind the standing grass. The road flattened, and in its first broad turn was the small, tired motel. Dulcie pulled up in front of the office. As she got out of the car, Neville asked her to be sure there was TV. A crevice of irritation appeared briefly between her eyebrows and she turned to the entrance. When she came back, she climbed in brusquely and threw the key on the seat. She gave him a long look and said, "Room seven," allowing her tongue to hang out slightly. Neville gave a small bounce to show he understood.

When the door closed behind them, they surveyed the room, its brown pipe bed, plastic curtains, and gloomy prints of the Custer massacre and the Blizzard of '86. Dulcie took it all in, and when she turned to Neville he was holding up one of his new condoms.

"Americans are coming together to stamp out HIV," he said, with touching sincerity. "Can you help me with this?"

Not at all self-conscious, Neville stripped and stood naked next to his pile of clothes, instantly erect. Dulcie lit a cigarette and knelt in front of him. There was nothing to do but apply the condom. Cigarette held in the V of her teeth, squinting against the rising smoke, she rolled it on deftly. "Now," she said, standing up, "I'll just go into the bathroom and get ready."

"Take your time," said Neville, moving instinctively for the television. As he watched it, she opened the door to the bathroom for an instant and took his picture.

"Memories." She smiled and closed the door again, wondering what the cops would make of a guy with nothing but a channel changer and a rubber. She created a bit of noise with the shower curtain, the faucets, and a cupboard door. It seemed like enough. She stood stock-still and listened. She thought someone else was in the room; then the realization that it was only the television made her doubt her sexuality.

Downhill Racer. Neville was Robert Redford. He locked his knees together and bent into every slalom, concentrating so thoroughly that the condom fell off. After a while, he began to miss Dulcie and rapped politely on the bathroom door. Neville wasn't stupid. He smiled to himself; he knew she wasn't in there. He got dressed and went outside. The bathroom window was wide open, the curtains hanging against the wall of the motel. The car was gone. He returned to the room and tried to kick the condom across the rug, but it just rolled up under his foot. He carried it dangling to the wastebasket and then stretched out to enjoy something reliable. Even the light of the TV flashing on the ceiling seemed pleasant. During the slow parts of the movie, he luxuriated in his relief. He couldn't fathom Dulcie and he wasn't even going to try. Nevertheless, out of fealty to his father, he would confide his intuition that she'd make a poor vice president. It was not out of a sense of having been betrayed but the unseemly picture of a vice president crawling out the window of a cheap motel. In this, he was well brought up, and he loved his poor, confused papa.

Dulcie was at the station house turning in her expense receipts, principally gas, motel, along with film, when they brought Neville Senior in for booking. He stared at her as they tugged him past. The cop at the desk didn't even look up as he stapled her chits to a large sheet. So Dulcie in effect spoke to no one when she said, "He bonds out, he settles, the beat goes on."

When Neville Senior dragged himself through the front door that night, Neville Junior was there to console him, having heard all about what had happened to his father on the local news. They fell into each other's arms. Senior's heart was overflowing, while Junior felt he was in a school play in which he had memorized the lines without knowing what he was saying.

Finally, Senior spoke. "I was lonely."

"Mom's dead," said Junior, in his odd blank way.

Neville's father explained his scheme so that his son at least would know that he hadn't been on some unseemly quest for his own carnal pleasure.

He had offered Neville Junior numerous pets in the years since his mother's death, hoping that greater familiarity with animals might help him understand his father's urges—and expenses!—but that had come to nothing, as Neville Junior found animals to be little more than a stream of unpredictable images and therefore unsettling. The dog was given away, the cat was given away, and the hamster bit an extension cord and was electrocuted.

"That Dulcie sure is mean!" he now cried. "It's just not right, Dad. I'm going to pay her back."

When the newspaper published his name as a patron of whores, Neville Senior lost his job at the bank. We've all been there, his friends and former colleagues told him, but they hadn't, nor had they forfeited their homes to their own bank as he had, though he was allowed to keep the rather fussy furniture his late wife had chosen. In time, that too would be sold and the funds applied to a rental house on the south side of town, where the homeless walking on their battered patch of lawn reminded the Smithwicks of just what might be next.

Senior's friends had gotten him a job as assistant greenskeeper at his old golf club, where the summer heat frequently laid him low as he tried to perform work for which he had little training. He was one of eighteen assistants, and when the chief learned the bunker crew on which he'd placed Neville Senior was ridiculing him with requests for car loans or mortgages, he reassigned him to moisture sampling, which allowed Senior to wander the golf course alone with probe and notebook under a hard prairie sun. The greenskeeper himself took subtle pleasure in lording it over someone who had fallen through the invisible ceiling that had separated them for so many years. A former caddie replaced by electric carts, he understood perhaps better than Neville Senior ever had how perilous is all employment, though as a workingman it was unlikely society would bother to take away his job for consorting with prostitutes, as there wasn't enough class separation to produce a stirring fall. In many places, whores were now "sex workers" moving freely between golf courses and no-tell motels like any other independent contractors.

Neville Junior's habits remained little changed, except that because of the danger of muggings his former acquaintances were reluctant to visit him. Since his father had not shared his plan to commit suicide, there was no reason for Neville Junior to imagine a time when the television would be shut off and he would have to bestir himself should he wish to eat or be sheltered from the weather. His father's decision was based equally on his failed career and his now-accepted inability to communicate with his son at any level.

He made his departure as uneventful as possible. For two straight days he watched shows with his only child, including uplifting sitcoms, sitcom reruns, and sitcom pilots that were seeing the light of day that very night. An agnostic, he retained a faint hope, magnified by overpowering loneliness, of meeting his late wife, and that gave him the courage—indeed, a certain merry determination—to gas himself in the garage. Before he went there to seal the windows and start the car, he needed final confirmation, and so he returned to the living room, whose shabbiness was emphasized by the prissy furniture. Neville Junior's head was outlined against the square of light of the television. "Tomorrow, I'll be gone," he said, but his son didn't hear him. "Goodbye, Karl." The consequences began: the discovery of the body, the unattended funeral, the eviction of Neville Junior, and the loss of all things familiar to him, including those he cared for most: the smell of lilacs and spring perennials filling the air, the sounds of pickup baseball in the park a few blocks away, and television.

Dulcie Jones's days were numbered.

ON THE FOURTH OF JULY, FOUR MONTHS AFTER THE PASSING of Neville Senior, Orval looked up the dirt road in front of his house toward the Cheyenne car garden, the crooked line of telephone poles, the mud puddles mirroring blue sky and thundercloud silhouettes, the watchful hawk in the chokecherry thicket, and saw a willowy man in old clothes coming toward him, a man whose bounding gait marked him as younger than his apparent circumstances might have suggested. Orval sensed he was coming to see him, and indeed he was. There was no reason for him to know that this was Neville Junior, or to know what brought young Neville to his ranch.

He removed his hat rather formally on arrival at Orval's porch, the hair under it looking wet and plastered down close around his small skull, while Orval eyed him suspiciously from his rocking chair. Neville's well-cared-for teeth gleamed through his beard, whose black bristles falsely suggested a hard life. "Mister," he said, "I'm in a bad way. Throwed a rod here a mile or two back and didn't have the do-re-mi to get it fixed. I need a job." Neville had the Appalachian accent routinely heard in westerns down pat.

"Not hiring."

"A little sumpin' to eat, place to sleep, and a TV; wouldn't have to pay me."

"Wouldn't have to pay you? What exactly is it you want to do for free gratis?"

"I'd work, but like I say you'd need to train me."

"But not pay you?"

"You heard right, mister. Just those things I mentioned."

The two swept out the old milk house, which had a two-stage concrete floor and a place for the creek to run through, though the creek had been diverted long ago and the room was dry enough. Then they assembled an iron bed and rolled out a thin mattress, which they beat until the room filled with dust. "No telling what's been living in here," said Orval, with an ingratiating smile. Neville threw up his hands in wonder. "But I guess that'll do you. Gon' have to."

"TV."

"What's that?"

"I said TV."

"I haven't got but one and it's up to my house."

"I told you when we started in on this," hissed Neville, "that I'd require a TV."

The reception was exceptionally poor in the milk house, but by adding aluminum foil to the rabbit ears they were able to get two channels, one all snowy with Greer Garson. The tension seemed to go out of Neville's body as he told Orval to call him for supper and then settled down on the pipe bed for some viewing, ignoring the dust that continued to rise and the perhaps-too-vigorous closing of the door by Orval.

In the morning, Orval was determined to see if he could get his money's worth out of this man, who had introduced himself as Karl "with a *K*." He could tell right away that Karl meant to stay, as he hurled himself into shoveling out the calving shed, a job requiring no experience whatsoever but a strong tolerance for grueling repetition. At one point, he went at this with such demonic energy that it caused Orval to tell him whoa-up, he had all day. Neville wiped his forehead, leaned on the shovel, and asked Orval if he had any family, smiling as he heard about Dulcie as though for the first time. Today he'd parted his hair in the middle, and with the dark beard he had the appearance of an old-time preacher, someone who could talk about Jesus with plausible familiarity. Orval thought he'd have to find him some other clothes if he worked out, something brighter, because he wasn't a hundred percent comfortable with the preacher look. There was always one going up the road with a Bible in the glove box supposedly to convert the dump bears but probably to check out the little squaws.

This one was here for vengeance. "She ever get out to see you?"

"Just on weekends."

"But that's tomorrow."

"The horse sees more of her than I do."

"Could be, now you got a hired man, there'll be more time for the two of you to visit."

"I'm available!"

It seemed like he spent half of Saturday, the set on mute, listening to her gallop up and down the place, wondering when she'd get the curiosity to come over and say howdy. Poor old Orval was doing the vigil thing in his rocker, Saturday beer in hand, but Neville could tell he wasn't getting much in the way of contact either—on a day made for family, a light breeze in the cottonwoods, the Cheyenne sleeping it off up the road, and the rare lowing of distant cattle. Springtime!

She knocked on the door.

Neville had a loose, gangly act ready for this, head tipped to one side, wire lightly wrapped around his left hand as he turned to let her in. Blue light from the silent television jerked around a room that smelled like concrete and once stored an ocean of purest milk. Dulcie wore jeans and tennis shoes, a snap-button western shirt with the sleeves cut off. She had on sunglasses. He liked her firm arms, the lariats and roses that decorated the pink shirt. She gazed at him and, crossing her arms behind her back, leaned against the door she'd just closed. She raised her forefinger to slide the sunglasses down enough to look over their top.

"I know who you are," she said.

"That's more than I can say!" Neville called out.

"May I turn that thing off?"

"No!"

"Well, I am. I'm turning it off."

Dulcie went past him and bent over the set, reaching for the controls. Neville had the wire on her in nothing flat, called her a low-down escort service. Though there was a spell of tumult—more like a rerun than anything new—it was the moment when movement stopped that finally produced surprise, and Neville was swept by desire at last. Everything in his life had led to this ravishing stillness. He knew who to dedicate this one to.

ORVAL WENT ON SITTING IN HIS ROCKER, STUBBING OUT HIS cigarettes in a tomato juice can. Sooner or later, Dulcie would have to put the horse up and come have a few words with him. At the same time, his new hired man wandered down the darkening road away from the little ranch, away from the Cheyenne and their old cars, weeping at the innocence now beyond his grasp, never to be a virgin again. It was great to feel something so strongly. He hoped to weep forever. If only his father could have been there to see him with tears streaming down his face. It would have been a beginning, something good. He could just hear his voice.

Well, son, I'll be damned. You feel pretty strongly about this, don't you?

MIRACLE BOY

W<small>E ALWAYS WENT BACK TO MY MOTHER'S HOMETOWN WHEN</small> someone was about to die. We missed Uncle Kevin because the doctors misdiagnosed his ruptured appendix, owing to referred pain in his shoulder. Septicemia killed him before they sorted it out with a victorious air we never forgave. The liverless baby was well before our time—it would have been older than my mother had it lived—but my grandfather's departure arrived ideally for scheduling purposes in the late stages of diabetes; we drove instead of taking the train and en route were able to stay over for an extra day at the Algonquin Inn in western New York, taking advantage of Wiener Schnitzel Night, and still make it in time for the various obsequies while reducing prolonged visits by priests. (My father was an agnostic and fought sponging clergy with vigor, remarking that he had "fronted his last snockered prelate" and adding, "Amazing how often it's Crown Royal.")

Before I relate the death of my grandmother, I have to summarize that of my grandfather, because that was where I acquired my short-lived reputation as a worker of household wonders. Ever since I have had great sympathy for those identified as seers or healers; my heart even goes out to those merely called lucky. Like someone drifting lazily down the Niagara River, the big fall is just a matter of time.

My grandfather, though a diabetic, went on occasional sweet binges, cherry pies at Al Mac's Diner, and he injected himself with insulin daily, to our agog fascination. He held in reserve giant sugar-filled jawbreakers in his pocket, and when I was too pressingly talkative a single one of those hunks would keep me silent for almost three hours. He was a quiet man, a volunteer fireman who played checkers in the open-fronted firehouse down whose brass pole I was sometimes allowed to slide. In his youth he had read in a newspaper that "Many people persist in making the cemetery a place of recreation, generally a foreign element prompted by ignorance," and thereafter he was a tireless promoter of public parks.

On the Fourth of July, while most of the family was at the parade on North Main Street, and after a midday meal of quahog chowder, swordfish, beet greens, and corn, he lay down on his big brown favorite couch and died. He'd never taken up more room than he needed, and in an essentially matriarchal household his death was mostly seen as foreshadowing my grandmother's, though it was widely celebrated among "the foreign element." This was not long after little boys were given dresses to wear, and my mother and aunts sent me off dressed as a hula girl for the Fourth of July parade, a debacle that ended in my breaking a white plastic ukulele with its Arthur Godfrey "automatic" chord changer during one of many clashes with Azorean native Joao Furtado—later known as Meatball—who called me, with sensible directness, "little girl." When I got home from the parade, my grandfather was dead. I studied the adults for clues. They were studying my grandmother for clues. She took to her bed. Three days later, she was still there.

Her absence brought the household to a standstill. My mother and aunts seemed entirely helpless without her ordering them around. She did not even seem to acknowledge them when they visited her room, and a meeting was called where it was decided to send me in. Her idealization of children was counted upon to bring her around before the house and its contents sank into the earth, an eventuality I could imagine to include the opaque projector in the attic with its pictures of long-dead baseball players, the cabinet full of Belleek china in the priest parlor, all the wildly squeaky beds and creaking stairs, the bookless "library" reeking of cigars, and even the souvenir Hitler Youth knife my uncle Paul had given me. As it happened I was the only child available for idealizing, standing around with my mouth open. And so I headed to my grandmother's bedroom, which was on the second floor, and there I acquired my reputation as a performer of miracles, setting myself up for a fall whose effects would never end. (When my father learned of my success, he began calling me Miracle Boy, later M.B.)

I let myself in without knocking, closing the door behind me. From her bed my grandmother followed me with her eyes. I started to say something in greeting, but the impulse died, and instead I looked around for a place to sit. The ornate brass bed was to the right as I entered; to the left was a vanity with its silver brush and mirror carefully arranged. At the far end of the room was a door to a small porch over Brownell Street, access to which we were all denied, as it sagged dangerously with dry rot. I took the chair from in front of the dresser, pulled it up beside my grandmother's bed, and sat down. I was perfectly comfortable. My grandmother had turned her head on the pillow to look directly at me, upon me, and I could tell that my presence was welcome. After a while, several formulaic remarks on the death of my grandfather passed through my mind, since even then I was capable of a modicum of glibness in the little-old-man style encouraged by my aunts. But those thoughts vanished and I gazed at my grandmother's long hair, gathered around her face in silver braids. My mind wandered again, and then I spoke.

"I was wondering," I mused, "if Grandpa left me any jewels."

My grandmother stared at me, sitting on my hands in her vanity chair, knocking the toes of my shoes against each other as the silence lengthened. Suddenly she began to laugh, from some deep place and loud enough that the scurrying of my mother and my aunts could be heard outside the door, where they must have been eavesdropping. Then my grandmother sent me away so she could rise, dress, and make our supper. Thus was born my reputation as a child healer, my personal albatross, Miracle Boy.

THE HOUSE WAS A TYPICAL TRIPLE-DECKER ON A VERY SMALL lot, hardly bigger than the footprint of the house itself, with a tiny yard bound by a severely rectilinear and humorless hedge. Any game in the yard had to involve the roof, usually winging a ball up there and guessing which side it would fall off. My uncle Paul, a veteran of World War II, was always willing to do this with me for hours on end; he never really seemed to have a job. Otherwise, all you could do in the yard was stand there and stay clear of the hedge. This being a corner lot, the windows on two sides gave a point-blank view of the faces of pedestrians, and the second- and third-floor windows were ideal for the launching of tomatoes, stink bombs, and rotten eggs. Once, when my constant adversary, Meatball Furtado, had chased me all the way from North Park, Aunt Constance was able to pour boiling water on him from the second floor, melting the cast on his recently broken arm. This unambiguous Irish-Portuguese skirmish pretty much reflects the fortress quality of the small neighborhoods of the town, with a church at the center and a pocket park for escalating ethnic conflict. In time, jicks, Portagees, and harps would be partners in law firms and especially in local politics. Then they'd move away and just be Americans—consumers, parents, drivers of minivans. I suppose it's a good thing.

Here in this small yard, on his reluctant and occasional visits from the Midwest, my father sat, reading *Yachting* and contemplating a global circumnavigation, though, he often told me with a conspirator's wink, he would not necessarily return to the same spot from which he'd gamely set sail—by which I guess he really meant he hoped one day to leave us. The closest he came to circumnavigating was a steel cabin cruiser that never left the dock and came with an oil painting of a busty woman walking through a crowded church. It was entitled *A Big Titter Rolled down the Aisle.* This vessel sat in a rental slip on a stagnant lake and served as a platform for cocktail parties. At the height of these gatherings, my father would start the engine and then look with authority over the transom to make sure the water pump was sending coolant out the exhaust. The feat was performed in silence and suggested that behind the revelry lay a serious world, the world of the sea.

Now my grandmother was dying, the death of a monarch. My father was going to have to visit my mother's cherished hometown and all his in-laws, a dreadful prospect, as he viewed my grandparents' house as a lunatic asylum; its bubbling humanity trained a cold light on behavior that had its roots in his own days as an Eagle Scout and piano prodigy in a four-block area south of Scollay Square, where he was the only pianist, thanks to his iron-willed mother, half paralyzed by an early stroke brought on by her terrible temper. My father hated to play the piano, hated even to see one, and forbade me to join the Boy Scouts.

Between my grandmother's first and second strokes, my mother and I set out in the Nash for this old lunch-bucket city and its mosaic of neighborhoods, the house-rattling trains and worn-out baseball diamonds; my father told my mother he would follow "in due course" for the funeral. She looked him in the eye and asked, "What if she recovers?"

I was inside my grandparents' house on the occasion of her second cerebral hemorrhage. My reputation as a wonder worker had lingered in the years since my grandfather's death, and at each crisis I worried that I would be asked to perform again. As the house filled with family members, including my physician uncle Walter, all gathered hopelessly around the door to my grandmother's bedroom, which seemed to glow with ominous beams of light. Walter came and went wearing a stethoscope, which he had never before done in this house. He was so handsome it sometimes made his sisters gasp, and with all power now in his hands he seemed like a god.

My mother ordered my father to get on the road immediately, and I worried that if his opinions got loose in this atmosphere every one of us would suffer. I was less focused on the impending demise of my grandmother than on seeing my favorite uncle, Paul, my grandmother's youngest, a man in his fifties who sold the occasional insurance policy from his bare office in the Granite Block. He lived in a rooming house named Mohican House after the old Mohican Hotel, and his habits had changed little in many years, consisting as they did of day-drinking and reading odd books from the public library. He collected printed mazes; some, he told me, were quite famous, like Welk's Reflection, Double Snowflake, and Jabberwocky. He was keenly interested in the tea clippers and had an old painting that he claimed to have fished out of some Yankee's garbage pail, a portrait of a Massachusetts sea captain dressed in embroidered robes like the emperor of China.

On our drive across Ontario and western New York, I listened again as my mother recited the saga of my grandmother, both hands on the wheel, cigarette in her mouth: the Saga of the Displaced Gael. Orphaned at twelve, Grandma worked a life-devouring job in the textile mills but managed a happy marriage to a fellow she met on the Narrows (Grandpa) between North and South Watuppa Ponds, where young people gathered. They were to enjoy fertile parenthood, modest gentility, economic sufficiency, and religious security only a block from their parish church; she did, however, occasionally cross the Quequechan River to attend Mass with French Canadian girlfriends she'd met in the spinning room at the Pocasset mill. My grandfather supplied special groceries to the side-wheelers of the Fall River Line, including the *Commonwealth*, the *Pilgrim*, and the fabulous *Princess*. His was a tiny business based on special arrangements with a fruit boat that brought bananas from Central America. My grandfather told me of the deadly spiders that sometimes arrived with this cargo, hinted at Spanish treasure from Honduras (probably the origin of my previously mentioned interest in "jewels"), and described the three great steering wheels in the pilothouse of the *Princess* and the chandeliers in its engine room. Even my grandparents' Yankee neighbors, who ranged from mill owners and bankers to broken-down fellows who delivered firewood by horse and wagon, accorded grudging admiration to this honest couple, especially as immigrants, got smaller and browner by the day. If my mother was too caught up in her story, she allowed me to drive on my learner's permit while she kept smoking or chewed her thumbnail.

The children grew up and took their respective places: teacher, policeman, physician, waitress, and finally occasional insurance salesman Paul, who came home from the war having lost his best friend to a German booby trap, a boy from President Avenue with whom he'd enlisted. Paul emphasized that the device was a Leica camera, which seemed to undercut the disparaging term for the thing that had killed his friend. After that Paul began to decline, and the gossip was that he wouldn't have taken the loss of his friend so badly if the pair of them hadn't been queer. But he was smart and resourceful and he managed to go on, usually by selling a policy to one of his drinking buddies. He was tall and well dressed, his auburn hair combed back straight from a high forehead in an elegant look that spoke of success. By evening, the look would change to something wild and slipping.

My mother had always seemed fearless; if she wasn't, she concealed her fear with spontaneous belligerence. But she strove for obedient perfection under my grandmother's eyes and when she fell short, usually in household matters like cooking or cleaning or religious matters like forgetting First Fridays, she responded to my grandmother's well-concealed wrath like an educated dog, performing as directed but with the faint slink of force training. This behavior was disturbing and made me ambivalent about my grandmother, who treated me like a prince. Behind the geniality of this tiny woman, I saw the iron fist. I wasn't sure I liked it.

Paul moved in and out of the house over the years, even had temperate spells. I remember some very pleasant times when my mother and I visited: he threw a baseball onto the complex of roofs for me to field with my Marty Marion infielder's mitt and tried to instill in me his passionate Irish sentimentality and diasporic mythology. The rest of the family was feverishly American and did not care to celebrate the Irish connection; in fact, Uncle Walter on traveling to Ireland announced that the place was highly disorganized and insufficiently hygienic, and that the garrulity of the people was annoying, especially the sharp cracks that were mechanical and tiresome and always about other people.

But Paul had archaic Gaelic jigs on 78s that he played at tremendous volume from his room next to his mother's, and, when drunk, he could roar along to various all-too-familiar ballads—"Mother Machree," "The Wearing of the Green," "When Irish Eyes Are Smiling," and so on—giving me a whack when I accompanied the great John McCormack with such invented lyrics as "my vile Irish toes" or "God bless you, you pest, you, Mother Machree."

Sometimes he tired of his old records and said it wasn't the potato famine that had driven the Irish from the land; they had left to escape the music. It really depended on what the Bushmills was up to. He also used me to practice his insurance pitch. "Good morning, Wilbur," he would begin—not my name—and it was always "morning" in these pitches even though he was incapable of rising early enough to make a morning pitch. Wilbur was an imaginary Yankee farmer, dull, credulous, yet wily. "Wilbur, we've known each other a good many years and, God willing, more to come with, let's hope, much prosperity and happiness. I know you to be a man, Wilbur, whose family stands just below the saints in his esteem, a man who thinks of everything to protect them from . . . from—*Christ!*—protect them from, uh—*the unforeseen!* Christ, of course! *The unforeseen!* But ask yourself, have you really thought of everything?" Here is where the other shoe was meant to drop, but, more often than not, Paul allowed himself an uncontrolled snort of hilarity before refilling his "martini." This was never a martini; it was invariably a jolt of Bushmills, but he called it a martini, and the delicacy of the concept compelled him to hold the libation between thumb and forefinger, which uncertain grasp sometimes caused the drink to crash to the floor, a "tragedy."

The fact that Paul and I got on so well would be remembered during my seventeenth year, when I was called upon to perform one more miracle. By my humoring him during his Irish spells, I had earned his faith. He'd taken me to see the Red Sox, Plymouth Rock, Bunker Hill, and *Old Ironsides;* he bought me lobster rolls at Al Mac's Diner, a Penn Senator surf-casting reel, coffee cabinets, and vanilla Cokes by the hundred. He made me call a drinking fountain a "bubbler," in the Rhode Island style.

Eventually, Paul moved back to his digs at Mohican House, evicted by Uncle Walter, who had replaced my grandfather for such duties. My grandmother was also a disciplinarian, but when it came to her youngest son she reverted to type and viewed him as troubled, broken by the war, while the rest of her offspring were expected to follow clear but inflexible rules. Irish tenors were replaced by radio broadcasts of ball games. For every holiday and the whole of summer, my mother continued to drag me from what she viewed as our place of exile in the Midwest to Brownell Street, which I might not have liked but for our almost daily trips to Horseneck Beach, where I had the occasional red-faced meeting with a girl in a bathing suit. I also made a new friend on Hood Street next to North Park, Brucie Blaylock, who could defend me against Meatball and his allies. Brucie was a tough athletic boy with scuffed knuckles and a perpetually runny nose whose beautiful eighteen-year-old sister had just married a policeman. The couple was still living in my friend's home awaiting an apartment and, while snooping through their belongings, we discovered a *gross* of condoms, which we counted, being unsure how many were in a gross. "This cop," said my friend, gazing at the mountain of tiny packages, "is gonna stick it in my sister a hundred and forty-four times!" My mind spun not altogether unpleasantly at this carnal prospect, and my fear of bathing-suit girls at Horseneck Beach rose starkly. From time to time, we would recount the condoms; by the time the number dropped below a hundred, my friend was suffering and I wandered around as if etherized by the information.

My aunts continued to adore and pamper me while reminding anyone who would listen of my capacity for working miracles. This would have been long forgotten but for the fact that the encouragement came directly from their mother, especially inciting my aunt Dorothy, who waitressed long hours at the Nonpareil diner downtown, and my aunt Constance, a substitute teacher who lived two houses away with her husband, a glazier. My uncle Gerry, who had joined the Boston mounted police solely to acquire a horse, was rarely around. Uncle Walter said the horse was all the family Gerry ever wanted. Dorothy's husband, Bob, made himself scarce, too, finding the constant joking around my grandparents' house exasperating. Theirs was a mixed marriage, the first in our family, as Bob was an English immigrant, a jick. It was customary for those of Irish extraction to mimic the accents of such people by singing out, "It's not the 'eavy 'aulin that 'urts the 'osses' 'ooves. It's the 'ammer, 'ammer, 'ammer on the old 'ighway." My grandmother outlawed this ditty out of deference to Bob, who, after all, might one day convert.

I seemed to have been forgotten during the early moments of the crisis, even by my mother. I seized on my brief obscurity to cook up reasons why I was now exempt from the miracle business: one, I was not the same boy who had stirred my grandmother to rise after the death of her husband; and two, it was not a miracle in the first place, except in the minds of my mother and her crazy sisters. I now sequestered myself in my room with *Road & Track*, Dave Brubeck Fantasy label 45s, and *True West* magazine. I was greatly absorbed by the events leading up to the gunfight at the OK Corral. No longer able to enchant me with accounts of the big baboon by the light of the moon combing his auburn hair, my mother tried upgrading my reading habits by offering me a dollar to read *Penrod and Sam*. I declined. But all this was distraction; I feared my call would come and I worked at facing it. I worried that by keeping to myself and playing the anchorite, I gave credence to my imputed saintlike powers; it behooved me to mingle with my relatives and strive to seem unexceptional, even casual. Being incapable of grasping the possible demise of my grandmother, I had no problem sauntering around the house seeing to everyone's comfort. No one suspected the terror in my heart. At one point, as I suavely offered to make cocktails, my mother jerked me aside and asked me if I thought this was the Stork Club. Thereafter, my attempts to disappear consisted of idly scratching my head or patting my lips wearily as I gazed out upon Brownell Street, where every parking spot was taken by my relatives' cars, all except Paul's, which he called a "foreign" car. Anyone pointing out that it was a dilapidated Ford was told, "It is entirely foreign to me." That car was not here, and if it was not over at the Mohican it could be as far afield as New Bedford or Somerset, whose watering holes provided what he called "acceptable consanguinity." These were terrible stewpots mentioned in the paper from time to time in an unflattering light, the one in New Bedford being, according to Uncle Walter, a bucket of blood haunted by raving scallopers and their molls.

My aunt Constance functioned as a kind of hall monitor. She had no legitimate authority, but she enforced the general rules as laid down by her mother, and at a time like this she saw to comings and goings, the hanging of visitors' hats, and the drawing of blinds and the pulling of draperies; she liked to catch me out in little infractions, since I had, besides the unearned affection of my grandmother, the fewest accrued rights around the place. This had to be undertaken discreetly, or there would be my mother to contend with, younger than Constance but spoiling for a fight with her. I'd once heard my father say that Aunt Constance's ankles were thick. One day she came to my room where, out of quiet desperation, I was committing self-abuse in consideration of the rate condoms were being consumed up on Hood Street by the homeless cop and his teenage bride. She told me through the door that she would be taking me to see my grandmother. There was a platitudinous tone she used, even when she addressed me as Elvis or when she reminded me that others needed the bathroom too or wouldn't it be nice if I picked up a few of my things so that others didn't have to do it for me. When I emerged, she gave me a stare that insinuated either that she knew what I'd just been doing or that I was unaware of the gravity of the situation. Is it Miracle Time? I wondered. I already had enough to fear, because I couldn't grasp what was happening to my grandmother. Well, I told myself, we aren't there yet.

As if I lacked sufficient power in my legs, Aunt Constance gave me a last little push into my grandmother's bedroom, then followed me inside. My mother was already there, red eyed and helpless. She was far the prettiest of the sisters and had been indoctrinated somehow in the idea, perhaps by the whole family, that handling crises would not be her strong suit. Years later, she would tell me that at the moment I'm now describing she wanted to curl up on the floor and break down completely; however, even semiconscious, her mother still had strong authority, and such behavior could fall under the proscribed category of "shenanigans."

My grandmother spoke my name with groggy satisfaction, her face lit by the candles surrounding a figurine of the Virgin Mary that rested on her bedside table, a cheerful statue, trophy sized and a lovely Bahamian blue. My mother appeared to have been there awhile, and sorrow transfigured her face in a way that I'd never seen it before, which upset me thoroughly. Aunt Constance fidgeted around, disturbed that my grandmother's mouth remained open. My mother caught Constance's briskness, and when she gently tried to close my grandmother's mouth, my mother hissed under her breath, *"Don't touch her!"* Constance's hand rested in midair, her eyes meeting my mother's with a kind of warning. It was like one of the showdowns I'd been investigating. Our awkward vigil didn't last much longer, as Uncle Walter soon arrived and shooed us out. We waited on the first floor for half an hour until Walter came down. He walked straight through us, speaking only as he went out the door: "I'll get the priest." He had a deep voice, and everyone in the family knew he was the law.

It was summertime. Our parish priest, Father Corrigan, had gone to the Cape for a few days, so we wound up with some alien in a round collar, Father Cox, whom Walter kept on call in the parlor, reminding us that Extreme Unction did not reside in persons. Meanwhile, a bulletin was sent out for Corrigan, who appeared the next morning with a raging sunburn and loftily dismissed his surrogate. Father Corrigan took me aside, to a quiet spot past the stove. I was alert. He looked at me gravely and asked if I had noticed that Birdie Tebbetts had been promoted to starting catcher for the Cleveland Indians. I admitted ignorance in a way that suggested that at another time I would have been better informed. Father Corrigan reminded me, "Birdie went to Providence College with your uncle Paul—say, where *is* Paul?"

"He couldn't make it," I replied impulsively, based on no particular knowledge. Everyone was relieved that Paul had declined to be here, although Aunt Constance had conveyed my grandmother's condition to him by a note to his landlord.

"What'd you do that for?" my mother demanded.

"Ma asked me to," said Constance contentedly.

Father Corrigan, handsome enough that his departure for the seminary had sown heartache, was a priest of old-fashioned certainties who saw nothing cheerless in the present circumstances. He had gone completely bald, not even any eyebrows, but he wore a wig, a small vanity that was considered to have humanized him. He had a redhead's complexion, and the wig was auburn. It didn't fit particularly well: the hairline was too emphatic around the front, and when he bent over, as he was usually careful not to do, it pried up from behind and exposed an eerie sanctum of white scalp.

As my grandmother's confessor, he knew she was bound for the ultimate destination, a place whose glory was beyond the descriptive powers of the most effusive travel agent. We fed off his optimism, sort of. He and Uncle Walter consulted away from the rest of us, who tried to read their lips from across the wide kitchen. Uncle Walter worshipped his mother, and it could not have been easy for him to recognize that she was ending her life in his professional hands.

Aunt Constance now brought her two girls, my cousins Kathleen and Antoinette, who viewed me as a corrupt hoodlum because of the then-ubiquitous blue suede shoes I wore. My uncle Gerry finally showed up too, in his glossy black trooper boots and Boston police uniform, which seemed thrillingly archaic, like something Black Jack Pershing might have worn. But Gerry was so shy and sweet, he could barely speak. "He gets it from the horse," said Walter. I retired quietly to my room, where I resumed my study of the Old West, a place where do-gooders and mad dogs alike lived free of ambiguity and insidious family tensions. At the moment, the

Earps and the Clantons were beginning the open movements of their mortal ballet.

By evening, our two authorities agreed that my grandmother would not live much longer, though she was conscious enough to make one thing clear: she wished to see her baby, Paul, before she died. My mother got on the phone and confirmed that my father had set out by automobile. "He'll be here in no time!" she said into thin air.

Uncle Walter departed for the Mohican. Bickering the whole time, Aunt Dorothy and my mother made a desultory attempt at cooking supper on the big gas stove from which my grandmother had so long and so majestically ruled: this time, macaroni and cheese. We were seated before our identical platters, my cousins studying my deployment of the silverware, when Uncle Walter returned and, entering the dining room, announced to us all, "He says no." After a suspicious glance at the macaroni, he turned significantly to the adults, who rose as one and left the dining room, leaving me with my cousins. We heard "bloody bugger" through the door.

Kathleen, who had snapping blue eyes and jet-black hair in tubular curls that hung alongside her face, announced, "We're awfully sad over at our house." Antoinette, a plainer brunette with a thin downturned mouth, looked on and remarked, "It's too bad your father isn't here to help. Why is it he never comes?"

I couldn't tell her that the household melodrama was unbearable to him or that he was busy, in my mother's absence, making the two-backed beast with his secretary. Instead, I replied, "He has a job. He's on his way now. How fast do you expect him to drive?" Both smiled: anyone who couldn't broil in an old mill town all summer long was to be pitied. I remembered with satisfaction the day this pair appeared at Horseneck Beach. They looked like two sticks in their bathing suits, no butts but the same superior smiles. Naturally, they started a shell collection, everything lined up according to some system.

I was preoccupied, having just reached the point where Doc Holliday was moving silently behind the corral planks with his sawed-off shotgun. Distantly, my mind was moving to the eventualities facing those men in that dusty patch of earth when the door opened and Uncle Walter summoned me with a crooked finger. I rose slowly to go out. My fears were aroused by the hauteur in the faces of my cousins, then confirmed when I saw my mother and my two aunts. I first pinned my hopes on the slightly skeptical expression of my aunt Dorothy, but when I saw my mother's pride and the phony look of general forgiveness on the face of my aunt Constance, I knew I was cooked. It was miracle time again. Father Corrigan gazed with detachment, wig tipped up like a jaybird: the services this family expected of me probably struck him as verging on sacrilegious.

I clapped both hands over Uncle Walter's car keys as they lightly struck my chest. "The Blue Roadmaster in front. Bring your uncle Paul. You're the guy that can get this done. Get Paul now and *bring him here.*"

Constance piped up. "He is your favorite uncle."

It was a straight shot to Mohican House, and at that hour there was enough room to park a thousand cars. The entire way, I was plagued by mortifying visions of unsuccessful parallel parking, but I was never tested. Spotted by pedestrians my own age—three swarthy males with ducktails—as I climbed out of the car, I adopted a self-effacing posture I hoped would make clear that I was not its spoiled young owner. Once it was locked, I plunged its incriminating keys into my pocket.

Paul answered the door to his apartment promptly, greeting me with the phrase "Just as I expected," and showed me in with a sweep of his arm. He wore a surprising ascot of subdued paisley foulard that complemented a sort of smoking jacket. His was what was once called a bed-sitting room, which perfectly described it. A toile wall covering with faded merriment of nymphs and sparkling brooks failed to create the intended atmosphere. "How'd you get here, Walt's car?"

"Yes," I said, as though it was obvious. Paul had a faint brogue this evening, a bad sign. I glanced around: his bed was beside the window that looked down into an alley and was made with military precision, including the hospital corners he had once demonstrated. There was a battered but comfortable armchair nodded over by a single-bulbed reading lamp, and on the other side a night table that held the only book Paul owned, his exalted *Roget's The-*

saurus, which he called "the key to success" and which Uncle Walter blamed for his inability to speak directly on any subject. A gray filing cabinet a few feet from the foot of the bed supported an artillery shell that served as a vase for a spray of dried flowers.

Paul poured each of us a drink, and when I courteously declined mine, he said, "Why, then, our evening is at an end."

"I don't think I should drink and drive," I said defensively.

"Do it all the time," he said, "an essential skill. Never caught unprepared. Learn it while you're young. Bluestockings have given it a bad name." He used the same voice on me that he employed in testing insurance pitches, brusque shorthand best for indicating the world of valuable ideas he had for your future, take it or leave it.

I had a sip and, after little pressure, finished my strong drink; whereupon I was coerced to accompany John McCormack and my uncle Paul in "Believe Me If All Those Endearing Young Charms," a performance that, under the responsibility of my family assignment, I found so disturbing that I accepted Paul's offer of another drink. Next Paul recited a poem about Michael Collins, how he left his armored car to walk laughingly to his death, after which a silence made it clear that Paul was ready to hear my pitch. I was emboldened and terrified by the alcohol, and not entirely sure who Michael Collins was or why walking to his own assassination cheered him up. I suppose this contributed to my disorientation. The record playing in the background was scratchy, and the orchestra accompanying the various tenors sounded like a bunch of steamboats all blowing their whistles; at the same time, I could see the appeal of being drunk.

There was no use telling Paul his mother was dying. Walter had already said that. Not only did I feel utterly burdened, but being here gave me such an enduring case of the creeps that, years later, I voted against Kennedy, switching parties for the only time in my life. I now admit that I feared the loss of my standing as a miracle worker and longed to find a way of preserving my reputation, partly because it was so annoying to my father, who considered my mother's first home a hotbed of mindless nostalgia and an impediment to her conformity and compliance. I couldn't appeal to Paul's values because I didn't know what they were and because I suspected that beneath his lugubrious independence lay some kind of awful bitterness that, if uncovered, might turn my world upside down.

I had no strategy, and my heart ached. It was important to my grandmother that I deliver Paul to her side, and the only thing I could think to do was to tell him what she meant to me. I began with a head full of pictures, my grandmother folding her evening paper to rise from her rocker and embrace me when I returned from a day in North Park, of the harmony of her household, the smell of pies arising from her second kitchen in the basement, the Sunday drives after Mass when she was taken around the perimeter of her tiny kingdom and to the abandoned mills where she had once worked. I even thought of our life in the Midwest, when I'd longed for her intervention in a family slow to invent rules for their new lives. I was with her on the first visit to her husband's grave when, looking at the headstone of their little boy right next to my grandfather's, she said, "I never thought they'd be together so soon." A half century between burials: "so soon." She bent to pat the grass in the next space. "No keening," she had warned her children at my grandfather's funeral. And indeed, it was a quiet American affair.

I imagined I could touch on a few of these points and move Uncle Paul to accompany me back to Brownell Street, but I never got started. I was seized by a force I'd barely suspected and astonished myself by choking on tears that spilled down my face while Paul watched impassively.

Once I pulled myself together, Paul stood and turned off the record player. He looked at me with chilling objectivity and then stated his position clearly. Moving to his filing cabinet, he began to rearrange the dried flowers in the artillery shell, awaiting my departure.

Driving the Roadmaster I became immediately hysterical. I saw myself rocketing through the railings of the Brightman Street Bridge and plunging into the nocturnal gloom of the Taunton River below. But the Buick rolled along like a ship, and my panic abated.

As I parked in the dark of Brownell Street and turned off the lights, I could see the faces in the window: time to take my medicine. I hoped their seeing me alone would make it unnecessary to explain that I had failed, but Paul could be just behind me in his foreign car. Walter, my mother, and my aunts would not give up so easily. Perhaps my quite legitimate expression of defeat would help, assuming no one noticed my unsteadiness.

Like a jury they were waiting for me in the kitchen. Knowing my grandmother still lived, I was strengthened. Entering the back door, sole entrance for anyone but a priest, gave access to a hallway and the choice of going straight upstairs, to my bedroom, or into the kitchen, where I was expected. The great blue presence of my uncle Gerry opened the door for me. Walter, Dorothy, Constance, and my mother stared without a breath or movement. I could state that I had failed; I could indicate that I had failed; I could make a paper airplane with a handwritten statement that I had failed and sail it at those faces; but until I did I was still a worker of miracles and reluctant to step down. The silence lasted long enough that my uncle Walter elevated his chin sternly, more pressure than I could withstand. I shook my head: no.

I didn't look up until Walter summoned me to the bookless library. His fingers rested lightly on my shoulder as though I might not be able to find my way. Once we were behind closed doors, he reached an open hand for his car keys, which I deposited therein. "Have you been drinking?" I nodded, meek but with rising surliness, concealed in the booze that was now thrumming in my eardrums. "I suppose it was a condition of your negotiations." I nodded again, this time modestly. "Well," said Walter, "I would like to know exactly what Paul said." I felt reluctant to convey this information, perhaps out of lingering loyalty to my favorite uncle, who had so often thrown the baseball on the tenement rooftops for me to field, but in the end I felt it wasn't mine to keep.

"He said to tell you all that . . . that sick people depress him."

I returned to my room reconciled to my lost sainthood. For now, there was the OK Corral and its several possible outcomes. But that night, my grandmother died at last and nothing in the story of Wyatt Earp suggested an appropriate response, as he of course was dead, too.

FOR THE SEVERAL DAYS OF THE VIEWING, THE WAKE, THE FU-neral Mass, it was as if we were troops following orders. My mother kept slipping off, trying to check on my father's progress. First it was a flat, then they wouldn't take a check for gas, then a distributor cap, then the magneto, and later, when she told Uncle Gerry about the bad magneto, he said, with all his big-cop innocence, "Jeez, Mary, they haven't had magnetos in twenty years!"

My father arrived on the day of the wake, a hot day more like August than late September. Greetings were fulsome, given the gravity of the occasion, Dorothy frayed with grief and worry and Constance somehow politicizing it and making the demise of my grandmother refer mostly to her own need for importance despite having married a Protestant. My father always seemed extraordinarily brisk, compared with my mother's relatives, and more capable of defusing social awkwardness with sunny confidence. He hugged my mother so long that her sisters grew uncomfortable and abandoned the porch. As the baby of the family, she might be more "advanced," but it was not their job to bear witness to the decline of standards. It was my turn with my father, and my mother followed her sisters indoors.

"Come here, Johnny," he said, leading me to the trunk of his big sedan, which he opened with a broad revelatory gesture. There was his leather suitcase with its securing straps and, next to it, a ten-horsepower Evinrude outboard motor. Looking over his shoulder left and right as though fencing loot, he said, "These worthies are all indoors men, unlike you and me. They see the sky about twice a year. Now that the inevitable has come to pass, we're going to rent a rowboat, attach this beauty to the transom, and run down to Fogland for some floundering."

I told him I could hardly wait, and he mussed my hair in approval. Later, I felt a pang at omitting to suggest that Grandma's departure was an impediment to floundering. I helped my father take his bag to Paul's old room and stayed with him for a short time because he seemed to forget that I was still there. He hung his clothes carefully and placed a bottle of Schenley's blended whiskey on the dresser. He lined up three pairs of shoes, in the order of their formality, walked to the window overlooking Almy Street, and heaved a desolate sigh. I left the room.

I suppose he was nearly forty by then and wore his liberation from what he considered the ghetto Irish with a kind of strutting pride. The circumstance of my grandmother's death was such that he would be forgiven for being a Republican and for condescending to the family with his obviously mechanical warmth. He was still remembered bitterly for summoning the family to the Padanaram docks to admire a Beetle Cat with a special sail emblazoned with I LIKE IKE. He now received news of Paul's disgrace with a serious, nodding smile. Aunt Constance, rushing about to prepare the funeral dinner for the family, brusquely and with poorly concealed malice gave him the job of opening a huge wooden barrel full of oysters. Standing next to me in the backyard, he confided, "Here I am in fifty-dollar Church's of London shoes, a ninety-dollar Dobbs hat, a three-hundred-dollar J. Press suit, *shucking oysters.* When will I ever escape all this?"

I was afraid to tell him that I was enjoying myself. He pointedly reminded me that he always made note of whose side I was on. "This group"—they were always a *group*—"ain't too keen on getting out of their familiar tank town." He liked bad English for irony but was normally painfully correct about his diction. He viewed himself as an outdoorsman, almost a frontiersman, based solely on having taught canoeing at a summer camp in Maine. "You'll find this outfit," he said, gesturing to my grandmother's house, "in street shoes." For my mother's family, the outdoors came in just one version: a baseball diamond. But his view of my mother's family could be infectious, and I went to our first meal with him now viewing them as a *group*, nervously calibrating the array of forces around the table.

My father never seemed particularly interested in me, except when my alliance offered him some advantage, or at least comfort, in disquieting settings like this household. My grandfather thought he looked like an Indian and once greeted him with, "Well, if it isn't Jim Thorpe! How are your times in the four-forty, chief? Leaving them in the dust?" Or, more succinctly, "How."

My grandfather drove the back wheels on the majestic American-LaFrance hook and ladder. "A good place for him," said my father. "Well to the rear."

I knew his stay here would be a trial, though it seemed the only voice that carried up through the floor, causing him to flinch, was

Father Corrigan's. Religion was an empty vessel to my father, a contemptible relic of the origins he hoped to escape.

"Now the keening begins," he said. "Your grandmother was a fine woman, but all the noise in the world isn't going to get her anywhere any faster. When you hear them in the parlor tuning up, you may think they've gone crazy. This stuff's about to go the way of the Model T. You'll be able to tell your kids about it. The sooner it's over, the sooner I can go back to America and try to make a buck."

"Will I see Grandma again?"

"That's the sixty-four-dollar question, isn't it? Ask Father Corrigan. Old Padre Corrigan never had a doubt in his life. He'll tell you it's only a matter of time. Me, I'm not so sure. He'll have Grandma crooking a beckoning finger from the hereafter even if you can't see it and he can. Poor fellow spent his life making promises to weavers with TB and loom mechanics with broken bodies. I guess he started believing it himself. You ought to hear him describe heaven. It sounds like Filene's Department Store."

Then he went off on the Irish. "Among the many misconceptions about the Irish," he said, "is that they have a sense of humor. They do *not* have a sense of humor. They have a sense of ridicule. The Ritz Brothers have a sense of humor"—I had no idea who the Ritz Brothers were, but he held them in exalted esteem—"Menasha Skulnik has a sense of humor. You think the Irish have a sense of humor? Read James Joyce. You'll have to when you go to college. I did. You'll ask yourself, Will this book never end?"

I always tried to agree with my father, even when I didn't understand him. "I see what you mean," I said, with an aching sort of smile.

"Here's a famous one," he said as the wailing started downstairs. "'If it weren't for whiskey, the Irish would rule the world.' Do I like this. They're *only* charming when they're drunk. When they're sober, they're not only not *ruling* the world, they're ridiculing its hopes and dreams." This was entirely true of my father himself. He was a merry boozer but a bleak observer of reality when sober. The present moment was a perfect example. He saw no legitimate grief in the response to my grandmother's death, only posturing and inappropriate tribal memory. "Rule the world, my behind," he added. "'If it weren't for blubber, Fatty Arbuckle would set the world record in the high jump.'"

My relatives were certainly not ruling the world, and they went about their lives with high spirits. While their certainties like everyone else's were soon to be extinguished by the passage of time, their ebullience was permanent, and I say this having seen two of them expire from cancer. My father, on the other hand, was grimly obsessed with his health, and for some reason I associate this with his flight from his origins. I recall him explaining to my mother that he had missed making his Easter Duty on the advice of his eye-ear-nose-and-throat specialist to avoid crowds.

I went downstairs and sat among my relatives, some of whom hadn't seen each other for a long time, especially the ones from Lawrence, who seemed to have in common straitened finances and sat in their overcoats watching the circulation of plates of finger food. My aunt Taffy, from Providence, wept copiously and in a manner that reminded everyone, I was sure, of the melodramatic nature so annoying to my grandmother that she pretended that Taffy longed to star in a soap opera. The Sullivans were there from across the street. Uncle Gerry, wearing his mounted policeman's uniform with its crossed straps and whistle deployed just under his left shoulder, stared straight ahead and moved his lips in authentic prayer. My physician uncle Walter maintained a look of dignified pragmatism, and I'm sure he knew we looked to him for deportment hints. We believed he understood life and death through actual experience and, unconvinced by Father Corrigan's merry certainties, wished he would say something about the afterlife.

Saddest of all was Aunt Dorothy, because her household meddling had expired with my grandmother and she was now wandering about without a self to give meaning to her acts. I thought of her with white holes for eyes, as in the standard depiction of zombies. She looked blank and confused and made clueless efforts to find chairs, answer the phone, and offer horrifying comfort to people she barely knew. Finally, Walter commanded, "You need a rest. I'm sure everyone will excuse you." At this she let out a somewhat lunar cry that made poor Mr. Sullivan, a surgical arch outlining the former position of his cigar, grab his wife and run for the door.

Aunt Constance served the funeral dinner with a kind of pageantry, abetted by her daughters, the two little shits Kathleen and Antoinette. Watching their stately entrance for each course, learned in that narcissistic training ground of First Communion, I could have, as Joseph Goebbels once remarked, "reached for my Luger." The meal was a tribute to my grandmother and featured all her favorite dishes—swordfish (my father confided these small steaks were doubtless from a skillygallee, an obsolete term for the less desirable white marlin), corn on the cob, parsnips, and apple pie—and represented a maudlin idea of grieving. "They're gonna milk it," he said, when he heard the menu.

We were seated, Walter at the head of the table, my mother, father, and I in a row, Dorothy sniveling into the canned consommé preceding the main course, Kathleen and Antoinette, half crouched in their pinafores and ready for duty, Gerry upright as a man of the law. As Walter said grace, I watched my mother closely; her melancholy smile was less occasional than chemical, produced by the pills she took, ostensibly to raise an abnormally low blood pressure, as well as straight shooters from the vodka tucked in her suitcase. Like many of their generation, my parents believed in the absolute odorlessness of vodka and applied to its consumption none of the restraint of the blends whose broadly familiar aroma marked the user like a traffic light. My father sported his customary deniable supercilious smile. When cornered, he'd lay it to gastric distress or the unaccountable prelude to heartbreak, as when my mother walked out on him and he couldn't wipe the grin off his face and had to explain it.

The front door was carelessly slammed shut and Uncle Paul walked in, wearing his drab woolen officer's uniform with obvious moth holes, and commented that we looked a bit gloomy. Father Corrigan rose to his feet, held his napkin between thumb and forefinger, and dropped it to the table. With infinitesimal authority, Walter indicated with his eyes that Father Corrigan was to take his seat again promptly. Constance appeared behind Paul and, leaning around him, said in a shrill voice, "Just making certain there's a place set."

"Grab me a beer from the fridge," said Paul. Constance froze, but my mother leaped up and chirped nonchalantly that she knew right where it was. My father patted her butt, eyes half lidded with private irony as she swept past, and Paul smiled at his favorite relative, my mother; Uncle Gerry, rendered huge in his uniform by the smallness of the room, strode to the sideboard to turn on the big Sunbeam fan. He'd begun to sweat. Seated again, he asked Walter about various old folks of our acquaintance. Most got good health reports, except Mary Louise Dwyer and Arthur Kelly, who had, he said in a significant voice, "been in to see me." As to Mr. Sullivan's lip cancer, "You couldn't hurt him with a tire iron."

"A corker," Gerry agreed.

Once my mother had deposited the beer in front of a greatly relieved Uncle Paul, Aunt Constance began to send in my cousins with a steady parade of dishes. Noticing my father, Paul nodded and said, "Harold." Constance shooed the cousins along from close behind, with no effect on their speed at all but reinforcing her position as culinary benefactress. She kept her husband behind in the kitchen as a kind of factotum and sous-chef; besides, he wasn't comfortable in what he not altogether humorously called Harp Central. He could have said it more clearly because no one cared what he said, all part of Constance's disgrace: she would have enjoyed greater standing if she'd been gang-raped by a hurley squad.

I'm not sure my father enjoyed much esteem either, and I think he knew it. He was well educated, hardworking, and ambitious, yet something set him apart, as though he had renounced a portion of his humanity to achieve his current station and had, moreover, abducted the baby of the family, my mother, to a dreary and stunting world where people made themselves up and were vaguely weightless. I realized with dread that, at this funeral meal, he was likely to take a stand.

"I wonder where she is now," Paul said, slurping his consommé.

"Where who is?" Walter asked coolly.

"Ma. Where Ma is."

Dorothy covered her mouth.

"Ma is in heaven," said Walter.

"You, as a man of science, say she is in heaven?"

"Absolutely."

"Well, good. I hear great things about the place."

Kathleen made a covert rotary motion with her forefinger at her temple; then, fearing she'd been observed, she pretended to adjust one of the tubular curls. She wouldn't look at me.

My father half rose from his chair, rather violently, shifting all attention to himself, as he reached across the table for a dish of lemons. "It's been a long time since I had a chance to enjoy a swordfish steak!" This fell discordantly upon me and anyone else who'd heard his theory of the skillygallee.

My mother said, "Wonderfully done, Constance, a beautiful meal." Constance gave a self-effacing curtsy. Dorothy stared at her food with white eyeholes and a half-opened mouth, and Gerry rubbed her back consolingly until she picked up her fork and prodded a parsnip. Since I eat too fast when I'm nervous, my mother put her hand on my forearm to slow me down. I looked up at her helplessly, wide eyed.

Walter smiled all round and said, "This would be a good time to remember all the happy times we've had at this table, especially when Pa would have been in my place. We saw very little of Ma then. She just came and went from the kitchen, long enough to look after us. She sure looked after us, didn't she? Generations of us. Me, Connie, Gerry, Mary, and you kids, right, Antoinette?"

Antoinette stood up from her seat. "My grandmother is a saint," she sang out, in a high mechanical voice. "She is being welcomed by the angels this very minute."

Paul blew up his cheeks and nodded.

"Kathleen?"

Kathleen rose and gazed around the room with her electric-blue eyes. "Our grandmother—"

I knew I was next, and I felt the ironic expectations of my father, who loved to see me on the hot seat. I never really believed it was the test of character he claimed.

"—brought to our family the highest standards of piety and family concern, especially as to her devotion to Holy Mary Mother of God." Even knowing they'd been prepped, I asked myself where the two little hussies had come up with this chin music. I hadn't long to think about it, though; it was my turn.

"Johnny?"

I sat dumbfounded, a weird tingling in my scalp. My father looked at me with a faint smile, and my mother gazed into her lap. Both seemed to understand I wasn't up to this. I had the whirlies.

"Why don't you stand up?" Uncle Walter said gently.

I rose slowly, the tightness in my throat making speech impossible. A glance at my father revealed ill-concealed hilarity. Uncle Paul was waggling his empty beer at Constance, who stood in the doorway bearing down on me with her eyes. The cousins looked like winners. Only a brief picture of my grandmother rescuing me from this, which she certainly would have, allowed me to break quietly into inarticulate tears.

Uncle Walter smiled sadly and said, "Thank you, Johnny. That's how we all really feel. You've done us all a big favor—thank you." As I sat down, my father's glance said he could hardly believe I'd pulled off this stunt. I could almost hear him saying, *Fast one there, M.B.*, or *Smooth*.

Uncle Walter turned his gaze to my father but quickly looked away; my father was fussing with the napkin in his lap and plainly intended to say nothing at all about the passing of my grandmother. My mother stared at the side of his head, and I knew that in more private circumstances she would have been ready to raise hell. He surely knew ahead of time how brittle any words of tribute might have seemed. My mother's family was great at seeing through things, and he wasn't about to walk into a trap. Paul stood a carrot in the mound of his mashed potatoes and hummed "The Halls of Montezuma," satire that seemed somehow directed at my father. Kathleen and Antoinette were still smirking at me for crying, and I consoled myself with napalm fantasies as their mother stood between them, urging them to clean their plates while tossing me an artificial look of bafflement that suggested I'd lost a step or two to her darlings.

As Aunt Constance turned somewhat loftily to return to the kitchen and another unwelcome course, my mother, always ingenious when it came to defusing tension with her chaotic sense of humor, asked, "Where you going, Constance?"

She stopped but did not look back. "To the kitchen, Mary. Why?"

"Wherever you're going"—she pointed to the uncanceled first-class stamp affixed to Aunt Constance's behind—"it's going to take more postage than that!"

So we got some relief, and Constance could do no more than smile patiently through the laughter before continuing to haul food. The cousins were bouncing their heels on the rungs of their chairs, and I hoped their waning patience would undo all their prissy decorum. In the past I had seen their pandering, obsequious grins turn into frustrated rage in a blink—ballistic in pinafores— and I could wish for that.

"Gerry, tell us about some crimes."

"Oh, Mary, nothing so exciting. Mostly just blocking jaywalkers with the horse. Ran down a purse snatcher on Sunday."

"That must have been satisfying."

"Yes, yes, it was. They slam into the old ladies to get the purses. We get a lot of broken hips, nice old ladies who might not walk again. When we catch the snatcher we take him up the alley and give him the same, couple shots with a paver."

We all admired this.

"What's the horse's name?" I asked.

Gerry lit up. "Emmett. From a farm in Nova Scotia." It was clear Gerry preferred Emmett's company to ours. Embarrassed to reveal so much emotion, he ran his finger around the tight collar of his uniform. "Seventeen-hand chestnut," he said in a choky voice.

"This is *real* food," Paul announced. "It's certainly not K rations and, by cracky, she's no international cuisine."

"What d'you mean *international cuisine*?" said my father. The rest of the family regarded him alertly. He seemed aggressive.

"Let me give you an example, Harold." Paul bounded back with startling volubility. "I was taken to a French restaurant in the city of New York with, if memory serves, a five-star rating from acknowledged experts in the field, and I don't mean Duncan Hines. Because there were four of us, all friends, I was able to sample each celebrated entrée, and I can report to you without prejudice that they all smelled like toilet seats. It gave me the fantods. I prefer a boiled dinner."

My father seemed ostentatiously bored. I had noticed the faint ripple of cheek muscles as he violently suppressed his yawns. His boredom became so pronounced it looked like grief and was probably taken for that. I knew better. I'd heard an argument start in his bedroom with my mother before dinner in which he stated that my grandmother was being "impetuously canonized," a claim my mother made no attempt to refute. She just called him a son of a bitch. "Ah," said he, "the colorful household vernacular."

Uncle Paul began to wail at the end of the table. It was astonishing. He looked around at his family and sobbed, not bowing or covering his head and face. A theory about traditional keening may have lain behind this, perhaps giving it a somewhat academic tone that didn't make it any less alarming.

"What's the matter, Paul?" my mother asked softly, which only raised the volume. I'd never seen anything like this before. I was thrilled at this splendid racket. Uncle Walter stood and placed his hands on Paul's heaving shoulders, giving them rhythmic squeezes, as the campaign medals tinkled. That seemed to calm Uncle Paul somewhat. Aunt Dorothy had begun a contrapuntal snivel, and Walter gently raised his palm for it to stop. Constance ran to the table with a glass of water, taking the position that Paul had something stuck in his throat. My mother held her cheeks, which streamed hot tears. Dorothy lowered the window, then the shade, and turned the Sunbeam fan up several notches until napkins began to flutter. Paul struggled to his feet, and Walter steered him slowly to the door as though fearing Paul would buckle.

My father jumped up and threw out an arm in Paul's direction with startling emphasis, a mariner spotting land. "For Christ's sake, tell him to pull himself together!" He was nearly shouting. There was something experimental in his exasperated tone.

Walter stopped, his back to us and his head bowed. He turned slowly, his head still bent, but when he was faced our way, I saw his eyes blazed.

"You would do well," he said to my father levelly, "to mind your own business." A terrible quiet followed.

Once Walter had steered a gasping, heaving Paul from the room, my father sat in the ensuing quiet and wiped his lips with his napkin in thought. "Exactly," he said as he rose and walked out of the room.

Constance soared in with the hot apple pie. I wondered why she always described things as being fresh from the oven, as she did again now. My mother had a terrific sweet tooth and fell on her slice with relish. Cocking her ear to a slight sound, she said, "He's heading up the stairs," and, at a series of thuds, announced, "He's packing his bag." She began to race through her pie. At the last mouthful, she grabbed my hand and stood me up. "We'd better see him off, or we'll never hear the end of it."

It was a moonless night, and the three of us gazed into the trunk of the sedan. My father slung his leather bag in and gave the Evinrude a comradely wiggle, looked at us, and smiled at the shabby building behind. "Goodbye," he said.

I THOUGHT MY MOTHER REALLY HAD NO CHANCE TO ABSORB the death of her own mother as long as my father was around. His general disapproval of her family and the ongoing need to argue about it must have drawn a veil over her feelings. I noticed too that though she had fallen nearly silent after my father's departure, she was also more efficient now in getting things done around the house, cooking and cleaning. She went to Mass every day, St. Joseph's, a short walk, and she usually brought me some little treat on the way home. She even had a carpenter come in to see to the sagging second-floor porch. Whatever tension was brewing between her and my aunt Constance must have come to a head, because Constance stormed out on her familiar slogan—"This is the thanks I get!"—and was not seen again before we left for home. Silence was not my mother's strong suit, but we spent a nearly wordless day where the Westport River opened onto the sea, wading in the salt mud for quahogs. "This is what I loved best when I was a girl" was nearly all she said. The clouds on the horizon made a band of light on the deep green Atlantic, and the breakers that lifted and fell with such gravity might have drowned our conversation, if there had been any. We must not have felt the need.

ALIENS

Homer newland, a partner and franchise specialist at a Boston law firm, had had a distinguished career and a very long one before retiring at seventy-five, when he was certainly still useful but had become more aware of the frequent need, when meeting new clients, of demonstrating that he still had all his marbles. So he indulged a lifelong dream and returned to live in the West, where he'd grown up but which in his long absence had made the place of his nativity hard to grasp.

For decades he had nursed his dream of going home, but when he moved back his dismay was all-consuming; Montana seemed like a place he had once read about in a dentist's office, and his daughter who lived there felt the pressure of his impending return. It reminded him of his early days in Boston, when he was always the only person anyone had met named Homer, and the name seemed to suggest risible rural origins. His internist, originally from Wisconsin, was named Elmer, and that seemed to help. Homer was a widower, after enjoying marriage for forty years to CeeCee, a pleasant alcoholic from Point Judith, Rhode Island. Their vacations were spent not in Montana, as he would have liked, but on the island madhouse of Nantucket, which he detested, as he did all seaside places. Too well bred to cause the fuss that might have led to intervention, Homer's wife had boozed her way right off the planet and was buried among kin in the Point Judith churchyard, and Homer was back home in Montana, not quite comfortable and blaming a scholarship to Harvard Law for turning his life upside down. His waning grief at CeeCee's death had been marked from the beginning by ambivalence; it was possible that either she or both of them were better off now that she was gone.

Twenty years ago, Homer sent their only child, Cecile, to a dude ranch, hoping to find a kindred spirit in his Montana romance, and it worked. Cecile met a local football star and settled down to raise two children, very much a local, soon treating her own father with that ambiguous humor reserved for out-of-staters. His grandchildren were precocious, in his opinion, and a bit crude, also his opinion. Cecile and her husband, Dean, were fairly crude themselves, always fighting and frequently separated. Homer had to make an effort to keep from finding everything somewhat crude in his old homeplace. Nevertheless, this further motivated him to retire there instead of visiting as he had been doing. He bought a nice place outside town with a view of the Absarokas, a long driveway, and a deep hundred-gallon-a-minute well. In his pleasantly interfering way, Homer could be quite forceful, causing more than a few unpleasant moments in his daughter's household, an ill-run enterprise at the best of times. He was determined to find his solace in nature but not having much luck at it.

The new quarters became in just a few years quite lonely. But Boston was long behind him, and he didn't know what to do with himself. Nor could he account for the decades spent in Boston leaving so little trace. He couldn't go back there, he didn't have a wife, and he read himself into a hole. He brought himself excruciatingly up to speed on national and world affairs. In two years he would be eighty, and of all things he'd have liked a fresh start. He was remarkably fit for his years; maybe that was the problem. Considering his prospects without the alibi of decrepitude kept him on edge. He snapped at the propane man, not out of the blue—the lout had backed his big truck over a lilac—but a loss of composure uncharacteristic of Homer. He had generally been solicitous, especially of tradespeople on whom he'd come to rely and of the key gossips around the post office. Next, he quit greeting the UPS man and just let him leave things on the porch. He felt that some birds were bullying others at the feeder and started to fret about stepping in, before recognizing that this might just be some geriatric absurdity. He had enough money to keep managed care at bay, and he was determined never to need it.

On his not-infrequent trips back to the city, he felt the extraordinary energy that seemed to emanate from the streets—staying only in hotels with thriving, even booming, lobbies—and on returning home he'd feel dissatisfied with land where all life seemed to have belonged to absent Indians and the blank faces of the neighbors.

Believing that the great beauty of the place would have a possibly sweeping impact on an out-of-towner, he began to think of inviting a lady friend for a visit, a benign calculation that enlivened him considerably. At his age, a smorgasbord of widows lay before him. Surprisingly hale, several had undergone a kind of spiritual tune-up with the departure of their husbands and had become wonderful, even creative, company. There were a few with whom he'd had flings as much as forty years before.

Madeleine Hall was particularly vivid in his memory. He might have been in love with that one. Well, he was and God knows he acted it out. Homer felt that, blessed by longevity, he could be in a position to take advantage of this sentiment, and he elaborated upon the idea without losing sight of the fact that it was really about avoiding loneliness. He dismissed any notion of answering isolation with some fellow sufferer, since the thought of a woman who was herself lonely put him off: needy females had repelled him even in his youth, when neediness was more in style. He married CeeCee for her toughness, but then the drink got her. His greatest disappointment at his wife's dipsomania had been the decline of her contentiousness as she grew supine and content in addiction. And so he began to stray a bit, his handful of city flings thrilling him with their conflicts and rage. Married in Montana, Cecile had lost all contact with her mother and was strangely unsympathetic to her plight, viewing the addiction strictly as an extravagance not everyone could afford.

It was quiet at home, and then very quiet.

Homer and Madeleine's wonderful fling back in the fifties included risk-filled lovemaking right under the windows of her husband, Harry, a fund manager and broad-bellied former Princeton football star, and once they'd done it in the very home of Homer's passed-out CeeCee. Homer had wished Madeleine's interest in him originated in distaste for Harry. Unfortunately, it was sex and sex only; she adored Harry, but he was now too fat, preoccupied, and plastered to fulfill what she considered a tiny part of her life. Madeleine's leggy tennis player's body was full of wanton electricity, and this memory was not entirely absent as Homer greeted a nice-looking old lady as she got off the plane. Her smile was the first thing that caught his eye—it was drawn off center—causing her to remark lightly, "I've had a stroke. Is it still okay?"

He took her in his arms and let the passengers find a way around them. He didn't quite understand his present desperation. His excitement to show her his house in the country, to introduce her to his daughter and grandchildren, had coalesced into uncomfortable urgency. The vacuum filled with a roar.

Madeleine had not been there long before she discovered Homer's neglect of the flower beds around the house, not that they amounted to much, nearly odorless rugosa roses for the most part. But she was not happy about the weeds in the hard ground that resisted her arthritic fingers, or about the signs of careless pruning. She could see that this was not anything Homer cared about. "I care about it," he protested, "but I'm not a gardener."

"We've got to get some water on them before I can do a single thing."

Homer tried to think of the implied time span of an improved rose bed and was apprehensive. "You see this," he said, indicating a faint ditch running around the perimeter of the beds. "This is how they were always irrigated. But it's a bit of trouble."

"How much trouble can it be?"

"You have to go up the river and turn some water into the ditch."

"And after that you've got water down here?"

"Yes."

"Then what's the problem? These roses are being tortured, and I can't get the weeds out of the ground."

Madeleine walked ahead of Homer as the trail progressed along the river and up through a chokecherry thicket. He was fascinated at her forthright progress, given that she did not know the way. He slyly let her lead them down a false trail that ended at the bottom of an unscalable scree slope, fine black rock shining in mountain light. She smiled to acknowledge that he probably knew the route better. At length they reached the headgate, an old concrete structure with 1927 scratched into the cement. In the bend of the river, it diverted water to ranches in the area, and in its steel throat snowmelt gurgled off to the east to meet with crops and fertilizer. Homer's place was not a ranch, but it still retained its small right to a share of water, just enough for a garden and a few trees. He seldom used it, but when he did he usually got a call from one of the neighbors who also used the ditch regularly and invariably addressed him as "Old-Timer."

Downstream from the headgate, another ditch branched off, back toward Homer's place; he pulled the metal slide that held back the water, and a small stream headed for his house. "This will be nice for the trees and flower beds."

"If it softens the ground, I can do something with it," said Madeleine. "You've just let things go, Homer. It looks like a transient has been squatting there."

"Madeleine, I'm doing something about it right now."

"How long will it take for the water to get there?"

"Not long." Actually, he didn't know.

Homer went back to the headgate, followed by Madeleine, hurrying along the path. He thought of that awful word "spry" and wondered why he imagined he might be exempt. "Spry" was supposed to be positive. It was awful.

A truck stopped on the road above them, a blue-heeler dog in back and rolled fabric irrigation dams piled against the cab. By the sound of the truck door being slammed, Homer knew this would not be a friendly visit. But he continued his adjustments, meant to preserve the water level of the ditch even after he had extracted his small share for the garden. Madeleine was looking up at the truck as its driver wheeled around the tailgate and started toward them. This was Homer's neighbor, Wayne Rafter, who raised cattle and alfalfa on the bench downstream. Wayne had a round red face, surmounted by a rust-brown cowboy hat with a ring of stain above its brim. He wore irrigating boots rolled down to the knee and carried a shovel over his shoulder.

He said, "What are you doing with the water?"

"We're sending a little down to the garden."

"You need to leave my headgate alone. You've got the whole valley screwed up."

Madeleine said, "That little trickle?"

"Stay out of this," said Wayne, without looking at her at first. When he did, he said, "What's wrong with your face?"

Homer answered that she'd had a stroke and was immediately

sorry he'd said anything at all. Wayne dismissed the explanation, saying that a lot of folks had had strokes. Homer felt a pressure he might not have if Madeleine had not been looking on.

"I do have a small water right attached to my property."

"Very small."

"But it is a right."

"Not if you don't use it. It reverts."

"I'm using it now."

"You're in the goddamn way."

"I wonder if we should get a ditch rider to allocate this water and not argue about it."

"Do you have any idea what that costs?"

"It might be necessary if you prevent me from taking my water. Shall I arrange it?"

"No, don't 'arrange it,' Old-Timer. Just play with the water if that's what turns you on."

At this, Wayne marched off with his shovel over his shoulder, and soon his truck was gone, the dog barking and running around in the bed.

Madeleine said, "Wow."

"Yep."

"Is that how they are?"

"Can be." Homer's insouciance concealed his humiliation.

Madeleine stared around herself into immediate space. Homer knew the remark about her face must have stung. Long ago, she'd been so careful about her looks, a little fashion driven for Homer's taste but always ready to be seen, always lovely. They started back toward the house quite depleted by the encounter.

"Harry was truculent," said Madeleine. They found candles and Madeleine made their meal, a nice salad and cold cucumber soup, good for a warm summer evening. "But I wouldn't say abusive. Abusive is when they focus on you. He just raged around, and whatever he might have done to me he did equally to the furniture."

In the sixties when, for whatever reason, CeeCee had started tying a scarf around her head, she acquired a reputation for heightened spirituality among acquaintances who didn't realize she was drunk. For them, she never passed out but was "transported." Part of this was abetted by CeeCee as an apparatus for her illness, and her conversation was increasingly ethereal as she discovered the allure of non sequiturs. Their neighbor, Dick Chalfonte, a thoracic surgeon, was enchanted, and Homer suspected that days spent out of town—some surreptitiously with Madeleine—allowed Chalfonte's fascination to be transmuted into something more tangible. Homer didn't like this thought at all but, because of Madeleine and his own fair-mindedness, found indignation unavailing; anyway there was some consolation if Dick Chalfonte was able to make contact with a soul drifting slowly to another world. It might have been that Homer wished he would take her away altogether, but of course this was unthinkable.

Madeleine rolled her napkin ring from side to side with her forefinger. "We used to think it was an affectation when you wore cowboy boots with your suit."

"And my Turnbull and Asser shirts. Of course it was an affectation. What else does a young man have? I was trying to make a name for myself, and in that town there didn't seem to be many possibilities left. Who's 'we,' anyway?"

"Harry and me, I guess. Harry thought you were a phony."

At night, they talked about poetry. Madeleine had a particular aversion to the poet H. D., whom she called "I. E." for what she thought was a perverse inability to say anything plainly. Homer feebly recited Wordsworth, to which Madeleine remarked she greatly looked forward to getting, spending, and laying waste her powers. And when Homer remarked that General Wolfe would have preferred to have written "Elegy Written in a Country Churchyard" than to have conquered Quebec, she urged him to stop thinking of poetry in terms of its public currency.

"I just read the funnies," said Homer.

They had twin beds with a reading lamp and nightstand between them, an easy distance for holding hands. The lamp could be adjusted so that Madeleine could read while Homer drifted off. She looked up from her book.

"Homer, are you afraid to die?"

"No."

"The Day of Judgment?"

"Nope."

"Homer, are you afraid of anything?"

"I'm afraid of rigor mortis."

She chuckled—"But exactly"—and went back to her book. It soon dropped to her lap. He watched her until she fell asleep, then slipped his hand free of hers and turned off the lamp.

Homer's daughter, Cecile—named for her mother, though unlike her in every way and never called CeeCee—phoned at about ten o'clock at night. Madeleine was asleep and Homer was setting out mousetraps, one for the cereal cupboard, one under the stove, and one in front of the refrigerator he hoped he would remember when he was barefoot in the morning. He didn't like this, but the humane traps were too humane to catch mice. He rotated the geranium on the windowsill to equalize its sun exposure and watched the grosbeaks and juncos scouring the ground under the empty feeder. Hawks sometimes killed juncos at the feeder; while nature might be red in tooth and claw, Homer worried about being complicitous in the death of the juncos. In fact, he'd twice moved the feeder to give the songbirds better cover from overhead but underestimated the hawks' capacity for swooping.

"Father, I'm having a yard sale tomorrow morning at ten. Can you help me look after the kids?"

"Cecile, I'm not so good at that." His tone was pleading.

"You'll be fine. They like you." This was a command. In fact, the children were quite distant with him. He thought he detected acid in her next remark. "You can bring your friend to help you." Cecile knew Madeleine's name perfectly well.

Homer was afraid of children. He could barely remember being one, and he really didn't understand them or why they acted as they did. He certainly didn't dislike children, but he found them emotionally opaque except when tribal or violent. Actually, he longed for Cecile's children to like him. But he was not always ready to test the idea, and they had rather peered at Madeleine on meeting her.

"You've got to do this. What's-her-name can help me with the sale. She'd just scare the kids. They don't know her."

"Why are you having a yard sale at all? Your furnishings are sparse now."

"Not sparse enough, buddy, not by a long shot. So get it together, Grandpa, and head on down here."

Cecile was always lightening her load, paring away at things, fixing a car that should have been traded, and he knew why: she was preparing for flight. She was readying herself for the moment when her life would change and she could escape. She had lost all her former levity, no longer introducing her father as a "forensic barber," and had recently had her breasts dramatically augmented, a move he viewed as panic inspired by those magazines at the checkout.

He helped Cecile prepare the yard sale while Judy and Ralph, seven and two, still slept inside and Madeleine waited for them to awaken. Cecile, a rag tied around her head, grunted enthusiastically as they hefted the NordicTrack to the sidewalk. A low egg-yolk-yellow September sunrise was stretching shadows across the street to lawns with uncollected morning newspapers. On the pavement an old steel porch glider rested, his lower back pain reminding Homer how it had arrived. Also: a bread box, an early microwave, percolator, a run of *National Geographics*, a yoga mat, a cactus, a birdcage, several of Cecile's college paintings in the once-universal style of Georges Rouault, a child's English saddle with jodhpurs and boots (Cecile's), scenic place mats, a standing ashtray with a lever that flushed the butts and ashes down a trapdoor, a silhouette of an Indian chief made with bullets, several rugs, a Monopoly game, a Parcheesi set, a Mille Bornes set, a double-deck card holder for canasta, a checkerboard—these last worried Homer, as it was hard to imagine Cecile without her games—incidental venetian blinds, canoe paddles, a Dutch oven, and a mosquito net. Here we hit the strata of the ex-husband, where lay the heart of the yard sale, as they announced Cecile's single status: commemorative whiskey bottles from Old Fitzgerald, I. W. Harper, Jim Beam, Ezra Brooks, and others, depicting Man o' War, a largemouth bass, a fire truck, Custer's Last Stand, the OK Corral, Elvis, W. C. Fields, a cat-and-dog, a rooster, a turtle, an Indian with a tomahawk on a white horse, a Florida gator, a black rotary phone, the Run for the Roses, a Siamese cat, a kachina doll, the Wyoming bronco, a raccoon, the Chevy Bel Air, Ducks Unlimited, Van Gogh's *Old Peasant*, and there was also a set of train-related decanters: engine, mail car, caboose, water tower. Homer found it dizzying, but Cecile assured him it would be the big draw, and she was right. One customer drove from Yakima, Washington, for the rotary phone, while a few more, drawn by the bottles, bought other items, mostly small cheap things to satisfy the urge for a transaction aroused by the bottles.

Cecile wanted to stay outside to guard the merchandise, so Homer waited in the living room with Madeleine for the children to awaken. They felt so apprehensive they hardly spoke, and Homer looked around at the room as if through Madeleine's eyes. Only the front window admitted much light, enough to bleach the rug but not enough to lend any cheer. The living room of a single mother, he reflected, is a sad room. This one, containing so many things CeeCee had sent from Rhode Island, hoping for a response from Cecile, was especially sad. Even the old Aeolian player piano seemed to refer to cheerful times long gone by. The furniture was sad, the curtains were sad, the strewn toys were sad, the chandelier was utterly sad, but the china cabinet with its unemployed crockery was tragic. Over the fireplace there was still a color-saturated photograph of Dean, Cecile's ex-husband, in a classic football pose: knee raised, twisting off the opposite foot, ball tucked under one arm, the other projected, fingers spread wide, barreling toward an imaginary tackler.

"That's my son-in-law."

"What became of him?" asked Madeleine.

"Still in town. He's a bit impaired. He had an accident. They're separated."

"What kind of accident?"

Homer thought. There was a long version and a short version. He elected the latter. "He fell off a building."

"Good grief. But he's out of the picture?"

"Sort of," said Homer, with meaning.

"I see. Once they're in the picture," said Madeleine, "they're never really out of the picture, are they?"

How could my daughter have all this weight on her shoulders? His view might have been colored by his relationship with his grandchildren. He tried hard to charm and amuse them despite their lack of fondness for him. Still, he gave Cecile credit for an outstanding job: Judy and Ralph were lively, curious, and confident. Also, they were calm. Judy was even a bit lofty. And why should they know him better? He never seemed to know exactly where he was, and the children could sense it. Ralph once asked him if he was an alien.

"Why are you here, Grandpa?" Judy stood in her doorway, wearing her pajamas. She had chosen not to see Madeleine at Homer's side, another alien. Homer had imagined a situation in which the children adored her on sight.

"I'm looking after you and Ralph while your mom has her yard sale." She was small with an oval face and burning black eyes. Homer's attempt to explain things had a whiny edge that he could tell annoyed her. Ralph wasn't paying any mind and looked dopey. "Can you say hello to Madeleine?" He wondered whether he should have introduced her as Mrs. Hall, but he was somewhat jealous of Harry Hall, long dead though he may have been.

"Me and Ralph are against the yard sale."

"Of course you are," said Madeleine merrily. "I dislike change, too. But how can we stop it?"

Judy stared at her as though she were nuts.

Ralph stood at Judy's side, still half asleep. To Homer, he resembled all two-year-old boys, though not nearly so fat as some. He had dark hair as his father once had, and it stuck out in a burr. He stared at Judy, awaiting her leadership. Then, as it was not forthcoming, he wandered to Madeleine and reached for her hand.

"Well, how does breakfast sound?" asked Homer, immediately recognizing the absurdity of the question, as breakfast had no sound. The new acuteness about diction, with Madeleine listening, produced this odd thought.

"Cheerios for me. Cap'n Crunch for him. Honey on mine. Sugar on his. The honey bear is over the toaster. It's on a paper towel because it was sticking to everything. The bowls are still in the washer. We don't use napkins, we use paper towels. Regular spoons, not soup spoons, and not too much milk."

It didn't take much for this to seem like drudgery. He was displeased by the cereal rustling from the waxed-paper liners of the boxes into the bowls. It looked like packing material. "You don't have to sit here and stare at us," said Judy pleasantly. Madeleine strayed back out to the yard sale, doubtless to warm things up with Cecile. Homer watched her go.

"I didn't mean to stare. My thoughts were wandering."

"Do you find us obnoxious?" Judy asked.

Now Homer was wide awake and attentive. "Judy, how can you ask such a thing?"

This was too plaintive. Her gaze darted over his face. "You seemed off in the clouds, Grandpa, probably thinking about your new girlfriend."

"It doesn't mean I find you obnoxious."

Ralph poured his cereal into Homer's lap and, when Homer jumped up, started wailing as if his grandfather meant to attack him. In a moment, while Homer knelt on the floor, a rag in his hand and an icy feeling in his crotch from the milk, Cecile came in with no particular look of concern, quieting Ralph and organizing another bowl of cereal. She pushed Ralph's chair very close to the edge of the table, which seemed to make his movements less random. Ralph just stared into his bowl, unsure what to do with it. Homer got up indecisively. Cecile said, "Your new friend is working the crowd." Ralph waved his spoon jubilantly and then looked around to gauge its effect.

"Let's spruce them up and take them to the sale," she said, "a little poignancy to drive up prices."

A wet washcloth and extraordinary efficiency in lifting limbs or whole bodies into the apertures of their clothes had the two children spiffy in very short order, though it left them dazed. With Homer in the lead, Cecile herded the children from behind. Homer immediately mingled with amiable body language among the skeptics looking at the merchandise. Suddenly, Cecile cried "Oh, no!" and whirled on Madeleine.

"What happened to the bottles?"

"A man came for them, a man in a wheelchair. He said they were his." Madeleine suddenly looked her age, with something comic about the makeup she'd applied so carefully.

"Did he pay for them?"

"He said they were his."

"Lady, I gotta tell you: this is a sale. You know, where objects are exchanged for money?"

"Yes, of course, I do know that."

"Who do you suppose got them?" Homer asked rather lamely.

Madeleine said, "He was in a wheelchair. I can't believe they didn't belong to him. In fact, I thought he said they were his."

"That cripple happens to be my husband. If you're around here long enough, you'll learn not to put anything past him." Cecile looked at the scattered offerings of her yard sale as though seeing them for the first time. She said, "I'm breaking down. Take Ralph and Judy to see the kittens. You can go with him, lady."

"Her name is Madeleine." Homer started to back toward the outside door, guiding Madeleine by the elbow, the rigidity of which let him know that she was getting angry. "Where are the kittens?"

"Judy, honey, please show Grandpa and his lady friend the kittens. *Now*, Judy, okay? Her name is *Madeleine.*"

When Homer looked back from the house, he saw that Cecile's interrogation of the customers must have been somewhat accusatory: they were fleeing.

Once in the house, he clapped his hands together and rubbed them briskly, as though he had a pleasant surprise in store. Judy's evaluating squint indicated his failure to convince. "Who would like to show me the kittens?" No answer. "Where are the kittens?" Let's try not making it a question. "I've been wondering how many kittens there are."

"There are two," said Judy, with authority.

"But I suppose Mrs. Hall and I can't see them. That's the feeling I'm getting from you, Judy."

After a moment. "You can see them. Follow me."

Towering behind Judy and Ralph across the living room, in the unaltered light, past the gut-wrenching china cabinet, through the kitchen, into the pantry, and out to the garage, Homer tried to emanate modest obedience for fear Judy would change her mind, but she strode along, an algebra teacher of the future, until they reached a storage closet, where she pointed to a latch she couldn't reach. Madeleine, who seemed to have lost all confidence, trailed behind, utterly lost. Ralph tried to crowd in front of Judy, but she moved him aside so that Homer could open the door. When he did, he felt around the inside wall for a light switch until Judy told him, "Reach up and pull the string." He did as he was told, and the resulting low wattage barely illuminated a room filled with discarded household goods: rugs, bath mats, cleaning rags, and worn-out towels. These formed a kind of rough nest next to which Judy sat, holding Ralph's hand to keep track of him. She looked up at Homer and said, "They're in there." Then she looked over at Madeleine and said, "You're allowed to look."

Homer had to get on all fours to make an adequate inspection, and when he peered around he quickly found a gray kitten with vivid black stripes and black ears. He cupped his hand over it and felt the little motor start as it lifted its head against his palm. "Here's one," said Homer, and Judy was at his side at once. He smiled up at Madeleine, hoping to draw her in, but her face projected only some indeterminate fear. His knees hurt and he was concerned that in getting back up he would stagger.

"Where's the orange one?" Judy demanded.

"What orange one?"

Homer lifted the gray kitten to make way for Judy's inspection and felt the needle claws pricking his palm. Judy crawled around, lifting wads of fabric and old towels, which cast shadows up the wall, all the way to the back of the closet, where she stopped suddenly. "Here he is!" she cried. "He's dead!"

Judy was seated with her back to him for a long time, long enough for him to see her shuddering with silent weeping. He crawled over and pulled her into his arms, at which point the sobs became audible, and Ralph, without any idea of why he was upset, joined in to make it deafening. Homer drew Ralph to his side, and soon the quiet was broken only by Judy's snuffling. Homer felt mucus run onto the hand that gripped her tight, and he looked up at Madeleine with an expression of helplessness. When Judy began to calm down, he spoke very quietly about how the kitten was in heaven and how we all hope to go there someday; thinking to close his argument, he said, "Kittens are like all creatures, including us, Judy. They don't live forever, and neither do we."

The effect of this was to amplify Judy's anguish. "I know that," she said, indignant in her grief, "but I thought we all went at the same time!" Strangely, Madeleine nodded in agreement.

Homer could think of nothing to say. He would have had to care about the kitten to have been inspired to the right remark; Judy seemed to see through his dissembling. Besides, nothing was up to Judy's profound statement, which hung in the air. "I wish we did," he said, "it would be so much better. I don't know why we don't all go at the same time, but we don't, and we have to accept that." That's that, he thought, take it or leave it. Besides, something troubled him about Madeleine's nod of agreement.

To make things worse, Madeleine's eyes began to fill, and Homer wondered if it was over that brute Harry Hall and his size 13 oxblood saddle shoes, ungainly even in death. Homer could almost hear his booming voice: *Come on in, Homer. You like gin? I've cornered the market!*

Judy no longer cried, but she was very somber and far away. "Someone is responsible," she said.

"God!" barked Homer with exasperation. "God is responsible!" This yard sale was about to kill him. "Madeleine, is there anything I can do to make you feel better?" he inquired coolly. She was touching each of the children unobtrusively. She didn't know how to comfort them. He didn't know how to comfort her.

"Let's go to the living room. Maybe we can think better there." The children followed Homer, who, aware of his waning desperation to make anyone happy, followed Madeleine. In the living room, he looked around briskly, as though trying to choose among several marvelous possibilities. "Here, come sit here," he said, and indicated the bench in front of the old player piano. Judy's grief kept her from seeing through his various efforts to entertain her. They obeyed with dull bafflement as he loaded a roll of music and started pumping the pedals. "Pretend you're playing!" he called out, over the strains of "Ida, Sweet as Apple Cider." Looking at each other, the children put their hands on the keys, which snapped up and down all around their fingers as Judy took over the pumping and Ralph howled like a dog; soon they were caught up in it.

Inexplicably, Madeleine began doing a graceful if somehow cynical foxtrot with an invisible partner. Homer stared at her, arms hanging at his sides. The noise was unbelievable. Into the space between Madeleine's arms, Homer placed Harry Hall and his big belly.

Homer darted out the front door to the yard sale, where Cecile was persuading a pregnant teenager that the light-dark setting on the toaster still worked. Four or five others grazed among the offerings, concealing any interest they might have had, though a middle-aged man in baggy khakis and an Atlanta Braves hat was bent in absorption over a duck-decoy lamp that had never been completed. "Darktown Strutters' Ball" poured from the house, stopped abruptly, then resumed with "I Want a Girl Just Like the Girl Who Married Dear Old Dad." Homer could hear Madeleine joining in with a sharp, angry contralto. When the teenager replaced the toaster on the card table and wandered off, Homer said, "One of the kittens died."

Staring at the unsold toaster, Cecile said, "You're shitting me. When it rains, it pours. *My God*, what's with the piano?" Holding a cigarette in the center of her teeth she blew smoke out of either side of her mouth.

"Go in and comfort Judy. I'll try to sell something till you get back."

"No reasonable offer refused." At this, two or three browsers cocked their heads, which Cecile noted. "Just kidding, of course." She went inside and Homer surveyed the prospects, holding his lapels like an expectant haberdasher. No one met his eye and, instead of rubbing his hands together, he plunged them into his pockets and considered the weather: low clouds, no wind. The player piano stopped abruptly and the shoppers all looked up with the silence.

Homer went over to the man still examining the duck-decoy lamp. "Why don't you buy it? It's beautifully made. It works. I can't imagine any home that wouldn't be improved by it."

"I'm just trying to picture the sort of people who wanted this in the first place," said the man. "This doesn't look like a duck, it looks like a groundhog. I hate it. I really hate it."

"The people who wanted it in the first place are my daughter and her husband," said Homer.

"My condolences," said the man, before he turned to go.

Homer stared hard and said, "Go fuck yourself." He could hardly believe he'd said it. It was like a breath of spring, such vituperation.

"Get in line, Pops."

Cecile returned and muttered, "Bugs Bunny on low. Usually holds them. Your friend is resting on the couch with a washcloth on her head. She looks like she's on her last legs." A very thin older man in a navy-blue jogging suit with a reflective stripe down the pant legs was interested in the NordicTrack. He had an upright potbelly, bags under his eyes, and a cigarette in his mouth that made him turn his head to one side to examine the distance meter on the machine. Homer watched Cecile approach within a foot of the prospect, but the man went about his examination without acknowledging her. He knelt to examine the bottom of the machine, then sat back on his haunches, removed the cigarette, and bethought himself. When he finally stood, he said something very brief to Cecile. She seized her head in both hands while he puffed and looked the other way. When she came back to Homer with some bills in her hand, she said, "I got creamed but it's gone." The new owner was trying out his new machine, the cigarette back in his mouth. A gust of wind showered Homer and his daughter with cottonwood leaves. Wild geese creaked above. Soon there'd be ice on the river.

"You seem to have gotten over the bottle collection," said Homer. He saw the American flag go up a pole across the street, a hedge concealing whoever raised it.

"Guess again."

"Why don't you go and ask Dean to give them back?"

"That's what he's trying to accomplish. The whole issue has been over him having anything I need."

"Does he?"

"Yeah, the bottles." She stared hard at him. "I know exactly what you're thinking, exactly. You're thinking, How can anyone lose themselves in such trivia?"

"Nope."

"Well, I'm not going to dignify this by fighting over it. But don't you ever look down your nose at me. Just because things haven't exactly worked out doesn't make us white trash."

"It's beyond me why you'd have such a hateful thought. Your mother would have felt the same way, if you had ever deigned to share your thoughts with her."

Homer had already decided that he would retrieve the bottles. By that time the sale would be over and the awful things would be part of the desolation of the living room again. When he asked his daughter why none of the other customers had mentioned the theft, she said, "The only one he had to fool was your friend, and I guess that wasn't too hard."

Homer just let it go. It was hopeless.

He went inside to check on Madeleine. Without removing her hand from over her eyes, she said, "I feel terrible for losing those horrible bottles," and when he tried to speak, she waved him away. He went back outside and watched the tire kickers and the idly curious begin to drift away, leaving four who looked like real buyers. Out of the blue, he wanted to make a sale. Homer thought they were couples but, after considerable study, could not match them up. He became fixed on this task as a difficult crossword puzzle, but finally he sighed and gave up. He was wary of misreading anyone as he had the duck-lamp guy. He couldn't believe the two redheads were together, because he'd never seen that before; which left the two short ones, and that pair seemed less unlikely. Their gazes crisscrossed like light beams, giving nothing away. Homer wondered whether they were like our ancestors, wary and footloose. The red-haired male took sudden notice of the American flag ripping away in the wind across the street, and Homer realized he was avoiding eye contact. No sale.

He returned to the house, where he found the children sitting on either side of Madeleine. "We're discussing their Halloween costumes," she said, her warmth restored. "Judy is going as a punk rocker and Ralph is going as a traffic cone."

Homer said, "Let's get out of here."

Cecile was still outside, cleaning up after the sale, tossing everything toward the garage. Madeleine and Homer paused on the sidewalk for a moment. It seemed not unreasonable that Cecile might say a word or two to them, but she didn't. Homer wondered whether his daughter had developed this awful carapace on account of being raised by a helpless mother. Once inside his car, he said, "Can I take you to dinner?"

"We're going to get those bottles," said Madeleine.

"Oh, you don't want to go there. That's a real can of worms."

"Bring it on."

Imagining for a euphoric moment that Cecile's ex-husband

would see the light quickly, Homer reluctantly agreed to go to Dean's house. Wait till she gets a load of this! was his uncharitable thought. It was getting dark as he started the car.

"I'll buy the bottles," Madeleine cried.

"That won't solve it."

She said, "I thought I'd seen everything."

He stepped up onto Dean's porch and rang the bell, nearly embedded in careless layers of house paint. He had a reassuring hand on Madeleine's back. There was some sort of somber music coming from within. The door began to open revealing the interior of what was little more than a cottage, single story by necessity, with the kitchen and living room adjacent to the front door. He wanted to help but knew that Dean liked doing this sort of thing himself. Then Dean rolled around into view. He had a smile on his big soft face, and the weight of his head seemed to be sinking into the expanding circles of his neck. One hand poised birdlike over the controls of his wheelchair. None of the waywardness was gone from his sky-blue eyes. On the television screen, an aircraft carrier was sinking with slow majesty. Homer was relieved to find that the dirge he'd heard at the door was not just something Dean was listening to.

Homer introduced Madeleine and Dean greeted her warmly, and they followed him into the house.

"That's a new wheelchair," commented Homer as he made his way past Dean. There was very little furniture but the gas fire log made a twinkling, habitable light, concealing the bareness of the room. "Brand-new," said Dean. "Haven't even knocked the paint off it." There were some trophies on an old library table and milk crates filled with paperbacks, a cheesecake calendar on the far door, which led to the bathroom. The young model, naked on a white fur rug, was holding an automobile muffler.

"Front-wheel drive. Watch this." Dean pivoted around the back side of the door and, with a graceful thrust of the chair's motor, swung the door to and latched it. "Onboard battery charger," he said, leading Homer into the living room. "Actually got to pick the color. That last chair wasn't nearly enough for quads, more for limited-leg-use folks."

Madeleine said, "I'll bet you can go anywhere you want." She seemed to like Dean. Maybe it was just for leaving Cecile. Homer was glad to see it. He knew Madeleine had had about all she could stand.

"Hell, I'm on the town again."

He wheeled over in front of the television, on which the funeral of Princess Diana played: it was an anniversary on an odd year. "Madeleine, check this out: here she is again!" Homer didn't know where this was headed, but he was encouraged by the friendliness with which Dean addressed Madeleine.

There were slow panning shots of Diana's cortege interspersed with scenes from happier times, including those with paramour Dodi Fayed at the beach; then the mayhem with the paparazzi and the fatal limousine chase with the drugged chauffeur, ending in underground calamity.

Moving to the side, Homer determined that the shaking he saw in Dean's body was caused not by grief but by laughter. Madeleine noticed and said sharply, "She died young!"

Dean said, "It's a start."

"What?"

Dean turned it off with his channel changer, and as the picture sank to a blue dot he said to Madeleine, "None of that would have happened if she'd been fat."

Two years earlier, Dean had attended an after-game Cats-Griz party at the Nez Perce Inn, a dependably rowdy annual uproar, and fallen from a second-floor balcony into the parking lot with a freshly opened beer in his hand. He woke up the next morning, hungover and paralyzed. He had been out of work, but now he was running for mayor.

The commemorative bottles were lined up on the floor next to the north wall, receiving the last light of the day. Dean said, "There they are."

"Let me take them back to Cecile," Madeleine said reasonably.

"Over my dead body." His lips were drawn flat across his teeth. He was quite menacing.

"Ohhkay."

Homer could see that Madeleine was not happy. She would bolt at the first opportunity. All the mean people, all the open space, seemed to be closing in upon him at once.

"I don't like disappointing you, Madeleine. Or Homer neither. But those bottles are mine."

"No doubt they are, but I'm the one who let you take them, and now it seems I'm in trouble. You ought not to have done that to a lady. Besides which, you have two beautiful children and you continue to poison your relationship with them over your bottle collection. I'm an out-of-towner and I don't get it. Cecile has quite a job with those children. She could probably use some help as opposed to battling over a collection of whiskey bottles." Homer was impressed at the practical way Madeleine swallowed what must have been her distaste for Cecile.

"I'm lucky she isn't feeding them sardines with the mother-seagull glove to make them think they can fly. Do tears embarrass you, Madeleine?"

"Not at all."

"Homer's seen all this before. I blubber, and he just goes with it." He swept his hand down his face, but it continued to glisten. "The bottles don't belong to Cecile. I bought those bottles full and I emptied them in my own home. They're a monument to better days. So, here's what you tell Cecile: No dice. Also, where's the phone decanter?"

"Yakima," Homer said, rather pleased he could supply this fact.

"I emptied that phone last New Year's Eve. Cecile was upstairs watching the ball come down on Times Square. When she showed up, do you think she wished me Happy New Year? No. She said, 'Shit-faced in a wheelchair is a look whose time will never come.'"

Madeleine gazed at Dean for a long moment, with wonder or compassion Homer couldn't say, though he struggled to understand. He seemed to expect that she would say something wise, should she finally speak, but all she said was "I give up. Perhaps the bottles are happier with you."

MADELEINE COULDN'T MAKE IT ALL THE WAY THAT NIGHT, but Salt Lake City was a hub and gave her several options for the morning, and there were shuttles to the hotels near the airport.

She assured Homer that she had loved visiting the West and learning firsthand that it was, as all had promised, breathtaking. And just think: once in Salt Lake, you could go direct or change in Memphis, Atlanta, Minneapolis, Chicago, Detroit, Cincinnati—all those cities!—and still get home. Homer seemed downcast at these prospects, but she assured him it had been a treat catching up.

THE REFUGEE

Errol healy was going sailing to evade custody in one of the several institutions recommended for his care. He believed the modest voyage from his berth in Cortez across the Gulf of Mexico to Key West was something he could handle. All therapeutic routes in which he was described as having a labile affect and deficient insight had proved ineffective, and friends and professionals alike felt the trip might help him reconstruct events in a way positive to his well-being. In particular, his boss at the orange groves urged him to pull himself together or else, and he realized with a panic that losing his job would, under current circumstances, not be endurable. In contrast to the skepticism he directed at mental health professionals, he ascribed almost supernatural powers of healing to an old woman in Key West, Florence Ewing, whom he'd not seen for so many years that it was questionable whether she still lived in Key West or lived at all. In many of his plans these days, he was reduced to superstition, and the mestizos he managed in the groves, who had won his friendship and peculiar loyalty, were superstitious about all things, hanging their charms everywhere, from their old cars to the branches of orange trees. Errol, quite sensibly, thought it was absurd to describe someone who was drunk all the time as having "a labile affect and deficient insight." Better to note that a do-or-die crisis seemed at hand and something had to be tried if body and spirit were to be kept together. His body was fine.

Years ago, he'd had a sailing accident. As a result, his closest friend, Raymond, was lost at sea, and the meaning of Raymond's death, nagging and irresolute, continued to consume him. The customary remedies were unavailing, and he intended to resort to this soothsayer of his past. His employer, the owner of numerous large orange groves, had agreed to this final shot: after that, he was on his own. This ultimatum was not offered lightly: Errol, a fluent speaker of Spanish, had a loyal crew who would disperse in the event of his firing. The employer, a patrician cracker who also owned a large juice plant in Arcadia, Florida, said something that really caught Errol and made him see his plight more clearly. "I just can't have someone like this. Not around here."

It was evening before Errol boarded *Czarina*, unfurling her jib to gain enough headway to sail the few yards to her mooring. Not far away, a big ketch with the steering vane and ratlines of a long-range cruiser tugged politely at her rode. Otherwise the tideway, lit by stars, was empty. He went below to the galley, turned on a lamp, and made a drink, then carried it to the cockpit, where he sipped and watched the clouds make their way in a moon-brightened sky. He brought the bottle with him and refreshed his iceless drink from time to time, feeling the deep motion of the boat as the incoming tide lifted her against the weight of her keel.

Errol awoke as the sun crossed the side of the cockpit. As usual, he was sick and disgusted but with the rare luxury of not being guilty over something he'd done the night before. He declined to throw the empty bottle overboard and sentenced himself to live with it a few hours more. He had wisely provisioned the galley already—wisely, because he hardly had the strength for a shopping trip now—but was in no mood for food. He remained stretched out, waiting for his mind to clear.

Errol made his way around the yawl, raising the mizzen first so that she swung on the mooring facing upwind. Raising the main seemed to take all his strength, the hard stretched halyard in his aching hands, but the sail went up and the halyard somehow found its way to a cleat and *Czarina* trembled under the steady luffing of the mainsail. Errol went forward and cast off the mooring, and *Czarina* began to drift backward toward the dock. Errol released the mizzen sheet and drew in the mainsail; *Czarina* bore off into the tideway. He trimmed the mizzen, and the yawl sank down onto her lines and beat across the harbor, tacking here and there to avoid anchored boats. Errol was glad she had no engine: an oily bilge would have been disastrous in his current state.

He sailed south in shallow water past islands covered with winter homes and islands which had been declared wildlife refuges. There was occasional traffic on the Intracoastal Waterway and to the east, towering from the mangroves, a baseball stadium. Cumbersome brown pelicans sailed on air currents, suddenly becoming arrows as they dove into schools of fish. *Czarina* was moving well, rail down and tracking her course insistently. A northwest wind was building, and Errol planned to evaluate the seas once he reached the pass. He would venture out into the Gulf and make a decision. The leeward side of the foredeck had begun to darken with spray as the wind increased, and he could hear the telltales on the leech fluttering. Exultation at the little ship's movement cheered Errol at last, and he went below to examine his larder. He cut up an apple into a bowl of dry cereal, then poured Eagle Brand condensed milk over it. *Czarina* had sailed herself contentedly in his absence, and he sat down to eat with an inkling of happiness.

The tide was falling through the pass, building up steep seas. A big new-moon tide, it sucked channel markers under and left streaming wakes behind them. Errol was anxious to begin his voyage and, nearly certain he would be turned back, he beat out toward the Gulf of Mexico and the dark sky to the west.

Because of the running tide, the faces of the waves were steep and the little yawl seemed to be ascending skyward before reaching their crests. The long slopes at the backs of the waves were almost pleasant as she ran down them, the centerboard humming in its trunk and a fine vibration coming through the tiller. But by the time he passed Johnson Shoals and began to contemplate a long trip in these conditions as opposed to the immediate sporting challenge, he grew apprehensive. There was green water on the deck racing toward the scuppers, the bottoms of the sail were dark and soaked, and he was getting shaky again. This development was something he meant to observe from afar.

He came about and headed downwind toward Cayo Costa, avoiding whatever temptation he might have had to press on in this small boat, and in the face of obvious peril that would have been the real loss of nerve. Better to shake himself miserable in a safe anchorage than abandon himself to the fatal and picturesque.

Pelican Bay was a protected anchorage in the middle of a state park, and its oceanic zephyrs were personalized with the smells of hot dogs and hamburgers from the many boats anchored there. Errol was ill equipped to cope with this banality, and he looked beyond the mouth of the bay to the increasingly raging seas of the Gulf with melancholy and regret. By tomorrow, the winds should have diminished and clocked around to the northeast, which would make the hundred-mile open-sea crossing to Key West one long reach. Meanwhile, the high-spirited shrieks of children made him furious. That the powerboats looked like huge tennis shoes only added to his general dissatisfaction with the world. Nevertheless, his belief that all his problems would go away once he reached Key West brought him a kind of grim cheer; recently and in an hour of unsurpassed bleakness, when the landscape of his failures seemed almost to afford death a dismal glamour, he'd had a kind of satori in which he'd either remembered or imagined an old woman of infinite wisdom who could see him on to a better place. In years past she'd done this for him and for several dissolute friends, among whom he remained the sole member whose life seemed to be slipping through his own fingers. The occasion of his vision was less than august: trying to please a new lady friend, he'd lost a toe while mowing her lawn at midnight, and the pain as he sat in a crowded emergency room, a bath towel around his foot, a tall to-go cup in his lap, seemed to summon forth a vision of a livable future spelled out by the old lady in Key West. He had to get there and he would, once the wind was in the northeast.

About fifty yards away, a man stood in the stern of a dilapidated launch, hands on his hips, playing Beethoven's Fifth Symphony from a boom box at high volume. He seemed to be challenging anyone who might wish to interrupt his attempt to educate water-borne vacationers. Errol was having difficulty ignoring this. Presently, a cigarette boat filled with young people pulled anchor and relocated near the loner in the old launch. They played rap music on their much more powerful sound system while mimicking the crablike moves of hip-hop. Errol ransacked his boat for booze and miraculously found a six-pack of warm beer made with water from the Rocky Mountains wrapped in a bundle of canvas in his sail-repair supplies. He tingled with the excitement of discovery as he remembered hiding it from a woman who'd come aboard one morning, an attractive woman who'd gone nuts, shouting invitations to a coast guard station in her underwear. Errol permitted himself to sample the beer. Feeling better, he mused over the old fellow's persistence in playing Beethoven; and with the second can, he began to enjoy the undulations of the half-clothed youths in the cigarette boat. The arrival of a private helicopter overhead, ruffling the entire surface of the harbor and tossing the smaller craft merrily, made him bless whatever gods had dropped off the six-pack. He retreated to the cabin and assumed the cooler view that would become necessary if the hilarity continued to spread over Pelican Bay. His simple ambition—to avoid insanity—seemed in danger of deteriorating into misleading annoyance. Still, he was smart enough to know that the curtain would fall again. It was only a matter of time.

After a short and troubled nap, Errol rigged a handline and small jig that he dangled from the side for only a short time before bringing a snapper aboard. He held it in front of him, its fins braced, bright eyes seemingly fixed upon his. He rapped it over the head with his cleaning knife, and as it stiffened, shivered, and died in his hand, tears filled his eyes. He cleaned it, placed the two fillets in a skillet on the single-burner alcohol stove, and, after examining the fleshless frame of the fish and thinking it looked like a good plan for a snapper, he threw it overboard. A seagull flew straight from the Beethoven boat, where it had been working the owner for snacks, and carried off the remains. The cigarette boat was now motoring slowly among the other anchored boats, treating them to the latest urban sounds. The helicopter was gone. "Why do we 'clean' fish?" Errol said aloud. "They are not dirty." He chuckled as though he'd made this remark for genteel company, then grimly contemplated pulling anchor and sailing for Key West. The wind had not come around sufficiently, but surely it would; staying in this public anchorage any longer would only put off the help he needed to avoid calamity and, more important, polishing off the beer would make it unavailable for the voyage, when its service to morale in stormy conditions would be invaluable.

Therefore, he raised the sails, pulling the halyards until they squeaked in the jam cleats. They luffed loudly as the boat drew back on the anchor rode, the boom bouncing against the mainsheet traveler, the tiller swinging from side to side as though the boat were being steered by a ghost. The anchor came up covered with turtle grass, and Errol laid it on deck, cleaning the weeds and throwing them overboard before lashing the anchor into its chocks and returning to the cockpit. He sat down and pushed the tiller to one side. The boat drifted backward and swung, until the sail filled and she reversed direction. *Czarina* then moved swiftly, rail down, toward the entrance to the bay.

As he sailed out the pass, he felt the slight easterly shift of the still-powerful winds. The faces of the waves were now tall but less abrupt, and the rudder never lost its bite as it had on his first crossing. The sky was gray, but it was higher and faintly light-shot to the west. He trimmed the sails until, at due south, there was no pressure on the helm, and the yawl sailed herself. His only job would be to adjust the sheets to keep this heading as the wind clocked around to the east.

The coast soon disappeared and he found himself making good progress in the open water; the Gulf of Mexico, and the greater regularity of the seas, uninfluenced by tide and shore, made the little boat lope along with a purpose. Errol had a few sips of his beer, but he could already tell he was not going to drink too much. He occupied himself with housekeeping, making up the pipe berth below, folding his oilskins and stowing them in their locker, draining the icebox into a bucket and pouring the water overboard. He pulled the floorboards and sponged out the salt water that had come on deck and gotten through the deck ventilator, which now poured fresh air through the cabin, arousing the smells of cedar and old varnish. On the bulkhead a framed photograph had discolored over time, a picture of himself much younger, a man, and a woman, the same age. Underneath, it said "Pals."

Back in the cockpit, he unspooled a handline with a large silver spoon and single hook over the stern. It danced and dove a hundred feet behind the boat and seemed to elevate Errol's spirits further. He wished he had some sort of flag to raise and then remembered that he did have just the thing. He dug around in the cockpit locker among dock lines, fenders, and life jackets until he found the flag of the Conch Republic, the imaginary nation of Key West from its days of hippie utopianism, an era Errol seemed to have trouble escaping. He raised it to the masthead on the flag halyard and liked seeing its pink-and-yellow conch and sunburst against an increasingly blue sky.

The compass indicated he was now heading for Yucatán and so further adjustment to the sails would be necessary. This was the result of the steady easterly shift of winds and clearing weather. The seas were ever less violent, and within an hour the skies had cleared entirely and the Gulf had regained its characteristic dusty-green placidity under towering white clouds. It occurred to Errol that his drinking days were behind him. Oh, joy! Not another shit-faced, snockered, plastered, oiled, loaded, bombed, wasted minute ever again! No more guilt, remorse, rehab, or jail! Free at last!

Calming down, he remembered that his hope lay in his visit to Florence Ewing, the good witch. She had seen right through him in days past and found something redeeming. She would again. He could have taken the bus and gotten there straightaway, but he had arrived by sea the last time she'd put him right, and though it was decades ago he was sure she could do it again. He knew better than to alter any of the details. His mestizos, trustworthy and industri-ous, would keep the cracker's groves in order until he returned.

A frigate bird followed him at a great altitude, a perfect flier that barely needed to move its wings, an elegant black zigzag watching his wake for baitfish. He daydreamed about what it would be like to be a bird like that, a seabird with that great altitude and hori-zon. No big thoughts, of course, just Where's the fish? Like being a fine athlete, everything vision and muscle memory, Ted Wil-liams watching the ball compress on the bat, no attitude, a simple there-it-is. Roar of the crowd same as wind or traffic, just worth-less noise. If I were a bird, that six-pack wouldn't glow like radium, a screeching come-hither.

The yawl was making wonderful progress. With the slowly clocking wind and more moderate seas, she sped along on a con-trolled reach that might scarcely need adjustment before Key West. The coast soon disappeared beneath the eastern horizon, and for a pleasant half hour a pair of young dolphins surfed in the quarter wave before peeling off for more interesting games. Huge schools of bait, shadows in the pale Gulf green, erupted like hail falling on the water as predators coursed through and terns dove at them from above. The leeward deck was dark with spray all the way to the transom.

In late afternoon, he sailed through a congregation of Louisiana shrimp boats, nets draped from trawling booms as they awaited nightfall. And at dusk a big ketch rail-down passed a couple miles to the north of him, heading for Yucatán. Errol lashed the tiller and went below to warm some soup over the blue alcohol flame. He ate it slowly, sitting on the companionway step and looking at the clouds swaying back and forth above the cockpit, their undersides pink at the approach of sundown. As he gazed south, he wished he could do this forever. Maybe once he'd been saved, it would be possible. At least he could go to the islands for a spell, which islands it was hard to say. What difference did it make? he thought irritably, as though being cross-examined about the islands. For a moment, he fretted about islands all running together and being required to distinguish between them. Now his ears were ringing.

Then it was dark, a comfortable dark with stars coming up in tiers, and a quarter moon hung outlined in haze. The tiller throbbed gently in Errol's hand and the lubber line on the compass rested quietly on his course of 180 degrees. It seemed that since his boat went in the water all things were sweeping him gently toward this destination. The hours slipped by until the loom of Key West lit the southwestern sky in a pale glow, calling for a "cocktail," a cause for celebration even Errol found suspicious. He might have felt misgivings.

Sails had to be trimmed again as he beat his way past the sea buoy and up the ship channel toward the bright skyline of the city. He didn't feel he had time to go all the way around Tank Island to get to Garrison Bight. Instead, he sailed on until he broke out into the Atlantic, and then broad-reached up Smathers Beach before turning in toward the desalinization plant and a dismaying number of bright lights and even automobile traffic. Dropping the mainsail, he lashed it to the boom and crept up the channel under the jib and mizzen between small anchored boats backlit on black water. Spotting an empty slip, he dropped the jib and mizzen and glided very slowly to the dock. As he stepped ashore to secure the yawl, he suddenly felt frightened, but the feeling passed. He was briefly without momentum, a situation efficiently solved by one of the beers. Furthermore, last call was still hours away.

He kept inhaling deeply, surprised after his long absence at the familiarity of Key West night air, the particular humidity, the scent of more flowers than occur in nature, salt water, and faint indications of humanity: tobacco, perfume, automotive exhaust. It was a perennial aroma occasionally subsumed by a single smell, new house paint or Sunday-morning vomit. All in all, it made his heart ache.

Key West seemed a most appealing landfall. Old-timers used to tell him that before the aqueduct and plentiful fresh water, the place was a kind of gooney-bird island, not much greenery and plenty of exposed caprock and coral. Now it was as lush as Hawaii, an easier sell.

The bartender had a deeply fissured, weathered face, a gold chain around his neck, de rigueur before Key West went literary; also, solidarity with the Cubans. He returned with Errol's drink.

"I quit drinking over eleven thousand days ago," said the bartender, whose name was something to do with dog: Coon Dog, Hound Dog, Blue Dog—Errol forgot. "And it was no mistake."

Dog-something seemed to be studying Errol, probably remembered Errol no better than Errol remembered him. Errol clearly recalled that the bartender drove in one day from Boston about a quarter century ago with a blue-eyed dancer he was very proud of and who wasted no time in absconding with one of the entrepreneurial hippies, a corrupt prep-school boy from Columbia, South Carolina, who was restoring a conch house.

"What about that Natalya? You still see her?"

"That was quite long lasting, wasn't it? No, I haven't seen her in ages." Natalya was from New Orleans, a beautiful girl with thick auburn hair who reminded everyone of Gene Tierney. She had a genuine New Orleans–Brooklyn–southern accent. She was languorous and virginal, with a promise of depravity so instinctive in New Orleans girls that it must have been devised by their ancestral mothers. Some logged feverish turns in town before going home, marrying Tulane doctors, and raising little magnolia aristocrats to replenish the Garden District. But Natalya was different from all the others; she and Errol had been engaged to be married. He hadn't cared about anything else at all. He stood beside his stool and said, "Well, I suppose."

"Nice seeing you."

"Same."

"You remember West Coast Anita?"

"I remember Anita."

"There were two Anitas, Anita and West Coast Anita."

Errol was anxious to go. Looking toward the door, he asked, "Which one had the flag in her tooth?"

"West Coast Anita."

"What about her?"

"Anita stayed too long at the fair. She had an out-of-body experience in the Turks and Caicos, and they had to take her down on the beach and shoot her."

Errol said, "I must be missing something." He counted out his tab on the bar. "Well," he said, "I'm off to see Florence Ewing."

He didn't know why he was not cordial to Dog-something, one of those citizens you can't quite remember, though he tells you that you and he go way back. Perhaps it was the sense that one was about to be drawn into something or discover that one had failed to recall a debt. A group strode in, three women and a man with low gray bangs who cried out, "But wait: right after the car crash, we come in with the Japanese flutes!" The women were awestruck as he swept his arm toward the table he had selected for them. One, forefinger to a dimple, hung back, contemplating the flutes in her imagination.

Night Dog! That was it!

From here he could see shrimp boats between the buildings on Lower Caroline Street. He and Raymond had backed the old ketch in here one winter to pull out the Vere diesel that had turned into a half ton of English rust in the bilge. They'd built a gallows frame of old joists they got when the Red Doors Saloon was remodeled, and all the wallets fell out of the walls from a century of muggings. They lifted the great iron lump on a chain fall and swung the dead engine to the fish docks. Thenceforth, they sailed her without the engine. She went that way into Havana, but Raymond was not aboard.

Florence Ewing lived on Petronia Street, a street frequently in the *Key West Citizen* for scenes of mayhem; but this was the more sedate upper Petronia, now part of a district renamed by realtors the Meadows, a tremendous leap of the imagination. Florence was born in the house over eighty years ago, and Errol's every hope was pinned on her being still alive.

She had gone to sea with her father, a turtle captain, when she was eleven and could still describe the Moskito Coast of Nicaragua in detail. By sixteen, she was a chorus girl in New York; she married at seventeen back home and stayed married for over sixty years to her physician husband. A precondition was that they never leave the Petronia house. Dr. Ewing, an Alabaman and a sportsman, struggled with this, turning the old carriage house into a kind of dominoes hall for his cronies, building a stilt shack past Mule and Archer Keys where he fished and played cards on weekends in his old Abaco launch. He delivered thousands of Key West babies, who stayed until the tourist boom pushed them up A1A to the mainland; some were even his own, begotten on lissome Cuban teens. When Raymond Fitzpatrick and Errol Healy went into partnership, they lived around the corner from Florence; and during some of the fraught hours of their business life, Errol found himself being quietly counseled by the very sensible and spiritual Florence Ewing. You could say they became close, cooking meals for each other or watching Johnny Carson. And it was not a matter of an old widow needing company. Errol needed the company; Florence was wholly self-sufficient. Errol was cautious about imposing on her, though he supposed he must at times have tested her patience. He never went there high, more consideration than anyone else got, and he tried to keep the more outrageous ladies from battening onto her and declaring her a role model. He didn't know how she created such peace. Others noticed and sought her out; they believed she had the power to sanctify and heal those who had lost hope. He marveled that she didn't run them all off or even judge them or, just once, tell them she was too tired. They were her subjects. For some she was an oracle; for a few a last chance. She had learned forgiveness and discovered its mighty power.

He made the trek from the bar in the fragrant early evening, taking enough time to gaze upon the laundromat still lifes, those all-night getaways where girls of yore rode the tumblers and fornicated on the washing machines. Notions and grocery stores still open were nevertheless somnolent. Here and there among the renovated houses miraculously a few remained tumbledown as before, with gutted refrigerator kingfish smokers in the backyard. Many of the houses were tall and attracted the eye, making you look upward at a sky that let you know that you were surrounded by the sea. Elsewhere, rainwater cisterns had been converted into atmospheric soaking tubs, leaves and rotting fruit were made to disappear, and services created to secure the things bound to fail when the city was astonished by some intrusion of nature, such as a storm. Life sometimes tested absentee owners. When, after a half year, remembering the fresh air and clean linens, the truce with vegetation, the ringless tubs and toilets, the owners returned to find fetor and mildew, the inconvenienced rats and fleeing roaches and bellicose fighting chickens who had moved into the lap pool, there was seldom anything so untoward as a demand for return of caretakers' fees. Slaves of their own vacations, the owners began by negotiating.

He cut through a lane behind the library on Fleming to gaze at a house where Natalya's friend Frances Mousseau had lived, working on a romantic play, a gnomish tale of Cajun high jinks set in the Atchafalaya Swamp. Errol thought Frances, a racist Creole from Plaquemines, too dull witted for passionate folly; nevertheless, upon learning she'd been disinherited, she jumped off an ocean liner. Had a passenger watching the moonrise from a cheap cabin not seen Frances go by his porthole, her absence might never have been noticed. While characteristic notions of the day included a dreamy version of suicide, Frances was quickly forgotten.

Errol walked to Fleming, where he had lived with Natalya and Raymond, at least one Anita, and a few others, sharing the rent and parceling out all the small rooms. He remembered believing this lack of privacy was assurance that his love for Natalya would remain undisturbed. But Natalya could make men find original ways to hurt themselves, even his late, great best friend Raymond. Holding the iron railing, he looked up at the old house, which had become a bed-and-breakfast, Fronds, with a sign in front: NO CHILDREN. NO PETS. In that house, Errol felt all he had left behind.

There was still light in Petronia, brighter along Georgia, and indeed in the garden at Florence's house someone was toiling late, a middle-aged man in khaki pants and work shoes whom Errol did not recognize. The grounds were in ominously poor shape. Though infinitely polite, Florence had always gotten a lot of work out of her people, some of whom were of remarkably little account, reverting to their torpid ways as soon as they left her.

When Errol told the gardener that he had come to see Miss Ewing, the man stood back from him uneasily.

"She's in there." He was inhospitable but could not have known how much Errol had riding on this. "And who are you?"

"An old friend from Fleming Street."

He gave this some thought. "You want to go in, go in."

"Yes, of course." So he went up the steps, and on the gardener's peremptory "Don't knock; she can't get to the door," he let himself in. He felt shaky.

Except for the soaring lines of the old shipwright's staircase and the few glints of a high chandelier, he couldn't see much of anything. Just this was enough to make him feel quieter as his soul expanded safely into Florence Ewing's sanctum, the house that turtles built, furnished from wrecks, including a grand piano made of African mahogany, said to have killed a man as it came aboard. Here, nearly a century ago, Florence was delivered by a black midwife from Great Inagua who, she claimed, taught her to conjure, a tale the young people made her tell again and again. Compared with the conventional mummery with which they had arrived, conjury held great attraction. Florence owned dozens of lacquered boxes, little private containers of silver and enamel that could furnish coveted storage for secret things, and sometimes she made gifts of them. Secrets were everything in Errol's circle, and they all worked at suggesting they were full of them. It was not for everyone and especially not for Errol and Raymond, who made a handsome living transporting souls from Cuba, their earnings disbursed not by driving big cars or hiring interior decorators but rather by throwing banquets.

Dividing the foyer from the living room was an old theater flat with a great big moon sparkling on an empty sea that created an obstruction to direct entry. Errol called out, "Florence," and got no reply. There was a blue spider with a body shaped like a pentagram lowering itself slowly on a single strand of silk; from afar came the sound of a ship signaling the harbor pilot. He stepped around the theater flat and wondered why he had waited so long. He felt weightless as he gazed, soaring and uncertain, at the ghostly figure of his redeemer.

The living room had become her bedroom, and the chandelier that Errol had glimpsed from the other side was seen to hang over her bed, an old gas-burning model that had been converted to electric and was now a garland of mostly expired little bulbs. He remembered best her big ormolu bed, formerly on the second floor, a table beside it supporting a water pitcher, a vase of anemones, and several small bottles. Florence was propped against many pillows and covered by the palest-blue counterpane. The room was fresh and the bedclothes looked buoyant and clean; someone must be looking after her. Errol wished he could have slipped in beside her, to begin pouring out his heart in crazy familiarity, to detach himself completely from his own story and watch it sail out into the air like a ribbon.

As he entered she gazed at him with eyes that were opalescent. He greeted her and told her who he was. She said nothing, and he drew up the only chair, one so straight-backed and uncomfortable that he wondered if she ever had visitors. Florence had grown so very old, with a diaphanous quality of something about to turn to powder. Yet she was as elegant as an ancient Spanish altarpiece. Errol almost wished some of the others were here, especially Raymond Fitzpatrick, of whom she was so fond. Or even Natalya, whom Florence disliked; here they could have all finally come clean. The last time Florence spoke to Natalya, she told her that she saw right through her, and Natalya gave her no chance to elaborate. Florence smiled until Natalya got up and left.

It didn't seem to matter that neither of them spoke. Errol was fascinated that he could slip back into Florence's house and feel that the fabric of consolation had never been torn. He decided then and there that he would just talk, just pour it out. He was far too desperate to do it conversationally, and she looked as though she might not have the strength. She could always ask him to stop, but it had been a long ride and he needed to talk.

"Florence," he said, "I've been gone a long time." He could see her eyes sharpen somewhat, and he wanted to get the mechanical tone out of his voice. "I moved up to Canada for a while." That reminded him: there used to be a number of French Canadians around town, Separatists in Speedos, who told the girls they'd planted the mailbox bombs in Montreal. It was a very effective line and kept the bulk of the Separatists out of inclement weather. "Now I'm in citrus. I'm responsible for four huge groves in Hendry County, frost-free high ground, the best. Natalya and I split up quite a while ago." He'd mistakenly thought this would induce a reply. "She's up in New Orleans, three beautiful kids. They all swim. Remember how crazy Natalya was about swimming? Jumping off the White Street Pier? And remember Jackie L. Dalton? Used to play his songs for you on the guitar? He's a huge hit, just huge, got his own jet plane." He caught himself mimicking with his hand the jet plane flying through the sky. "Fills big stadiums," he added weakly.

For an instant his head was empty. Then he wanted to talk again.

"Those days seem so long ago. But that's nothing to you, is it? Not when you've seen Cay Sal from the deck of a schooner. Really, I think all of us were just pitiful, just homeless and pitiful. Didn't know anything. Worse came to worst, declare yourself a carpenter. There was that awful song, 'If I was a carpenter and you were a lady,' started all that mess. Then some people couldn't get out of it, and after they left here they couldn't ask you, so a lot of them took off more or less empty-handed. It wasn't your fault and I don't know what you got out of listening to all that, and here you are doing it again and I'm starting to feel better already. I'll be honest with you; I had to come here. In a way, it's my last chance. I said to myself, Miss Florence Ewing will not permit me to go on like this.

"I didn't really move to Canada, I just said that. I didn't move anywhere. I moved my body several times but nothing else moved. I was like that four-hundred-pound lady bouncer at the Anchor they called Tiny. We were there a thousand times and nobody ever saw Tiny move. I'm kind of like old Tiny, but in my case the body is the only thing that *did* move. Let me clear that up: I went to Canada, I went to Red Deer, Alberta, but it just didn't work out, and anyway Canada won't let me back in. It's not like I meant to mislead you about that.

"By the way, it's sure nice nobody smokes in here. I can smell all that longleaf pine just like the day your granddad nailed it up. When you used to get us to do a little work around here, we'd run into those gumbo-limbo joists and break our tools and you'd just laugh. I think me and Raymond pretty much covered that old turtle route in that black Nova Scotia ketch we had together, a real little ship. We probably saw as much of the tropics as anybody."

He looked off to one end of the room where the tall windows had darkened and a breeze lifted the long curtains. The four live bulbs in the chandelier were little help and Errol was at the point of thinking Florence had passed away.

"That last trip, coming across the stream in a northern gale, a big wave took Raymond right off the helm and away. I came up for my watch and there was no one at the wheel. Not a soul." He delivered a hearty laugh, but there was a scream buried in it. "I realize there are plenty of people who said it didn't exactly happen that way, and I hope you believe me. But I got the boat home, got her tied up at the desalinization plant, and walked to Natalya's house. She wasn't there. She wasn't going to be there. Well, what do you know about that, Florence? I'll bet you imagined you were through with all that. I kind of wish you'd answer me or say something. I'll bet you figured we had used you about up. Surprise, surprise. You know what? Just goes to show you, Raymond is the legend we all knew he would be. I can tell you that I have failed to make—uh, to make an appropriate accommodation. I am a drunkard and I really felt I better get back down here for a little visit, see what you had to say about all this, help a person more or less sort of stand it."

Florence Ewing did not say a word. Errol could feel her opal eyes enter his soul. He knew that if he did not tell the truth she would not offer him absolution, and even then there was no certainty, no promise, no assurance that her powers would work or that he would ever be whole again. It had been half his life since he'd known what hope felt like. In Florence Ewing's face it seemed everything was accepted as morning accepted light. He was joyous that he'd had enough mother wit left to make the trip, to place himself in the way of this illumination.

"Florence, you don't have to talk."

He rose from his chair and sat at the corner of her bed and thought. Carter and Castro were going to show the world we could be friends and they declared a race from Key West to Cuba. Errol and Raymond entered the race with no hope of winning, and they agreed they wouldn't try to bring any souls back with them. The manifest showed just the two of them in both directions: Errol Healy and Raymond Fitzpatrick.

Errol couldn't tell if he was talking or just thinking. Florence's eyes took him in with even-greater opalescence, and he wondered whether she was reading his mind. He thought he could hear himself speaking, maybe just part of this dream, a disquieting dream that suggested the possibility that he wasn't even here at all, that he would be awakened by an attendant of some sort, someone he would be unable to recognize. He never wanted to be in any form of custody.

ALL THE BOATS KNEW A GALE WAS PREDICTED. EVERYONE leaving the ship channel at sundown thought they would reach the middle of the stream sometime after midnight. There was a crowd by the coast guard dock, all the sunset watchers and dogs and jugglers there to see them off, grand prix yachts and cruisers and local dope captains in anything they could lay hands on, from J24s to backyard trimarans. It had the feeling of a big parade, with Errol and Raymond's the only ship customarily dedicated to profiteering at the misfortune of refugees.

They were going to Cuba! The sun set behind them kind of cold, and for a few hours right into the darkness they were on a beam reach in fifteen to eighteen knots from the north, and the ketch had her rail right at the water, pulling a quarter wave higher than the transom. They had an overlapping jib that was almost too much for her, but this was perfect sailing for a heavy English ketch, and her rock-elm ribs creaked under her. They had a bottle of Courvoisier to sip, and Errol chattered about all the good things in their lives, all their tax-free money, and about Natalya and sailing forever and someday settling down with her, with their own crabbing pier for the kids, with a flounder light and maybe a picture album of the days when Raymond and Errol were young in a dangerous trade, when everyone they did business with had a gun.

At some point, Errol realized that Raymond hadn't said a word. He was a very direct man, an honest man. He never spoke for effect, and Errol had long ago learned that something was coming when he was quiet like this. Well, something was coming. Raymond said that he had never intended to join this race. He came so he could talk to Errol man-to-man. And what he had to say was that when they got back to Key West, he and Natalya were moving to New Orleans. That by the time they got back she would already be gone.

"Raymond was at the helm and I was sitting in the footwell with my back to the companionway. I could see all the way to the last glow on the horizon, and Key West was under the western horizon except for the loom of its lights. I felt I should say something. I actually felt I should say something *out of our friendship.* But nothing would come. I kept trying to picture Natalya, and she would come to me all outlined; it's hard to explain. But I couldn't say *anything.* I guess I thought we should go back, but if I said we should go back, that would really make it . . . really make it official. So I never said, Let's go back, and we pushed on toward Cuba.

"At about two in the morning, the gale was rising and we put a double reef in the main, a real adventure because she had an old-fashioned boom that overhung the transom by ten feet, and getting the bunt tied in all the way to the leech was dangerous." Again, the thought returned that he was not actually speaking and this was only a dream, but Florence's gaze seemed to indicate absorption and whether he was thinking or speaking seemed not to matter. In fact, this is how he remembered it was with Florence Ewing. It was what they'd all looked for: the trance she'd cast from her past mysteries.

"The wind really came up fast, and since it was blowing against the direction of the stream the seas were bad. At first we could see the spreader lights of the other yachts, and then we couldn't even see that and all around us it was just the black wave faces in our running lights. Without saying anything, I changed places with Raymond and took the wheel. He went below and stayed there for a long time as the seas built and the ketch began to groan under the strain and yaw worse and worse, especially as we came down the faces. Several times I could feel her try to broach, but I was able to head up and keep her on her feet. I later heard the seas had been over twenty feet. Boats were dismasted and *Black Magic,* a Great Lakes yacht, killed her helmsman in a standing jibe. One of the dope captains on a Stone Horse disappeared entirely, the only boat out there without a self-bailing cockpit. No one ever found the tin cans full of money he'd buried all over Key West, but his girlfriend went around in a haze, carrying her shovel and knocking on doors, trying to get in people's yards.

"Raymond came partway up the companionway and I could barely hear him over the storm. He said, 'The jib's got to come off before we lose control.' I knew it was true, but all this time I had been thinking, and I wasn't sure if I cared whether we controlled the boat or not. As it was, I had trouble. Even twenty-five tons of oak and lead seemed to lose traction in those seas.

"Typical Raymond, he went forward hand over hand toward the foredeck. I kept her on course until he eased the halyard and the jib started down. I turned her upwind and the jib collapsed, Raymond on top of it lashing it with wild, violent exertions of his arms. I bore off, and as I did so we were lifted on a huge wave. We stayed atop it for a long moment, Raymond facedown on the foredeck, and then we started into the trough, which was just a long, bottomless hole. What had made me change direction? I felt the boat pick up speed as we went down, and it had begun to yaw as the sea hissed out behind the keel. It seemed like it yawed harder and harder. The spokes on the wheel just tore at my hands, and either I lacked the strength or I—or I—it got away from me. The wheel got away from me . . . and we broached. The next wave buried us from starboard, and the bow went under, beyond the forward hatch, then over the brow of the house. She stayed like that for a long time, and when she came up, the ocean was pouring off the crown of the foredeck. There was no one there.

"The Cuban came aboard in Havana and read the crew manifest. He said, Where's the *otro hombre*? I said I came by myself. He left and came back with another guy in a green uniform with a machine gun. He spoke English. I said there had been a language problem with the first guy. I told him the *otro hombre* washed overboard on the western edge of the stream where it changed color. He believed me. I don't think it's that unusual to Cubans to wash overboard."

The gardener came quietly into the room. Errol couldn't tear his gaze away from Florence, because he felt any second now she might speak. He was hoping she would. She pulled herself up and looked at him intently, all phosphorus gone as her eyes blackened and some beads rolled off the counterpane and tinkled to the floor. Errol could tell she was going to say something.

"Are you with the termite people?" she asked. Errol didn't reply and Florence repeated her question, this time with some agitation.

The gardener pushed past him and leaned over Florence so she would be sure to hear him. "They can't come without they tent the place," he said to her. "And they can't tent the place if you in it, 'cause they pump it full of poison." She let out a moan. The gardener spoke in a more conciliatory voice. "The exterminator been every week," he told her, as if he was singing her a song. She seemed crushed at the news.

"Is he the one with his car all fixed up like a rat?" asked Florence urgently. "Has big ears on it like a rat?"

The old house on Fleming was the obvious choice, as long as they had a room with a tub available. He stopped first at Tres Hermanos for some supplies. The front door was wide open to the air, and a desk had been set up in the front hall. Here sat the clerk reading the newspaper, his treated blond hair swept forward from a single spot. Without looking up, he asked how he could help and Errol told him he wanted a room with a tub.

"No can do."

"No rooms?"

"Not with a tub."

"There's a tub in the last room on the second floor."

"That's a *suite*. You said you wanted a *room*."

"I'll take the suite."

"It's not the same *price* as a room."

"I understand."

The clerk looked up finally. He regarded the paper bag from the Cuban *tienda*. "Is that all you have to your name?"

"Yes."

"Usually, when we rent the suite, it's to someone with a *suitcase*."

"I'll bet that's right." The clerk had no idea what a problem lay before him.

Despite all the heavy, almost-operatic furniture and tasseled drapery, the room was recognizable. He remembered its old bare wooden bones, the sparse secondhand furnishings of that time, the Toulouse-Lautrec poster and its rusty thumbtacks. The names were streaming at him. The gardener had told him he was wasting all that noise on Miss Ewing; he declared that Miss Florence Ewing had upped and cleared out during a previous administration and wouldn't know him from Adam.

The water made a deep sound in the old tub. Errol pulled a chair next to it and placed the bag where he could reach it. He filled the tub, calculating how deep it could be without the mass of his body overflowing it. The water looked so still, so clear, with light steam arising. He undressed and got in, sliding down until the water was as high as his throat. Errol remembered taking bread scraps to the birds in the small town where he grew up; and when he reached toward the chair next to the tub, he saw the birds again, how they rose in a cloud. He was alert enough to enjoy this slide into oblivion, to picture a million oranges rotting on trees as his mestizos dispersed into Florida barrios, and at first he confused the shouts he heard with those of his boss, the cracker, the juice king of Arcadia and citrus oligarch who made his life so wearisome. A cloud of blackbirds rose from the rotting oranges around a small man shouting in the grove . . .

It was the desk clerk and two police officers, but the desk clerk alone, soaking wet, was doing all the shouting. "He ruined my beautiful hotel!"

One of the officers, a small portly Cuban, asked, "You call this a hotel?"

"Get him out of here! Pump his stomach, do something!"

To the skeptics in the emergency room, Errol said, "Must be some kind of bug."

Grisly days at Keys Memorial passed slowly. The nurses knew what he had done, and several considered it a mortal sin, a view that produced grudging service and solitude beside otherwise busy corridors. At checkout, the accounting office having assumed indigence expressed surprise at his Blue Cross. He started to explain, but he was too numb to speak and wondered whether he had done himself permanent harm. Perhaps I am now feebleminded, he thought. But really his heart was lighter for having survived the outcome of a long obsession.

HE SPENT THE REST OF THE MORNING BUYING PROVISIONS. The yawl was just as he had left it, but for a light coating of ash from the island's heroic burning dump. A fishing boat was being swabbed down by two Cubans in khakis and white T-shirts who from time to time tossed a fish from the scuppers to a pelican waiting modestly on the transom. The tide had dropped, leaving a wide band of barnacles around the pilings, and Errol moved his spring lines until the boat stood away from them. Provisions were stowed in the galley; the water he had acquired on the mainland was still in good supply. He washed the deck down with seawater, sweeping the ash over the stern, and checked his watch. The bars had just opened. He stepped off the boat and headed uptown, stopping at a phone booth to call his employer, the owner of the groves and juice plant. He told him he'd gotten a much-needed rest and would be back among the oranges in no time flat. He'd left the Latino crew detailed instructions sure to see them through every waking moment. "I'll just bet," the grove owner said, adding, "You're the damnedest feller I ever met."

"Anyway, you said you'd go along with me on this," said Errol.

"To a point," said the cracker. "There's a limit to everything."

ALL HE REMEMBERED WAS WALKING THROUGH THE DOOR OF the Bull and Whistle Bar and not much of that. He had sufficiently conquered disgust to realize he was in the Gulf Stream, the sun just rising, and he felt a bleak pride that he could manage the yawl in his present condition. He sank and rose among the ultramarine troughs and saw golden strands of sargasso weed at eye level. Flying fish skittered off breaking wave edges, and the three that landed on deck he gutted and laid in the sink. By the end of the ten days promised him by the cracker, the mestizos would be gone and jobless. The oranges would fall and fruit wasps would rise in a cloud. He couldn't let that happen. He couldn't let himself put words to his dismal pride in belonging to the manager class, but he clung to it nonetheless.

Wherever it was going, the little yawl was sailing well. Errol stood on the deck hanging on to the backstay and looked down into the Gulf Stream and the almost-purplish depths. The rudder made a long trailing seam at the surface; he could see all the way to the end of the blade as it vibrated under the force of the boat's progress. The sun had dried the decks, and only the leeward side remained dark with sea spray.

Errol started to search out details of the previous night but nothing came. He had a good many of these blanks now. Sometimes they unexpectedly came to life, filled with detail. He called them "sleeping beauties" in an attempt to assign some value amid what he realized was simple creeping oblivion. He even knew that his current behavior—indifference to where he might be headed—was customary following a blackout, and not unrelated to his frivolous attempt to do away with himself; the feeling would soon give way to extreme concern for his situation and all-round fearfulness. As strength returned he would be amused by these comical swings, even a bit jubilant, and the cycle would begin again, its force undiminished by familiarity. His excuse was that life was repetitious anyway, without quite realizing that the source of despair's enduring power was that it was always brand spanking new.

The yawl climbed each swell toward its breaking crest with steady progress, its thin wake like a crack in glass, until a moment when the view from the helm was blue sky and the whitest sea clouds; then hissing down the back slope into the trough to begin the climb again. In one ascent, he saw in the thinnest part of the rising wave a big iridescent fish that vanished as the sea swelled around it.

He merely wondered where he was going.

By afternoon, he more than wondered. The pleasant breeze from the southeast had gone round to the southwest and picked up considerably. Moreover, his spirits had sunk and he began to picture his restive mestizos, the towering cracker unfurling from his Mercedes to shout dismay at the ground covered with rotting oranges. But there was still time before all that happened, before the mestizos dispersed to the work camps at Okeechobee and their cramped prospects. He hadn't really been their friend, but he spoke their language and they shared his whiskey, and that was enough, relatively speaking.

The blue of the sea was still reflected by the clouds, but instead of gliding down the backs of waves, the yawl seemed now to push its way down them, the wind driving the bow deeper and deeper until only inches remained before seawater came aboard. It was time to reef.

Errol turned the yawl into the wind and she stopped, wallowing in the rolling ocean, the boom jumping from side to side until he sheeted the mizzen in and she held quietly, nose to wind. With eagerness and relief, Errol went from thinking to doing this work: releasing the main halyard to lower the mainsail, securing the first reef at the luff cringle, and then drawing down the leech until the sail was a third smaller. By tying in each of the fifteen reef points, he secured the loose stretch of decommissioned sail hanging below the boom in a tight, efficient bunt. The main halyard was raised until it hardened; he eased the mizzen, trimmed the jib and main, and the yawl resumed her course for an unknown destination, once again gliding down the waves with her nose up and her decks dry.

Back at the tiller, he regarded the sweat pouring off his body as a result of his exertions and knew it carried poison away. He first thought it behooved him never to land, but awareness of his limited stores made him reject this foolishness. As misery approached, the romance of annihilation seemed to recede, and he wondered why his bouts of self-destruction always occurred on a rising tide of self-love. He knew that the worse he felt the harder he would try to get somewhere and survive. First he had to find out where he was. He had missed his chance at a noon shot of the sun with the sextant and would have to wait for the stars.

The erasure of the previous night left him with no information about his departure; all he knew for certain was that he was in the Gulf Stream, heading for either Cuba or the Bahamas. At this rate, he would reach one or the other during the night, and he really ought to find out which one it was.

He lashed the tiller and went below to cook the flying fish on the alcohol stove, frying them until they were crunchy and taking them back to the cockpit on a tin plate, where he watched the white top of each wave racing along a blue edge before turning into white spume and blowing away. Overhead terns hunted fish and rained down onto baitfish pushed to the surface by predators beneath, mostly unseen but sometimes showing a dark fin slicing through the turbulence.

Lying back, Errol watched the mast move against the sky, a repeated crossed loop, the infinity sign. He had begun to feel sick. It started as pain just behind his forehead and spread down his spine; as the pain moved into his limbs over the next several hours, he began to tremble. By sundown his entire body was shaking and he began dragging things from the cabin—sail bags, an army blanket, the canvas cockpit cover—covering himself with these to the height of the coaming so that only his face showed and the arm that connected him to the tiller. These too were shaking, and unless he kept them locked his teeth rattled audibly. His course was taking him to some part of the vast world of rum, and his mind traced a path between this universe and a wallet still fat with banknotes. This wallet, pressed uncomfortably against his buttock, could have been left in the cabin, but the prospect of misplacing it on arrival in the land of rum was such that he wished to verify its whereabouts continuously by the discomfort it produced. Sunken eyed and desolate, he watched the stars rise from the sea, and he knew he was meant to find out where he was. But the sextant in the far end of the cabin with the sight tables might as well have been on the moon; he knew he couldn't hold it steady enough to take a fix. Instead, he made a crude estimate in his mind of where he might be. The wind was in the first part of the southwest shift; hence the building seas after the quiet of the prevailing southeasterly. He knew he sailed on a starboard tack perhaps ten or fifteen degrees east of the wind, which meant only that he was headed for islands of various sizes, histories, and languages and not the open Atlantic. Beyond that he couldn't say how far he'd gone since he'd departed from a hole in time somewhere behind him.

He vomited the flying fish onto the sole of the cockpit and moaned as malodorous drool poured from the corner of his mouth. His hand on the tiller was a claw by now and the shaking had grown sufficiently violent that he heard himself thump against the cockpit seat, where he stretched out under the heap of things he'd brought from the cabin. He recognized that he wouldn't be able to steer much longer and wished that, while he'd had the strength, he'd heaved to and stopped the boat until a better hour. It was too late now. He lashed the tiller in place and let the wind pick his course out of a hat. The one advantage of this much misery was that he could quit caring, a welcome detachment from his suffering, suffering that would end in the Isles of Rum. At this point, he heard a bitter laugh fly from his mouth, a raspy bray that produced another just like it, then another as they fed off one another, and finally a picture of himself braying at a colossal rum bottle, which inspired bleak masturbation on the cockpit floor. After that, he could only hold his head up by resting his teeth on the seat.

A calming spell of defeat overtook him as he lay on his back looking up at the sail as it passed the stars. Though he recognized them all, he was somewhat absorbed as they flowed in one side of the sail and out the other with a purpose—though not his, of course; he had no purpose. He was not purpose, he was pulp. He cast about for consolation, grimly congratulating himself for being childless. But he remembered that his mestizos trusted him. Of course, they were grateful to anyone who learned their language in this coldhearted nation. But more. He worked beside them, made sure they were paid, while the cracker often inclined to contrive withholdings. The mestizos knew Errol was not so devious, and a working alcoholic appealed to their sense of shared desperation and defensible self-destruction. Indeed, they shook their heads in sympathy when he came to the groves sick, picked things up when he dropped them, carried his ladder. In the depths of his misery, this was all Errol could find, but under the circumstances it seemed quite a lot. Perhaps he was beginning to turn the corner, but first there was more vomiting to be done and the last of the flying fish went over the side. Miguel, Delfin, Juan, Machado, Estevez, Antonio, were their names. Good men.

He slept, but lacked the humanity to dream.

The yawl sailed on into day without his attendance. For hours the decks shone bright with dew and then dried as the sun arose. The telltale streamed from the masthead in the freshening breeze, and the water was no longer purple, as she had crossed the stream;

now she pulled her thin seam of wake across the blue water of a new sea, one that grew steadily paler until the yawl's own speeding shadow on the bottom preceded her, then rose to meet her when she ran aground.

Unavailing curses poured from the companionway as Errol emerged to view his misfortune. The jib, the main, and the mizzen displayed their same wind-filled curves and emphasized the sheer peculiarity of the boat's lack of motion. Looking in every direction, he could see only more bars and the dark shapes of coral heads, any one of which would have sunk the boat. Noon was rapidly approaching, and he dug out his sextant to take a sight of the sun, though he mirthlessly noted the irony of having two pieces of information, latitude and the proximity of the bottom.

The sight reduction from his battered book of tables gave him to conclude that he was somewhere in the western Bahamas. He should pride himself on his effortless crossing of the stream, he thought sardonically. Once he'd accepted that he was immobile, he felt an unexpected wave of security at the calm translucent waters around him, the coral gardens that were pretty shadows beneath them, and he marveled at having sailed so far into this gallery before going aground on forgiving sand. The full moon was a few days away. If he was not too surely embedded on this bar, he had an excellent chance of floating free on a spring tide. He had enough food and seemed to exult in this absence of choices; he explored the idea that he was content to be stuck.

THE DAYS BEGAN TO PASS, EACH MORE PEACEFUL THAN THE last. He had begun to think of his boat as an island, and in fact he could walk all around it or swim among the coral heads where clouds of pretty reef fish rose and fell with him in the gentle wash. He caught lobsters and boiled them in salt water while Radio Havana played from the cabin. He stretched out in the cockpit and read Frantz Fanon, experiencing pleasant indignation. After the first night, he had dragged a mattress from atop the quarter berth into the cockpit, and he slept there, watching expectantly as the moon grew full to bring the big tides that would float him off. Then, for better or worse, his life would resume. The boat had begun to float tentatively, lifting slightly at the bow only to ground again when the tide fell, but release would come soon.

The last day Errol knew that at high tide, a few hours from now, the yawl would float, free to sail away. He took the opportunity to give the bottom a good scrubbing, breaking down the new bar-nacles with the back of his brush and then sweeping them off. Down tide, hundreds of tiny fish gathered in a silver cloud to eat the particles of barnacle. With the full moon, the weather changed and dark clouds gathered against the western sky. He would have to look for shelter as soon as he was under way, or at least find enough seaway to heave to. A storm was coming.

He waited in the cockpit into the afternoon, and around three, with a light grinding sound, the yawl lifted off and turned into the wind. The anchor line, which had hung slack when he'd walked the anchor out into the shallows, rose and grew taut. If this were a safe anchorage, he would wait out the storm, but the anchor wouldn't have to slip much under the force of the wind to put him atop the coral. He reduced the mainsail before ever departing, taking the sail down at the second reef to a cleat on the mast. The line lead-ing to a cringle on the leech he wrapped onto the reefing winch and drew that down until the main was little more than a storm trysail. He brought the anchor aboard, hand over hand, the rode dropping into the anchor locker until the anchor was at the stem-head, streaming turtle grass and small snapping creatures; there he secured it and returned to the mast to raise sail before the yawl could make much sternway.

Once sail was up, the yawl began to move obediently. Errol stood at the tiller, carefully conning his way through the dark coral heads in their white circles of sand. The shadow of the boat scur-ried alongside him on the rippled bottom. Gradually the shadow shrank, then vanished, as he found blue water. With a rising thrill, Errol set sail for the unknown. He knew that any piece of land at all was on the trail to hell, and that this ocean road put a good face on oblivion. A bad storm was coming; he meant to embrace it. The first passage would be fear, but the other side—if he could get there—was what interested him as being the country of death or freedom, unless it turned out they were the same thing.

It was the season of equinoctial storms, and the halo around the sun made Errol see in this something of a larger plan for him. Still, the little yawl was indifferent to such things, a thought whose absurdity he recognized without quite believing. Like most sailors, he did not regard his ship as inanimate and extended his senses out to all her parts the better to understand the whims of the sea. This impulse came of a great desire to survive that he was not sure he owned. Nevertheless, he believed his ship wished to live, and perhaps he would defer to her out of respect for the adage that a good ship is one which, when her master can no longer take care of her, takes care of her master.

Her purposeful obedience let Errol work his way through the coral heads to the dark blue of deeper water. Once she had way on, she never hesitated in stays—unless the man at the tiller was entirely lacking in skill—and moved from tack to tack like one of the domino players at the Cuban-American Hall in Key West. She'd been built forty years ago by a tidal creek in St. Michaels, Maryland, with a bottom of yellow pine from a church made by slaves, the marks of whose axes could still be found inside a hull so thick and hard that screws had to be drilled first; the topsides were single-length planks of Atlantic white cedar, frames of sawn white oak, the deck of native pine and canvas, Sitka spruce spars that had come on a train from Oregon a long time ago. When he reviewed her various attributes, as he often did, Errol began to feel responsible for her, and he recognized its absurdity without believing it. Whatever juju he believed her to possess was not mitigated by the fact that her previous owner was shot in a card game and she had sunk into desuetude at Garrison Bight until Errol rescued her for past-due dock fees and a modest bribe to the city council. He'd never find another boat with the marks of slaves' axes in her timbers. She went up on jack stands at Stock Island, neglected sculpture among the shrimp boats, slowly returned to life by Errol and friends until launching day, when in an alcoholic crisis he sailed her away to the Dry Tortugas, anchoring in Mooney Harbor under the shadow of Fort Jefferson, to await a new day. His gratitude toward his little ship was evident in his belief that she had treated him like a cherished dependent and hung on her anchor, keeping a fresh breeze across his bunk until such time as he could return to the tiller like a man. When that day came, he sailed right past

Key West and all his previous sins and fetched up at Cortez, his current berth, where he met the cracker at a party on the latter's sixty-foot Hatteras; and there he began his apprenticeship in the orange groves, where his command of Spanish was put to service exploiting the cracker's laborers. Errol suffered no more than most over the plight of his fellow man, yet this was a bit of a problem. Some of the men were refugees from violence, and their children, though occasionally visited by well-meaning social workers from the State of Florida, clearly expected massacres at any time and so avoided anyone who was not obviously a mestizo peasant. One way or another, the oranges continued to head for the juice plant at Arcadia, and Errol came to be trusted by these lost souls, who forgave his being a *perro enfermo* or perhaps even liked him because of it.

The job now was to get to deeper water and plenty of it before getting knocked around by the storm. He had no destination other than the knowledge that in this ocean you could not go far before striking some community or another, a bit of shelter, perhaps some refreshments. The problem was that his slowly clearing mind wasn't sure it wished to arrive. The gradual illumination—cramps, headaches, and diarrhea notwithstanding—was a substantial reward in itself, and the reattachment to reality bore a religious quality, or at least rootless excitement. He imagined the storm as a cascade of invigorating challenges.

A set of line squalls formed across the horizon, driving columns of seabirds before it, a thunder-filled cross-winded trough of weather. He traversed five miles of broken sea to sail right into them, lightning jumping around over the spar, an uprush of fragrant supercharged sea in omnidirectional winds. Each cell had its own weather and light, from near darkness and pandemonium to a fluorescent stillness walled by rain. Thus far, a pleasant exercise, for he sailed right through the squalls for a better view of the gray sky beyond, scudding clouds and building seas where a barometric trench made the rules.

Foresight suggested that he feed himself in the time available. He lashed the tiller and went below to light the alcohol stove, dumping a can of chicken noodle soup into a pot. The yawl's steady progress had acquired a kind of leaping motion, and he stirred the soup impatiently, as though that would shorten the time it took to heat it. He raised and lashed the weather cloths beside the bunks and stowed the few loose objects in their Pullman nets: a bottle of aspirin, a notepad, the Frantz Fanon book, a Key West telephone directory, spare winch handle, and flashlight. When he returned to the stove, a wisp of steam rose from the soup, but there was no time to enjoy it as the yawl was knocked onto her beam ends by the crush of wind, imprisoned in a bad angle by the lashing on her tiller. When Errol looked up through the companionway, a graybeard arose in the dim light, its top blowing off into spume, and subsided. It was a grim black-and-white movie, *Down to the Sea in Ships*, Clara Bow the It Girl and dying whales. This sort of respite from reality had previously been his accommodation; but for better or for worse, reality would be back, plowing irony before it.

Errol half crawled into the cockpit from the companionway and snapped on his lifeline. Once the tiller was free again, the boat rose to the gusts and relieved some of the lateral pressure that had her on her side. The pool of water in the self-bailing cockpit roared through the scuppers and emptied quickly. The frontal storms that had met his requirements for a manageable challenge were beyond him now; in their place, the wind came in an unimpeded fetch from open ocean in a scream. The incessant movement of the boat gave him the sense that they were being chased by the increasingly enormous waves, whose breaking crests gleamed unpleasantly. A cabinet burst open in the galley, discharging all his canned goods, and when Errol looked below he could see the food racing about on the floor.

The yawl rose as each great sea swept past with an uncanny hiss. His steering the boat now consisted entirely in keeping the stern presented to the waves and preventing the yawl from broaching as she sped down their backs. Thankfully, he detected a rhythm in this and, being able to feel the rise of sea without looking, made the proper adjustments through the memory of his muscles. Though reefed to a fraction of its original size, the mainsail seemed hard as iron and its leech buzzed like an electric saw. The black faces of approaching waves were so steep that Errol quit looking back; they were at the height of the spreaders and it seemed another degree or two of pitch and they must fall on him. If they did, they did: he wouldn't watch that.

A rain began, and then a pelting rain, which after a time flattened the sea. Now the yawl whistled along, seeming to enjoy its velocity undeterred by the recent mountains of water, the speed of wind for the moment little more than an inconvenience. Errol took this opportunity to go below and confront the disorder of the cabin. It was mostly canned goods and he stowed them frantically, knowing the calming rain wouldn't last.

When the violent motion of the ship resumed, he was reluctant to go above. He pretended the cabin was insufficiently tidy and lingered over trifles, the charts that needed rolling, the celestial tables that had somehow landed on the wrong shelf; he even renewed the paper towel on its roller. All this housekeeping betrayed a grim comedy as he was flung about performing it.

A boarding sea fell with a thud on the cabin top. He watched the water roar through the cockpit, overwhelm the scuppers, and pour over the transom and the untended helm. He felt the weight of it press against the little yawl's buoyancy in repeated attempts to overwhelm it. Recognizing a plausible run-up to drowning, Errol was swept by lethargy, not the same as peace but fatalist stupefaction. He was not afraid to die but very frightened of drowning, of filling his lungs with seawater and sinking to the bottom of the ocean; nothing could be more alien unless it was on another planet. That of course was just how his friend Raymond had departed, having once remarked that it would be an appropriate end for anyone who had trafficked in refugees. This thought produced in Errol an unexpected return of the heebie-jeebies. He forced himself into the cockpit, and there he saw that the great waves had begun to cascade and he was sure the end was at hand. This gave him some peace at least. He went about his business managing the ship, exercising what few options remained.

He replaced the reefed main with a storm trysail, now the only sail on the boat. He'd thought that the double-reefed main would be good enough, but it wasn't. If it had loaded up with seawater, it would have been big enough to take out the mast. Amid gusts that sounded like gunshots, he sheeted the trysail to leeward, lashed the tiller in the opposite direction, and produced a plausible version of heaving to: the yawl drifted and forged slightly into the wind, fell off, forged, and fell off again. The sea was now covered by fly-ing spindrift, a gruesome fuzz that extended to the glittering wave tops. Errol could bear to see no more and went below and crawled into a bunk but was soon flung onto the floor where the oozing bilge emerged between the planks. He crawled in again, lashed up his weather cloth so he was secured in the bunk, laced his fingers behind his head, and entertained himself with ideas of death while disdaining those of drowning, fish eating his flesh, descent to a lightless sea bottom, et cetera. In the Pullman net beside him was a Cuban statuette of the Madonna, the gift of a refugee physician; he turned it until it faced him. "Our Lady," he said. He liked her face. She looked a bit Cuban, actually; he was pleased she was not so universalized as to seem inhuman. He stared into the tiny face as the senseless chaos of the sea tried to destroy his home. The face grew larger and came toward him. He was falling in love.

It was time to go topsides once again. He didn't realize how peaceful the cabin had been until he was in the cockpit. The hove-to yawl seemed to follow a cycle. At the bottom of the troughs there was a kind of peace. This created a leeward eddy that moder-ated some of the more fearsome violence. At the same time, the troughs were so deep they actually protected him from the wind. Once the yawl rose to the crests again, the full force of the wind and its attendant shrieks could be felt.

It was with welcome detachment that he observed the behavior of his boat and concluded that there was no more he could do for her; she had managed thus far, and to be ready to cope with any great change in conditions he would have to sleep. He hoped that the cooler sea temperatures outside the stream would restrain the storm, but there was as yet no sign of that. He went below once again and secured himself in his bunk, feeling, as he fastened the weather cloths that kept him from rolling out, an odd coziness that he guessed came from his now-rapt gaze upon his Madonna. It was not that he possessed a single religious conviction, but knowing millions worshipped her was consoling. He wished to be among the millions, and this was a start. If he lived till daybreak, he would address his gratitude to Allah as well as Our Lady, and to their millions of worshippers, his fellow humans.

First, he asked her forgiveness for not helping Raymond back into the boat. True, he had not pushed Raymond overboard. The ocean had done that: the jib boom had come adrift and was beating a hole in the deck; Raymond had gone forward without his lifeline; the bow buried in a green sea, and when it came up, in a white cloud of spindrift, Raymond was no longer there. He floundered alongside the passing hull, reaching toward Errol. The split second of ambivalence—as though Raymond were being swept to New Orleans with Natalya—was all it took, and Raymond was gone. Natalya had had her fling with pirates and was careful the next time to latch on to someone with a future and an office.

He asked to be forgiven. Natalya was raising beautiful children in the Garden District, driving them to their swimming lessons from her home on Audubon Street, and Raymond, who had not known homeownership, was at the bottom of the sea. Errol understood that he was being shriven by the same sea and held the statuette in his fist, praying for forgiveness. Expecting his boat to crack open at any time and release him to his fate, he believed his request was legitimate. Certainly he'd never felt anything quite like it before. Such sobbing pleas were something he'd never heard from himself, as though he were being disemboweled by his own voice. His grief was possession and infancy, far more urgent than the storm and something of a deafening joyride. At one odd moment, he burst into laughter.

He wished to live. He stared into the face of the little statue, absorbed by her high Latin coloring and carmine lips; she was devouring him with her eyes. He felt himself sink farther into his bunk supinely awaiting her kiss. "You gorgeous bitch," he murmured.

IF HE COULD TELL BY THE WEIGHT IN HIS LIMBS, HE HAD awakened from a long sleep. He moved his eyes and took in his surroundings warily. It required some time for him to understand what had changed so completely: the boat was still. As the cabin was sealed against breaking seas, he could not see outside, and the air within had become sultry and fetid. He untied the weather cloths and swung his feet out onto the sole, glancing at the gimbaled lamps that had swung so violently in the night. They were motionless, though their oil was splashed around underneath him, indicating to his relief that he had not imagined the storm. He reached a hand gratefully to the cedar planks of the hull, still cool, still fragrant, perhaps still trees. Pines and oaks and cedars had carried him safely.

He was always given one more chance: it was frightening. The sight of the Madonna, moreover, gave him a queasy feeling. It reminded him of awakening in the bed of a woman who clearly didn't remember meeting him. But the Madonna didn't say a word. He got to his feet, startled that he was wearing no clothes; he looked around and discovered them tossed on the opposite bunk. He pulled on his shorts and went topsides.

"The Dawn of Creation," he thought, with a giddy impresario's flourish: the sea, ultramarine and pierced by sunlight, was still in every direction, no birds, no fish, no clouds, just the blue of heaven as it awaited completion. It crossed Errol's mind that by existing he intruded upon all this vacant magnificence. He preferred this more solemn view of so heroic and empty a vista. He considered his pill-gobbling episode in Key West with shame as trivializing the question posed by this empty sea, where eternity had stored the materials for a fresh start.

Errol went below and directed his optimism toward feeding himself. He had a beautiful round McIntosh apple, which he sliced carefully on the galley sideboard, and a piece of Canadian cheddar. He disguised the staleness of a hunk of Cuban bread by toasting it over the alcohol flame of his stove and basting it with tinned butter. The coffee soon bubbled in the percolator and filled the cabin with its wonderful smell. As he pictured Raymond sweeping past the hull, he could nearly imagine forgiving himself. But when he speculated on how many miles astern Raymond might have been before he drowned, he failed to add relief or prospects for forgiveness to his detachment.

His mood didn't last as he discovered how wide ranging his

hunger was. He gazed about at his breakfast and inventoried the other things he might eat. The tea cake, in the cabinet under the sink, excited him, as did the small tinned ham whose container he vowed to respect as long as necessary. The cornucopia of food that he had stowed here and there—even the pineapples under the floorboards!—unconsidered during the storm, began to re-form in his mind.

Admiring Natalya as she hung her bathing suit on the line behind the house on Fleming, Raymond had said, in a reflective tone, "I love 'em with that hunted look, don't you?"

After a moment, Errol had said, "No."

It came to him now: here resided one of the roots of hesitation as Raymond swept past the ketch. A boat that weighed almost fifty thousand pounds would not stop on a dime; there was that. Or turn in fewer than several of its own lengths. Even luffing up, the ketch would forereach farther than a man could swim in those seas. That knowledge could have been embedded too—couldn't it?—the sort that produces indecision, and indecision produces hesitation, and hesitation produces unfortunate accidents as opposed to murder.

At noon, he took a perfect sight of the sun. The boat was unmoving and the horizon a hard clean line. With the sextant to his eye, he measured the elevation and then went below to try for a signal on the radio direction finder. Haitian Baptist Radio was in its customary spot, and by combining its direction from the boat with the noon sight of the sun, he knew for the first time where he was. The information was sickening.

When Raymond was lost over the side, Errol reported the accident to the coast guard and gave them his position. Was it not right here? He went back to the cockpit and looked around the yawl at the stillness of the sea and its plum blue depths under a quiet sky as though he would recognize the scene of many years ago. This, he knew, was absurd. Surely he had simply superimposed the two pieces of information in an unreliable mind. He pounced on the idea that the accident had happened in the stream, and clearly this was not the stream. He had the celestial fact that the stream lay to the east of his current position, information that should have protected him from the sense that he had been directed to revisit the site of the misfortune. But the Gulf Stream moves like a great blue snake and there were times when this spot on the planet was indeed in its trail. Still, he didn't believe it.

Recently, Errol had become more superstitious, and as he was at base a practical man he ascribed the change to two matters: alcohol and hanging around with peasants who buried things at work sites as health talismans or to ward off accidents. On occasions of birth and death, his workers tied ex-votos in the orange trees. He had twice visited a palm reader in an old strip mall on the Tamiami Trail, a service he took sufficiently seriously to pay for it. Dressed in a bronze-colored gown decorated with sequins and designs from the horoscope, she had a snubby Scandinavian face and the flat *A*s of Minnesota. When he pointed out that her interpretations of his Life line were diametrically different on separate occasions, that his Heart line on one visit indicated that he was devious and unreliable while on another that he was courageous in the face of impediment, she called him a motherfucker without a moment's hesitation, then, relenting, told him his barred Sun line made him vulnerable to jealousy and that he must always exercise caution. He paid her grudgingly but thought about her remarks as he stood before the tattoo parlor next door while tourists battled for position on Route 41.

He was prepared to consider that he was back at the scene of the accident, and only recently this would have been enough to cast him into a black hole. But his guilt was changing. His superstition had begun to be attached not to the consequences of Raymond's being swept away but to the belief that trafficking in refugees had given rise to Raymond's death and his own long slide toward the abyss. When he remembered the myriad plastic Madonnas in the jalopies at his groves, like little scenes of lynchings, hanging from rearview mirrors or from the branches of orange trees, and the impure thoughts aroused by the little *chicas* who brought food to their men in the groves as well as a tremor of excitement among them, feral gusts of flesh and spirit, he began to realize that you pay for all your sins, and if that was superstition, then so be it. It was the implied lesson of the mestizos. What he should have done for his friend no longer mattered; he was guilty of everything. The wish to be forgiven poured from him as a moan directed to the sea;

he could think of no one else. Still, there was a glimmer of solace in acknowledging his superstition that every bird, every cloud, every flash of light, had a message for him, now and in eternity.

A breeze, a zephyr, arose from the southeast, and Errol could smell some sort of vegetative fragrance, some hint of land. He untied the reef nettles and reefing lines and raised the main. Its folds were full of freshwater from the storm, and it showered down on him as the sail went up. There was just enough air to pull the boom into position, and the jib barely filled, but a serpentine eddy formed behind the transom, and the boat was moving once again.

He sailed half the day at this slow pace and the water grew paler blue as the bottom beneath the hull came near. There were more birds now, and when the horizon thickened with the mangrove green of land, it was as he expected. He kept on in this direction, now recognizing that he couldn't live on the open sea. He would have to make his way home to his grove workers, who would fare less well without him under the cracker and to whom he owed his last allegiance. In this, time was running out: he would reprovision, look for a hole in the weather, and sail home, determined to find there the strength to withstand evil.

A scattering of cays lay before him, Cuban, Bahamian, it didn't matter; both were far from empire. As he drew nearer, he was surprised to see stands of coconut palms emerge from the mangrove shoreline. These cays were more substantial than he had guessed they'd be—a better chance to take on some water, a nicety he'd overlooked during his Key West tear, a better chance of finding some helpful souls. He stopped the boat before he was much closer, as a bar arose before him bright with its reflective sand bottom. Beyond it he could see a protected turtle-grass sound but, at first, no way through to what would be a superb anchorage. Where the palms were concentrated at the shore, boats were drawn up, and after he'd tacked back and forth for an hour, unsuccessfully looking for an opening, he saw two figures at one of the boats pushing it into the water. One of the men sat in front, elbows on his knees, face in his hand, while the other sculled vigorously from the stern with a long oar.

Errol watched with rising apprehension, not so much at what these two might have in mind for him but at the fact they were humans at all. In a short time, they were alongside, two tall black men, shirtless, barefoot, in a crude plank skiff with a coconut-shell bailer, a grains for gigging lobster. Errol bade them good afternoon, as the man in front reached a hand to the rail of the yawl to keep the skiff from bumping. This man replied inaudibly and Errol determined only that he'd said something in Spanish and that rather shyly. Errol decided he would not let on that he too spoke Spanish until he had a better idea of what these fellows had in mind for him. The man holding the rail, with the refined features of an Indian, kept his eyes downcast while his companion boldly boarded the yawl. The miserable detachment with which Errol had long encountered people he didn't know had somehow disappeared—perhaps during the storm—and he greeted his uninvited guest somewhat heartily as he asked in English what he could do for him. Putting his hand on the yawl's tiller and wiggling from side to side, the man explained in pidgin Spanish, which Errol pretended not to understand, that if he wished to land he would have to be piloted over the bar. For an instant, Errol thought of revealing his Spanish but thought better of it. Instead, he made some obtuse gestures indicating the boat, the land, the water; at which the man at the tiller—a dignified and classically African-looking man, older, Errol now saw, than he'd first thought, even maybe the father of the other man—said in exasperated Spanish to the man still in the skiff that he didn't know what this white man wanted but that if he wanted to go to the inside anchorage, he would need their guidance. At this, with disconnected and resolute stupidity, Errol gestured around at the boat in general and then pointed to the island, where water and some of the consolations of dry land awaited him. He could stay on the boat and incur few obligations by mingling with these people.

The two men understood, and at this the fellow in the boat secured the painter of the skiff to a stern cleat of the yawl and came aboard with a shy nod to the owner. The older man glanced about the deck of the boat to determine how the rigging ran and then drew the jib sheet in and cleated it. The yawl eased into motion once more, not much as the wind was faint, swung around, and, as the man at the tiller made several more adjustments with a smile and a shrug directed at Errol, sailed straight at the bar, tugging the skiff behind. As Errol stiffened, the helmsman shook his head and measured a distance to the floor with his hand, suggesting plenty of water, then waving into space as if to shoo all cares away. Errol could see nothing but the gathering shallows, changing color alarmingly as they sailed forward. He resigned himself that they would be aground in minutes, hoping his shipmates knew of a rising tide.

At the moment of impact, a miraculous thread of dark green appeared in the bar, barely wider than the yawl, and the man at the helm followed it quickly and efficiently like a dog tracking game as he crossed the bar into the small basin. He continued sailing nearly to the shore and then rounded up, stopping the boat. Errol went forward and let go the anchor. *Czarina* dropped back slowly until the rode tightened and she hung in the light breeze. "A well-behaved vessel," said the helmsman in Spanish. Errol gave him a puzzled smile. The three went toward shore, passing a post driven into the bottom to which was tethered a huge grouper, arriving at a long dock so decrepit it resembled part of a Möbius strip. The black men led, waving Errol along, and he followed on a path between old shell mounds and soon came to a clearing with several houses made of salvaged timbers and monkey thatch, then around those houses to a well. "Wada," said the older man with a smile. Errol looked down the well, not more than fifteen feet deep, with a bucket on a wooden windlass contraption and various ladles, two of which were cut down Coca-Cola bottles and the others coconut shells like the bailer in the skiff. When they went back to the clearing, Errol following obediently, several people, probably family members, had appeared from the houses, two women of indeterminate age, a very old man, and a teenage boy with dreadlocks. All smiled. At this, Errol turned to his hosts and told them in Spanish that he was quite comfortable speaking Spanish. The two men laughed and pounded his back.

"You were espying on us!" said the younger.

On reflection, the older man seemed less pleased with this deception. "What besides water do you wish from us?" he asked rather formally.

"I'm not sure I even need water. I was looking for a place to rest. I've been in that storm, you see."

"Yes, that was a storm."

"I'm a bit tired."

"Of course you are tired. One hardly drifts about in such a situation. Great exertion is called for."

"I have to admit, I nearly lost my nerve."

"Evidently you didn't, for here you are. You have a safe anchorage, and this place is good for rest if nothing else."

Caught up in this colloquy, Errol was reduced to a small bow.

"You're our only guest," said the younger man. "We ate the others."

General laughter.

"Wrong ocean," said Errol. General appreciative laughter except from the very old man, who seemed a bit disoriented. Errol had a whorish need to include all in admiring his wit and rested his glance on the old man long enough to determine that he was blind.

It was agreed that he would go on sleeping on the yawl and borrow the skiff for transport. One of the women, tall and Indian looking, with a bright yellow-and-black cloth tying her hair atop her head, informed him in English that when dinner was ready someone would come to the shore and make a noise. Noting his pause at her choice of language, she said, "I from Red Bays."

The older of the two men who'd brought him said, back in Spanish, "You'll come, of course."

Errol bowed all round and said, "Enchanted."

All replied, "Equally."

Errol returned to his boat, rowing past the great fish swimming slowly around its stake, tying the skiff alongside and climbing back into the yawl and the security it offered, especially after its latest and probably worst storm. He found himself disturbed and so particularly dreading the dinner that he made himself sit in the cockpit and puzzle over his aversion to such companionable people, an aversion so strong that he only abandoned the thought of sailing off when he admitted he'd never find the way back over the bar. Isolation seemed to have the attraction of a drug, and he reluctantly intuited that he must not give in to it. He'd have been less apprehensive about that dinner if it had been at the White House, but he believed, if he could pass this small social test, he could begin to escape the superstitions and fears that were ruining his life.

He had a short rest on the quarter berth with its view of blue sky over the companionway. The stillness of the yawl was a miracle, and he laid his palms against the wooden sides of the hull in a kind of benediction, or at least thanksgiving. For now it gave him the feeling of home.

He smelled buttonwood smoke. The sun was going down and he had to close the companionway screen to keep out the mosquitoes that always seemed particular to their own area: these were small and quick, produced a precise bite that was almost a sting, and couldn't be waved away. Presently, he heard someone beating on a piece of iron. Poking his head out the hatch, he saw the younger of the two men announcing dinner with two rusty pieces and gave him a wave, upon which the man retired up the path between the shell mounds. A fog of buttonwood smoke lay over the water at the mangrove shoreline.

He pulled the skiff onto the beach and secured its painter to a palm log, which, judging by the grooves worn in its trunk, was intended for that purpose. He pulled his belt tighter and straightened his shoulders before heading up the path for dinner. Excepting the woman from Andros, the group, including the blind old man, was sitting by the fire watching strips of turtle roast over the glowing coals, which the older of the two men raked toward him. The remains of the turtle were to one side, heaped within its shell, and seemed to have concentrated a particularly intense cloud of mosquitoes. When Errol saw the rum being passed around, he reassured himself that the supply would be limited. No liquor stores out here! he thought, with creepy hilarity.

The unhesitating first swallow made everything worthwhile and was followed by an oceanic wave of love for his companions. When the Andros woman came to the fire with plantains to be roasted, he reached the rum out to her. The younger of the two, Catarino, seized his hand, said, "No," and took the bottle himself. The woman from Andros cast her eyes down and went on preparing the plantains. At Errol's bafflement, Catarino explained, "She is our slave."

Looking at the bottle of rum and wondering why Catarino was so slow in raising it to his lips, Errol asked, "How can that be?" He wondered if he had misunderstood the Spanish word, but he repeated it, *esclava*, and had it confirmed. He reached for the rum, but it went on to the old blind man.

Catarino patiently explained further, "As you can see, she is black."

Errol emitted a consanguineous giggle lest his next statement give offense and dispel the convivial atmosphere and—he admitted to himself—result in the withholding of the rum. "But all of you are black, aren't you?"

The blind man threw his head back and in a surprising rumble of a baritone asked incredulously, "Black and Spanish?" Catarino looked at him sternly.

"We are as white as you, sir. I hope this is understood."

"Oh, it is, it is," said Errol, with rising panic.

The older of the two men, Adan, gazed at him with a crooked smile and said, "You must be hungry."

Not seeming to hear him, Errol asked, "Will she eat with us?"

"Clearly not," the blind man rumbled. "The American would do well to turn to our repast and that which makes all men brothers." He held up the bottle. Errol decided not to express his thought, Except the slaves, again less out of principle than a fear of causing the rum to be withheld. When the Andros woman came back to the fire, Errol asked her in English what her name was, and she told him Angela. The others nodded their incomprehension but encouraged this foreign talk with smiles.

"I'm told you're their slave."

"They believe that," she said complacently.

"And it's because you're black?"

At this, she stopped and gave voice to what was evidently dispassionate consideration. "How amusing I find this. I am a Seminole Indian. My great-grandfathers came to Red Bays in cayucos. Why else would the University of Florida send us so many anthropologists? We are all Indians in Red Bays. Why else would they bring us T-shirts from the Hard Rock Cafe and expensive tennis shoes to earn our trust, if we were not Indians?"

The others nodded happily; they were enjoying her indignation and seemed to understand that it was based on a discussion of her slave status.

"These disgraceful Spaniards don't understand that they are blacks. They think their language protects them. How they'd love to be Indians!"

"Were you captured?"

Angela couldn't control her mirth. She held the turban around her head with both hands and jiggled from head to toe with laughter. The others united in what seemed to be real pleasure, and she looked at them and rolled her eyes at the absurdity of the white man. This rather calmed things because, as his fellow whites, the Spanish-speaking blacks did not want to throw in their lot with their slave too emphatically. They wished to project that they were compassionate slaveholders who followed the dictates of humanity.

The rum landed back in Errol's hands, and all the others, including Angela, generously relished his enthusiasm as he raised it to his lips and kept it there for a long time, not fully understanding how ravenous he was. But when he lowered the bottle something in his gaze caused them to fall silent. The moment passed as interest turned to the turtle and plantains. Noticing that Angela sat by herself on the step of one of the driftwood shacks, Errol asked her if she thought of herself as a slave.

She replied, "Don't be a fool."

"Oh, well," said Errol, in odd contentment. Confusion could be pleasant when you were drinking; it kept the mind whirring agreeably. He began to eat, taking pieces of turtle from spits over the sputtering buttonwood coals. The teenager with dreadlocks was wholly focused on the food and neither laughed with the others nor in any way seemed to know he was not alone. The only other woman, a heavyset Spanish-speaking black, watched Errol with sullen attention as though he were there to present a bill or a summons. The blind man staring with white eyes across the fire into the darkness cupped his hands in front of him, into which Adan and Catarino placed pieces of food. Catarino asked Errol if he was enjoying his meal.

"I certainly am!"

"And the rum suits you, does it not?"

"Very agreeable."

"Sometimes it is more important than food, no?"

"Sometimes," said Errol.

Adan smiled at his food and asked, "Sometimes?"

Errol waited before answering. "I believe that is what I said."

Catarino gave Errol a jovial thump on the back and returned the bottle to him. The wind had shifted slightly, and Errol moved closer to the buttonwood smoke to be free of the vicious little mosquitoes. When he glanced at Angela, sitting away from the fire, Catarino explained that mosquitoes didn't bother black people.

"How is it that she is your slave?" Errol asked. At this, the blind man spoke in a surprisingly firm voice.

"Her man drowned."

"Is that so?"

"Yes, that is so," said Adan. All except Angela seemed quite sad to reflect upon this event. "We didn't take her back to her country. That would be against the law. Those blacks have laws no one can understand. With her man dead, she wished to throw in with us, but we were barely surviving as it was. You see how it is. We offered to let her come and be our slave, as that is entirely natural and appealing to blacks. As you see, she accepted."

"Which only proves our point," Adan added.

Errol took another slug of rum and gazed around at his companions, who seemed to him, as best as he could tell, to all be black. Then he thought of something. "What color do you think I am?" The three looked at one another. It was Catarino who finally spoke, his smile full of accommodation.

He said, "We haven't decided."

"I can't take mosquitoes at all," said Errol nervously. "Never could. They drive me nuts!"

The blind man said, "Have some more of that aguardiente. To enjoy your meal, you must calm your nerves."

Adan looked pensive. "They served wine at the Last Supper. If we had not been prepared to offer refreshment to our guests, perhaps the turtle would not have offered himself to us. All things are connected. Even you, sir, are connected to us, if only in that we share a clearing which we made of sufficient size with our machetes as to offer you a place at our meal." He smiled pleasantly. "Surely we knew you were coming."

Errol's expression of gratitude was interrupted by a burp, which brought a change of mood, and all went about eating with a purpose, all except Angela, who paced about, desperately waving away the mosquitoes.

THE SUN MUST HAVE AWAKENED ERROL, BALLED UP NEXT TO the extinguished fire, the sun that caused the mosquitoes to retreat into the mangroves. Errol didn't seem to remember where he was, and indeed his body was disagreeably unfamiliar. No parts of it seemed to fit together any longer and all were consumed by burning and itching. He felt his face with swollen fingers. His lips were drum tight, his eyelids so thick he could see them, and his cheeks lumpy with bites. He had lost his shoes, then remembered they'd been laced. Someone had taken his shoes. In any case, his swollen feet would no longer be contained by them. He lay back, let his mouth fall open, and gazed at the sky.

Once there was sufficient water in his boat, he could call it provisioned and begin the voyage home. He had handlines and a shoebox full of diamond-shaped silver spoons: he would have fish and freshwater and that was enough. All this horror, this misshapen body, was temporary. Steps toward atonement had been taken; more could be promised. He remembered his mestizos and the groves. He tried reckoning how long he'd been away, but no exact answer was required. The cracker's deadline had come and gone: he had broken his covenant with the mestizos and by now they were dispersed, thrown once again to fate, to wander the labor camps at Immokalee or Belle Glade, offering the days of their lives for sugar, citrus, and white men. His, like theirs, were the inconveniences of hell.

Certainly it lay in his power to arise, thank his hosts, sail away, and, against the cadences of wind and sea, sort through his many failings and the invoices for atonement that accompanied them. There was no mess so great it could not be broken down into a manageable sequence, a bill of lading for debts to oblivion.

As he stood, his buttocks abraded each other in special misery. My God, he wondered, how did they get in there? He began scratching himself all over. He hurried from one place to another as no sooner did he palliate some mad insistence than it appeared in another place. He was writhing and dancing without leaving his small spot in the dirt.

Something caught his eye.

Angela, arms wrapped around her sides, was lost in shaking, silent mirth. He stopped and stared at her through indignant, swollen eyes. He walked over to her, the pressure of edema squeezing up his calves with every step. She smiled at him when he arrived. She had unwound her turban and twisted it around her hands, allowing her hair to spring out in all directions. In his present condition, that hair struck him with its terrible vitality. There was something thrilling about it. She said, "I tink it will rain. And dis is my great day. Dey have freed me."

"That's nice," said Errol sarcastically. His disfigured lips distorted this offensive speech, but Angela seemed not to notice. "Are they still sleeping?"

"Oh, dey gone."

Errol could not lose his snide tone. "Where exactly is there to go?"

Angela answered him imperturbably. "Miami." Errol considered this for a remarkably short time.

"They took my boat?"

"Oh, yes."

Errol seemed unsurprised. He considered levelly that he was without choices. His despair was such that the possibility of solace could only lie in the evaporation of all his options. Never before had he sensed himself greeting his destiny with so little resistance. It was an odd luxury to contemplate this, pants unbuttoned to accommodate his itches, spread fingers hanging at his sides, and a face whose risibility could now be enjoyed only by Angela, who had the upper hand of observing him.

An implement of sorts leaned against the shack. A corner of salvaged iron had been secured to a hardwood limb from which the branches had been removed with many wraps of rusting wire. Angela handed this to Errol and ordered him to follow her up the path through the mastic and wild palms. As they walked, Angela told him of the brothers' dream of taking their father, the blind man, to Miami, where they had been told you could buy eyeballs on the black market. There had been much in the air about family values, but Errol had never imagined they'd be honored at his expense. Perhaps he didn't really mind as he followed Angela with his new implement. Musing on the current arrangement, he wondered whether she was his owner and what color they each were, since the evidence of his eyes had proved insufficient.

Bright-hued birds flashed through the opening made by the path; near the flowers of tall vines, clouds of hummingbirds rose and sank, competing for nectar with surprising ferocity. A bananaquit, an urgent little yellow bird, danced down the path ahead of him, landed, and then scurried off like a mouse.

The path opened atop what Angela said was an old burial mound, and there he saw a garden under the morning sun. Errol briefly wondered what sorts of people were buried here but doubted that Angela knew. She showed him how things were arranged, the peppers, the tomatoes, the staked gourds, the new melons concealed under dark leaves glistening with dew. A pleasant smell arose from the tilled ground. A tall palm hung over the scene, and from its crown of leaves the sound of parrot nestlings descended.

At the still-shaded end of the garden, wild vegetation had encroached on the perimeter. She showed him where he must start.

GALLATIN CANYON

THE DAY WE PLANNED THE TRIP, I TOLD LOUISE THAT I didn't like going to Idaho via the Gallatin Canyon. It's too narrow, and while trucks don't belong on this road, there they are, lots of them. Tourist pull-offs and wild animals on the highway complete the picture. We could have gone by way of Ennis, but Louise had learned that there were road repairs on Montana Highway 84—twelve miles of torn-up asphalt—in addition to its being rodeo weekend.

"Do we have to go to Idaho?" she asked.

I said I thought it was obvious. A lot rode on the success of our little jaunt, which was ostensibly to close the sale of a small car dealership I owned in the sleepy town of Rigby. But since accepting the offer of a local buyer, I had received a far-better one from elsewhere, which, my attorney said, I couldn't take unless my original buyer backed out—and he would only back out if he got sufficiently angry at me. Said my attorney, Make him mad. So I was headed to Rigby, Idaho, expressly to piss off a small-town businessman, who was trying to give me American money for a going concern on the strip east of town, and thereby make room for a rich Atlanta investor, new to our landscape, who needed this dealership as a kind of flagship for his other intentions. The question was how to provoke Rigby without arousing his suspicions, and I might have collected my thoughts a little better had I not had to battle trucks and tourists in the Gallatin Canyon.

Louise and I had spent a lot of time together in recent years, and we were both probably wondering where things would go from here. She had been married, briefly, long ago, and that fact, together with the relatively peaceful intervening years, gave a pleasant detachment to most of her relationships, including the one she had with me. In the past, that would have suited me perfectly; it did not seem to suit me now, and I was so powerfully attached to her it made me uncomfortable that she wasn't interested in discussing our mutual future, though at least she had never suggested that we wouldn't have one. With her thick blonde hair pulled back in a barrette, her strong, shapely figure, and the direct fullness of her mouth, she was often noticed by other men. After ten years in Montana, she still had a strong Massachusetts accent. Louise was a lawyer, specializing in the adjudication of water rights between agricultural and municipal interests. In our rapidly changing world, she was much in demand. Though I wished we could spend more time together, Louise had taught me not to challenge her on this.

No longer the country crossroads of recent memory, Four Corners was filled with dentists' offices, fast-food and espresso shops, and large and somehow foreboding filling stations that looked, at night, like colonies in space; nevertheless, the intersection was true to its name, sending you north to a transcontinental interstate, east into town, west to the ranches of Madison County, and south, my reluctant choice, up the Gallatin Canyon to Yellowstone and the towns of southeast Idaho, one of which contained property with my name on the deed.

We joined the stream of traffic heading south, the Gallatin River alongside and usually much below the roadway, a dashing high-gradient river with anglers in reflective stillness at the edges of its pools and bright rafts full of delighted tourists in flotation jackets and crash helmets sweeping through its white water. Gradually, the mountains pressed in on all this humanity, and I found myself behind a long line of cars trailing a cattle truck at well below the speed limit. This combination of cumbersome commercial traffic and impatient private cars was a lethal mixture that kept our canyon in the papers, as it regularly spat out corpses. In my rearview mirror, I could see a line behind me that was just as long as the one ahead, stretching back, thinning, and vanishing around a green bend. There was no passing lane for several miles. A single amorous elk could have turned us all into twisted, smoking metal.

"You might have been right," Louise said. "It doesn't look good."

She almost certainly had better things to do. But looking down the line of cars, I felt my blood pressure rising. Her hands rested quietly in her lap. I couldn't possibly have rivaled such serenity.

"How do you plan to anger this guy in Rigby?" she asked.

"I'm going to try haughtiness. If I suggest that he bought the dealership cheap, he might tell me to keep the damn thing. The Atlanta guy just wants to start somewhere. All these people have a sort of parlay mentality, and they need to get on the playing field before they can start running it up. I'm a trader. It all happens for me in the transition. The moment of liquidation is the essence of capitalism."

"What about the man in Rigby?"

"He's an end user. He wants to keep it."

I reflected on the pathos of ownership and the way it could bog you down.

"You should be in my world," Louise said. "According to the law, water has no reality except its use. In Montana, water isn't even wet. Every time some misguided soul suggests that fish need it, it ends up in the state supreme court."

Birds were fleeing the advance of automobiles. I was elsewhere, trying to imagine my buyer, red faced, storming out of the closing. I'd offer to let bygones be bygones, I'd take him to dinner, I'd throw a steak into him, for Christ's sake. In the end, he'd be glad he wasn't stuck with the lot.

Traffic headed toward us, far down the road. We were all packed together to make sure no one tried to pass. The rules had to be enforced. Occasionally, someone drifted out for a better look, but not far enough that someone else could close his space and possibly seal his fate.

This trip had its risks. I had only recently admitted to myself that I would like to make more of my situation with Louise than currently existed. Though ours was hardly a chaste relationship, real intimacy was relatively scarce. People in relationships nowadays seemed to retain their secrets like bank deposits—they always set some aside, in case they might need them to spend on someone new. I found it unpleasant to think that Louise could be withholding anything.

But I thought I was more presentable than I had been. When Louise and I first met, I was just coming off two and a half years of peddling satellite dishes in towns where a couple of dogs doing the wild thing in the middle of the road amounted to the high point of a year, and the highest-grossing business was a methamphetamine tent camp out in the sagebrush. Now I had caught the upswing in our local economy: cars, storage, tool rental, and mortgage discounting. I had a pretty home, debt-free, out on Sourdough. I owned a few things. I could be okay. I asked Louise what she thought of the new prosperity around us. She said wearily, "I'm not sure it's such a good thing, living in a boomtown. It's basically a high-end carny atmosphere."

We were just passing Storm Castle and Garnet Mountain. When I glanced in the mirror, I saw a low red car with a scoop in its hood pull out to pass. I must have reacted somehow, because Louise asked me if I would like her to drive.

"No, that's fine. Things are getting a bit lively back there."

"Drive defensively."

"Not much choice, is there?"

I had been mentally rehearsing the closing in Rigby, and I wasn't getting anywhere. I had this sort of absurd picture of myself strutting into the meeting. I tried again to picture the buyer looking seriously annoyed, but I'd met him before and he seemed pretty levelheaded. I suspected I'd have to be really outlandish to get a rise out of him. He was a fourth-generation resident of Rigby, so I could always urge him to get to know his neighbors, I decided. Or since he had come up through the service department, I could try emphasizing the need to study how the cars actually ran. I'd use hand signals to fend off objections. I felt more secure.

Some elk had wandered into the parking lot at Buck's T4 and were grazing indifferently as people pulled off the highway to admire them. I don't know if it was the great unmarred blue sky overhead or the balsamic zephyr that poured down the mountainside, but I found myself momentarily buoyed by all this idleness, people out of their cars. I am always encouraged when I see animals doing something other than running for their lives. In any case, the stream of traffic ahead of us had been much reduced by the pedestrian rubbernecking.

"My husband lived here one winter," Louise said. "He sold his pharmacy after we divorced, not that he had to, and set out to change his life. He became a mountain man, wore buckskin clothes. He tried living off the land one day a week, with the idea that he would build up. But then he just stuck with one day a week—he'd shoot a rabbit or something, more of a diet, really. He's a real-estate agent now, at Big Sky. I think he's doing well. At least he's quit killing rabbits."

"Remarried?"

"Yes."

As soon as we hit the open country around West Yellowstone, Louise called her office. When her secretary put her on hold, Louise covered the mouthpiece and said, "He married a super gal. Minnesota, I think. She should be good for Bob, and he's not easy. Bob's from the South. For men, it's a full-time job being southern. It just wears them out. It wore me out, too. I developed doubtful behaviors. I pulled out my eyelashes and ate twenty-eight hundred dollars' worth of macadamia nuts."

Her secretary came back on the line, and Louise began editing her schedule with impressive precision, mouthing the word "sorry" to me when the conversation dragged on. I began musing about my capacity to live successfully with someone as competent as Louise. There was no implied hierarchy of status between us, but I wondered if, in the long run, something would have to give.

West Yellowstone seemed entirely given over to the well-being of the snowmobile, and the billboards dedicated to it were anomalous on a sunny day like today. By winter, schoolchildren would be petitioning futilely to control the noise at night so they could do their schoolwork, and the town would turn a blind eye as a cloud of smoke arose to gas residents, travelers, and park rangers alike. It seemed incredible to me that recreation could acquire this level of social momentum, that it could be seen as an inalienable right.

We came down Targhee Pass to Idaho, into a wasteland of spindly pines that had replaced the former forest, and Louise gave voice to the thoughts she'd been having for the past few miles. "Why don't you just let this deal close? You really have no guarantees from the man from Atlanta. And there's a good-faith issue here too, I think."

"A lawyerly notation."

"So be it, but it's true. Are you trying to get every last cent out of this sale?"

"That's second. The first priority is to be done with it. It was meant to be a passive investment, and it has turned out not to be.

I get twenty calls a day from the dealership, most with questions I can't answer. It's turning me into a giant bullshit machine."

"No investments are really passive."

"Mutual funds are close."

"That's why they don't pay."

"Some of them pay, or they would cease to exist."

"You make a poor libertarian, my darling. You sound like that little puke David Stockman."

"Stockman was right about everything. Reagan just didn't have the guts to take his advice."

"Reagan. Give me a break."

I didn't mind equal billing in a relationship, but I did dread the idea of parties speaking strictly from their entitlements across a chasm. Inevitably, sex would make chaos of much of this, but you couldn't, despite Benjamin Franklin's suggestion, "use venery" as a management tool.

Louise adjusted her seat back and folded her arms, gazing at the sunny side of the road. The light through the windshield accentuated the shape of her face, now in repose. I found her beautiful. I adored her when she was a noun and was alarmed when she was a verb, which was usually the case. I understood that this was not the best thing I could say about myself. When her hand drifted over to my leg, I hardly knew what to do with this reference to the other life we led. I knew it was an excellent thing to be reminded of how inconsequential my worldly concerns were, but one warm hand, rested casually, and my interest traveled to the basics of the species.

Ashton, St. Anthony, Sugar City: Mormon hamlets, small farms, and the furious reordering of watersheds into industrial canals. Irrigation haze hung over the valley of the Snake, and the skies were less bright than they had been just a few miles back, in Montana. Many locals had been killed when the Teton Dam burst, and despite that they wanted to build it again: the relationship to water here was like a war, and in war lives are lost. These were the folks to whom I'd sold many a plain car; ostentation was thoroughly unacceptable hereabouts. The four-door sedan with a six-cylinder engine was the desired item, an identical one with 150,000 miles on it generally taken in trade at zero value, thanks to the manipulation of rebates against the manufacturer's suggested retail. Appearances were foremost, and the salesman who could leave a customer's smugness undisturbed flourished in this atmosphere. I had two of them, potato-fattened bland opportunists with nine kids between them. They were the asset I was selling; the rest was little more than bricks and mortar.

We pressed on toward Rexburg, and amid the turnoffs for Wilford, Newdale, Hibbard, and Moody the only thing that had any flavor was Hog Hollow Road, which was a shortcut to France—not the one in Europe but the one just a hop, skip, and a jump south of Squirrel, Idaho. There were license-plate holders with my name on them in Squirrel, and I was oddly vain about that.

"Sure seems lonesome around here," Louise said.

"Oh, boy."

"The houses are like little forts."

"The winters are hard." But it was less that the small neat dwellings around us appeared defensive than that they seemed to be trying to avoid attracting the wrath of some inattentive god.

"It looks like government housing for Eskimos. They just sit inside, waiting for a whale or something."

This banter had the peculiar effect of making me want to cleave to Louise, and desperately, too—to build a warm new civilization, possibly in a foolish house with turrets. The road stretched before me like an arrow. There was only enough of it left before Rigby for me to say, perhaps involuntarily, "I wonder if we shouldn't just get married."

Louise quickly looked away. Her silence conferred a certain seriousness on my question.

But there was Rigby, and, in the parlance of all who have extracted funds from locals, Rigby had been good to me. Main Street was lined with ambitious and beautiful stone buildings, old for this part of the world. Their second and third floors were now affordable housing, and their street levels were occupied by businesses hanging on by their fingernails. You could still detect the hopes of the dead—their dreams, even—though it seemed to be only a matter of time before the wind carried them away, once and for all.

I drove past the car lot at 200 East Fremont without comment and—considering the amount of difficulty it had caused me in the years before I got it stabilized and began to enjoy its very modest yields—without much feeling. I remembered the day, sometime earlier, when I had tried to help park the cars in the front row and got everything so crooked that the salesmen, not concealing their contempt, had to do it all over again. The title company where we were heading was on the same street, and it was a livelier place, from the row of perky evergreens out front to the merry receptionist who greeted us, a handsome young woman, probably a farm girl only moments before, enjoying the clothes, makeup, and perquisites of the new world that her firm was helping to build.

We were shown into a spacious conference room with a long table and chairs, freshly sharpened pencils, and crisp notepads bearing the company letterhead. "Shall I stay?" Louise asked, the first thing she'd said since my earlier inadvertent remark, which I intuited had not been altogether rejected.

"Please," I said, gesturing toward a chair next to the one I meant to take. At that moment, the escrow agent entered and, standing very close to us, introduced himself as Brent Colby. Then he went to the far end of the table, where he spread his documents around in an orderly fan. Colby was around fifty, with iron-gray hair and a deeply lined face. He wore pressed jeans, a brilliant white snap-button shirt, cowboy boots, and a belt buckle with a steer head on it. He had thick, hairy hands and a gleaming wedding band. Just as he raised his left wrist to check his watch, the door opened and Oren Johnson, the buyer, entered. He went straight to Louise and, taking her hand in both of his, introduced himself. It occurred to me that, in trying to be suave, Oren Johnson had revealed himself to be a clodhopper, but I was probably just experiencing the mild hostility that emanates from every sale of property. Oren wore a suit, though it suggested less a costume for business than one for church. He had a gold tooth and a cautious pompadour. He too bore an investment-grade wedding band, and I noted that there was plenty of room in his black-laced shoes for his toes. He turned and said it was good to see me again after so long. The time had come for me to go into my act. With grotesque hauteur, I said I didn't realize we had ever met. This was work.

Oren Johnson bustled with inchoate energy; he was the kind of small-town leader who sets an example by silently getting things done. He suggested this just by arranging his pencils and note-pad and repositioning his chair with rough precision. Locking eyes with me, he stated that he was a man of his word. I didn't know what he was getting at, but took it to mean that the formalities of a closing were superfluous to the old-time handshake with which Oren Johnson customarily did business. I smiled and quizzically cocked my head as if to say that the newfangled arrangements with well-attested documents promptly conveyed to the courthouse suited me just fine, that deals made on handshakes were strictly for the pious or the picturesque. My message was clear enough that Louise shifted uncomfortably in her chair, and Brent Colby knocked his documents edgewise on the desk to align them. As far as Oren Johnson was concerned, I was beginning to feel that anyone who strayed from the basic patterns of farm life to sell cars bore watching. Like a Method actor, I already believed my part.

"You're an awfully lucky man, Oren Johnson," I said to him, leaning back in my chair. I could see Louise openmouthed two seats away from Brent Colby, and observing myself through her eyes gave me a sudden burst of panic.

"Oh?" Oren Johnson said. "How's that?"

"How's that?" I did a precise job of replicating his inflection. "I am permitting you to purchase my car lot. You've seen the books: how often does a man get a shot at a business where all the work's been done for him?"

Brent Colby was doing an incomplete job of concealing his dis-taste; he was enough of a tinhorn to clear his throat theatrically. But Oren Johnson treated this as a colossal interruption and cast a firm glance his way.

"It doesn't look all that automatic to me," he said.

"Aw, hell, you're just going to coin it. Pull the lever and relax!"

"What about the illegal oil dump? I wish I had a nickel for every crankcaseful that went into that hole. Then I wouldn't worry about what's going to happen when the DEQ lowers the boom."

"Maybe you ought to ride your potato harvester another year or two, if you're so risk averse. Cars are the future. They're not for everybody."

Oren Johnson's face reddened. He pushed his pencils and note-pad almost out of reach in the middle of the conference table. He contemplated these supplies a moment before raising his eyes to mine. "I suppose you could put this car lot where the sun don't shine, if that suits you."

Johnson having taken a stand, I immediately felt unsure that I even had another buyer. Had I ever acknowledged how much I longed to get rid of this business and put an end to all those embarrassing phone calls? I wanted to hand the moment off to someone else while I collected my thoughts, but as I looked around the room I found no one who was interested in rescuing me—least of all Louise, who had raised one eyebrow at the vast peculiarity of my performance. Suddenly, I was desperate to keep the deal from falling apart. I gave my head a little twist to free my neck from the constrictions of my collar. I performed this gesture too vigorously, and I had the feeling that it might seem like the first movement of some sort of dance filled with sensual flourishes and bordering on the moronic. I had lost my grip.

"Oren," I said, and the familiarity seemed inappropriate. "I was attached to this little enterprise. I wanted to be sure you valued it."

The deal closed, and I had my check. I tipped back in my chair to think of a few commemorative words for the new owner, but the two men left the room without giving me the chance to speak. I shrugged at Louise and she, too, rose to go, pausing a moment beneath an enormous Kodachrome of a bugling elk. I was aware of her distance, and I sensed that my waffling hadn't gone over particularly well. I concluded that at no time in the future would I act out a role to accomplish anything. This decision quickly evaporated with the realization that that is practically all we do in life. Comedy failed, too. When I told Louise that I had been within an inch of opening a can of whup-ass on the buyer, I barely got a smile. There's nothing more desolating than having a phrase like that die on your lips.

It was dark when we got back to Targhee Pass. Leaving town, we passed the BeeHive assisted-living facility and the Riot Zone, a "family fun park." Most of the citizens we spotted there seemed unlikely rioters. I drove past a huge neon steak, its blue T-bone flashing above a restaurant that was closed and dark. There were deer on the road, and once, as we passed through a murky section of forest, we saw the pale faces of children waiting to cross.

"What are they doing out at this hour?"

"I don't know," Louise said.

I made good time on the pine flats north of the Snowmobile Capital of the World, and I wondered what it would be like to live in a town that was the world capital of a mechanical gadget. In Rigby, we had seen a homely museum dedicated to Philo T. Farnsworth, the inventor of television, which featured displays of Farnsworth's funky assemblages of tubes and wire and, apparently, coat hangers—stuff his wife was probably always attempting to throw out, a goal Louise supported. "Too bad Mama Farnsworth didn't take all that stuff to the dump," she said.

We had the highway to ourselves, and clouds of stars seemed to rise up from the wilderness, lighting the treetops in a cool fire. Slowly, the canyon closed in around us, and we entered its dark flowing space.

The idyll ended just past the ranger station at Black Butte, when a car pulled in behind us abruptly enough that I checked my speed to see if I was violating the limit, but I wasn't. When the car was very close, the driver shifted his lights to a high beam so intense that I could see our shadows on the dashboard, my knuckles on the steering wheel glaringly white. I was nearly blinded by my own mirrors, which I hastily adjusted.

I said, "What's with this guy?"

"Just let him pass."

"I don't know that he wants to."

I softened my pressure on the gas pedal. I thought that by easing my already moderate speed I would politely suggest that he might go by me. I even hugged the shoulder, but he remained glued to our bumper. There was something about this that reminded me strongly of my feeling of failure back in Rigby, but I was unable to put my finger on it. Maybe it was the hot light of liquidation, in the glare of which all motives seem laid bare. I slowed down even more without managing to persuade my tormentor to pass. "Jesus," Louise said. "Pull over." In her accent, it came out as "Pull ovah."

I moved off to the side of the road slowly and predictably, but although I had stopped, the incandescent globes persisted in our rearview mirror. "This is very strange," Louise said.

"Shall I go back and speak to him?"

After considering for a moment, she said, "No."

"Why?"

"Because this is not normal."

I put the car in gear again and pulled back onto the highway. The last reasonable thought I had was that I would proceed to Bozeman as though nothing were going on; once I was back in civilization my tormentor's behavior would be visible to all, and I could, if necessary, simply drive to the police station with him in tow.

Our blinding, syncopated journey continued another mile before we reached a sweeping eastward bend, closely guarded by the canyon walls. I knew that just beyond the bend there was a scenic pull-off, and that the approaching curve was acute enough for a small lead to put me out of sight. Whether or not this was plausible, I had no idea: I was exhilarated to be taking a firm hand in my own affairs. And a firm foot! As we entered the narrows, I pinned the accelerator, and we shot into the dark. Louise grabbed the front edges of her seat and stared at the road twisting in front of us. She emitted something like a moan, which I had heard before in a very different context. Halfway around the curve, my tormentor vanished behind us, and although my car seemed only marginally under control, the absence of blinding light was a relief as we fled into darkness.

When we emerged and the road straightened, I turned off my lights. I was going so fast I felt light-headed, but the road was visible under the stars, and I was able to brake hard and drop down into the scenic turnoff. Seconds later, our new friend shot past, lights blazing into nowhere. He was clearly determined to catch us; his progress up the canyon was rapid and increasingly erratic. We watched in fascination until the lights suddenly jerked sideways, shining in white cones across the river, turned downward, then disappeared.

I heard Louise say, in a tone of reasonable observation, "He went in."

I had an urgent feeling that took a long time to turn into words. "Did I do that?"

She shook her head, and I pulled out onto the highway, my own headlights on once more. I drove in an odd, measured way, as if bound for an undesired destination, pulled along by something outside myself, thinking: Liquidation. We could see where he'd gone through the guardrail. We pulled over and got out. Any hope we might have had for the driver—and we shall be a long time determining if we had any—was gone the minute we looked down from the riverbank. The car was submerged, its lights still burning freakishly, illuminating a bulge of crystalline water, a boulder in the exuberance of a mountain watershed. Presently, the lights sank into blackness, and only the silver sheen of river in starlight remained.

Louise cried, "I wish I could feel something!" And when I reached to comfort her she shoved me away. I had no choice but to climb back up to the roadway.

After that, I could encounter Louise only by telephone. I told her he had a record as long as your arm. "It's not enough!" she said. I called later to say that he was of German and Italian extraction. That proved equally unsatisfactory, and when I called to inform her that he hailed from Wisconsin she just hung up on me, this time for good.

WEIGHT WATCHERS

I PICKED UP MY FATHER ON A SULTRY MORNING WITH HEAVY, rumbling clouds on the horizon. My mother had thrown him out again, this time for his weight. She'd said that he was insufficiently committed to his weight-loss journey and that if he hit two-fifty she wouldn't live with him anymore. She seemed to know he'd be heading my way: I had been getting obesity-cure solicitations over the phone, my number doubtless supplied by her. I was tired of explaining to strangers that I wasn't fat and of being told that a lot of fat people don't realize how fat they are or wrongly assume that they can do something about it on their own, without paying.

By the time my father got to me, he was well over Mom's limit, and he wanted to go somewhere to eat as soon as he got off the plane. He was wearing a suit, rumpled from his travels, but his tie was in place: a protest against the rural surroundings. I took him on a little tour of the town—the rodeo grounds, the soccer field by the river, the old-car museum. He was happiest at the railroad shops, the smell of grease rising from a huge disabled locomotive, mechanics around it like Pygmies around an elephant. "When's she go back to work?" he asked, his eyes gleaming. The mechanics didn't look at him; they looked at one another. My father was undismayed: they assumed he was management, he said.

At the diner, he asked if the chicken sandwich on the menu was actually made of chicken or was "some conglomerate." A blank stare from the waitress. He ordered the sandwich. "I'll just have to find out myself." He insisted on buying our lunch, but when the cashier counted the change too rapidly for his taste he pushed it all back toward her and said, "Start over."

A man in a suit was an uncommon sight around here, and the responses to him indicated bafflement. In the afternoon, I rowed him down the river, still in the suit. He brought along some pie from the restaurant and asked me not to hit it with the oars; he held both hands over the pie as though to protect it.

I made dinner at my house, a place he plainly considered a dump. He sat at the card table in a kind of prissy upright way that indicated a fear that the dump was about to rub off on him.

"What's this stuff?"

"Tofu."

"Part of the alternate lifestyle?"

"No, protein."

I hated to tee him up like this, but he couldn't go home unless I got some weight off him.

Dad owned a booking agency for corporate and private aircraft and had to act as if he could afford what he booked, but just watching him handle my thrift-shop silverware you could tell that he was and always would be a poor boy. He felt that he had clambered up a few rungs, and his big fear was that I was clambering back down. As a tradesman—I run a construction crew—I had clearly fallen below the social class to which my father thought I should belong. He believed that the fine education he'd paid for should have led me to greater abstraction, but while it's true that the farther you get from an actual product the better your chances for economic success, I and many of my classmates wanted more physical evidence of our efforts. I had friends who'd trained as historians, literary scholars, and philosophers who were now shoeing horses, wiring houses, and installing toilets. There'd been no suicides so far.

My father believed that anything done for pleasure was escapism, except, of course, when it came to seducing his secretaries and most of my mother's friends. He and my mother had been a glamorous couple early in their marriage; good looks, combined with assertive tastemaking, had put them on top in our shabby little city. Then I came along, and Mother thought I'd hung the moon. In Dad's view, I put an end to the big romance. When I was a toddler, Dad caught Mom in the arms of our doctor on the screened back porch of the doctor's fish camp. (Though there must have been some ambivalence about the event, because we continued to accept perch fillets from Dr. Hudson's pond.) A few years later, when the high-school PE teacher caught the doctor atop his bride and shot him, Mother cried while Dad tilted his head to the side, elevated his eyebrows, and remarked, "Live by the sword, die by the sword."

As an only child, I was the sole recipient of my parents' malignant parenting. Their drinking took place entirely in the evening and followed a rigid pattern: with each cocktail they became increasingly thin skinned, bristling at imaginary slights. When I was young, they occasionally tried to throw me into the middle of their fights ("I don't believe this! She actually bit me!"), but I developed a suave detachment ("The Band-Aids are in the cupboard behind the towels"). In a real crisis, my mother brought in our neighbor Zoe Constantine for consolation, unaware that Pop had been making the two-backed beast with Zoe since I was in fifth grade—which happened to be the same year that my mother superglued Dad to the toilet seat, so perhaps she had her suspicions.

I asked about her now, not without anxiety. "She's in bed with a bottle and the poems of Edna St. Vincent Millay," my father said. He was proud of this remark—I'd heard it before. Although my mother read a lot, she was never "in bed with a bottle." Most likely, she was out playing golf with her friend Bernardine from the typing pool over at Ajax.

My mother comes from a southern family, though she's always lived in the North, and she has a tiny private income that has conditioned the dialogue since my childhood. Like a bazillion others of southern origin, she is a remote beneficiary of some Atlanta pharmacist's ingenuity: Coca-Cola—not a big remittance but enough to fuel Dad's rage against entitlement. That money had much to do with his determination to keep my mother within sight of smokestacks all her life. As did his belief that everything outside the Rust Belt was fake. To him, the American Dream was a 350-pound interior lineman from a bankrupt factory town with five-second forties, a long contract with the Colts, and a bonus for making the Pro Bowl.

IN THE MORNING, WE WENT OUT TO MY JOB SITE, AND I FELT happy at once. Everything there seemed to buoy my spirits: the caked mud on the tires of a carpenter's truck, the pleasant oily smell of tools, the cool wind coming through the sage on the hill, a screaming Skil saw already at work, the smell of newly cut two-by-fours, a nail gun going off in the basement, three thermoses on an unfinished ledge.

The doctor who'd hired me wanted a marshy spot behind the house excavated for a pond, and I had my Nicaraguan, Ángel, out there with a backhoe, trying to find the spring down in the mud so that we could plumb it and spread some bentonite to keep the water from running out. So far, all we'd found was mud and buffalo skulls, which Ángel was piling to one side. I told Dad that this had once been a trap made by Indians, but he wasn't all that interested. He was drawn to the Nicaraguan, whom he considered someone real on a machine—despite the heavy Central American accent, Dad had found his Rust Belt guy out here among all the phonies in cowboy hats. And Ángel was equally attracted to Dad's all-purpose warmth. He slid back his ear protectors and settled in for a chat.

Evidently, I'd had a flat tire as I pulled up to the site, left front, and it was a motherfucker getting the spare out of a three-quarter-ton Ford, the Ford jacked up on the soft ground, and the whole muddy wheel into the bed to take to town. At the tire shop, Dad looked weird in his slacks and loosened tie, amid all the noise from impact wrenches and the compressors screaming and shutting down, but nobody seemed to notice. He gazed admiringly at the big rough kid in a skullcap running a pry bar around the rim and freeing up the tire. The kid reached inside the tire, tugging and sweating, and presented me with an obsidian arrowhead. I nearly cut myself just taking it from his hand. "Six plies of Jap snow tire and it never broke," he said. I went up front and paid for the repair.

THE NEXT DAY, A COLD, RAINY DAY, DAD STAYED AT MY PLACE while I took my crew up to Martinsdale, where we'd hired a crane to drop the bed of an old railroad car onto cribbing to make a bridge over a creek. We'd brought in a stack of treated planks for the deck, and I had a welder on hand to make up the brackets, a painfully shy fellow with a neck tattoo who still had his New York accent. Five of us stood in the downpour and looked at the creek rushing around our concrete work. The rancher stopped by to tell us that if it washed out he wasn't paying for anything. When he was gone, Joey, the welder, said, "See what a big hat can do for you?"

I'd left Dad at loose ends, and I learned later that he'd driven all the way to Helena to see the state capitol and get a lap dance and then slept it off at a Holiday Inn a half mile from Last Chance Gulch.

I've been told that I come from a dysfunctional family, but I have never felt that way. When I was a kid, I viewed my parents as an anthropologist might view them and spent my time as I sometimes spend it now, trying to imagine where on earth they came from. I was conceived soon after Dad got back from Vietnam. I'm not sure he actually wanted to have children, but Mom required prompt nesting when he returned. I guess Dad was pretty wild back then. He'd been in a lot of firefights and loved every one of them, leading his platoon in a daredevil manner. He kept wallet pictures of dead VC draped over the hood of his jeep, like deer-camp photos. His days on leave had been a Saigon fornication blitz, and it fell to Mom to stop that momentum overnight. I was her solution, and from the beginning Dad viewed me skeptically.

One night, I crept down the stairs in my Dr. Denton footies to the sound of unusually exuberant and artificial elation and, spying from the door of the kitchen, saw my father on his knees, licking pie filling from one of the beaters of our Sunbeam Mixmaster, tearful and laughing, his long wide tongue lapping at the dripping goo. The extraordinarily stern look on my mother's face above her starched apron, as he strained upward to the beater, disturbs me to this day.

I have a million of these, but disturbance, as I say, is not trauma, and besides I moved away a long time ago. I came to Montana on a hiking trip with my girlfriend after college and never went back. I've left here only once, to join a roofing crew in Walnut Creek, California, and came home scared after two months. I saw shit at parties there that it'll take me years to forget. Everyone from the foreman on down had a crystal habit. I had to pretend I was using just to get the job.

———

DAD RETURNED FROM HELENA AND SAT IN MY KITCHEN WITH his laptop to catch up on business while I met with Dee and Helen Folsom out on Skunk Creek, leaving the whir of the interstate and veering into real outback within a quarter mile. I was building the Folsoms' first house, on a piece of ground that Dee's rancher uncle had given him. Not a nice piece of ground: it'd be a midwinter snow hole and a midsummer rock pile. The Folsoms were old enough to retire, but, as I mentioned, this was their first home. They were poor people. Dee had spent forty years on a fencing crew and constantly massaged his knotty, damaged hands. Helen cooked at the high school, where generations of students had ridiculed her food. I could see that this would be a kind of delayed honeymoon house, and I wanted to get it right.

The house was in frame, and Helen stood in what would be the picture window, enchanted by not much of a view—scrub pine, a shale ledge, the top of a flagless flagpole just below the hill along the road. Her expression would not have been out of place at the Sistine Chapel or on the rim of the Grand Canyon. One hand was plunged into the pocket of her army coat while the other twirled a pair of white plastic reading glasses. Dee just paced in his coveralls, happy and worried, pinching the stub of his cigarette.

I had cut this one to the bone—crew salaries and little else. The crew—carpenter, plumber, electrician—sensed the tone of things and worked with timely efficiency. Dee had prepared the site himself with a shovel and a wheelbarrow. We had a summer place for a plastic surgeon under way at Springhill, and if I'd looked a little closer, I might have seen it bleeding materials that managed to end up at the Folsoms'.

While I was at work, Dad was wandering the neighborhood, talking to my neighbors. After a few days, he knew more of them than I did, and I would forevermore have to be told what a great guy he was. But by the time I got home, he was in his underwear with the portable phone in his lap, nursing a highball and looking disconsolate. "Your mother called me from the club," he said. "I understand there was some dustup with the manager over the sneeze shield at the salad bar. Mom said she couldn't see the condiments, and it went from there."

"From there to where?" I inquired peevishly.

"Our privileges have been suspended."

"Golf?"

"Mm, that, too. Hey, I'll sort it out."

I nuked a couple of Rock Cornish hens, and we sat down in the living room to play checkers. Halfway through the game, my father went into the guest room and called my mother. This time she told him that she'd bought a car at what she thought was the dealer's cost. Dad shouted, "Asshole, who got the rebate? I'm asking you, goddamn it, who got the rebate?" I heard him raging about the sneeze shield then, and after he quieted down I heard him say plaintively—I think I heard this—that he no longer wished to live. I always looked forward to this particular locution, because it meant that they'd get back together soon.

I'm not lacking in affection for my parents, but they are locked into something that is so exclusive as to be hermetically sealed to everyone else, including me. Nevertheless, I'd had a bellyful by then. So when my father came back to finish the checkers game, I asked him if he'd enjoyed the lap dance.

"'Enjoy' isn't quite the word. I'm aware that the world has changed in my lifetime and I'm interested in those changes. I went to this occasion as . . . as . . . almost as an investigator."

"You might want to withhold the results of your research from Mom."

"How dare you raise your voice to me!"

"Jump you and jump you again. Checkers isn't fun if you don't pay attention."

"I was distracted by the club thing. I'm red, right?"

At some point, I knew he would confide that he and my mother were considering a divorce. They've been claiming to be contemplating divorce for half of my lifetime, and I have found myself stuck in the odd trope of opposing the idea just to please them. I don't know why they toss me into this or if only children always have this kind of veto power. I do care about them, but what they don't know, and I would never have the heart to tell them, is that the idea of their no longer being a married couple bothers me not at all. My only fear is that, separate, no one else would have them, that I'd get stuck with them one at a time or have to watch them wither away in solitude. These scenarios give me the fantods. Am I selfish? Yes and no. I'm a bachelor and hope someday to be an old bachelor.

My father picked at a bit of imaginary dust on his left shirt cuff, and I suspected that this was the opener to the divorce gambit. Cruelly, I got up and left the game half finished.

"Can you pardon me? I was slammed from daylight on. I'm all in."

"Well, sure, okay, good night. I love you, Son."

"Love you, too, Dad." And I did.

WHEN MY FATHER CAME HOME FROM THE WAR, HE WAS JUBI-lant about all the violence he'd seen. Happy to have survived, I suppose. Or perhaps he saw it as a game, a contest in which his platoon had triumphed. He worked furiously to build a business, but there was something peculiar about his hard work. He seemed to have no specific goal.

When I was fourteen, my mother said, "Do you know why your father works so hard?"

I thought I was about to get a virtue speech. I said, "No."

She said, "He works so hard because he's crazy." She never elaborated on this but left it in play, and it has remained with me for more than a quarter of a century.

The only time my father ever hit me was when I was fifteen and he asked if I was aware of all the things he and my mother had done for me. I said, "Do you have a chart I could point to?" and he popped me square on the nose, which bled copiously while he ran for a box of Kleenex. His worst condemnation of me was when he'd mutter, "If you'd been in my platoon . . . ," a sentence he always left unfinished.

My mother was a scientist; she worked in an infectious-disease lab until my father's financial success made her income unneces-sary. Even then, she went on buying things on time, making down payments, anxiety from their poorer days leading her to believe that she wouldn't live long enough to pay off her debts, even with her Coca-Cola money. Once they were comfortable with afflu-ence, they became party people, went to the tropics, brought back mounted fish, and listened to Spanish tapes in the car. But they were never truly comfortable away from the smoke and rust of their hometown.

The last year I lived with them, my father came to the bizarre conclusion that he lacked self-esteem, and he bought a self-help program that he was meant to listen to through headphones as he slept. From my bedroom, I could hear odd murmurings from this device attached to his sleeping head: "You are the greatest, you are the greatest. Look around you—it's a beautiful day." You can't make this shit up.

WE WERE NEARLY DONE WITH THE PLASTIC SURGEON'S VACA-tion home. I had a big crew there, and everyone was nervous about whether we'd have someplace to go next. We had remodels coming up, and a good shot at condominiumizing the old Fairweather Hotel in town, but nothing for sure. I met with Dr. Hadley to lay out the basement media room. He was a small man in a blazer and bow tie, bald on top but with long hair to his collar. I asked him, "Are you sure you want this? You have beautiful views." Indeed, he had a whole cordillera stretched across his living-room window. He was gazing around the space we were inspecting, at the bottom of some temporary wooden stairs. Push brooms stood in a pile of drywall scraps in the corner. There was a smell of plaster. He lifted his eyes to engage mine, and said, "Sometimes it rains." One of the carpenters, a skinny cowboy type with a perpetual cigarette at the center of his mouth, overheard this and crinkled his forehead.

No checkers tonight. Dad was laying out his platoon diagram, a kind of spreadsheet, with all his guys, as he called them, listed. "When I can't fill this out, I'll know I have dementia," he said. It was remarkable, a big thing on butcher paper, maybe twenty-five names, with their specialties and rankings designated—riflemen, machine gunners, radiomen, grenadiers, fire-team leaders, and so on. There was, characteristically, a star beside my father's name, the CO. Some names were crossed out with Vietnam dates; some were annotated as natural-cause eliminations. It was all so orderly—even the deaths seemed orderly, once you saw them on this spreadsheet. I think this was how Dad dealt with mortality: when a former sergeant died of cirrhosis in his sixties, Dad crossed out his square on the spreadsheet with the same grim aplomb he'd used for the twenty-somethings in firefights; it was all war to him, from, as he said, "the erection to the Resurrection."

Although he complained all the time, Dad lost weight on my regimen. When he got below the magic number, Mom didn't believe my scale or my word, and we had to have him weighed at the fire station, with a fireman reading the number to her over the phone while Dad rounded up a couple of guys to show him the hook-and-ladder. He'd made it by a little over a pound.

When I came home from the plastic surgeon's house that night, Dad was packing up. He had a glass of whiskey on the nightstand, and his little tape player was belting out a nostalgic playlist: Mott the Hoople, Dusty Springfield, Captain Beefheart, Quicksilver Messenger Service—his courting songs. My God, he was heading home to Mom again!

"Got it worked out?" I said, flipping through one of the girlie magazines he'd picked up in Helena, a special on "barely legals."

"We'll see."

"Anything new?"

"Not at all. She's the only one who understands me."

"No one understands you."

"Really? I think it's you that nobody understands. Anyway, there are some preliminaries in this case that I can live with."

"Like what?"

"I can't go to the house. I have to stay at a hotel."

"And you're okay with that?"

"Why wouldn't I be? A lot of surprising stuff happens at a hotel. For all intents and purposes, I'll be home."

AND NOW I HAVE TO FIGURE OUT HOW TO WORK AROUND DEE and Helen Folsom, who are on the job site continuously and kind of in the way. One night, they camped out on the subflooring of what will be their bedroom, when we barely had the sheathing on the roof. The crew had to shoo them away in the morning. I think the Folsoms were embarrassed, dragging the blow-up mattress out to their old sedan.

I have no real complaints about my upbringing. My parents

were self-absorbed and never knew where I was, which meant that I was free, and I made good use of that freedom. I've been asked if I was damaged by my family life, and the answer is a qualified no; I know I'll never marry, and, halfway through my life, I'm unable to imagine letting anyone new stay in my house for more than a night—and preferably not a whole night. Rolling over in the morning and finding . . . let's not go there. I build houses for other people, and it works for me.

I like to be tired. In some ways, that's the point of what I do. I don't want to be thinking when I go to bed, or if there is some residue from the day, I want it to drain out and precipitate me into nothingness. I've always enjoyed the idea of nonexistence. I view pets with extraordinary suspicion: we need to stay out of their lives. I saw a woman fish a little dog out of her purse once, and it bothered me for a year. It's not that there's anything wrong with my ability to communicate: I have a cell phone, but I only use it to call out.

THE HOUSE ON SAND CREEK

W HEN MONIKA AND I WERE FIRST MARRIED WE RENTED A house on Sand Creek, sight unseen, because Monika wanted to live in the country, and nothing else was available within reach of town. Everything we had been told was true: the house was a furnished ranch house with two bedrooms, two baths, near a quiet grove of aspens. It had been repossessed from a cowboy and his wife, who had gone on to Nevada or Oregon—somewhere in the Great Basin. The man at the bank said that he was an old-time rambling buckaroo, who'd stopped making his mortgage payments because "he was looking for a quit." Monika turned to me for an explanation, but I just wanted to get the deal done and move in. "It might not be exactly to your taste," the banker said, "but nothing says you can't tweak it."

It was an absolute horror. Skinned coyote carcasses were piled on the front step, and a dead horse hung from its halter where it had been tied to the porch. Inside was a shambles, and there was one detail we couldn't understand without the help of the neighbors: shotgun blasts through the bathroom door. Apparently Mrs. Old-Time Buckaroo used to chase Mr. Old-Time Buckaroo around the house until he ran into the bathroom, locked the door, and hid in the bath. The sides of the tub were pocked with lead.

Monika, who had seen the dead horse, said that it was a shame the wife had failed and that the two of them were now in the Great Basin, living out their lives. This is a bit of an understatement—at the time Monika broke into sobs and begged to be taken away. "Is this how you treat your wife?" she turned on me. "Stop calling me your princess, you bastard." I never quite got used to these flare-ups or to Monika's sometimes-misleading passion for fresh starts.

Monika was not only not a westerner; she was not even an American. She had been stranded in architecture school by the uproar in the former Yugoslavia, and by the time it was safe for her to go home, we had met and planned to marry. Which we did. And now we were in that house. Monika was commuting to architecture school, and I was running an underemployed law office that five years earlier had done thirty real-estate closings a month and now did at most two and often none. Booms in real estate came and went, like weather, except that there always seemed to be plenty of weather.

I am aware that my ability to wittily point out things like this, and to describe the house the way I am describing it, has a lot to do with the fact that Monika left soon after we'd moved in. She abandoned what she contemptuously described as "the western lifestyle" to return to her parents in Bosnia-Herzegovina. There, she found herself a nice house with no dead horses or coyotes, and a nice man and a nice baby—a twofer in the fresh-start business. Ours had been a poor excuse for a marriage, borne on an ill wind from the start.

I was still in the house, which we had painted in such a hurry that we'd rolled right over the outlets and floor moldings in uneven lines, giving one the feeling that the interior had somehow been draped in paint. For a long time, the sight of the walls kept Monika in my mind, even when womenfolk came for a visit, always short. Something—either me or the house—seemed to give them the willies.

I first met Bob when he came to congratulate me on "getting rid of that Croat." Like many other men in the area, Bob wore cowboy boots and a big hat and described himself as a former cowboy. This phenomenon interested me, and I began to put the stories together a bit. For example, Bob, a retired electrician, had not been a cowboy for at least forty-five of his sixty-two years. Further investigation suggested that his cowboy years had occurred somewhere between the sixth and seventh grades and may have lasted just under a month. I had always imagined cowboys, former and otherwise, to be laconic men, who, if they overcame their reluctance to speak at all, did so without much expression. Not Bob. Bob never shut up, and his facial movements had more in common with those of Soupy Sales than John Wayne. A surprising number of his anecdotes culminated in his telling people off, especially members of his own family. "My mother's in her eighties and she keeps talking about when I was in her belly. Ever hear anything more disgusting? I finally had to tell her to shut her trap." Or "I got fed up with my son. I told him to go fuck himself. He said he'd give it his best shot. Never at a loss for words, that boy." Or "They're all driving me crazy: my wife, my mother, my son, all his noisy friends. All the guys I worked with. Too much time on their hands. They need to get a life and quit cluttering up mine."

Mail addressed to Bob was once mistakenly delivered to my box, so I took it up to his place. It was clear that he was living alone. In time, I learned that he had been living alone for years and that all his stories of telling people off were just wishful thinking. Bob's relatives had put plenty of distance between themselves and him long ago. The only car that was ever in his driveway was his, an obsolete six-cylinder Bel Air with plenty of gravel cracks in the windshield. But at least Bob had integrity: he was mad at the world, if not yet at me. If I didn't wind sprint to my car or work on weekends, I was in for long visits. Still, something about him touched me.

Bob and I had really started to settle in—with Bob tracking my movements to make sure that I was home from work for at least ten minutes before he showed up—when Monika called me from Belgrade. She had written occasionally since leaving, but this was the first time I had spoken to her in a couple of years. I found it painful in the extreme and didn't quite keep track of the conversation, uncertain why I should care that she had money from the sale of her house or that little Karel already slept through the night and was such a happy boy. Monika must have detected my confusion because she suddenly asked, "Are you following this?" and I had to admit that I was a bit lost. She filled me in: she wanted to come back. What had happened to her new man? I asked her. "Out the window!" she said.

Monika spoke nearly perfect English, but she always managed to alter our colloquialisms slightly. My favorite was her description of a problem as "a real kink in the ointment." I tried to correct this to "fly in the ointment," but with a blank look on her beautiful face she asked me what a fly would be doing in ointment. I let it go. I had been raised to think that loving your spouse was a requirement. "Love is a job," my mother had snarled at our wedding as she gazed at Monika, who was wearing some sort of shocking Eastern

European headdress. Thus, I loved Monika even after she left me and until the day she announced her return, a baby under her arm by someone I had never met.

ON THE FIRST DAY OF THE BOZEMAN SWEET PEA FESTIVAL, Monika got off the plane and handed me little Karel. "For you. Have I aged? I don't seem to turn heads the way I used to." She wore some sort of gown that fit her like a giant lampshade, a grand cone that went from her neck to the ground. "Is that a dirndl?" I asked.

"No, it's a dashiki. Oh, God, you haven't changed."

I was in shock. As for little Karel, now in my arms, he was clearly black. I had an unworthy thought: Wait until Bob gets a load of this. Turned out I was wrong to worry about it because when Bob met Karel he thought he had a skin condition of some kind and expressed his sympathy.

In the parking lot, Monika said, "What are you doing with this tiny car?"

"I've been single, Monika. It was all I needed."

"Well, I'm back." She worked her way into the passenger seat while I held little Karel, who was gazing into my eyes confidently. "And this put-put will prove inadequate."

The feeling came back to me, from the days of our marriage, that I was doomed in life to take a lot of shit and make weak jokes in response.

We made love as soon as we got to the house. Monika bounced me around and remarked that I seemed out of it. Across her lower back was a mysterious architectural tattoo, which turned out to be Le Corbusier's plan for the High Court of Chandigarh, India. As I drifted off into postcoital tristesse, Monika raided the icebox. She was perfectly candid about her enthusiasm for food, explaining that her ex was a glutton. "Often when people come from lands of scarce resources their response to abundance is gluttony."

"A big fellow, is he?" I asked weakly.

"In every way," she said with a laugh. "You know what a Mandingo is?"

"Is it something to eat?"

"No, idiot! A Mandingo is an African warrior. You're thinking of a mango!"

"Oh. Is he an African warrior?"

"Hardly. He's a Nigerian neurosurgeon. But Olatunde has the sort of Mandingo traits that I hope Karel inherits. He's actually Yoruba."

I looked over at Karel. He didn't seem to possess any Mandingo traits. He was just a little baby waving his arms around. When Monika collapsed with jet lag, I took him out to the sofa and let him play on my chest until he fell asleep. And then I fell asleep. The last thing I saw was a bird trying to get in the window. Monika's luggage was still sitting in the living room, unopened.

Bob must have figured out that Karel did not have a skin condition because there was certainly a theme to the gifts he brought over. "He already had a baby shower in Belgrade," Monika said, but that didn't stop Bob. A children's biography of Martin Luther King Jr., James Brown's *Greatest Hits,* and a pretend leg of fried chicken made out of some rubberlike material. "He can actually teethe on it!" Bob said.

When he was gone, Monika said, "My dream was of a new life here, but this may be impossible."

"I think Bob meant well," I said.

"Ah, make no mistake: that was not Bob speaking and bringing his symbolic gifts. That was America speaking through Bob."

Meanwhile, Karel teethed contentedly on his rubber drumstick, his little chin glistening as he hummed.

AS PART OF MONIKA'S FIRST ASSIGNMENT ON HER RETURN TO architecture school, she began to design some alterations for our house, a wing here, a wing there: I was terrified that she would actually want me to have these things built.

"Why do we need a loggia?"

"Why do I even talk to you?"

Bob continued to visit some mornings for coffee. If he arrived before Monika left for school, she fled to her car. "Always in a hurry, that gal," Bob said. "Someday she'll be designing skyscrapers, and we'll brag we knew her back when." Whenever Bob drove

Monika from the house, it fell to me to care for Karel until the babysitter arrived in her white tennis shoes and loose shorts that made the vanishing of her thighs into them a matter of urgent mystery. I loved to start the day by playing with Karel in bed. He'd sit on my stomach, and we'd play hand games that always ended with this merry little boy tipping over onto the pillows only to arise and crawl on top of me again to resume the battle with a shout. If Bob was still there, we did this on the living-room rug, scurrying around until I had rug burns on my knees. When Bob wasn't launching into some complaint about his overindulgent mother, he was wonderful with Karel. I could leave the two of them together while I dressed for work, and whatever Bob did always had Karel squealing with delight. The arrival of the babysitter, nubile Lydia, would put an end to all this: I went to work; Bob went home.

I have lived in this town for a long time, but I was raised in Bakersfield, California, a town I was longing to flee by the age of ten. I coughed up out-of-state tuition, went to law school, then settled here, at first alone and then with Monika. I mention all this because my colleague, Jay Matthews, who has lived here all his life, told me that Bob's mother could hardly be driving him crazy: she died when he was a boy. "Got to be fifty years ago."

"I must have misheard him."

"Yeah, Bob was an only child, and his mom was single. Ole Bob was a bubble and a half off plumb, even back then. That's why he's always fit right into this godforsaken town."

Life went on. Karel's father, Olatunde, called every week, sometimes talking to me and sometimes to Monika. His attempts to talk to Karel came to nothing, as Karel drooled and stared at the receiver. Olatunde spoke in measured tones in a deep voice, which, combined with his cultivated, slightly fusty British accent, seemed to come from a tomb. Nonetheless, his melancholy over the absence of his little boy could be discerned. He wished me luck with Monika and said that I was going to need it. His, he said, had run out.

Bob and Karel became so close—Karel singing in his presence and crying out in delight when he arrived—that Monika and I consulted about dispensing with the babysitter and using Bob instead. I wasn't sure about this. The babysitter was getting ready to start college and needed the money, and, besides, I was sweet on her and thought she was starting to come around, recklessly bending over to pick up Karel's toys in my presence. Monika noticed this once and started braying with sardonic and distinctly Slavic laughter. The time had come for me to take the bull by the horns. I followed Lydia to her car and told her that any fool could see how beautiful she was and I was no fool. She started but failed to reply. "You—you—you—" She got into her car and roared off. I thought it best to maintain a sphinxlike expression on my way back into the house. Monika smiled at me as I entered. "Turn you down?"

"Seems to be running okay. I can't think why she thought the ignition was going out."

Gales of laughter. "Oh, good one. Stick to your weapons."

The moment blew over, with the usual residue, but in the end I was furious with Lydia for having wiggled around the house on the assumption that I wouldn't notice. Entrapment, pure and simple. Another few steps down that trail, and Lydia could have owned my law firm. These youngsters look right through you, unless their gaze falls on something they might need. I should have held my wallet aloft with one hand while pointing at my crotch with the other, but I simply lacked the nerve. So (a) babysitter leaves, and (b) here comes Bob. The convenience and economy of this arrangement appealed even to Monika, who allowed that he was "not a bad chicken egg after all."

Obviously, we made several forays into marriage counseling, during which we turned each of our counselors into helpless referees. I always felt that these sessions were nothing more than attempts by each side to win over the counselor, with charm, cajoling, whatever it took. In the end, Monika decided that everything that had led to the idea of counseling—Freud, Jung, Judeo-Christianity—was spiritually bankrupt. Therefore, she was going to look back thousands of years and seek the help of a shaman, now resident in Missoula. This shaman, she explained, had the benefit of ten thousand years of human spiritual experience, as opposed to the Johnny-come-latelies of psychoanalysis, and she intended to partake of that knowledge. I listened thoughtfully and replied that it sounded promising so long as she didn't fuck the shaman.

Thus began our decidedly parallel lives: Monika and her shaman and her architecture, me and my law practice, Bob and Karel. Monika came home in the evening with long rolls of paper under her arm, and I with my briefcase, containing few briefs in these straitened times, to the happy home of Bob and Karel. When Bob left for the night, I held Karel's rigid little body as he wailed and reached frantically in the direction of Bob's departure. "Give him something to eat," Monika remarked on her way into the bedroom.

One afternoon, Monika and I had a rather sharp exchange in the presence of Bob and Karel. I asked innocently if it was absolutely necessary for her to keep using her boarding pass as a bookmark.

Monika said, "None of your business."

"I suppose it helps to remind you of that shithole where you grew up."

"It reminds me that they still have airplanes that go back there."

"Everyone wants to go to Yugoslavia," I said, "where shooting your neighbor is the national sport."

"Oh, you're awful. You're just so awful. My God, how truly awful you are."

Karel started to cry, and Bob took him outside. Soon I could see the chains of the swing flashing back and forth and hear Karel's delighted cries.

Monika had recently undergone an abrupt sartorial change from dark Euro-style clothing to Rocky Mountain chic: hiking boots, painter pants, bright yellow down jacket, and a wool cap with strings hanging down the sides. Now screwing a mountaineer, I thought ungenerously. Her exhaustion, I assumed, owed more to her shagging the mountain man than to anything she was doing in the world of architecture.

It should come as no surprise to anybody that the day came when Monika and I returned from work to find Bob and Karel missing. Having read *Huckleberry Finn,* she remarked that Bob had "lit out for the territory" with Karel. I don't want to overstate the ghastly nature of our response, as we were both crying—though whether at the loss of Karel or at the feeling that we deserved to lose him and Bob deserved to have him, I couldn't say. When I attempted to cheer Monika up by saying that when life gives you lemons you must make lemonade, she slapped my face. I almost fought back, and you can only imagine how that would have seemed under the circumstances.

Instead, I called the police in town. Monika called Olatunde in Yugoslavia and put me on the phone. "You tell him."

"Good morning, Doctor. It's afternoon there already? Well, I have news, well, not news exactly. One of our neighbors here has . . . kidnapped Karel." Dr. Olatunde was understandably slow in absorbing this announcement but not in any other way, and it fell to me to pick him up at the airport a day and a half later.

These were terrible hours. Monika stayed home as we awaited word from the police, her drawings laid out on the kitchen table. She showered me with reproaches, the recurrent one being that Karel would never have "slipped through her hand" if I hadn't chased the babysitter away with my ogling. Pointing at the drawings, I said, "I see the loggia stays."

"Yes, and a pergola."

"I hadn't noticed."

"There are none so blind as those who will not see."

I MET DR. OLATUNDE AT THE BAGGAGE CLAIM THOUGH HE had only a carry-on. He was the sole African among all the skiers, and he drew a bit of attention to himself for that and for the suit he wore, a nice English cut, rumpled from the long trip. He was not at all the big Mandingo glutton I had pictured but a small, precise man with a slightly receding hairline and a friendly but crisp manner. He said, "You were kind to come for me."

"You must be tired."

"Not so bad, really."

"Well, I have marvelous news for you. Karel has been found."

"Is that so?"

"I hope you don't feel the trip was wasted."

"Nothing could compare to this. Is he well?"

Bob and Karel had not gone far, at least not far enough to give plausibility to a charge of kidnapping. They were in the first motel on the way into town. Their loud music had given them away. Bob was belligerent about what he described as the hostile atmosphere of our home, and we felt that by pressing charges we would only bring his version into the public eye. Karel responded to his father, whom he could hardly have been expected to remember, much as he responded to Bob: he was always drawn to someone who looked straight at him as though making a delightful discovery. I spell this out because it was against all odds that we allowed Bob to come back again and let ourselves be compensated by Karel's squeals of delight. More and more, he stays over at Bob's anyway, which Monika and I hope will give us some room to work things out.

GRANDMA AND ME

My grandmother lost her sight about three years ago, just before she turned ninety, and because it happened gradually, and in the context of so much other debility, she adapted very well. Grandma's love of the outdoors combined with her remarkable lucidity and optimism to keep her cheerful and realistic. And she could get on my ass about as good as she ever could. She was now greatly invested in her sense of smell, so I tried to put fresh flowers around her house, while Mrs. Devlin, her housekeeper of forty-one years, kept other things in the cottage fresh, including the flow of gossip and the newspaper under Chickie, a thirty-year-old blue-fronted parrot that had bitten me several times. When Grandma goes, Chickie is going into the disposal.

Grandma did a remarkable job of living in the present, something I'd hoped to learn from her before going broke or even crazier than I already was. I'd been away for over a decade, first as a timekeeper in a palladium mine, then dealing cards, downhill all the way. Three years in a casino left me so fucked up I was speaking in tongues, but Grandma got me back on my feet with pearls of immortal wisdom like "Pull yourself together." And while I waited for her to give me a little walking-around money, a pearl or two would come to me, too, like "Shit or get off the pot."

Grandma owned several buildings in the middle of our small town, including the old hotel where I lived. I looked after them, not exactly as a maintenance man—I don't have such trade skills—but more as an overseer, for which Grandma paid me meagerly, justifying her stinginess with the claim that I was bleeding her white. Another building housed an office-supply shop and a preschool, where I was a teaching assistant. That is, a glorified hall monitor for a bunch of dwarfs. I also tended bar two nights a week—the off nights, when tips were scarce, but it was something to do and kept me near the hooch. Grandma had bought the bar, too, back when it was frequented mainly by sheepherders. Sheep have mostly disappeared from the area since being excluded from the national forest, which they had defoliated better than Agent Orange. I didn't see much point in tending an empty bar, but Grandma required it. It was part of my "package," she said, and besides she was sure that if we closed it down, it would become a meth lab. Grandma was convinced every empty building housed a meth lab.

The preschool thing was another matter. Mrs. Hessler, the teacher, considered me her employee, and I played along with this to keep the frown off that somewhat-shapeless face she had crowned with an inappropriate platinum pixie. I regularly fed her made-up news items from imaginary newspapers, and she always bought it.

"Drone Strike on a Strip Club," for example. In return, Mrs. Hessler made me wear clothes she supplied and considered kid friendly: loud leisure suits and sweatpants, odd-lot items that gave me the feeling I was at the end of my rope.

Barring weather or a World Series game, on Sundays I'd pick up a nice little box lunch from Mustang Catering and take Grandma someplace that smelled good. I was often in rough shape on Sunday mornings, so a little fresh air helped me dry out in time for work on Monday. We'd have our picnics in fields of sage and lupine, on buffalo-grass savannas north of town, on deep beds of spruce needles, and in fields of spring wildflowers. I'd have enough of nature pretty quick, but we stayed until Grandma had had her fill; she told me it was the least I could do, and I suppose she's right.

Today's nature jaunt turned out to be one for the ages: we went to a bend in the river near Grandma's and set up our picnic under the oldest of cottonwoods, so that the eastbound current raced toward us over pale gravel. It smelled wonderful. Once out of the car, I led Grandma with a light touch on the elbow, marveling at how straight and tall she was—how queenly she looked with her thick white hair carefully piled and secured by Mrs. Devlin with a broad tortoiseshell comb. I had just settled Grandma on her folding chair and popped open our box lunch when the corpse floated by. Though facedown, he seemed formally attired, and the tumult of current at the bend was strong enough to make him ripple from end to end, while his arms seemed lofted in some oddly valedictory way, and his hair floated ahead of him. The sunlight sparkling on the water made the picture ghastly.

"Oh!" said Grandma as though she could see it.

"What?"

"That divine smell, of course! I can still smell snow in the river!"

The corpse had rotated in such a way that I could now see the heels of its shoes and the slight ballooning of its suit coat. Just then I remembered that cheap Allegiant flight I'd taken back from Las Vegas. I'd lost so much money, I got drunk on the plane and passed out, and someone scrawled LOSER on my face in eyebrow pencil, though I didn't see it until the men's room at the Helena airport. Was I so far gone I was identifying with a corpse?

"What an awful child you were," Grandma said. "Already drinking in the sixth grade. What would have become of you if I hadn't put you in Catholic school? It was your salvation and thank goodness the voodoo wore off in time. It wasn't easy humoring those silly nuns. They never took their hands out of their sleeves the whole time you were there."

"Uh, Grandma, excuse me, but I have to see a man about a horse." I jogged along the riverbank until I was well out of earshot, and lighting a cigarette, I called the sheriff's office on my cell. I let the dispatcher know who I was and asked if the sheriff or one of the deputies was available. "I'll check. What's the topic?" The dispatcher's tone let me know how they felt about me at the sheriff's office.

"I'm down on the river, and a corpse just went by. Across from the dump. It's going to pass under the Harlowton Bridge in about ten minutes."

"There's no one here right now. Marvin has a speeder pulled over at the prairie dog town. Maybe he could get there."

"Next stop after that is Greycliff. Somebody'd have to sit on the bridge all day."

"Please don't raise your voice. Any distinguishing features?"

"How's 'dead' sound to you?"

I went back to find Grandma lifting her face in the direction of the sun and seeming contented. A few cottonwood leaves fluttering in a breath of wind onto the surface of the river revealed the speed of the current. Every so often people floated by on rafts, blue rafts, yellow rafts, their laughter and conversations carried along on the water like a big, happy wake following a corpse.

"Are you ready to eat?" I asked.

"In a bit, unless you're hungry now. It smells different than when we were here in August. I think something happens when the leaves begin to turn, something cidery in the air, and yesterday's rain stays in the trunks of these old trees." It had rained for about two minutes yesterday. Grandma's got all these sensations dialed in as though she's cramming the entire earth before she croaks.

I walked down to the river, took off my shoes and socks, and rolled up my pant legs. I waded in no more than a few inches when I heard my phone ring. I turned just in time to see Grandma groping for it next to where I left the box lunches. Oh, well. I kept wading and noticed three white pelicans standing among the car bodies on the far side of the river. I'd have thought they'd have gone south by now. I dug a few flat stones off the bottom and skipped them toward the middle of the river. I got five skips from a piece of bottle glass before going back to Grandma.

"That was the sheriff's office."

"Oh?"

"They wanted you to know that it was a jilted groom who jumped into Yankee Jim Canyon on Sunday. What day is today?"

"Wednesday." Must have averaged a couple miles an hour.

"Why would they think you'd care about a jilted groom jumping into Yankee Jim Canyon?"

"Idle curiosity," I said sharply.

"And the sheriff was calling just to fill you in? I don't understand one bit of that, not one bit."

I wasn't about to let Grandma force me to ruin her outing by telling her what I had seen. So I opened the box lunch, spread a napkin on her lap, and there I set her sandwich, sliced cucumbers, and almond cookie. She lifted half of the sandwich.

"What is this? Smells like deviled ham."

"It is deviled ham."

"Starving."

Must have been: she fucking gobbled it.

"I see where you had another DUI."

You didn't see that, you heard it, and I could reliably assume that Mrs. Devlin made sure of it. "Yes. Grandma, drunk at the wheel." Of course I was making light of this, but secretly I thanked God it had stayed out of the papers. When you work with young children, it takes very little to tip parents into paranoia—they are already racked with guilt over dropping their darlings off with strangers in a setting where the little tykes could easily get shot or groped.

In families like mine, grandmothers loom large as yetis. I always thought having Grandma had been a blessing for me, but still I have often wondered if it wasn't her vigor that had made my father into such a depressed boob. He was a case of arrested development who never made a dime, but Grandma supported him in fine-enough style for around here and at the far end of her apron strings. He was devoted to his aquarelles—his word. The basement was full of them. His little house has remained empty, except for the flowers, bunnies, puppies, and sunsets on every wall. Grandma says it's without a doubt a meth lab.

Perhaps I felt some of his oppression as Grandma sat bolt upright holding that half a sandwich ("I trust you washed up before handling my food") and inhaling the mighty cottonwoods, the watercress in the tiny spring seeping into the broad green and sparkling river. I thought about the drowned bridegroom sailing by, his arms fluttering like a bat. It was Grandma who'd taught me that every river has its own smell and that ours are fragrant while others stink to high heaven, catch fire, or plunge into desert holes never to be seen again.

I think that at bottom some of these reflections must have been prompted by the mention of my latest DUI, which was a frightful memory. I knew it wasn't funny. I had left the Mad Hatter at closing, perfectly well aware that I was drunk. That was why I went there, after all. From the window at the back of the bar, as the staff cleaned up, I watched the squad car circle the block until I had determined the coast was clear. I ran through the cold night air to my car and headed up the valley. I hadn't gone far when I saw the whirling red light in my rearview mirror, and there's where I made a bad decision. I pulled over and bolted out of the car and ran into a pasture, tearing my shirt and pants on a barbed-wire fence. I didn't stop running until I fell into some kind of crack in the ground and broke my arm. That light in my rearview turned out to be an ambulance headed farther up the valley. I crawled out of the crack and got back into the car to drive to the emergency room back in town. I soon attracted an actual policeman and hence the DUI, the cast on my arm, and this latest annoyance from Grandma, who may in fact be the source of my problems. I knew that thought was a tough sell which defied common sense, but it was gathering plausibility for me.

I looked across the river at the row of houses above the line of car bodies. I heard a lawn mower over the whisper of river. A tennis ball came sailing over the bank, a black dog watching as it disappeared into the river.

Grandma said, "When you were a little boy, I thought you would be president of the United States." I got that odd shriveling feeling I used to get when our parents couldn't handle us and she would have to come to our house. I decided to give her the silent treatment. She didn't notice. I watched as she took in all she could smell and hear with the same upright posture and air of satisfaction. I unexpectedly decided that I was entitled to a little liquid cheer and began tiptoeing in the direction of my car a good distance away; wasted tiptoeing, I might add, as Grandmother said, "Bye-bye."

I have no idea why starting the car and putting it in gear gave me such a gust of exhilaration that the quick stop for a couple of stiff ones seemed almost redundant. But that's what happened, and I felt all the better for it as I walked into the sheriff's office just as Deputy Crane was leaving. I caught his sleeve and asked about the corpse. I could tell by his expression that he could smell the adult beverage on my breath. "They pulled it out of the water at the Reed Point Bridge. I'm headed there now."

"Oh, let me ride along."

"What's the matter with you?"

Deputy Crane would have to get up earlier in the morning if he wanted to be rid of me. By the time he pulled out of town, I was hot on his trail. The interstate followed the river, and we sped along doing seventy-five, the river intermittently visible on my left. Thus far the bridegroom had outrun us.

Pulling off the interstate and down into a riverside trailer park, I was convinced that euphoria was the rarest of all prizes, and being as good as anyone at cherishing mine, I started to fear that seeing the corpse up close might be a buzzkill. A small crowd had formed at the riverbank, and the squad car was parked close by. I pulled up next to the deputy, who got out and, spotting me, said, "Jesus Christ." The small crowd parted at the sight of the uniform, and I pushed through in its wake, rudely asked to stop shoving. There within the circle of gawkers was the dead bridegroom. Either his wedding clothes were too small for him or he was seriously water-logged. I don't know why they laid him out on a picnic table. The well-trimmed mustache seemed misplaced on the broad moon face whose wide-open eyes were giving me such a bad feeling. The gawkers would look at the face, then at one another searching for some explanation. People with sideburns that long were inevita-bly from the wrong side of the tracks, where me and my family, excepting Grandma, had all lived. I couldn't say why I felt a corpse shouldn't have a mustache and long sideburns. It seemed about time to buck up with some more artificial elation. But first I thought it only right to inform this group that it was I who had first spotted our friend floating past. This fell on deaf ears. I looked around me with a bleak, ironic smile undaunted by their indignation.

Somebody at the Mad Hatter had told me there was going to be midget wrestling at the Waterhole. There was a van parked in front with the logo SUPPORT MIDGET VIOLENCE, but no midgets in sight unless they were asleep inside. Two horses stood tied to the hitching rack in front by the trough and beside them four pickup trucks with so much mud on the windshields that the drivers could only have seen through the wiper arcs. Between two of the trucks was a bloodred Porsche Carrera with New Mexico plates and a King Charles spaniel at the wheel. I was able to get what I wanted without giving the others the impression that I cared to mingle. The bartender was a compulsive counter wiper, and when I got up, the tip I left there disappeared. He pretended to find the bills under the rag as I departed, giving the entire crowd a laugh at my expense as I pushed through the doors. I thought of going back and raising hell but found the Porsche unlocked and released the spaniel instead. It was dark, and all I could think of was one word, "Grandma!" The dog headed off through the houses with their lighted windows as I was swept by uneasiness.

Something was making me drive this fast. I was trying my best to reckon where those little units of time had gone. Whatever trouble I was headed for, it didn't feel like it was entirely my fault, just because someone decided to send a corpse through my day. If he'd lived on Grandma's side of town, he would have enjoyed more options with no sideburns to maintain.

It was not easy to find our picnic site in the dark, and I wouldn't have been sure I'd found it if I hadn't spotted the remains of the box lunch. I ate the other deviled-ham sandwich, the hard-boiled egg, the spicy pickle, and the cookie, and staring at the large expanse of the river, breathing mostly with my abdominal muscles, I tried to collect my thoughts and ward off hysteria.

The chair was gone. So she didn't jump in the river. Can't have more than one corpse a day. Somebody must have found Grandma and taken her home. This thought gave me an especially sharp pain, as it suggested one more person looking down on me, the oaf who left his blind grandmother on the riverbank.

I drove back across the Harlowton Bridge, through town heading for Snob Hollow, where Grandmother lived. My watch has a luminous dial, but I was afraid to look, fearing yet another buzzkill. By the time I stopped in front of Grandma's, I was having palpitations. I rifled the backseat in search of the minis sometimes scattered there but found only a mocking handful of empties. I stared through the windshield at the pair of juniper hedges leading to the door. My mind was so inflamed that when I got out of the car I thought I saw a face. I approached the front door and knocked, and then knocked again. Blood rushed to my head when I heard something within.

Mrs. Devlin was fastening her terry-cloth wrapper at the neck. She was no girl herself, and those big teeth and accusing eyes only subtracted from any impression of innocence. She had led a blameless life and wouldn't say shit if she had a mouthful, but when backed by Grandma's authority she could be dangerous.

"You," she said.

"Just checking in on Grandma."

Then in the dark behind Mrs. Devlin I heard Grandma ask, "Is that him?"

"Yes, it is, Adeline."

"Mrs. Devlin, kindly slap his face for me." It sure stung.

I imagined saying, *Try this one on for size,* before throwing Mrs. Devlin a roundhouse, but of course I just stood there as the door was slammed in my face. I headed back downtown, which in the dark looked abandoned, with so few lights that their silhouettes showed against the night sky, the blank face of the derelict mercantile, the bell cupola of the fire station with its mantle of cold stars. I returned to my room at the hotel, and the view of the mountains through the empty lobby, the old billiard table on which a century ago some surgeon treated the victim of a gunfight, the smells of mahogany and matted carpet, the dimmed lights gleaming off the souvenir cabinet. On my wave of booze and self-pity, one more nobody for the rest of the world to kick around. I pictured myself as the last survivor of my family, except for Grandma, who was left to contemplate what she had achieved over the generations. The thought lulled me into a nice sleep. I awakened to the sound of the breakfast dishes clattering in the restaurant, and for me a brand-new chance for success. As usual, whether I made the most of it or not, it would be fun just to see what happened, because, say what you will, I'm a glass-half-full kind of guy.

There wasn't time to eat before going to work, Mrs. Hessler being a Nazi about punctuality. I was careful to avoid a long look at myself as I brushed my teeth and glanced at my watch. I pulled on one of my work shirts, the one that says YOUR COMPANY NAME HERE at the top, YOUR LOGO HERE in the middle, and ONE CHILD AT A TIME at the bottom. Mrs. Hessler had gotten them in some close-out sale and expected to see them.

When I first went to work for Mrs. Hessler, it was just after my casino years and, knowing about my résumé, she got me to teach her Texas Hold'em. She was pretty good but soon got overconfident and went off for a gambler's weekend to Vegas and lost her ass. Naturally she blamed me. That set the tone. I told her that in a world where sperm donors are expected to pay child support, anything could happen.

Hooray for me! I was actually early. I let myself into the playroom and realized I had never cleaned up on Friday. I had been in some haste to get to the Mad Hatter, and so now, with so little strength, I would have to put everything in order before Hessler let me know by her silence how unhappy she was with me, her drone. *Back to the barracoon, darky!* I told her I'd read that some archbishop staying at a five-star hotel in the Seychelles got his ass scorched on a rogue bidet. She didn't even crack a smile. Chutes and Ladders was all over the floor, and I got dizzy picking up all the pieces. Moronic instruments for tiny mites—drums, tambourines, ocarinas—all would have to go on the music shelf. The GOD MADE ME SPECIAL poster had broken free of its thumbtacks. I didn't remember so much chaos on Friday—motivational ribbons and certificates, birthday crowns, star badges, alphabet stickers all over the room—but then my mind had been elsewhere.

Frau Hessler made the rounds of the refrigerator, counted out the snacks in a loud voice, put the removable mop heads back in the closet, gave her own YOUR COMPANY HERE shirt a good stretch, and greeted the first mother at the door. It was on. They came in a wave of noise as Hessler and I checked each other's faces for the required cheer. I had mine on good but felt like my teeth were drying out. Two mothers asked for the containers of their breast milk to be labeled and were quite abrupt telling me that Post-its would fall off in the fridge. The room was full of children, nearly babies, little boys and girls thematically dressed according to the expectations of their parents, little princesses and tiny cowboys, some still in pajamas. Hessler always seemed to know exactly what to do and began creating order. I dove into the sock-puppet bins, trying to find one that felt right, pawing through the Bible-themed puppets, the monster puppets, the animal puppets. I was fixated on getting one I was comfortable with, since I'd ended up with Saint John the Baptist the previous week, and Hessler rebuked me for failing to come up with relevant Bible quotes. Realizing I was running out of time by Hessler standards, I just snatched one randomly and found myself wearing an African American fireman and wiggling the stick that operated the hand holding the hose, all for the sake of a surly four-year-old named Roger. Roger was not amused and after a long silence called me poopoo head. I offered up some goofy laughter, and Roger repeated the remark. "In ten years, Roger," I muttered, "you'll be sniffing airplane glue from a sandwich bag." I dropped the fireman on the bench and moved on to nicer children. I made it until time-out, when I left the playhouse for a cigarette. A cold wind stirred the last leaves on the old burr oaks at the corner. Up on the hill, where Grandma's house stood, the sun was already shining. Mrs. Devlin would be setting out her midmorning tea, and Grandma was sure to feel that things were in perfect order.

HUBCAPS

By late afternoon, Owen's parents were usually having their first cocktails. His mother gave hers some thought, looking upon it as a special treat, while his father served himself "a stiff one" in a more matter-of-fact way, his every movement expressing a conviction that he had a right to this stuff, no matter how disagreeable or lugubrious or romantic it might soon make him. He made a special point of not asking permission as he poured, with a workmanlike concentration on not spilling a drop. Owen's mother held her drink between the tips of her fingers; his father held his in his fist. Owen could see solemnity descend on his father's brow with the first sip, while his mother often looked apprehensive about the possible hysteria to come. Owen remembered a Saturday night when his father had air-paddled backward, collapsing into the kitchen trash can and terrifying the family boxer, Gertrude. Gertrude had bitten Owen's father the first time she saw him drunk and now viewed him with a detachment that was similar to Owen's.

In any event, the cocktails were Owen's cue to head for the baseball diamond that the three Kershaw boys and their father had built in the pasture across from their house, with the help of any neighborhood kids who'd wanted to pitch in—clearing brush, laying out the baselines and boundaries, forming the pitcher's mound, or driving in the posts for the backstop. Doug, the eldest Kershaw boy, was already an accomplished player, with a Marty Marion infielder's mitt and a pair of cleats. Terry, the middle son, was focused on developing his paper route and would likely be a millionaire by thirty. Ben, the youngest and sweetest, was disabled and mentally handicapped, but he loved baseball above all things; he had a statistician's capacity for memorizing numbers and had learned to field a ball with one crippled hand and to make a respectable throw with the other. To Owen, Ben's attributes were nothing remarkable: he had his challenges; Ben had others.

It was rare to have full teams, and occasional lone outfielders started at center field and prepared to run. Eventually, Ben was moved off first base and into the outfield. With his short arms, he couldn't keep his foot on the bag and reach far enough for bad throws. Double plays came along only about three times a summer, and no one wanted to put them at risk. So long as Ben could identify with a renowned player who had played his position—in this case, Hoot Evers—he was happy to occupy it, and physically he did better with flies than with grounders.

Owen was happy with his George Kell spot at third base, and he didn't intend to relinquish it. He was a poor hitter—he was trying to graduate from choking the bat, though he was still not strong enough to hold it at the grip—but his ability to cover stinging grounders close to the foul line was considered compensation for his small production at the plate. He had learned to commit late to the ball's trajectory—grounders often changed angles, thanks to the field's irregularities—and he went fairly early when they chose up sides. Chuck Wood went late, despite being the most muscular boy there, as he always swung for the fence in wan hope of a home run and was widely considered a showboater. Ben was a polished bunter and could run like the wind, assuring his team of at least one man on base. He was picked early, sometimes first, but never got to be captain, because in the hand-over-hand-on-the-bat ritual for choosing sides, his hand wouldn't fit anywhere below the label. In the beginning, Mrs. Kershaw had stuck around to make sure that he was treated fairly, announcing, "If Ben doesn't play, nobody plays." But now he belonged, and she restricted her supervision to meeting him as he got off the school bus and casting an authoritarian glance through the other passengers' windows.

After a game, the equipment was stored on the back porch of the Kershaw house, where Terry ran his newspaper operation and often recruited the players to help him fold for the evening delivery. The Kershaws' small black schipperke dog, Smudge, watched from a corner. Doug put a few drops of neat's-foot oil in the pocket of his mitt, folded a ball into it, and placed it on the broad shelf that held shin guards, a catcher's mask, and a cracked Hillerich &

Bradsby thirty-four-inch bat that Mr. Kershaw thought could be glued. It had been a mistake to go from oak to maple, he said. Eventually, Mrs. Kershaw would appear, mopping her hands on her apron before making an announcement: "Kershaw dinner. All other players begone." Owen and the other boys would rush out, with ceremonial doorway collisions, looking up at the sky through the trees: still light enough to play.

Owen would walk home, reflecting on the game, his hits, if he'd had any, his errors and fielding accomplishments. His parents dined late and by candlelight, in an atmosphere that was disquieting to Owen and at odds with thoughts about baseball. He eventually gave up on family dinners altogether and fed himself on cold cereal. Sometimes he arrived home in time for an argument, his father booming over his mother's more penetrating vehemence. There were times when his parents seemed to be entertaining themselves this way, and times when they seemed to draw blood. Owen would flip his glove onto the hall bench and slip upstairs to his room and his growing collection of hubcaps. He'd still never been caught. He had once been on probation with the Kershaws, though: Doug, hiding in the bushes with a flashlight, had caught him soaping their windows on Halloween, but winter had absolved him, and by baseball season he was back in their good graces. He still didn't know why he had done it. The Kershaws' was the only house he'd pranked, and it was the home of people he cherished. He'd wanted contact with them, but it had come out wrong.

OWEN SAT WITH BEN ON THE SCHOOL BUS EVERY MORNING. Half asleep, his lunch box on his lap, he listened to Ben ramble on in his disjointed way about the baseball standings, his mouth falling open between assertions—"If Jerry Priddy didn't hold the bat so high, he could hit the ball farther"—and his crooked arms mimicking the moves he described: George Kell's signature scoop at third or Phil Rizzuto's stretch to loosen his sleeve after throwing someone out. Only Ben, whose bed was like a pass between two mountains of *Baseball Digest* back issues, would have remembered that Priddy had torn up Rizzuto's fan letters. Yet in almost every other way, he was slow and easily influenced by anyone who took the trouble: Chick Terrell lost a year of Kershaw baseball for sending Ben on a snipe hunt.

The MacIlhatten twins, Janet and Janice, sat at the back of the bus, two horsey, scheming freshmen who dressed alike, enjoyed pretending to be each other, and amused themselves by playing tricks on Ben, hiding his hat or talking him out of the Mars bar in his lunch box. They laughed at his blank stare or repeated everything he said until he sat silent in defeat. Idle malice was their game, and, because they were superior students, they got little resistance from adults. Not entirely pretty themselves, they were brutal to Patty Seitz and Sandy Collins, two unattractive girls unlucky enough to ride the same bus, who quietly absorbed the twins' commentary on their skin, their hair, their Mary Jane shoes, and their Mickey Mouse lunch boxes. Only Stanley Ayotte, who was often suspended, except during football season, when he was a star, stood up to the twins, and to their intervening mother, actually calling them bitches. They flirted with Stanley anyway, though he ignored it.

Owen felt the twins' contemplation of his friendship with Ben: they were watching. At school, they disappeared down the corridor and forgot about him, but on the bus at the end of the day they resumed their focus. His rapt absorption in Ben's recitation of baseball statistics seemed to annoy them, but, because they understood nothing about the subject, he had been safe so far.

The school knew about Ben's love of sports. His schoolwork was managed with compassion, but water boy for the football team was the best the teachers could come up with on the field. Still, it was a job he loved, running out in front of the crowded bleachers with a tray of water-filled paper cups.

CHURCH. OWEN HATED CHURCH AND FIDGETED HIS WAY FROM beginning to end. Or maybe not all of it, not the part where he stared at some girl like Cathy Hansen, the plumber's beautiful daughter. The moment when Cathy turned from the Communion rail, her hands clasped in front of her face in spiritual rapture, took Owen to a dazed and elevated place. He wondered how such a girl could stand to listen to a priest drone on about how to get to heaven. Cathy must have registered his attention. After Mass, she sometimes tried to exchange a pleasantry, but Owen could only impersonate disdain from his reddening face, his agony noticed with amusement by his mother, when she wasn't gazing down the sidewalk in search of a good spot for a cigarette. After contemplating the suffering of Christ, she needed a bit of relief. Owen's father had slipped an Ellery Queen novel into the covers of a daily missal; he kept his eye on the page, presenting a picture of piety. He saw his presence at the weekly service as an expression of his solidarity with the community, sitting, standing, or kneeling following cues provided by the parishioners around him.

The slow drive home after church was a trial for Owen, who could picture the game already under way on the Kershaws' diamond. Slow because they had to creep past the Ingrams' driveway. Old Bradley Ingram had married the much-younger Julie, who claimed to have been a Radio City dancer but was suspected of having been a stripper at the downtown Gaiety Burlesque House. Now they were separated. Bradley had moved into the Sheraton, and Julie was still in their home, receiving, it was said, all-night visitors. Julie did not mingle locally, and so no information could be gotten from her. The best Owen's parents could do was check out her driveway on the way home from church.

His father stopped the car so that they could peer between the now-unkempt box hedges. His mother said, "It's a Buick Roadmaster."

"I can't see the plates. I don't have my glasses."

"They're Monroe."

"That tells us nothing."

"Really?" His mother blew smoke at the ceiling of their Studebaker. "Last week it was a Cadillac."

"She's coming down in the world."

"Not by much," his mother said, and they drove on.

Owen was required to stay at the table for Sunday lunch, which went on until the middle of the afternoon. Usually, he missed the game.

IN THE HARDWOOD FOREST, A SHALLOW SWAMP IMMERSED the trunks and roots of the trees near the lake. Owen and Ben hunted turtles among the waterweeds and pale aquatic flowers. The turtles sunned themselves on low branches hanging over the water, in shafts of light spotted with dancing dragonflies. Ever alert, the creatures tumbled into the swamp at the first sound, as though wiped from the branches by an unseen hand. The wild surroundings made Ben exuberant. He bent saplings to watch them recoil or shinnied up trees, and he returned home carrying things that interested him—strands of waterweed, bleached muskrat skulls, or the jack-in-the-pulpits he brought to his mother to fend off her irritation at having to wash another load of muddy clothes. Once, Owen caught two of the less vigilant turtles, the size of fifty-cent pieces, with poignant little feet constantly trying to get somewhere that only they knew. Owen loved their tiny perfection, the flexible undersides of their shells, the ridges down their topside that he could detect with his thumbnail. Their necks were striped yellow, and they stretched them upward in their striving. Owen made a false bottom for his lunch box with ventilation holes so that he could always have them with him, despite the rule against taking pets to school or on the school bus. He fed them flies from a bottle cap. Only Ben knew where they were.

One afternoon, Owen came back from the swamp to find the flashing beacon of the town's fire truck illuminating the faces of curious neighbors outside his house. He ran up the short length of his driveway in time to see his mother addressing a small crowd as she stood beside two firemen in obsolete leather helmets with brass eagles fixed to their fronts. She looked slightly disheveled in a housedress and golf-club windbreaker, and she spoke in the lofty voice she used when she had been drinking, the one meant to fend off all questions: "Let he who has never had a kitchen grease fire cast the first stone!" She laughed. "Blame the television. Watching *The Guiding Light.* Mea culpa. A soufflé." Owen felt the complete bafflement of the neighborhood as he listened. Then her tone flattened. "Look, the fire's gone. Good night, one and all."

Owen's father's car nosed up to the group. His father jumped out, tie loosened, radiating authority. He pushed straight through to the firefighters without glancing at his wife. "Handled?" The shorter of the two nodded quickly. His father spoke to the neighbors: "Looks like not much. I'll get the details, I'm sure." Most had wandered off toward their own homes by then, the Kershaws among the last to go. Owen's father turned to his wife, who was staring listlessly at the ground, placed his broad hand on the small of her back, and moved her through the front door, which he closed behind him, leaving Owen alone in the yard.

When Owen went in, his parents were sitting at opposite sides of the kitchen table, the *Free Press* spread out in front of them. The brown plastic Philco murmured a Van Patrick interview with Birdie Tebbetts: it was the seventh-inning stretch in the Indians game. Owen's father motioned to him to have a seat, which he did while trying to get the drift of the interview. His mother didn't look up, except to access the flip lid on her silver ashtray. She held a Parliament between her thumb and middle finger, delicately tapping the ash free with her forefinger. His father flicked the ash from his Old Gold with his thumbnail at the butt of the cigarette and made no particular effort to see that it landed in the heavy glass ashtray by his wrist. Commenting on what he had just read, his father said, "Let's blow 'em up before they blow us up!"

"Who's this?" his mother said, but got no answer. Instead, she turned to Owen. "Your father and I are going to take a break from each other."

"Oh, yeah?"

"We thought you'd want to know."

"Sure."

His father lifted his head to glance at Owen, then returned to the paper. Owen knew better than to say a single word, unless it was about the weather. He wanted his parents to be distracted, so that he could fit in more baseball and get any kind of haircut he liked, but he worried about things falling apart entirely. He was unable to picture what might lie beyond that. School, of course, out there like a black cloud.

His mother said, "Ma said she'd take me in."

At this, his father raised his head from the paper. "For God's sake, Alice, no one is 'taking you in.' You're not homeless."

"Why don't *you* go someplace, and I'll stay here? Maybe someone will take *you* in."

"I'll tell you why: I've got a business to run." His business, which dispatched plumbers and electricians to emergencies, was called

Don't Get Mad, Get Egan and made the sort of living known as decent. With tradesmen on retainer, he worked from an office, a hole-in-the-wall above a florist's shop. An answering service gave the impression that it was a bigger operation than it was.

"Ma will think you've failed."

"Well, you tell Ma I haven't failed."

"No, you tell her, sport."

"I'm not calling your mother to tell her that I haven't failed. That doesn't make sense. Owen, where have you been? You look like you've been in the swamp."

"I've been in the swamp."

"Would you like to add anything to that?"

"No."

His mother stubbed out her cigarette and said, "I think you owe your father a more complete answer, young man."

"It's nothing more than a little old swamp," Owen said. "Mind turning that up? It's the top of the eighth."

Nobody was going anywhere except back to the newspaper.

MR. KERSHAW WAS AN AGRICULTURAL CHEMIST FOR THE state—a white-collar position that was much respected locally—but, despite his sophisticated education and job, he was a country boy through and through, with all the practical and improvisatory skills he'd acquired growing up on a subsistence farm. He wore bib overalls on the weekends and had a passion for Native American history. He was interested in anything from the remote past. He had a closet full of Civil War muskets that had been passed down through his family and a cutlass given by a slave on the Underground Railroad to a forebear who had run a safe house on the route to Canada. This same forebear, by family legend, while pretending to help find a runaway, had pushed a Virginia slave hunter out of a rowboat and held him off with an oar until he drowned.

When baseball was rained out one Saturday, Mr. Kershaw took Owen aside. "How's everything at your house?"

"Great," Owen said suspiciously, assuming he was being asked about the grease fire in the kitchen.

Mr. Kershaw looked at him closely and said, "Now, Owen, after it rains I hunt arrowheads. The rain washes away the soil around them, and if you're lucky you can see them. My boys don't care, but maybe you'd like to come along."

THEY DROVE A FEW MILES TO A FARM THAT BELONGED TO A friend of Mr. Kershaw's. The long plowed rows in front of the farmhouse stretched to a line of trees that shielded the fields from wind off the lake. A depression, not quite plowed in, ran diagonally across the main field, from corner to corner.

"That was a creek, Owen. The Potawatomi hunted and camped along it. Their palisades were right over there, where you see the stacks of the electric plant. So you go down the left side of the old creek, and I'll go down the right. If you have anything at all on your mind, you will never find an arrowhead."

The two walked in close sight of each other, staring at the ground. From time to time, Mr. Kershaw stooped to examine something, while Owen strained to catch sight of an arrowhead among the stones. At length, Mr. Kershaw summoned him to look at a broken point. Owen was amazed to see how its symmetrical flakes distinguished it from an ordinary stone. When Mr. Kershaw called him over again, he had an arrowhead in his hand, perfect as a jewel. "Bird point," Mr. Kershaw said, and Owen stared in possessive longing. Mr. Kershaw dropped it into his shirt pocket with a smile. "Don't think and you'll find one," he said.

Owen resumed the search with greater intensity as they approached the row of trees, whose tops were ignited by lake light. Sticking out of a clod was a pale-white object that Owen picked up and gazed at without recognition. "What've you got there?" Mr. Kershaw called. "Bring it here." Owen crossed the depression and handed it to Mr. Kershaw. "Oh, you lucky boy. It's a"—he shook dirt from it—"French trade pipe. Indians got them from the trappers such a long time ago. Want to swap for my arrowhead?"

"Which is worth more?"

Mr. Kershaw laughed. "Probably your trade pipe, but that's a good question. So good, in fact, that I'll give you my arrowhead.

Perhaps I'll find another." He reached into his shirt pocket, removed the arrowhead, and dropped it, warm, into Owen's palm, where its glittering perfection nearly overwhelmed him.

The ground had dried, and by the time Owen got back to the diamond the other boys were choosing up sides. Mike Stallings was captain of one team and Bobby Waldron captain of the other. Owen wanted to put his finds in a safe place; he ran toward his house, a hand pressed over the lumps of arrowhead and clay pipe in his shirt pocket, the late sun starting to flash from the windows of the neighborhood, a lake freighter moaning as it passed to the east.

THE EARLY FOOTBALL GAME WITH FLAT ROCK A WEEK LATER was played under lights and in the mud from another afternoon rain. It was a bloody affair from the start, with poorly understood game plans and pent-up, random excitement among the players. At the end of the first quarter, Ben dashed out with his tray of water, tripped, and fell in a melee of paper cups. The stands erupted in laughter. Owen ran onto the field and squatted beside Ben to pick up the mess, stacking wet cups while Ben stood by, helpless and ashamed. The players waited, hands on hips, while Ben and Owen carried the remains back to the sidelines. The game resumed, and Owen wandered behind the bleachers, hoping that Flat Rock would kick the home team's asses and give the handful of visitors something to cheer about. He headed over to the parking lot, thinking he might spot some Oldsmobile spinner hubcaps to steal for his collection but settled for a set of Pontiac baby moons, which he stashed in the bushes to be picked up later. The car didn't look quite the same with its greasy wheel studs exposed, and he really wanted to stop there, but then he saw Bradley Ingram's Thunderbird and soon had all four of its dog-dish ten-inch caps.

On the bus the next morning, the twins were arguing with each other, a welcome change, as it kept their attention away from others. Ben watched them with delight, despite all their teasing. The twins were as knowledgeable about radio hits as Ben was about baseball, and he was drawn to their statistical world. Also, he had begun to notice girls. These days he often sat at the back of the bus by the twins, who seemed to regard him as a trophy stolen from Owen. They sensed that Owen's popularity was falling, and they enjoyed seeing him sitting by himself. On good days now, Ben was their playmate, their mascot. They alone—thanks to their status— could make liking Ben fashionable. Owen used his new privacy to peek into the false bottom of his lunch box and check on the well-being of his turtles. He liked finding his bottle cap empty of flies. The safety patrol, an unsmiling senior with angry acne and an attitude that went with the official white belt across his chest, had been steadily expanding his list of prohibitions from standing while the bus was in motion to eating from lunch boxes and arm wrestling. He had never bothered Owen but appeared to watch him in expectation of an infraction. Owen watched him back.

The low autumn light left barely enough time for a few innings after school. The chalk on the base paths had faded into the under- lying dirt, and a ring of weeds had formed around third base. Horse chestnuts were strewn across the road between the Kershaws' house and the diamond. Somehow, partial teams were fielded, though even the meagerest grounders ended up in the outfield, to be run down by Stanley Ayotte, who was proud of his arm and managed to rifle them back. Shortstop had been eliminated for lack of candidates. The score ran up quickly.

Owen's father appeared and boomed that an umpire was needed. He hung his suit coat on the backstop, tugged his tie to one side, stepped behind the catcher, folded his arms behind him, and bent forward for the next pitch. There was no next pitch. The players saw his condition, and the game dissolved. As Owen started to walk home with his father, Mr. Kershaw, observant, came out his front door and gave them a curt wave. Owen tried to think of hub- caps he didn't have yet while his father strode along, looking far ahead into some empty place toward home.

On the school bus the next day, Owen fielded questions about "the ump" and sat quietly, sensing the small movements of the turtles in the bottom of his lunch box, which was otherwise filled with the random sorts of things his mother put in there—Hostess Twinkies, not particularly fresh fruit, packaged peanut butter and crackers. Ben was sitting on the broad bench seat at the back, between the twins, who tied things in his hair and pretended to help him with his homework while enjoying his incomprehension. He must have begun to feel rewarded by his limitations. The twins whispered to each other and to Ben and made his face red with the things they said. Then Ben told the twins about Owen's turtles, and the twins told the safety patrol, who towered over Owen's seat and asked to see his lunch box.

"Why do you want to see it?"

"Give it to me."

"No."

The safety patrol worked his way forward to the driver and said something, then returned. "Give it to me or I'm putting you off the bus."

Owen slowly handed the lunch box to him. The safety patrol undid the catch, opened the lid, and dumped the food. Then he pried out the false bottom and looked in. "You know the rules," he said. He gingerly lifted the turtles out of the box, leaned toward an open window, and threw them out. Owen jumped up to see them burst on the pavement. He fell back into his seat and pulled his coat over his head.

"You knew the rules," the safety patrol said.

Life went on as though nothing had happened, and nothing really had happened. Ben was the twins' plaything for several months, and then something occurred that no one wanted to talk about—if one twin was asked about it, the question was referred to the other—and Ben had to transfer to a special school, one where he couldn't come and go as he pleased, or maybe it was worse than that, since he was never seen at home again or in town or on the football field with his water tray. Owen continued to attend the football games, not to watch but to wander the darkened parking lot, building his hubcap collection. As time went on, it wasn't only the games: any public event would do.

ON A DIRT ROAD

I'D HAVE THOUGHT WE WOULD HAVE MET THE JEWELLS sooner, since we all had the same commute down the long dirt road to the interstate and thence to town and jobs; to say they never reached out would be an understatement. The first year they didn't so much as wave to either Ann or me, a courtesy conspicuously hard to avoid given that passing on our road is virtually a windshield-to-windshield affair, and an even slightly averted gaze is a very strong bit of semaphore. That we could see their faces in extraordinary detail, his round and pink with rimless glasses, hers an old bohemian look with stringy hair parted in the middle, hardly seemed to matter. He looked sharply toward us while she just stared away.

"It's just fine with me," Ann said. "We don't spend nearly enough time with the friends we already have."

"Oh, baby, we need new ones."

"No, not really. We've got good friends."

"Like the vaunted Clearys?" I was egging her on.

"That wasn't great, I'll admit," she said. "Maybe they need another chance." This was a reference to a dinner celebrating the Clearys' seventeenth wedding anniversary. The big party on an odd year was their idea of a joke. They had us wearing paper hats and twirling noisemakers, all part of their bullying cheer, which made us feel they were making fun of us. I wouldn't have put it past a guy like Craig Cleary, regional super-salesman and fireworks mogul, with a Saddam Hussein mustache that somehow matched the black bangs his dour wife wore down to her eyebrows. Before we even went, I had told Ann that I'd rather go to town and watch haircuts, but she pronounced the whole thing clever. "Cleary's an oxygen thief," I pleaded. "You can hardly breathe around him."

Unneighborly though they were, the Jewells had the fascination of mystery, but that was likely due to the extent of their remodeling project. For half a year, tradesmen were parked all around their house, the familiar plumber and electrician, but also the wildly expensive Prairie Kitchens people must have been there for two months, with those long slabs of polished black granite in the front yard lying under a tarp that blew off regularly and was just as regularly replaced. "It's granite," I said. "Stop worrying about it."

Ann said, "Could they be building a restaurant?"

The Jewells would keep us wondering, and I thought we agreed about the Clearys. So after a perfectly pleasant ride home through the tunnel of cottonwood one night, I met Ann's announcement of the Clearys' invitation that we meet them at Rascal's for pizza with regrettable thoughtlessness: "No fucking way," I think is what I said. Or "Fuck no." Or "Is this a fucking joke?" Something like that. As I say, thoughtless. Ann didn't take it well.

"If memory serves, you were the one clamoring to get out more."

"I wasn't 'clamoring.' What's more, these people aren't promising." All I wanted was my chair and the six o'clock news, not pizza peppered with Craig Cleary's rapid-fire hints as to how I might turn my career around.

"You're not even a little tempted?"

"No."

"But I accepted!" I was thunderstruck and all too mindful of how lovely she looked as she primped for this pizza outing in town, a wholly inauspicious occasion to which she seemed excitedly committed. She wore the flowered silk skirt with the delicate uneven hem that she knew to be my favorite and the linen shirt with pleats, another of my favorites, both of which had been hibernating in her closet. All these preparations for pizza with two boors? When I caught her taking a final glance in the hall mirror, I detected distinct approval. As she left, she chortled, "I hope you don't feel stuck!"

"We have two cars," I said cheerfully.

I admit that I was aware of our isolation and in a way glad to see her take the lead in freshening things up. But we'd been through at least one so-called social occasion with the Clearys, and I thought our disapproval was solid. I remember asking Ann on the way home, "How about the 'Moroccan cuisine'? We should have called them on it: *Moroccan? Moroccan how?*"

Ann had said, "But exactly." At that time.

So finding myself at loose ends because of the Clearys of all people came as a surprise. I pulled open the door to the refrigerator
hoping to ignite my appetite, but I got no farther than lifting a piece
of Black Diamond cheddar to my scrutiny before returning it and
closing the door. I went into the mudroom and looked at my car
through the window, trying to think of something I could do with
it. I really wasn't used to Ann going off like this on her own. I have
a way of extolling peace and quiet in theory without enjoying it in
practice and end up fending off the idea that I've been abandoned.
As I've grown older, I've begun listing my more regrettable traits,
and this one has always made the cut. I think the list was supposed
to help me improve myself, but it's turned out to be just another
list alongside yard chores, oil changes, and storm windows.

I've been out of the legislature for over a year, and it has not
been the best thing in the world for our relationship, though I
just hate to use that word. I served one term and made my values
plain to the voters—respect for the two-parent household, preda-
tor control, and reduced death taxes for the family farm. When I
ran for a second term, fringe groups twisted everything I'd said,
and the net result was this Assiniboin half-breed named Michelle
Red Moon Gillespie cleaned my clock, leaving her wigwam for the
capitol in Helena while I, unwilling to resume my job as a travel
agent, headed home to try to figure out what was next. I kept my
office in town on the theory that something would come along, but
nothing did. It allowed me at least to keep Ann at bay while I tried
to think, and we went on referring to it as "my job." Eventually,
my weakened state was something she could smell, and once or
twice I caught her regarding me in a way I never saw when she was
frisking around the Governor's Ball or any other time when I was a
senator. We talked about the early days of our marriage, before the
travel agency, before state politics, before we learned there would
not be children. We were going to get the fuck out of Montana and
buy a schooner. We even flew to Marina del Rey to look at it parked
there among thousands of other boats that never went anywhere. I
said, "You know, I just can't see it."

Ann said, "You're not serious! I've heard nothing but 'schooner'
for the last five years!"

"It was only a dream."

"I'll give you dream. Don't do this to me again."

The captain came out of the cabin in a cloud of marijuana smoke to ask if we were interested. He said he was tired of life at sea and was going to carry the anchor inland until someone asked him what it was. There he would settle down, find himself a gal of Scandinavian heritage, and raise a family. He kept looking hungrily at Ann, then back at me with an expression that said, *What's she doing with you?*

We flew home, and Ann began tap-dancing lessons. One day when I'd forgotten, she told me to flush the toilet immediately, adding, "In this matter, timeliness counts. I can't be expected to review your diet at this remove." That was one of the low points and yet another hint that my idleness was so complete that I no longer remembered to flush the toilet.

By way of placating my instantaneous loneliness in Ann's absence, I decided to visit the Jewells and find out why anyone would get so involved in remodeling such a plain house, one probably built on the cheap to judge by the rusty stovepipe sticking out the top. Their place was so close, I almost didn't need to drive, though I did so very slowly, without listening to the radio or anything else as I thought about why I was doing this at all. I figured that it was a bit like having a drink, just a matter of changing gears. I didn't know why Ann would want to join the Clearys. Was she that bored? Did I bore her? I certainly wasn't entertaining myself. So going to visit the Jewells was not just a matter of breaking the ice with inscrutable neighbors but, frankly, to get myself out of our settled cottage with its old trees and vines, even for a short journey to what looked like remodeling hell a mile down the road. Would the Jewells peek at me through a crack of their front door and ask what I wanted? Would they pretend they weren't at home? Either way it would be more interesting than killing time while I waited for Ann to return. A pleasant jolt of the unfamiliar ought to have been within my capacities. I might cook it up as an enchanting tidbit for Ann.

I felt newly alive as I looked for a place to park in front of the Jewells' house amid the building supplies, camper shell, cat travel crates, cement mixer. Two things struck me: the drawn curtains and pirate flag fluttering from the pole in the front yard. Also, the manufacturer's stickers on the plate-glass windows had not been removed. As I passed the upended canoe going to the door, several cats ran out, one climbing the only tree in the yard. When I knocked, the door opened so quickly as to confirm that I'd been observed.

"How did you find a place to park in all that junk?"

Jewell's teeth were big for his face, or he was just too thin for them, but his smile was intense and welcoming all the same. We were nearly the same height, so his eager proximity was especially notable. I found myself leaning back. He was very glad to see me!

"I thought we'd never meet!" he cried. "Bruce."

"Well, here I am!" I exclaimed, sounding exceptionally stupid. "Bruce."

"You can say that again!" Was Jewell being ironic? The all-knowing look you get when you buy rimless glasses seemed at odds with his guileless enthusiasm. I was confused. "We don't allow smoking," he added. For just a moment, I thought Jewell was fucking with me, but the thought passed as I followed him into the house, his windmilling arms leading the way. That he was barefoot was not so remarkable given that he was at home, but it seemed at odds with his somewhat-spiffy attire, slacks and smoking jacket. Bruce was a little younger than me, and painted toenails might have been a generational thing I missed.

"What's with the pirate flag?"

"Oh, Nell and I have a kind of game. I pretend I'm a pirate, and she's a royal prisoner." Jewell shifted into a guttural "pirate" voice: "You look after the old lady and I shall see to the daughters."

"Is that Blind Pew?" I asked.

"Oh God, no. Anyway, at first we were going to be cowboys—here's my study—and then astronauts. At the moment, it's pirates, but who knows. Nell, thank goodness, has a private income. Being a programmer was more a matter of my personal dignity, but oh well, what's the use of that? Life is short, don't you agree, might as well enjoy it."

Opening the door to the study, Jewell called out, Ed McMahon style, "Heeeeeere's, Nell!" And indeed there she was in a prospect of piled Lego pieces, with a large picture of the finished model thumbtacked to the wall next to her: the Leaning Tower of Pisa. "She's already done Big Ben. So she's ready to move up the Architecture Series. This one got a great review in Eurobricks, didn't it, Nell?" Her face had no expression of any kind, and she was wearing a wash dress of the sort seen in WPA photographs. "We got sidetracked by the Royal Baby Series when Kate's little Prince George of Cambridge was commemorated with a fifty-five-brick pram."

"I want a baby!" boomed Nell.

Jewell seemed not to have heard and introduced us. Nell struggled to respond. There was something wrong with Nell, big-time. Retarded, I think, but healthy otherwise and rather pretty. She stood up and smiled, quite a nice smile, and said with extraordinary deliberation, "Hullo."

Jewell said, "Why don't I just leave you two for a moment and let you get acquainted."

I instinctively turned as though to follow Jewell out the door, but it was gently closed in my face. Nell said, "We don't serve drinks in here."

"Ah."

"But we do have healthful snacks."

"Thank you, but I'm okay."

"This puzzle is very time-consuming."

She had a gentle, crooning voice that, once I absorbed its strangeness, was so soothing as to be almost hypnotic. She told me the puzzle didn't really interest her and that before her accident she had seen the real Tower of Pisa and that hadn't interested her either. I began to ask what sort of accident, to which she answered preemptively, "Bicycle," before going on to tell how on Tuesday she got lost in the woods behind the house and that it didn't bother her but it bothered "Bruce" and, because it had, she was sad all day, until "Bruce" made her pancakes with blueberry syrup and after that they were fine about the woods and what she was doing there.

The door opened and Jewell, now shod—they looked like bowling shoes—entered briskly and said, "Just that little bit past name and face makes everyone more comfortable. So you're Hoyt, right? Okay, Hoyt, I was going to throw something together for Nell and me. Care to join us? Not promising a lot because the kitchen is a work in progress, to say the very least."

This is when lightning struck. I glanced at Jewell in his suspenders and bowling shoes, and at Nell in her clean Depression shift, and said, "Why don't we run down to Rascal's and split a pizza? My treat."

Before Bruce could answer, Nell clapped her hands and bayed, "I love pizza!"

"You really want to take us on, Hoyt? We've only just met, and we can be a handful. Nell is very active, aren't you, Nell?"

I had enough on my hands to understand why I had cooked up the invitation at all. My hands were already pretty full trying to figure out what I could have been thinking in the first place. I tried to sell myself the idea that this would be a rescue operation to save Ann from the wearisome Clearys, but that still left me with the original bafflement as to why she wanted to meet them at all. Nevertheless, everything would be quite clear when the Jewells sat down at the table. The introductions would be interesting, and Nell versus the pizza menu could be a real hoot, since Rascal's had about a hundred toppings.

Nell made me promise to help her with the puzzle later, and when I agreed she looked at me quite pointedly and said that she was not a vegetable. I assured Nell that indeed she was not, and Jewell smiled his assent. We stood around for a bit while he set the burglar alarms, an exercise I failed to understand. The Jewells must have come from someplace where this was necessary. Their clothing seemed rural, backwoods almost, but had something of the costume about it. "Pizza!" said Jewell. "What an idea! Nell, when was the last time we had pizza?"

"Two Thanksgivings ago," said Nell sternly.

"Did we enjoy it?" asked Jewell.

Nell said, "How should I know?"

I wanted to get in on this somehow and asserted that you could get turkey as a topping at Rascal's, but the two just gazed at me thoughtfully as though the meaning of this would come to them if they were patient.

In any case, we'd have to hurry along if we were going to catch Ann and the Clearys. Afterward, once she got her face out of the pizza, she could pitch in on her Legos. Ha! These were brave thoughts: I still couldn't believe she'd prefer dinner with the Clearys to codependent nattering with me in our enchanted cottage with its vine-crowded windows.

We took my car; in fact I didn't see one at the Jewells'. En route, I let them in on the setup: "My wife, Ann, is dining with the Clearys, and I thought it might be fun to join them as a kind of surprise and give you a chance to meet not only Ann but the Clearys, Craig and Bonny, because Craig runs an international fireworks company right from his house, and Bonny heads up the county commissioners, in case you need some rules bent."

Nell said, "Can I play the radio?"

"We're talking, Sweet Pea, can't you see that?"

Nell looked puzzled. "I can hear you talking . . ."

"Hush, now," Jewell said to her rather more firmly. We were at highway speed when Nell rolled down the window and stuck her head out, the wind inflating her cheeks. Our mail and several documents I'd left in the backseat were now whirling around the inside of the car. Jewell raced to batten them down, but Nell just kept hanging her head out, her hair streaming all the way past the rear window. "Guy clipped her and kept going. Forget about the helmet. Shattered like an egg. We're talking former Miss Utah runner-up." I thought about this and then sought to change the subject.

"What's your business . . . ?"

"Bruce. I sold my original business and ten-thirty-oned it into self-storage. Now my job is limited to welcoming receipts."

"Your original business was?"

"Nutritional supplements, weight-loss products, essential oils, pet vitamins, the usual. I ran it right here in town. Now it's in a portfolio somewhere, probably Bahrain." Bruce pulled Nell back into her seat by her shirt collar and rolled up the window. She slumped and stared at the dark radio dial.

"Where is your car?"

"Do we have a car?"

Nell said, "We have a car. Ours is a sedan."

What would have unnerved me otherwise, I welcomed: Wait'll I load this duo onto Ann and the Clearys. "Why can't she listen to the radio."

"She can listen to the radio but not while we're talking. We've covered the main stuff. Now she can listen. There's a time and a place for everything." I rejoiced at this clodhopper's philosophy.

Nell turned the radio on, dialing around until she found a classical station and the mournful sound of an oboe, which seemed to settle her down. As though speaking only to herself, she said that she had never been to Bahrain, either in a sedan or any other way. "It's across the ocean," barked Jewell.

Nell said, "A truck hit me."

"Poor Nell."

"A small red Japanese truck with Idaho plates and a woman driver."

"See what bubbles up?" said Jewell.

Nell said, "Handel Oboe Concerto in G Minor," and raised the volume, cupping her hand over the knob so that no one would be able to interfere. Her brows raised, eyes bright, mouth wide open, she was in awe.

Jewell said, "As discussed."

After listening to the music intently for several minutes, Nell said, "Bruce only likes stupid hillbillies. I take him for what he is."

I was confused: Nell was mentally challenged, underappreciated, and had a killer body. A guy could get into a world of hurt with such mixed signals. I concentrated on the road and reflected that nothing would alleviate my present anxieties like a bulletproof spell of adultery. The ex-Miss-Utah-runner-up thing had an enticing ring of prestige as well, and I was up for leaning into her Tower of Pisa problem.

"What are you, anyway?" she asked her husband.

I pulled into the parking lot of Rascal's Pizzeria and found a slot between a rusted-out Pontiac GTO and a home-oxygen supply van with a kayak rack on top. A light rain had begun to fall, and when Nell got out, she danced around, head thrown back, tongue wiggling and palms up. It was crazy but kind of infectious. Jewell caught her eye, raised a warning finger, and her arms dropped to her sides. Then Bruce pivoted toward the front door. "We surf the toppings." Nell and I followed, and I was startled when she sought my hand, like a child. I thought I'd extract it, then thought I'd just let it ride and watch for Ann's reaction. Even in the shift, Nell was eye-catching and would remain so until her behavior was observed.

Looking around the half-filled room, I said, "Let me see if I can spot them." Rascal's had turned into something of a sports bar, with armatured TV screens hung all around the room, speakers blaring. Servers in the lavender Rascal's uniform hunched over beers while keeping eyes on the screens, some of which showed a demolition derby in Wyoming; one was playing an interview with A-Rod as to his health, and yet another displayed a girl weeping in some jungle setting, holding a revolver. I regarded each of these as a distraction, ground clutter keeping me from finding my wife. Jewell was right in front of me, thumbs in his suspenders. "What say we eat?"

"Sure, Bruce, grab a table. We can always move."

"Not once I tuck into a family size. I could eat a horse."

"I'm soooooo hungry!" cried Nell.

They weren't here, and I was very abruptly frantic. I kept checking my watch as though it could tell me something. I made sure the ring and vibrate features were both activated on my cell phone, probably taking too much time doing so, since before I knew it both the waitress and the Jewells were eyeing me impatiently. I ordered a small house pizza automatically, just to dispel the awkwardness.

"Not even going to check out the toppings?" asked Jewell.

"Got it," said the waitress and sped off.

Jewell said, "You all right?"

"Me? Sure. It's just that I—"

"Maybe she ran away with the circus! Ha-ha-ha!"

"Yeah, that must be it," I mumbled, instantly aware of what must have been my disquieting delivery. In any case, they saw nothing funny and gazed at me quietly, Nell with her own fervor and concern. "The circus," I added.

Why was I so preoccupied? Because I had been deceived by my wife and she had invested some serious planning in this deceit. To what end? To meet someone who was not me and as I awaited a pizza I would have enormous trouble choking down while sitting with two idiots. These were not happy thoughts.

Then it hit me! The Clearys were too good for a pizza joint, and they had changed restaurants. No doubt, one of their children would be happy to tell me which one they had chosen. I excused myself and went outside with the smokers and called the Clearys' house. Craig Cleary answered. "Oh, Craig, hi, Hoyt here. Wasn't tonight the night Ann and I were to meet you at Rascal's?"

"I don't eat at Rascal's. Is that where you are?"

"No big deal. We'll just grab something to go."

"Rascal's! How's Ann taking this?"

"I think she's fascinated in a kind of ironic way."

"Fascinated! What's fascinating at Rascal's?"

I struggled, finally blurting, "The toppings." I disliked this treatment by Craig, and so I repeated firmly, as though training a dog, "The toppings, goddamn it!"

When I got back to the table, Jewell remarked, "Your face could turn wine into vinegar." I took it in stride. I had to. My head was spinning. There was a numb spot on my leg, and my mouth felt like it had been years since my last cleaning. There was only one thing to do: get home before Ann.

"Why is the food taking so long?"

Bruce asked, "First time ordering a pizza, pal?"

"I just found out on the phone that Ann sprained her ankle—"

"Oh, how?"

"Gopher hole."

"A gopher hole!"

"Jesus Christ, do you have to challenge everything?"

"Oh. Oh. Oh. Say, I don't like the way this is heading at all."

"People, people," Nell implored, "let's just simmer on down."

My head was full of a picture of my wife, random and dangerous as a Scud missile. I told the waitress about my emergency, and we soon had the pizzas, packed to go. I grabbed a menu from the counter. Neither of the Jewells spoke as I drove hell-bent back up the dirt road, trees rushing through the side windows, nor when I shoved their pizzas across the seat at them as I parked in front of the darkened house. Jewell said, "Thanks, neighbor," as he got out. "Thanks, a bunch." Nell already in flight across the pea rock that served as a lawn. I was soon home with a drink in hand and thinking, perhaps too much, about Ann with someone else, intimate, of course, but also covered with sweat. How much did I want to know? I seemed to be doing all right with bourbon and abstraction at least not having seen her yet. Fortunately, there was a built-in time frame, since last call at Rascal's would dictate the faux chronology. In this sense, I felt I had my ducks in a row and relaxed for the time being, perusing the Rascal's menu.

As part of financing her education, Ann had served in the navy, where I have no doubt she was the darling of the fleet. When we were courting, I could hardly avoid colliding with one of her amatory enthusiasms, especially the one called Shelley, with his collar-length hair and crew-neck sweaters. Shelley was no seaman; Ann believed him to be a filmmaker. It turned out he was a drug dealer, which remained unclear to Ann until formal charges had been filed. I don't know how that would have turned out if Shelley hadn't gone to prison, where he was rehabilitated as a nurse. He's now at a regional hospital outside Omaha. I refilled my drink and started killing moths to pass the time. At the edge of my consciousness, the mystery of Ann's whereabouts reared its head as often as I could chase it away. I couldn't tell if the whiskey was helping or not; on the one hand, it seemed to numb me to the escalating misery; on the other hand, it made the drama of it more florid. I was like a dog trapped in a hot car. The temptation was to drink more and throw the matter into greater relief on the theory, masquerading as fact, that I would thereby handle the situation with more equanimity, or at least not start a fight that could only enlarge my suffering while making sure Ann shared it. In the end, I realized it wouldn't pay to be drunk, and I dumped my latest refill, taking up instead some microwave popcorn, which I ate from a bowl in the armchair I had positioned to face the front door. I pictured this as a prosecutorial touch, which it might well have been if I'd had any guts. I was still at some remove from recognizing that I was terrified of the truth, and when I thought of the way Ann used emery boards as bookmarks, I felt myself choking with emotion.

Ann came in the door with a blaze of energy and a wildly insincere "Honey, I'm home!" She was a little taken aback to find me hunkered down in the armchair, bowl of popcorn and pizza menu in my lap. And there must have been something in my tone when I asked her about the evening, since she paused with the coat halfway off her shoulders. I could have pressed my face to her crotch and busted her on the spot, but this was not my way. "It was okay," she said. "How good could it have been with the Clearys?"

"Did you stuff yourself?"

She paused before saying, "I've never been that excited about pizza."

"Mozzarella and pepperoni? The usual?"

"Yep."

I raised the menu to my eyes. "Didn't feel like trying the sun-dried tomatoes, anchovies, porcini mushrooms, prosciutto, eggplant—"

"Where'd you get the menu?"

"Rascal's. I thought I'd join you."

Ann finished hanging her coat and came over to where I sat with the bowl.

"Did you put butter on this?"

I felt the shift like a breath.

"No."

Ann took a single piece of popcorn and raised it to her mouth.

"So, how shall we leave it?"

A LONG VIEW TO THE WEST

THE WIND FUNNELED DOWN THE RIVER VALLEY BETWEEN the two mountain ranges, picking up speed where the interstate hit its first long straightaway in thirty miles. Clay's car lot was right on the frontage road, where land was cheap and the wind made its uninterrupted rush whatever the season of the year. Before winter had quite arrived to thicken his blood, while the cattle trucks were still throwing up whirlwinds of cottonwood leaves, the wait between customers seemed endless. He couldn't even listen to the radio anymore. In the snowy dead of winter it was easier somehow. Now, face close to the window, and one hand leaning against the recycled acoustic tile that lined the walls, he stared down at the roofs and hoods of used vehicles in search of a human form.

When, just before lunch, a rancher came in about a five-year-old three-quarter-ton Dodge that Clay had sold him, Clay was glad even to receive a complaint. Barely over five feet tall in his canvas vest and railroad cap, the rancher held a pair of fencing pliers as an invitation to mayhem. He shouted, "It's a lemon!" Clay, trying to lighten the mood, said, "The space shuttle was six billion, and it's a lemon." But he ended up getting sucked into a retroactive guarantee just to keep the guy's business. With my luck, thought Clay, I'll end up throwing a short block into it, or a rear end. Once the rancher, a friend of Clay's father, had the repair deal in hand, he asked, "How's the old man? Gonna pull through?"

"He's just about dead," said Clay emphatically, and went back into the shack with its telephone, cash drawer, and long view of the vehicle lot. At the end of the frontage road, where it met Main Street, a newspaper tumbling through plastered itself against the boarded-up frozen-yogurt stand. The metal sign on wheels in front of the tire-repair shop was flapping back and forth. The Dodge pulled back onto the road and went by the shack. The rancher, barely able to see over the wheel, gave Clay a wave, and Clay smiled broadly, saying "Eat shit!" behind his teeth.

IT WAS REALLY NO LONGER A HOSPITAL, JUST A PLACE PRO-viding emergency care until an ambulance or helicopter could take you to Billings. Three nurses and a doctor were on call. Clay got his father admitted there on the strength of being one of three ranchers who had founded the little hospital when it actually served the rural population then flourishing. It had the advantage of being close to home, with views that meant something to the old man, like the one of the big spring where they'd watered cattle for a century. There was not a lot to be done for him, at least not here. About all anyone could do was listen to his stories, and that seemed enough. Clay of course had heard them all, so there remained only to notice the thickening of detail with each retelling, assuming he could stand to hear his father express yet again his love for the life he'd lived while Clay pondered his own peaked existence at the lot. Should you interrupt the telling, the hard look would return, the face of a man who, throughout his life, had called all the shots that really mattered. Seeing his father in the bed, Clay could hardly help thinking about the ease that lay ahead for him and his sister, even as guilt tore at him. Times had changed all right, but that didn't excuse much.

Weekdays Clay listened for as long as he could; and on weekends his sister, Karen, came over from Powderville, sometimes with one of her kids. There were three boys, but two were too wild for that long a ride. Karen said that while she was gone they always got up to something obnoxious if their dad couldn't find time to come in off the place and kick their asses.

The hospital sat right in the middle of the old Matador pasture, where the longhorns coming up from Texas had recovered from the long trail. Clay's great-grandfather had been one of the cowboys, and the story was that when they first arrived the Indian burials were still in the trees, and the ground was covered with stone tepee rings. A picture of that first roundup crew, with the reps from five outfits lined up in front on their horses, was Bill's most cherished possession, and he fretted constantly about its safekeeping when he was gone. He seemed to feel that no one in his family cared anything about it. That was probably true. Either that or they were sick of hearing about it.

It had begun to rain, and with the rain came the smell of open country. Karen was supposed to have been there already, and Clay really wanted to get back to the lot. No matter how often intuition betrayed him, he could still convince himself that someone was going to come along and buy a car today. Apart from that he felt a little angry, but at what he wasn't so sure, maybe everything.

"I don't know what's keeping her," he said to his father.

"Probably had to wait for Lewis to get out of school or find someplace to stash them two other little shits."

His father couldn't see as far as the door. So when Karen appeared there, she was able to summon Clay discreetly. For a small brunette, in her jeans and boots and hoodie she could be as emphatic as a trooper telling you to pull over. She was proud to be married to a cowboy.

"I've got to take Lewis in for a shot. He got bit by a skunk and, now, the poor little guy is going to have to have that series. So you need to hold the fort."

"My God, Karen, I can't stay anymore. I've been here all morning." He couldn't say he'd been fucked over by that sawed-off rancher just half an hour past breakfast, because Karen had zero sympathy so far as his job was concerned.

Karen said, "You're going to have to," and just walked on out. By the time it had occurred to him to offer to take Lewis for the shot, his sister was gone and his father was awake. What good had it been, the old man herding thousands of cattle over all those years only to wind up with his arms like Popsicle sticks and pissing through a tube. Nothing to show for his trouble but stories his son would have to hear all over again, with no relief but the chance of picking up something new about Leo the Illegal or O.C. or Robert Wood or some horse plowed under way back when. Sometimes during these tales, Clay would think about pole dancers or money pouring out of a slot machine or some decent soul appreciating something he'd done, such as that time he acquired the nearly new fire engine the government had bought because the Indians on the

Rez didn't want it, since they already had a bunch just like it they hadn't gotten around to wrecking. The town enjoyed a lot of use out of that engine, even though no one seemed to remember who found it for them, or even that day the big red beauty first rolled down the street, sirens blazing and blinding chrome all over it. So much for quiet acts of heroism. Maybe it was time to start drawing attention to himself. A Ford dealership in Great Falls was having a Christian fund-raiser with TV stars on Saturday, and something like that might well be in his future. Or just toot his own horn down at the chamber of commerce.

IT WAS THE LAST MOTHER'S DAY BEFORE WORLD WAR II. YOU and Karen was just little bitty. Your ma and me drove into the ranch yard, and Leo, the illegal who worked for me then (*Here we go*, thinks Clay), said some old fellow had arrived about sundown on a wild horse and rolled out his bedroll under the loading chute, put his head on his saddle, and gone to sleep. I had this feeling that it was old Robert Wood, and sure enough it was. (*Yep!*) Of course I caught him before he fell asleep, just caught his eye to tell him I would see him in the a.m. I pretty much knew what he was after. (*So do I.*) He had a band of mares up on the mesa behind our mares, and they were running out with wild horses there. Folks from town had come out from time to time to chase them around, and they was absolutely wild. I had been hoping for the chance to gather them for Robert when we had enough hands, because it wasn't going to be easy at all. (*And what a bitch it would turn out to be.*)

Clay's only defense against these onslaughts was the things he couldn't say aloud.

Several months before this, Robert went out into the sagebrush to catch his red roan stud, which was running with some draft horses by the springs. He came with nothing but a little pan of oats and a lariat. (*Wait'll you see how good this trick works.*) Just as he got his stud caught, one of the draft horses bites the stud, and Robert gets hung up in the rope and dragged. Your uncle O.C. Drury was plowing up wheat stubble about two miles away and saw the dust cloud from where Robert was being hauled. At his age, Robert really never should have lived, but he did. He was in the hospital all winter.

I ran into him after he'd healed some, and he said to me in his kind of whiny voice, "Bill, I been laid up. Can you carry me to the place?" I went with him into his little shack of a cabin, and he stripped down to his long underwear. He pulled back the covers of his bed, and there was a great big nest of mice, just full of little pink babies. He carefully moved them to one side and got in next to them, pulled up the covers, and nodded thanks for the lift. (*Set your watches for hantavirus.*)

Gradually, I heard rumors that he was back at work pulling up his poor fence and halfway cowproofing it. He brought back his black baldies and his bulls. He was even seen crawling around the cockleburs packing a sprayer with a full tank and a rag tied across his face. He had always lived and worked alone and was still on the place where he was born. (*Same dog bit me.*)

Robert was an old-time spade-bit horseman. His horses were quick and bronc-y, and the only safe place around them was on their backs. But they were quiet in a herd of cattle and had the lightest noses in Montana. O.C. Drury hauled cattle as a sideline, and he hated to haul Robert's calves. Invariably, he'd arrive in the ranch yard mid-October, and Robert would complain, "O.C., I'm so shorthanded just now. Would you catch up that bay and help me bring these cattle in?" O.C. would feel obliged, and he'd crawl on the old bay or the old sorrel, both of which would know right away it wasn't Robert Wood. So one false move, and the bronc ride was on. (*Nice way to treat someone helping you out.*)

So I let Robert sleep through the night, and by the time I woke, just before sunup, I could smell his fire and coffee. Then in a bit I could hear Leo's voice, and I knew the two of them were working on a plan. I threw on the lights and got dressed, went into the kitchen, and started cooking. I knew I didn't want to put on a breakfast for everyone. I was buying time, and I was still hoping I could talk Robert out of his dangerous plan to bring these horses off the mesa with such a small crew. Leo came in with Robert, who had to be helped up the steps, and we shared a big breakfast, and then we smoked and shot the shit. Leo was a little Indian-looking feller from Sonora, with black bangs over his face. You couldn't joke with him, because he was always serious, but he could work like nobody's business and make any kind of a horse do like he said, even the ones you'd rather not get on. (*Why would he have a sense of humor? Wasn't nothing around there that was funny.*)

Robert had an old-fashioned, long-nosed face, and you could see a little blue vein in the thin skin of his forehead. He was a puncher who had outlived his time. (*Sound familiar?*) He hated farming and especially alfalfa, which he thought was the enemy of the Old West. I suppose he was seventy-five. The hat he wore was just the way it came out of the box—no crease, no nothing. He wore it year-round. He said a straw hat was a farmer's hat. He said that was what you wore when you went out to view the alfalfa.

We always laid our plans at breakfast, except if I was sitting on the john writing out the day's work on a matchbook cover. Robert wanted us all to go up the switchback together all the way to the mesa. "When we get there," he said, "I'll ride around to the crack." The crack was a deep washout, and Robert didn't want the horses to get past it and escape. Instead, he'd hide in the brush and keep them from getting there. Once they were out on the flat, we'd just ride on past them and turn them down toward my corrals.

That crack was deep and steep, and personally I didn't think Robert was going to be able to turn them there. I felt sure this herd of canners would jump the crack even if it meant breaking their necks and no horse or rider would consider following them. If it had been me, I'd just fog them off toward the neighbors' and gather them up when we had us a big-enough crew. (*Why take a knife to a gunfight?*) But Robert didn't think a lot of our horsemanship after all his years on the N Bar and Niobrara. So I thought better of voicing my doubts.

He looked pretty stove up leading his sorrel mare out of the pen behind the scales and tied her to a plank of the chute, just his kind of horse, sickle hocked, good withers, short pasterns, low crouped, and coon footed, a real mutt of a cow horse you wouldn't take to a halter class. (*In short, the whole reason God invented cars.*) Robert looked barely strong enough to throw his old Miles City saddle up on her or reach over to pull the Kelly Brothers grazer into her mouth. He led her around to the front of the chute, threw one rein up around the horn, and looped the other around the corner post.

She had her nostrils blowed out and white all around her eyes, but then all his horses looked half loco.

Robert limped around to the holding pen, squeaked open that old gate, went inside, crawled up the chute, out the end, and sorta fell onto his horse. She snorted, backed away stretching out that one rein until he could reach down and retrieve it, plait them both through the fingers of his left hand, which he lifted a tiny bit, and the mare sat down on her hocks and backed across the ranch yard. Robert lifted his hand, and she stopped, straightened up, and looked around for some work to do.

Karen came in with Lewis, who wanted to talk about his rabies shot, but Karen raised a finger to her lips, and now all three of us had to hear this damn thing all over again. Lewis at least had a coloring book, and Karen could tap around on her smartphone. I was dying for a cigarette.

Ramrod straight as we go single file up the trail, Robert had his boots plumb home in iron oxbows; he turned to look us over. It wasn't long before we were on top. Leo loped out to the west and made a little dust. His small form sank and then nearly disappeared as he made a big ride around the horses. They had wheeled up to watch him and only began to disperse and feed as the circle he made came to seem too grand to concern them. I was able to ride straight back to the far side of the mesa, and by the time I got there, Leo was closing in my direction and those horses, two miles off, had already begun to drift away.

We rode straight at them, and in two jumps they were smoking. Our horses caught their wildness and for a minute or two were pretty hard to handle, kicking out behind and trying to run slap through their bridles until we got the best of them. (*I admit this is scary.*) The mares had such a cloud of dust behind them it just seemed to drift off into that day's weather, like from a grass fire. We'd seen Robert just float out of there to remind us how coarse broke we had our ponies.

Robert was nowhere in sight, and there was no possible way to turn them down the road the way we had planned. We knew the mares had winded him somewhere because they suddenly slowed down and blew out their nostrils. The crack, which was big enough to be an earthquake fault, was the place to turn them, so long as they didn't try to jump it. All we could do then would be to throw them down the slope and let them play hell with the farming on all those little ranches along the river. What a mess. (*Here comes the part I still like hearing even if I sometimes wish I could have been there.*)

Then, everything changed. Way past the crack, Robert broke out of the brush on his horse. Hell, we didn't even know he was in there, and Leo on the back of his sweaty gelding just looked at me. The mare came out in a flurry, greasewood stobs racking off in the air around her. Those wild horses froze. Either they would leap that crack and fly past him, or Robert could jump it himself and turn them down toward the house. I couldn't see doing much of anything to save this wad of cayuses, Roman noses, and big feet. Back at the time of the Boer War, some remount outfit had turned draft studs to put some size on them, but it turned up in all the wrong places. Leo looked like they hurt his eyes.

They boiled back toward us, and we whooped and hollered at them. Leo took down his slicker and got them bunched up once more toward the trail, where they didn't want to go, but Robert kept yelling for us to drive them. They advanced his way like a bright cyclone; and just before they broke around him, Robert spurred his horse straight at the huge crack like he was riding into hell, but the mare burned a hole in the wind, and when she reached that yawning gap, she just curved up, into the air, Robert easing back into the saddle with his stirrups pushed out in front, the mare's legs reaching toward the far shore. I saw them land, but Leo had his eyes covered.

I guess when the wild horses challenged Robert to raise them, he just raised them out of their chairs, because as he leaned up in his saddle, deep slack of reins hanging under the sorrel's neck, taking time to count them, they were just the quietest most well-behaved herd of critters, ready to jog on home to my corrals. When we had them locked in, Robert said, "There, done. I was afraid we might have trouble with them." He rode over to where he left his bedroll and said to me, "Mind if I ask your Mexican to cheek this mare while I slide off? She's bad to paw at you when you get down. Man'd rather piss down her shoulder than go through that."

In the hall, Clay admired some of Lewis's coloring before following Karen to the cemetery to pick out a plot, leaving Lewis in the car with an electronic game he played with his thumbs. They strolled through the old part with a kind of Boot Hill of wild old-timers, before they hit some of the kids they'd gone to school with, Charlie Derby (gored by a rodeo bull), Milly Makkinen, homecoming queen (overdose), and so on.

They selected a plot near two trees and a long view to the west. "Well," said Karen, "at least we got that out of the way." Efficiency was always her tonic; Clay felt rotten. He stopped to see his father before he locked up at the car shack. He was surprised to find him back so soon. Clay tried to make light of it. He said, "So, I interrupted something? What're you doing?" He wished he hadn't asked.

"Dying. What's it look like?"

Clay didn't know what to say, so he said, "And you're okay with that?"

"How should I know? I've never done it before."

Clay was surprised to feel so shaken. He'd known when he'd brought his father here that it was the end of the trail, but hearing him admit it reminded Clay that he was more frightened than his father was. Soon he would be gone and the stories with him. Maybe he'd be able to remember them during hard times or, really, whenever he needed them. Maybe he needed them now.

THE CASSEROLE

W E WAITED UNDER THE COTTONWOODS FOR THE FERRY TO come back across the Missouri River. But the heat still throbbed from the metal of our car, and it turned out to be better to stand close to the water. The river seemed so big, its incongruous whisper belying its steady speed. Clouds of swallows chased insects over the water, and doves rested in the shadows. My wife kept touching her forehead with a Kleenex and staring across at the ferry, as if to hurry its return. We could see the ferryman chatting with his passengers, which only increased her agitation. We were heading from our home in Livingston to Ellie's family ranch to celebrate our twenty-fifth wedding anniversary. Twenty-five years and no children: her parents had stopped interrogating us about that. They assumed that it was a physical problem that some clinic could solve, but we didn't want children. We lacked the courage to tell them that. We both liked children; we just didn't want any ourselves. There were children everywhere, and we saw no reason to start our own brand. Young couples plunge into parenthood, and about half the time they end up with some ghastly problem on their hands. We thought we'd leave that to others. But my in-laws were elderly, and they had the usual views of hereditary landowners: they longed for an heir. They had acquired their land from my wife's grandfather and, with it, a belief in family values that did not stand up to scrutiny, since most ranches these days were the scene of bitter inheritance battles. But even if my wife had had siblings, she would not have been part of this sort of trouble, as she had never—at least, not since adolescence—wanted to pursue ranch life, rural life, agricultural life. She would have said to a sibling, *Take it! It's all yours. I'm out of here.* There would have been an element of posturing in this, because she was very attached to the land; she just didn't want to own it or do anything with it. Neither did I.

The thing was that we were quite poor. We were both grade-school teachers, and owning a house had been the extent of our indulgences. We loved our house and our work and were suitably grateful for both, though Ellie felt that if I hadn't been so hell-bent on retiring the mortgage we might have done a few more things for fun. My in-laws couldn't believe that we had no interest in owning a ranch that was worth millions. But they wouldn't have allowed us to sell it. We'd be stuck with it if we went along with them, which we weren't about to do, and so now they were stuck with it: cows, farming equipment, fences—the whole enchilada. And they were getting old.

The ranch was going to eat them alive, and they knew it. The fences would fall down; the cows would get out; the neighbors, old friends, would start to think of them as a problem. Once across this river, we'd be heading for a very sad story.

Well, not that sad. They'd had their day, and it was almost over. That's how it is for everybody. They liked to be seen as heroic strivers, alone on the unforgiving prairie, but they could have handed the ranch over, no strings attached, and headed for Arizona; after the sale, there would have been plenty for everybody. I had an extensive collection of West Coast jazz records, including the usual suspects, Gerry Mulligan, Chet Baker, Stan Getz, and so on—not everybody has Wardell Gray and Buddy Collette, but I did—and if I'd had a bit more dough I could have added a room on to our house specifically to house this collection, with an appropriate sound system. But when I complained about things like this to Ellie, she just said, "Cue the violins."

It looked as though our appallingly high-mileage compact car was going to be the only one going on the ferry. My wife and I sat in the front, while the backseat was filled with her belongings, as was the trunk. I had no idea why she'd felt called upon to bring this exalted volume of luggage, unless it was to store things on the ranch that were cluttering up our little house. I could have asked, but I just didn't feel like it.

"I think he's turning around," Ellie said, and I came out of my trance. The cable groaned next to us, and, across the river, I could see the ferry finally moving our way. Ellie was looking forward to this visit. I certainly was not. The ranch was where she had grown up, a nature lover. Despite all its deficiencies, it was her place on earth.

We watched the ferry tack across the Missouri, tugging at an angle to the cable, then landing with a broad thump on the ramp. The ferryman, who was far too young for the wide red suspenders he affected, motioned us forward, and I drove our piece-of-shit car onto the dock.

While we crossed, my wife stood on the ferry deck, looking out at the river, smiling and sighing at the swallows circling the current. I told her that they were just after the bugs. She said she understood that, but they looked beautiful whatever they were doing, all right? I've long had trouble with people picking out some detail of the landscape and pretending it's the whole story, as though, in this case, the blue light around those speeding birds could do anything to mask the desolation of the country north of the river, a land I traverse holding my nose.

"Aren't you going to get out of the car?" she asked.

"Who's supposed to drive it off the ferry?"

I looked away from my wife and turned on the radio: no signal. I thought about her peculiar cheer today. I supposed it was the prospect of seeing her mother and father, of revisiting the scenes of her childhood, which she had done often enough to prove the utter heroism of my patience. Though, in recent times, we had talked less and less, which begged the question: What was there to talk about? We worked and we saved. We saved quite a bit more than Ellie would have, had she been in charge of things. What was becoming a comfortable nest egg would have disappeared in jaunts to Belize or some other place, where Ellie could show more of the body she was so proud of to anyone and everyone. She once had the nerve to point out that all this saving up for old age was remarkable for someone who had so much contempt for the elderly. I said, "Ha-ha-ha." She was going to have to settle for wiggling her butt in the school corridors until the inevitable day when the damn thing sagged.

At last we landed, and I drove off. Ellie was having a lively chat with the ferryman, and she took her time getting back in the car. I stared straight through the windshield until she got around to it. When she climbed in, with a sort of bounce, she exclaimed, "He grew up on the neighbor's place, the Showalters'. He's a Showalter. Graduated from Winnett, where I went."

"Ah, so."

The ranch was no more than half an hour from the ferry. Ellie's excitement grew along the route. Here is a sampler of her exclamations:

· "Look at all the antelope! There must be a hundred of them!"
· "Oh, I can smell the sage now!"
· "This road looks like a silver ribbon!"
· "Those are all red-tailed hawks, just riding that thermal!"
· "Larkspur!"
· "What a grass year! Can you imagine what Dad's calves will look like?"

To this last, I said, "No." I honestly thought she was getting manic as we approached the ranch. Ellie is an enthusiast, but this went well beyond her usual behavior. I don't know if she detected my concern, but she seemed to catch herself and clam up; she was talking less, but I could still feel her glee from my position at the wheel. I wondered if the situation called for a pill.

I drove under the ranch gate, with its iron brand hanging overhead—two inverted Vs, known in the graceful local vernacular as the squaw tits. Dad, as I had long felt obliged to call him, and his wife, Mom, stood at the edge of the yard, framed from behind by their bitter little clapboard house. Dad was in full regalia: Stetson hat, leather vest, cowboy boots, and—this was new—a six-gun. Mom was dressed more conventionally, except for the lace-up boots with her wash dress and the lunch pail she was holding. Believe me, it was Methuselah and his bride at the Grand Ole Opry.

There was something about their expressions that I didn't like. It was my turn to keep busy as I tried to elicit signs of life from this tableau, which now included my somber wife. Dad helped me unload Ellie's considerable luggage, and, once it was all out on the ground, Mom handed me the lunch pail. "What's this?" I asked.

"Something to eat on the way home. A casserole."

I turned to Ellie. Tears filled her eyes. I felt that this could have been handled in another way—without Dad's hand on the gun and so forth. I think, at times like this, your first concern is to hang on to a shred of dignity. If I had a leg to stand on, it was that Ellie was upset and I was not. What kind of idiot puts a casserole in a lunch pail?

After I got back on the ferry, the thought that I was headed . . . home—well, I was not entirely comfortable with this thought, and I didn't enjoy the ferryman staring at me, either, or asking if someone had shot my dog. I just stared out at the river, hardly a ripple in it, and miles to go before the next bend.

MOTHERLODE

In the hotel mirror, Dave adjusted the Stetson he so disliked before pulling on the windbreaker with the cattle-vaccine logo. He was a moderately successful young man, one of many working for a syndicate of cattle geneticists in Oklahoma, employers he had never met. He had earned his credentials from an online agricultural portal, the way other people became ministers, and was astonishingly uneducated in every respect, though clever in keeping an eye out for opportunity. He had spent the night in Jordan at the Garfield, ideal for meeting his local ranch clients, and awoke early enough to be the first customer in the café, where, on the front step, an old dog slept with a gum wrapper stuck to his butt. By the time Dave had ordered breakfast, several ranchers had taken tables and were greeting him with a familiar wave. Then the man from Utah, whom he'd met at the hotel, the one who said he'd come to Jordan to see the comets, appeared in the doorway, looking around the room. He was small and intense, middle-aged in elastic-top pants and flashy sneakers. He caught the notice of several of the ranchers. Dave had asked the elderly desk clerk about the comets. The clerk said, "I don't know what he's talking about and I've lived here all my life. He doesn't even have a car." Though he'd already ordered, Dave pretended to study the menu to keep from being noticed, but it was too late: the man was looming over him, laughing so hard his eyes shrunk to points and his gums showing. "Don't worry. I'll get my own table," he said, his fingers drumming the back of Dave's chair. It gave Dave an odd sense of being assessed.

The door to the café kept clattering open and shut with annoying bells on a string. Dave enjoyed all the comradely greetings and gentle needling, and even felt connected to the scene, if loosely. Only this fellow, sitting alone, seemed entirely set apart. But he kept attracting glances from the other diners. The cook pushed plate after plate across his high counter as the waitress struggled to keep up. It was a lot to do, but it lent her star quality among the diners, who teased her with personal questions or air-pinched her bottom as she went past.

Dave kept on studying the menu to avoid the stranger's gaze and then resorted to making notes about this and that on the pad from his shirt pocket.

The waitress, a yellow pencil stuck in her chignon, arrived with his bacon and eggs. Dave gave her a welcoming smile in the hope that when he looked that way again, the man would be gone. But there he was still, now giving Dave a facetious military salute, then holding his nose against some imaginary stink. The meaning of these gestures eluded Dave, who was disquieted by the suggestion that he and this stranger knew each other. He ate and went to the counter to pay, so quickly the waitress came out from the kitchen still wiping her hands on a dishcloth and said, "Everything okay, Dave?"

"Yes, very good, thanks."

"Put it away in an awful hurry. Out to Larsen's?"

"No, I was there yesterday. Bred heifers. They held everything back."

"They're big on next year. I wonder if it does them any good."

"Well, they're still in business, ain't they? No, I'm headed for Jorgensen's. Big day."

Two of the ranchers, done eating, leaned in their chairs, their Stetsons back on their heads while they picked their teeth with the corners of the menus. As Dave pushed his wallet into his back pocket he realized he was being followed to the door. He didn't turn until halfway across the parking lot. When he did, the gun was in his belly, and his new friend was in his face. "Ray. Where's your ride?"

"You robbing me?"

"I just need a lift, amigo."

Ray got in the front seat of Dave's car, tucked the gun into his pants, and pulled his shirt over it, a blue terry-cloth shirt with a large breast pocket full of ballpoint pens. The top flap of the pocket liner was courtesy of "Powell Savings, Modesto, CA."

"Nice car. What're all the files in back?"

"Breeding records, cattle-breeding records."

"Mind?" Without awaiting an answer, he picked up Dave's cell phone and began tapping in a number. In a moment, his voice changed to an intimate murmur. "I'm here, or almost here," he said, covering the mouthpiece as he pointed to the intersection: "Take that one right there." Dave turned east at the intersection. "I got it wrote down someplace, east two hundred, north thirteen, but give it to me again, my angel. Or I can call you as we get closer . . . No cell service! Starting where? Never mind, a friend's giving me a lift"—again he covered the mouthpiece—"your name?"

"David."

"From?"

"Reed Point."

"Yeah, great guy, Dave, I knew back in Reed Place."

"Reed Point."

"I mean, Reed Point. Left the Quattro for an oil change, and Dave said he was headed this way. Wouldn't even let me split the gas . . . So, okay, just leaving Jordan now. How much longer is that gonna be, Morsel? . . . Two hours! Are you kidding? . . . Yeah, right, okay, got it, I'm just anxious to see you, baby, not being short with you at all. No way."

Ray turned away and murmured softly, lovingly, and then lifting his eyes to the empty miles of sagebrush, snapped shut the phone and sighed. "Two fucking hours." Except for the gun in his pants, Ray could have been any other impatient lovebird. He turned the radio on: *Swap Shop* was playing: "Broken refrigerator suitable for a smoker." Babies bawling in the background. He turned it off. Dave was trying to guess if he was a fugitive, someone Dave could bring to justice for a reward or just the fame, which might be good for business. He had tried every other promotional gambit, including refrigerator magnets with his face beside the slogan DON'T GO BUST SHIPPING DRIES.

"Wanna pick up the tempo here? You're driving like my grandma."

"This is not a great road. Deer jump out all the time. My cousin had one come through the windshield on him."

"Fuckin' pin it or I'll take the wheel and drive it like I stole it."

David sped up slightly. This seemed to placate Ray, who slumped against the side window and stared at the passing landscape. An old pickup went by the other way with a dead animal in back, one upright leg trailing an American flag.

"Ray, do you feel like telling me what this is all about?"

"Sure, Dave, it's all about you doing exactly as you're told."

"I see. And I'm taking you somewhere, am I?"

"Uh-huh, and waiting around as needed. Jesus Christ, if this isn't the ugliest country I ever seen."

"How did you pick me?"

"I didn't pick you, I picked your car. You were a throw-in. If I hadn't a took you along you'd of had to report it stolen. This way you still got it. It's a win-win. The other lucky thing for you is you're now my partner."

The road followed Big Dry Creek, open range with occasional buttes, mostly to the north. "I guess this is the prairie out here, huh, Dave? It's got a few things going for it: no blood on the ground, no chalk outlines, no police tape. Let's hear it for the prairie!" Ray gaped around in dismay, then with rising irritation sought something that pleased him on the radio. After nearly two hours, passed mostly in silence, a light tail-dragger aircraft with red-and-white-banded wings overtook them and landed about a quarter of a mile down the road. The pilot climbed out and shuffled their way. Dave rolled down the window to reveal a weathered angular face in a cowboy hat, sweat stained above the brim. "You missed your turn. Mile back turn north on the two-track." Ray seemed to be trying to convey a greeting that showed all his teeth but was ignored by the pilot. "Nice little Piper J-3 Cub," Ray said, again ignored.

The pilot strode back to the plane and taxied straight down the road. Once airborne again, he banked sharply over a five-strand barbed-wire fence, startling seven cows and their calves, which ran into the sage scattering clouds of pollen and meadowlarks.

Ray said, "Old fellow back at the hotel said there's supposed to be a lot of dinosaurs around here." He gazed at the pale light of a gas well on a far ridge.

"That's what they say."

"What d'you suppose one of them is worth, like a whole *Tyrannosaurus rex*?"

Dave just looked at Ray. They were coming on the two-track. It was barely manageable in an ordinary sedan. Dave couldn't imagine how it was negotiated in winter or spring, when the way was full of the notorious local gumbo. He'd delivered a Charolais bull somewhere nearby one fall, and it was bad enough then. Plus, the bull tore up his trailer, and he'd lost money on the deal.

"So, Dave, now we're about to arrive I should tell you what the gun is for. I'm here to meet a girl, but I don't know how it's gonna turn out. I may need to bail, and you're my getaway. The story is, my car is in for maintenance. But you're staying until we see how this is going, so you can carry me out of here if necessary."

"Let's say I understand, but what does this all depend on?"

"It depends on whether I like the girl or not, whether we're compatible and want to start a family business. I have a lot I'd like to pass on to the next generation. Plus, I got a deal for her that's even more important than the ro-mance."

The next bend revealed the house, a two-story ranch building barely hanging on to its last few chips of paint. "He must have landed in that field!" said Dave while Ray gazed at the Montana state flag popping on an iron flagpole.

"*Oro y plata.*" He chuckled. "Perfect. Now, Davey, I need you to bone up on the situation here. This is Weldon Case's cattle ranch, and it runs from here for the next forty miles or so of bad road that leads right into the Bakken oil field, which is where all the *oro y plata* is at the moment. I'm guessing that was Weldon in the airplane. I met his daughter Morsel through a dating service. Well, we haven't actually met in person, but we're about to. Morsel thinks she loves me, so we're just gonna have to see about that. If she decides otherwise, she still may want to do the business deal. All you need to know is that Morsel thinks I'm an Audi dealer from Simi Valley, California. She's going on one photograph of me standing in front of a flagship Audi. You decide you want to help, you may see more walkin'-around money than you're used to. If you don't, well, you've already seen how I make my wishes come true." He patted the bulge of blue terry cloth.

Dave pulled up under the gaze of Weldon Case. Before turning off the engine, he saw Weldon call out over his shoulder to the house. Dave rolled down the windows, and the prairie wind rushed in. Weldon stared at the two visitors, returning their nearly simultaneous greetings with a mere nod. "It's the cowboy way," muttered

Ray through a forced smile. "Or either he's retarded. Dave, ask him if he remembers falling from his high chair."

As they got out of the car, Morsel appeared on the front step and called out in a penetrating contralto, "Which one is he?" Dave emerged from the driver's side affecting a formality he associated with chauffeurs. A small trash pile next to the porch featured a couple of spent Odor-Eaters. Ray climbed out gingerly, hiding himself with the door as long as he could, before raising his hand and tilting his head coyly and finally calling to Morsel, "You're looking at him." Noting that the gun was now barely concealed, Dave quickly diverted attention by shaking Weldon's hand. It was like seizing a plank. He told Weldon he was pleased to meet him, and Weldon said, "Likewise." Dave lied about his own name, "Dave" all right, but the last name belonged to a rodeo clown two doors down from his mother's house. He had never done such a thing in his life.

"Oh, Christ," she yelled. "Is this what I get?" It was hard to say whether this was positive or not. Morsel was a scale model of her father, lean, wind weathered, and, if anything, less feminine. She raced forward to embrace Ray, whose chronic look of suave detachment was briefly interrupted by fear. A tooth was not there, as well as a small piece of her ear. "Oh, Ray!"

Weldon looked at Dave with a sour expression, and Dave, still in his chauffeur mind-set, acknowledged him formally as he fell into reverie about the money Ray had alluded to. But then Dave could see Weldon was about to speak. "Morsel has made some peach cobbler," he said in a lusterless tone. "It was her ma's recipe. Her ma is dead." Ray put on a ghastly look of sympathy that persuaded Morsel, who squeezed his arm. "Started in her liver and just took off," she explained. Dave, by now comfortable with his new alias, thought, *I never knew "Ma" but good riddance.* Going into the house, Weldon asked him if he enjoyed shooting coyotes.

"I just drive Ray around." And observing Ray tuning in, he continued obligingly, "And whatever Ray wants I guess is what we do . . . whatever he's into." But to himself he said, *Good luck hitting anything with that shit pistol.*

He didn't volunteer that he enjoyed popping the bastards out his car window, his favorite gun the .25-06 with the Swarovski rangefinder scope and tripod he bought at Hill Country Customs.

Dave lived with his mother and had always liked telling her of the great shots he'd made, like the five hundred yarder on Tin Can Hill with only the car hood for a rest, no sandbags or tripod. So much for his uncle Maury's opinion: "It don't shoot flat, throw the fuckin' thing away."

Dave, who also liked brutally fattening food, thought Morsel quite the cook. Ray, however, was a surprisingly picky eater, sticking with the salad, discreetly lifting each leaf until the dressing ran off. Weldon watched him with hardly a word, but Morsel grew ever more manic, jiggling with laughter and enthusiasm at each lighthearted remark. In fact, it was necessary to dial down the subjects—to heart attacks, highway wrecks, cancer, and the like— just to keep her from guffawing at everything. Weldon planted his hands flat on the table, rose partway, and announced he was going to use the tractor to tow the plane around back. Dave, preoccupied with the mountain of tuna casserole between him and the cobbler, hardly heard him. Ray, small and disoriented beside Morsel, shot a glance around the table looking for something else he could eat.

"Daddy don't say much," said Morsel.

"*I* can't say much," said Ray, "not with him here. Dave, you cut us a little slack?"

Dave, using his napkin to conceal a mouthful of food, managed to say, "Sure, Ray, of course." Once on his feet, he made a lunge for the cobbler, but dropping the napkin he decided just to finish chewing what he already had.

"See you in the room," Ray said sharply, twisting his chin toward the door.

Weldon had shown them where they'd sleep by flicking the door open without ceremony when they'd first walked past it. There were two iron bedsteads and a dresser atop which sat Dave's and Ray's belongings, the latter consisting of a JanSport backpack with the straps cut off. Dave was much the better equipped, with an actual overnight bag and Dopp kit. He had left the cattle receipts and breeding documents in the car. He flopped immediately onto the bed, hands behind his head, then got up abruptly and went to the door. He looked out and listened for a long moment and, easing it shut, darted for the dresser to root through Ray's things. Among them he found several rolls of cash in rubber bands; generic Viagra from India; California lottery tickets; a passport in the name of Raymond Coelho; a lady's wallet, aqua in color and containing one Louise Coelho's driver's license, as well as her debit card issued by the Food Processors Credit Union of Modesto; a few Turlock grocery receipts; a bag of trail mix; and of course the gun. Dave lifted it carefully with the tips of his fingers. He was startled by its lightness. Turning it over in his hand he saw that it was a fake. At first he couldn't believe his eyes, but he was compelled to acknowledge that there was no hole in the barrel. A toy. Carefully returning it to where it was, he fluffed the sides of the backpack and leaped to his bunk to begin feigning sleep. He was supposed to be at Jorgensen's by now, with his arm up some cow's ass. But opportunity was in the air. He'd need to get rid of the smile if he wanted to look like he was asleep.

It wasn't long before Ray came in, making no attempt to be quiet, singing "Now Is the Hour" in a flat and aggressive tone that hardly suited the lyrics, "'Sunset glow fades in the west, / Night o'er the valley is creeping! / Birds cuddle down in their nest, / Soon all the world will be sleeping.' But not you, huh, Dave? Yeah, you're awake, I can tell. We hope you enjoyed Morsel's rendition of the song, lyrics by Hugo Winterhalter."

At length, Dave gave up his pretense and said, "Sounds like you got the job."

"Maybe so. But here's what I know for sure: I'm starving."

"Must be, Ray. You ate like a bird."

"Couldn't be helped. That kind of food just grips the chambers of my heart like an octopus. But right behind the house they got a vegetable garden. How about you slip out and pick me some. I've already been told to stay out of the garden. But don't touch the tomatoes; they're not ripe."

"What else is there?"

"Greens and root vegetables."

"I'm not going out there."

"Oh, yes you are."

Ray wasted no time reaching for his JanSport to draw the gun.

"Here's a meal that'll really stick to your ribs," he said.

"I'm not picking vegetables for you or, technically speaking, stealing them for you. Forget it."

"Wow. Is this a mood swing?"

"Call it what you want. Otherwise, it's shoot or shut up."

"As you might guess, I prefer not to wake up the whole house."

"And the body'd be a problem for you."

"Very well, very well." Ray went to his pack and put the gun away. "But you may not be so lucky next time."

"What-ever."

Dave rolled over to sleep, but his greedy thoughts went on unwillingly. He had planned to head out in the morning. He was expected at ranches all around Jordan. As it was, he'd have to explain himself at Jorgensen's. He had a living to make, and were it not for his morbid curiosity about Ray and Morsel, to say nothing of the possible business deal, he might have snuck out in time to grab a room in Jordan for the night. But the rolls of money in Ray's pack were definitely real, and his hints of more to come made him wonder how anxious he was to go back to work.

"Ray, you awake?"

"I might be. What d'you want, asshole?"

"I just have something I want to get off my chest."

"Make it quick, I need my z's."

"Sure, Ray, try this one on for size: the gun's a toy."

"The gun's a what?"

"A fake. And, Ray, looks to me like you might be one, too."

"Where's the fuckin' light switch? I'm not taking this shit."

"Careful you don't stub your toe jumping off the bed like that."

"Might be time to clip your wings, sonny."

"Ray, I'm here for you. But I'm not an idiot. Just take a moment so we can agree about your so-called gun, and then we can have some straight talk."

Ray found the lamp and paced the squeaking floorboards. "I gotta take a leak," he said, heading out to the porch. "Be right back." Dave wondered whether he'd been too harsh, sensing defeat in Ray's parting remark. Dave could see him silhouetted in the moonlight in the doorway, a silver arc splashing onto the lawn, head thrown back in what Dave took to be a posture of despair. Surely, he could squeeze this guy for something.

By the time Ray walked back in he was already confessing. "...
an appraiser in Modesto, California, where I was raised. I did
some community theater there, played Prince Oh-So-True in a
children's production of *The Cave of Inky Blackness,* and thought
I was going places. Next came *Twelve Angry Men*—I was one of
them—which is where the pistol came from. Then I was the hang-
man in *Motherlode.* Got married, had a baby girl, lost my job, got
another one, went to Hawaii as a steward on a yacht belonging to
a movie star who was working a snow-cone stand a year before
the yacht, the coke, the babes, and the Dom Pérignon. I'd had to
sign a nondisclosure agreement. Eventually, I got into a fight with
the movie star and got kicked off the boat at Diamond Head, just
rowed me to shore in a dinghy. I hiked all the way to the crater,
where I used the restroom to clean up and got some chow off the
lunch wagon before catching a tour bus into Honolulu. I tried to
sell the celebrity-drug-fueled-orgy story to a local paper, but that
went nowhere because of the thing I'd signed. Everything I sign
costs me money. About this time, my wife's uncle's walnut farm
went bust. He took a loan out on the real estate, and I sold my
car, a rust-free '78 Trans Am, handling package, W72 performance
motor, solar gold with a Martinique-blue interior—we're talking
mint. We bought a bunch of FEMA trailers off the Katrina deal
and hauled them to California. But of course we lost our asses. So
the uncle gases himself in his garage, and my wife throws me out.
I moved into a hotel for migrants and started using the computers
at the Stanislaus County Library, sleeping at the McHenry Mansion, where one of the tour guides was someone I used to fuck in
high school. She slipped me into one of the canopy beds for naps.
Online is where I met Morsel. We shared about our lives. I shared
I had fallen on hard times. She shared she was coining it selling
bootleg OxyContin in the Bakken oil field. It was a long shot: Montana. Fresh start. New me. But, hey. I took the bus to Billings and
thumbed the rest of the way. By the time I made it to Jordan I had
nothing left. The clerk at that fleabag almost wouldn't let me have
a room. I told him I was there for the comets. I don't know where I
come up with that. I had to make a move. Well, now you know. So,
what happens next? You bust me with Morsel? You turn me in? I
can't marry her anyway. I don't need bigamy on my sheet."

"You pretty sure on the business end of this thing?" Dave asked with surprising coldness. He could see things going his way.

"A hundred percent, but Morsel's got issues with other folks already being in it. There's some risk, but when isn't there with stakes like this."

"Like what kind of risk?"

"Death threats, the usual. Heard them all my life. But think about it, Dave. I'm not in if you're not. You really want to return to what you were doing? We'd both be back in that hotel with the comets."

Ray was soon snoring. Dave was intrigued that these revelations, not to mention the matter of the "gun," had failed to disturb Ray's sleep. Dave meanwhile was wide awake, and he began to realize why: the nagging awareness of his own life. So many risks! He felt that Ray was a success despite the wealth of evidence to the contrary. What had Dave accomplished? High school. What could have been more painful? Yet, he suffered no more than anyone else. So even in that he was unexceptional. There was only generic anguish, persecution, and lockdown. He didn't have sex with a mansion tour guide. His experience came on the promise of marriage to a fat girl. Then there was the National Guard. Fort Harrison in the winter. Cleaning billets. A commanding officer who told the recruits that "the president of the United States is a pencil-wristed twat." Inventorying ammunition. Unskilled maintenance on UH-60 Black Hawks. "Human resource" assistant. Praying for deployment against worldwide towelheads. Girlfriend fatter every time he went home. Meaner, too. Threatening him with a baby. And he was still buying his dope from the same guy at the body shop who was his dealer in eighth grade. Never enough money and coveralls with so much cow shit he had to change laundromats every two weeks.

It was perhaps surprising he'd come up with anything at all, but he did: Bovine Deluxe, LLC, a crash course in artificially inseminating cattle. Dave took to it like a duck to water: driving around the countryside (would have been more fun in Ray's Trans Am) with a special skill set, detecting and synchronizing estrus, handling frozen semen, keeping breeding records, all easily learnable; and Dave brought art to it. Though he had no idea where that gift had come from, he was a genius preg tester. Straight or stoned, his rate of accuracy, as proved in spring calves, was renowned. His excitement began as soon as he put on the coveralls, pulled on the glove lubed up with OB goo, before even approaching the chute. With the tail held high in his left hand, he'd push his right all the way in against the cow's attempt to expel it, shoveling out the manure to clear the way, over the cervix before grasping the uterus, now that he was in nearly up to his shoulder. Dave could detect a pregnancy at two months, when the calf was smaller than a mouse. He liked the compliments that came from being able to tell the rancher how far along the cow was, anywhere from two to seven months, according to Dave's informal system: mouse, rat, cat, fat cat, raccoon, Chihuahua, beagle. He'd continue until he'd gone through the whole herd or until his arm was exhausted. Then he had only to toss the glove, write up the invoice, and look for food and a room.

Perfect. Except for the dough.

Morsel made breakfast for the men—eggs with biscuits and gravy. At the table, Dave was still assessing Ray's claim of reaching his last dime back at Jordan, which didn't square with the rolls of bills in his pack. And Dave was watching Weldon watching Ray as breakfast was served. Morsel just leaned against the stove. "Anyone want to go to Billings Saturday and see the cage fights?" she said at last, moving from the stove to the table with a dish towel. Dave alone looked up and smiled; no one answered her. Ray was probing the food with his fork, still under Weldon's scrutiny. The salt-encrusted sweat stain on Weldon's black Stetson went halfway up the crown. It was downright unappetizing in Dave's view and definitely not befitting any customer for top-drawer bull semen. Nor did he look like a man whose daughter was selling dope at the Bakken either.

At last Weldon spoke as though calling out to his livestock.

"What'd you say your name was?"

"Ray."

"Well, Ray, why don't you stick that fork all the way in and eat like a man?"

"I'll do my best, Mr. Case."

"Daddy, leave Ray alone. There'll be plenty of time to get acquainted and find out what Ray enjoys eating."

Weldon continued to eat without seeming to hear Morsel. Meanwhile, Dave was making a hog of himself and hoping he could finish Ray's breakfast, though Ray by now had seen the light and was eating the biscuits from which he had skimmed the gravy with the edge of his fork. He looked like he was under orders to clean his plate until Morsel brought him some canned pineapple slices. Ray looked up at her with what Dave thought was genuine affection. She said, "It's all you can eat around here," but the moment Dave stuck his fork back in the food, she raised a hand in his face and said, "I mean: that's all you can eat!" and laughed. Dave noticed her cold blue eyes, and for the first time he thought he understood her.

She smiled at Ray and said, "Daddy, you feel like showing Ray 'n' 'em the trick." Weldon ceased his rhythmic lip pursing.

"Oh, Morsel," he said coyly, pinching the bridge of his nose with thumb and forefinger.

"C'mon, Daddy, give you a dollar."

"Okay Mor', put on the music." A huge sigh of good-humored defeat. Morsel went over to a low cupboard next to the pie safe and pulled out a small plastic record player and a 45, which proved to be a scratchy version of "Cool, Clear Water" by the Sons of the Pioneers. At first gently swaying to the mournful dehydration tune, Weldon seemed to come to life as Morsel placed a peanut in front of him and the lyrics began, luring a poor desert rat named Dan to an imaginary spring. Weldon took off his hat and set it upside down beside him, revealing the thinnest comb-over across a snow-white pate. Then he picked up the peanut and with sinuous movements balanced it on his nose. It remained there until near the end of the record, when Dan the desert rat hallucinates green water and trees, whereupon the peanut dropped to the table, and Weldon just stared at it in disappointment. When the record ended, he replaced his hat, stood without a word, and, dropping his napkin on his chair, left the room. For a moment it was quiet. Dave felt he'd never seen anything like it.

"Daddy's pretty hard on himself when he don't make it to the end of the record. But," she said glumly, thumbing hair off her forehead as she cleared the dishes and went into the living room to straighten up, "me and Ray thought you ought to see what dementia looks like. It ain't pretty and it's expensive." Soon they heard Weldon's airplane cranking up, and Morsel called from the living room, "Daddy's always looking for them cows."

Dave had taken care to copy the information in Ray's passport onto the back of a matchbook cover, which he tore off, rolled into a cylinder, and stashed inside a bottle of aspirin. And there it stayed until Ray and Morsel headed to Billings for the cage fights. She'd left Dave directions to the Indian small-pox burials, in case he wanted to pass the time hunting for beads. But at this point, by failing to flee in his own car, Dave admitted to himself that he had become fully invested in Ray's scheme. So he seized the chance to use his cell phone and 411 connect to call Ray's home in Modesto and chat with his wife or, as she presently claimed to be, his widow. It took two tries a couple of hours apart. On the first, he got her answering machine, "You know the drill: leave it at the beep." On the second, he got Mrs. Ray. He had hardly identified himself as an account assistant with the Internal Revenue Service when she interrupted him to state in a voice firm, clear, and untouched by grief that Ray was dead. "That's what I told the last guy, and that's what I'm telling you." She said he had been embezzling from a credit union before he left a suicide note and disappeared.

"I'm doing home health care. Whatever he stole he kept. Killing himself was the one good idea he come up with in the last thirty years. At least it's prevented the government from garnishing my wages, what little they are. I been all through this with the other guy that called. Have to wait for his death to be confirmed or else I can't get benefits. If I know Ray, he's on the bottom of the Tuolumne River just to fuck with me. I wish I could have seen him one last time to tell him his water skis and croquet set went to Goodwill. If the bank hadn't taken back his airplane, there wouldn't have been even that little bit of equity I got to keep me from losing my house and sleeping in my motherfuckin' car. Too bad you didn't meet Ray. He was an A-to-Z crumb bum."

"I'm terribly sorry to hear about your husband," said Dave mechanically.

"I don't think the government is 'terribly sorry' to hear about anything. You reading this off a card?"

"No, this is just a follow-up to make sure your file stays active until you receive the benefits you're entitled to."

"I already have the big one: picturing Ray in hell with his ass *en fuego.*"

"Ah, speak a bit of Spanish, Mrs. Coelho?" said Dave, who would have rather heard mention of some *oro y plata.*

"Everybody in Modesto speaks 'a bit of Spanish.' Where you been all your life?"

"Washington, D.C., ma'am," said Dave indignantly.

"That explains it," said Mrs. Ray Coelho, and hung up.

Dave could now see why Ray was without transportation when they met. Wouldn't want to leave a paper trail renting cars or riding on airplanes. He got all he needed done on the library computers in Modesto, where he and Morsel, two crooks, had found each other and planned a merger.

Apart from the burial grounds there was nothing to do around there. He wasn't interested in that option until he discovered the liquor cabinet, and by then it was almost early evening. He found a bottle labeled HOOPOE SCHNAPPS with a picture of a bird, and he gave it a try. It went straight to his head. After several swigs, he failed to figure out the bird, but that didn't keep him from getting very happy. The label said the stuff was made from mirabelles, and Dave thought, Fuck, I hope that's good. Then as his confidence built, he reflected, Hey, I'm totally into mirabelles.

As he headed for the burial grounds, Dave, tottering a bit, decided he was glad to have left the Hoopoe schnapps back at the house. Rounding the equipment shed, he nearly ran into Weldon, who walked by without speaking or even seeing him, it seemed. Right behind the ranch buildings a cow trail led into the prairie, then wound toward a hillside spring that didn't quite reach the surface, evident only from the patch of greenery. Just below that was the spot Morsel had told him about, pockmarked with anthills. The ants, she'd claimed, would bring the beads to the surface, but still you had to hunt for them. Dave muttered, "I want some beads."

He sat down among the mounds and was soon bitten through his pants. He jumped to his feet and swept the ants away, then crouched, peering and picking at the hills. This soon seemed futile, and his thighs ached from squatting; but then he found a speck of sky blue in the dirt, a bead. He clasped it tightly while stirring with his free hand and flicking away ants. He gave no thought to the bodies in the ground beneath him and continued this until dark, by which time his palm was full of Indian beads, and his head of drunken exaltation.

As he crossed the equipment shed, barely able to see his way, he was startled by the silhouette of Weldon's Stetson and then of the old man's face very near his own, gazing at him before speaking in a low voice. "You been in the graves, ain't you?"

"Yes, just looking for beads."

"You ought not to have done that, feller."

"Oh? But Morsel said—"

"Look up there at the stars."

"I don't understand."

Weldon Case reached high over his head. "That's the crow riding the water snake." He turned back into the dark. Dave was frightened. He went to the cabin and got into bed as quickly as he could, anxious now for the alcohol to fade. He pulled the blanket up under his chin despite the warmth of the night and watched a moth batting against the windowpane at the sight of the moon. When he was nearly asleep, he saw the lights of Morsel's car wheel across the ceiling, before going dark. He listened for the car doors, but it was nearly ten minutes before they opened and closed. He rolled over against the wall and pretended to be asleep but watching as the door latch was carefully lifted from without.

Once the reverberation of the screen-door spring had ended, there was whispering. He perceived a dim shadow cross his face, someone peering down at him, and then another whisper. Soon their muffled copulation filled the room, then paused long enough for a window to be opened before resuming. Dave listened more and more intently, comfortable in his pretended sleep, until Morsel laughed, got up, and left with her clothes under her arm. "Night, Dave. Sweet dreams."

The door shut, and after a moment, Ray spoke. "What could I do, Dave? She was after my weenie like a chicken after a June bug." Snorts and, soon after, snoring.

IN THE DOORWAY OF THE HOUSE, TAKING IN THE EARLY SUN and smoking a cigarette, was Morsel in an old flannel shirt over what looked like a body stocking that produced a lazily winking camel toe. As Dave stepped up, her eyes followed her father crossing the yard very slowly toward them. "Look," she said, "he's wetting his pants. When he ain't wetting his pants, he walks pretty fast. It's just something he enjoys."

Weldon came up and looked at Dave, trying to remember him. He said, "This ain't much of a place to live. My folks moved us out here. We had a nice little ranch at Coal Banks Landing on the Missouri, but one day it fell in the river. Morsel, I'm uncomfortable."

"Go inside, Daddy, I'll get you a change."

Once the door shut behind them, Dave said, "Why in the world do you let him fly that plane?"

"It's all he knows. He flew in the war, and he's dusted crops. He'll probably kill himself in the damn thing. Good."

"What's he do up there?"

"Looks for his cows."

"I didn't know he had any."

"He don't. He hasn't had cows in forever. But he looks for 'em long as he's got fuel, then he comes down and says the damn things was brushed up to where you couldn't see 'em."

"I'm glad you go along with him. That's sure thoughtful."

"I don't know about that, but I gotta tell you this: I can't make heads or tails of your friend Ray. He was coming on to me the whole time at the cage fights, then he whips out a picture of his ex-wife and tells me she's the greatest piece of ass he ever had."

"Aw, gee. What'd you say to that?"

"I said, 'Ray, she must've had one snappin' pussy, because she's got a face that would stop a clock.' I punched him in the shoulder and told him he hadn't seen nothing yet. What'd you say your name was?"

"I'm Dave."

"Well, Dave, Ray says you mean to throw in with us. Is that a fact?"

"I'm sure giving it some thought."

"You look like a team player to me. I guess that bitch he's married to will help out on that end. Long as I never have to see her."

Sometimes Dave could tell that Ray couldn't remember his name either. He'd say "pal" or "pard" or, in a pinch, "old-timer," which seemed especially strange to someone in his twenties. Then when the name came back to him, he'd overuse it. "Dave, what're we gonna do today?" "Dave, what's that you just put in your mouth?" "I had an uncle named Dave." And so forth. But the morning that Morsel slipped out of their room carrying her clothes, he summoned it right away: "Dave, you at all interested in getting rich?"

"I'm doing my best, Ray!"

"I'm talking about taking it up a notch, and I'm fixing to run out of hints."

"I'm a certified artificial inseminator," said Dave, loftily. If he had not already scented the bait, he'd have been home days before. But this was a big step, and he knew it was a moment in time.

AT LEAST ON THE PHONE SHE COULDN'T THROW STUFF AT HIM.

"The phone is ringing off the hook. Your ranchers wanting to know when you'll get there."

"Ma, I know, but I been tied up. Tell them not to get their panties in a wad. I'll be there."

"David," she screeched, "I'm not your secretary!"

"Ma, listen to me, Ma, I got tied up. I'm sparing you the details right now, but trust me."

"How can I trust you with the phone ringing every ten seconds?"

"Ma, I can't listen to this shit, I'm under pressure. Pull the fucking thing out of the wall."

"Pressure? You've never been under pressure in your life!"

He hung up on her. He knew he couldn't live with her anymore. She needed to take her pacemaker and get a room.

MORSEL WAS ABLE TO GET A CUSTODIAL ORDER IN MILES CITY based on the danger to community presented by Weldon and his airplane. Ray had so much trouble muscling him into Morsel's sedan for the ride to assisted living that Dave's hulking frame had to be enlisted to bind Weldon, who tossed off some antique curses before collapsing in defeat. But the God he called down on them didn't count for much anymore. At dinner that night, Morsel was still a little blue, despite the toasts, somewhat vague, to a limitless future. Dave smiled along with them, his inquiring looks met by giddy winks from Morsel and Ray. Nevertheless, he felt happy and accepted, at last convinced he was going somewhere. Exchanging a nod, they let him know that he was a "courier." He smiled around the room in bafflement. Ray unwound one of his wads. Dave was going to California.

"Make sure you drive the limit," said Ray. "I'll meanwhile get to know the airplane. Take 'er down to the oil fields. Anyway, it's important to know your customers." He and Morsel saw him off from the front stoop. They looked like a real couple.

"Customers for what exactly?" Dave immediately regretted his question. Not a problem, as no one answered him anyway.

"And I'll keep the home fires burning," said Morsel without taking the cigarette from her mouth. Dave had a perfectly good idea what he might be going to California for and recognized the advantage of preserving his ignorance, no guiltier than the United States Postal Service. "Your Honor, I had no idea what was in the trunk and I am prepared to affirm that under oath or take a lie-detector test, at your discretion," he rehearsed.

Dave drove straight through, or nearly so, stopping only briefly in Idaho, Utah, and Nevada to walk among cows. His manner with cattle was so familiar that none ran from him but gathered around in benign expectation. Dave sighed and jumped back in the car. He declined to be swayed by second thoughts.

It was late when he drove into Modesto, and he was tired. He checked into a Super 8 and awoke to the hot light of a California morning as it shone through the window onto his face. He ate downstairs and then checked out. The directions he unfolded in his car proved quite exact: within ten minutes he was pulling around the house into the side drive and backing in to the open garage.

A woman in a bathrobe emerged from the back door and walked past his window without a word. He popped the trunk and sat quietly as he heard her load then shut it. She stopped at his window, pulling the bathrobe up close around her throat. She wasn't hard to look at, but Dave could see you wouldn't want to argue with her.

"Tell Ray I said be careful. I've heard from two IRS guys already." Dave said nothing at all.

Dave was so cautious, the trip back took longer. He overnighted at the Garfield again so as to arrive in daylight, getting up twice during the night to check on the car. In the morning, he was reluctant to eat at the café, where some of his former clientele might be sitting around picking their teeth and speculating about fall calves or six-weight steers. He was now so close that he worried about everything from misreading the gas gauge to getting a flat. He even imagined the trunk flying open for no reason. He headed toward the ranch on an empty stomach, knowing Morsel would take care of that. He flew past fields of cattle with hardly a glance.

No one seemed around to offer the hearty greeting and meal he was counting on. On the wire running from the house to the bunkhouse, a hawk flew off reluctantly as though it had had the place to itself. Dave got out and went into the house. Dirty dishes sat on the dining-room table, light from the television flickered without sound from the living room. When Dave walked in he saw the television was tuned to the shopping network, a close-up of a hand modeling a gold diamond-studded bracelet. Then he saw Morsel on the floor with the remote still in her hand.

Dave felt an icy calm. Ray had done this. Dave patted his pocket for the car keys and walked out of the house, stopping on the porch to survey everything in front of him. Then he went around to the shop. Where the airplane had usually been parked, in its two shallow ruts, Ray was lying with a pool of blood extending from his mouth like a speech balloon without words. He'd lost a shoe. The plane was gone.

Dave felt trapped between the two bodies, as if there was no safe way back to the car. When he got to it, a man was there waiting. He was about Dave's age, lean and respectable looking in clean khakis and a Shale Services ball cap. "I must have overslept," he said. "How long have you been here?" He touched his teeth with his thumbnail as he spoke.

"Oh, just a few minutes."

"Keys."

"Oh right, yes, I have them here." Dave patted his pocket again.

"Get the trunk for me, please." Dave offered him the keys.
"No, you."

"Not a problem."

Dave bent to insert the key, but his hand was shaking so that at
first he missed the lock. The lid rose to reveal the contents of the
trunk. Dave never felt a thing.

AN OLD MAN WHO LIKED TO FISH

THE SMITHS WERE A VERY OLD COUPLE, WHOSE LIFELONG
habits of exercise and outdoor living and careful diet had resulted
in their seeming tiny—tiny, pale, and almost totemic—as they
spread a picnic tablecloth on my front lawn and arranged their
luncheon. Since I live with reckless inattention to what I eat, I
watched with fascination as they set out apples, cheese, red wine,
and the kind of artisanal bread that looks like something found in
the road. The Smiths were the last friends of my parents still alive.
And to the degree we spend our lives trying to understand our
parents, I always looked forward to Edward and Diana's visits as a
pleasant forensic exercise.

Edward was a renowned fisherman, much admired by my
father, and me, but given his present frailty, it was surprising that
he thought he could still wade our rocky streams. He had a set rule
of no wading staff before the first heart attack, and as he had yet to
suffer one, he continued picking his way along, peering for rises,
and if he ran into speedy water in a narrow place, he'd find a stick
on the shore to help him through it. My father, by contrast, had
always used a staff, an elegant blackthorn with a silver head that
was supposed to have belonged to Calvin Coolidge.

Diana had been an avid golfer and considered fishing to be an
inferior pursuit, with no score and thus no accountability. Furthermore, I feel sorry for the fish. She never followed Edward along the
stream, instead taking up a place among the cottonwoods, where,
with her binoculars, she quietly waited for something to happen
in the canopy, hopeful of seeing a new bird for the list she kept in
her head. She had done this for so many years that she felt empow-
ered to report the rise and fall of entire species, extrapolating from
her observations in the cottonwoods. This year she announced the
decline of tanagers; last year, it was the rise of Audubon's warblers.
Lately, she would too often describe her sighting of Kirtland's war-

bler, which occurred thirty years ago on Great Abaco. Not a good sign. At the last iteration, I must have looked blankly, because she said "wood warbler" in a sharp tone. Still, her birding represented mainly an accommodation of Edward, enabling her to stay close by while he fished, though he had never made a secret of his disdain for golf, golfers, and golf courses.

I fished with Edward for an hour or so, just to be sure that he could manage. He lovingly strung up his little straw-colored Paul Young rod, pulling line from the noisy old pewter-colored Hardy reel. Holding the rod at arm's length, sighting down the length of it, he announced, "Not a set after forty years." But I could see the leftward set from where I stood ten feet away. His casts, on the other hand, were straight as ever: tight, probing expressions of a tidy stream craft, such simplicity and precision. They took me all the way back to my boyhood, when from a high bank on the Pere Marquette, at my father's urging, I had first observed Edward with utter rapture at seeing it all done so well. Now watching him hook an aerial cutthroat from a seam along cottonwood roots, I concluded he would be just fine on his own. He gave me a wink and cupped the fish in his hand, vital as a spark, before he let it go. I could see the fish dart around in the clear water, trying to find its direction before racing to midstream and disappearing. Edward held the barbless fly up to the light, blew it dry, and shot out a new cast. "I'm sorry your father isn't here to enjoy this," he said, keeping an eye on his fly as it bobbed down the current.

"So am I."

"We had quite a river list. He was the last of the old gang, except for me and the wives." Edward laughed. "The Big Fellow is starting to get the range."

"My dad was a great fisherman, wasn't he?"

"Oh, not really, but nobody loved it more." My father and I hadn't gotten along, so I was surprised to find myself feeling defensive about his prowess as a fisherman. But it was true: his style of aggression was ill suited to field sports. He had played football in college, and I could recall feeling that baseball, my sport, was a little too subtle for him. And slow.

Edward promised that when the sun got far enough to the west to put glare on the water, he'd head back up to the house, and meanwhile he hoped that I would be patient with Diana. She had begun to slip further, something that I had noticed but not much worried about, because she could still be talked out of the most peculiar of her fixations. I had seen the very old—my aunt Margaret, for example—slide into dementia good-naturedly, even enjoying some of its comic effects or treating the misapprehensions as amusing curiosities. But Diana demanded to be believed, and so perhaps her progression had not been so pleasant. Edward did say that they'd had to light the flower beds at home when she began to see things there that frightened her.

Edward said, "Well, I'm going to keep moving. I want to get to the logjam while there's still good light." He looked down at the bright water curling around his legs. "Amazing this all finds its way to the sea."

Edward wasn't seen again. That's not quite accurate: his body turned up, what was left of it, in a city park in Billings, on the banks of the Yellowstone. It had gone down the West Fork of the Boulder; down the Boulder to the Yellowstone, past the town Captain Clark had named Big Timber for the cottonwoods on the banks; down the Yellowstone through sheep towns, cow towns, refinery towns; and finally to Two Moon Park in Billings, where it was found by a homeless man, Eldon Pomfret of Magnolia Springs, Alabama. In a sense, Edward had gotten off easy.

At sundown, Diana came out of her birding lair and asked, "Have you seen Edward?" She had binoculars in one hand and a birding book in the other, and her eyes were wide. I was still in the studio, and her inquiry startled me.

"Maybe he stayed for the evening rise or—"

"I wonder if you should go look for him. He doesn't see well in the dark. It will be dark soon, won't it? What time is it, anyway?"

"I don't have my watch, but I'll walk up and see how he's getting along."

"Don't bother him if there are bugs on the water. He gets furious. What time did you say it was?"

"I left my watch on the dresser."

"What difference does it make? We can tell by the sun."

"Okay, here I go."

"And if he's intent, please don't disturb him."

"I won't."

"He gets furious."

When I got back, I sat with Diana on the sun porch waiting for the sheriff. She was weeping. "He's with that woman."

"What woman, Diana?"

"The one with those huge hats. Francine. I thought that was over."

I refrained from noting that Edward would have had no means of conveyance to "Francine." Perhaps, she knew more than I thought and was escaping into this story. As time went on, "Francine" came to seem something portentous. Diana hung on to the idea even after the sheriff arrived, who seemed to us old folks an overgrown child, bursting out of his uniform. He listened patiently as Diana explained all about Francine. He nodded and blinked throughout.

"She met him in the lobby of the Alexis Hotel in Seattle and lured him to her room. That was back in the Reagan years, and she has turned up several times since."

"Ma'am," said the sheriff—and I remember thinking that this big, pink, kindly, bland child of an officer was the right person to say "ma'am" as slowly as he did—"ma'am, I can't really comment on that other lady, but this creek comes straight off the mountain, and we're a long way from town." Diana watched him closely as he made his case. She was quiet for a moment.

"He's dead, isn't he. I knew this would happen." Diana turned to me. "I suppose that settles it." I couldn't think of one thing to do except wrinkle my brow in affected consternation. "Well," said Diana. "I hope she's happy now."

PRAIRIE GIRL

When the old brothel—known as the Butt Hut—closed down, years ago, the house it had occupied was advertised in the paper: "Home on the river: eight bedrooms, eight baths, no kitchen. Changing times force sale." The madam, Miriam Lawler, an overweight elder in the wash dresses of a ranch wife, beloved by her many friends, and famous for having crashed into the drive-up window of the bank with her old Cadillac, died and was buried at an exuberant funeral, and all but one of the girls dispersed. Throughout the long years that the institution had persevered, the girls had been a constantly changing guard in our lively old cow town. Who were they? Some were professionals from as far away as New Orleans and St. Louis. A surprising number were country schoolteachers, off for the summer. Some, from around the state, worked a day or two a week but were otherwise embedded in conventional lives. When one of them married a local, the couple usually moved away, and over time our town lost a good many useful men—cowboys, carpenters, electricians. This pattern seemed to land most heavily on our tradespeople and worked a subtle hardship on the community. But it was supposed by the pious to be a sacrifice for the greater good.

Mary Elizabeth Foley was the one girl who stayed on after the Butt Hut closed. She retained a pew at the Lutheran church, just as she had while working for Miriam. No one sat with her at first, but gradually people moved over, with expressions of extraordinary virtue. The worldly old pastor must have cited some Christian duty. It fell to Mrs. Gladstone Gander—not her real name but a moniker bestowed by others with less money—to ask the aggressive but traditional local question: "Where are you from?"

Mary Elizabeth replied, "What business is it of yours?"

Where was the meekness appropriate to a woman with her past? It was outrageous. From then on, the energy that ought to have been spent on listening to the service was dedicated to beaming malice at Mary Elizabeth Foley. Even the men joined in, though it was unlikely that they had entirely relinquished their lewd fantasies. Soon she had the pew to herself all over again and greeted it each Sunday with happy surprise, like someone finding an empty parking spot right in front of the entrance to Walmart.

The rest of the town was suspicious of Lutherans, anyway, and would have been more so if Gladstone Gander—not his real name—hadn't been president of the bank that was the only lending institution in town, and if his wife had not been the recognized power behind the throne. Mary Elizabeth was a depositor at the bank and would have enjoyed modest deference on that basis, but everything changed when she eloped with Arnold, the son and only child of the banker and his wife, whose actual names were Paul and Meredith Tanner.

Since it was a small town, and functioned reliably as a Greek chorus, the Tanners had never been free of the pressure of being the parents of Arnold, a gay man. Now that Arnold had married, appearances were much improved, or would be once time had burnished Mary Elizabeth's history. In town, there were two explanations for the marriage. The first held that Mary Elizabeth Foley had converted Arnold by using tricks she had learned at the Butt Hut. The second was that she intended to take over the bank. Only the second was true, and the poor Tanners never saw it coming. But it wouldn't have worked if Arnold and Mary Elizabeth hadn't been in love.

Mary Elizabeth was an ambitious woman, but she was not cynical. In Arnold she saw an educated lost soul. She had great sympathy for lost souls, since she thought of herself as one, too. She lacked Arnold's fatalism, however, and briefly thought that she could bring him around with her many skills. Once she realized the futility of that, she found new ways to love him and was uplifted to discover their power. She delighted in watching him arrange the clothes hanging in his closet and guessing at his system. He had ways with soft-boiled eggs, picture hanging, checkbook balancing, and envelope slitting that she found adorable. She could watch him stalking around the house with his flyswatter in a state of absorbed rapture. He brushed her hair every morning and played intelligent music on the radio. He had the better newspapers mailed in. Mary Elizabeth was not a social climber, but she did appreciate her ascent from vulgarity and survival. They slept together like two spoons in a drawer, and if she put her hands on him suggestively and he seemed to like it, she didn't care what he was imagining. She had been trained to accept the privacy of every dream world.

When they returned from their elopement, in Searchlight, Nevada, the Tanners welcomed them warmly. After a preamble of Polonian blather, Paul Tanner said, "Mrs. Tanner and I are both pleased and cautiously optimistic going forward. But, Mary, wouldn't your father have preferred to give you a big, beautiful wedding?"

"Possibly."

"I don't mean to pry, but who, exactly, is your father?"

"What business is it of yours?"

This could have been a nasty moment, but the Tanners' eagerness to sweep Junior's proclivities under the rug resulted in their pulling their punches, which was much harder on Mrs. Tanner, who was bellicose by nature, than on her husband. At times like this, she gave out a look that suggested that she was simply awaiting a better day.

The luxury of sleeping with someone threatened Arnold's punctilious habits. It was his first experience of sustained intimacy, and it had its consequences, which weren't necessarily bad but were quite disruptive. Arnold was a homely man, and one local view had it that his homeliness was what had driven him into the arms of men. He had big ears and curly hair that seemed to gather at the very top of his head. He had rather darty eyes except when he was with Mary Elizabeth or when he was issuing instructions at the bank. His previous love had been the only lawyer in town who had much of a standing outside of town, and whatever went on between them did so with fastidious discretion. Their circumstances made it certain that they would never have any fun.

"Where is he now?" Mary asked.

"San Juan Capistrano."

"And that was the end of your affair?"

"Here."

"You know I don't mind." And she didn't. The sea of predators who had rolled through the Butt Hut had seen to that.

"I'd like to be a good husband."

Arnold was the vice president of the family bank and dressed like a city banker, in dark suits, rep ties, and cordovan wing tips. He had a severe, businesslike demeanor at work that put all communications, with staff and customers alike, on a formal basis. He and Mary Elizabeth lived thirteen blocks from the bank, and Arnold walked to work, rain or shine. If the former, he carried an umbrella, which was an extremely unusual object in town. Everyone knew what an umbrella was, of course, but it seemed so remarkable in this context that, on rainy days, it was as though the umbrella, not Arnold, was the one going to work. In any case, what anyone might have had to say about Arnold in town, no one said to his face. People were confused, too, by the motorcycle he rode on weekends. He did a fifty-yard wheelie down Main Street on a Saturday night that really had them scratching their heads. When Mary asked him to wear a helmet, he replied, "But then they won't know who it is."

THE LAST THING PAUL TANNER DID BEFORE HE DIED WAS SEND Mary off to be trained in banking skills. She'd told him that she wanted to work. She went to a loan-officer and mortgage-broker boot camp and returned to town well versed in the differences between FHA, VA, and conventional forward mortgages, as well as reverse mortgages and loan models. And she was going to have a baby. Arnold said, "I hope he's a nice fellow."

"We don't even know if it's a boy or a girl!"

"I mean, the father."

"Sweetheart, that was a joke."

"Okay, but who is he?"

Mary said, "What business is it of yours?" But she quickly softened and said, "You, Arnold, don't you see?"

Paul Tanner died in his sleep, of an embolism—or something like that. Arnold wasn't sure. He and his father had never been close and had viewed each other with detachment since Arnold was in kindergarten. Paul had been so anxious to see Mary's baby that Arnold concluded that his father's hopes were skipping a generation and was more pissed off than ever. But now Arnold was president of the bank, which was merely a titular change, as he had run the place for years and run it well, with a caution that allowed it to avoid some of the ruinous expansions that had recently swept the banking community. With Paul gone, Mrs. Tanner was slap in the middle of their lives, and Mary knew from the beginning that Mama was going to need a major tune-up if they were to live in peace.

It happened when Mary's water broke and labor commenced. Arnold promptly took her to the hospital and sat by her bed, grimacing at every contraction. His mother arrived in a rush and with a bustle and consumption of space that indicated that she intended to be in charge. After she had removed her coat and scarf, tossed them over the back of a chair, and bent to pull the rubbers from her red shoes, she made a point of seeming to discover Mary and said, "Breathe."

"I'll breathe when I want to breathe."

"Of course you will, and no one is at their best going into labor." Mrs. Tanner went to the window and raised her arms above her head. "I'm about to become a grandma!"

Arnold and Mary glanced at each other: it was ambiguous. Was Mrs. Tanner happy to become a grandmother? Hard to say. Mary groaned through another contraction unnoticed by Mrs. Tanner, who was still at the window, craning around and forecasting the weather. Arnold was keeping track of the contractions with his wristwatch while Mary dutifully gave a passing thought to the stranger at the loan-officer school who was about to become a father. She hoped that Arnold was having a fond thought for his friend in San Juan Capistrano and that the arriving child would help to sort out all these disparate threads. Family-wise, Mrs. Tanner already stood for the past, and it was urgent that she bugger off ASAP. Arnold knew of Mary's aversion to his mother and had survived several of Mary's attempts to bar her from their home. "We can't just throw her under the bus," he said. This was an early use of the expression, and Mary took it too literally, encouraged that Arnold thought such an option was in play.

Mrs. Tanner turned from the window, beaming at everything and animadverting about the "new life." Arnold winced at these remarks as sharply as he did at Mary's contractions. Mary was just disconcerted by the number of unreciprocated statements, more bugling than dialogue. Arnold held her hand, and then leaned across so that he could hold both of her hands, while Mrs. Tanner strode the linoleum. He loved to hold Mary's hands: they were so strong. He thought of them as farmer's hands.

Mary owed her hard hands and a confidant horsemanship to her childhood on a ranch a mile and a quarter from the Canadian border, a remote place yet well within reach of the bank that had seized it and thrown Mary and her family into poverty. The president of the United States had told them to borrow, borrow, borrow for their business; thus, the bank had gotten the swather, the baler, the rock windrower, the tractor, the front-end loader, the self-propelled bale wagon, and eight broke horses and their tack, while the family had hit the road. Mary used to say that "bank" was just another four-letter word, but eventually she'd put that behind her, too.

"Mrs. Tanner," Mary said, "I seem to be oversensitive tonight. Could you stop talking?"

"Is it a problem?"

"Is it a problem?" Mary repeated. Arnold's face was in his hands. "Mrs. Tanner, it is a huge problem. This is a time when people want a little peace, and you just won't shut up. I'm about to have a baby, and you seem rambunctious."

Mrs. Tanner reassembled her winter clothes and departed. Mary looked at Arnold and said, "I'm sorry, Arnie."

THE BOY WAS BORN AT TWO O'CLOCK IN THE MORNING. MARY was exhausted and so was Arnold, who was both elated and confused but truly loving to his bedraggled wife. They had never chosen a name for the baby, thinking that it was presumptuous to do so before seeing whether it was a boy or a girl. They agreed that a list of gender-based alternatives was somehow corny. But Mary's suggestion, based on a sudden recollection of the aspirant at loan-officer school, startled Arnold.

"Pedro? I don't think I'd be comfortable with that, Mary."

They settled on Peter, which left Mary with her glimmer of ratio-nale and pleased Arnold, who liked old-fashioned names. Mary's affectionate name for him, however, would always be Pedro. And, without question, he had a Pedro look to him.

Mary bought a horse and, as Peter grew, Arnold spent more and more time in San Juan Capistrano; the day came when he told Mary that he would not be coming back. As foreseen as that must have been, they both wept discreetly to avoid alarming Peter, who was in the next room. They tried to discuss how Arnold would spend time with Peter, but the future looked so fractured that they were forced to trust to their love and intentions.

"Will I always be able to see Peter?" Arnold sobbed. Mary was crying, too. But she knew where to put her pain. She had her boy to think of, and where to put pain was a skill she'd learned early on.

"The house is yours, of course," Arnold said with a brave, gener-ous smile that suggested he was unaware that he was speaking to a loan officer who had already begun to do the numbers in her head. She couldn't help it. It was her latest version of tough.

"Thank you, Arnold."

"And my owning the bank with my mother means that your job is assured."

Mary loved Arnold, but this airy way of dispensing justice hur-ried her agenda.

"Don't you find that a little informal?"

"You must mean divorce."

"I'm not the one going to San Juan Capistrano. You are."

"No doubt we'll have to get something written up."

"This is a no-fault state. When couples split the sheets, they split them fifty-fifty." Mary laughed heartily. "I could keep you on at the bank, Arnold, but not from California."

He'd let Mary see his origins, and Mary had reminded him of hers. Arnold sighed in concession.

His mother was not pleased when she learned of her new part-nership. Her mouth fell open as Mary explained the arrangement, but Mary reached across the conference-room table and gently lifted it shut. News of all this was greeted warmly as it shot around the bank.

Mary learned more about banking every day. Mrs. Tanner, despite her claims at the beauty parlor, however, knew nothing except how she had come to acquire what equity she had, and she spent more and more of her time and money on increasingly futile cosmetic surgery. As a figurehead at board meetings, she wore costumes and an imitation youth that contrasted with the professionalism of Mary Elizabeth Tanner, who ran the bank with evenhanded authority. Over time, there came to be nothing disreputable about Mary whatsoever. Wonderful how dollars did that, and Mary had a little gold dollar sign on a chain around her pretty neck.

Considering the hoops he had to jump through, Arnold did his very best to be Peter's father, virtually commuting from California. This was even more remarkable once he had sold his share of the bank to Mary, since this occasioned a rupture with his own mother. Peter was consoled by the fact that his parents were now sleeping together once a month, and Arnold called him Pedro at intimate moments. He never let on to his friend in California how much he enjoyed these interludes of snuggling with Mary.

Peter was already a star at little-guy soccer. Mrs. Tanner came to the games, and Peter ran straight to Grandma after each game, which softened the smirk on her well-stretched face. Finally, Arnold and his mother reconciled, under the leafless cottonwoods shadowing the battered playing field, during a 3–1 win over the Red Devils of Reed Point, Montana. All the fight went out of Mrs. Tanner, who never made another board meeting but spent her life estate as she saw fit, letting her face sag and reading bodice rippers on her porch, from which she could watch the neighbors during the warm months, and by the pool in San Juan Capistrano during the cold.

Arnold got out of banking and into business, at which he did well. Arnold always did well: no one was more serious about work. Peter had a girlfriend, Mary's hair was going gray, and Arnold's domestic arrangements were stable most of the time, except during the winter, when his mother interfered.

"She's driving me nuts," Arnold complained to Mary.

"You'll have to stand it," Mary said. "She's lonely, she's old, and she's your mother."

"Can't Peter do winter sports? What about basketball?"

When Mrs. Tanner's advancing dementia and prying nature made Arnold's companion, T.O.—tired of her referring to him as a "houseboy"—threaten to leave, Arnold popped her into assisted living, and that was that. Mrs. Tanner did not go easily; as T.O., a burly Oklahoman, drawled, "She hung on like a bulldog in a thunderstorm."

"She's my mother!" Arnold cried without much feeling.

BEFORE PETER LEFT FOR COLLEGE, MARY DECIDED TO TAKE him to see the place where she had grown up. This was a reward, in a sense, because Peter had always asked about it. No doubt he had heard rumors concerning his mother, and he wanted to confirm her ranch origins. This was straightforward curiosity, as Peter was the furthest thing from insecure. Well brought up and popular, he was the first in his family to trail neither his past nor his proclivities like a lead ball.

They set out in the middle of June, in Mary's big Lincoln, heading for the great, nearly empty stretches of northern Montana, where underpopulated counties would deny the government's right to tax them, attempt to secede from the Union, and issue their own money in the form of scrip. Some radicalized soothsayer would arise—a crop duster, a diesel mechanic, a gunsmith—then fade away, and the region would go back to sparse agriculture, a cow every hundred acres, a trailer house with a basketball backboard and a muddy truck. Minds spun in the solitude.

Peter said, "Where is everybody?"

"Gone."

"Is that what you did, Mom?"

"I had to. We lost the place to the bank. I liked it where I was. I had horses."

"Don't you wish you'd gone to college?"

"I got an education, Peter, that's what matters. And now I can send you to college. Maybe you can go to college in California, near Pop."

"Where did your brothers go?" Mary understood that Peter would have liked to have a bigger family.

"Here and there. They didn't stay in touch."

"Did you ever try to find them?"

Mary didn't say anything for a moment. "I did, but they didn't want to stay in touch with me."

"What? Why's that?"

"They had their reasons."

"Like what?" Peter could be demanding.

"They didn't like what I did for a living."

"What's wrong with working at the bank?"

She thought for a moment. "Well, a bank took away our home."

Peter said, "I still think it's totally weird. They'd better not be there."

Mary glanced over from the wheel, smiled a bit, and said, "It was a long time ago, Peter."

She watched him as he looked out the window at the prairie. She thought that he was beautiful, and that was enough. It didn't hurt that the car was big and smelled new and hugged the narrow road with authority. She said to herself, as she had since she was a girl:

"I can do this."

THE GOOD SAMARITAN

Szabo didn't like to call the land he owned and lived on a ranch—a word that was now widely abused by developers. He preferred to call it his property, or "the property," but it did require a good bit of physical effort from him in the small window of time after he finished at the office, raced home, and got on the tractor or, if he was hauling a load of irrigation dams, on the ATV. Sometimes he was so eager to get started that he left his car running. His activity on the property, which had led, over the years, to arthroscopic surgery on his left knee, one vertebral fusion, and mild hearing loss, thanks to his diesel tractor, yielded very little income at all and some years not even that—a fact that he did not care to dwell on.

He produced racehorse-quality alfalfa hay for a handful of grateful buyers, who privately thought he was nuts but were careful to treat his operation with respect, because almost no one else was still producing the small bales that they needed to feed their own follies. They were, most of them, habitués of small rural tracks in places such as Lewistown or Miles City, owners of one horse, whose exercise rider was either a daughter or a neighbor girl who put herself in the way of serious injury as the price of the owner's dream. Hadn't Seattle Slew made kings of a couple of hapless bozos?

Szabo was not nuts. He had long understood that he needed to do something with his hands to compensate for the work that he did indoors, and it was not going to be golf or woodworking. He wanted to grow something and sell it, and he wanted to use the property to do this. In fact, the work that he now did indoors had begun as manual labor. He had machined precision parts for wind generators for a company that subcontracted all the components, a company that sold an idea and actually made nothing. Szabo had long known that this approach was the wave of the future, without understanding that it was the wave of his future. He had worked very hard, and his hard work had led him into the cerebral ether of his new workplace: now, at forty-five, he took orders in an office in a pleasant town in Montana, while his esteemed products were all manufactured in other countries. It was still a small, if prosperous, business, and it would likely stay small, because of Szabo's enthusiasm for what he declined to call his ranch.

It wasn't that he was proud of the John Deere tractor that he was still paying for and that he circled with a grease gun and washed down like a teenager's car. He wasn't proud of it: he loved it. There were times when he stood by his kitchen window with his first cup of coffee and gazed at the gleaming machine in the morning light. Even the unblemished hills of his property looked better through its windshield. The fact that he couldn't wait to climb into it was the cause of the accident.

The hay, swathed, lay in windrows, slowly drying in the Saturday-morning sun. Szabo had gone out to the meadows in his bathrobe to probe the hay for moisture and knew that it was close to ready for baling. The beloved tractor was parked at the foot of the driveway, as though a Le Mans start would be required once the hour came around and the moisture in the tender shoots of alfalfa had subsided, so that the hay would not spoil in the stacks. Szabo, now in jeans, tennis shoes, hooded sweatshirt, and baseball cap, felt the significance of each step as he walked toward the tractor, marveling at the sunlight on its green paint, its tires nearly his own height, its baler pert and ready. He reached for the handhold next to the door of the cab, stepped onto the ridged footstep, and pulled himself up, raising his left hand to open the door. Here his foot slid off the step, leaving him briefly dangling from the handhold. A searing pain informed him that he had done something awful to his shoulder. Releasing his grip, he fell to the driveway in a heap. The usually ambrosial smell of tractor fuel repelled him, and the towering green shape above him now seemed reproachful. Gravel pressed into his cheek.

AS HE LAY IN RECOVERY, THE MORPHINE DRIP ONLY PRO-longed his obsession with the unbaled hay, since it allowed him to forget about his shoulder, which he had come to think of not as his but as a kind of alien planet fastened to his torso, which glowed red like Mars, whirling with agony, as soon as the morphine ran low. It was a fine line: when he wheedled extra narcotic, his singing caused complaints, and he got dialed back down to the red planet. Within a day, he grew practical and managed to call his secretary.

"Melinda, I'm going to have to find somebody for the property. I've got hay down and—"

"A ranch hand?"

"But just for a month or so."

"Why don't I call around?"

"That's the idea. But not too long commitment-wise, okay? I may have to overpay for such a limited time."

"Whatever it takes," Melinda remarked, producing a mystification in Szabo that he ascribed to the morphine.

"Yes, sure," Szabo said. "But time is of the essence."

"You can say that again. Things are piling up. The guy in Germany calls every day."

"I mean with the hay."

Melinda was remarkably efficient, and she knew everyone in town. Her steadiness was indispensable to Szabo, who kept her salary well above temptation from other employers. By the next day, she had found a few prospects for him.

The most promising one, an experienced ranch hand from Wyoming, wore a monitoring ankle bracelet that he declined to explain, so he was eliminated. The next most promising, a disgruntled nursery worker, wanted permanent employment, so Szabo crossed him off the list, ignoring Melinda's suggestion that he just fire him when he was through. That left a man called Barney, overqualified and looking for other work but happy to take something temporary. He told Melinda that he was extremely well educated but "identified with the workingman" and thought a month or so in Szabo's bunkhouse would do him a world of good. Szabo called Barney's references from his hospital bed. He managed to reach only one, the wife of a dentist who ran a llama operation in Bozeman. Barney was completely reliable, she said, and meticulous: he had reshingled the toolshed and restacked their large woodpile in an intricate pattern—almost like a church window—and swept the sidewalk. "You could eat off it!" she said. Szabo got the feeling that Mrs. Dentist had been day-drinking. Her final remark confused him. "Nobody ever did a better job than Barney!" she said, laughing wildly. "He drove us right up the wall!"

Szabo took a leap of faith and hired him over the phone. The news seemed not to excite Barney. "When do you want me to start?" he droned. After the call, Szabo gazed at his phone for a moment, then flipped it shut. His arm in a sling, his shoulder radiating signals with every beat of his heart, he returned to his office and stirred the things on his desk with his left hand. Eventually, he had pushed the papers into two piles: "urgent" and "not urgent." Then there was a painful reshuffle into "urgent," "not that urgent," and "not urgent." Melinda stood next to him. "Does that make sense?" he asked.

Melinda said, "I think so."

"I'm going home."

Barney, who looked to be about forty, with a pronounced widow's peak in his blondish hair and a deep dimple in his chin, was a quick study, though it took Szabo a while to figure out how much of his instruction the man was absorbing. Barney was remarkably without affect, gazing at Szabo as he spoke as if marveling at the physical apparatus that permitted Szabo's chin to move so smoothly. At first, Szabo was annoyed by this, and when Barney's arm rose slowly to his mouth to place a toothpick there, he had a momentary urge to ask him to refrain from chewing it while he was listening. It was the sense of a concealed smirk behind the toothpick that bothered Szabo the most. But once he'd observed Barney's efficiency, Szabo quickly trained himself not to indulge such thoughts. Some of the hay had been rained on, but Barney raked it dry, and soon the shiny green tractor was flying around the meadows making beautiful bales for the racehorses of Montana. This gave Szabo something of a heartache, but he praised Barney for the job he had done so well. Barney replied, "That's not enough hay to pay for the fuel."

Szabo tried to ride his old gelding, Moon, a tall chestnut half thoroughbred he had been riding for thirteen of the horse's sixteen years. One armed, he had to be helped into the saddle. He could get the bridle over Moon's head and pull himself up from the saddle horn, barely, but the jogging aroused the pain in his shoulder so sharply that he quickly gave up. Barney looked on without expression.

Szabo said, "I really need to ride him regularly. He's getting old."

"I'll ride him."

"That would be nice, but it's not necessary."

"I'll ride him. There's not much else to do."

Barney rode confidently but without grace of any kind. Moon's long trot produced a lurching sway in Barney's torso, exaggerated by the suspenders he always wore, that was hard for Szabo to watch. And it was clear from Moon's sidelong glances that he, too, was wondering what kind of burden he was carrying. But the sight of Barney's lurching exercise rides seemed a small price to pay for the skilled work he provided: repairing fences, servicing stock waterers, pruning the orchard, and even doing some painting on the outbuildings. One day, as he rode Moon down the driveway, Barney said to Szabo, who had just pulled up, "By the time you get the sling off, I'll have your horse safe for you to ride." From the window of his car, Szabo said, resisting the impulse to raise his voice, "As I recall, he's been safe for me to ride since he was a three-year-old colt." Barney just looked down and smiled.

When Barney restacked the woodpile, Szabo decided to treat it as an absolute surprise. He stood before the remarkable lattice of firewood and, while his mind wandered, praised it lavishly. He was reluctant to admit to himself that he was trying to get on Barney's good side. "It's one of a kind," he said.

SZABO'S MOTHER LIVED IN A GROUND-FLOOR APARTMENT across the street from a pleasant assisted-living facility. She had stayed in her own apartment because she smoked cigarettes, which was also what seemed to have preserved her vitality over her many years. Further, she didn't want to risk the family silver in an institution, or her real treasure: a painting that had come down through her family for nearly a century, a night stampede by the cowboy artist Charlie Russell, one of very few Russell night pictures in existence, which would likely fetch a couple of million dollars at auction. The old people across the street would just take it down and spill food on it, she said. When Szabo was growing up as an only child, his mother's strong opinions, her decisive nature, had made him feel oppressed; now those qualities were what he most liked, even loved, about her. He recognized that when he was irresolute it was in response to his upbringing, but caution, in general, paid off for him.

Barney enjoyed tobacco, too, smoke and smokeless. One afternoon, Szabo sent a shoebox of pictures and two much-annotated family cookbooks to his mother by way of Barney, who was heading into town to pick up a fuel filter for the tractor. Later, Szabo cried out more than once, "I have only myself to blame!"

In a matter of weeks, Szabo was able to discard the sling and to exercise his shoulder with light weights and elastic strips that he held with one foot while feebly pulling and releasing, sweat pouring down his face. The next morning, three bird-watchers entered the property without stopping at the house for permission and were all but assaulted by Barney, who chased them to their car, hurling vulgar epithets until they disappeared down the road with their life lists and binoculars.

"But, Barney, I don't mind them coming around," Szabo said.

"Did they have permission, yes or no?"

There was no time for Szabo to explain that this didn't matter to him, as Barney had gone back to work. At what, Szabo was unsure, but he seemed busy.

Szabo had to be in Denver by the afternoon. He took an overnight bag and drove to town, past Barney, lurching from side to side on Moon, who bore, Szabo thought, a fresh look of resignation. He stopped on the way to the airport to see his mother, who sat in her living room doing sudoku in front of a muted television, a cigarette hanging out of the corner of her mouth. On a stand next to her chair, her cockatiel, Toni, hunched in the drifting smoke.

"I'm off to Denver till tomorrow, Ma. I'll have my cell if you need anything." She looked up, put down her stub of pencil, and moved the cigarette from her mouth to the ashtray.

"Nothing to worry about here. I've got a million things to do."

"Well, in case you think of something while I'm—"

"Lunch with Barney, maybe drive around."

"Okay!" Luckily his mother couldn't see his face.

Melinda had things well in hand, had even reduced some of the piles on his desk by thoughtful intervention where his specific attention was less than necessary. She was a vigorous mother of four, barely forty years old, happily married to a highway patrolman she'd grown up with. They were unironic enthusiasts for all the mass pleasures the culture offered: television, NASCAR, cruises, Disney World, sports, celebrity gossip, and local politics. Szabo often wished that he could be as well adjusted as Melinda's family, but he would have had to be medicated to pursue her list of pleasures. And yet she was not just an employee but a cherished friend.

It was a tested friendship with a peculiar intimacy: Szabo's former wife, Karen, an accomplished ironist, had made several stays at the Rimrock Foundation for what ended up as a successful treatment for alcoholism—successful in that she had given up alcohol altogether. Unfortunately, she had replaced it with other compulsions, including an online-trading habit that had bankrupted Szabo for a time. Once it was clear that Szabo was broke, she had divorced him, sold the house, remarried, and moved to San Diego, where she was, by the reports of their grown son, David, happy and not at all compulsive. What does this say about me? Szabo wondered obsessively. Maybe she was now on a short leash. Szabo had met her husband, Cliff: stocky, bald, and authoritarian—a forensic accountant, busy and prosperous in the SoCal free-for-all. His dour affect seemed to subdue Karen. In any case, Szabo had loved her, hadn't wanted a divorce, and had felt disgraced at undergoing bankruptcy in a town of this size. He'd sunk into depression and discovered that there was no other illness so brutal, so profound, so inescapable that made an enemy of consciousness itself. Nevertheless, he had plodded to the office, day after day, an alarming, ashen figure, and there he had fallen into the hands of Melinda, who dragged him to family picnics and to the dentist, forged his signature whenever necessary, placed him between her and her husband at high-school basketball games as though he might otherwise tip over, taught him to cheer for her children, and occasionally fed him at her house in the uproar of family life. When, once, as she stood by his desk in the office, he raised a hand to her breast, she amiably removed it and redirected his attention to his work. By inches, she had restored his old self, and solvency seemed to follow. He began to see himself as someone who had returned from the brink. He liked making money. He liked visiting his little group of suppliers in faraway places. He liked having Melinda as a friend, and her husband, Charlie, the highway patrolman, too. Charlie was the same straight-ahead type as his wife: he once gave Szabo a well-deserved speeding ticket. Now Szabo's only argument with his ex-wife's contentment in San Diego was that it seemed to prove to David that it had been Szabo who drove her crazy.

As Szabo headed away from the Denver airport, he could see its marvelous shape at the edge of the prairie, like a great nomads' camp—a gathering of the tents of chieftains, more expressive of a world on the move than anything Szabo had ever seen. You flew into one of these tents, got food, a car, something to read, then headed out on your own smaller journey to the rapture of traffic, a rented room with a TV, and a "continental" breakfast. It was an ectoplasmic world of circulating souls.

On a sunny day, with satellite radio and an efficient midsize Korean sedan, the two-hour drive to the prison that had held his son for the past couple of years flew by. Szabo was able to think about his projects for the ranch—a new snow fence for the driveway, a mouseproof tin liner for Moon's grain bin, a rain gauge that wouldn't freeze and crack, a bird feeder that excluded grackles and jays—nearly the whole trip. But toward the end of the drive his head filled with the disquieting static of remorse, self-blame, and sadness, and a short-lived defiant absolution. In the years that had turned out to be critical for David, all he had given him was a failing marriage and a bankrupt home. I should have just shot Karen and done the time, Szabo thought with a shameful laugh. The comic relief was brief. Mom in California, Dad in Montana, David in prison in Colorado: could they have foreseen this dispersion?

Razor wire guaranteed the sobriety of any visitor. The vehicles in the visitors' parking lot said plenty about the socioeconomics of the families of the imprisoned: Szabo's shiny Korean rental stuck out like a sore thumb. The prison was a tidy fortress of unambiguous shapes that argued less with the prairie surrounding them than with the chipper homes of the nearby subdivision. It had none of the lighthearted mundane details of the latter—laundry hanging out in the sun, adolescents gazing under the hood of an old car, a girl sitting on the sidewalk with a handful of colored chalk. The place for your car, the place for your feet, the door that complied at the sight of you, were all profoundly devoid of grace—at least, to anyone whose child was confined there.

David came into the visiting room with a promising small smile and gave Szabo a hug. He had been a slight, quick-moving boy, but prison had given him muscle, thick, useless muscle that seemed to impair his agility and felt strange to the father who embraced him. They sat in plastic chairs. Szabo noticed that the room, which was painted an incongruous robin's-egg blue, had a drain in the middle of its floor, a disquieting fact.

"Are you getting along all right, David?"

"Given that I don't belong here, sure."

"I was hoping to hear from you—" Szabo caught himself, determined not to suggest any sort of grievance. David smiled.

"I got your letters."

"Good." Szabo nodded agreeably. There was nothing to look at in the room except the person you were speaking to.

"How's Grandma?" David asked.

"I think she's doing as well as can be expected. You might drop her a note."

"Oh, right. 'Dear Grandma, you're sure lucky to be growing old at home instead of in a federal prison.'"

Szabo had had enough.

"Good, David, tell her that. Old as she is, she never got locked up."

David looked at his father, surprised, and softened his own voice. "You said in your letter you'd had some health problem."

"My shoulder. I had surgery."

Szabo knew that the David before him was not the David on drugs, but, now that the drugs were gone, he still hadn't gone back to being the boy he'd been before. Maybe it would happen gradually. Or perhaps Szabo was harboring yet another fruitless hope.

"Melinda still working for you?"

"I couldn't do without her. She stayed with me even when I couldn't pay her."

"Melinda's hot."

"She's attractive."

"No, Dad, Melinda's hot."

Szabo didn't know what David meant by this, if anything, and he didn't want to know. Maybe David just wanted him to realize that he noticed such things.

"David, you've got less than a year to go. Concentrate on avoiding even the appearance of anything that could set you back. You'll be home soon."

"Home?"

"Absolutely. Where your friends are, where you grew up. Home is where your mistakes can be seen in context. You go anywhere else—David, you go anywhere else and you're an ex-con. You'll have to spend all your time overcoming that, when everyone at home already knows you're a great kid."

"When I get out of here," David said in measured tones, "I'm going to live with Mom and Cliff."

"In California?"

"Last time I checked."

Szabo was determined not to react to this. He let the moment subside, and David now seemed to want to warm up. He smiled faintly at the blue ceiling.

"And, yes, I'll write Grandma back."

"So you heard from her?"

David laughed. "About her boyfriend, Barney. I think that's so sweet. A relationship! Is Barney her age?"

"Actually, he's quite a bit younger."

As Szabo drove back to the airport, he tried to concentrate on the outlandish news of Barney's role in his mother's life, but he didn't get anywhere. He couldn't stop thinking about David, and thought of him in terms of a proverb he had once heard from a Mexican man who had worked for him: "You have only one mother. Your father could be any son of a bitch in the world." That's me! I'm any son of a bitch in the world.

He did have a mother, however, there in God's waiting room with a new companion. His late father, a hardworking tradesman, would have given Barney a wood shampoo with a rake handle. But my standing, thanks to my modest prosperity and education, means that I shall have to humor Barney, and no doubt my most earnest cautions about the forty-year age gap between Barney and my mother will be flung back in my face, Szabo thought. Suddenly tears burned in his eyes: he was back to David.

Drugs had swept through their small town one year. They'd always been around, but that year they were everywhere, and they had destroyed David's generation. The most ordinary children had become violent, larcenous, pregnant, sick, lost, or dead. And then the plague had subsided. David, an excellent student, had injected the drugs between his toes, and his parents had suspected only that he suddenly disliked them. Instead of going to college, he had apprenticed with a chef for nearly a year, before heading to prison. David didn't think that he would go back to drugs when he was released, and neither did his father. But his bitterness seemed to be here to stay, fed, likely, by his memory of the things that he had done in his days of using. Perhaps he blamed himself for the failure of his parents' marriage. The body he had acquired in the weight room seemed to suit his current burdened personality. The way he looked, he could hardly go back to what he had been.

THE TRACTOR WAS WET AND GLEAMING IN THE BRIGHT SUN-light. Barney was gathering stray bits of baler twine and rolling them up into a neat ball. He hardly seemed to notice Szabo's arrival, so Szabo carried his suitcase into the house without a word. Once inside, he glanced furtively through the hall window at Barney, then went back out.

"Good morning, Barney."

"Hi."

"This shoulder thing is behind me now. I think I'm ready to go back to work here." Barney looked more quizzical than the situation called for. "So let's square up and call it a day."

"Meaning what?" Barney asked with an extravagantly inquisitive look.

"Meaning the job is over. Thank you very much. You've been a great help when I needed it most."

"Oh?"

"Yes, I think so. I'm quite sure of it."

"It's your call, Szabo. But there's something about me you don't know."

"I'm sure that's the case. That's nearly always the case, isn't it, Barney?"

Some ghastly revelation was at hand, and Szabo knew that there would be no stopping it. "But I'd be happy to know what it is, in your instance."

Barney gazed at him a long time before he spoke. He said, "I am a respectable person."

Szabo found this unsettling. Clearly, it was time to have a word with his mother. He asked her out to lunch, but she begged off, citing the new smoking rules that, she said disdainfully, were "sweeping the nation." So he took her to the park near the river. Her size had been reduced by tobacco and her deplorable eating habits. She scurried along briskly, and any pause on Szabo's part found her well ahead, poking into garden beds and uprooting the occasional weed to set an example. They found a bench and sat. Mrs. Szabo shook out a cigarette by tapping the pack against the back of her opposing hand, then raising the whole pack, with its skillfully protruded single butt, to her lips. There the cigarette hung, unlit, while she made several comments about the weather and dropped the pack back into her purse. Finally, she lit it, and the first puff seemed to satisfy her profoundly.

"How did you find David?"

"Fine, I think. The way I get to see him down there . . . it's uncomfortable. Just a big empty room."

"Is he still angry?"

"Not that I could see."

"He was such an angry little boy."

"Well, he's not little anymore, Mom. He's got big muscles."

"Let's hope he doesn't misuse them. He got that attitude from your wife. The nicest thing I can say about her is that she kept on going."

"She married a decent, successful guy."

"What else could she do? She didn't have the guts to rob a bank."

"You forget what David was like before his problems. He didn't have an attitude. He was a nice boy."

He could see she wasn't listening.

"Barney said you told him he was no longer needed."

"He knew it was temporary from the start."

"Well, he's certainly got my place pulled together. My God, what a neatnik! And he made me insure the Russell, which I should have done a long time ago. He thinks that David's in this pickle because he got away with murder while he was growing up."

"What? He's never met David!"

"Barney's a very bright individual. He doesn't have to know every last thing firsthand."

"I think his views on how Karen and I raised David would be enhanced by actually meeting David."

"Why?"

"Jesus Christ, Mom."

"Of course you're grumpy. Barney does so much for me, and you want me all to yourself. Can't you just relax?"

Telling people to relax is not as aggressive as shooting them, but it's up there. The first time Barney had driven the tractor, he'd nearly put it in the irrigation ditch. Szabo had cautioned him, and Barney had responded, "Is the tractor in the ditch?" Szabo had allowed that it was not. "Then relax," Barney had said.

THERE WAS NOTHING LIKE IT: LEANING ON HIS SHOVEL NEXT to the racing water, the last sun falling on gentle hills crowned with bluestem and golden buffalo grass, cool air rising from the river bottom. Moon grazed and followed Szabo as he placed his dams and sent a thin sheet of alpine water across the hay crop. The first cutting had been baled and put neatly in the stackyard by Barney. The second cutting grew slowly, was denser in protein and more sought after by owners trying to make their horses run faster. All the way down through this minor economic chain, people lost money, their marvelous dreams disconnected from hopes of success.

Once winter was in the air, Szabo spent less time on his property and made an effort to do the things for his business that he was most reluctant to do. In November, he flew to Düsseldorf and stayed at the Excelsior, eating Düsseldorfer Senfrostbraten with Herr Schlegel while pricing robotic plasma welding on the small titanium objects that he was buying from him. The apparent murkiness of Germany was doubtless no more than a symptom of

Szabo's ignorance of the language. He wondered if all the elders he saw window-shopping on the boulevards were ex-Nazis. And the skinheads at the Düsseldorf railroad station gave him a sense of historical alarm. After a long evening in the Altstadt, Szabo found himself quite drunk at the bar of the Hotel Lindenhof, where he took a room with a beautiful Afro-Czech girl, called Amai, who used him as a comic, inebriated English instructor, her usual services being unnecessary, given his incapacity. Since Szabo appeared unable to navigate his way back to the Excelsior, Amai drove him there in return for the promise of a late breakfast in the Excelsior's beautiful dining room. Afterward, she asked for his address so that they could stay in touch once he was home.

From Germany, Szabo flew directly to Denver. He slept most of the way and awoke to anxiety at the idea that this was probably the last visit he would have before David was released. In the chaotic year that preceded his son's confinement, he had never known what David was doing or to what extent he was in danger; in the last weeks of his marriage, he and Karen had admitted to feeling some relief, now that David was in jail, simply at knowing where he was. Perhaps it was that relief that had allowed them to separate. Yet Cliff's prompt appearance had aroused Szabo's suspicion: he sensed that California had beckoned while his marriage was still seemingly intact.

David was warmer toward his father this time but more fretful than he had been on the previous visit. Szabo understood that David was probably as afraid of his impending freedom as Szabo was on his behalf. He seemed, despite the muscles, small and frightened, his previous sarcasm no more than a wishful perimeter of defense. And the glow of anger was missing. Szabo wondered if jet lag was contributing to his heartache. He hardly knew what to say to his son.

"In two weeks, you'll be in California," Szabo said.

"That was the plan."

"Is it not anymore?"

"Mom and Cliff said they didn't want me. I've got to go to plan B."

"I'm sorry, David. What's plan B?"

"Plan B is I don't know what plan B is."

"What made your mom and Cliff change their minds?"

David smiled slightly. He said, "I'm trying to remember how Mom put it. She said that a new relationship requires so many adjustments that introducing a new element could be destabilizing. It was sort of abstract. She left it to me to figure out that I was the destabilizing new element. Then Cliff got on the phone and said that unfortunately closure called for the patience of all parties."

"Did you say anything?"

"Yes, Dad, I did. I told Cliff to blow it out his ass."

Szabo could have taken this as evidence of David's unresolved anger. Instead, he enjoyed the feeling that they were in cahoots. "How did Cliff take that?"

"He said he was sorry I felt that way. I told him not to be. I told him I didn't feel anything at all."

They were quiet for long enough to suggest the inkling of comfort. Finally, David said, "Tell me about Barney."

"Barney! What about him?"

"Why did you send him here to see me?"

Startling as this was, Szabo did not react at first. He was quiet for a long and awkward moment. Then he asked quite levelly, "When did Barney show up?"

"While you were still in wherever. He said you sent him."

"Not exactly. Perhaps, based on our conversations, Barney thought it might be something I wanted him to do."

Szabo had no idea why he was dissembling like this, unless it was to buy time.

He suddenly recalled, from David's childhood, the purple dinosaur toy called Barney that was guaranteed to empower the child, a multimillion-dollar brainstorm for cashing in on stupid parents. "Did he explain what he was doing here? How did he get here?"

"He came in your car."

"Of course. Well, that was cheaper than flying. What was the purpose of his trip?"

"Are you asking me?"

"David, cut me some slack. I've been halfway around the world."

"Did you sleep in those clothes, Dad?"

Now Szabo was on the defensive, still in the clothes of his Düsseldorf night with Amai, whom, in this moment of bewilderment, he was certain he should have married. Escape was not so easy. If he hadn't fallen off a tractor and injured himself, this squirrel Barney wouldn't be in the middle of his life. What would he be doing? Living in Germany with Amai, siring octoroons and trying to keep her out of the bars? "I'm afraid I underpacked, David. I wore this suit at meetings and slept in it on the plane. So, Barney was here . . . for what?"

"I guess for counseling of some kind, to prepare me for the outside world."

David winced at these last two words.

"Why would Barney think he was in a position to counsel you?"

"If you don't know, Dad, I'm sure I don't either. At least he has a Ph.D."

"Is that what he told you?"

"Dad, I'm not following this! I didn't send him here—you did!"

"I know, I know, and I'm sure it's all to the good. Was Barney helpful?"

"You tell me. He said I should go home and take over the ranch."

"It's hardly a ranch, David. It's just some property. What made him think you should do that?"

"Nothing you need to hear."

"What do you mean by that? I want to hear what some jackass with a Ph.D. had to say."

"You won't like it."

"David, I'm a big boy. Tell me."

"He said that you're incompetent and that it's only a matter of time before you break your neck doing something you have no business doing."

Furious, Szabo took this in with a false thoughtful air. Karen had said almost exactly the same thing. But her words had been motivated by a wish to replace the property with a winter home in San Luis Obispo, a town that had ranked number 1 in a *Times* survey of residential contentment.

"I trust you told Dr. Barney Q. Shitheel that you were not interested."

"I didn't tell him that, Dad."

"What did you tell him?"

David smiled at his father. "I told him I wasn't welcome there."

"You could have come there anytime you wanted."

"Right."

"What's this? Dave, why are you crying?"

David wiped his eyes with the back of his hand and spoke with odd detachment. "I knew I would never understand business, but I worked on a lot of ranches in high school. I was good at that."

Not all the fight was gone out of Szabo. Nor had he given up on the story he'd been telling himself. But even as he asked his derisive question he was reminding himself how he might have been absent for his own child. "Did you think selling drugs was a way of learning business?"

David looked weary. He didn't want to play anymore. "You're right, Dad. What was I thinking?"

"I'm not saying I'm right."

"No, Dad, you're one hundred percent right."

"Well," he said, "I'm right some of the time."

This exchange, more than anything, troubled Szabo. Here was David, broken down, imprisoned, soon to be released with his stigma. And Szabo was only adding to his insecurity, instead of trying to make the situation better.

THERE WAS PLENTY TO DO WHEN HE GOT HOME. AND THERE was something to learn when he visited his mother: Barney had absconded with the Charlie Russell painting. The next morning, Szabo met the detective who was interviewing his mother while fanning away the smoke with his clipboard. She only glanced at Szabo, crestfallen, defeated. From the detective, a handsome fellow in a short-sleeved shirt, too young for his mustache, Szabo learned that his ranch hand's name wasn't Barney; it was Ronny—Ronny Something. Ronny's gift was for slipping into a community with one of his many small talents: the sculptural woodpile had taken him far. The painting would go to a private collector, not likely to be seen again. "This isn't Ronny's first rodeo," the detective said. "The only thread we've got is the Ph.D. There is no actual Ph.D., but it's the one thing Ronny drops every time. There's been a string of thefts, and they all lead into the same black hole. I don't know why everyone is so sure that Ronny wants to help them."

When Szabo repeated this to Melinda and saw her wide eyes, he just shrugged and shook his head. Maybe to change the subject, she asked after David, and Szabo told her that he would soon be coming home.

STARS

Only the very treetops caught the first light as Jessica started up Cascade Creek, a sparkling crevice in a vast bed of spruce needles. As she walked, the light descended the trunks and ignited balsamic forest odors, awakening the birds and making it easy to find stepping-stones to cross the narrow creek. She'd found this trail on a Forest Service map; the contour lines had suggested a climb she could manage, and by scrutinizing images on Google Earth she had seen the small watershed open into what looked like a meadow or a strip of saturated ground. Jays were foraging in the hawthorns and, as day emerged, the hurrying clouds signaled fast-changing weather. Jessica's pack held a spare down vest, a windbreaker, and an apple.

She came to a spot where the creek fell through a tangle of evergreen roots to form a plunge pool. Sitting for a moment, she followed the movement of bubbles into its crystalline depths, lost in her thoughts, free of history. Time was not the same dimension here that it was in the rest of her life, and floating like this was something to be savored. The bubbles in the plunge pool reminded her of the stars she had fallen in love with so long ago, years before she became an astronomer and began to spend her days analyzing solar data from the *Yohkoh* satellite or the RHESSI spectroscopic imager. The stars were no longer a mystery to her; these bubbles would have to do.

After the plunge pool, the trail became steeper, and it pleased Jessica to feel her attention shift to her aching calves. She surprised a hawk on a low branch, not a soaring hawk but one that flashed through trees and seemed to take her with it. As she followed its search for an opening wide enough to ascend through, she saw a bright, grassy area ahead, a gap of light in the evergreens. She would explore there, then retrace her steps down the creek.

Once she'd reached the edge of the meadow, she stopped, unable at first to understand what she was seeing: two figures, proximate and mutually wary, one circling the other. Without moving, she grasped that a man, pistol dangling from one hand, was contemplating a wolf he had trapped; and the wolf, its foreleg secured in the jaws of a trap, was watching the man as he looked for a shot. Then the wolf turned and faced the forest in what seemed a despairing gesture. Jessica began to shout, running toward the man. She called, "You're not going to do that!"

The man turned, startled. "I sure am," he said gently. He was of an indeterminate age, tall and bareheaded in a canvas coat. His lace-up boots had undershot heels. A hat lay on the ground by his foot; his face was slick with sweat. "If this isn't something you'd like to watch, you might just want to be elsewhere."

Jessica was taken aback by his soft voice and by his peculiar tidiness. She noticed a mule tied in the trees, plywood panniers lashed to its ribs. Looking back at the terrified wolf, which was trying now to fling itself away from the trap, she heard herself say, "I'd rather shoot you than that animal."

"Oh? I don't think you know how hard it is to pull a trigger," the man said. "You have to feel pretty strongly about anything you kill. My old man used to tell me that you have to kill something every day, even if it's a fly, or you lose the knack."

He handed her the gun, and Jessica took it readily, surprised at how warm it was in her hand. She had a sense that some kind of power might shift to her, if she knew what to do with it.

"You obviously don't read the papers," she said. "People aren't having any trouble pulling the trigger these days."

"I'll take it back now, thank you," the man said patiently. "I need to go about my business, and it doesn't look to me like you feel any big need to save this animal." The wolf was on its belly now, staring at the trees, its trapped leg drawn out taut in front of it.

"I'm going to shoot you," Jessica said.

She could almost see these words go out of her mouth.

"You think you're going to shoot me."

"I know I am."

"Just wait until you try to turn him loose. That wolf isn't going to be very nice to you."

When the man seized the barrel of the gun, she felt as if she might fall, but she let him pull it away. Later, she felt that she hadn't struggled hard enough. "You need to picture this thing a little better," the man explained in his thoughtful voice. "I'm going to make a rug for my cabin out of his hide. I'm going to make jewelry out of his teeth and claws. I'm going to sell them on eBay."

Jessica started to laugh miserably, and by the time the laughter got away from her the man had joined in, as though it were funny. The wolf was watching them, up on its haunches now. The man wiped his eyes. "Honest to gosh," he said. "Where would we be without laughter?"

Maybe the laughter was an opening. Jessica tried to explain to the man that the wolf stood for everything she cared about, everything wild. But he laughed and said, "Honey, can't you hear those chain saws coming?" Her confession had gotten her nowhere.

The wolf made no attempt to escape as the man walked over and killed it.

IT WAS THE ONLY PLACE YOU COULD GET COFFEE AT THAT hour—sunrise had barely lit the front of the building—and the customers were already lined up right to the door. The young woman at the cash register, too sleepy to interact with anyone, made change mechanically, while her colleague, a young man in a woolen skullcap, seemed to hang from the levers as he waited for the coffee to pour. Jessica kept her hands in the sleeves of her sweater as she awaited her turn behind four people staring absently at their phones. Once she had the coffee, she put a second paper cup around it, went out into the morning, and felt a minor wave of optimism, ascribable to either caffeine or the sunrise.

Customers emerging from the shop were quickly absorbed by the town. As Jessica walked to Cooper Park to watch the morning dogs, the sunlight caught her, and she blew silver steam from her mouth. She had still been able to see a few stars when she left home, but they were gone now. The diehard dog people were already at the park, with others trickling in from the old houses around the neighborhood. This was the world of the cherished mongrel—rescue dogs, shelter dogs, strays that had dodged euthanasia: a part border collie that made an exuberant entrance, then spun away from any dog that wanted to play, a dignified Labrador with its nose elevated, a greyhound missing a tail, a terrier that kept getting overrun by the others only to bounce up again in furious pursuit. They all froze in tableau at the call of a crow, a distant siren, or the arrival of another dog. The owners sat at the perimeter watching, as if at the theater. It occurred to Jessica that she might have been happier as a dog. Then again, she didn't play well with others.

She had always had the stride of a country girl and felt that she had to cut through people to get anywhere. She walked at such a clip that someone asked, "Where's the fire?" On her way to the university, she bumped into an unyielding clutch of trustafarians, gathered for the day's recreation in front of Poor Richard's, and one called her a douche cannon. A woman swiped at her from behind with an umbrella. She stopped only to pet dogs or to side-slip between children. In a clear stretch, she tended to run. She seemed to be clashing with everything.

Walking was how she'd met Andy Clark, on the trail along Bozeman Creek. Later, it occurred to her that it was odd for someone to hike the way he did, with his hands in his pockets. Andy was thirty years old, looked about twenty, and was in no hurry. No hurry was Andy all over. He was good-natured and full of ideas, but Jessica suspected that there was something behind that—not concealed, necessarily, but hard to know, and possibly not all that interesting. Still, Andy's boyish momentum and playfully forceful suggestions had made him good company at a time when she needed cheering up; and for a while, at least, he hadn't gotten on her nerves. It was eventually reported to Jessica that, during the production of an independent film in the city the previous summer, Andy had hung around the actresses so much that he was referred to locally as "the sex Sherpa to the stars." When Jessica brought this up, she was exasperated to see that it pleased him.

It was unclear whether Andy had a job, though he did have an office with a daybed for what he called "nooners." Jessica didn't learn this appalling term until she'd already experienced it, stumbling absently onto the daybed with him. Her previous affairs had been grueling, and she had promised herself not to do grueling ever again. She saw Andy, initially, as a kind of homeopathic remedy. But then something got under her skin. Maybe it was the kara-oke machine in his bachelor apartment or his unpleasant cat or the Ping-Pong matches he pressured her into; the way he darted around in a crouch at his end of the table made it clear to her that she'd never sleep with him again.

This was something of a pattern with Jessica. Whatever interest she may have had or whatever not particularly spiritual need she felt impelled to satisfy was soon drowned by a tide of little things she would have preferred not to notice. By the time she encountered the wolf, she was sick of Andy. And that would have been that, if he hadn't continued to pursue her and if she hadn't had some creeping sadness to escape.

A few days after her hike to Cascade Creek, Andy invited Jessica to dinner at his father's house, on a ridge high above the M north of the city. She went reluctantly. On the winding road there, a white-tailed buck trotted in front of the car, wearing its horns like a death sentence. Andy led Jessica with a slight pressure on her elbow through the front door to his waiting father, who seemed to have positioned himself well back from the door he'd just answered.

"Dad, please meet Jessica Ramirez," he said. And, in a get-a-load-of-this tone, "She's an astronomer!"

Mr. Clark was a tall, thin, sallow widower in an oversize cardigan, whose pockets had been stretched by his habit of plunging his fists into them. His upper lip seemed permanently drawn down, as if he were shaving under his nose. He led them to the living room in a house that appeared to be all windows. The mountains were just visible in the last of the sunset. Mr. Clark didn't look back or speak a word in their direction, confident that they were following appropriately.

In the living room, which had an adjoining bar, Mr. Clark made them drinks with a perfunctory "I hope that suits you." Jessica sniffed hers, and Andy's father aimed a hard, questioning beam at her. "Okay?"

Jessica said, "No top brands?"

My God, she thought, what is the matter with me?

Mr. Clark turned his querying look on his son, who glanced away, and by some unspoken accord the three headed over to the picture window. It was dark now, and only the lights of the city

were visible. Jessica felt as if she were hovering among the con-
stellations, and that lifted her spirits. The way that geologists are
liberated in time, she thought, astronomers are freed by space.
Mr. Clark touched her glass with his. He wore a piece of eight on
a chain around his neck. "Well, stargazer, what's happening in the
firmament today?"

"Nothing new," she said. "Some seasonal star clusters and nebu-
lae. Are you interested?"

Mr. Clark said, "I'm afraid I miss out on all that. I'm a day guy or
I'm in bed. Trout fishing is my thing. I have a collection of bamboo
rods, by all the great makers. Would you like to see them?"

"No."

Mr. Clark turned abruptly and left the room. Andy gazed after
him thoughtfully, before saying, "He's not coming back."

"Seriously? Because I didn't want to see his fishing poles?" Andy
let a censorious silence fill the air. It worked. She briefly thought of
ways to make amends, but it was too late now to pour love on the
fishing poles.

Andy didn't speak as they made their way back down the winding road where they'd seen the deer. Finally, he asked, "What would
you like me to do, Jessica?"

"Drop me off," she said.

JESSICA'S CLOSEST FRIEND AT THE UNIVERSITY WAS DR. TSIEU,
a fellow astronomer, barely five feet tall in generous shoes. When
Dr. Tsieu's baby boy was born, Jessica was nearly the first to the
maternity ward; Dr. Tsieu seemed too small to have accomplished
such a thing. When Jessica got to her lab, Dr. Tsieu asked her out to
lunch, but she said that she wanted to go for a walk, that she needed
the exercise—which she did after a morning in front of her computer screen. But her walk up and down Olive Street and around
the post office was so restless and agitated that it didn't provide
relief from anything. Of course, she could not possibly have pulled
the trigger. Why even go over it in her mind? Why? Why again?
And what on earth had made her so sullen with Andy's father and
his blasted fishing poles? She deliberated over this transgression
as though it had the same importance as her failure to shoot that

man. She wondered if she was just too inflexible. In time, would she become one more peevish old spinster in the hideous rest home behind the Walmart?

She drove to the mall and, without more of a plan than getting through the lunch hour, wandered into a shoe store. A lone customer stood at the display rack turning the shoes over, one after another, to look at their soles. Jessica recalled the proverb "Hell is a stylish shoe." A salesman greeted her at the door, a young man with a shaved head and a black turtleneck. Too intimate from the start, he held each selection so close to her face that she had to lean back to get a better look. She felt his breath as he pressed some studded, sparkly sneakers on her. Jessica found it fascinating that he thought she would want these, or the next pair he held up—stiletto-heeled jobs that seemed lewd, as did his smirk. The salesman didn't conceal his disappointment when she bought a pair of marked-down Vera Wang flats. She bought them because they seemed so pedestrian. Men preferred women teetering, so she chose to walk like a Neanderthal.

Traffic was thick on North Seventh, and she timed the lights wrong. Glancing at her watch, she failed to notice one turn green and heard a loud horn blast. In the mirror, she saw a cowgirl in a pickup truck giving her the finger. When she moved forward, the truck tailgated her, inches away. Jessica peered sharply into the rearview mirror, stabbed at the brakes, and the truck plowed into her. The two vehicles pulled to the side of the road.

The door of the truck burst open, and the cowgirl came wheeling toward Jessica's car. Jessica was on the phone calmly telling the secretary at her department the reason for her delay. She rolled the window down slightly and addressed the raging cowgirl. "Let's wait for the police. Do you have insurance?"

The police arrived in a pageantry of flashing lights—a single officer, who got out and chatted familiarly with the cowgirl as she held her thick braid with both hands. Isn't it nice that they're friends? Jessica thought. There was no denying her malice, no matter how she tried to stand apart from it. Then the officer came over to Jessica's car, hardly needing to duck in order to peer into her window. "What'd you do that for?" he barked. Jessica contemplated her steering wheel. "You caused that accident by braking suddenly!"

"You know the law. She rear-ended me."

"Don't you lecture me, lady," he shouted.

Jessica gave him time to settle down before raising her eyes to his and asking, "What is this really about, Officer? Is it because you're short?"

THE NEXT DAY, JESSICA WAS SILENT AT THE DEPARTMENT meeting but asked Dr. Tsieu, the only other woman in their group, to stay afterward. Dr. Tsieu tilted her head, hands laced over her stomach, always keen to listen. Jessica said, "I'm going to take a leave."

"And?" Dr. Tsieu hardly seemed surprised.

"I'm losing my marbles."

"Anger or disgust?" Dr. Tsieu asked. "Despair, malaise, detachment, loss of purpose?"

She's trying to cheer me up, Jessica thought, complying with a grin that felt idiotic.

"It's à la carte."

There was an anger specialist right there in town, and Jessica arranged to see him, since anger was at least one component of what she was experiencing, and she was unaware of a therapist who specialized in disgust or any of the other things on Dr. Tsieu's list. A friendly giant, the therapist was dressed like an outdoorsman, in Pendleton items that were far too warm for his office. Jessica had never had counseling before and was startled to find the man so interactive. She made a summary of her concerns, and he mugged through every one of them. It seemed that he intended to cure her through his facial expressions. The prickly feeling of confinement she had in his office, the colorized photograph of his wife and children, the diplomas, the complimentary pharmaceutical notepad, and his gooberish attempts to forecast calm all convinced her that this wasn't going to work. At the end of the session, he asked her to see the receptionist, but she went sightless through the lobby.

She decided to stick to walking. If that didn't work, she would turn herself over to some program. There were now customized rehabilitation programs that combined therapy with kayaking, weight loss, and makeovers. It was part of her problem, she thought, that she could foresee a stream of self-evident lectures and desolating group sessions with people who knew why they were angry or disgusted, while her disappointment seemed to be rooted in humanity in general. In college, she had read Faulkner's Nobel Prize speech, in which he asserted that mankind would not only endure but prevail; these days, she thought that this was the most depressing thing she'd ever come across. She no longer had any idea why she had become an astronomer. Had she expected to live in space?

She walked day after day in the hills and mountains around town, in the Bridgers, the Bangtails, and the Tobacco Roots. It was autumn now, and the chokecherry thickets and hawthorn breaks were changing color. Sometimes she went with other hikers, but she rarely spoke to them. At night, she treated her blisters and planned the next day's walk. Once, she fell asleep with her shoes on, to the static of a radio station gone off the air. The phone messages piled up until her voice-mail box was full. Ho, ho, ho, she thought, this is a crisis. Before sunrise, she lay in bed staring at the window for the first signs of light. Andy's last message suggested that she go to hell. She saved that one, suspecting that she might already be there.

She ran into Dr. Tsieu at the food co-op and, feeling comradely, told her about the hikes. Dr. Tsieu smiled supportively and said, "I feel sorry for your shoes." By that time she was traveling to more-remote areas to walk, distant prairie hills and wilderness foothills. She got lost more than once and only just made it out of the hills, in flight from hypothermia. Her eyesight grew exceptionally sharp, and she could see ravens in the dark, the shadows of animals in brush, and the old footprints of her predecessors. In this state, her own hands seemed to glow, the stars fierce and the moon more than usually banal.

Jessica kept walking into winter. Twice, Andy tried to join her, jumping out of his little car at the trailhead, but the chill drove him back, shivering and waving her on in disgust. It was only a matter of time before she came to her senses, he told her the second time. He yelled something else, but he was too far away by then for her to hear.

In the gathering dark and the swirling snow, she began to imagine voices and distantly wondered if she could still see the trail. She stopped to listen more closely, hoping to hear something new through the wind. A pure singing note rose, high and sustained, then another, in a kind of courtly diction.

Wolves.

SHAMAN

THE RILEYS LIVED ON A SMALL PIECE OF LAND, THE REMAINS of a much-bigger property that had been diminished over the generations; but what was left was a lovely place: the two-story clapboard house, built in 1911 in an old grove of cottonwoods, was fed crystalline water by a hillside spring and graced by morning sun in the kitchen and a shelter belt of chokecherry and caragana. On the benches above the creek, the evening sun revealed old tepee rings from when the land had all been Indian country. The doorstop at the front entrance was a stone hammer for cracking buffalo bones. Good hard coal from Roundup filled the shed, and on a painted iron flagpole the American flag popped in the west wind until it was in ribbons and had to be replaced. The house had a hidden fireplace vented by a center chimney, in which, during Prohibition, Pat Riley's grandfather had made whiskey, which he sold from the trunk of his Plymouth at country dances. He was thus able to reverse the contraction of the property, for the time being, which soon resumed under Pat's father, a small-time grain trader, usually described as "a fine fellow, never made a dime." The Plymouth remained, with two rusty bullet holes, the shots fired from the inside during a hijacking attempt, and was now embedded in an irrigation dam serving two neighbors, since the Rileys had lost the water rights. The property, Pat's birthright, was the Rileys' pride and joy. The point of all their work, however tedious, was to keep them on the place.

Pat was a physical therapist who made the rounds of the small hospitals and rest homes and clinics in southwest Montana. Pat loved his job, feeling that he helped people every day he worked, mostly with postoperative rehabilitation and the debilities of age. He found the residents at the rest homes especially interesting: old cowboys, state politicians, a veteran of the Women's Army Air Corps, and so on. His wife Juanita's job at the courthouse was tiresome: reconciling ledgers, posting journal entries for accruals and transfers, tracking grant revenues and expenditures, and filing, filing, filing! So it was that, on the occasion of Pat's overnight trip for a case in Lewistown, Juanita was ripe for the visit of the shaman. As a point of fact, she fancied him before even knowing he was a shaman. She just figured he was looking for a ranch job, but she never found a chance to tell him there hadn't been a cow on the place in forty years.

Juanita hardly knew what a shaman was and would have pictured someone on the Discovery Channel, feathered, painted, beaded, perhaps belled—certainly not someone dressed like this or presenting a calling card. His name was Rudy, and he seemed like an Olympian in his tracksuit and Nike shoes. He explained that he was an anthropologist and arid lands botanist, whose work had led him to discover a spiritual being living under a sandstone ledge on the Medicine Bow River, also named Rudy. It had taken seven years for the two Rudys to track each other down and become the united Rudy now standing before Juanita and touching a button of her blouse for emphasis. Juanita felt the heat rise. "I was out in the prairie. It was a hot day. All I could hear was wind and crickets or birds. Then the grass seemed to creak under my feet and I could feel the other Rudy was near and coming to me. The wind stopped as Rudy arrived. It was a lighthearted moment, Juanita. I said, 'Welcome aboard.' And that quick, I was unified. I was undivided, united as one, the one and only Rudy. But now there was . . . something else." He seemed disturbed by Juanita's hard, restless gaze. She let him follow her into the house, where she dug her phone out of her yellow, fringed purse hanging on the doorknob. She called her husband. "Pat, I've got a shaman here at the house. When are you coming home? You heard me. How on earth should I know? He says he's a shaman." She cupped the phone and said to the stranger, "What exactly is a shaman?"

"That's a long story. I—"

"He says it's a long story. Okay, sure, see you in a few."

She hung up. It would not be a few minutes, more like a day, before she saw Pat. But the ruse had an immediate effect on Rudy the shaman: panic.

"Does he mean literally 'a few minutes'?"

"Maybe five. He has to stop for cigarettes."

Rudy the shaman burst through the door at a dead run. Juanita watched him windmill down the driveway and out onto the county road, stooping to pick up some kind of pack at the corner. She grabbed the phone again.

"As soon as I told him you were about to arrive, he ran for it."

"Juanita, listen to me, you need to call the sheriff."

"And tell him what? I had a shaman at the house?"

"What does that even mean?"

"Pat! I don't know. I told you that."

"Well, call anyway and then call me back. Or I'll call them. No, better you, in case they need a description."

"Aren't you just assuming this guy is a criminal?"

"Maybe that's all a shaman is, for Chrissakes. Just call and then call me back."

At first, Juanita resisted making the call, then, realizing Pat wouldn't let it go, she picked up the phone. Sheriff Johnsrud was at a county commissioners' meeting, but she was put through to Eric Caldwell, his deputy.

"Hi, Juanita."

"Eric, some strange guy stopped by here. Said he was a— something or other. When I told him Pat was due home, he ran out the door in kind of a panic."

"That doesn't sound good."

"I don't think it's a big deal, but Pat insisted I call."

"Pat has a point. Describe this guy, would you, Juanita? What'd you say he was?"

"I can't remember, but he was wearing kind of a tracksuit, good-looking guy, maybe thirty-five, odd but with nice manners and one of those big watches tells you how far you walked, wavy brown hair, and talked educated like."

"Whoa, Juanita, you did get a pretty good look!"

"That'll do, Eric."

"Okay, we'll check it out. Wavy hair. Got it."

"Do me a favor, call Pat on his cell or he'll fret."

Afterward, Juanita had to piece the story together. Sheriff Johnsrud came back from the commissioners' meeting and joined Eric in scouring the area between the Riley place on the county road and the edge of town, down by the Catholic church and the ball field. They confronted Rudy just past the Lewis and Clark Memorial. When he went for something in his backpack, Sheriff Johnsrud shot him. Looking at the body, Johnsrud said, "He's done. Stick a fork in him." Eric pushed the backpack open with his foot and said there was no gun. Neither spoke until Johnsrud mused that they should go get one, and Eric nodded. "That way," said the sheriff, "it's a senseless tragedy."

Rudy, a low-risk mental patient, had just walked out of the Warm Springs hospital. The backpack contained pebbles, a dead bird, and a book on teaching yourself to dance. There hadn't been a cloud in the sky for a week in Rudy's hometown on the Wyoming border. He could have walked there in half a day.

It had been too obvious that Rudy was harmless. The doctors at the Warm Springs hospital made such a huge point of it that the whole town was embarrassed. Otis Sheare at the Ford dealership said it was like they had shot the Easter Bunny, "Town Without Pity," and so forth. So Sheriff Johnsrud conceded the terrible misfortune and took full responsibility. After all, he had fired the shot. But eventually Johnsrud changed, or everyone thought he had, though some admitted they would've changed, too, if such a thing happened to them, or else they concluded they were only imagining the sheriff was any different than he had always been. Eric, however, who had been born right there in town, moved away. Eventually people quit asking where Eric had got off to, just assuming he had landed on his feet somewhere. Probably his sister still heard from him. She lived over where the first post office burned down, giving her a great view of the mountains.

When, sitting under the Dos Equis beer umbrella, Pat joked that Eric had left law enforcement, Juanita startled herself by spitting in his face. Things had started to go wrong for them, though it didn't seem so at first and not really for a while afterward, because the Cancún trip had provided needed relief, especially for Juanita, who found she could still turn a few heads on the beach. "Oh God, we're not really going back to Montana," she said on the last day. Pat said,

"I hate to think how much we'll miss these warm sea breezes," but that wasn't what she meant at all, at all, at all.

During a pensive moment in the airport, while waiting to board, Pat said, "Tell me honestly, Juanita, why did you spit in my face?"

"I admit I thought about it."

"Darling, you didn't think about it, you did it. You spit in my face."

"I did?"

Juanita found this very disturbing. She knew she'd thought about it but . . . really?

Winter went on well into April, and they both were working very hard, trying to become a "unit" again, but the word itself had lost its meaning. They had been one for so long they couldn't comprehend why it had become so hard. They couldn't understand what was happening to them in other ways either. For example, Sandy Hayes, the sheriff's dispatcher, who worked at the courthouse down the hall from Juanita and was just about her best friend, right out of the blue told Juanita to her face that she was a bitch on wheels. Juanita was astonished.

"What can you possibly mean!"

"Isn't it obvious, Juanita?"

Juanita shrank into the files and deeds of her musty corner and went off to lunch with her head down. She didn't want to dignify Sandy's remark by asking further what it meant, and as a result it just hung over her like a cloud. She quit going to the window and staring in the direction of their house, almost visible beyond the poplars at the fairgrounds. Oddly, she became more efficient. The small annoyance she once felt at being confined to this room was gone. There was a kind of relief in feeling she belonged here, as though the fight had gone out of her. And what good had that been anyway?

Pat's situation had become more precarious. While rehabilitating an old priest after rotator cuff surgery, he had been a bit zealous, causing a new tear. It was quickly repaired, but the surgeon appeared at physical therapy and rebuked Pat, who would remember the vehemence, if not the words particularly, and the fact that the surgeon, still in his scrubs, wore the most beautiful pair of oxblood loafers, slippers almost, with the thinnest of soles. Pat was so friendly with the staff that he was ashamed to have been scolded in front of them like a dog or a child. They couldn't look at him.

The exceptionally long winters—the drifted driveway, the circles of ice in the windows, the days that abruptly ended in afternoon— might have had something to do with it, but that same hard April they decided to put the place on the market. They made no secret of thinking it a case of good riddance and didn't mind letting the neighbors and their former friends know it. They put up a FOR SALE BY OWNER out front and awaited results.

At the courthouse, Juanita held up their deed for Sandy the dispatcher to see. "This will have a new name on it for the first time in ninety years. It's only a matter of time."

"Where do you think you're headed?"

"I'll let you know."

Sandy went back to her desk opposite the front stairs. There wasn't any point in talking to Juanita anymore. Pat used to be so much fun, too. Now he was a regular sad sack; so maybe Juanita came by this new disposition honestly. The truth was, they didn't know where they were headed, but since they had never before known liquidity, they were sure it would come with ideas they didn't yet have, ideas resembling hopeful points on the map. This confidence came and went, and there was little to be gained by mentioning the dread that seemed to seep out of nowhere.

Someone pulled up into the driveway in a brown four-door. It was the same shade of brown as Pat's grandfather's shot-up Plymouth rip-rapping the irrigation dam upstream. They watched from the edges of the front window, careful not to seem eager. The driver's door opened, and a pair of narrow legs in old farmer pants swung out, resting on the ground. The driver gingerly slid out and shut the door: a woman perhaps just entering old age and remarkably unkempt, the wild gray hair pinned off her forehead with a red plastic comb, her barn coat done about the waist with twine. Walking unsteadily, she stared hard toward the house; she did not have the look of a prospect.

Pat and Juanita opened the door before the woman could knock. She made no attempt at introducing herself. "Yes?" said Juanita, Pat at her side attempting, "How can we help you?"

"I'm not sure you can," she said distantly, looking from one to the other, and then just stopped. She had green eyes. Later, when Pat and Juanita remarked on them to each other, it seemed to start a conversation that went nowhere.

"What brings you here?" Pat asked like some sort of radio announcer too hearty for this small stalemate.

"A glass of cold water out of that spring behind the house."

"Why, most certainly! You know, it's piped right to the faucet. So why don't you come in. I'll bet you're thirsty."

"For some of that spring water."

"You shall have it!" said Pat in that same hale voice, causing Juanita to glance quickly at him.

"How did you know about the spring?" Juanita chirped.

"I was told about it."

They sat the woman down at the kitchen table made of cottonwood planks from the old stall barn. Pat had fitted the planks together with perfect joints when they were first married. This encumbrance they also intended to leave behind, because, as Juanita said, "It weighs a ton." Pat felt they could have taken it but didn't want to argue.

Juanita went to the sink and filled her tallest glass, and as she started to turn toward the refrigerator, the woman said, "No ice," so Juanita turned back and set the glass of water before her. The woman nodded thanks. Pat sat at the far end tilting back his chair, hands behind his head in a pantomime of nonchalance.

The woman drained the glass and held it to eye level as though to look through it. Staring thus, she said, "I'm Rudy's mother, the dead boy."

Pat pulled his chair upright and set his hands close to him on the table. Juanita grinned with pain. "I'm so sorry."

Pat said, "We're both so sorry."

"Oh?"

After a long silence, Juanita asked, "Is there anything we can do?"

"Sure," she said, fishing a cigarette out of her coat and lighting it with a beat-up old Zippo. Pat and Juanita refrained from mentioning how much they hated smoking. The woman held the cigarette between her second and third fingers, as if in the middle of her hand. "You can tell me about his last day here."

"I can do that," said Juanita, getting braver. "He—Rudy—really just turned up and immediately started talking about his life like I had known him before."

"You had known him before?"

"No, I don't think so."

"Okay."

"Oh yes, and then, uh, we were just chatting in general, well, really it was quite brief, and he told me he—"

"He gave you some reason to call the law?"

"Well, ma'am, I have to be honest, he kind of frightened me the way he, the way he was talking." Juanita was startled to hear her own voice rise so quickly. "How he knew things."

The woman took the cigarette from her mouth but kept it in her hand in front of her face. "Rudy was a shaman."

"We don't even know what that is!" cried Pat.

The woman got up and dropped the cigarette hissing into the nearly empty water glass. "I just feel like you made a big mistake, but I guess time will tell if it hasn't already."

At the door they assured her they felt just as bad as she did. She shook her head slightly; she seemed to wonder at them. "I wouldn't have done that," she said. "I'd of had more sense."

They watched her go to her car. They expected her to say something or glance back, but no. In the house, when Juanita said she had eyes like a cat, Pat didn't seem to pick up on it, remarking instead that she must have been a great beauty in her day. He left the room, and Juanita emptied the cigarette butt into the sink before going to the window. The car was already gone.

CANYON FERRY

John's wife, Linda, hadn't remarried, but she was in a stable relationship with a reliable man, while John, laid off from the newspaper a year by then, was living alone in a way to suggest he always would—all of which made visitations a study in contrasts for their son, Ethan. John could have found another newspaper job—downsizing had only marginally trumped his proficiency—but it would have meant moving away, in preference to which he stayed in town and taught welding, his former hobby, to nontraditional students at the college. And two days a week, he met with the former host of a TV "blooper" show, helping him write his memoirs, an entirely lugubrious tale of imagined suffering. The ex-host was determined for posterity to know that belying those forty years of guffawing at the pratfalls of others, he had known real anguish and been misunderstood from the day he was born in the back of a taxi, his first recollection the foldout ashtray on the back of the driver's seat.

It might have seemed that Linda and her Lucifer—actually his name was Lucius, only John called him that—would supply at least a semblance of family life, while John the bachelor, led by his tuning fork into the hungry thickets of the town, would struggle to make time for Ethan. In actuality, Linda and Lucius found their bliss as two purposeful suits, both on the way up. It made John feel that his marriage of almost ten years had served as Linda's think tank for an eventual assault on the future, an unkind and somewhat-unwarranted version of facts, because she'd always said she wanted to work. She was pretty, and her life with John was meager, while Lucius was a rising star in banking, land, cattle, natural gas, and hydropower. John would learn only long after it mattered that the two had been exhausting their erotic urgency over four vigorous years of infidelity prior to the separation, which left John struggling to catch up in one sad purlieu after another, and feeling as a father nihilistic and unworthy. The three women he bedded during the proceedings were impossible to avoid, and when he ran into them, whether at the post office, the bank, or the Safeway, he just apologized. But each of these was a single unmarried woman and John was attractive, so they hardly knew how to take his contrition. If John had learned anything, it was that, once the threshold of venery was crossed, and all the furies unleashed, the aisles of the Safeway were no longer safe. A baffled if indignant former paramour in Cereals could loom with ominous incomprehension.

For the regular handoff, John appeared at Linda's new house with its wonderful view of the snowy massif of the Bridger Ridge. The moment was rarely less than painful despite that it had gone on for more than a year. This time, Ethan was already dressed in a red snowsuit and an insulated hat slightly too big for him. Linda hugged herself against the cold. It was easier all around to meet her ex-husband on the front step than have him come inside. Ethan's arms hung at his sides, and he glanced at his mother several times; she responded by resting a hand on his head. Ethan peered out from beneath that shelter while John stared at Linda with hopeless longing.

"I'll have him back by supper." He didn't want to say he'd have him "home" by supper but should have known that the struggle with that terminology was long lost.

"Perfect. You guys will have fun. Right, Ethan?" Ethan nodded grimly. His mother laughed at his posturing. "He'll be fine once you get going." Reflexively she touched her lips with her forefinger, which she then touched to Ethan's, then to John's.

John led Ethan by the hand to the car. He turned to give Linda a wave, but she was already gone behind the door. It was too cold for ceremonial lingering, though Ethan, too, stared at the door before getting into John's car with a boost.

"Do you want to take off your snowsuit?"

"No."

"Do you want to unzip it?"

"No. I want to listen to the radio."

"Can we just talk a little bit?"

"Okay."

It was quiet before John, his voice thick with emotion, spoke. "Do you like doing stuff with me?"

"It's okay."

"Because today we're going fishing."

Ethan looked startled and scrutinized his father with interest. He said, "But everything is frozen." They were following a Brink's truck changing lanes without signaling.

"We're going ice fishing. You drill a hole in the ice and drop your line through."

"Are there fish under there?"

"We're going to find out."

Canyon Ferry Lake, an impoundment of the Missouri River, spread before them as a vast sheet of ice that ended at a seam of open water, perhaps the old river. John parked across the ice from Confederate Gulch at the "silos," the tall brick towers for storing grain. The Big Belt Mountains rose against a blue sky marbled with cirrus clouds streaming toward them from the Gate of the Mountains. Ethan, suddenly excited, ran around the car helping John with their gear. An iron spud for making a hole in the ice stuck out of the trunk. Ethan tried to carry it, but it was too heavy. John had spent a bewildering hour at Sportsman's Warehouse and come away with only the minimal kit but all that he could understand. He could have spent a fortune on a gas-powered ice auger, heated shelter, and underwater cameras attached to TV monitors, which, said the salesman, would set him up "good as the next guy." But John settled for a box of assorted hooks and jigs, the spud, and a skimmer to clear slush from the hole.

Ethan carried these things while John toted a coffee can of night crawlers, two plastic buckets to sit on, and the iron spud. They headed out onto the ice, and John was immediately struck by a complete lack of topographic clues as to where to spud a hole; the fish could be anywhere in such a featureless and white expanse.

One other human was visible, pulling a black plastic sled heaped with all the things that John had seen at the store. Holding Ethan's hand, John waited for him on the near-shore ice. He stopped him to ask a few questions and show the man his gear.

"You got another tip-up?"

"Nope."

"You got just one?"

"Yes, that's right." He didn't want this guy giving Ethan the idea they weren't adequately equipped.

"Ooooohkay . . . ," said the fisherman, then suddenly, "Don't touch them fish, son." Ethan's hand recoiled from the man's bucket, and he looked at his father. "Why don't you go right there where I was at," the fisherman said. "I augured nine holes in a row. Counting from this side, hole number five was where most of the fish were. Put your tip-up there, but if I was you I wouldn't stay long. The wind comes up in about an hour, and it's a dad-gum typhoon. Black clouds come up past them hills right over there. When they do, you need to be long gone."

The fisherman continued on with his sled, his ice crampons allowing him a full and crunching stride, while John and Ethan slipped and skidded out onto the lake halfway to the thin black line of open water before they found the nine precise holes made by the fisherman's power auger. Together, they counted off until they reached number 5, and there they set down their buckets and gear. The holes had already begun to fill in, but John had acquired that skimmer, with which he quickly scooped out the slush to reveal the surprisingly mysterious black surface of the deep water.

He put out a bucket for Ethan to sit on, round and red as an apple in his puffy snowsuit, while his father fiddled with the tip-up rig until he understood how to bend the springy wire with the tiny flag into its notch and lowered the line adorned with a sparkling green jig and baited with a twisting night crawler. It seemed he was unspooling line forever before he reached bottom. He spread the braces across the span of hole and arranged the wire and flag that would spring up when they had a bite. Inverting his white bucket, he sat down opposite Ethan and waited with his hands stuffed up opposing sleeves.

"How long will this take?" asked Ethan.

"I wish I knew, Ethan."

"Is fishing always like this?"

"I guess you could say it's different every time."

Ethan thought for moment. "I wish fishing would hurry up."

"Are you warm enough in that thing?"

"It's boiling in here."

"How about your feet."

"They're boiling, too."

John, who could have used another layer of clothes himself, stood from time to time to bounce on the balls of his feet and clap his mittens together, at which sight Ethan nearly laughed himself off his pail. When John sat down again, he gazed around the shore, off toward the mountains; every now and then the light caught a car on the road to Helena, a quick flash, but otherwise the lake and its surroundings seemed completely desolate.

"What do you call Lucius?"

"I don't know."

You could call him Lucifer, thought John. Lucius, as John saw it, had tempted away his lively but somewhat-flaky wife and turned her into a career woman fit to stand beside him at the Consumer Electronics Association. They hadn't come out as a couple for a whole week before she was talking about the glass ceiling. Lucius was fifteen years older than Linda, who, though contented with the relationship, had shown no interest in becoming his fourth wife, something Lucius expected to happen sooner or later, as indeed it did. Lucius would tell his friends that the wedding was to be small and intimate; he wouldn't be inviting them this time. They'd slap him on the back and offer to come to the next one. This, with Linda on his arm. She seemed to take it in stride. Her eyes had by now opened to a much-larger world, if weekly trips through airport security were a gateway to such a thing. She must have thought so, because in an unguarded moment after she'd remarried, she called John a bump on a log. He felt betrayed. He'd always thought he'd been doing fine right up until his paper was restructured. But greater than his hurt was his worry about what place there would be for Ethan in Linda's new life.

The small red flag popped up, and Ethan was so startled he tumbled from his pail. John was able to lift him to his feet by a handful of snowsuit at his back. He set the tip-up to one side and felt the tautness on the line slowly traveling from the spool. He gave the line to Ethan who grasped it in both hands and smiled in amazement to feel the life in it. At John's direction he pulled fist over fist, the loose line falling behind him until with a heave the fish flew out of the hole into the air then bounced around on the ice. John held the fish, a yellow perch, close to Ethan who stared at its keen eye. "Throw him back?"

"Yes, please, back in the hole," said Ethan. John unhooked the perch and slipped it back in. Ethan leaned close and peered into the blackness. "He's gone."

John reset the tip-up and noticed that Ethan was more concentrated on its operation now that he had seen it work. He asked a few questions after he thought about the fish and its friends and what there was to eat down there. Then he said his feet were cold.

"Mine, too. Let's jump up and down." The two hopped around the fishing hole, and then Ethan fell on his back laughing until John picked him up by the front of his red one-piece like a suitcase. "Put your mittens on."

"Okay."

"And tell me if you get too cold."

"Oh-oh-kay."

"Are you cold now?"

"Okay."

"Ethan, be serious, are you cold?"

"No-kay. What is that?"

"What is what?"

"That black thing."

To the northwest, a storm cloud was climbing fast, dark and full of turbulence. John glanced at their fishing rig hoping the flag would pop up soon; he could see Ethan was eager for another fish. But then the wind was upon them, picking up with startling speed, sweeping shards of ice toward the seam of open water with an unremitting tinkle.

"Ethan, I think we should reel this thing up. This weather is—I don't know what this weather is doing."

John bent over the hole in the ice and was carefully spooling in the line, when he saw the little flag flutter in the corner of his eye. Just then a fish grabbed the bait and began pulling the line again. "Uh-oh, Ethan, we've got another one," he said as the wind rose to a screech. "I'm going to have to break it off. I hope that's okay—" No answer. "Okay, Ethan? Ethan, okay if we just let it go?"

John looked up and saw the boy forty feet away, tumbling like a leaf in the wind. He dropped the fishing line and stood, barely able to keep his own balance. Ice particles chimed in the air accompanying Ethan's jubilant laughter. John made for him, the wind pushing him forward, and each time Ethan got to his feet, crouching arms held apart for balance, he tumbled forward and skidded some more. John hurried but Ethan kept sliding faster. The black cloud roared like an engine overhead bringing a whirl of heavier snow that made Ethan harder to see as he slid yelling joyfully toward the open water. Trying to overtake him, John fell again and again, now with only the sound of laughter to guide him. He no longer knew where the water was, whether it was even in the general direction in which he was stumbling. He fell and crawled until he became aware of the stickiness of blood on his hands. Certain he had lost his way he stopped to listen, straining to distinguish any sound in the din of the storm. He had no idea which way he should go. Every impulse to move was canceled as soon as it arose.

The cloud passed overhead to the south and the Missouri River valley. The wind died as the remaining snow was sifted onto the ice, slowly unveiling a blue sky. Some forty feet away Ethan was clear as day in his red snowsuit. He was sitting crossed-legged next to the open water. "Daddy! Let's fish here!" As they crossed the ice toward the car, John saw his son look back toward the black line of water, and he knew he was troubled.

Linda met them at the door. Lucius was out. Ethan jumped into her arms, and John handed her the bundled snowsuit. "Mom, we had so much fun! We caught a fish and went sliding, with Daddy trying to catch me!" But looking back at his father in confusion, he seemed about to cry.

Linda asked, "Where was this?"

"Over toward Helena."

"A pond?"

"Not really."

"Oh, well, never mind. It sounds like a great place."

"I'll take you sometime."

Linda smiled, looked into his eyes, and gently rapped his chest with her knuckles. "Time to move on, Johnny, you know?"

John glanced away, pretending to look for Ethan. "Where'd he go?"

———

HOAGY BROWN, THE TV HOST, HAD LOST INTEREST IN HIS memoirs. He let John see the sex and fart bloopers that could not be broadcast; but after the sufferings of his deprived childhood had been recounted in full, he found he hardly cared about revisiting his later life, his several wives or his son, a La Jolla realtor. To John he seemed tired of living, having used up all the Schadenfreude that had propelled an illustrious career. He still had a dirty mind, though that too was fading, or perhaps he noticed John's lack of enthusiasm for his tales of conquest among women, most of whom were, even by Hoagy's account, dead anyway.

John didn't expect to be paid now that he was leaving the project, and Hoagy never offered it. Instead, he followed John to his car and said, "You're brushing me off, aren't you?"

"Not in the least, Hoagy, but I don't think at this late stage I have much to offer you."

"What late stage? I'm just getting started."

By then it was his time to have Ethan with him again, and he was excited about his plan for a hot-air-balloon ride, arranged and paid for at a popular "balloon ranch" in the foothills south of town. He paused before knocking on the door, a great oaken thing with a letter slot. On last year's Christmas card it had been adorned with a splendid wreath, in front of which Linda and Lucius beamed, with Ethan in the foreground between them in a little blazer and bow tie. John had felt some incomprehension at the assertive formality of this scene and wondered what it was about the heavy front door that even now made him feel affronted.

He knocked, and Lucius answered. "Oh, John, what a pleasure. Let me get Ethan. Ethan! It's Dad, get your things!"

Lucius ducked out of the doorway with a small, self-effacing bob that nevertheless left John waiting on the step looking into the hall. There he remained for a long time, his impulse to shut the door against the draft suppressed at the thought of again facing the letter slot and the expanse of varnished wood.

At length Lucius reappeared, wearing a frown of concern. He faced John silently in his cardigan, one arm clasped across his waist, the other holding his chin in deep thought. "I gather, John, that last week's experience at Canyon Ferry was pretty darn frightening for Ethan. Is that how you understand it, Linda?"

Linda answered from someplace inside. "It is."

"Linda's trying to watch Mary Tyler Moore," Lucius explained. "Some classic episode."

"And, what, Linda?" John called to her.

"And he doesn't want to go with you," came Linda's voice in reply. "Do you mind? Why prolong this?"

"May I speak to Ethan?"

"If that's what you require. Ethan, come speak to your father!"

Lucius seemed to be twisting with discomfort. He looked straight overhead and called out, "Please, Ethan, right now."

Linda said, "Sorry about not coming to the door, John, but I'm not decent."

Ethan appeared in flannel pajamas, a bathrobe, and rabbit slippers, head hung and glancing offstage in the direction of his mother. Lucius rested a hand on his head. John said in a voice of ghastly jocularity "What d'you say, Ethan? Aren't we going to have our day together? I've planned something you'll really like."

Ethan said, "I don't want to go with you."

John was amazed at his directness.

JOHN GOT INTERVIEWS AT SEVERAL PAPERS. HIS RECORD WAS good, and the owners all apologized for the pay. Three of the seven made the same remark: "It's a living." And so without great conviction, John found himself in charge of the news in Palmyra, North Dakota, which served an area identical in size to the principality of Liechtenstein, or so the *Herald*'s owner liked to say. Over the course of many years, John learned all there was to know about Palmyra, and almost nothing of the place he'd left, except that Linda had died, that Ethan had finished college and lived in Fresno, at least according to the last update he'd received quite some time ago. John assumed he was still around there somewhere—Ethan, that is. Lucifer could be anywhere.

RIVER CAMP

"Anytime you're on the Aleguketuk, you might as well be in heaven. I may never get to heaven, so the Aleguketuk will have to do—that, and plenty of beer! Beer and the river, fellows: that's just me.

"Practical matters: chow at first light. If you ain't in the chow line by oh-dark-thirty, your next shot is a cold sandwich on the riverbank. And don't worry about what we're going to do; you'll be at your best if you leave your ideas at home.

"Now, a word or two about innovation and technique. You can look at these tomorrow in better light, but they started out life as common, ordinary craft-shop dolls' eyes. I've tumbled them in a color solution, along with a few scent promulgators distilled from several sources. You will be issued six of these impregnated dolls' eyes, and any you don't lose in the course of action will be returned to me upon your departure. I don't want these in circulation, plain and simple.

"The pup tent upwind of the toilet pit is for anyone who snores. That you will have to work out for yourselves. I remove my hearing aid at exactly nine o'clock, so snoring means no more to me than special requests. From nine until daybreak, a greenhorn can be seen but not heard.

"Lastly, the beautiful nudes featured on the out-of-date welding-supplies calendar in the cook tent are photographs of my bride at twenty-two. Therefore that is a 1986 calendar and will not serve for trip planning. Besides, she left me and I'm only a little suicidal. Ha, ha!"

Marvin "Eldorado" Hewlitt backed his huge bulk out of the tent flap, making a sight gag of withdrawing his long gray beard from the slit as he closed it. Sitting on top of their sleeping bags, the surgeon Tony Capoletto and his brother-in-law Jack Spear turned to look at each other. Tony said, "My God. How many days do we have this guy? And why the pistol?"

Tony, the more dapper of the two, wore a kind of angler's ensemble: a multipocketed shirt with tiny brass rings from which to suspend fishing implements, quick-dry khaki pants that he'd turned into shorts by unzipping them at the knee, and wraparound shades that dangled from a Croakie at his chest. His pale, sharp-featured face and neatly combed hair were somewhat at odds with this costume.

"I have no idea," Jack said. His own flannel shirt hung loose over his baggy jeans. "He seemed so reasonable on the Internet."

Some sharp, if not violent, sounds could be heard from outside. Tony crawled forward in his shorts, carefully parting the entry to the tent to look out. Jack considered his friend's taut physique and tried to remember how long he'd had his own potbelly. Tony was always in shape—part handball, part just being a surgeon.

"What's he doing, Ton'?"

"Looks like he's chopping firewood. I can barely see him in the dark. Not much of the fire left, now."

"What was that stuff he made for dinner?"

"God only knows."

The tent smelled like camphor, mothballs; the scent was pretty strong. When Jack let his hand rest outside his sleeping bag, the grass still felt wet. It made him want to take a leak, but he didn't care to leave the tent as long as Hewlitt was out there.

Tony went back to his sleeping bag. It was quiet. A moment later his face lit up with blue light.

"You get a signal?"

"Are you kidding?" said Tony. "That would only inspire hope."

Tony's wife—Jack's sister—was divorcing him. There were no kids, and Tony said the whole thing was a relief, said that he was not bitter. Jack was quite sure Tony was bitter; it was Jack's sister who was not bitter. Jack had seen Gerri at the IGA, and she'd been decidedly unbitter—cheerful if not manic. She'd hoped they would have an "outtasight" trip. This was part of Gerri's routine, hip and lively for a tank town. Tony might have been a bit serious for her, in the end. Maybe he needed to lighten up. Jack certainly thought so.

Jack's wife, Jan, was one of the sad stories: having starred, in her small world, as a staggeringly hot eighteen-year-old when Jack, half cowboy and half high-school wide receiver, had swept her out of circulation, she had since gone into a rapid glide toward what could be identified at a thousand yards as a frump, and at close range as an angry frump. Gerri and Jan had driven "the boys" to the airport for their adventure together, each dreading the ride home, when in the absence of their men they would discover how little they had to talk about. In any case, they could hardly have suspected that they would never see their husbands again.

But the divorce wasn't the reason that Tony was so bent on a trip. He'd made some sort of mistake in surgery, professionally not a big deal—no one had even noticed—but Tony couldn't get it out of his mind. He'd talked about it in vague terms to Jack, the loss of concentration, and had reached this strange conclusion: "Why should I think I'll get it back?"

"You will, Ton'. It's who you are."

"Oh, really? I have never before lost concentration with the knife in my hand. Fucking never."

"Tony, if you can't do your work in the face of self-doubt, you may as well just quit now."

"Jack, you think you've ever experienced the kind of pressure that's my daily diet?"

Jack felt this but let it go.

Marvin Eldorado Hewlitt was now their problem. Jack had tried plenty of other guides, but they were all either booked or at a sportsmen's show in Oakland. He'd talked to some dandies after that, including a safari outfitter booking giraffe hunts. At the bottom of the barrel was Hewlitt, and now it was getting clearer why. So many of the things they would have thought to be either essential or irrelevant were subject to extra charges: fuel for the motor, a few vegetables, bear spray, trip insurance, lures, the gluten-free sandwich bread.

"But Marvin, we brought lures."

"You brought the wrong lures."

"I'll fish with my own lures."

"Not in my boat."

Lures: $52.50. Those would be the dolls' eyes.

"Marvin, I don't think we want trip insurance. I'm just glancing at these papers—well, are you really also an insurance agent?"

"Who else is gonna do it? I require trip insurance. I'm not God, but acts of God produce client whining I can't deal with."

Trip insurance: $384.75.

"Tony, give it up. There's no signal."

Tony looked up. "Was that a wolf?"

"I don't think it was a wolf. I think it was that crazy bastard."

The howl came again, followed by Marvin's chuckle.

"You see?"

Tony got out of his sleeping bag and peered through the tent flap.

"He's still up. Sitting by the fire. He's boiling something in some kind of a big cauldron. And he's talking to himself, it looks like. Or it's more like he's talking to someone else, but there's no one there that I can see. We're in the hands of a lunatic, Jack."

"Nowhere to go but up."

"You could say that. You could pitch that as reasonable commentary."

Jack felt heat come to his face. "Tony?"

"What?"

"Kiss my ass."

"Ah, consistency. How many times have I prayed for you to smarten up?"

Jack thought, I've got him by forty pounds. That's got to count.

The two fell silent. They were reviewing their relationship. So far, Tony had come up only with "loser," based on Jack's modest income; Jack had settled for "prick," which he based on the entitlement he thought all doctors felt in their interactions with others. This standoff was a long time coming, a childhood friendship that had hardened. Probably neither of them wanted it like this; the trip was supposed to be an attempt to recapture an earlier stage, when they were just friends, just boys. But the harm had been done. Maybe they had absorbed the town's view of success and let it spoil something. Or maybe it was the other thing again.

Outside, by the fire, Marvin was singing in a pleasant tenor. There was some accompaniment. Jack said, "See if he's got an instrument." Tony sighed and climbed out from his sleeping bag again. At the tent flap, he said, "It's a mandolin." And in fact at that moment a lyrical solo filled the air. Tony returned to his bag, and the two lay quietly, absorbing first some embellishment of the song Marvin had been singing and then a long venture into musical space.

Shortly after the music stopped, Marvin's voice came through the tent flap.

"Boys, that's all I can do for you. Now let's be nice to one another. We've got our whole lives ahead of us."

In a matter of minutes, the camp was silent. Stars rose high over the tents and their sleepers.

MORNING ARRIVED AS A STAB OF LIGHT THROUGH THE TENT flap and the abrupt smell of trampled grass and mothballs. A round, pink face poked through at them, eyes twinkling unpleasantly, and shouted, "Rise and shine!"

"Is that you, Marvin?" Tony asked, groggily.

"Last time I looked."

"What happened to the beard?"

"Shaved it off and threw it in the fire. When you go through the pearly gates, you want to be clean-shaven. Everybody else up there has a beard."

The flap closed, and Jack said, "I smelled it. Burning." Then he pulled himself up.

Jack fished his clothes out of the pile he'd made in the middle of the tent. Tony glanced at this activity and shook his head; his own clothes were hung carefully on a tent peg. He wore his unlaced hiking shoes as he dressed. Jack was briefly missing a shoe, but it turned up under his sleeping bag, explaining some of the previous night's discomfort.

Tony said, "It's time for us to face this lunatic if we want breakfast."

The sunrise made a circle of light in the camp, piled high with pine needles next to the whispering river. Hewlitt had hoisted the perishable supplies up a tree to keep them away from bears; a folding table covered by a red-and-white-checkered tablecloth was set up by the small, sparkling fire. Stones on either side of the fire supported a blackened grill, from which Hewlitt brought forth a steady stream of ham, eggs, and flapjacks.

Jack rubbed his hands together eagerly and said, "My God, it's like Chef Boyardee!" Tony rolled his eyes at this and smiled at Hewlitt, whose surprisingly mild and beardless face had begun to fascinate him. The beard, it was explained, was something Hewlitt cultivated for sportsmen's shows: he hated beards.

"I'm not ashamed of my face," he said. "Why would I hide it?"

Hewlitt had already eaten, and so Jack and Tony sat down at the table while he headed off toward the trees. Halfway through the meal, Jack noticed the man making slow, strange movements. Tony, thoroughly enjoying this breakfast, which was miles off his diet, hadn't looked up yet.

Finally Jack said, "I think the guide is having some kind of a fit."

Tony glanced up, mouth full of unsaturated fats.

"No, Jack, that's not a fit. That's Tai Chi."

"Like in the Kung Fu movies, I suppose."

"No, not even."

They continued to eat in a less-pleasant silence until Hewlitt bounced over and joined them. Tony smiled as though they were old friends and asked, "Chen?"

"Uh-uh," said Hewlitt.

"Yang?"

"Nyewp."

"I'm out of ideas," Tony admitted modestly.

"Wu," said Hewlitt, in subdued triumph.

"Of course," said Tony. "What was that last pose?"

"Grasp-the-Bird's-Tail."

Jack listened and chewed slowly. He let his eyes drift to the other side of the river: an undifferentiated wall of trees. The water seemed so smooth you'd hardly know it was moving at all if it wasn't for the long stripe of foam behind every boulder. Invisible behind the branches, a raven seemed to address the camp.

Fried eggs on a metal plate. Jack ate more cautiously than usual: Tony was always on him about his weight. But then Tony was a doctor, and Jack felt he had his well-being in mind despite the often-annoying delivery. It was pleasing to notice these signs of old friendship, such as they were. Jack knew he should take better care of himself, and he had complied when Tony had wanted him to give up the cigarettes. It had been hard, and they were never completely out of his mind. In an odd way, that had been his own gesture of friendship, despite Tony's main argument having been that financially Jack really couldn't afford to smoke.

Tony was telling a story to Marvin that Jack already knew. He'd heard it a hundred times.

"We went on vacation to Mexico one year, and I brought back these little tiny superhot peppers to cook with. We had Jack and his wife, Jan, over for dinner one night, and I told Jack what I just told you, that these were the hottest little peppers in the world. Well, Jack, he's had about five longnecks in a row, and he says, 'Nothing's too hot for me!' right before he puts a spoonful of them in his mouth. Buddy, that was all she wrote. Tears shoot out of his eyes. His face turns . . . maroon. His head drops to the table, and what do you think he says?"

"I don't know," said Hewlitt.

"He says, 'Why is it always me?'"

Hewlitt stared at him for a moment. Then he said, "What's the punch line?"

Tony's face fell with a thud. Hewlitt got up to feed the fire.

"Our host doesn't seem to have much of a sense of humor," Tony said, when the man was gone. Jack just smiled at him.

There were a lot of Italians around the meatpacking plant, and that's where Tony's people had settled. He had come a long way. Jack's family was cattle, land, and railroad: they'd virtually founded the town but hadn't had a pot to piss in for generations. Gerri liked to point out that half of her and Jack's relatives were absolute bums, which generally made Jack's wife respond that Tony's family was right off the boat. Nobody crossed Jan: she wasn't witty; she was angry. He may be a doctor to you, but he's a wop to me. Jack was fundamentally too fragile for this kind of badinage, unfortunately, because he had to admit that Tony and Gerri were far less snippy when Jan was around. She'd say to Jack, "You want respect, you better be prepared to snap their heads back." Or she'd put it the way Mike Tyson did: "Everybody's got an attitude until you hit them in the face."

Jack's roots in town were so deep that he thought that Jan's bel-licosity was just a result of having grown up somewhere else. She was from Idaho, for crying out loud. This was before he found out Jan had had a slipup with Tony back in the day, while Jack was off doing his time with the National Guard.

When Tony and Gerri took them to New York to see *Cats*, that's when it really hit the fan. Tony had made a big thing about *Cats* winning a Tony Award, which Jan thought was such a hoot because Jack had no idea what a Tony Award was. He'd thought Tony was flirting with Jan again, with his so-called humor. Jack and Jan moved to their own hotel, leaving the room Tony had paid for empty. In their new room, Jan went on the defensive and blamed alcohol for the flirtation. She seemed to think that with this cita-tion, the issue was settled. Jack didn't buy it, but he'd never been willing to pay the price for taking it further. Instead, he absorbed the blow. Having Tony know he just took it was the hardest part.

But somehow the problem between the two of them evapo-rated when they were back in town. "New York just wasn't for us," Tony said, and Jack accepted this gratefully. Jan, however, twisted it around; she took it to mean that she and Jack just weren't good enough for New York.

"Who wants to go there anyway?" she'd say. "All those muggers, and that smelly air!"

Meanwhile her slipup was consigned, once again, to history. Full stop. Jack couldn't stand any of it.

THEY ALL PITCHED IN TO TIDY UP THE CAMP, AND THEN THEY headed for the boat. It was tied to a tree, swinging in the current; a cool breeze, fresh and balsamic, was sweeping up the river. Hewlitt carried a Styrofoam chest—their lunch—to the shore and put it aboard. Fishing tackle had been loaded in already.

A moment later the three men climbed in, and Hewlitt started the engine. Once he was sure it was running properly, he stepped ashore and freed the painter from the tree, sprang aboard again, and turned into the current. Tony said, "This is what it's all about."

Jack nodded eagerly and then felt a wave of hopelessness unattached to anything in particular. Maybe catching a fish, maybe just the day itself. Hewlitt gazed over the tops of their heads, straight up the river. He seemed to know what he was doing.

He had looked more competent when he'd still had the beard. Now he looked like a lot of other people. God was always portrayed with a beard—for Jack it was impossible to picture him without one, even if he strained to imagine what he assumed would be a handsome and mature face. The only time you ever saw Jesus without a beard, he was still a baby. Tony had grown his own beard right after med school. Sometime later Jan had told Tony that he needed to get rid of it; that was one of the worst arguments Jack and Jan had ever had. Jack had said it was for Gerri to say whether or not she liked the beard, since it was her husband. Jan said that a person was entitled to her own opinions.

"Who taught you to cast?" Tony said. They had started fishing.

"You did," Jack replied.

"Obviously you needed to practice."

Jack just shrugged it off. He was still getting it out there, wasn't he? Maybe not as elegantly as Tony, but it shouldn't have made any difference to the fish. The casting was just showing off. It seemed to have impressed Hewlitt, though, because he took Tony upriver to another spot, leaving Jack to fish where he was, even though nobody had gotten a bite. Jack thought it was probably a better spot, this new one, and of course it was perfectly natural that Hewlitt would take Tony there, since it was Tony who was paying for the trip. Nevertheless, after another hour had passed, he felt a bit crushed and no longer expected to catch a fish at all. He thought, None of this would be happening if I had more money.

The sun rose high overhead and warmed the gravel bar. Jack's arm was getting tired, and eventually he stretched out on the ground with his hands behind his head. The heat felt so good, and the river sounded so sweet this close to his ear. Let Tony catch all the fish, he thought; I am at peace.

"How are you going to catch a fish that way, Jack?"

Tony was standing over him. He hadn't even heard the motor.

"I'm not. Did you catch anything?"

"No."

"See? You could have had a nice nap."

Tony sat down next to Jack on the gravel and glanced over at Hewlitt, who was carrying their lunch box from the boat to the shore. "You know what old Eldorado did before he was a wilderness outfitter? Guess."

"Lumberjack?"

"Way off. He was a pharmacist."

"I'm surprised they even had them up here."

"This was in Phoenix."

Jack thought for a moment, and then asked, "Do you think he knows what he's doing?"

"No."

"Are we going to catch fish?"

"It seems unlikely."

They were interrupted by a cry from Hewlitt, whose rod had bent into a deep bow.

"Jesus. I didn't even see him cast," Jack said.

The two men hurried over. Hewlitt glanced at them and said, "First cast! He just mauled it."

The fish exploded into the air and tail-danced across the river.

"Looks like a real beauty," said Tony grimly, his hands plunged deep in his pockets.

After several more jumps and runs, Hewlitt had the fish at the beach and, laying down his rod, knelt beside it, holding it under its tail and belly. It was big, thick, and flashed silver with every movement as Hewlitt removed the hook. Tony and Jack craned over him to better see the creature, and Hewlitt bent to kiss it. "Oh, baby," he murmured. Then he let it go.

"What'd you do that for?" Tony wailed. The fish was swimming off, deeper and deeper, until its glimmer was lost in the dark. "We could have had fresh fish for lunch!"

Their guide, in response, got right in Tony's face. "Don't go there, mister," he said with an odd intensity. "You don't want that on your karma." Then he walked back to the boat and dragged the anchor farther up the shore.

"My God," Tony said. "What have we got ourselves into?" But Jack was simply pleased with everything.

A few minutes later, he even made a possibly insincere fuss over the bologna sandwiches. "Is there any lettuce or anything?"

"Doesn't keep without refrigeration. Where do you think you are?"

"The Aleguketuk. You already told me."

"Nice river, isn't it?"

"I wish it had more fish," said Tony. "Although it's obviously not a problem for you."

"Nyewp, not a problem."

As Hewlitt went to the boat to look for something, Tony said, "Ex–pill salesman."

"But fun to be with."

Jack had gone through times like this with Tony in the past: just be patient, he knew, and his friend would soon be chasing his own tail. It had already started. Tony had come unglued once when both couples had gone to a beginners' tennis camp in Boca Raton—thrown his racket, the whole nine yards. Jack had just let it sink in with Jan, what she had done with this nut. He knew he shouldn't feel this way: Jan had made it clear she regretted the whole thing, but he felt doomed to rub it in for the rest of their lives, or at least until she quit marveling over how fit Tony and Gerri were. He always suspected she included Gerri only as camouflage when she mentioned it. He'd seen this fitness language before: buns of steel, washboard abs, power pecs—all just code for Tony hovering over Jan like a vulture. And now, because Tony and Gerri were divorcing, Jack feared that further indiscretions might be on tap.

Tony threw his bologna sandwich into the river. "I can't eat it."

Hewlitt had his mouth full. "Plan on foraging?"

Tony sat down on the ground, elbows on his knees, and held his head in despair.

No other fish were caught that day, and neither man slept well that night. The next day a hard rain confined them to their tent; Tony read *Harvey Penick's Little Red Book: Lessons and Teachings from a Lifetime in Golf,* and Jack did sudoku until he was sick of it. The weather finally lifted in time for the third night's evening fire, and Hewlitt emerged wearing only his long underwear to prepare the meal, which was a huge shish kebab with only meat the entire length of the stick. When it was cooked, Hewlitt flicked the flesh onto their tin plates, which were so thin you could feel the heat through their bottoms. Afterward Hewlitt recited a Robert Service poem—"There are strange things done in the midnight sun"—so slowly that Tony and Jack were frantic at its conclusion.

"Where exactly was that drugstore you worked in?" Tony asked.

Hewlitt stared at him for a long time before speaking. "A pox on you, sir."

Back in the tent, Jack asked, "Aren't you concerned that he'll confiscate the impregnated craft-shop dolls' eyes?"

"What difference does it make? They haven't worked so far."

"Tony, it was a joke. Jesus, for a fancy doctor with a five-thousand-square-foot home on the golf course, you sure haven't kept your sense of humor."

"Fifty-two hundred. Get some sleep, Jack. You're getting crabby."

Jack had worked for the county all those years since the National Guard. In '96 he had denied Tony a well permit for his lawn-sprinkling system, and Tony had never gotten over it. It was pay-back for the little nothing with Jan, he was convinced, even though in reality it was no more than a conventional ruling on the law, which Tony, as was often the case, thought should be bent ever so slightly. Jack had explained the legal basis for his decision without denying that it was pleasant seeing Tony choke on this one. Tony had put his hand in Jack's face and said, "This is for surgery, not for holding a garden hose."

"You might want to tone down the square footage, if your time is limited," Jack had replied. "That's an awful lot of lawn."

"What the fuck are you talking about!" Tony had shouted back. "You don't even have a lawn, you have fucking pea rock!"

Hewlitt must have been throwing more wood on the fire. You could see the flare of the flames through the walls of the tent. From time to time, he laughed aloud.

"Do you suppose he's laughing at us?" Tony asked.

"Things can still turn out. We have time."

"At least we got away together," Tony said. "We used to do more of this. It's important. It makes everything come back. We're kids again. We're who we used to be."

"Not really," said Jack. "You used to be nicer to me."

"You're joking, aren't you?"

Jack didn't answer. He wished he hadn't said such a thing, and his throat ached.

"What about Cancún in 2003? It didn't cost you a nickel."

Jack didn't know how to reply. He was in such pain. The tent fell silent once more. When Tony finally spoke, his voice had changed.

"Jack. I don't have another friend."

Jack wanted to make Tony feel better then, but it wasn't coming to him yet. Tony was right about one thing: they were who they used to be. Jack was still doing okay in his little house, and Tony was still just as lonely by the golf course as he'd been by the meat-packing plant. He had to take it out on somebody.

IN THE MORNING, THERE WAS FROST ON EVERYTHING. JACK and Tony, arms stiff at their sides, watched as Hewlitt made breakfast and merrily reminisced about previous trips.

"Had an English astronaut here for a week, just a regular bloke. Loved his pub, loved his shepherd's pie, loved his wee cottage in Blighty."

Tony and Jack glanced at each other.

"Took a large framed picture of the Queen Mother into space. Ate nothing but fish-and-chips his whole month in orbit, quoting Churchill the entire time."

Tony whispered to Jack, "There were no English astronauts."

"I heard that," Hewlitt said, standing up and waving his spatula slowly in Tony's face.

"Did you? Good. Stay tuned. There's more."

Hewlitt resumed cooking in silence. The silence was worse. He served their meal without a word, then went to his boat with his new bare face, and in his hand he grasped a handful of willow switches he had cut from the bank. With these, he scourged himself. It was hard not to see this as a tableau, with the boat and the river behind him and Hewlitt, in effect, centered in the frame. His audience, Jack and Tony, turned away to gear up for a day of fishing and standing with their rods at their sides like a sarcastic knockoff of *American Gothic*.

Right out of the blue, Hewlitt stopped his thrashing and turned to fix them with a reproving gaze. "I've spent my entire life as a liar and an incompetent," he said.

"Don't be so hard on yourself, Eldorado," Tony said, with poorly concealed alarm.

"Bogus vitamins on the Internet? How about swingin' doors and painted women?"

"That's all behind you, now."

"If only I could believe you!" Hewlitt cried.

Tony was paralyzed by the strangeness of this, but Jack stepped forward and snatched the willow switches away. He got right in Hewlitt's face.

"How much of this do you think we can stand?"

"Well, I—"

"We're not on this trip to hear about your problems. We don't even know you. I came here to be with my friend because we need to talk. This is a freak show, and we shouldn't have to pay for it. We thought we'd catch some fish!"

This seemed to sober Hewlitt, who replaced his look of extravagant self-pity with one of caution and shrewdness.

"I'm the only one who can get you out of here, son. No brag, just fact. You make me feel respected or you're SOL. I'd like to be a fly on the wall when you try backing this tank down a class-five rapid. That's the only way home, punk, and I'm unstable."

"Jesus," said Tony. "This is insane! This trip was my reward as a vassal of Medicare!"

Hewlitt responded by pretending to play a violin and whistling "Moon River." Jack raised a menacing finger in his face, and he stopped. Then Hewlitt was talking again.

"How about you try going broke on eating-disorder clinics to wake up to find your wife still gobbling her food? Forty K in the hole and she's facedown on a ham!"

Jack turned back to Tony. "I don't know what to do."

Hewlitt's lament rushed onward. He had dug deep in his pharmacist days to throw a big wedding for his daughter, apparently; she had married way above their station thanks to her big blue eyes and thrilling figure. It was, in Hewlitt's words, a hoity-toity affair with the top Arizona landowners, the copper royalty, and the developers, and Hewlitt's caterer food-poisoned them all. Several sued, his wife and daughter blamed him, and in this way Hewlitt found himself at the end of his old life and the beginning of the new. He took a crash course in wilderness adventures at an old CCC camp in Oregon, graduating at the top of his class and getting a book on the ethics of forestry in recognition. Hewlitt seemed to think that this was all an illusion, that no one really cared about him at all.

Tony and Jack maintained compassionate, respectful smiles throughout this tirade. By the end Hewlitt was so upset his cheeks trembled. When he finished, Jack raised an imploring hand in his direction, but to no avail: Eldorado Hewlitt walked past them and into his tent.

"Doesn't look like a fishing day," Jack said.

Once they were back in the tent, Jack stretched out on his sleeping bag, and Tony turned to grab a thick paperback from his pack, a book about zombies with the face of someone with white eyeholes on the cover. He slumped back on his bedroll, drew his reading glasses from his shirt, and was on the verge of total absorption when Hewlitt flung open the tent flap. Tony slowly lowered the zombie book.

"Sorry to disturb you," the man said, though there was no evidence of that. "I have to ask: What is your problem? 'Old friends'? Is that what you are, 'old friends'? Grew up together in the same little town? I know I have problems; I'm famous for my problems. I'm told by qualified professionals that I have ruined my life with my problems, but these few days with two 'old friends' have completely unnerved me. What did you two do to each other? Where is this bad feeling coming from? I'm terrifically upset, and I don't know what it is. But it's coming from you two, I've figured out that much. Can't you work this out? You're killing me!"

Hewlitt hurled down the flap and left. Jack and Tony looked at each other, then quickly glanced away.

"What was that all about?" Tony asked, unpersuasively.

Jack said nothing. He had found his box of lures and was lifting one up as though to examine it. A blue frog with hooks.

After a minute he got to his feet. He went out of the tent, looked around, and came back in with their rods. He made a show of breaking them down and putting them back in their travel tubes. Tony, staring determinedly now at a single page of his zombie book, barely lifted his eyes to this activity, which caused Jack to raise the intensity of it. He held up a roll of toilet paper in his hand. Tony couldn't look at him.

"Might as well take a shit. Nothing else to do around here."

Tony kept his eyes on the book and gave him a little wave.

A short time later, the toilet paper flew back into the tent, followed by Jack. He slumped on his bedroll with a sigh.

"I've got another book," said Tony.

"I hate books."

"No, you don't. You loved *The Black Stallion*."

"I was twelve."

"So don't read. Who cares?"

"What's the other book?"

"*Silent Spring*."

Jack snorted. "Thanks a bunch."

Tony dropped the book to his chest. "Jack, what do you want?"

"In the whole world?"

"Sure."

"I'd like you to tell me in plain English what my wife saw in you."

Tony exhaled through pursed lips and looked at the ground. "We did this a long time ago. Either you shoot me or throw her out, but otherwise there's nothing more to say. The whole thing is both painful and negligible to me, and kind of an accident and kind of ancient history. We have managed to stay friends despite my very serious personal crime against you. It is a permanent stain on my soul."

"What do you mean by that?" Jack said. "You don't even believe you have one."

"Well, you do, and you're innocent. I have a soul that is blemished by shame. All right? I'm not proud of myself."

Jack lay facedown on his bedroll, chin on laced fingers, and looked miserably toward the tent flap. He fell asleep thus, after a while, and so did Tony, glasses hanging from one ear. Hours later, they were awakened by the cooling tent and diminished light.

Jack got to his feet abruptly, seeming frightened, and rifled through a pile of clothing until he found his coat.

"You going to find us something to eat?" Tony asked.

"I am like hell. I'm going to have a word with our guide."

Tony raised a cautioning hand. "Jack, we're dealing with a very unstable—"

"Well put, Tony. That's exactly what I am, but I plan to do something about it. I'm upset. And it's his fault."

"Jack, please—"

But Jack had already gone. Tony slumped back with his hands over his face. It went through his mind that patiently putting up with Jack was an old habit. That's what had started their mess. Jack had done something dumb—gotten drunk and driven his car on the railroad tracks, in fact, nearly ruining it—that had caused Jan and Tony, in an accidental encounter at the post office, to commiserate with each other, and the next thing they knew they were in bed, bright sunlight coming through the thin curtains of the Super 8. It wasn't anything, really, but Jan threw it into an argument with Jack the next year during the Super Bowl, and the half-life was promptly extended to forever.

Jack came back in through the tent flap, slapping it open abruptly. He crouched down, staring at Tony. Then he said, "He's dead."

Tony sat up. The zombie paperback splattered on the floor. He stood and walked straight past Jack, out through the flap, then came back in, kicking the book out of his way, and lay down again.

"He sure is," he said.

"So what happened?"

"He took something."

"Jesus. Did you see this coming?"

"I thought it was an act."

"Is the food in there with him?"

"He hauled it back up the tree. Where the bears couldn't get it."

"Bears. Jesus, I forgot about bears." Jack dashed out of the tent once more. When he returned, dangling Hewlitt's gun by its barrel, he had a wild look in his eyes. Tony knew what it was and said nothing.

"I'll get a fire going," Jack said. "We've got to eat something. Why don't you get the food down and see what we've got."

Outside they felt the strangeness of being alone in the camp, the cold fire, Hewlitt's silent tent. The boat meant everything, and separately they checked to see that it was still there. Tony ended up crouched by the fire pit, shaving off kindling with his hatchet, while Jack puzzled over the knots on the ground stake: the rope led upward over a branch, suspending the food supplies out of reach. Once the rope was free, he was able to lower the supplies to the ground and open the canvas enclosing them: steaks, potatoes, onions, canned tomatoes, girlie magazines, schnapps, eggs, a ham. He dragged the whole load to the fire and stood over it with Tony, not quite knowing what to do next.

"If I'm right about what's ahead, we go for the protein," Tony said.

It was getting darker and colder; the flames danced over the splinters of firewood. Jack was quite still.

"What's ahead, Tony?"

"The boat trip."

"Oh, is that what you think?"

"That's what I think."

Jack looked up at the sky for a moment but didn't reply. Instead, he lifted two of the steaks out of the cache and dropped them onto the grill.

THE BEDROLLS BECAME COCOONS WITHOUT REFUGE. THEY were in a dead camp with a dead fire and a corpse in a tent. They thought about their wives—even Jan's misery and Gerri's demand for freedom seemed so consoling now, so day-to-day. Tony's small slip with the scalpel was now nothing more than a reminder of the need for vigilance—a renewal, in a sense. Jack had a home and all his forebears buried on the edge of town. He could wait for the same. No big deal, wink out. Nothing about this bothered him anymore. He had sometimes pictured himself in his coffin, big belly and all, friends filing by with sad faces. He belonged.

They couldn't sleep, or they barely slept; if one detected the other awake, they talked.

"I don't know what the environmentalists see in all these trees," Jack said.

"Nature hates us. We'll be damn lucky to get out of this hole and back to civilization."

"Well, you want a little of both. A few trees, anyway. Some wildflowers."

"You try walking out of here. You'll see how much nature loves you."

There was no point worrying about it, Tony said; they would have the whole day tomorrow to work on their problems.

"So what do we do with the body?" Jack asked.

"The body is not our problem."

It couldn't have been many hours before sunrise by the time the bears came into the camp. There were at least three; they could be heard making pig noises as they dragged and swatted at the food that had been left out. Tony tried to get a firm count through a narrow opening in the tent flap while Jack cowered at the rear with Hewlitt's gun in his hands.

"It's nature, Tony! It's nature out there!"

Tony was too terrified to say anything. The bears had grown interested in their tent.

After a moment of quiet they could hear them smelling around its base with sonorous gusts of breath. At every sound, Jack redirected the gun. Tony tried to calm him, despite his own terror.

"They've got all they can eat out there, Jack."

"They never have enough to eat! Bears never have enough!"

Tony went to the flap and tied all its laces carefully, as though that made any difference. But then, as before, the sound of the bears stopped. After a time he opened a lace and looked out.

"I think they're gone," he said. He hated pretending to be calm. He'd done that in the operating room when it was nothing but a fucking mess.

"Let's give them plenty of time, until we're a hundred percent sure," Jack said. "We've got this"—Jack held the gun aloft—"but half the time shooting a bear just pisses him off."

Tony felt he could open the flap enough to get a better look. First light had begun to reveal the camp, everything scattered like a rural dump, even the pages of the girlie magazines, pink fragments among the canned goods, cold air from the river coming into the tent like an anesthetic.

Tony said, "Oh, God, Jack. Oh, God."

"What?"

"The bears are in Hewlitt's tent."

Jack squealed and hunkered down onto the dirt floor. "Too good, Tony! Too good!"

Tony waited until he stopped and then said, "Jack, you need to take hold. We've got a long day ahead of us."

Jack sat up abruptly, eyes blazing. "Is that how you see it? You're going to tell me to behave? You're a successful guy. My wife thought you were a big successful guy before she was fat. So tell me what to do, Tony."

"Listen, start by shutting up, okay? We're gonna need all the energy in those big muscles of yours to get us out of this."

"That's straight from the shoulder, Tony. You sound like the old guinea from down by the meat processor again."

"I'm all right with that," said Tony. "Up with the founding families, piss poor though you all are, it must have been hard for you and Jan to know how happy we were."

"Somebody's got to make sausage."

"Yes, they do."

"Linguini, pepperoni, Abruzzo. Pasta fazool."

"I can't believe you know what pasta fazool is, Jack."

Jack imitated Dean Martin. "'When the stars make you drool, just like pasta fazool.' Asshole. Your mother made it for me."

He was gesturing with the rifle now. When the barrel swung past Tony's nose, the reality of their situation came crashing down on them as though they had awakened from a dream. Jack, abashed, went to the front of the tent and peered out. After a moment, he said, "All quiet on the western front."

Tony came to look over his shoulder, saw nothing.

"They're gone."

The two men emerged into the cold, low light, the gray river racing at the edge of the camp. There was nothing left of the food except a few canned goods scattered among the pictures of female body parts. The vestibule of Hewlitt's tent was torn asunder, to the point that the interior could almost be inspected from a distance. Jack clearly had no interest in doing so, but Tony went over gingerly, entered, then came out abruptly with one hand over his eyes. "Oh," he said, "Jesus Christ."

They picked through the havoc the bears had left until they'd found enough undamaged food for a day or so in the boat. They put their bedrolls in there, too, but the tents they left where they were. Any thought of staying in camp was dropped on the likelihood of the bears returning at dark.

"We'll start the motor when we need it," Tony said. "All we're doing is going downstream until we get out."

Jack nodded, lifted the anchor, and walked down to the boat, coiling the line as he went.

THE RIVER SEEMED TO SPEED PAST. AS THEY FLOATED AWAY, Tony thought that this was nature at its most benign, shepherding them away from the dreaded camp; but Jack, looking at the dark walls of trees enclosing the current, the ravens in the high branches, felt a malevolence in his bones. He glanced back at their abandoned tents: already, they looked like they'd been there for hundreds of years, like the empty smallpox tepees his grandpa had told him about. This might be good country if someone removed the trees and made it prairie like at home, he thought. With the steady motion of the boat, he daydreamed about the kinds of buildings he'd most like to see: a store, a church, a firehouse.

Tony said, "My dad was a butcher, and I'm a surgeon. I'm sure you've heard a lot of jokes about that around town."

"Uh-huh."

"The funny thing is, I didn't want to be a surgeon—I wanted to be a butcher. The old second-generation climb into some stratosphere where you'll never be comfortable again. Where you never know where you live."

"I don't think you'd like it back there at the packing plant."

"Not now—I've been spoiled. But if I'd stayed . . . I don't know. Dad was always happy."

"And you're not?" Jack asked.

"Not particularly. Maybe after Gerri goes. Now that I'm used to the idea, the divorce, I can't wait. I think I'm overspreading my discomfort around."

"Jan and I don't have the option," Jack said. "There's not enough for either one of us to start over on. We're stuck together whether we like it or not." He was thinking of how life and nature were just alike, but he couldn't figure out how to put it into words.

Boulders, submerged beneath the water, could be felt as the boat rose and fell, and the river began to narrow toward a low canyon. In a tightening voice, Tony said, "Most of humanity lives beside rivers. By letting this one take us where it will, we'll be delivered to some form of civilization. A settlement, at least." He reached inside his coat and pulled out a wallet. "I thought we better bring this."

"Is that Hewlitt's wallet?"

"That's not his name. There are several forms of identification, but none of them are for a Hewlitt." He riffled it open to show Jack the driver's licenses and ID cards, all with the same picture and all with different names.

"He had a lot of musical talent," Jack said, and let out a crazy, mirthless laugh.

"See up there? I bet those are the rapids he was talking about."

"Oh, goody. Nature."

Indeed, where the canyon began, and even from this distance, the sheen of the river was surmounted by something sparkling, some effervescence, a vitality that had nothing to do with them. Shapes appeared under the boat, then vanished as the river's depth changed, the banks and walls of trees narrowing toward them and the approaching canyon walls. You couldn't look up without wanting to get out through the sky.

At the mouth of the canyon was a standing wave. Somehow the river ran under it, but the wave itself remained erect. A kind of light could be seen around it. Tony thought it had the quality of authority, like the checkpoint of a restricted area; Jack took it for yet another part of the blizzard of things that could never be explained and that pointlessly exhausted all human inquiry. Carrying these distinct views, their boat was swept into the wave, and under; and Jack and Tony were never seen again.

LAKE STORY

GLENDIVE WAS UNBEARABLY HOT IN AUGUST, AND FOR HALF of it I rented a cottage on the western shore of Flathead Lake, a little getaway in sight of Wild Horse Island and built a long time ago between two rocky points barely thirty yards apart, the lawn between them leading down to a pebbly shore and the deep green water in a kind of pool. The place was only available because the neighbor whose starter castle towered over the next small bay had died in the spring. A Kansas City resident who had made a fortune trading carbon credits and ringtones, he owned the kind of craft normally at the service of drug runners, a vastly powerful cigarette boat whose daily thunder made the nearby rental cottages uninhabitable. Pleas went unacknowledged, the petition thrown out as the smell of fuel continued to drift up from his dock. So after the boat owner died, concluding a prolonged battle with pancreatic cancer, Memorial Day in the small surrounding neighborhood was given over to celebrating his death. The jubilant air persisted as FOR SALE signs appeared on his property, then through its deterioration, especially as islands of quack grass started pushing up through the clay tennis court. Suddenly the small cottages, each with its tiny green bay and an evergreen-crowned rocky ridge running to the lake, were all back in business. I felt very lucky to have scored one of them on short notice, a one-bedroom clapboard house with a mossy shingled roof and overstuffed chairs fished out of winter homes elsewhere, before the age of dedicated cottage furniture. The fireplace was made of round stones from the lakeside, and a huge incongruous print of Niagara Falls was the main room's only decoration. "Were these people all short?" Adele asked, noticing that every lamp lit us at waist level unless we slumped into one of the low-slung chairs to thumb the swollen copy of *Redbook*. At night, above these lamps, all was darkness.

I was having an affair with Adele, a married woman whose availability was also made known to me at the last moment. We'd been doing this for nine years, nine short-term rentals, each begun just as her husband finalized his schedule, which included an annual visit to his mother in rural South Africa, where communications were conveniently, if uncertainly, faulty. Adele and I otherwise avoided deceit of any kind, operating on a don't-ask-don't-tell basis, each suspecting that ours was the kind of flourishing relationship that would wither in the full light of day. Sunlight may be the best disinfectant, but it fades passion like everything else. I'm a widower with grown children, but Adele's were of an impressionable age, and God forbid they ever found out about us. They couldn't possibly have understood. We relished this covert life and didn't mind in the least that we could be deceiving ourselves, lost as we were in its pleasures and logistics.

Usually, we arrived in separate cars, but this time Adele came on the train from Seattle, where she'd gone for a design show. I picked her up at the station in Whitefish, observing our customary artifice—"You never know who you'll run into in Montana"—before we took a look around from inside my car and began kissing. By now, there was no need for any foreshadowing in these early pecks: we knew what was coming. As I drove out and turned onto the highway for the lake, Adele said, "Seattle was wonderful, but then it's summer. You smell salt water, and there are cranes and freighters and container ships like a real seaport. You don't get that in San Francisco. And I met the coolest cowboy, a professional rodeo cowboy, and he could talk about anything. He was reading a book!" Adele looked great in a cotton summer dress, this one blue with tiny silver zigzags.

"And?" I asked.

"He was too big for a Pullman berth."

I didn't know if she was serious. I don't think she was. It's possible she had a wild side, but you wouldn't know it by our relationship, which had almost nothing wild about it. Perhaps monogamous cheaters were commoner than I thought.

I loved Adele, and Adele loved me, but we were not in love, and she couldn't make me jealous, though that principle was untested. I once pretended to be in love with her, and my saying so was greeted by silence arising from contempt. It was instructive. I barely made up for it by deferring ejaculation for about ninety minutes, which left me stooped for two days with lower back pain. I took some ibuprofen, and Adele read to me from *Tartarin of Tarascon* in recognition of my sacrifice. When we got to the part where Tartarin is unable to decide whether to cover himself with glory or with flannel, we closed the book and fell asleep with plenty of room between us on the bed, where we always left whatever we'd been reading and, lately, our reading glasses.

That evening at the lake, we sat out on the weathered deck and watched the blue twilight dwindle until the broad silver of its surface was lit with stars. Perhaps Adele glanced at me, or I at her, but some wordless signal passed between us, and we entered by the screen door, just a crack, so as to exclude the moths, and made for the bed, which proved a squeaking seismograph that registered the tiniest movement. Even reaching to turn off the lamp produced a cacophony. This bed was good for nothing, and so we dragged the mattress to the floor, where there were only our own sounds to contend with. I touched her with my fingertips.

"You're tracing. You can't remember me from one year to the next?"

"I like being reminded."

"You're looking for change."

"Nope."

In the morning, I caught several very small cutthroat trout from the dock, using a child's rod found in the garage and worms from beneath the paving tiles that ran from the house to a tiny garden shed. Adele woke up to fried eggs, fresh trout fillets, and sourdough toast served in bed. This was all a bit easier for me, as I lived alone, while Adele was married, happily married, to a very nice guy about whom I should have felt some guilt except that he was known for straying himself and had caused Adele a bit of pain over this. I mean, you looked at these things and you could see possible retribution in every direction, if that's what you wanted, but I didn't. Besides, some of my pleasure consisted in just having company.

WE READ ON THE SHORE UNTIL LATE MORNING, WHEN IT WAS warm enough for a swim. That is, the air was warm enough: the lake is never warm, but we dove in naked, paddled for a very short time, floating on our backs and gazing up at the cheerful little clouds over the Mission Range, then clambered out into the warm air, and had dried off by the time we fell into sex on one of the Adirondack chairs at the bottom of our sunny ravine, the glare on the cottage windows suggesting a steady stare. When we stood up, we laughed at the sight of each other before Adele, glancing back at the chair, said, "Eww, I'll get it." That's when I had the idea that ruined everything.

The cottage came with a battered aluminum boat, an old Scott-Atwater motor on its transom and a litter of things strewn in its bottom, life jackets, a mushroom anchor and line, a net with a broken handle, a Maxwell House bailing can, one oar, and a sponge. I looked into the red gas can; it was full, and the fuel smelled fairly recent. "I say we make a run across the lake and have lunch in Big Fork." In my defense, it was a perfect day for it, windless and sunny, the mountains to our east wonderfully green and regular. Summer traffic glinted from the highway for miles across the water and along the ripening cherry orchards.

The motor started on the first pull. Adele in her summer dress and white-framed sunglasses sat facing forward atop a life jacket, while I, with an arm behind me on the motor's handle, maneuvered us out of our little bay into the open water. I tried to memorize the position of the cottage in the landscape so we could find our way home, knowing as I did it wouldn't be long after lunch that we'd be longing to drag the sagging mattress onto the floor again. We tended to overdo these exertions in what time we had, even though, as Adele reminded me, it's not something you could store for later. I supposed that was true, as there was nothing routine about each renewal of ardor, though we did get better at it every year. If we were not as attractive as we once had been, we had the advantage of knowing what we liked with greater certainty, even as it had grown more unmentionable in polite company.

The surface of the lake sparkled green, and its placidity belied the occasional squall that popped unexpected out of the mountains, drowning kokanee fishermen, whose bodies sank like stones in the cold water. Now it was as delightful as a rain forest on a sunny day. I gave the pressure bulb on the gas line an extra squeeze, and Adele, sensing my movement, turned to smile, then rolled her eyes heavenward in bliss over our surroundings. Leaving a bubble trail and a straight wake, the little Evinrude pushed us slowly to the other side.

"We're a long way from shore. Want to fuck in the boat?"

"No, I want lunch."

I resumed cruising speed, and in a short time we were at the dock south of the golf course. I tied up without interference from the marina staff, who may have been eating. We climbed from the boat, Adele straightened her dress as she looked around, and with my hand on the small of her back, I led her to a pathway along the Swan River, where youngsters were swimming off docks in front of well-kept cottages nearly lost in greenery. By now we were uncomfortably hungry and followed a boardwalk to the nearest restaurant, which looked popular, at least with locals. The obvious tourists were pouring into a bigger place across the street with water views and outside dining. Once seated, we were encouraged by the originality of what was on the blackboard menu. They seemed especially proud of something called MISSION RANGE BASIL TOMATO GREEN CHILI MEAT LOAF. That item ran the length of the board, unlike FRIED CHICKEN OR SOUP OF THE DAY. We ordered it and received startlingly sincere congratulations from the waitress, a rawboned brunette with a cigarette behind her ear and a shamrock tattoo on her forearm. I was glad to get our orders in, because the restaurant was filling up, and already other couples were standing in front waiting for a table. Adele remarked that we became an ordinary couple once a year, the South African part of the year; when we relied on ordinary opportunity, we were just garden-variety adulterers. "There was a good bit of that at the design show, I think. Trade shows seem mostly for that. Couples just getting acquainted, regret in their faces. Getting out of town. Departing duty for desire."

"Sounds like a bus route," I said.

"For some, it is a bus route."

"We're solitary travelers. Smartphones, a boat, meat loaf."

With the dining room full, the noise picked up, and Adele and I drew closer. Our food arrived. My state was such that I could feel the least adjustment of her chair in my direction. Someone waiting outside for a table was smoking a cigarette, and our waitress closed the door in his face. Adele held a forkful of meat loaf in front of her and said, "Eat up, get the bill, and take me back to the cottage." My heart raced at how effortlessly she could reduce all else to preliminaries.

A heavyset woman dining alone walked toward the cash register holding her bill like a specimen. She glanced our way, then glanced again, and then headed toward us. Adele didn't see her coming until she was nearly at our table, by which time Adele went white and jumped to her feet, clutching her napkin in grotesque exuberance. "Esther!" It came out as little more than a croak at which she clutched her throat, as if to blame an unchewed bit of food for the strange sound. By the time I was on my feet, wiping my mouth, causing a shower of crumbs from my napkin, I knew I was hosed. Esther, Adele's sister-in-law, a woman in late middle age, was possessed of a kind of authoritarian face, an effect unrelieved by her close-cropped yellowish hair and a red summer blazer. I was a "colleague" from Glendive.

"You didn't go to South Africa with Marty?" Esther said.

"I was at a design show in Seattle. With Marty away, I thought I'd take a leisurely train ride here, grab something to eat, and rent a car to drive home. Walked in and here he was. Old Home Week." I guessed that was me, though Adele was pointing in case there was doubt.

"Matching meat loaf!" I cried stupidly. Esther, evidently no fan of wordplay, gave me a bit of a look.

"What brings you here?" Adele asked with a grimace.

"Damage control: one of our legislators got drunk and T-boned a travel trailer with his speedboat. Ran it right off the lake into the middle of an RV park."

"Esther does PR for . . . who exactly?"

"Anyone with American money. Looks like you're nearly finished. Ride home with me and save on that rental. I can wait for you in the car. No hurry."

"Are you sure you won't join us?" I asked, but Esther laughed grimly, perhaps tellingly, and went out the door without another word.

"I hate her," said Adele. "Three hundred fifty miles in a white Honda Civic is not what I had in mind. And she's got breath like kerosene." The waitress brought the check.

Adele stared into my eyes. "I'm sure you could see, as I could see, that she's onto us."

"I'm not particularly intuitive but, yes, I thought there was something there."

"Something unpleasant as if . . ."

"We'd been nabbed."

"Well, maybe not so clear as that but suspected, perhaps. Can I ask you a favor?" she said.

"Of course."

"Don't ever do this to me again."

"And all this time, I thought it was mutual." I didn't know what else to say, or why I more or less sang these words. I'd never seen Adele angry before, and I was startled at the transformation.

"This strikes you as a good time for irony?!"

"Adele, people are staring."

"Staring! I'd love to be able to worry about stares."

Esther appeared in the doorway and came toward us in big strides, like a forest ranger. "Everything okay?" She glanced back and forth between us with transparently insincere concern. Adele's mottled face made an implausible attempt at reply.

"Just winding up here, Esther. I'll be right along. Sorry to hold you up."

Esther backed away giving us a good long look at her quizzical expression, then strode out the door again. I perhaps felt less vulnerable than Adele and believed that while Esther was happy to exhibit her intuitions, hers was still a theory masquerading as a fact. She had nothing to go on.

"I'd better leave."

I didn't dare try an affectionate farewell given Esther's circling. I said, "Well, kiss, kiss."

Adele said, "Same." She got up, gave me a small waist-level wave, and went out. I wasn't proud of the speculating I began. I barely knew Adele's husband, Marty, a petroleum geologist originally from South Africa and something of a lady's man, as I said. There might be a tiny contretemps just on principle, with some awkwardness on those rare occasions when we met again; or the shit might really hit the fan, with Adele winding up out on the street and Marty drawing me into fisticuffs, for which I have no particular talent. I was cringing at how quickly my erotic stream of consciousness had evaporated into a haze of measliness and fear. Adele came back and sat down.

"Screwed. She left. She's going to turn me in."

"Adele, honestly I doubt it."

"I'm toast, and you know it."

Part of me wanted to exploit this heightened state erotically, but that seemed a dangerous idea, and so in the end we made a gloomy pair heading across the lake to the cottage, Adele facing the bow while I steered. The lake was still quiet except for cat's-paws and the wakes of birds. Just past midway, I could smell the piney breeze from shore as I dwelled on Adele's shape through her blue dress, and as she braced herself on the seat. Her hair was loose, stirred around her shoulders by the air moving across the boat. I thought that at some point she might look back at me, but she never did. In our nine years of meeting I had given her very little to go on, and now I could see that it wasn't enough.

I tied the boat up and tilted the engine on the transom. Adele was already walking up the dock but stopped halfway, her forefinger crooked and pressed it to her lips in thought. "Maybe I'm overreacting." I followed her partway, encouraged that she was taking a more hopeful view of things; but what I had to say put an end to that.

"Deny everything. Esther wasn't here. Marty wasn't here. Tell them their data is corrupt."

Adele's arms fell to her sides in disgust as she walked the rest of the way to the cottage. I could only follow and then watch her throw her belongings into her suitcase. I may have breached the bedroom door too enthusiastically; it banged against the wall behind it, causing Adele to look up sharply from her packing. "Is this your James Cagney moment?"

"No, no, it isn't," I said mildly.

"I'm so sorry," she said tearfully. "This has always been inevitable. I should have taken it better. I love Marty. What the fuck have I been doing?"

I had a flippant answer for that, too, but it would have only revealed my bitterness. I hardly needed to be reminded of her love for Marty, who had always seemed pretty and bland and devious to me, although I probably made that up. All I really knew of Marty was that women found him presentable. I thought his expensive clothes were odd on a petroleum geologist, and that to me suggested a real slyboots in his finery. But I also knew my inferences were utter crap.

Either Adele didn't want to be seen with me on arrival in Glendive, or the long ride together would have been too fraught; either way, we ended up at the nearer Kalispell airport to rent her a car, a Kia that made her seem bigger than she was as she gave me a forlorn wave and departed. Kaput.

I moped around the cottage for another day and headed out. The day I got home, Esther and I met for coffee at her request. She hadn't abandoned Adele at the restaurant after all; she'd gone for gas. When she returned and discovered us gone, she searched frantically for Adele and finally gave up and drove to Glendive. I suppose she was aware of what we were up to together; but taking Adele away must have seemed the perfect chance to break it to her that Marty wasn't coming back anytime soon. He'd met someone in South Africa, an English girl working at a branch office of Deutsche Bank.

I had dinner with Adele that winter at Walkers American Grill in Billings, always crowded with local suits, but now it didn't matter who saw us together. She was working hard and living alone, her marital situation still unresolved. She blamed herself for everything but placed her hopes on Marty's irresolute arrangement with his girl in Johannesburg. "He honestly doesn't know where it's all going," she said, smiling uncertainly. "He told me he just wants to live it out."

I guess I'll have to wait. Esther thinks I'm being a dope, but she's so instinctively protective I can't take her seriously. She's a specialist in damage control, adequate company, and may see more in me than is actually there. We're kind of in the same boat.

CROW FAIR

Kurt was closer to Mother than I. I faced that a long time ago, and Mother pretty well devoured all his achievements and self-aggrandizements. But there came a day when the tide shifted, and while this may have marked Mother's decline, it was a five-alarm fire for Kurt. He had given Mother yet another of his theories, a general theory of life, which was the usual Darwinian dog-eat-dog stuff with power trickling down a human pyramid whose summit was exclusively occupied by discount orthodontists like himself. Kurt had successfully prosecuted this sort of braggadocio with Mother nearly all his life; but this time she described his philosophy as "a crock of shit." This comment had the same effect on Kurt as a roadside bomb. His rapidly whitening face only emphasized his moist red lips.

Kurt and I put Mother in a rest home a few months back. I don't think you can add a single thing to putting your mother in the rest home. If ever there was an overcooked topic, popping Ma in the old folks' home has to be a leading candidate. Ours has been a wonderful mother and, in many ways, all the things Kurt and I aren't. We are two tough, practical men of the world: Kurt is a cut-rate tooth straightener; I'm a loan officer who looks at his clients with the view that it's either them or me. The minute they show up at my desk, it's stand-by-for-the-ram. Banks love guys like me. We get to vice president maybe, but no further. Besides, my bank is family owned, and it's not my family. Kurt goes on building his estate for Beverly, his wife, and two boys, Jasper and Ferdinand. Jasper and Ferdinand spent years in their high chairs. Beverly thought it was adorable until Ferdinand did a face plant on the linoleum and broke his retainer. What a relief it was not to have them towering over me while I ate Beverly's wretched cuisine. Her Texas accent absolutely drove me up the wall. Kurt has lots of girlfriends in safe houses who love his successful face. His favorite thing in the world is to make you feel like you've asked a stupid question. Beverly has some haute cuisine Mexican recipes no one has ever heard of. She has to send away for some of the ingredients. She says she'd been in Oaxaca before she met Kurt. Some guy with his own plane. It was surprising that Kurt and I turned out like we did. Our dad was a mouse, worked his whole life at the post office. In every transaction, whether with tradespeople or bankers like me, Dad got screwed. To make it even more perfect, his surgeon fucked up his back. Last three, four years of his life, he looked like a corkscrew and was still paying off the orthopod that did it to him.

But Mother—we never called her Mom—was a queen. Kurt said that Dad must have had a ten-inch dick. When we were Cub Scouts, she was our den mother. She volunteered at the school. She read good books and understood classical music. She was beautiful, et cetera. Like I said. This is the sort of shit that happens when kids fall in love in the seventh grade, brutal mismatches that last a lifetime. Dad's lifetime anyway, and now Mother's in God's waiting room and going downhill fast. Kurt and I always said we hoped Mother cheated on Dad, but we knew that could never possibly have happened. She was above it, she was a queen, and despite our modest home and lowly standing, she was the queen of our town. She gave us status, even at school, where Kurt and I had to work at the cafeteria. People used to say, "How could she have had such a couple a thugs?" meaning me and Kurt. Some words are born to be eaten.

Kurt and I have lunch on the days we visit her in assisted living. These are the times we just give in to reminiscence, memories that are often funny, at least to us. In the seventh grade, Mother took all of our friends to the opera, *La Bohème,* in her disgraceful old Pontiac, five of us in the backseat chanting, "Puccini, Puccini, Puccini." She was worried as she herded us into our seats under the eyes of frowning opera fans. We stuck our fingers in our ears during the arias. One little girl, Polly Rademacher, was trying to enjoy the show, but Joey Bizeau kept feeling her up in the dark. Mother would've liked to have enjoyed herself, but she had her hands full keeping order and succeeded almost to the end. When Mimi dies and Rodolfo runs to her side, we shrieked with laughter. The lights came up, and Mother herded us out under the angry eyes of the opera patrons, tears streaming down her face. It was a riot.

THE PARKWAY WAS A NICE BUT SHORT-LIVED RESTAURANT that didn't make it through the second winter. Before that we just had the so-called rathskeller and its recurrent bratwurst, but it had turned back into a basement tanning parlor with palm-tree and flamingo decals on its small windows. While we still had the Parkway, Kurt was picking at his soufflé as the waiter hovered nearby. Kurt shook his head slightly and sent him away. Kurt has natural authority, and he looks the part with his broad hands and military bearing. He rarely smiles, even when he's joking: he makes people feel terrible for laughing. I'm more of a weasel. I don't think I was always a weasel, but I've spent my life at a bank; so I may be forgiven. "Remember when she got us paints and easels?" We laughed so hard.

Several diners turned our way in surprise. Kurt didn't care. He has a big reputation around town as the guy who can get your kid to quit looking like Bugs Bunny; no one is going to cross him. It was a tough call selling our crappy childhood home, but it helped pay for assisted living. Mother would've liked to have had in-home care—that is, when she was making sense—but the day was fast arriving when she wouldn't know where the hell she was, unless it was the chair she was in. Anyway, we've got her down there at Cloisters. We just hauled her over there. It's okay. Kurt calls it Cloaca.

Mother's days are up and down. Sometimes she recognizes us, sometimes not, but less and less all the time. Or that's what Kurt thinks. I think she recognizes us but isn't always glad about what she sees. When she is a little lucid, I sometimes feel she is disgusted at the sight of us. I mean, that's the look on her face. Or that we're hopeless. Or that I am: she never could find much wrong with Kurt. This used to come up from time to time, a kind of despair. She once screamed that we were "awful" but only once, and she seemed guilty and apologetic for days, kept making us pies, cookies, whatever. She felt bad. If she'd had any courage, she'd have stuck to it. We were, and are, awful. We will always be awful.

We were in Mother's room at the center. I won't describe it: they all have little to do with the occupant. Me and Kurt in chairs facing Mother in hers. Her face is pretty much blank. Someone has done her hair and makeup. She still looks like a queen, keeps her chin raised in that way of hers. But she just stares ahead. Kurt bangs on about a board of supervisors meeting; then I do a little number about small-business loans, naming some places she might recognize. Mother raises her hand to say something.

She says, "I gotta take a leak."

Kurt and I turn to each other. His eyebrows are halfway to his scalp. We don't know what to do. Kurt says to Mother, "I'll get the nurse." I stole around in front of Mother to get the call button without alerting her. I couldn't find it at first and found myself crawling down the cord to locate it. I gave the button a quick press and shortly heard the squeak of the approaching nurse's shoes. Kurt and I were surprised at how hot she was, young with eye-popping bazongas. Kurt explained that Mother needed the little girls' room. Ms. Lowler winced at the phrase. Kurt saw it, too. He's quicker to take offense than anyone I know, which is surprising in someone who so enjoys making others feel lousy. When Mother came back from the bathroom, she was refreshed and a little communicative. She knew us, I think, and talked a bit about Dad, but in a way we hadn't heard before. She talked of him in the present tense, as though Dad were still with us. "I knew right away he wasn't going anywhere," she said. We were thunderstruck. Mother yawned and said, "Doozy's tired now. Doozy needs to rest."

Outside, Kurt splayed both hands and leaned against the roof of his car. "Doozy? Who the fuck is Doozy?"

"She is. She's Doozy."

"Did you ever hear that before?"

The door was open to Ms. Lowler's office, which was small and efficient and clean, and refreshingly free of filing cabinets. Little uplifting thoughts had been attached to the printer and computer. Have-a-nice-day level. I took the initiative and asked if we could come in. "Of course you can!" she said with a smile and hurried around to find us chairs. Kurt introduced himself, booming out "Doctor" and I made a small show of modesty by just saying, "I'm Earl."

"Your mom has good and bad days in terms of her cognition generally, but she never seems anxious or unhappy."

"She got any friends?" said Kurt.

"I think that's a bit beyond her. Her friends are in the past, and she mostly lives there."

Kurt was on it. "Who's this Doozy? That name mean anything to you?"

"Why, yes. Doozy is your mother. That's her nickname."

"Really?" I said. "We've never heard it."

"Doozy is the nickname Wowser gave her."

"Wowser? Who's Wowser?"

"I thought it might be your dad."

I just held my head in my hands. Kurt asked if this had gotten out. Ms. Lowler didn't know, or didn't want to know, what he was talking about.

Kurt and I love to talk about Mother because we have different memories of her before she lost her marbles, and we enjoy filling out our impressions. For example, Kurt had completely forgotten what a balls-to-the-wall backyard birder Mother was. We went through a lot of birdseed we really couldn't afford. Dad shot the squirrels when Mother was out of the house. By holding them by the end of the tail, he could throw them like a bolo all the way to the vacant lot on the corner. Naturally, Mother thought the squirrels had decided the birds needed the food more and had moved on.

Kurt remembered her gathering the cotton from milkweed pods to make stuffing for cushions. He was ambivalent about this because we both loved those soft cushions, but it seemed to be a habit of the poor. Dad was the one who made us feel poor, but through her special magic Mother made us understand that we had to bow our heads to no one. By being the queen she transformed Kurt and me into princes. It stuck in Kurt's case. Wowser and Doozy put all this at risk.

TWO WEEKS LATER WE WERE SUMMONED BACK TO THE HOME by Ms. Lowler, who this time wore an all-concealing cardigan. She'd had enough. It seems Mother had been loudly free-associating about her amorous adventures in such a way that it wasn't always best that she occupy the common room during visiting hours. She had a nice room of her own with a view of some trees from her window and a Bible-themed Kinkade on the opposite wall and where she couldn't ask other old ladies about whisker burn or whatever. That's where we sat as before, except this time I located the call button. Kurt and I were in coats and ties, having come from work, Kurt shuffling the teeth of the living, me weaseling goobers across my desk. She smiled faintly at each of us, and we helped her into her chair. Kurt started right in. I kind of heard him while I marveled over the passage of time that separated us from when Mother ruled taste and behavior with a light but firm hand and left us, Kurt especially, with a legacy of rectitude that we hated to lose. Kurt was summarizing the best of those days, leaning forward in his chair so that his tie hung like a plumb bob, his crew cut so short that it glowed at its center from the overhead light. Mother's eyes were wide. Perhaps she was experiencing amazement. As Kurt moved toward what we believed to be Mother's secret life, her eyes suddenly dropped, and I first thought that this was some acknowledgment that such a thing existed. Kurt asked her if she'd had a special friend she'd like to tell us about. She was silent for a long time before she spoke. She said, "Are those your new shoes?"

I followed Kurt into Ms. Lowler's office. "I would like to speak to you, Ms. Lowler, about our Mother's quality of life."

"What's wrong with it?"

"She's no longer here at all, Ms. Lowler."

"Really? I think she's quite happy."

"Ms. Lowler, I'm going to be candid with you: there comes a time."

"Does there? A time for what?"

"Ms. Lowler, have you had the opportunity to familiarize yourself with the principles of the Hemlock Society?"

"I think it's quite marvelous for pets, don't you?"

Later, when Mother started thinking Kurt was Wowser, he really got onto the quality-of-life stuff. I waited before asking him the question that was burning inside of me. "Have you ever done it?"

"I've never done it but I've seen it done."

There were times when Mother seemed so rational apart from the fact that what she told us fitted poorly with the Mother we used to know. She said, for example, that Wowser always wore Mr. B collars with his zoot suit.

Kurt told me that he never knew what would happen when he visited Mother. Lately she's shown an occasionally peevish side. Today she suggested that he "get a life." This was about a week after Mother had started confusing Kurt with Wowser, and a few days after Kurt had started addressing Mother as Doozy in the hopes of finding Wowser before he could add his own stain to our family reputation. "You're in a different world when your own mother doesn't recognize you, or thinks you're the stranger who gave her a hickey."

This brought up the Hemlock Society all over again. I told Kurt to forget about it. "Why?" said Kurt. "That's the only way we get our real mother back. The human spirit is imperishable, and Mother would live on through eternity in her original form and not, frankly, as 'Doozy'. They really should weigh the spirit just to convince skeptics like you. I see the expression on your face. You could weigh the person just before and just after they die. Then you'd see that the spirit is something real. Scientists have learned how to weigh gravity, haven't they? It's time to weigh the spirit."

I'd give a million dollars to know why Kurt is in such a lather about our "standing" in town. Does anyone actually have "standing" in a shithole? Well, Kurt thinks so. He thinks we have standing because of Mother's regal presence over the decades, which, I will admit, was widely admired but which seems to be under attack via these revelations about Wowser and Doozy. I shudder to think what would happen if Kurt found out who Wowser is. Sadly, we know who Doozy is. Doozy is our mother.

I SAID TO THE SHINING YOUNG COUPLE ACROSS MY DESK, "IF you take this loan, at this bank's rates, at this point in your lives, you could find yourselves in a hole you'd never dig out of." Was this me speaking? This was an out-of-body experience. I didn't tell them that if I went down this road I'd be in the same mess I was recommending they avoid. Feeling my heart swell at the prospects of this couple was more than a little disquieting. From their point of view—and it wasn't hard to see it in their eyes—I was just turning them down. They would have liked me better if I'd hung this albatross around their necks and let them slide until we glommed the house. After they were gone, I slumped in my chair—a butterfly turning back into a caterpillar. I hadn't felt quite like this since I repeated ninth grade with Mrs. Novacek busting my balls up at the blackboard doing long division.

Kurt has this habit of picking up his napkin between thumb and forefinger as though letting cooties out. It's his way of showing the restaurant staff that nobody is above suspicion. He was on his third highball when I said, "There were times when Mother could be pretty hard."

"Where do you come up with this shit?"

I felt heat in my face. "Like when she was den mother."

"Of course she was hard on you. You were still a Bobcat after two years. What merit badges did you earn?"

"I don't remember . . ."

"I do. You earned one. Handyman. You earned a handyman merit badge. I never ever knew anyone who even wanted one. I had athlete, fitness, engineer, forester, and outdoorsman in year one. And Webelos. I didn't find Mother hard, ever. Unless you mean she had standards. Where are you going? You haven't even ordered!"

After the lunch I missed, Edwin, our bank president, came to my desk for the first time since spring before last and asked when I would start moving product like I used to. The young couple must have complained.

VISITING MOTHER WITH KURT WAS GETTING TO BE TOO HARD. The last time we tried, Mother got a mellow, dewy look on her face, and at first Kurt thought it was her pleasure at seeing us. Then he seemed to panic: "She calls me Wowser, I jump out the window."

Mother said, "Wowser."

Kurt was blinking, his nose making a tiny figure eight, but he didn't jump out the window. So I started seeing Mother on my own. I didn't try to make anything happen when I was with her, and we mostly just sat in silence. She would look at me for a long time with a watery unregistering look, and then, once in a while, I'd see her eyes darken and focus on me with a kind of intensity that lasted for a good long time. I think I knew what was going on, but I was darned if I would start yammering at her like Kurt did to get her to put into words what couldn't be put into words and only produced some crazy non sequitur from her deepest past. Of course if it featured Wowser, Kurt was on the warpath. If she just chattered about this, that, and the other without naming names, then Kurt would announce she was talking about Dad. But mostly he couldn't handle her obvious mental absence.

"Mother, I just heard the sprinklers go off. Now that's summertime to me. Mother! Are you listening to the sprinklers? It's summertime!"

"Kurt," I said. "It's not registering."

"Mom! The sprinklers! Summertime!"

Kurt had a brainstorm, and it turned out very badly. I say this not knowing how it went down, but I know it wasn't good. He decided that since Mother was mistaking him for Wowser, he would just go ahead and be Wowser—"Wowser for a day." He came home shattered. I really don't know what happened, unless it was Mother's golden boy turning into some vanished adulterer, a role in some ways similar to the one he'd been playing around town and in his safe houses for years. Finally, and without telling me anything, he calmed down. He said, "I think I have a headache. Do I? Do you think I have a headache?" It was getting to him.

When we were young, I was always a little stand-offish. That is, I was a social coward. But not Kurt. By the time he was twelve, he'd be sticking out his big paw and telling grown-ups, "Put 'er there." They liked it, and it kind of made me sick. Now he revealed an uncertainty I hadn't seen before; but it didn't last. He was soon on the muscle again. Kurt: "I see literally—literally—not one thing wrong with my taking on the identity of Wowser in pursuit of truth."

Mother's love of excellence was not something I always embraced. It certainly raised Kurt to the pedestal to which he had become accustomed, but it unfairly cast my father in a negative light. Truth be told, I was far more comfortable with Dad than with our exalted mother. What you saw was what you got. He was a sweet man, and a sweet old man later, who was not at war with time. He noticed many things about life, about dogs and cats and birds and weather, which were just so many impediments to Mother. Kurt was right: left to Dad we would have probably not gone very far, nor been nearly so discontented.

I'm on the hot seat looking into the piercing eyes of my boss: "Earl, how long have you been with the bank?"

"Twenty-two years."

"Like to see twenty-three? Not much coming over your desk except your paycheck. Desks like yours are financial portals. You know that."

"My, what big teeth you have." I was fired that day.

WHERE HAD I BEEN ALL MY LIFE? I HAD GROWN UP UNDER SO many shadows they were spread over me like the leaves of a book. Only Dad and I were equals, just looking at life without being at war with it. There was no earthly reason I should have been a banker beyond serving the shadows. By all that's reasonable, I should have been at the post office like Dad, taking packages, affixing stamps. Reciting harmless rules, greeting people. I loved greeting people! In my occupation, you had to screw someone every day, even if it was your own family.

I went to see Mother on my own on a beautiful day with a breeze coming up through the old cottonwoods along the river and cooling the side street where the rest home sat in front of its broad lawn and well-marked parking spaces. The American and Montana flags lifted and fell lazily. It was hard to go indoors. A few patients rested in wheelchairs on the lawn, the morning sun on their faces. I recognized old District Court Judge Russell Collins. He had no idea where he was, but his still-full head of hair danced in the breeze, the only part of Judge Collins moving. The others, two women who seemed to have plenty to talk about, barely glanced at me.

I sat with Mother in her room. It seemed stuffy, and I got up to let in the air. A glance at the spruces crowding the side lawn made me want to run out into the sun as though these were my last days on earth. I was unable to discern if Mother knew I was in the room. She rested her teeth on her lower lip, and each breath caused her cheeks to inflate. It was very hard to look at, which doesn't say great things about me.

I'd had enough of these visits to feel quite relaxed as I studied her and tried to remember her animation of other days. Why had she married Dad? Well, Dad was handsome and for thirty-one years held the Montana state record for the 440-yard dash. He looked like a sprinter until he died. His luck and happiness as a successful boy lasted all his life. Even Mother's provocations bounced off his good humor when she attempted to elevate his general cultivation with highbrow events at the Alberta Bair Theater in Billings. Dad liked Spike Jones, "the way he murders the classics." I remember when he played "Cocktails for Two" on the phonograph when Mother was at a school board meeting. I loved the hiccups, sneezes, gunshots, whistles, and cowbells, but Kurt walked out of the house. I thought Dad held his own with Mother. Kurt thought she made him look like a bum.

Kurt asked me to come over and help him get some things out of his garden, a jungle of organic vegetables that he plundered throughout the season as part of his health paranoia. He said that he intended to share some of this provender, as though to suggest that I would be suitably compensated. He was pouring with sweat when I got there, shirtless, his ample belly spilling over the top of his baggy shorts. He had on some kind of Japanese rocker shoes that had him teetering down the rows and doing something or other, strengthening his calves or his arches, I don't know. He took me to a cucumber trellis that was sagging with green cylinders of all sizes and told me to take my pick. I had a big brown shopping bag, and I started tossing cukes in there until he insisted on picking them himself, giving me the worst ones, ones with bug holes and brown blemishes.

"Doozy has completely confused me with Wowser."

"I think you're encouraging that, aren't you?"

"I'm learning way too much about Wowser, Earl. All their adventures. Roadhouses, et cetera. God-awful barn dances in the boonies. I imagine Dad is spinning in his grave."

Maybe Dad strayed, too. I didn't think so, and it wouldn't really fit for him. Dad was as plain as a pine board; but Mother, with her art and opera and shiny pumps—well, I could see it. Ambition is never simple. "Kurt, she has dementia. She could be making this all up."

Then he was right in my face. I could feel his breath as he rapped my elbow with a trowel. "How little you know. Dementia means she *can't* make it up."

Kurt wanted me there to knock down his potato pyramid: he'd start his plants in an old car tire, and as they grew he began stacking tires and adding dirt until the whole assemblage reached eye level. Now was the payoff, and he wanted me there. "Ready?" I said I was, and he pushed over the stack of tires, spilling dirt and hundreds of potatoes at our feet. He put his hands on his hips, panting, and smiled at the results. "Take all you want." I took a few. He'd be hiking up and down the street giving the damn things away.

I had a sudden insight. "Kurt," I said, "you seem to be competing with Wowser."

He slugged me. The cucumbers and potatoes fell from my hand. He must have fetched me a good one because I could hardly find my way out to the street.

I let it go. I can't believe it, but I did. I just wanted to keep these things at a distance. Kurt continued to press the staff at "Cloaca" about whatever Mother might be saying that others would hear. He was obsessed by the unfamiliar nature of her coarse remarks, which he said reflected the lowlife thrills she had experienced with Wowser. I had dinner with Kurt and his wife at the point that things seemed to be deteriorating. Their two boys were displeased to have me, their uncle, even in the house. These are two weird, pale boys. I don't think they've ever been outdoors. I always ask if they've been hiking in the mountains. They hate me. Beverly was quite the little conversationalist, too. She asked why I didn't have any girlfriends.

"They just haven't been coming along."

"They may find you drab. I know I do."

Beverly had made some desultory attempt at meal preparation. She'd been drinking—nothing new—and there was not much left of her former high Texas sleekness besides her aggressive twang. Kurt always looked a bit sheepish around her and was anxious when, over the sorry little meal, she brought up Mother, a subject Beverly found hilarious. Years ago when Mother was at her best, she had made no secret of her disapproval of Beverly, whom she called a tart. Local wags said that she and Beverly were competing for Kurt, and there may have been something to it, as I could bring around a rough customer with a gold tooth or neck tattoo and Mother would greet her like a queen. Of course I resented it, and of course I was pleased when Beverly, having gotten wind of Mother's new interest in Junior, said, "Old Doctor Kurt got his tail in a damn crack, ain't he?" I haven't really liked Beverly since the day of their marriage, when she called me a disgrace. There'd been a bunch of drugs at the bachelor party, and I had an accident in my pants; the word got out, thanks to Kurt.

"It's just all part of the aging process, hon," Kurt said pandering to Beverly. "The sad aging process."

"That right, Doc? Just don't drag your mama over here and give her a shot."

Like I said, she'd been drinking.

MOTHER HAD NEARLY HIT BOTTOM. SHE WAS STILL FOLLOW-ing things with her eyes, like a passing car or a cat, but not much. No, not much. I continued to see her, but I didn't know why. No, it's hard to say why I went. I'd say now that she was damn near a heathen idol, propped here or there, in a window or facing something, a picture, a doorway; it didn't seem to make much difference. It wasn't pretty at all. But Kurt kept at it until something went wrong. Evidently he broke some furniture, kicked down a door, shouted, cried. Police were involved on the assumption he was drunk. Fought the cops, got Tased, booked, released, and then a day later fucked up his rotator cuff yanking on a venetian blind. It was a week before I felt I could go near him. I thought it might be best to quietly approach Ms. Lowler.

"It has been a nightmare," she said. "And not just for me. The other residents were terrified. We've had the doctor here for them. It's a full moon, and they don't sleep well anyway. Ever since your brother started pretending to be your mother's boyfriend, she has become more and more agitated. I personally think it has been quite cruel. Then he wanted to move her to his own house, which seemed I hardly know what."

He wanted to put Mother to sleep like an old cocker span-iel. I don't know why this agitated me so; she was all but asleep anyway—I suppose it was the unexpected memories that rushed back at the thought of her no longer existing—Mother hurtling along in our old Econoline with a carload of kids, bound for a dinosaur exhibit, an opera, a ball game, or off to Crow Fair to watch the Indian dancers and eat fry bread. Crow Fair was right in the middle of when Dad and I liked to fish the Shields, which I would have preferred, while Kurt was happy to drink in all the culture with the possible exception of Crow Fair, which he considered just a bunch of crazy Indians. Maybe not fishing with Dad was why my memory was so sharp.

Or why it came to me: Mother was herding a little mob of us like a border collie through the tepees and concessions, thousands of Indians and spectators, smoke drifting from campfires, Crow elders in lawn chairs talking in sign language, young dancers running past us to the competitions in a rush of feathers. Our guide was Mr. White Clay, who helped Mother lead us to the rodeo grounds, the powwow, the fry-bread stands, and the drumming of the Nighthawk Singers. Mr. White Clay looked more like a cowboy than an Indian in his jeans, snap-button shirt, and straw hat. He was tall and dark like many Crows, and it was surprising how Mother deferred to him and how well they seemed to know each other. He had quickly familiarized himself with our group and was vigilant in rounding up anyone who strayed. It was wonderful to see Mother so relaxed, so willing to let Mr. White Clay handle things. We kids had to call him Mr. White Clay. Mother called him Roland.

My face was burning. I cut my conversation with Ms. Lowler so suddenly she was startled. I went home, burst through my front door, and picked up the phone. I called information for Crow Agency and requested a number for Roland White Clay. He answered. He answered! I told him who I was, who my mother was, who my brother was, how old we were then. Mr. White Clay was silent. I asked if we could come to see him, and he said with odd formality, "As you wish."

I had found Wowser.

I will never know why I told Kurt, but that's what I did. It took him a while to absorb this and determine for himself if I was imagining it. But he remembered, too. He remembered. He said that when he was "Wowser," "Doozy" had given him the impression that after the war Wowser no longer belonged in a tepee. Kurt said, "In case you hadn't noticed, I have forensic skills." I told him I hadn't noticed; but he went on rather plausibly. Evidently Wowser's stationing in Southern California had briefly transformed him from Plains Indian to Zoot Suiter; and more troublingly, Mother had gone from den mother to tart. Maybe they had fun. But Kurt wasn't happy. He said it looked like he would have to move. My brother move away? After all these years? I couldn't possibly face that. Kurt was there at the Grass Dance with Mother on that far-away and now sadly beautiful day. He said, "We're gonna drag that Indian back up here and let him and Mother have a grand reunion. That's when this Wowser retires."

We drove to the Rez in his little MG, which he stores most of the year. I couldn't think of a worse car to drive on a hot day on the interstate, our hair blowing in the heat, our faces getting redder. Kurt thought it would cheer him up, but by the time we got near Laurel, where fumes from the refinery filled the little two-seater, tears were pouring from his eyes. At first I thought it was the appalling conditions of driving this flivver among the sixteen-wheelers, pickup trucks, and work-bound sedans. But that wasn't it. He was remembering throwing a fit at assisted living. Surely I knew that. I waited until we slowed for the Hardin exit to ask him what happened. He unexpectedly swerved onto the shoulder. Our dust cloud swept over our heads and dissipated downwind. Kurt stared at me.

"She came on to me."

"It's your own fault!" I shouted.

"Searching for the truth about our mother? You're actually calling that my fault? To my face? You never cared about Mother!"

"Mother never cared about me!"

Kurt lowered his voice. "Earl, there was a problem of course. The problem was that you were uneducable."

"Ah. I thought Dad was uneducable. That's what she said. What luck she had you."

"I think she felt that way," he said with a slight toss of his head.

"Was this when she was fucking the Indian?"

"You need to be careful, Earl." I could see violence rising in Kurt's face. "You need to be very, very careful."

"Just asking, Kurt. It shouldn't be controversial. I'm only trying to establish a time frame."

"'Fucking the Indian' is not a time frame. It's ignorant. Remember John Wayne in *Hondo*, where he plays a half-breed army scout? My point is he has a hard time being accepted by Indians and whites, per se."

"Are you saying we might be half-breeds?"

"Not per se. We just don't want any questions like that hanging over us."

"Can we stop for water? What happens if we have mechanical problems on the Rez? You can't even buy tires for this thing." I was trying to change the subject, and I guess I was successful because Kurt started the motor and pulled back onto the highway, the tiny four-banger sneezing under the hood. I knew perfectly well that I didn't pass inspection around our house except with Dad. Kurt was trying to see himself in the mirror, his hair windmilling around in the heat. Then he'd look at me like a dermatologist. It didn't take me long to figure out that he was wondering if we were half-breeds.

ROLAND WHITE CLAY WAS SOME KIND OF EMERITUS TRIBAL chairman. His office was at the end of a corridor past the drinking fountain, and sparsely furnished, a military portrait behind the desk. He wore a sport coat over his jeans and a sky-blue western shirt, his Stetson resting upside down on his desk. He met us with cordial suspicion and occasionally glanced out of his window as we met, seemingly anxious to be outdoors again. Kurt and I sat in front of his desk, as though interviewing for a job.

"Chief—do you mind if I call you Chief?"

"Suit yourself," said White Clay with a wintry smile.

"Chief, I read all the Montana and Wyoming papers pretty much every day, and I see an issue that affects Indian people very negatively." Here White Clay perked up. "And that is: rolling cars. My research indicates that with each six inches of wheelbase, the likelihood of rollovers is reduced by eighteen percent." I spotted this as bullshit from the get-go. "My thought is to appeal to the automobile industry as an altruistic salute to Native American culture to manufacture special editions of their standard vehicles with wider wheelbases to help prevent rollovers." The acid look in White Clay's face was a wonder to behold. White Clay spoke after a long silence.

"If you think I should," said White Clay, "I can have tribal council sit in."

"No," said Kurt. "We're just trying to learn more about our mother. She has dementia and she's slipping away."

He gazed at us. "Well, we were close."

"How close?" said Kurt. You could hear the demand in his voice. White Clay mused comfortably as he looked back at him. Finally, he smiled. Just then three little boys ran in: White Clay's grandchildren. He introduced them. All had short, crisp names, Chip, Skip, and Mick. He reproached them affectionately for their muddy jeans and T-shirts. They tagged White Clay and shot out as quickly as they'd come.

"I never married," he said.

"That's all you're going to say?"

"That's all I'm going to say."

The photograph behind the desk, grainy from being blown up, showed a smiling GI on a riverbank, propped against his M1. I couldn't tell if it was White Clay or just another Indian kid. We had deferments, which Kurt said was the only way to go if there was nothing more to fight than gooks. My asthma exempted me, but Kurt could easily have been drafted if Mother hadn't gone to the board. She had something on the woman who was running it.

"Is Caroline suffering?"

Caroline. When had someone last called Mother that? "No," I said. "Except during her so-called good spells when she is confused." I didn't say a word about what she might have been going through while Kurt was impersonating him, not when we were sitting across the desk from the genuine Wowser.

"Whose idea was it to come and see me?"

Kurt barked an artificial laugh. "We just thought you might want to see her. Might do her a lot of good."

A truculent cloud crossed Kurt's face. "Our mother enjoys an unparalleled and dignified standing in our community that will never change." All I could think was that if he took a stand at this moment he could plan on being Wowser for the rest of Mother's life. White Clay picked the Stetson up off his desk and thrust it onto his head. He stood, still tall if bowlegged, but broad shouldered and erect. "Caroline and I were . . . there wasn't room for it. I'll come to see her, if you think it would help. Might help me!"

One look at Kurt's MG and he said he'd take his pickup. Going back in that hot headwind was awful. It nearly stopped that silly little car, and our faces roasted as we headed into the afternoon sun. "How about the three papooses that showed up in the chief's office? What'd he call 'em? Snap, Crackle, and Pop? Something like that."

"CAROLINE," SAID WHITE CLAY. "IT'S ME." HER EYES MOVED slightly in White Clay's direction, and Kurt threw his head back and mouthed some words to the ceiling. For him, it was all over. White Clay just moved his head very slightly from side to side, as if saying no. In a while he got up, bent over, and kissed Mother on the cheek. You couldn't tell if she noticed. White Clay turned to speak to us. He said, "You were a couple of cute little boys. I understood why your mother wouldn't go off with me. Now I see you again, and you are grown men. I must tell the truth. There doesn't seem to be much to either one of you." He nodded to me and went out. Then Kurt left, leaving me alone. I sat and watched Mother. There was nothing in her face, nothing like life, nothing except the rise and fall of her breathing. It felt safe, after so long, to ask her if she loved me. It was just the two of us. No reply. I didn't expect one.

I met with Kurt at his clinic in the old ice-cream plant that had been stylishly renovated to house fashionable new businesses, but fashionable new businesses failed to arrive except for a doomed florist and a malodorous brisket palace. I couldn't wait to speak to him, and sitting in one of his examination chairs, I felt I was confessing after a long interrogation. Kurt, who is never off duty, wandered around in his white tunic inspecting his weird tools while I told him the story.

"I spent almost three hours with Mother, and don't ask me why, she was pretty lucid."

"Lucid about what?"

"I'm going to tell you. Maybe the visit from White Clay, I don't know, but she was kind of excited, kind of agitated, you could say, and I just sat there, and finally I said, 'What's on your mind?'"

"You think she has one?"

"Kurt, honestly."

"All right, so go on."

"Remember when Dad had his gallbladder surgery?"

"And the septicemia?"

"Exactly, and do you remember when it was?"

"No."

"Well, I'll tell you when it was. It was the same week as Crow Fair, one year later."

"Earl, that's not something I would ever remember. And in some ways it speaks to some of your issues, always looking back, always regretful."

I ignored this. I felt it was important that Kurt hear the story and that it would maybe change his views of Mother and help him realize she was only human. "Well, when Dad was in the hospital you remember his sister Audrey came out from Spokane to help care for him. And Mom felt it was kind of insulting, and she went off by herself."

"I vaguely remember. As I recall, Audrey was a hell of a cook. But repetitious."

"Oh, you thought it was a big improvement. That's another thing that may have gotten Mom, this big fuss over Audrey. Anyway, she left."

"Where did she go?"

"Crow Fair," I hissed.

"You heard this today? What did they do?"

"I'll tell you what they did. They took two horses and went on a day's ride up the Bighorn River and camped under the stars."

"They camped under the stars."

"They camped under the stars. They ate antelope. Mom said it tasted just like chicken."

"It's like you're reading a fucking poem. Antelope doesn't taste like chicken."

"They swam in the Bighorn and gathered wild berries. He took her to the secret graves of the warriors. They dried their clothes on the willows." Kurt winced, clutching a dental tool. "In two days, she was back at Dad's bedside."

Kurt said with feeling, "Our mother was a cheating housewife."

I hoped my story provided a gentler interpretation of our mother and the choices she made. Of course I made the whole thing up. My only regret was some bucktoothed kid coming in and finding himself in the hands of an agitated orthodontist. But. It may have been a mistake. Kurt didn't take it at all as I had intended. It made him see our dad as a victim. "He's there recuperating from surgery eating that awful stuff Audrey kept making over and over." Now Audrey was a bad cook. I thought it would be strategic to egg him on. Dishes we called shit-on-a-shingle and buffalo balls.

"Dad definitely was getting the short end of the stick. Mom out there in the tepee." What tepee? I could see he was moving his allegiance to Dad. Soon I'd be an orphan.

Kurt had a big job and had all the time in the world to work through our family history. I was broke and out of work. Also, my phone had been turned off. I thought I knew why, but at first I was unwilling to borrow someone's phone to find out. In the end I put on my game face, borrowed an office at my old bank for a morning, and, braving a gauntlet of smirks, arranged an interview at a bank in Miles City and put several hundred miles of prairie between Kurt and me.

It was my luck that the president of the bank in Miles City, who wore a cowboy hat at all times, regarded the president of the bank that fired me as a "pilgrim and a honyocker." I didn't entirely follow this but sensed it was in my favor; and indeed it was. I was offered the job on my word alone. In middle age, I had the chance to move away from home for the first time. I was terrified because it meant leaving Mother in Kurt's hands. Soon I was at a very similar desk doing very similar things with the same clients but with more cowboy boots. I was clawing for volition and tried to develop a personal algorithm that would predict the date I would be fired all over again. I developed a garish fantasy life for what my last stop would be and came up with cleaning porta-potties at Ozzfest.

Then Kurt called to tell me that he had instigated a forensic inquest into the finances of Ms. Lowler that revealed minor malfeasance, easily challenged. But Ms. Lowler wouldn't stand for it and quit. I knew what was next: he was taking Mother to his home. "She gave so much, it's time to give back."

"She'll be lucky to make it a month," I said. I was paralyzed.

Kurt said, "Never be ruled by hatred."

"And forfeit the merit badge?"

In the last five weeks of Mother's life, I really should have been fired, but the staff at the Miles City bank was just fascinated by my torpor, wishing to see how far I might go toward complete ossification. In some way I was kind of fun for them. They were like happy children watching a frog.

I had the oddest feeling going to the funeral and at the funeral itself a kind of helium levitation. Kurt and his loudmouth wife, Beverly, were there gaping with fascination at the sight of me. I never spoke to them. There were lots of people there, lots of elderly people mostly, and some others, too. It was a crowd. It seemed like they were underwater, and I alone had a boat, such a nice little boat. I was pretty much sunning myself and the waves were gentle. Occasionally, I looked over the side. I was sailing away.

I rose rapidly at the bank, if you call five years rapid. I grew fond of Miles City and bought an old Queen Anne house on Pleasant Street. I loved banking so much—funneling the universal lubricant—and led our expansions to five midsize cities. Lately, I've been riding a carriage at the annual Bucking Horse Sale, waving to everyone like an old-timer, which I guess is what I'm getting to be.

TANGO

L. RAYMOND HOXEY BOUGHT AN OLD MANSION IN LIVINGS-ton, Montana, and converted the third floor into a delightful apartment with views of several mountain ranges, including the Absarokas, the Bridgers, and the Crazies. The second floor kept his print collection in archival conditions, with humidifiers and air-quality equipment. The first floor was divided into two apartments, one of which housed his assistant, Tessa Larionov, and the other, in the summer, a textile historian, employed by the Metropolitan Museum in New York, who was also a trout fisherman.

The year the historian died, I was still premed and was painting houses to support myself; I moved into the vacated apartment. Acknowledging that there is a difference between being naïve and being innocent, I will say that I was entirely naïve back then. My parents lived only a few miles away, but we weren't getting along, and I needed some distance, despite the fact that my mother was sick and often ranted about God. How was I to know that she was about to die? Like most aspiring to study medicine, I planned to get rich, but I wasn't rich yet; I was just a poor housepainter, out of work and hoping for something to come along, and, despite all other evidence, I feared that I would be one forever, packing a great wheel of color chips from one indifferent house to another. I don't mean to suggest mild insecurity here: by any reasonable standard, I was losing my mind.

Tessa Larionov was the daughter of a Russian engineer who had immigrated to the United States in 1953 and found his way to Choteau, Montana, where he set up business building bridges for the railroad. Tessa's mother was not Russian; she may have been Italian. She had met Tessa's father in New Jersey, when he first landed. Tessa was a powerfully built but attractive woman, with black hair, black eyes, and the look of a Tatar—humorous and a little dangerous. She was liked by everyone who knew her. Trained in library science, she had worked as an archivist at some very august places, including the Huntington, in San Marino, where she'd met her employer and our landlord, L. Raymond Hoxey, who had let her talk him into retiring to Montana with his rare-prints business, which she was now helping to run. Hoxey was eighty-one years old, and his arrangement with Tessa was really just a way of avoiding assisted living. She was very fond of him but had wanted to move home, and this arrangement worked for them both. Tessa was exactly thirty, still single, though she had enjoyed an active love life, leaving behind only grateful hearts, or so she said. "They're all still crazy about me—that's why I left California," she told me. Settling down was of no interest to her; the prints were her life, and she wanted to keep her eye on Hoxey. I was twenty, but she treated me as if I were even younger—a salute to my retarded behavior, I'm sure.

My father was a pipe fitter for the Northern Pacific Railroad. (In the world of corporate takeovers, the railroad had actually changed its name several times, but "Northern Pacific" was the one that stayed in all our minds: it meant something; "Burlington Northern" meant nothing.) My mother was a hairdresser and, because of her big mouth, she had enemies all over southwest Montana and very few customers. As an only child, I was driven back and forth between our house and the less fashionable grade school in the area, then the local high school, where I was anonymous, never having been allowed by my overprotective mother to learn a sport. But I liked to fish. I'd fish anywhere there was water; I fished in a lot of ditches where there was no hope of success. I commuted to college and lived like a monk, on a small scholarship. I now understand that I was a weirdly underdeveloped human being for my age, ripe for just the sort of encounter that I would have with Tessa Larionov. Even my mother noticed my immaturity; she was always telling me, "Stop staring at people!"

It was Hoxey whom I got to know first. The day I arranged to rent from him, he happened to have received several Reginald Marsh prints, of which he was very proud. I acted as if I'd heard of Reginald Marsh. I didn't know one painter from another, but I had a hunger for this sort of information—I was sure that it would be useful later, when I was rich. Hoxey was a pleasant old man who must have once been very fat, because he had loose flesh hanging from him everywhere and as many as seven chins. I always tried to count them while he was speaking to me, but then something in his remarks would break my concentration. This physicality, which bespoke a lifetime of phlegmatic living, gave his discourse on prints the authority that a weathered desert rat would have if he told you about cactus. I remember Hoxey carefully unpacking one of the prints—a kind of crazy thing with blank-faced people swarming in and out of doorways, no one reacting to anyone else. He said that it was the calmest Reginald Marsh he'd ever seen. "No *Moonlight and Pretzels* in this one!" he cried. I could see both that he'd be an agreeable landlord and that many health issues lay before him. As someone studying medicine, I could make a little game of guessing which one would kill him.

A few days after I moved in, Tessa asked me over for drinks. She had done a beautiful job of making her apartment habitable, with old, comfortable furniture that she'd bought cheap and re-covered. She also had a good many of Hoxey's prints on loan, though, as she explained, she was really just providing storage for them, and her collection changed as things were sold. She made a little face when she told me that she couldn't afford to get attached to any of the prints, a particular trial for her as she loved the art of all nations. Cocktails and art, I thought—maybe I'll get into her pants. I'm sure that I had a big goober smile on my face as I contemplated such an outcome.

"Because I work upstairs, I've had to become a walker just to get outside," she told me, as she mixed our drinks in a blender. "You start getting curious about different neighborhoods—where the railroaders lived, where the ranchers retired, where the doctors and bankers live. In the winter, when the wind starts up, I have to tie a scarf over my face. Anybody you see in the street is ducking for a building, kind of like in the Blitz."

As I listened, I found that I was leaning forward in my chair with my hands pressed between my knees. It was only when she stopped to look at me that I realized that my posture was strange. I pretended that I was just stretching and leaned back in an apparently casual but quite uncomfortable position. As Tessa came toward me with a brightly colored drink, it seemed as though both she and it were expanding, and when she handed me the glass I wasn't sure that I was strong enough to hold it. I felt suddenly as if everything were bigger than me, as if I were in over my head, trying to handle the kind of situation that, when I was rich, I would take to like a duck to water. But things settled quickly once she sat down, and I was glad to have the drink because I was a bit cotton-mouthed. I had gone from my first impulse to get into her pants to fearing that she'd try to get into mine.

I'm not much of a drinker; water would have served as well. That summer I'd made an experimental jaunt into a local bar. I felt that I needed to learn to be more social. I struck up a conversation with a somber, middle-aged fellow in a rumpled suit. He looked so gloomy that I regaled him with what I felt were uplifting accounts of my struggles at school. He stared at me for a while, until I sensed that all the timing was going out of my conversation. Finally, he said, "Hey, boss, I got to go: you're creeping me out."

"Now," Tessa said, "let's start at the beginning: what do you think being a doctor will do for you?"

"I don't know." My answer came out so quickly she looked startled. She leaned back into the sofa—she was at one end, I at the other—with her elbow propped and her fingers parting the hair on the side of her head.

"You don't know?"

"I wish I did. *Sorry.*" I involuntarily sang out this last word.

"No, that's all right. That's fine. If you don't want to talk about it, I'm okay with that."

I didn't share the image I had of myself: still dark haired but with a graying mustache, marching up the gangplank of a yacht. I kept looking into my drink as if it were a teleprompter and I were the president of the United States. The colorful liquid seemed like something I had found and would have to turn in. I don't know why I made people so uncomfortable. As a kind of icebreaker, I thought to ask her a question.

"When people use the expression 'Rest in peace,' do you think they have some basis for saying it, or is it just wishful thinking?"

I can't imagine what made me think that she'd have the answer to this doleful conundrum. But surely my mother's poor health was on my mind.

"You mean, about *the dead*?"

"Sure."

Tessa looked at me for a very long time before saying anything.

"You know, let's try this another time. Maybe it's you, maybe it's me, but at this point in time and space it's just not happening."

I backed out of there like a crab. I felt sorry for Tessa; she'd probably have trouble sleeping after this weird visit from the new neighbor. I just didn't know what to do about it—an apology from me would have made it all seem even weirder.

Thereafter, we sometimes ran into each other in the hallway between our apartments, and things did not get any less awkward. I made increasingly maladroit attempts to be cordial, attempts that were received with growing skepticism, even revulsion. Finally, upon seeing me, Tessa would dart into her apartment and slam the door. What was strange is that whenever I lingered in the hallway after she'd gone inside, I always, moments later, heard her phone ring.

Once she said to me, "I know you're tracking my movements." And another time, "Don't think you're fooling me." And another, a cry: "Please *stop*!"

"Stop *what*?"

A mirthless laugh followed and a slammed door.

I made every effort to avoid these encounters. Indeed, I did start tracking her movements, in order to avoid her. She headed upstairs to work for Hoxey at exactly nine, out for the mail at ten-thirty, lunch with Hoxey in his apartment, catered by Mountain Foodstuff, Monday, Wednesday, and Friday, out to lunch Tuesday and Thursday but always back by one-thirty, UPS and FedEx and other outbound packages at four o'clock, and then her workday was over. On the weekends, I really didn't have a pattern of her activities and nervously came and went from my apartment. When she had men over, they seemed to linger around my door as if they were on the lookout for me. One afternoon, a strapping man positioned himself as though to actually block my way. I gave him a big smile and pushed past. He smelled like motor oil. He said, "Hello, Doc." Tessa must have told him that I was premed. I said hello. I was glad to get inside and, when I looked through the little spy hole in the door, I was looking into his ear.

Concentrating on the help-wanted ads calmed me down. I had discovered that I needed to look for work in other towns, as people in Livingston knew who I was and—this really is very funny—held my studies against me.

"You can't paint my house," Mrs. Talliafero said. "You're going to be a doctor!"

"Not necessarily!" I said in my warmest tone, while hers cooled markedly. I have no idea why I answered her that way. I was sure that I was going to be a doctor, but when I was under pressure to make conversation it was as if all my life plans went up in smoke.

I kept studying the paper. I recognized the real opportunities that exist for those who wish to sell cars or apply siding, but the trouble I was having with my communication skills made me fear that those occupations might not be my line. I really thought that once I got my timing back—and it *was* a timing issue—I'd be able to look into a different set of prospects. I was very much focused on my chances of being unexceptional; if I had any opportunity to keep my head down, I meant to take it.

I got a job working for a very nice guy, or so I thought, named Dan Crusoe. He was an attorney in Billings who specialized in whiplash and owned a cute little turn-of-the-century cottage in Harlowton, which he used as a weekend place—or, rather, somewhere to get away with his secretary, who did not enjoy the same legal standing as his wife. "Lawyers like me make doctors leave the profession every day!" he joked. "Stick to painting houses." But he was an amiable fellow with a big laugh that led one's attention away from his shrewd, close-set eyes. His dark curls were so uniform and regular they suggested the work of a beautician. When I asked him if they were natural, he told me to mind my own business with such vehemence that I actually jumped back. The previous owner of his cottage had used stolen Forest Service paint for the trim and shutters, and Dan wanted it all yellow, "like sunshine, get it?" I was rehearsing what I thought to be the appropriate style for my current position when I said, *"No problema,"* but Dan seemed to detect some awkwardness in my delivery, for his eyes grew narrow and he just said, "Right."

I rented a pressure washer, masked everything, used a quality primer, and picked my weather for the final coat. The house looked much better, but Crusoe never responded to the bill I sent, nor to the second or the third notice. Live and learn. I wasn't much interested in exploring my remedies, and, since other revenues were unassured, I sold my car and went on a grocery binge. Also, to celebrate my first two months in the apartment, I bought a bed and put it out in the middle of the living room, where I could luxuriate in all that space and gaze east, west, and south, but not north, out of fine windows at prospects that were better than any painting, in that they were full of those moving, changing parts called Life.

One morning, I heard a timid knock on my door and called, "Enter!" I was stretched out on my new bed in my shorts, reading a newspaper I'd found in the doorway of the bank, when I learned that my visitor was the chief of police. I was really pleased to see him, so pleased that I easily set aside my worries about the reason for his visit. I suppose that I was lonely. In a decent society, the chief of police is the one stranger you should be able to welcome into your home without reservation. But the first thing he told me was that I'd better get dressed, as I was going to jail. He gazed at me with sad knowingness. He had a big, warm face; it shouldn't be misunderstood if I state that he looked like Porky Pig, with all that guileless amiability, the same pink complexion.

"Tessa Larionov"—he gestured with his head in the direction of Tessa's door—"has charged you with making obscene phone calls to her."

"Oh?" I said. "I don't have a phone."

For one miraculous moment, there were people passing all three windows and the chief remarked that I needed curtains.

"How bad were these calls supposed to be?" I tried to picture myself as the twisted man dialing her number. In a weird way, it seemed plausible.

"They were not nice."

It comes as a great surprise to anyone who spends some time in a small-town jail that it is a remarkably stress-free environment. If your reputation is of no concern, your troubles are behind you. The Livingston jail was as good a place as any in which to unravel all the causes for the state I was in. In a rare moment of lucidity, I suggested a wiretap. The chief didn't take my idea seriously, but tomorrow was a new day because Tessa would inform him that the calls had continued while I was in jail, and so the wiretap came into play after all.

It soon paid off. Hoxey had been making the calls. Tessa declined to press charges, and it all went down as a lovers' quarrel, once you swallowed the fifty-one-year difference in their ages. Tessa's routine remained the same, except that her phone no longer rang so much after her workday was done. I finally ran into her in the hallway one afternoon, just as she was coming down with the packages. She stopped in her tracks, arms loaded, and regarded me quizzically. "Hello," she said. I waited before replying. I wanted her to think about what she had done to me. But she didn't seem worried, and the longer I waited the less worried she looked.

"Hello," I said.

"You look like you've been painting."

"Yes, I've been painting a house."

"Here in town?"

"Yes, a doctor's house on Third."

"How funny. But you're going to be a doctor."

"Yes, I'm going to be a doctor."

"I don't suppose we'll ever get to the bottom of that."

"No, probably not."

"If you were sick, would you go to a doctor, or treat yourself?"

"Oh, I'd go to a doctor. I'm not a doctor yet."

"I mean if you already were . . . Oh, never mind. Can you help me with these?"

We took the packages to the post office and I stood outside on the steps while she shipped them. I watched a grackle walk between parked cars, one of which had an American flag on its antenna. A strong young man was wheeling a cart of pies into the back of a restaurant. He looked too powerful to wheel pies. My mother drove past, blowing her horn and revealing her colossal agitation through the windshield. People in town enjoyed such scenes.

Once Tessa had sent the packages, she commended me for having taken the jailing episode with such good grace. I told her that I didn't know how I could have done otherwise, which she mistook for some form of courtesy. I used both speech and body language to indicate that I mostly understood, and that what I didn't understand I forgave.

I had been brought up to believe that time delivers our dreams and quietly carries our nightmares away, and that most of what lies before us is welcoming and serene. This was part of the strange but cozy world of my home, with God in the role of Mr. Goodwrench. Or, at least, that's how I looked at it, peering out from the cocoon of my oddly sheltered Pentecostal household, where the only thing I had to worry about was the flames of eternal damnation, which didn't seem like all that much. I saw Satan as just another person who could be bought after my career took off. My mother was always telling me how deceitful the devil was, but that only made me feel that I could handle him.

Tessa soon took charge of my life, and she decided that it would be good if we were to do something together, just for fun. "Mr. Hoxey feels terrible about all that has happened," she said. "He wants to treat us to a night on the town."

That Friday, we signed up for a tango lesson.

Tessa and I and six other couples entered the Elks Hall, with its terrible acoustics and all-pervading clamminess. We were conventionally dressed; I wore a secondhand sport coat and wide tie, Tessa a black sheath that struggled to control her well-muscled shape. The others were more South American in style—hot-red lipstick on their small-town faces, tortoiseshell combs in their swept-back hair. Some of the men had gone with a pomaded look that betrayed their sense of mission. They seemed to smolder in anticipation of their future proficiency.

Our instructor was Juan Dulce, or just Dulce, a genuine Argentine who worked his way around the American West giving lessons. He had created a real interest in the tango in the most unlikely places—cow towns, oil towns, uranium towns, coal towns—where this hint of another kind of life carried a special allure. He was perhaps sixty, as thin as a herring, and wore striped pants, a formal black coat, a ruby cravat, and stacked heels. His hair, slicked to his skull, emphasized eyes that seemed to belong to a marine creature of some sort. He was without humor and he effectively conveyed the sacredness of his task. I doubt that I shall forget the sight of him standing on a Pepsi crate and pouring out his introduction in a deep and vibrant voice that seemed to make the room hum.

"When I am fifteen in Buenos Aires I am longing for love and suffering and, above all, success—the hope of becoming a legend of our hot and drowsy tango. I underwent numberless deprivations, but success would reward the sensual designs that I demonstrated in many venues. Now the money I earn is exchanged for my fatigue, but I have no other way to go, and there are days I awaken upon wretchedness. Once I converted my dancing of three weeks' duration by a pocket ruler into three hundred seventy-two kilometers. Still, tango is all! Without tango my face inspires doubt. Therefore, my advice is press your tango to great advantage! And now we begin."

He turned on the big sound system, which had hitherto been employed to enlarge the voices of prairie politicians bent on higher office and nostalgic Scandinavian chorales with cow horns on their heads. The system had astounding capacity, and the room was soon filled with the somber, inevitable cadences of this prelude to intercourse. (As a student, I had not only enjoyed several instances of actual copulation—albeit with Mr. Goodwrench staring down at me—I had seen the act explained on huge blackboards, so that there could be no doubt about what was going on.)

We began to learn the steps, in the chest-to-chest Argentine style. We arrayed ourselves counterclockwise and concentrated on the spacing between us and the other couples. My exhilaration at Tessa's great power soon gave way to apprehension, as though I were riding an unruly horse; and, when I failed to comprehend the crossover steps as described by Dulce, Tessa used her might to drag me into position with a determined expression on her face. To avoid potential humiliation, I attached myself to her flying carcass with a wiry grasp. Her cry of alarm brought Dulce to our side and the other dancers to a stop just as I was beginning to enjoy myself.

"*Señor!* Grappling has no place in our national dance!"

"I cannot follow her movements," I explained in an accent identical to Dulce's, which I found unexpectedly infectious.

"You are not to follow—you are to lead!"

"It's my fault," Tessa said. "I lost patience with him during the first abrazo. He just seemed lost. I'll try to do better."

"Perhaps this is the time to work on our syncopation," Dulce said sternly to both of us, "with greater respect for the movements of each other."

"The music is unfamiliar," I explained. "You don't happen to know 'La Bamba'?" He held his head and moaned as though he'd been shot.

The other couples had deftly caught on to the oddly triangular chests-together, feet-apart position. An older pair of bottle blonds, obviously trained in various kinds of ballroom dancing, made an effort to dance past at close range. The woman had a fixed and toothy Rockettes smile, and when she swept by she caught my eye and called out, "Piece of cake!"

I gave Dulce my word that I would syncopate respectfully, and I began to dance in earnest. At first, Tessa complimented me on my "good hustle," but she soon proved unequal to my speed and dexterity. Whatever had been going on in my life up to that point poured into my tango, and the exultation I began to experience was interrupted only when Tessa let out a real showstopper of a screech. Then Dulce came between us and made the mistake of laying hands on me. Insofar as I retained a modicum of male pride, this contact quickly devolved into a dustup on the floor, oddly accompanied by the raucous music of Argentina and the sounds of angry interference from the other students. With their help, I was flung into the street. "*Good night,* Doctor!" I realized that Tessa had told the others that I was already out of medical school and that she was no cradle robber.

I recall feeling breathless and completely without direction as I allowed Tessa to take charge of our stroll. She stopped momentarily, between two old commercial buildings, not far from the railroad yard, looked straight at me, and said, "Boo. Hiss." We went on. "I'm lucky you didn't request Mannheim Steamroller," she added. I was defeated.

"Now, don't be offended and, more important, don't walk in front of that car," she said. "I realize you aren't attracted to me, are you?"

"That's not the real story," I replied. "I need encouragement." These two sentences were uttered with such sincerity that I could see Tessa respond with visible happiness.

"Then let me tell you my own fears. Why? Because you're adorable. Of course you're a complete idiot but, within that, there is a certain appeal—I've felt it before in pet shops. But I have fears, too. Isn't that real friendship, to tell someone your fears? You could have been extremely disagreeable over those phone calls."

"What good would it have done?"

"None, but few people would have recognized that. I sense that you have a good heart, a good heart trapped in a self that is a hop, skip, and jump from needing day care. Obscene phone calls from a stranger are intolerable. But when they come from someone you know, particularly a deluded old walrus like Hoxey, well, they don't arouse quite the same wrath. You had the right to revenge and you declined to take it. Hoxey and I are in your debt."

I had a strong glimpse here of the sensible side of Tessa, and I had a sudden hunch that she would end up a friend, which rather worried me because she was the sort who might anchor me and teach me to accept reality, such as it was then emerging.

"How about you just walk me home?" she said finally. "That work for you?"

"Of course."

We paused at the railroad tracks to watch a big northern express rip through. She watched intently and I positioned myself behind her in such a way that it looked as if the train were pouring in one of her ears and out the other. I knew then that I would kiss her.

I suppose it took ten minutes for us to get back to the house, during which time Tessa did her level best to tell me her hopes and dreams, which were honest and simple: ride old man Hoxey into the ground and clean out his estate. That wasn't how she put it, naturally. Her motive, as she expressed it, was a passion for aesthetic rarities. "No one knows the inventory as I do. No one cares as I do, and no one knows the importance of getting it into strong and caring hands as much as I do." I didn't say anything, and I suppose she found my silence censorious.

We entered her apartment. Before pulling the door closed behind her, she said, "At the end of the day, it is what it is." I wondered what that meant. Of course it is what it is, and it didn't even have to be the end of the day to be what it was. I couldn't understand this sort of thing at all, and in a way kissing someone who said things like that was like kissing air. When I did, it was with the kind of apprehension one feels on placing an open mousetrap in a promising location. Afterward, she held me at arm's length and looked at me with what one of my professors had called the copulative gaze. She seemed all-consuming. I thought of the big-bang theory, wherein a tiny speck of matter and energy mysteriously explodes, expanding into the universe.

I said, "What do you think?" My heart pounded.

She said, "Let's give it a whirl."

We made love on the couch. I performed in a state of amazement at all that skin. Skin everywhere! At one point, she said, "I wonder if you could change your expression. I can barely do this." When I reached that moment to which all our nature ascends and by which the future of the species is assured in spasm after spasm, she remarked, "Never a dull moment."

OVER THE EIGHT YEARS THAT FOLLOWED, AS I MADE MY WAY through medical school and graduated, I'd occasionally see Tessa going about the affairs of Hoxey. She had acquired a questionable reputation around town by then, as he was now sick and demented, and she was seen as exploiting him. Then Hoxey died, and whatever worries I might have had for her were briefly allayed, as it seemed that she had inherited the business.

She made an appointment to see me at the clinic. I had forgotten just how large and burningly vital she was. Her hair, piled atop her head and held there by a bright-red plastic comb, seemed to represent fulminating energy. She had a white streak, which she attributed to "trauma."

"Hoxey's henchmen have put me on the street," she told me, "with little more than the clothes on my back."

"Tessa, I find this very hard to picture."

"Perhaps a few prints, a watercolor or two."

"Who exactly are these 'henchmen'?"

"His children. Grown daughters. I never factored them in. They arrived on the scene like Valkyries hovering over the battlefield in search of corpses."

"I'm terribly sorry to hear this."

"At a difficult time in your life, Doctor, I offered you companionship and sexual healing."

"What can I do? Medication is my line, but I don't think that's what you're looking for."

"I plan to stay here, and I'll have to start looking for work. I hope you'll recommend me."

I reached for a pen, poised to join the millions who have made their way out of a difficult spot by providing a letter of recommendation. But Tessa said, "Not now. I'll let you know."

That, more or less, was the end of our appointment. She seemed happy with my response, taking my hand in both of hers. I suppose that she was just checking to see whether I was still on her side.

Tessa went downhill fast. Within two years, she had spells of homelessness, punctuated by temporary jobs, none of which became permanent because of her imperious nature, her contempt for owners and bosses. She never left a job—she stormed out of it. She took over the homes where she was briefly a guest. Even as her fortunes fell, Tessa didn't lose her rakish airs, though they began to seem just a bit automatic as she strode around town in worn clothes.

I was one of several people who helped in little ways, but I rarely saw Tessa. By this time, I had established the small-town practice that would not make me rich, though it might make me happy. Hoxey had long ago returned to California in powder form, leaving nothing behind. Those years seemed to have allowed me to awaken from my own background and, without boasting, I can say that I had become somewhat less of a fool, though I was constantly aware that my foolishness could recur at any time, like a virus that lies dormant at the base of the spine. I can't say that I saw Tessa as my responsibility; nor can I claim to have quite gotten her out of my mind.

The December night on which I was celebrating my fortieth birthday with a cake in the emergency room, an ambulance arrived with Tessa: into her abdomen she had plunged a serrated bread knife, an item she continued to clutch on the gurney that conveyed her. I took it from her hand and, feeling on me the heat of her eyes, I quickly began dealing with her wound. I knew that if she were admitted to the clinic itself she would be subjected to what I viewed as diagnostic imprudence—laparotomy and other explorations that experience had led me to associate with increased morbidity. Though I would later have a chance to review these judgments, I honestly feel that they didn't alter the way things turned out. In effect, I was keeping Tessa to myself. I had hoped that this was only a cry-for-help injury—the timing, during my shift, aroused my suspicions—but the knife, it turned out, had pierced the skin, the subcutaneous layer, the linea alba, and the peritoneum; I could only hope that it had gone no farther—that is, into the viscera. Over the next four days, attending Tessa around the clock while she stared at me without speaking, I failed to contain the major spillage, the uncontrolled peritoneal contamination, the necrosis, and an infection that laughed off antibiotics in a general cascade. She was looking right through me when she slipped away.

Aren't there things that your parents should tell you? After my mother died, I'd gone to my childhood house and found her reading glasses. I'd sat on our old sofa by the window overlooking a stunted row of odorless roses, still knowing, after all those years, which part of the sofa I could sit on without feeling the springs. I put my mother's glasses on. The earpieces were too short for me, and I had to press them down on my nose uncomfortably. It didn't matter: I could barely see through them.

THE DRIVER

Mrs. QUANTRILL LIVED IN A BEAUTIFUL OLD PRAIRIE-STYLE house built in the twenties, which she'd restored to its original splendor with Mr. Quantrill, a patent attorney attached to the burgeoning natural-gas industry. She'd then raised all kinds of hell getting it listed in the National Register of Historic Places. The Quantrills were known for their philanthropy and their elegant parties, featuring such high jinks as horses in the living room and mock gunfights on the lawn. Hereditary landowners, they no longer lived on their land but plied it for energy leases. They did hang on to their cattle brands long after the last cow had gone down the road, beautiful single iron brands from Territorial days. When their son, Spencer, inherited the house many years later, he demolished it and replaced it with storage units. Even these fell into disrepair, and it was hard to know if they produced any income when Spencer, who had temporarily lived in one of the units, eventually moved away.

Such was her standing that Mrs. Quantrill's appearance in the grade-school principal's office, with nine-year-old Spencer in tow, required a bit of fanfare, which she provided with an abrupt doffing of her coat and the slower removal, a finger at a time, of her lovely gloves. Back then, before such people took to concealing their station, it was not unusual to dress up even for minor occasions. Mrs. Quantrill was the tallest in the room and very thin, with unblinking blue eyes. Spencer hovered beside her as Mr. Cooper, the principal, in a tan suit and referee's whistle, directed them to two chairs, before sidling behind his desk to sit down, fingers laced under his chin.

"Hi, Spencer."

"Hi."

"Thank you for coming, Mrs. Quantrill. Spencer's struggling. Aren't you, Spencer?"

"I guess so."

Spencer sat with his tennis shoes one atop the other and pushed his hair across his forehead. He seemed not to know what to do with his feet, his eyes, or his hands.

"Struggling how?" Mrs. Quantrill asked sharply.

"You describe it, Spencer."

"Can't pay attention?" He looked to his mother to see if that was the correct answer.

"What's the whistle for?" she asked the principal.

Mr. Cooper picked up the whistle as though seeing it for the first time and declined to answer. "I think Spencer wants to participate and be a part of things, but he often seems . . . stunned."

"Stunned?" Mrs. Quantrill said. "Hardly." Spencer restacked his tennis shoes, this time with the left foot on top of the right.

"Anyway, I think it might be in Spencer's best interest to let him enjoy a spell in special ed—get the pressure off him a bit and let him spread his wings."

"*Special ed?*" Mrs. Quantrill got to her feet, eyes flashing, plucked her coat from the back of her chair, and said, "Over my dead body."

"I see. What do you think is best?"

"I'll raise his standards in my own way. I have tickets to Bayreuth and I shall take Spencer with me this year. No one leaves Wagner unimproved."

"Where?"

"Wagner!"

"Ah."

IN THE CAR, MRS. QUANTRILL SPOKE NONSTOP. SHE GLANCED down Main Street and remarked, "What a hole." It was nearly dark and most of the small-business owners were closing up shop. "Mr. Cooper means well, Spencer. He wants to help you and he's correct in noticing that your grades are not as they should be . . . That wretched waterbed outlet is finally going out of business! . . . But we all develop at different speeds, and though I was tall and strong and popular at your age, your father was small and fearful, and just look how he turned out. The mighty oak, little acorn, and so forth. Oh, my angel, you're going to love Bayreuth, this year especially, because we will see *Parsifal* and you'll find out why Mommy calls you that, and you will be strengthened and return to school with something new that will be felt by everyone—students, teachers, and even nice Mr. Cooper, with that dopey whistle, who thought you should be in special ed. So, let's break the news to Daddy: we're off to Bavaria. Look, Spencer, there's where Daddy bought those Italian snow tires. Why do you suppose he thought Italians would know about making snow tires? Well, when he slid off the road in front of the airport you can bet he found out how much they know! You probably think I was pretty rude to the principal, what's his name, but no, Spencer, I was only being direct. I'm not a mean person. I simply thought the faster he knew my feelings the better. I'm just going to let this policeman pass me. I don't like being followed, no matter who it is. Spencer, you're too quiet, it makes me feel judged. Are you asleep back there?"

AFTER WATCHING HIS MOTHER LEAVE THE PARKING LOT without him, Spencer first considered going back into the school, but trying to explain to Mr. Cooper or anyone else how his mother just got caught up in her thoughts seemed beyond him. He was sure that if he waited she would eventually realize her lapse, but meanwhile if he just stood there alone people would start wondering about him, so he set out walking, though it was almost dark and getting cold. If she hadn't driven off so fast, he would have been in his bedroom by now with his aquarium light turned on, the guppies and angelfish swimming around the bubbler or darting for the flakes of food he dropped.

He hadn't seen this street before. Of all the houses along it, only two had lights bright enough to show where the sidewalk was. Spencer looked back and tried to remember how many turns he had made and why he thought he had been heading toward more lights instead of fewer. He stopped. His hat was in his desk at school, and his head was getting cold, but the idea of knocking on a stranger's door to ask for a hat overswept him with shyness and desperation.

A car turned onto the darker end of the street and, as its headlights hit Spencer, it slowed to a crawl. Its lights were so bright that he covered his eyes, until the car drew alongside him and stopped. Still blinded, Spencer could see no more than the outline of a man's head in the driver's window. It seemed a long time before the driver spoke. "Hello, mister, you look like you could use a ride. Care to hop in?"

When Spencer opened the door to get in, the interior light came on, revealing an older man with a white crew cut that stood straight up and a cardigan with an elk embroidered on its wool. Spencer caught only a quick look, because once he closed the door the light went off and the man was only an outline again.

"Where are we headed, young man?"

Spencer didn't know what to say and so said nothing.

"Better tell me where or I'll run out of gas idling here like this."

Spencer felt anxious trying to come up with a plausible answer. The driver had put the car in gear but took it out again and sat back and crossed his arms. Under pressure, Spencer wanted to blink. Finally, he said, "Bayreuth."

"Buy-Rite? Jeez, that's way on the other side of town. And it's closed. Is someone picking you up at Buy-Rite?"

Spencer couldn't speak.

"I wish you'd say something. You want to play the radio? You want me to play the radio? Okay, no radio."

It occurred to Spencer that this was like school; he was always tongue-tied just when people wanted to help him. This would all get worked out at Bayreuth, he told himself, even if it was closed at this hour. His mother would take over the situation. She hadn't meant to forget him and would soon have him back with his aquarium. Today was Thursday, and sometimes on Fridays his father brought him a fish in a water-filled Ziploc bag. Last time it had been a Siamese fighting fish, but it was floating upside down in the bag and it had to go into the toilet. Then his dad did some research and explained to Spencer that, until they got a better bubbler, they really couldn't get another fish. So they wound up getting the one with a little deep-sea diver with bubbles coming out of his helmet, but so far no new fish.

The car stopped under the LIVE WELL—PHARMACY—PHOTO CENTER sign. "Is this it?" No one in sight. The pulsing red neon reflected off the dashboard and lit the side of the driver's face. Spencer needed his mother here to do the talking.

He managed, "Maybe not."

"Son, you gotta help me. Where do you want to go? I was supposed to be at the legion ten minutes ago."

"Maybe back to the school?"

"School is closed, too! Okay, please don't cry. I shouldn't have raised my voice, but this is getting to be a problem. There's a Buy-Rite Auto on the frontage road. That sound like it? No?" The driver gripped the wheel hard, then rested his head on it. "*Please* tell me where to take you. Wait. Stop, don't open the glove compartment!"

"Is it loaded?"

"Yes, yes, put it back now. I have a permit for that. I need it. I'm a traveling salesman. Thank you."

"Someday I'll have a gun." And a big mustache, he thought.

"When you're old enough and have received proper training. So now where are we headed? Son, tell me the truth, do you actually want to go home?"

"There's the road," Spencer said, pointing to a road that angled off to the west, a road he had never seen before.

"How far?"

"It's quite a ways."

Soon all the houses dropped away into the dark. It was possible to see the shapes of bluffs and, well back from the road, barely different from the stars, the occasional yard light at a ranch. A jackrabbit paused, lit up in the headlights, then vanished. For a while, the only sound was the pop of bugs against the windshield. The car came to a stop in the middle of the road, and the driver scratched his crew cut frantically with both hands, then covered his face. "I see it now: kidnapping, child molester, the whole nine yards. Son, you have to get out of the car." When he uncovered his face, Spencer was playing with the gun again.

"Oh, boy, how were you raised, anyway? That's not a plaything." The man reached over and took the gun from Spencer. "I tried to help you. My conscience is clear. Out you go." Spencer gripped the seat and wouldn't budge. He wanted to keep going down the road. The man's voice came in a roar. "Get the fuck out now before I hit you over the head! You're starting to scare me."

Spencer opened the door, hoping the driver would change his mind, then got out and closed the door. He had wanted to speak, but as he searched his mind nothing came to him. It was wonderful how the night smelled and how huge the stars seemed as the car pulled slowly away, pushing open a strip of road with its headlights. Once the sound of its motor had faded, a roar of insects filled the emptiness. Spencer was very still as he followed his happiness to its source and smiled to think, No one knows where I am. The driver was a nice man, but maybe this is better.

Then the lights of the distant car seemed to circle, and Spencer saw that it was coming back. He looked quickly to his left and to his right, but he couldn't move.

The driver leaned over to thrust open the passenger door. "Get in."

Spencer did so and closed the door.

"Son, I can't leave you out here by yourself. Something might happen to you."

"I wasn't scared."

"You don't know enough to be scared! God almighty!" As the car pulled forward, Spencer looked longingly into the dark. He thought of his mother and wondered if she would remember to feed the fish. He pictured them at the surface of the aquarium looking up at him, expecting to be fed. "As soon as we get to some town, I'm going to find a phone. Yes sirree, Bob, I'm gonna find me a phone and figure out where you belong."

They crossed a creek on a noisy bridge where telephone poles had been stacked. Just beyond was an empty house and a car on blocks, then the road climbed slowly on a straightaway toward the first lights they had seen in a long time. As they approached, the driver slowed down, holding the top of his head with one hand: a sheriff's car was parked there and several officers stood on either side of the road near it. "An accident? Doesn't seem like there's enough cars to have one." The driver rolled his window down. "But this is good, son. Maybe you'll talk to these fellers."

Two officers came to the driver's door. They looked hard through the window at Spencer, glanced at each other, pulled open the door, dragged the driver onto the road, and handcuffed him behind his back. The opposite door opened, and Spencer was swept into the arms of a burly deputy. There were lights everywhere, and Spencer cried, but not for the reasons the worried lawmen believed.

ON THE RADIO, IN THE PAPERS, BUT MOSTLY IN PEOPLE'S mouths, news of the kidnapper ballooned. In town, the driver's relatives were dismayed to learn of this side of his character and anxious to put some distance between themselves and him. The interrogator from Helena was delayed by a passing hailstorm, and, by the time he got to the town jail, the driver had done away with himself, an expression that Spencer failed to understand but which his mother explained by using her hands to illustrate a bird flying away. Even so, he knew that he was being misled. Now the newscasters were filled with questions as to whether it had been mothball- or golf-ball-sized hail. A widow up at Ten Mile was on TV with a hailstone the size of a grapefruit, but subsequent investigation revealed it to be something from her freezer.

PAPAYA

Errol healy should have retired by now from his marine-insurance business, but it was such a going concern that it was hard to let go, and anyway he feared retirement. He was widowed and his only child, Angela, named for a friend in the Bahamas, had gone up to Gainesville, graduated, and moved with her husband, a marketing consultant with a great job at the Seattle Art Museum. Each year, Errol traveled to Seattle to see Angela and her husband, Dylan, and lately his granddaughter, Siobhan. But Key West was always and intensely home, where his life had resumed, and it amused Angela to see his rush to get back. She missed Key West not at all, certain that having survived Poinciana Elementary and Key West High was as much as she needed despite having been elected Miss Conch in the eleventh grade. She'd been a conventional sorority girl at Florida, and if a word could describe her life thus far it would be "smooth."

It was more than peculiar that Errol had made a career insuring ships and boats, mostly commercial fishing boats, trawlers, long liners, northern draggers, and even a processing ship half a world away. He had begun as the janitor to two old Conchs named Pinder and Sawyer, who had been insuring shrimp boats for half a century and were part owners of a chandlery. When Pinder and Sawyer died in successive years, seemingly in response to the shrimp boats leaving Key West for good, Errol, with his modest understanding of how the business ran, was the last man standing, and he made the most of it. To this day, he loved salt water, and his only recreation was sailing his old boat *Czarina*, stolen long ago but recovered, a derelict tied to a piling in the Miami River, repaired ever since at unreasonable expense.

He was attached to her not only because he'd nearly lost her in a gale in the seventies, and to theft in the Bahamas while running from his problems, but because she had carried him on to the life he had led ever since. He had been a boy of his time and place, Florida in the latter third of the twentieth century, one among thousands who thought he could sail away to happiness, either tropical escape or riches, bringing home square groupers from Cartagena. Wooden sailboats with light air rigs, acoustic guitars, and reckless girls, the reckoning was always a bit closer in time than he and his cohorts quite imagined, but at that age a little time seemed like a lot. Now all that was long ago and far away, while the layers of familiarity at home and among friends were plenty good enough. He watched his own rising complacency with amusement and contempt. Today the dreadlocks of his youth would be viewed as cultural appropriation. He had annoyed his late wife with all his versions of "Funny How Time Slips Away": Joe Hinton, Al Green, Willie Nelson . . . Enough! she cried. I got it!

Personal summarizing was often Errol's indulgence on his numerous visits to Dr. Higueros's office on Flagler, to which he always took a big paper bag from Fausto's market to bring home mangos from the effulgent tree that shaded the doctor's driveway and eventually made it slippery with rotten fruit. Errol used them in his breakfast smoothies, staple of his widower's life and one of many reasons to visit a friend he'd known since their days as refugees, Dr. Higueros and his wife from the north coast of Cuba, Errol from a kind of detention in the Bahamas.

Today was a good day to see the doctor, a wet squall from the Gulf bending the palms along the street to Higueros's office, people hunching from awning to awning. The recurrent problem of wax in his ears, substantial buildup affecting his hearing, required Dr. Higueros's attention, hydrogen peroxide to dissolve the impaction and then vigorous syringing over a white ceramic bowl, something Errol found stirring as the wax fell into the water and leftover peroxide. It took time, since the fluid had to bubble in his ears, and as he awaited blasts of the warm water syringe, he talked with Juan, as he called the doctor, about things big and small, big like Mrs. Higueros's advancing dementia, small like the latest car models, of which Juan was a devoted fan. He told Errol, chopping his desk with his hand, that he was "over SUVs" as being too hard to park in Key West's intense street scene and was waiting for the Tesla to come down in price so that he could recharge at home rather than beating his way across town for gas. He had the same roughly ten-block life radius as Errol, who rarely left it, except to go to his boat or Dr. Higueros's, or to his club to play dominoes.

Out of friendship with Juan, Errol had learned to play dominoes, though his limited Spanish vernacular kept him a bit detached at the various iterations of the Centro Asturiano. He eventually quit but kept his cigar habit. The Higueroses also had a daughter, Jaquinda, an ophthalmologist at Green Cove Springs on the St. Johns. When Jaquinda was a teenager, Errol had stayed away from the Higueros household for perfectly good reasons: briefly a wild high schooler, Jaquinda had shared with him her little supply of cocaine, and things very nearly went off the rails before Errol sensibly fled to his insurance office. He saw her again when she was out of school, and she displayed a jocose formality toward him that he found quite brilliant in its way, and a relief. He took her new husband sailing, and when Jaquinda joined, he mused about time slipping away in his curiously segmented life.

Just when Juan thought he'd syringed enough, Errol urged one more shot because he could still sense his right ear was occluded. This time the doctor gave it a good blast of warm water, and a real gold nugget fell into the ceramic bowl to the great satisfaction of them both. It was, as they had devised, lunchtime; and they sent out for *masita de cerdo,* their favorite pork dish, which arrived in a big flimsy Styrofoam carton and which they split on paper plates with plastic forks, washing it down with beer from Dr. Juan's fridge. Then they settled in as usual, Juan's turn to pick the topic. Dr. Higueros believed his problem getting to the United States had been unlike Errol's. "You were stranded, but you were stranded in a friendly country, not fleeing *los barbudos.*"

"My boat had been stolen. I had nowhere to go. I was running away and I didn't want to go back. It was nothing to be proud of."

"You were a slave of that black woman!"

"I must have needed it." Errol raised his arms, palms opened. "More than that, really!" He left his arms wide like that as though beholding something neither he nor the doctor could see.

———

THE MEMORY WAS CLEARER TO HIM NOW THAN NEARLY ANY-thing since. When he had awakened in the sand, hungover, tormented by sand flies amid the extinguished buttonwood coals and smell of old meat, the Bahamian woman helped him understand that he had been robbed, his boat stolen. The news had the effect of emptying his mind entirely. He was not able to imagine what might be next while Angela, the Bahamian woman, seemed to find his bewildered appearance entertaining. "Boat gone!" she cried happily. The momentum was hers, and Errol found a bleak luxury in being taken over. Angela led Errol to a shack at the top of a ravine overlooking the papaya fields and gave him the task of cleaning the palm rats' nests out from under the sagging pipe bed. The window had been painted black, and Angela laughed as she pointed it out, saying, "You might want privacy! I am tellin' you, there could come a time! Woo-hoo!" She made a little furrow between her eyes to offset her teasing off-center smile. She had never seen a white boy with Rasta braids before, and if someone hadn't stolen his little sailboat, she would never have seen this one.

"Where's the nearest town?"

"Why you want a town for?" Angela tipped her head skeptically. She looked into the middle distance and asked, "Town?"

"Maybe have a drink with friends."

"Ha. Ha! You don't have no friends here! I'm your friend."

Errol thinks: No drink. The papaya trees, once Errol got out among them, struck him as a bit creepy—barkless, branchless, but lovely in the evening in their otherworldly shapes against the stars and oceanic clouds. He managed a fitful sleep before Angela arrived with porridge and half of a papaya, whose black seeds she scooped and flung outside his door. She brought a wheelbarrow, a cumbersome thing with an iron wheel and stripped branches for handles. Inside rested a square-headed shovel, its handle polished by long hard use. His job would be hauling bat guano from the cliffs above the papaya grove to fertilize the trees.

He was weary before he got to the cave and had to rest, but the elevation revealed some settlement to the south and a glimpse of the sea to the west. He felt a familiar pull at seeing this strip of blue above the green highlands and succeeding karst ledges, some of which seemed to have bigger caves than the one he had been directed to. The sea was so close. But what good would it do him to get to it? Still, that's what he wanted.

He entered the cave, pushing the wheelbarrow on its noisy iron wheel. Arawak petroglyph swirls were cut into the walls, and the nitrogen stink of guano was overwhelming. He was already sick from life, and this was too much: he let himself spew onto the floor. Then he began to dig, filling the wheelbarrow a shovelful at a time, staring from the shadows at the hard light outside the cave.

As he started back downhill to the papayas, he lost control of the wheelbarrow and had to refill it from the rough ground. He poured with sweat, and his eyes stung. Hands on her hips, Angela watched from below; and when he reached the grove, she directed him as he deposited the guano around a few of the trees. Then she gave him a drink of water. "Two more," she said, "and then I will bring you some food."

Errol considered the ways he could put this all to an end, but the third night in his shack as he plucked pieces of scorched pig from a piece of greasy paper, he found himself liking the clarity that pushed through the ache of his muscles. Then he stretched on the bunk and congratulated himself on declining Angela's offer to bring him a Kalik with his meal. He asked again for water. Not long after, it was dark. He had managed to get the blackened window open and the fragrant square of stars consoled him as he drifted off. One night a mongoose stood in his doorway like an amiable visitor, then hopped off for better prospects.

"What day is today?"

"Why you want to know?"

"Why don't you just tell me."

"What I tell you for? You want it to be the weekend?"

"I just wondered what day it was."

"You needing a day off?"

"I need a bath."

"Of course you do!" She fanned her face with rolled eyes.

Angela took him to her quarters, the first time he'd seen them, a wooden house on cinder blocks, a concrete cistern, very tidy, laundry on a line, and chickens in the yard. On the edge of the trees a pen held a nursing sow and her piglets. Angela lit a propane

flame beneath a copper coil and directed him to a faucet beside
the cistern, saying she'd be on the porch. A plastic cover from a car
battery, nailed to a tree, held the soap. Errol undressed, glancing
warily; after washing himself under the warm sprinkle, he quickly
put his clothes back on to sit on the porch with Angela, foursquare
in a homemade blue dress that came to her calves and some kind
of recycled military boots. Her hair was tied in a tall topknot with
a strip of blue rag.

"You been working like a mule. Ain't give out?"

"Not yet." Errol laughed. She stared at him rather than share the
laugh.

"Aks you something. What wrong with you? Look like something eat you up."

"Doing okay. Changes I'll let you know."

Errol merely smiled at the thought of a rant his dad would go on
about blacks and the many children of the poor and the hopelessness of improving their circumstances through education: "We've
been educating the sonsabitches for a hundred years and it has done
no good whatsoever. We're gonna have to spray them. Now that I
think of it, let's not spray them. Aviation fuel has gone through the
roof." His cousins in Missouri were even worse, "nigger"-this and
"nigger"-that, and if he argued with them, they told him he was
plumb ate up with the dumbass.

"Look here," said Angela. "You keep goin' up to the cave with
your wheelbarrow until you figure out what's the matter with you,
and then I'll try to get you on home."

"I'm fine!"

"Sure you is, li'l man!" Is it that funny? Errol wondered. "You
haves a home anyway?" Errol felt like arguing, but the feeling
passed.

It seemed that by the time he had fertilized each papaya tree
and gotten to one end of the grove, it was time to start at the beginning again. He had hauled hundreds of pounds of fertilizer, fanning away disgruntled fruit bats as he worked shirtless—hardest
part being to stabilize the load on an iron wheel as he worked his
way down the hill, zigzagging around sloping ledges and trying,
not always successfully, to keep the whole thing from toppling. On
one such failure, he found himself crying "Bat shit it's just bat shit

is all it is" to the firmament, then thinking how funny it was that it could have easily applied to him rather than the guano he hauled daily to these damn trees. Possibly he had acquired a degree of detachment now from this condition. At a bare minimum he recognized some of it was funny.

One night a storm came in from the sea, and because so many parts of his shack were minimally adjoined it made a tremendous noise until finally his anxiety grew. Lying abed he could see parts of the ceiling moving. Summoning figures from the past he masturbated, and when he reached his end a huge piece of tin blew off his roof to reveal clouds racing against a yellow moon. He heard the tin tumble away and pulled the flimsy blanket over his head. Who was that last one? He troubled himself over the image of a girl who bit her tongue during intercourse. It was . . . New Port Richey was as far as he got before nodding off, awaking abruptly to No, Crystal River! and falling asleep again, still without a name—wait: Homosassa? But no dice, a desirable girl lost to memory. When he awoke in the morning, the storm had passed, and a glistening white egret stood in the opening overhead looking down at him past its jet-black beak. His fingers were sticky from ejaculating into his hand.

That's when he remembered her, Chattanooga and her name was Denise. They'd been headed to Jazz Fest in Nola and wound up where there wasn't shit-all going on unless it was hillbilly clog dancing. There would be no reason she'd remember him now, probably got off drugs and had a Ph.D., living in a mansion with a litter of King Charles spaniels and driving a German car. Time to fix the roof, and he struggled to drag that sheet of tin from the Brazilian pepper seedlings and love vines where he found it entangled. Reaching up, he wedged the piece into the rooftop to keep it from sliding off, setting a jar of nails and a claw hammer beside it before using the window ledge to climb up. He saw his shoes aligned next to the bed, covers crumpled from struggles over the lamented Denise on her way to Jazz Fest via Chattanooga to hear Professor Longhair and Clifton Chenier.

He had trouble holding the tin in place while he tried to nail it down. Every time he started a nail, the tin moved and he lost the nail, which fell with a clink to the floor below him by the bed. He put some nails in his mouth, clutching the hammer in one hand

and easing his weight onto the tin to secure it. But as he reached for a nail, the tin shifted under his weight and he wound up sliding out onto the dirt yard twenty feet in front of the shack, where he continued to lie moaning until discovered by Angela, with her hands characteristically on her hips as she surveyed the scene, shaking her head from side to side, and marveled, "Good night!" He gazed back at her but said nothing.

"Can you move?"

"I don't know why I would."

"Do you want to be examined?"

"I suppose, but everything seems to work. I'm quite sore, it says here."

"Let me help—" Angela stood him up, though he was aware that he was crouching, not standing, and he seemed to be testing all parts of his back as he straightened it. "There. Or—"

Angela put him in bed and told him in so many words that she would review his condition at the end of the day but bring him something to eat meanwhile. He looked up at the leaves of a tall palm that swayed against a sky so attractive it enlarged his sense that he was missing something. While Angela fussed about the shack, he searched for what he missed until he found that it was his wheelbarrow. He sorely missed his wheelbarrow and its noisy iron wheel, and the weight of the fertilizer. He fell asleep.

He was awakened by the arrival of three of Angela's sons, Winston, Benson, and Isaiah, who introduced themselves as they peered at him in bed, eliciting broadly awkward responses and toothy embarrassed smiles. Shrinking back was a young woman, well along in her pregnancy. No one introduced her. Except for Benson, the eldest and a carpenter, the boys, both approaching young manhood, were fishermen—powerful youngsters all, they charged the shack with their energy. Benson had brought tools, and Errol could see his rusty Japanese truck in the doorway. Errol's father would have sprayed these fellows given aviation fuel at the right price. His Missouri cousins didn't bear thinking about. When he sat up and offered to help, Isaiah said, "We got it, mon. Stay where you at." So Errol lay amid all this activity like something inanimate, listening to the hammering and squeak of the corrugated tin as it was shoved into position. When they signaled they were done by the ostentatious dusting off of their hands, Winston reached to Errol and helped him to his feet; then Isaiah led the pregnant girl into the shack. She grinned shyly as the men helped her into bed while Errol, crouching in pain, tried to smile solicitously. "And you are—?"

"Pregnant."

"No, your name."

Benson called out, "Dat Shonda. Shonda havin' me baby!"

Then the three men swept Errol out the door and into the truck, Winston at the wheel, Benson and Isaiah riding in back with tools and lumber. "Where are we going?" asked Errol to gales of laughter. Finally, Winston said, "Get you some tomatoes."

"Tomatoes?"

"You don't like tomatoes?"

"I do like tomatoes, but why are you taking me for tomatoes?"

Benson said with extraordinary solemnity. "You better off wit' dem. You be rollin' in tomatoes."

Errol got a first look at the settlement, a handful of tiny homes made of assorted scavenged materials, driftwood, parts of wrecked boats—two had roofs like the tops of cabin cruisers—and surrounded by substantial piles of crawfish traps. When people could be seen in yards, Winston blew the horn of the truck and the merriment thus occasioned suggested a real event. At the settlement wharf, other small rusty Japanese trucks were gathered at the last stages of loading a low-slung forty-foot wooden boat with tomatoes, most in boxes but some in loose piles. At the stern of the boat was a modest pilothouse beneath which a smoky diesel engine rumbled and spat cooling water from a pipe at the stern. An old man stood in the pilothouse, cigarette hanging from the center of his mouth; occasionally he removed it, leaning to one side to call out orders for the loading of the vessel.

Errol and the others climbed from the truck, and one of them propelled him toward the boat with light fingertips at the small of his back, just coercive enough that Errol turned to look at him. A stern elder in a weathered Miami Dolphins cap gestured to the group, indicating that Errol was to be brought to him. This was the fellow in the pilothouse who'd directed the loading. Errol boarded the boat and shook the horny hand of what must have been the captain. Glancing back Errol saw that Angela had joined her sons and was blowing him kisses perhaps a bit sarcastically, elbowing one of the boys to share her point of view. Since he wasn't sure how to take this, Errol returned the gesture, and the resulting comic uproar confirmed it had been sarcasm. Observing this, the captain said, "Nothin' bettah to do," and identified himself as Wellington. Then he shouted, "Behave! And cahst me off." The three sons scurried obediently and untied the ropes from the rusty bollards, tossing them onto the boat with a thud. Wellington engaged the engine, and as the boat moved away from the dock toward a dark green channel in the pale shallows, Japanese truck horns blared farewell. Angela was still blowing kisses but now toward the houses where others returned the gesture, sharing some joke about who it was that was really departing.

Errol was not uncomfortable being led about like this, even onto an outbound vessel of dubious seaworthiness, but it did seem time to ask where they were going. "To West Palm to sell dese tomatoes."

"Are those people always trying to be funny?"

"Dey nevah busy. Angela make dem rich."

Errol saw they were headed for the Gulf Stream and thought early on he could make out its purple light. Wellington was not talkative and only replied with ill-concealed annoyance as he kept an eye on the compass and tried to steer in a way protecting the tomatoes from sea spray. Errol was exalted to be on the ocean again and could tell that while Wellington took his perfunctory glances at the compass he would regularly pick a cloud to steer by, using the plunging stemhead as a sight.

The laden hull created a steep stern wave, and in the first miles, dolphins slipped up its face and somersaulted back into the sea, skimming barely under the surface with electric energy between vaults. They angled off into a shower of flying fish and were gone. Checking the compass, Wellington raised his eyes to a better cloud.

Errol was tired and sore from his nighttime struggles and asked if there was a place he might stretch out. Wellington suggested he go forward and find a place among the crates. Errol left the pilothouse for the rush of ocean breeze and mist and the intense smell of the tomatoes. He found a place where lengths of cordage had been stowed, probably for the anchor, and lay down feeling bottomless physical relief. He laced his hands behind his head and, watching a frigate bird high above, immediately fell asleep, awakening only occasionally to change position and twice from imagining he heard voices. Once he was sure he had but talked himself out of it and fell into an even-deeper sleep, glancing up to the stars wondering vaguely when night had fallen.

He was awakened by the silence of the engine and the roll of the boat and concluded by its motion that they had crossed the stream. Sitting up, he could make out the loom from the lights of Florida on the far horizon, and he could hear Wellington speaking on the radio. Looking forward in the light from the moon and stars, he could see two figures. Wellington emerged from the pilothouse and seeing Errol awake said, "Say hello to Mr. and Mrs. Higueros. Is dat how you say it?"

"Yes," said the gentleman forward.

"I'm Errol Healy."

The Higueroses were dressed as though for a business meeting, he in a gray suit of an early broad-shouldered style ill befitting his small shape, and Mrs. Higueros in a kind of black jumper with a wide-winged white shirt that seemed like a schoolgirl's uniform. They were not very old.

Silence. Wellington returned to the pilothouse and sat by the radio, which squalled presently, bringing him out on deck again with something in his hand. He pulled sharply downward from it, and a flare shot up, parachuting an umbrella of white phosphorous. It was dark again except for starlight. They waited in expectant silence until a mobile speck of light appeared in the west at sea level, enlarging steadily until it became the running light of a low blue-gray race boat, entirely open except for the helm and windshield, behind which stood two men in night-vision goggles, one with his hand on the binnacle and the other resting on a machine gun attached to a clip on the side of the console. They slid their boat alongside deftly. The man at the wheel said, "Morning, Wellington," shutting the engine off to drift alongside. "Hugo here will do the banking. Who's that third guy?"

"Called Air Roll."

Errol made a rather feeble gesture of greeting.

"He staying with you?"

"He going with you."

"Angela didn't say nothin' about him."

"She just put him on, say you wouldn't mind."

"But I do mind, Wellington."

"It up to you. I can take them all to West Palm."

"They'll be arrested."

"It up to you," said Wellington firmly, easing toward the pilothouse.

"Naw, goddamn it, Wellington, come here." Errol could spot this amiable abuse as roughneck stuff racists used with blacks. Wellington went to the gunwale, balancing against it with his waist, and reached out his hand. Hugo began counting out money into it. When he went too fast, Wellington raised the palm of his free hand to slow things down. Hugo said, "That's a lot of U.S. dollars."

"They still good," said Wellington blithely. "More next time. I don't want to count it, I want to weigh it."

"Make sure Angela gets hers. Don't need to be hearing from her."

Wellington and I helped the Cuban couple, frightened and clinging to each other, into the boat. The pilot put the boat in reverse and it chugged backward in the wash around the tomato boat, turning ninety degrees, and was immediately up on plane in the thrust of its big engines. Once out of sight of the tomato boat, the race boat stopped again, and Hugo brought a hamper of clothes to Mr. and Mrs. Higueros. "*Oye,* change into these," he said, "you don't need to look so fuckin' *balsero.*" Mr. Higueros cut his eyes at Hugo, but nothing came of it. Hugo returned to the stern, and the three turned away while the Higueroses changed. To Errol, he said, "Cubans. If they got the money, honey, I got the time." When it was polite to do so, they looked back: the transformation was remarkable. Both wore baggy shorts and logo fishing shirts, Mrs. Higueros sporting a leaping blue sailfish and Mr. Higueros a livid map of the Caribbean with associated fishes and on his back, COME ON DOWN AND KICK SOME FIN! They had identical ball caps from the Dania greyhound track and beheld each other with comical admiration. Errol glimpsed right away that these were clever people.

Back to full speed: standing next to the driver and glancing at the GPS, Errol knew they could not be far from the coast. The fathom lines on the screen rolled past swiftly showing a virtual roadway, a long narrowing yellow band ending at the word JUPI-TER. The boat seemed to touch the water only delicately, a kind of lengthwise flutter beneath the hull, and the engine sound seemed astern of them. "How did you get on this load, Air Roll?"

"Friend of Angela's." He had no idea how it had happened or why he had not resisted or where he was even going exactly.

"Old Angela, man, she makes it happen. I don't know where she's burying all the money unless it goes to West Palm under a load of papayas." He jerked his head toward the passengers. "Slipped this duo out of Camagüey. Doctor and his wife. Relatives paid for it. Gotta hand it to 'em, don't none of 'em stay po' long."

"Are you planning to drop them off on a beach?"

"Naw naw naw, we go right into the marina"—he tapped Hugo on the shoulder and wiggled his finger at the machine gun; Hugo took it from the side of the console and stowed it in a side locker—"where nobody's worried about nothin'. The little doc's gonna be just fine. He probably speaks better English than we do. Hey, what's with the dreads? You a octoroon or something? I have a octoroon cousin, only he don't admit it. Hey, this is America, we gotta get along." He let it ride, Air Roll the octoroon.

In a while the well-lit coast grew clear, and the motion of the boat changed with the waves on the shelving bottom. Errol saw that the running lights were no longer on; the boat and its passengers just seemed part of the darkness. At length, the corners of an inlet emerged with long breaking rollers flowing to the interior, and at much-reduced speed they struggled to the top before sliding down inside the wave as the bow plunged with the elevation of the stern and the whine of cavitation. Increasingly house and yard lights massed on either side, until the boat slowed to steady idle, then abruptly turned into a wilderness of docks and finger piers. They seemed to vanish between rows of yachts, then on to less occupied docks until turning into one and shutting everything off. The new quiet seemed to go along with the huge shapes of the vacant boats all around them. At the base of the dock the windows of a black Lincoln Town Car shone in the security light. Hugo and the driver helped Dr. and Mrs. Higueros onto the dock. The minute their feet touched down, all the lights of the Lincoln went on. The Higueroses tossed off perfunctory kisses and hurried to clamber into a rear door, which had barely shut as the car drove off, away and gone. "New Americans," said Hugo. "I hope they like it." He shook his head and climbed out with Errol, and started to secure the boat with bow-, stern-, and spring lines. As Errol helped tie off the boat, the pilot came forward, glanced, and said, "Man knows how to tie a knot. Someone coming for you? No? So where are we taking you?"

"A1A."

Errol got a ride right away in a dry-cleaning van that took him as far as Homestead and could have taken him to Key Largo if he hadn't got out early, abruptly, at a stoplight. He had been closely watched for miles in sidelong glances and gazes by the driver, a large, somewhat-handsome man who, with his carefully combed hair and clueless lopsided smile, resembled the young Ronald Reagan. Errol's discomfort mounted until he felt compelled to explain his dishevelment. "I lost my boat, all my clothes and supplies. I'm afraid I'm a mess until I can get a shower and a change." The man smiled at him for a long time before speaking.

"It don't matter, son," he said in an easy drawl, "I'm gonna fuck you anyway." He spoke with relaxed confidence. Errol thought it best to consider this a settled plan until he could collect his thoughts. When the man reached toward him, Errol took his wrist and replaced it, saying, "Not now." Watching the approaching stoplight, he asked, "Mind if I play the radio?"

"Baby, knock yourself out."

Errol reached for the dial and wound around until he found one of several ranting evangelists. At the stoplight, he lifted the door handle and twisted the volume knob high. The radio poured out the screech to the hell-bound out yonder in radio land: Repent! The driver covered his ears, and Errol stepped onto the Dixie Highway with a grateful wave. Acknowledging him with a grim nod, the driver of the dry cleaner's van turned down the volume, followed by a hand flap of dismissal, bent to see up to the light, and drove off on green.

He walked for a while until he came to the old stone castle, a mess of erratic limestone shapes he had once visited with Denise because of its reputation as the work of either (1) space aliens or (2) a Latvian immigrant. The latter proved to be the case, and the banality of his achievement was enhanced by the theory that it was a "monument to unrequited love." That is why Denise made the wry suggestion in the first place, and she successfully searched the grounds for a cranny where intimacies were possible. He hadn't really thought of her since he'd jacked off in his hand back on the island. They once sat in adjoining rocking chairs made entirely of limestone, so heavy that once you started them rocking they would go on without you. But just seeing it again—the huge stone gate, the rocks shaped like zodiac signs, and Florida vegetation taking it all back—gave Errol a hard-to-define heartache, time, time, time slipping away.

He had not gone far down Old Dixie Highway when he found a homeless shelter and the smell of food. He hesitated and then thought he wouldn't last long without nourishment, so he went in to be promptly and cheerfully questioned by a nun at the front desk. He said he was hungry, and she said, "We'll get to that once we issue you an ID tag!" She made one up on the spot and pinned it on him, ERROL HEALY, IN TRANSITION. She asked if he needed assistance recovering identification papers, if he would like some foot lotion, a phone card, legal advice, a place to sleep, or mail service. He wailed, *"I want something to eat."*

"Our casserole program is just winding up. Head down the corridor; double doors on the right."

"Where're you from?" he asked to allay the effect of his cry for food.

"God loves us wherever we're from," she said with a laugh. "But okay, Green Bay, Wisconsin. I came for the climate."

The dining hall was almost empty, but the sound of silverware stopped as he entered. Maybe twelve elderly people in two groups, one black and one Cuban, separated by language and folding chairs. A casserole remained on the steam table, and Errol cut himself a piece, cheese, sausage, tomato, which he gobbled despite its blandness, followed by glass after glass of sweet iced tea. A corrugated shield had been pulled down behind the steam table, and raucous voices could be heard from behind it. The fluorescent tubes lighting the room had a tremor that seemed connected to something inside Errol, and he glanced around wondering if some bulbs were better to sit under than others. He ate more than he wanted, hoping the calories would last and keep propelling footsteps or awkward conversations if he found rides.

Refreshed altogether, he walked past the front desk, where the same nun, working at a ledger, said, "Go Packers," and he dropped off his ID tag. She smiled without looking up, and he was back in the rising heat of Route A1A, the Old Dixie Highway. He stood with his thumb out in front of streaming southbound traffic, cars, vans, motor homes; the police slowed but didn't stop. The reflected heat from the pavement had begun to make him dizzy when a black Lincoln pulled over, well ahead of him by the time it got itself out of traffic; it wasn't until he was already in its backseat that he saw Dr. and Mrs. Higueros, still in their anomalous sportfishing togs. Dr. Higueros at close range was still young, but quite old fashioned and friendly in a courtly way. They'd overnighted at a Super 8 in Pompano and showed him postcards: the Barefoot Mailman, bathing beauties picking oranges.

"Where are you going?" the doctor asked with a smile.

"Where are *you* going?" Errol shot back. Mrs. Higueros smiled rigidly; the decision to pick up a dirty stranger had not been hers, and Errol felt it when she muttered something to her husband about "'ippies."

"To our family in Key West. Can we drop you along the way?"

Errol said, "Key West would be fine."

DR. JUAN HIGUEROS LOVED TO MAKE THE NOISE OF CRUSHING the Styrofoam with both fists as he gathered the debris from their lunch. His raft had been made buoyant with Styrofoam, and he sometimes spoke of his love of Styrofoam with a wistful grin as he added that his family had always collected Styrofoam. "Did you put this on a tab?" Errol asked. Juan nodded. "Let me get one. I'm behind."

"Sure, and what's going on with Angela?"

"All good. Nothing new. I don't know how they can stand it there. The sun never comes out. I get a cold just from visiting."

"You're a new grandpa. You have to go. You only need warmer clothes and lots of them." This went all the way back to catching a ride with Dr. and Mrs. Higueros, when the doctor spoke just enough English to gently needle the dirty hippie in the backseat.

LITTLE BIGHORN

In a four-door clunker that would have perfectly served a salesman from State Farm Insurance, Coral and I drove from Ohio through what I think of as the Old Midwest, small colleges on the only hill in town; farmhouses with neglected woodlots and haunted outbuildings, like the writhing structures in Burchfield paintings; towns that had lost their caregivers but were still inhabited by the old, shuffling along unrepaired sidewalks to a post office they hoped would not be taken away; ostentatious courthouses with pigeons in the empty windows and vacant doorways. I'm not sure Coral cared about this extravagant pathos. This was her last trip before law school, and she wanted to keep it light.

"That was a bank," said Coral. A tattoo parlor now. Coral had a tattoo, a little one, rarely seen. I'd seen it. I didn't know who else had. She got it in Prague. "How about it? Something for your neck?" Across the way was a cannon, fetched home from the Civil War, even as the bodies were left in the ground down south. My thoughts lingered on the soft-blue skies and clouds of Ohio that must have once cheered these little places. A roadside marker celebrating the optimism of Johnny Appleseed just seemed cruel. Coral, fanning herself with the road map, and staring at yet another Evangelical church, asked if Jesus was making these people fat. The harder light of the Dakotas would be less melancholy, fewer people to fill the air with their vanished hopes. The windshield and satellite radio would press everything but the flattened images of landscape into the background. I don't know why I felt this way. Perhaps, it was a foreboding based on leaving home and the whole idea of Idaho.

We had only taken one long road trip before, and it ended in disaster. I think she may be claustrophobic, but in any case, she went on a rant about absolutely everything. That was one of those autumn–in–New England trips, and the truth is neither of us was very interested in anything about New England, especially the little towns and churches. I remember a lot of Halloween shit in doorways; so that's when it was—November—and no sunshine. We started by arguing about what to have on the radio, and it went on to some sort of irrational abhorrence of New England itself, altogether ridiculous, as we know zip about New England, but we couldn't stop arguing. In a chowder joint near Portsmouth, New Hampshire, road weary and tired of talking, I asked Coral how she felt about the witchcraft trials, and thinking I was referring to her, she blew sky high. I said, "That's it, I'm driving home." And Coral said, "*Hasta la vista.*" And I left, car and all. I so seldom feel actual rage that I might have been a tad pleased with myself. Anyway, the gauntlet was down, and she had credit cards. The next stop was to have been Salem, but if she figured that out, I never heard about it.

A short time afterward, she went off to Europe with a sly frat boy from Denison. They made several stops before coming home: Versailles, the Hermitage in Russia, Prague, and a Battle of the Bulge tour, which must have been a real hoot: the only evidence of the trip I ever saw, a photograph of Coral and Mr. Slyboots in front of a German tank. I took her back, though we don't say that these days. Perhaps, Coral returned herself to me. Do such things clear the air? Hardly, but we were doing quite well, considering.

I was headed to my new job in Boise, but on the way we would visit old friends Niles and Claudia in Montana, who were joining us on a trip to the Little Bighorn Battlefield. Our shared past seemed a big part of our lives, and maybe they'd restore some of the excitement of earlier days. I suppose it was my idea that we needed restoration. Coral had little interest in the visit, and anyway, from Boise she'd be flying back to school, and so we'd have to find a way to work it out. Time with friends from more ardent times would help to carry us over.

In college, Niles and Claudia were hard-partying style mavens who seemed to live on the edge of disaster. Now it was wood-stoves, homemade clothes, and life off the grid. Niles acquired found-art things, like a decommissioned iron lung from a medical museum in Youngstown, Ohio. They were each from different parts of the upper South, Niles from a family of recently risen professional people—two doctors and a judge—and Claudia from old, landholding, jobless, bourbon aristocrats and dilettante politicians with ancestors in the Confederate Congress. Sometimes, when they talked about home and their "people," you sensed Claudia thought Niles's family was all toadies no matter what they'd achieved, while Niles thought Claudia's people were parasites who had pauperized themselves with alcohol, horses, and quail. Sometimes Claudia made up stories about the sources of Niles's family's wealth, the most farfetched that they had made a fortune by patenting an African American folk remedy for stool softener, the only family in West Tennessee with a porta-potty in their coat of arms.

Coral and I, pallid midwesterners, spent less time partying and more time in bed in our garret above the knitting store with its view of the tire repair shop, practicing as much safe sex as schoolwork allowed. My father and grandfather were anxious for me to join their fading iron-ore business and from time to time sent their viceroy, an alcoholic CPA with tobacco-stained teeth, to urge me to "take advantage of my advantages." The old mine would barely provide a living. I needed a job.

The Black Hills were lovely out of nowhere, and after resisting roadside invitations to powwows, cave tours, and cliff diving, we stopped to eat at a café with a handwritten menu and Cinzano awnings. We had the luncheon special, called Aces and Eights after the cards held by Wild Bill Hickok when he was killed, elsewhere known as a cheeseburger with fries. Soon back in our car, we drove in silence for nearly one hundred miles. Then Coral said, "It's not travel, it's not anything."

"Go ahead and roll down the window. Let's see if there's any reception." I was daydreaming about Claudia and her air of mischievous promise. "Prick tease with a drawl," Coral had once said.

We crossed the Montana line, and it looked the same as South Dakota. We knew that it got better up ahead, but so far our impatience compressed everything. We drove as though we were beating our heads against the same freeze-frame; Coral wasn't taking it well. She leaned against the door and moaned. She nodded to herself and asked, "Is that the arms of our Lord behind those clouds?" She fluttered her lips with her forefinger to suggest derangement.

Niles went on to graduate school while Claudia worked answering the phone in a nail salon; but she still said "Yay!" a lot. And "Boo!" I thought it was cute, Coral not so much. We watched the presidential elections together, and every time Tim Russert put up a card representing the delegate count from one state or another, Claudia yelled either "Yay" or "Boo." By the time we learned who the new president was, Coral and I were ready to jump out of our skins. We just wanted one of these goobers to win and put us out of our misery. Every other night Russert praised his father, Big Russ, who was a saint, wise, generous, self-effacing. After one too many anecdotes about Big Russ's goodness, Claudia drawled, "If big Russ doesn't fuck the babysitter, I'm gonna kill myself." One more election and Coral would be a lawyer; in two more, a judge; by then Niles and Claudia would be back in Tennessee with other people. Nothing we could possibly have imagined.

Coral was at the wheel as we turned in at their mailbox, and I was riding shotgun with a huge bag of caramel corn on my lap. It rained a little, and the dirt road up to their house, mostly dark except where overhanging trees had kept it dry, was cut into the side of a hill and wound upward until suddenly it opened on a clearing with a view of the valley and the scattered small town below. In the middle of the clearing stood their house, an old bungalow with various modern appurtenances: attached greenhouse, solar panels, and, flapping away, the customary Tibetan prayer flags. A weathervane on the roof seemed to have been modeled on Sputnik, spinning around without pointing anywhere.

When you haven't seen people for a long while, even old friends, dauntingly precise adjustment is required, something akin to acting. The struggle to get out of my side of the car caused me to upset the generous sack of caramel corn. Coral cut her eyes at me. But by now Niles was on the porch, I was standing in the caramel corn, and Coral was calling out that I had made a big mess as usual. Claudia stood a pace behind Niles so that she could gaze directly at me.

Niles viewed our arrival without enthusiasm. Claudia stared

into the middle distance. Coral muttered from the safety of her open car door, "What on earth is going on here? They're staring at us. Let's appear puzzled. Show them your puzzle face!"

We strode up and hugged them as though whatever was missing we would replenish by the vehemence of our greeting. We squeezed away at the lifeless couple, and then held them at arm's length like two fish we had just caught. Niles, head thrust from the top of his turtleneck, said, "Here's the news: Claudia and I are not getting along. We thought we could sort it out before you got here but, well, we didn't." Later I would picture this thrusting head and high-colored face. "Doubtless," Niles continued, "Claudia is as vexed with me as I with her." Mystified by Niles's diction, I asked what we should do about the caramel corn. I just couldn't think of what else to say.

"We need some space," recited Niles. His turtleneck suggested a maddening jauntiness. "If you could take Claudia with you, it would do us both a world of good. Would you consider it?" He smiled in the way of comedians who wished to convey that they weren't sure this was a joke. "Would you? Pretty please?"

"Why not?" said Coral. It didn't sound like her. It was just a squawk and seemed directed at me. She knew as well as I that we were hosed. I kept nodding without saying anything.

"This is friendship," said Niles, discovering some lint on his woolen carpenter's vest. He frowned skeptically as if his own observation had been foisted on him, then smiled abruptly. "Guys, I can't believe you're doing this. As I recall, your last road trip went badly." I looked to Coral for a response, but it was not forthcoming.

We went back down the same highway heading for the Little Bighorn Battlefield. Claudia in the backseat with her small suitcase said, "We'll be fine. Niles is a bore, but I'm used to it. People like that come out of nowhere." Coral swapped moisturizers with Claudia to lighten the atmosphere, then touched the end of her nose in thought. "Honestly, we've just been in that awful place too long. An audience of one, the shack nasties. Too many books, especially that long one about the Danube. Ask me anything about the Danube." She turned to me and asked if my teeth were mine while I recalled "The Blue Danube Waltz" thinking it would contain a hint about where the fuck the Danube was. "They seem brighter than before. Niles collects stuff no one wants. He thinks that if he dislikes something it will soon be valuable. He moved the iron lung into the living room. He gets in it and thinks about the stock market while it breathes for him. Coral, how would you like ten years with a premature ejaculator?"

"Is that an Indian?" asked Coral of the hitchhiker standing beside the Canyon Creek on-ramp. Best to ignore Claudia who was playing around in her purse.

"Indians don't dress like Indians," said Claudia. "That's a hippie. I realize it was an awkward question." She swept her lips with a ChapStick.

"Do they still have those?" Coral asked as she picked caramel corn from the floor mat. I think she meant hippies.

"They do here," Claudia said.

"It's too hypothetical."

"You have to spot them before it's too late. Eliminate the ones in cowboy hats. Then move to the turtlenecks, car buffs, and southern new money."

Coral, wincing slightly, experienced this as noise. Finally she asked, "Claudia, you and Niles, how big of a deal is it actually, would you say?"

"Honey, it's as big as I need it to be."

We had arrived: motel, vacant lot, chain link, Walmart bags in the lilacs. I secured adjoining rooms and keys. We took Claudia to the café at the Trading Post and ate tacos made with Indian fry bread and buffalo burgers. We were right across from the battlefield where Sitting Bull had made so many beautiful memories. Claudia and Coral discussed leaving home, letting me scrutinize the four Frenchmen at the table near the service entrance, including one who'd bought a war bonnet in the gift shop, causing mock eagle feathers from assorted poultry to flutter in the ceiling fan. Claudia gazed at us. "Are you two always this happy?"

"That's a joke, right?" said Coral.

"You just seem a bit complacent. To me. But what do I know?"

"We long for complacency." The sudden widening stare from Coral alerted me to possible danger.

Claudia said, "Hey, I was just reaching out. Is all it was." She now wanted to buy something for Niles and made a detour through the gift shop, returning with a Custer's Last Stand coffee mug wrapped in tissue. She held it against her cheek and smiled at us. "'Complacent' was a poor choice of words."

"You want to make it a little clearer?" said Coral.

"No, Miss Coral, I don't. I'll leave it at that. Just another chapter. It's so nice we've grown up. Do you remember the crazy stuff we used to do?"

"No."

"Oh," said Claudia, holding the Custer mug very still. She smiled at the odd silence in the room and said, "So that was then, and this is now?"

We paused before saying good night, moths batting around the lights by our doors. In the parking lot, an elderly Indian in an oversize and tattered suit coat lit his companion's cigarette. She waved away the smoke and smiled at him. It made me happy to notice it. Once in our own room, Coral sat heavily on the bed and said, "I'm taking her out. How did she come up with this so-called complacency?"

I said, "She's confusing it with contentment." It was utter bullshit. When placating Coral, I could lay this stuff on with a trowel. I don't know why I bothered, because when I look back, there's the Indian in the suit coat waving away the smoke from his companion's cigarette while Coral and I are just getting used to the idea that we were hardly meant for each other. It must have been a relief, because the rest of the trip was much more fun. We packed up, checked out, and headed to the Little Bighorn Battlefield in our quiet car, so quiet in fact that I turned on the radio while we drove and listened to cattle prices. We strode out onto the battlefield in the fresh morning air, the smell of prairie, a sky streaked with altocumulus clouds. Among the headstones where the troopers of the Seventh Cavalry fell, we came to the very spot where Custer died and where his small headstone was remarkably no bigger than anyone else's. Claudia read the inscription, looked up, and cast her eyes across the battlefield. Coral and I were lost in our thoughts.

Really, it's all good. I hated Boise (it took three years) and went home to the badly shrunken family iron-ore business and somehow made a living only slightly smaller than the one I'd made in Boise. One year I managed to ignore a ton of parking tickets and ended up in Coral's court. "You again!" she said and threatened me with an ankle monitor. I paid the tickets.

KANGAROO

Named for a father never to be seen again, Patrick Howell identified as Latvian—his mother had described his face as the "map of Latvia," the country of her birth—and was a veteran parole officer in the city of Issaquah, an amiable fat man who belted his pants above his belly and wore short sleeves in all weather, his pocket liner kept full of pens. His years on the job had made him the skeptical but compassionate soul now hanging around the Pier 86 grain terminal, watching from what seemed a safe distance as his charge—Scott or Travis or whatever name he was now going by—stood beneath an empty container ship from China until the package fell from the four-story slab of a vessel into his arms. Howell was very sad to see this and rarely went to this much trouble to keep his parolees on the straight and narrow; but Scott or Travis had touched him as only a few young men—often ingenious but troubled or wounded, and on their way to lives as career criminals—had done. They were hard to turn around, quite unlike his murderers, whose problems often went away the minute they pulled the trigger. Travis or Scott was almost umbilically connected to container ships and the shifting populations of their crews. These ties had been forged in the bars of Ballard, where no matter how drunk you were or how persuasive your companion, you could still smell the ships and waters of the North Pacific. Howell thought he understood the addiction, but his idea that it might be in remission in Scott/Travis's case was, he acknowledged, delusional.

When, after its long fall from the side of the ship, the package landed in Scott's arms, it nearly brought him to his knees, though it failed to knock the furtiveness out of him, an aspect oddly accentuated by his scrawny frame. He remained in a feral crouch, gazing slowly all around himself to see if he had been observed, and just catching Howell turning away. Too late: he had violated probation, the membrane between him and a possible return to prison. Until then, he had had no interest in visiting his hometown in connection with his mother's death only days ago. But now he decided he would go despite having promised himself to never set foot there again.

He scurried to the first green can, lifted the heavy steel lid, and dumped 150 counterfeit Rolexes before turning in the direction of Howell's last position, with his hands raised to show they were empty. He was panting, but Howell was gone.

Scott left Issaquah and began driving, a trip that could be accomplished without a stop if he made all the lights. Because a modest inheritance was involved, a run-down house, someone had bothered to inform him about his mother. He felt he couldn't have what he truly wanted, which was never to arrive and never run out of gas. She had been a negligent mother, and he had spent long spells of his childhood in foster care, known by his baptismal name, Travis; but his life since had gone well enough, thanks to numerous lucrative if fishy enterprises trafficking low-end contraband, and there were times when he had even begun to imagine how his mother might have turned out as she had, a disheveled custodial case and worn-out party girl. Anyway, it was too late. If she had thought about him at all at the time of her death, she would have guessed that he had turned out bad. He had inherited her house and all the unpaid taxes that amounted to more than it was worth—besides which, it was in the floodplain, so not much use tearing it down for the lot. It was just one of the places he had lived as a child, when he had served as ring bearer at one of her numerous weddings. The groom had given her a gift certificate for a white-dove release, and at the ceremony, conducted by a friend wearing a priest's collar made of cardboard, the guy from the dove outfit released a pair of the birds from a miniature Taj Mahal to cheers; then the shit hit the fan. They played a 45 rpm record, "Open the Door, Richard," until fights broke out with the customary weapons, tire irons, sash weights, and razors. As he drove east, he guessed that no one would realize he'd gone home, and by simply disappearing, any guilt at letting Howell down was blurred. Besides, Howell had no business taking these things personally, and he had told him so to his face at Denny's. Still, it hurt to disappoint maybe the only person who'd ever actually cared about him.

He drove over the Cascades, the ShitMobile, his half-dead oil-smoke muscle car, barely managing the climbs; and he pulled into Cle Elum Farm & Home Supply, where he bought a bolt cutter to remove the ankle monitor. Just past the Sunset Highway exit, the interstate crossed the Yakima River. Scott pulled over, clambered down the bank, and threw the monitor and bolt cutter into the river. Up on the highway, an old Corolla with Idaho handicap plates and one headlight, stopped to see if Scott was having car trouble. The driver, a perilously skinny old lady wearing a red beret, got out and looked at Scott's empty car. Then the passenger door opened, and what must have been her husband climbed out very slowly and in a crouch. He wore the dashboard overalls of a farmer and a visor that read FREE MUSTACHE RIDES. When they'd looked over the bank and seen Scott, the old woman remarked, "Threw something away." Grandpa snorted. "Hope it weren't no baby."

Once back in the ShitMobile, Scott was careful to drive the speed limit as the sun slowly set behind him. Living near the north coast, you felt the sun just sank into the Pacific Ocean, no reason to feel it went on. He didn't want to leave the coast. The ocean was a happy place, and all those people in the interior where he was headed would end up by the ocean, sooner or later, or hate themselves. He had no reason to believe his mother had seen the ocean, though one of her boyfriends had been a chief bosun's mate on a saltwater tug that hauled hundred-ton crawler cranes to bridge projects. He wound up in Montana fucking Scott's mom because he *didn't* like the ocean.

At that moment, courtesy of Verizon cell towers, Howell could have known one of two things: Scott had either jumped into the Yakima and was gone, or Scott had thrown the tether into the Yakima. Unfortunately, Verizon would also have told of the tampering, and Howell would conclude that Scott had flown the coop, the only other explanation being that he had chosen not to die wearing a monitor, but Howell was no romantic. "Onward!" Scott exhorted the ShitMobile as he forged his way east. He forgot to check the odometer when he gassed up, and Howell, who had once ridden in Scott's car, mused, "Who knows how far that piece of junk will go anyhow. Better put 'hitchhiker' in the bulletin."

He listened to country radio on the long drive up the Columbia Basin, over the top, and down to the prairie towns below. The bumper sticker on the side of his Plymouth Hemi's fake turbo scoop read IN TWANG WE TRUST. Once a girl trap at drive-ins, for fifteen years it had been nothing but a chick repellent with a V-8 and was now too conspicuous for a getaway car. If somebody'd only leave another unlocked that he could hot-wire, he'd get him a new one. Heartsick and trailing smoke and tappet noise across the grain fields of the Palouse on a nineteen-way psycho crossroad, things surely had to improve. The Styrofoam coffee cups accumulated on the floor. If he could only shoot up, he could make the time fly, but no such luck: the road crawled at him and the little towns hardly looked like dope bazaars even if he'd had extra money, which he did not. He always disliked assessing his resources, but this time it was necessary. Should've kept a few Rolexes.

At dusk his hometown emerged from the foothills with an extraordinary ghastliness until he conceded no town was actually as grim as this parade of grain towers, railroad sidings, the blood-colored county courthouse, and meager houses drawn back on their yards. He felt a ferocious pride at having escaped this dump. If it had not been his hometown, it might have seemed an ordinary backwater village, not unpleasant, well kept and with enough trees. As it was, even jail seemed a reasonable option.

His various foster parents had overfed him, and Scott was pleased that the fat Travis anyone in this tank town might have recognized had been replaced by the slender, health-conscious, "commodities trader" Scott, a fucked-up gym rat. Awkward conversations were improbable. By "awkward," he meant ones likely to arouse guilt over the so-called abandonment of his mother. Scott was not buying that at all, and so far, no one had suggested it. They didn't know his new name and they didn't know his record. For all they knew he was an accountant at the Seahawks' head office. "Just a little cog," he had often informed the credulous who were drawn to the false modesty of this affable crook. Looking straight at him, they believed it was an accountant with a box seat at the King-dome before their very eyes. The motel was embedded in a truck stop, and the all-night noise made his sleep intermittent at best, but he got enough, and the café breakfast and coffee helped with his recovery. His sedan was the only car wedged among the trans-continental trucks, and he ate among exhausted men. He noted that it was a beautiful day and, with one quick phone call to the only funeral home in town, confirmed that he was not interested in viewing the body. His vehemence was remarkable and not well understood by the woman directing the mortuary: "I don't want to see it. You want to see it, you see it. Count me out because no way is it something I need to see." Taking offense at such aggression, she would have answered back, but he'd hung up on her.

HOWELL HAD A PRETTY GOOD IDEA OF WHERE SO-CALLED Scott might be headed, and he accepted the police sniper the department had stuck him with, and which Howell usually resisted in the case of a nonviolent criminal fugitive. In essence, the sniper was a throw-in. Howell had known Scott was problematic, but des-peration might be a new development; anyway, it might be better to be safe than sorry. It was a long ride and the sniper, a former shoe salesman, spent the time playing with his gun in the backseat while Howell enjoyed the quiet of the nice big black unmarked Ford Interceptor. As the sniper fooled with his Tikka T3x, or rather cud-dled it, which was why he was in the backseat, he would roll down a window and look at things through the super-clear Leupold scope. Howell forbade him to shoot it from the car, no matter how far out in the country they might be. He'd already ragged him about hav-ing a desert-tan stock in the Pacific Northwest and had the sniper pretty well under his thumb while noting his peevishness. How-ell tossed his cell phone over his shoulder and told the sniper to get the Montana weather, exactly at the moment when the sniper took a shot, jacking into the air a white plastic paint bucket about a thousand yards away in an empty pasture. "People need to pick up after themselves." That was the sniper's message.

"Jesus God my ears are ringing."

"It'll do that. It's like sex with strangers: you should wear protection."

The immediate effect of shooting the plastic bucket was to slightly adjust the power dynamic within the police car; Howell gazed through the side window and then thought about the sniper shooting from the car, which he had banned. Was it worth a confrontation?

"What makes you think he actually gives a shit his mother died?" inquired the sniper. He was always looking all around, even when asking questions.

"You got something better?"

The sniper settled into the backseat and gently lay his rifle across the floor, giving it a little pat. With one hand behind his head, he looked at his phone. "You ever try Under Armour?" No reply. "The best. Under Armour is *the* best. You could pave Iraq with Under Armour. They steal it and make shit out of it. I've seen them put curds in Under Armour trying to make cottage cheese. Supposed to be some new Under Armour shirt that'll collect data."

"What the fuck's that mean," shouted Howell, "a shirt collecting data?" Whatever Howell had been feeling came out this way. It made no sense.

"I don't know!" wailed the sniper. "That's not in my wheelhouse, but it don't make it impossible. Probably goes to an instrument like your phone. Bluetooth or USB."

"You're lost now."

This was the first raising of voices, and it silenced the car for a while until the sniper said, "Oh my God, are we near the Columbia Gorge?"

Howell said, "North of here."

"Get a load of this"—reading from his tablet—"'members of the Rainbow People, wished to give birth while bungee jumping.'" He looked up. "It actually worked! The baby was born high over the gorge, but the mother kind of lost track of it. I guess the dad was able to swoop in and make a landing with the baby, but the mom couldn't stop bungeeing and flew out over the gorge on this rubber band screaming, 'My baby!' All three ended up safe on the ground. But when papers interviewed them, they were so bummed. They wanted a girl!"

THOUGH DRAB, THE TOWN SAT WITHIN SWEET COUNTRYSIDE, a splendid valley surrounding a blue river winding through meadows, and now Scott was actually glad to be visiting it again, recognizing that it would be the last time, unless he found he liked it better with his mother dead. There had been a day, after all, when it comprised most of his happiness or at least escape, as a ward of the community who appeared in the local paper at Christmastime in proudly donated new clothes, inciting his mother to snatch him back from foster care, annually declaring, "*I'll* dress him," cigarette dangling from the corner of her mouth. "And I'll dress him good," tears in her eyes. "Ask around." It hurt to remember this.

On a fine day with hawks above the cliffs and the sky blue as ice, he drove up the river to a country bar once popular with his schoolmates. He felt equable enough to listen to the radio but thought a beer, or two, was nevertheless an excellent idea, since he was either excited to be on home turf or else just needed something to settle his nerves. He was surprised to find himself so on edge and looked abruptly from side to side as though he might be seeing things. Ranches were burning ditches, and the spring air was tangy with the grass smoke. For reasons he was unwilling to explore, he thought it best not to talk to anyone, and at this hour it was not likely anyone would be at the bar. If he was being followed from Issaquah he wouldn't have to hear about it.

At the sight of a truck and horse trailer parked in front, Scott considered turning back to town, then thought better of it and parked. Utah plates on the truck and trailer. He remembered his mother telling him that if he didn't do his homework he'd end up in Utah, like she actually gave a shit if he did his homework or if some particular state was a bigger dump than Montana. He turned off the radio and the engine, congratulating himself on his jittery nonchalance while glancing around the corners of the building as if Howell could be lurking behind that mountain of bar trash.

He noticed the movement of an animal through the aluminum slats of the horse trailer, most likely a horse. He felt a nudge of nostalgia, remembering cowboys stopping here after gathering cattle, saddle horses growing restive in old trailers while their owners had a beer before heading home to supper. His mom was always into cowboys, any cowboys; and Scott had long, and not implausibly, fancied himself the son of a cowboy. Perhaps he had startled the animal, and he moved close to reassure it. He pressed his face to the side of the trailer and looked in.

A kangaroo gazed back at him through the slats. It looked like a deer, a sort of candid fearless deer with hindquarters so substantial as to give it the appearance of being seated in a chair, forepaws curled close to its chest offering its service. Once he had accepted that it was not a horse, Scott was surprised at how great it was to look at a real kangaroo, and he had to pull himself away. A what? He looked again.

A cowgirl in a Qantas Air windbreaker, a black Stetson drawn down over her face, sat at the bar securing a drink with a couple of fingers around the glass. You couldn't sit far enough away to avoid contact, but she didn't seem to want it anyway, so Scott ordered a Rainier and gave the bartender a quick nod. The bartender looked off into space and the cowgirl stared straight ahead. "That your kangaroo?"

"Uh-huh."

"Heading to Utah?"

"Any business of yours?"

"I've always wanted to meet a girl with a kangaroo, but I've never gone to Utah and believe you me I never will."

"Looks like your lucky day." She gazed at him for a long moment. "Are you African American? Looks like you got you a drop or two."

"Well, my mom was sure white enough. Could of been something in the woodpile." He pressed his hand against the spring of his hair. "Just died, n'that. I'm supposed to go down there and pick up the . . . whatever."

"Don't look too broke up."

"It's been a week."

"So who's your dad? Where's he at?"

"No idea. Four lane with a divider ran right behind our house and guys'd come down off the highway."

"Musta been wasn't too white come off that highway. Look to me like she could of fixed your teeth."

With that, she got up, slapped down some money, and walked out of the bar. Scott thought it was just the two of them day-drinking the afternoon away with a shot at getting lucky. Anymore, you couldn't come on to them: you had to build a trap and watch them fall in, but not today. Scott, suddenly talkative, directed a question to the bartender. "What do you suppose she's doing with a kangaroo?"

"I know what she's doing," said the bartender, inspecting his row of bottles. "Charging people to look at him. In other words she stays broke."

A CONFLICT BETWEEN HOWELL AND THE SNIPER RESULTED from Howell's attempt to humanize Scott as just an American kid trying to make a buck. The sniper was having none of it, saying his job would be impossible if he went there. In Iraq, an insurgent on a Vespa was no different than a clay pigeon; his job had its source in marksmanship not psychology. In America's future, intoned the sniper, the only survivors would have a thousand-yard stare: he was glad he'd got his early and avoided joining the collaterals. "Let the collaterals elect the president. I'm into survival."

Howell just let this pass: why bust this drip's balls, knowing perfectly well that he was nothing but a local gun nut who had wheedled his way onto the force and had never been to Iraq or really anywhere outside the state of Washington, except on that one trip to Idaho to shoot a Paiute holed up in a Chuck E. Cheese with a BB gun. "Why negotiate when you can perforate," the sniper had remarked to big approval around the cop shop.

SCOTT WAS READY TO HEAD TO THE MORTUARY. CALVES WERE frolicking in the pastures along the road, and he called to them, "Live it up, you got a year to go!" What a marvelous day, he thought. Birds flew over the car, their wings glinting on the hood. His spirits began to sink again. He thought, Oh my God, I've had such a terrible life.

Scott's grieving didn't really begin until he had to negotiate the cremation, which required temporary retrieval of the name "Travis," and even so he wouldn't identify it as grief so much as something that was engulfing Travis, child of the deceased. He pictured himself as a newborn in the arms of a young, pretty mother. I'm sure she loved me, he thought. He tried to imagine how her voice might've gone, *I love you baby, Travis.* No, he thought, I was just any old baby that smelled like tobacco and Guckenheimer discount rye.

The undertaker was a middle-aged woman with a picture of herself on her office wall indicating that she had once participated in a beauty pageant. Seeing that she still hadn't lost the fight with gravity, Scott felt that it was too soon to cross her off. She said, "Do I know you?" and he said no so abruptly she was taken aback before settling down to speak warmly about his late mother, loss, and grief. There was little latitude in these recitations, but they still succeeded: he liked doing it and it felt recreational to think up shit about his mom. The undertaker gave him the feeling that she cared very much about his needs while trying to sell him things, cremation jewelry, deluxe urns, and a coffin that was going to burn up anyway. Scott was already worn out from the legal business of getting his mother released to the funeral home, but he was sufficiently atop things to pick the optional cardboard coffin and indignantly declined viewing the cremation itself. The former beauty said, "Oh? Travis, I wouldn't miss it for the world." Not until then had he noticed that she was losing her looks.

"Really?" said Scott. "You're sick." He paid no attention to the urn slide show nor to the undertaker's suggestion that his mother's size might run things up a bit. He hadn't realized she'd put on so much weight before the undertaker invoked the surcharge. Since Scott had declined embalming, the refrigeration fee was unavoidable, payable on receipt of ashes, and so what? It would all be mailed anyway and nothing prevented him from supplying a false address. Maybe he'd give Goody Two-shoes Howell's. Because his mother was without friends, the viewing took place in the anteroom of the furnace and, desperate to avoid being swept away by his feelings, Scott focused instead on the packing tape employed to hold the cardboard coffin together. There was a minor kerfuffle about his debit card, and he left with his hands over his ears, in case the roar of the furnace could be heard in the parking lot. Without question, Scott was not doing well, and he regretted failing to point out that while his mother may not have had friends at the moment, she'd once had tons of them. She'd been a curious person, and he would have loved telling her about the kangaroo and the carrots it ate from the Hutterite Colony up past Martinsdale. Oh God, he thought, oh God.

Still, he felt ready to see his school, the big test he hoped to pass before returning to Issaquah, and drove to it hunched over the steering wheel, uncertain where it was; but he got there so directly, so swiftly, as to feel like his own slightly unwilling passenger. He noticed the truck and trailer parked at the school yard, the cowgirl leaning on the hood, hands in the pockets of her quilted vest, talking to some older students. He didn't know what sort of luck it was to see her there again. The kangaroo was out on the playground.

He stood among the children happy at the antics of the kangaroo. My mother loved animals! She would have loved a kangaroo! She lived hard and never had the chance to see one, not even in a zoo. Never saw one fucking kangaroo her whole life! By now the kangaroo was hopping in a big circle, the children skipping behind it. Scott was instantly caught up in this scene and skipped along with them. Old Howell oughta see me now. They didn't like this and began drifting off, looking back over their shoulders at him. One small boy with a homemade crew cut turned and waved goodbye. The children drifted toward the school, and Scott found himself alone on the windy playground; even the kangaroo was leaving, hopping toward its trailer and a refill of carrots. The cowgirl was smiling at him, but it was unclear what she meant by it.

Scott began walking, hardly picking a direction, but the effort took him past the Carnegie Library. Not the worst idea, getting out of this town. But he wasn't ready to go yet, and the town seemed changed with a kangaroo in it. No one recognized him as he sat on a bench next to a planter filled with red and white petunias. He diverted himself thinking how much he hated petunias. Yes, he thought with anguish, this is my issue: hatred of petunias as I run from the law. An old woman stopped and bent to smell them. Scott said, "There's no smell, they're petunias." She stood sharply and hurried off. Scott whistled to himself and looked up and down the street as though the kangaroo could appear at any time. Scott thought he could mention some things he'd done in these lost years, if only someone would recognize him. Eyes closed, head in his hands, he heard a voice.

"You all right?" It was the cowgirl. She looked at him skeptically, fist to her cheek.

"I inherited my mother's house. I can't look at it. Follow? That's where she died."

When she lifted her hat, her hair fell out. "Why can't you look at it?"

"How about you get outta my face?"

"You need to look at that house. How many mothers do you think you had?" It felt like a month that she stared at him without saying anything. Finally, "I need a house. I'm about to get kicked out because of him."

Back in Issaquah he'd be able to picture the kangaroo kicking over the motherfucking furniture. Possibly, a rent-to-buy but off his hands anyway. He had little interest in entanglements, but the opportunity to help a kangaroo touched the quizzical part of him that was the good part of an otherwise criminal mind. He was drawn to plans like this one that had no chance of working out. He gets her in the house; there's gratitude, et cetera.

HOWELL AND THE SNIPER SPENT THE NIGHT IN TOWN AND had breakfast at the farmer-rancher hangout. The sniper thought the biscuits and gravy "were enough to gag a maggot." They were immediately spotted as strangers and talked quietly to keep the hicks out of earshot. The sniper enjoyed catching people staring so that he could fix them with an intimidating penitentiary eye-lock. He had the tightly wound body that Howell, a big fat guy with wet lips, associated with the sniper's imaginary deployment. They had already driven past Scott's inherited new home and noted squatters bolting the new ownership and the mess, but they would wait for the situation to ripen, open up a bit, so they could see into it and, like, act.

Howell was disappointed in himself for getting made at the pier and giving Scott the idea that absconding was his best option. He should have stayed out of sight and let him keep the knockoff Rolexes: now that Howell had fished them from the green can, he didn't know what to do with them; stocking stuffers, he guessed. In this he disagreed with the sniper who felt that a convicted felon who cuts off his tether is a dangerous criminal and should be treated as such, and given the smallest possible margin of error. Those container ships were all rubbish. What difference did it make how it got distributed?

"I'll pop him in the jail here, and we can extradite him later. He was just running crap off container ships. Never made enough money to fix the ShitMobile. Cased sake, motor parts, sex toys. All the time it took to fence he could have made a better living stocking shelves at Wally World. He's a petty criminal, garden variety. We don't shoot those."

The sniper called to another table, "I know you?" Farmer shaking his head. "Didn't think so."

In the patrol car—fun watching the farmers at the window: It *is* a police car—Howell said, "You are very, very aggressive, beyond what I think suits the situation."

"I'm forceful but in a measured way."

"Oh God, it's on me for mentioning it, you're so full of shit."

"Roll yours down, please, it's all steamed up. You need to just let things be, Howell. It's all about peace on earth."

THE NEXT DAY SCOTT PICKED UP HIS MOTHER'S ASHES. THE old beauty presented him with a measly urn with its embossed harp containing the remains. Scott wanted to break the ice despite getting zero warmth from this washed-up contestant. "You live around here?"

"What's it to you?"

"Nothing, I guess." Scott felt as he had in recent days, days of freedom after all, rising defeat, something he didn't remember feeling but that seemed to look toward a kind of void. He stared again at the urn and wondered what it was made of, a granular surface that seemed of some vegetable material. "What is this—this is like a—is it a locket or what?"

"It's an eternal embrace heart," she nearly shouted.

"Why would anyone want that?"

"You wanted the cheap urn! That's the cheap urn! It's papier-mâché. It comes with the eternal embrace heart *period*. Cheaper you get a shopping bag." She must have realized she'd gone too far with this last and made a final attempt to draw his attention to the embossed lilies before pulling herself up, crossing her arms, and with a stiffened face gazing toward the door. Scott gathered up his urn leaving nothing on the desk but a book of golf tips, an emery board, and a picture of her cat.

"I assume my mother died in peace . . ."

"Yes. In bed. Goodbye."

He was bent on driving by the house, the one down by the river, not the one by the tracks and not the one forty fucking yards from the loading docks of the elevator and certainly not the one up in Snob Hollow, where, when he was eleven, the bony chain-smoker had dressed him up like a girl while her husband was at the Cats-Griz game because she'd always wanted a daughter. Those were foster homes. Ma's home was downwind of the stockyards. Scott was seeing some sort of payoff for his three-year Gold's Gym certificate, this foster kid the chain-smoker had called a pencil-wristed weenie. Remembering that caused to him to daydream of the cowgirl. The three of them could—hey! this is way down the road—move into his old house, a real fixer-upper, no lie, but with possibilities. Most landlords probably weren't overjoyed about kangaroos, but he was different. He was the landlord, he felt drawn to them.

No problem getting in the house: the front door was open. Scott stood in the doorway without entering, surveying slowly as though something would jump him, then walked in—a mess, intense tobacco smell, broken glass that looked like bong remains, and no immediate sign a family had ever lived here. Did I live here? Someone had painted a swastika on the Farrah Fawcett poster covering the chimney hole where the heater had stood. Not his mother's work, maybe a vandal. Mousetraps that hadn't been emptied of their victims, Tony Orlando and Dawn album sleeve, Crock-Pot full of sludge. By turning himself around in the near-empty space of the living room, he was just able to identify doorways: bathroom, his old room, his mother's room. He awaited feeling something other than a sensation he had hit his head or had snorted something questionable. He didn't go into his old room but remembered vividly being really fat in there and being Travis. He'd kissed fat Travis goodbye a long time ago. He tried his mother's room where the sagging bed must have been where she died. She was never alone, so nothing too macabre about that. Maybe the bedclothes beside it were where somebody had cleared the decks to lift her out. A couple of items caused him to cover his face, bend over, and make gruesome noises: his Tonka T-Bucket Roadster and his Evel Knievel wheelie lunch box. How many years must she have saved them? How many? How many? How many?

PAT HOWELL AND THE SNIPER SAT IN THEIR CAR BEHIND A shelter belt of Russian olives and looked in the direction of Scott's inherited house. "It never was a nice house," said Howell. "And now it looks like it will fall in. Maybe he doesn't have to claim it. It's obviously a hazard."

"Yes," said the sniper, "just like the new owner. He ought to set fire to it and stay inside when she goes up." But he was too stupid for that to have been a prophecy.

SCOTT WAS SORTING THROUGH A CIGAR BOX FULL OF OLD postcards when the rooms lit up with a white phosphorous light and the first bullhorn blasts were heard from outside. Howell's amiable voice, grossly magnified, came through the walls. *"Scott, Pat Howell here. I guess you know what's up—big help to both of us if we take this nice and quiet and head back to the coast. We've got a lot to talk about. I know we can work something out. I got an eager-beaver sniper with me. Let's not give him anything to do."* Scott pushed over a curio cabinet filled with the worthless things his mother had gathered over the years and was walking through broken porcelain. *"—have explained to my backup here that I've known you a long time and this is going to be very very very uneventful—"* Scott fought off the soothing effect of Howell's voice, such a nice fat man and Scott had let him down again. *"Scott, is that you? Scott, it never had to come to this. Scott? Jared, put it down please?"*

"Looks like to me we're gonna sit this one out."

"No prob," said the sniper, "I'm on the clock."

Howell thought, based on what he knew about Scott's impatience, that the run time on this deal would be short, except for possible mind games, which he also knew Scott enjoyed. He was inclined to think of Scott as a waste, but then he was inclined to think of himself as a waste. That was the trouble with this job. If you cared about helping these guys, the distance between you and them disappeared. You were warned against this. There were enablers all through the system, and it wasn't always about money. The job was easier when you were dealing with an actual terrible human being. They'd usually been in a long time. They were hard; they were cold; they saw through you. You'd be lucky to keep them from cutting one more throat. They never got on your side of the desk. The Scotts of this world? Another story entirely, propelled down a crooked road by their own crooked history, a closed system, a carnival ride, only happy when they're scared.

The fire started somewhere well inside the house but quickly poured out the windows, then licked up the outer walls until it illuminated the whole yard and caused the scrawny trees to cast long shadows. The sniper said, "We've reached an end to the story, but which end we will have to wait and see. Your little friend is either burning himself up or producing a distraction so that he can bolt to his jalopy. I can only address the latter—" He raised the rifle, flipped down its legs, and settling in around it aimed for the driver's seat of the ShitMobile. "Two scenarios. Both successful."

Fire trucks arrived, but the fire was out of control and wouldn't be extinguished until only the appliances stood above the rubble and all else was smoking mud. The sniper wanted to stay and explain why the ShitMobile had Washington plates, but Howell said, "They'll work it out. We're going. Get in the fuckin' car now."

"Oooh man, I'm sensing a mood swing here."

Howell hardly spoke, damned if he was gonna let some turd know how he felt, explain himself to some gun nut who'd lost his chance to kill someone. He dropped the sniper off at his house, left him with his rifle dangling, and drove off without returning Jared's baffled stare.

He went to his office in the morning on little sleep, his exhaustion unresponsive to a hot shower and all his daily meds, his Prilosec, his beta-blockers, his multivitamin, his baby aspirin. He drizzled Visine into his bleary eyes. Why did I think I could help this guy, shunted from Seattle and Shoreline probation offices into *my* world? Trusted him, gave him my cell, fuckin' *reached out*. Howell took his reserved spot in front of the King County district courthouse that some sick city planner put way out on 220th Avenue for the inconvenience of all parolees, walked past reception and down the corridor to his office. "How did you get here?" he asked.

Scott said, "I moseyed."

Moseying wasn't quite it: risking immolation, Scott had slipped into the trees behind the house and relinquished the ShitMobile on the theory that the sniper would be training his dick extender on the driver's seat. Hitched a ride to Billings, where he caught an outbound dog to Seattle. He slept for a bit and checked shipping on his phone, when he saw a Korean Ro-Ro ship with a load of Kias coming into Seattle within the week. The crew would have something he could use, things that needed new owners, undeclared stuff you could drop over the side.

First, Howell was mad, then he wasn't so mad, and what was the use. "You almost got shot."

"I've been playing with house money all my life."

"This one wasn't smart."

"My mother died," said Scott.

"I'm aware of that. You gave the undertaker a phony debit card. You're going to have to make good on it."

"Not a problem, my ship will come in. How about the death of my mom?"

"What about it?"

"Is it mitigating?"

"Could be," said Howell. "It'll take work."

They were like mirror images, chewing their thumbnails in the silence. Finally, Scott spoke: "Nice watch."

Howell withdrew his thumb and smiled. "Thanks. It's just a knockoff."

VIKING BURIAL

I HADN'T LIVED VERY LONG IN BOLINAS, UP ON THE MESA with a glimpse of the town below, the serration of San Francisco to the south and its much-grander view, the one I liked best, of the open Pacific. I was helping an old hippie with a hopeless project and getting paid a low wage, though in the American money I was so short of, plus a room and meager board. We wasted a lot of time smoking dope and taking noon sights of the sun with a plastic sextant to get a real fix on the eucalyptus under which we sat watching the changing light on the ocean. In our minds, we were finishing a thirty-five-foot Lodestar trimaran, which Miles, the old hippie, planned on sailing to Micronesia. Arthur Piver, designer of the boat, a boon to do-it-yourselfers in that day and age, had drowned in one of his own creations along the wild coast of California, trying to qualify for the OSTAR. His body was never found, but his bibles stayed in print for dreamers who went on starting trimarans, few of which were eventually launched. Miles's trimaran never would be: we were on the third hull twenty years after he'd started the boat, and the first hull was already rotten. But Miles wanted me to build the rudder and dagger board as though this were really happening. Was it cynical of me to go on taking his money? I could claim that I was only modestly compensated for keeping the dream alive; that in the service of his illusion, I was confined to a mountain of boat-work material, epoxy tubs, fiberglass cloth, paint trays, and bits of rigging, snaps, shackles, indeterminate lengths of bronze and stainless rods, salvaged sheet winches, an old bosun's ditty bag with sail-repair items, a fid, a palm, waxed thread, and curved sailmakers' needles. The splicing knife was rusted into a single unusable mass, and after throwing it away I had to deal with him looking for it and proclaiming its sentimental value (Sea Scouts, 1949).

In the big picture I had not misled Miles. I said to him one day while under the eucalyptus eating the fabulous snacks and sand-wiches his wife made for us—I realize now to get him out of the house and keep him out as long as possible—I said, "This is a hare-brained scheme. We are building an unsafe thing or should I say an ill-advised thing that has little chance of going far enough to get anyone into trouble."

"Sinking as we launch?"

"Exactly." It made him smile. What a nut. I was crazy about him and his benign eccentricities. I could see he was not in particularly good health, and that helped entitle him to his ways.

"You're so negative. We won't let that happen. Or possibly we will press on without betraying the present. This is West Marin, boyo! These are the cards we have been dealt, and you are helping me play this hand. Nothing would be gained by a better or more seaworthy boat beyond accelerating an outcome whose virtue is that it is unforeseeable." NorCal at its most inscrutable: I was get-ting used to it. "We must put our heads down and do the work before us." From this experience I learned something lasting, if I could just put my finger on it.

Miles had a small private income. His father, a traveling doll salesman, had left him enough to get by. He was a nice man, quite erudite, but notional in every matter of living. When I first met him, he had paid for some genealogical research that revealed an Indian ancestor, very remote, a granduncle or some such, but it left him entirely preoccupied with "coming to grips with my Native American heritage." He was still burning herbal wisps when I first appeared to help him revive his sailing dream, but he gave it up soon after. He was hard of hearing, and you had to face him to talk; he'd tried a hearing aid a while back, an advanced one that elimi-nated background noise with cutting-edge directional features to capture what was important. But when he went to catch a bebop quartet at a San Francisco jazz club, the device homed in on the drums, leaving Miles momentarily traumatized. At first he blamed the whole thing on bad dope, but in the end he forswore the tech-nology and resumed his head-tilted lipreading. "God wants me to trust the ears he gave me," said Miles the confirmed atheist.

I'd gone to the University of California on a baseball scholar-ship. My father, a lawyer and judge in Billings, was a bully. He bullied my twin brother, my sister, and my mother, but it didn't work on me. By the time I was eleven I considered him a nuisance and, by mutual assent, college would alienate us permanently. So great was my mother's oppression, she never acknowledged his part in the matter and blamed me alone for our estrangement. Working at a flower farm, three years out of college and into the string of odd jobs that my degree in U.S. history had prepared me for, I was living in Santa Rosa with somebody or other when I received a small heavy box via UPS. It contained a note from my mother: "Remember that guy you never bothered to call?" I tried and really meant to throw away my father's ashes, but I held on to them as I traveled here and there on my old BSA Gold Star; now they were stowed in the first hull of Miles's trimaran. My father was Norwegian and loved the idea of a Viking burial: it was the longship idea at its most ridiculous, as I believed that one day it would be necessary to burn Miles's worthless boat. My mother vacated our old house on the Rims in Billings and moved to Lewistown next door to her sister. I haven't been to her new house but expect I will see it this year when I get home. This is duty, since I'm not all that fond of her either. But I *remember* being fond of her.

I lived with Miles and his wife, Adelaide, about four houses up from the wharf, doing home repairs in exchange for my space in the attic. It was a modest old cottage on a lot that, a century earlier, had come as a bonus with a subscription to the San Francisco newspaper. The Jefferson Airplane had bought a place closer to the water, but they hardly ever seemed to be around. Flower children swarmed on the weekends, and the old beatniks kept out of sight up on the mesa with a couple of aged Hells Angels and the Catholic anarchists. Miles and Adelaide never went over the hill to Marin, even to shop, on the grounds that it was a "breeding ground for suits."

Adelaide was a locally common bohemian earth mother and sometime hostess to the local poets: Lew Welch or Philip Whalen, with occasional celebrity appearances by Allen Ginsberg. Robert Duncan came as well; the only one with good manners, he also had the fewest affectations. He recited "My Mother Would Be a Falconress" for us over Adelaide's spaghetti and meatballs. Miles ran from these scenes as from a burning car, taking me with him to work on the doomed trimaran, sometimes in the dark, especially when Adelaide and the others were "Oming" in the backyard or working on their imaginary novel, *Conchita, Pastry Chef to the Stars*. Sometimes I would listen to them tossing dialogue back and forth. God knows they were having fun, however inscrutable to anyone else.

One night when the whole party seemed to have lost their minds, I walked past the dining room to get something from the refrigerator. Adelaide was standing at the table with a water tumbler of wine in her hand, quite agitated. "Wait, wait!" she yelled. "I *am* Conchita, the pastry chef!" The speech was celebrated beyond all reason, as the poets and artists manqué lost the boundary between laughter and sobbing. You couldn't help being disturbed, all those gaping mouths and the god-awful noise.

Adelaide was a big woman with wiry hair and sturdy feet protruding from an Indian-print dress that reached to the floor. She seemed to frighten Miles, and I soon learned that part of my job was to keep him away from the visiting artists, including the young fellow who wanted my room in the attic. Adelaide introduced him to me, suggesting that he had nowhere to sleep except the sofa on the front porch. Gesturing to the little fellow beside her, this Dirk, directing a complacent gaze my way, she explained, "He's an actor: stage, screen, television. He does it all. In between at the moment." She then walked out into the yard, leaving us to work it out. Dirk was direct. He told me I best be moving along; he needed the room. I told him I couldn't see it. He said I was the only one in the house not making a contribution. "A contribution to what?" I asked.

"The scene," said Dirk.

Bolinas then still seemed like a West Coast fishing village with the ubiquitous Pacific mongrels, the brindle dogs of Sitka and Baja, an out-of-the-way place where motorcycle gangs appeared every so often to beat people up or bask in the light of the local illuminati, who thought Hells Angels were quite marvelous.

In my abundant free time, I sometimes wandered out on Duxbury Reef at low tide, among the kelp beds and shale ledges where there were usually people hanging around hoping for a stranded fish or abalone. One Saturday afternoon under low gray skies, I came upon Adelaide and her entourage killing an octopus they had dragged out of a tide pool with the plan to eat it at one of their stormy dinner parties. An octopus has a remarkably sentient eye, and this one seemed to observe its own death as the blows of the artists rained down upon it. I must have let out an unhappy noise when I departed, because Adelaide watched me go with hands on her hips as she called out, "Delicious!"

Though I never went to these things anyway, the night of the octopus dinner I was rather formally disinvited, befitting my perceived censure of the gleeful killing. Adelaide had laid down a rule about water waste, and the toilet was to be flushed only as absolutely needed, a baffling directive that resulted in an appalling flotilla of turds, which backed up the thing at the most inopportune time, the night of the octopus dinner. As the water closet was adjacent to the dining room, the artists got what they deserved, and during a long deification of Louis Zukofsky by an older icon of the San Francisco art scene in a white Mohawk, everyone ran outdoors to get some air, leaving the icon, alone in the fetor, feeling he'd said something amiss about the poet.

Miles's mood was sinking, and he was eating by himself in the kitchen with me as he looked at charts of the seas he would never sail. Aligned before him were all the vitamins meant to ward off whatever was wrong, but his frailty seemed only to wax by the day. Our work on the boat had grown desultory, and each morning as we began, I'd gaze across the small cabin at the port-side hull, which, though hopelessly rotted, still contained my father's ashes. Finally, the day came when we had to assess its condition, and it was only when I showed Miles that I could pull handfuls of dry rot out of the frames that his accustomed volubility failed him. "I see the problem," he said. "I'm not stupid. We'll just rebuild it."

"You'll have to get help."

"I have help. I have you."

"I've got stuff to do."

"Saying you're quitting?"

"I need to get on with my life." I didn't want to tell him that I was starting to feel his despair as the folly of his escape plan was beginning to dawn on him. From where we worked under the grove of fragrant eucalyptus, it seemed cruel that the open Pacific sparkled before us, stretching toward the Farallon Islands and beyond, really beyond.

"I'll launch it myself then and trust to luck."

I knew it would never come to that. He was stuck, and it was a blessing that he didn't seem to know it. But I saw something as he gazed at the boat. I saw hope, a peculiar thing to see on the face of someone who didn't appear to have long to live.

It came to me that I couldn't afford to leave Miles. My problem was that I had no place to live now that Adelaide had replaced me with Dirk, and so I pitched my mountaineering tent beside my motorcycle, near the trimaran, and prepared to eat from my old Igloo cooler with the concert stickers and the decorative macramé handles fashioned by that person I lived with in Santa Rosa, sharing what was known as a crash pad, its only privacy a treetop platform made of pilfered construction-site planks. The inconvenience didn't keep ardent couples from climbing up and down the tree like orangutans, their love cries wafting from above. We enjoyed training flashlights on them.

FOR A SHORT WHILE, MILES SLEPT IN THE MIDDLE HULL OF the trimaran, effectively segregating himself from the hilarity of the Adelaide crowd, and by the withdrawal of his private income, he slowly began starving wife and crowd both out of the cottage. I managed to rise above my shame and go on taking the hourly wage for working on his hopeless sailboat, living in my tent and smoking dope.

Not long thereafter, Adelaide and Miles clashed in court, the sparks continuing to fly until Adelaide became our postmistress. She moved into rooms near the PO, while Miles occupied the old cottage by himself, ownership to be determined, moot because he soon missed Adelaide and the uproar and persuaded her to move back in, but without the revelers, who took a dim view of her bourgeois federal paycheck. The house was now filled with tradespeople and realtors. Miles loved the scene, but I'd had enough and went into the city in search of a real job.

Representing myself as a boatwright based on my days pulling handfuls of plywood out of Miles's rotten hull, I signed on to the crew of a fifty-seven-foot sloop built in Finland and helped deliver it to Hawaii. Such tiresome sailing with monotonous diurnal wind shifts had me praying for a typhoon per Conrad. The crew was mostly delivery professionals: a navigator, a helmsman nearly retired by the autopilot, a couple of well-built winch monkeys, and a kitchen girl, whom the navigator, a cunning fellow whose shameless ogling had done the trick, persuaded to share the forepeak while she waited to start graduate school which she would do once the equinoctial storms curtailed yacht deliveries.

Flown straight home, we were put on a downwind sled, a Santa Cruz 50, destined for San Felipe on the Baja Peninsula of Mexico. We had just left our first overnight port after San Diego, still on the Pacific side, when we were forced to wait out hurricane-force chubascos in a desert sea canyon stinking of guano. We were sitting around the cabin, trying to escape the abrasion of wind-driven sand, when I received a call from Adelaide on our satellite phone. Miles was dead. He'd left me the trimaran. She knew it was worthless but wanted to know what to do. I told her to burn it. After that, the wind abated, and we sailed on.

GHOST RIDERS IN THE SKY

> A Western Ranch is just a branch of Nowhere Junction
> to me.
> > —*Dinah Shore,* "Buttons and Bows"

ONCE A YEAR, MY SISTER, EMILY, AND I MET IN KEY WEST, where she now lived, usually in the winter for a long weekend at her tiny house amid other old metal-roofed frame cottages with cisterns and aging citrus trees on a street leading to the cemetery. I would only stay a few days. Emily never remarried after her divorce as a young woman; and after mine, neither did I. We were fed up with marriage but spent the brief time I got out of snowy Montana trying to understand our parents. Once, about twenty years ago, Emily visited me there but had no nostalgia for our old home, and so once was enough. I, however, seemed to cling to it. I don't know why. I'm still in the house we grew up in. It's hard to picture a fifties ranch-style house in the suburbs as a ghost house, but that's what it is.

Generally, we studied our long-dead mother and father in terms of their contrasting personalities, but really the mystery was their divorce, since they had always gotten along so well. Why would they have gone their separate ways, ending as solitary as Emily and me? Visiting them one at a time during our college years really scrambled our late upbringing; but we got through it and never felt that either of them was anything but blameless. Nevertheless, on our long weekend vacations in Key West we always did our best to add another fragment to the puzzle. This year we hit on our aunt Ada's visit to Montana as a clue, a vein of rich insight or non sequitur, we couldn't say, but it seemed to lead somewhere, a sort of clicking on the Geiger counter we were training on the marriage.

Aunt Ada had never been out west. I'm not sure she'd ever been outside the state of Maine or far from Lewiston, where our family had immigrated back when the place had big textile mills on the Androscoggin River and the families lived in ethnic enclaves that hardly exist anymore. Aunt Ada had two siblings, not counting Eloise, who had died as an infant: my mother and my uncle Martin. Martin drank himself to death, though he'd had an interesting life as a tennis player and a decorated OSS officer in the Second World War. Ada stayed in Lewiston, taught art at St. Dominic's, and cared for my grandparents until they died, sacrificing her own life and happiness without complaint. She was a homely old maid. If she was bitter, we couldn't tell, but that didn't mean she wasn't. It comes with disguises, and there was the feeling that it lay hidden in her energetic dowdiness.

My mother was a beauty and had modeled seasonal fashions at department stores in Maine while still a teenager. Ada, much older, had practically raised her, doted on my mother as though she were her own child, while my mother felt guilty all her life, as if her good looks and luck were to blame for Ada's want of either. I do know that when my mother went off into marriage there was some pain, for both of them. They wrote each other, Ada sending "news from home" years after Montana was our mother's home, and the latest from Lewiston, Maine, was painfully uneventful; though in retrospect our mother might not have felt that way at all.

My father was from Billings, Montana. My mother met him at a college dance in Boston, where both were students, she at a sort of finishing school that no longer exists, and he at MIT. My mother and her friends thought that since he was from Montana he must be a cowboy, and in fact he acted like one with many swaggering habits he had picked up from westerns. But he was a business-minded heir to a small scrap-iron fortune, anxious to strike out on his own and escape his social isolation as a Jew in Montana. He never gave up either his rakish cowboy habits or the clothing styles he had learned in Boston, remaining a tweedy Jewish cowboy, a horseman, a hunter, and a very keen businessman. My mother was a little too crazy about him and stood out in her own way with her imperishable Maine accent. Locals with defensive and shallow regional identity were quick to notice such things. By "a little too crazy about him" I mean there was an invisible wall of intimacy around them as a couple, which nobody, not even we children, ever quite broke through.

We revered our aunt Ada, my sister and I, when we visited her in Maine and from afar when we were home in Billings. She seemed to be a part of the place where she had lived her entire life, a keeper of ancestral graves and teacher of children. I remember thinking that she even dressed according to a Maine color scheme: brown, green, and a blue cloche, not a merry blue but a blue as dark as the local sea. Lobster-pot buoys hung around the doorway of the family home, a rusty old cottage, cozy enough in its day but too big for Aunt Ada, who rattled around inside its vacancies. The house was scantily decorated, with two formal photographs of our grandparents, Ada's own oil painting of a fleet of catboats with multicolored sails, and plates hung, for some reason, as though they were pictures—lots of stuff referring to an idealized nautical past, though my grandfather had worked for the B&M Railroad, a greasy denizen of the switching yards.

Our home in Billings was so antic with my father's high spirits, my mother's follies, and my sister Emily's cartoon addiction that I found something romantic, as well, about the solitary condition of Ada's life. Until I reached the eighth grade I'd planned to be a commercial fisherman! My mother said, "Stick to lobster rolls and call it a day." By the time of Ada's only visit to Montana I no longer dreamed of being a man of the sea and had moved on to carrier-based fighter pilot. The TV always showed a war, and I gloated over all catastrophes befalling the enemy, particularly those produced by airpower.

We met Ada at the Billings airport back when passengers still descended from the plane on a kind of stairway—all of us, my father, whom she both admired and suspected, dapper in summer business wear; my mother in clothes so up to date they were misunderstood; my sister and me, annoying teenagers in fad-driven regalia.

Ada descended lugging a huge needlepoint valise, the everlasting cloche seized in one hand. We had never seen anything like it in this context, the spraddled gait, the oddly challenging gaze. My sister, Emily, later said with understandable but inappropriate precision that Ada looked like a Martian. Her face was mottled with excitement as she threw back her head to inhale the mountain air, of which there was very little, and replaced the cloche.

This year in Key West we revisited that scene, starting with Ada's descent from the plane like—what?—something strange; but we loved her, didn't we? Surely we did. I had a tattered little cabana deployed on the beach by the range light. My sister and I sat inside it furrowing our brows, with swimmers, families, dogs, wandering past. We felt pressured to pursue our suspicion.

We watched Ada cross the runway in the heat of a High Plains summer. We rushed to her in the terminal and embraced her, dislodging the cloche while my father made a swooping bow to help with the needlepoint valise. "I thought I'd never get here! The crowds at the airport in Chicago, everyone pushing and shoving. The gate agent, why she was a big, rude hog! I asked her a simple question and she snatched my ticket, answered me as though I was retarded, then shoved it back at me. I considered giving her big snout a twist!"

"Air travel is not what it used to be," my mother offered with tense blandness.

"What's in here, B?" my father asked, hoisting the valise with a self-effacing grin. We were a little startled by Ada's vehemence about her travel experience, and my father was trying to lower the temperature. "Rocks?" was the wrong question, meant in good humor, but she merely looked at him. We knew what that look, well below our father's altitude, meant: our mother had married the wrong guy. He still called her A, having long ago mistakenly called her Anna. *"Ada's m'handle,"* Aunt Ada had said icily. So "A" it was, not to immortalize the correction, but out of my father's fear of making the same mistake again. I'd once overheard him mutter, "Lots of names start with *A.*"

By now Ada was leading us through the terminal, my father, usually in command, bringing up the rear with the big purse. My little sister, Emily, ever intuitive, whispered, "Man the parapets."

Looking back, I wonder if we should have ever pried Ada out of Maine with our persistent invitations. A gentle feature of the landscape by the currents of the Androscoggin, she was a guided missile in the desiccated atmosphere of Montana. An elaborate welcome dinner, two days away, was when she would show her stuff, a last and most vivid illustration of how nobody in my mother's family could hold their liquor, with Ada laughing gaily at interior jokes only she could hear and which we worried were directed at us. We were pretty sure we were the targets. We could only gaze at her crinkled eyes streaming tears of merriment as she reviewed some private comedy, forgotten by morning, alongside our alarm.

In the first days of Ada's visit we entertained her, driving her around the countryside, which she did her best to appreciate; but soon we realized that what we relished as open space Ada saw as vacancy. She was very nice about our mountains, rivers, and prairie; she complimented them formally but somehow conveyed that they were beside the point, gaping at them as though they didn't make sense or remarking that the trees seemed too far apart. Before we knew it, my sister and I were rhapsodizing on the smell of the sea, the winding lanes and weathered shingles. It was the beginning of the dissonance we felt at having Ada in the house. My mother ate up the hometown anecdotes while we—my sister, father, and I—sat through them; though still in thrall to my lobster-ridden future, I was well on my way to the ambivalence which is, as they say at Tiffany's, the house style.

"I hope you will come to see me in Maine," said Ada firmly.

"For sure, Aunt Ada," said my sister, Emily. She said "Ont," not "Ant." I took it as a ridiculous attempt to bond with her Maine relative. Ada grasped Emily's shoulders, approving this ersatz moment, and said she would skip lunch and thought a nap would do her good. My mother had put her in the guest room on the north end of the house, with its own bathroom and a nice view of my father's tomato garden. The rest of us dined together, a rarity at midday, when we were usually scattered. My father said, "Ada looks a bit out of place."

"What exactly do you mean by that?" said my mother.

"Only that, really. We usually see Ada on home ground."

"I would think this was home ground," said my mother. "We *are* her family."

You could cut it with a knife. My sister and I hardly ate and were soon off to preferable activities—my sister with her friends or on the phone, me playing pickup baseball—before it got any worse, but we were trailed by my poor father's forlorn gaze. We left him alone at the table, palms up, as we fled.

On the beach at Key West that day, Emily said, "Mom still hung on to that Maine thing. She was a modern girl. She wasn't going to give it up just because she got married."

"And moved out west?"

"So what? It's still America." I didn't take that up. I had no intention of arguing with my own sister. "Remember when Mrs. Halstead said Mom was 'not from here,' and Mom said, 'Who the hell would *want* to be from here?'"

My sister and I had a few small jobs around the property. I was big enough to mow the lawn and clean the eave troughs; she took care of the marigolds that surrounded my father's tomato patch. My father's concern about my mother's complete lack of interest in country things occasioned these small tasks around dirt. The marigolds planted to deter cutworms failed to do so. We had to go through the rows and pick the weirdly active slugs off the plants and drop them into a coffee can full of water. They horrified and fascinated Emily, especially since, on removal from the tomato plants, they twisted themselves into anguished Cs, which my sister imitated covering her face. The progress of the tomatoes through the summer until their apogee, when they lay heavy in the palm, broad and fragrant under my father's slicing knife (a special one for tomatoes), was a rhythm that ended with frost-burned hanging leaves heralding long winter days of confinement. We hated school. Emily did well; I did poorly. I loved my teachers; she despised hers. They loved her. Mine hated me. During our long winters they prepared us behind darkened windows for life, and that's what we were in now, one end of it, by the sea, whatever.

When we showed the worms to Ada, she said, "Mm-mm-mm. We don't have those." And when I mentioned to my father that back in Maine they didn't have cutworms like that, he responded with startling vehemence. "Do they not? Well, I will tell you what they do have. They have big red-horned tomato worms that would give your poor sister nightmares." I didn't see the point of this, given that my sister was unlikely to ever see a Maine tomato worm. I already understood that my father took a dim view of my mother's native state; but I didn't see why he would impugn their tomato worms in comparison with ours, not then.

MY FATHER WAS TAKING ME TO BASEBALL PRACTICE ON HIS way to work. Ada stood next to the driver's window and said, on a perfectly clear morning, that it would rain by afternoon. "She's an old soul," said my father sourly, turning on the radio. "She's been here before." And drove off.

It rained.

Ada had brought with her a videocassette of a silent movie, *Down to the Sea in Ships,* and we watched it in the dining room, twilit by the long day of northern summer. She was fascinated by Clara Bow, who played a rambunctious gamine in New Bedford, hoping to grow up to be a whaler. "A whaler?" asked my father, and my mother cut her eyes at him. He crossed his arms, hunched his shoulders, and continued watching. None of us could figure out how Clara Bow was also rumored to be on a wagon train heading up the Oregon Trail, as though turning her back on the whaling dream. It was just a ruse. We really were lost, but Ada had seen it many times and was able to mouth along with the silent actors while the rest of us drowsily took in the captions. We were startled into wakefulness when Ada cried out, "That's the Apponegansett Meeting House!" One of the actors harpooned a whale and converted to the Quaker faith. When I asked Emily how she got through it, she said she pretended to be at the dentist's. During the show, my father moved to the kitchen, stranded there, really, pulling things out of his briefcase and looking at them in a perfunctory way. When the lights came up, my mother went into the kitchen, and we heard her ask him why he hadn't paid attention to the movie. My sister and I listened and didn't move. If my father replied, I didn't hear it.

My mother crossed the living room on her way to bed and said good night to us, noting that my sister was gazing at her with her mouth open. "I'm at the dentist's," said Emily. Then my father came through, dutifully following the same trail.

"'Night kids, 'night A. Thanks for sharing that very historic cinema. Sorry that I was tied up getting ready for my meetings tomorrow. Were you able to bring any other movies?"

Ada didn't reply. This was war. There was another movie, *Wake of the Red Witch,* which she would leave behind on the guest dresser. I don't think that was a mistake.

From then on my father made less of an effort to conceal his annoyance when Ada said that people around here seemed to have no expressions on their faces. "Do they have an interior life?" she asked no one in particular.

"That's an excellent question, Ada," my mother replied.

Ada stayed the short time of her original plan. I think we mostly enjoyed the visit, though we had to adjust to the rising formality that assured us of comfort while putting paid to the idea of any further visits to the West.

By the years of my Key West weekends, Emily and I were more than up to date on life's accounts, and if the pleasures of this beach, the merry clouds, the misty blue sky, the children and dogs standing in the rollers, are any indication, we are well suited to approaching old age.

RIDDLE

I MUST HAVE BEEN RENTING A PLACE ON H STREET IN LIVING-
ston at the time so that I could meet clients in town. (My home was
several miles up the valley toward Gardiner.) I had a model of Frank
Lloyd Wright's Fallingwater I'd built in school on a library table
in the front room. Most of my clients thought it was my own
design. The H Street house was on an elevated lot facing the old
sewing-machine store. I never went in there, but I recall that they
sold machines with a foreign name that were said to hem, darn,
baste, and stitch—back when people did those things instead of
just throwing stuff away. Eventually, the place went out of business.
I had only the ground floor of the house; the upstairs was occupied
by a schoolteacher, who entered her apartment by way of a very
unsafe-looking exterior staircase that undulated and squealed with
her steps.

After drinking at The Wrangler until closing time one cold
November night, I wandered around to Main Street, which was
empty at that hour except for a crippled old cowboy who was making his way toward the railroad yards. There weren't many of these
fellows left, the ones whom horses had broken so often in accidents far from help, their hands still hard as lariats. They kept their
worn-out Stetsons so you wouldn't confuse them with railroaders. I had stopped to watch the old man, perhaps wondering how
far he'd make it in his condition, when a young boy, an urchin,
appeared from an alley and called out to him, "Jack! Hey, Jack!," and
the old man turned toward the voice. I don't know if I can put my
finger on it after all this time, but the excitement or joy, or whatever it was that these two experienced when they saw each other
has never left me. That's all I can say about it. It was late at night on
an empty street. Any euphoria I may have accumulated at the bar
was gone. The pair met up and spoke in an animated way, though

I couldn't hear them from that distance. It doesn't matter. I moved on before they did, and the boy is probably middle-aged by now, the old cowboy surely dead. Somebody later told me that he was born on the Cherokee Strip and had worked for Benny Binion. I'm not sure if that makes any sense.

We don't remember everything, but I'd love to know who's in charge of what we forget. If there's a system, it escapes me. I still remember that old cowboy and the boy's enchantment when I walk down Main, because heading home I was in a kind of trance that made me wonder later if I had dreamed the rest of the evening. I had not, of course, but it had that quality and it's hardly certain where dreams leave off.

My head was clear as I drove home, out Old 89 under the stars. My home was some miles south toward Gardiner, a two-story frame house, built in 1905, with a still incorporated into the fireplace, in which the owner had made bottles of hooch to sell at country dances during Prohibition. My ears were still ringing from various Doobie Brothers covers by locals who'd learned rock and roll at an air force base in Spain. The earliest houses in the valley were set close along the road for easy access in deep snow. Their lights were off at that hour, and I could just make out their shapes as I drove; up on the ridges, new homes glowed with yard lights and long driveways, their owners indifferent to weather. I turned on the radio, in case my post-Wrangler Bar attention wavered. Walking in the door by myself at three in the morning would make me long for someone to live with—anyone—but I'd soon be asleep, and in the morning I'd be glad to be alone again and would remind myself that I had to keep better hours if I was going to get any work done.

Just south of the cemetery, where the road starts down into the Suce Creek bottom, was a car upside down and two people, a man and a woman, standing beside it. The beams from my headlights carved a garish hole in the dark. I could see that the man was holding and trying to calm the agitated woman, who was pointing toward a vacancy of brush and prairie. I turned off the radio, so as to concentrate on, and try to understand, what I was seeing. I pulled up behind the overturned car without any sense that the couple was looking to me for help. On the contrary, the man was waving harshly at me to turn off my lights. When I did, I could no longer see them very well, and it was unclear whether they wanted me to stay or whether there was something private about the woman's anguished wails that I should respect. The glimpse I'd had of them with my headlights on had suggested that they were uninjured. I don't know why this encouraged my bafflement or diffidence, but I just sat in my car waiting to be asked.

Finally, that didn't make sense either. I couldn't just sit there but I really couldn't go on. I got out of the car, risking the parking lights, which didn't seem to offend the man as my headlights had. Now he beckoned me over, but with the same kind of authoritarian gestures with which he had ordered my lights extinguished. When I reached the couple, the man stared me straight in the face in a disquieting way. He was not big but seemed fit, with close-cropped hair and noticeably long sideburns. He shook his head to indicate either that this entire situation was a mess or that there was nothing to be done about the dramatic noises coming from the woman, a remarkably small person in a cotton dress that went all the way to the ground, who was still directing her cries toward the grass and underbrush. The man put his hand on my shoulder and moved me to a spot away from the noise.

"She's crying for her baby," he said in an oddly confiding tone almost as though he was selling me the idea. When I asked if the child had been thrown from the car, he said, "There is no baby. She's crazy. Just play along." His gaze was very direct. "I think you can do that."

At this, the woman rushed over to us and stood just at the level of my chest so that the peculiar arrangement of her hair, piled atop her head with a comb thrust through it, drew my exhausted scrutiny.

"He don't believe me! Timmy was throwed from the back window. Out in the pickers."

The man was staring at her. She touched a finger to a button on my shirt. I thought it was a curious gesture for someone in her position. Her diction, too, was in contrast to the refinement of her face and the delicacy of her clothing. The man watched her as though he'd never heard her speak before.

"Will you look for him? *He* don't believe me, and I got no shoes on."

The man tilted his head and nodded, and I concurred that there was no harm in going along with this. It seemed entirely possible that there was a baby. As I looked back, I wondered whom I believed.

I stumbled through the brush and weeds, my eyes not quite adjusted to the starry night. I thought something like a five-minute loop would demonstrate my willingness to help, but at the same time I listened for the sound of a child. I hadn't gone far before I stepped into a badger hole and fell; by the time I got the dirt out of my eyes and my mouth, I was annoyed. I thought of the old cowboy and the boy back on Main Street and how there was something important about them that I couldn't put my finger on. I was in no hurry as I stood up to pick the thistles out of my left palm.

It was thus that I observed my car drive away, two little red taillights, and this threw me into a strange reflective state, in which my dissolute night at the Wrangler and my ensuing exhaustion, the cowboy and the boy, the two crooks who had just stolen my car, my remote house and its unconquered air of vacancy, all seemed to have equal value, that is, no value. I have gone back to this idea since, because I feel it was a clue to my eventual burden, this set of random data points by which I simply moved across some screen before being faced with a connivance that I couldn't understand though it seemed to belong to me. The flashing light on a remote radio tower across the valley looked almost like a beacon, and I recall thinking that I could head for that as easily as go back to the road, where I no longer had a car. Later, misusing these memories to impress some girl, I would try pitching the idea that this descent into the abyss was hilarious, but I hardly laughed at the time.

When I got back to the road, scuffed up, fingernails packed with clay, I looked both ways as though I might be run over on this empty highway. I knew where I was, just at the rise toward Deep Creek, Pine Creek, Barney Creek, and so on; I could smell the irrigated hay fields on the night air. I was more than ten miles from my house on a little-traveled road. The Absaroka Range made a sharp silhouette against the starlight.

A car approached from the north, a pair of lights wobbling

on the uneven pavement. I stood at the edge of the road, arms at my sides. The car pulled up beside me, and from within I heard a woman's anxious voice. "Are you all right? You're lucky to be alive!" I made an effort to sweep the dirt from my clothes before opening the passenger door; it gave me the moment I needed to understand this interesting development. Then I got in, flinging myself back against the seat. "Yes," I breathed. "Very lucky indeed, thank you. I just need to get home."

"Shall I call someone, the—someone?" She held up her phone. A pretty face, sharply focused very dark brown eyes, shone in the thing's green light. I said I didn't think it was necessary. I supposed my own phone was traveling somewhere in the night, probably headed south, in my car. I tried to make conversation as we drove on. "Is that Cassiopeia?" She didn't know—she was trying to watch the road. I remembered the groceries I'd had in the trunk of my car—some apples, orange juice, Lean Cuisine, two tins of Science Diet cat food, a fifth of George Dickel. I knew what was going to happen: it was three in the morning. We didn't even get upstairs. We fucked on the couch with the front door open. The cat was all over us. She started laughing and soon left. I carried my clothes upstairs, threw them on the floor, and went to bed.

Karen was her name. I don't know if she got mine or not. She was an emergency-room doctor and smelled like surgical tape. She was tired from work and on her way home. I'm surprised she took the time with me. I believe I enjoyed the experience, but I really couldn't stop thinking about the old cowboy and his young friend. She did tell me that her job was grim and had taught her to "live it up." Maybe that explained it, as if an explanation was required.

I AWAKENED HUNGRY, BUT IT WAS ALMOST MIDMORNING. I had work to do! One of my skills was making models for other architects' projects. I was in far greater demand for these models than I was for my own designs. In fact, they pretty well ate my career. I was making one now for a glamorous house in Bridger Canyon. It looked like a spaceship, with rooms cantilevered over a spring-fed pond. I could just picture it below the gorgeous massif of the Bridger Range, a real piece of shit. Oh well, it was a living.

When I was this weary, I'd do various mindless things to get myself ready for the day, which necessarily demanded physical deftness. I was trying to drop two halves of a Lender's onion bagel into the slots of the toaster simultaneously, a tough hand-eye maneuver: I'd nail one and the other would flop out onto the counter. I was further distracted by the beauty of the morning, visible above the sink, a crowd of finches in the lilacs beside the kitchen window, through which came the most ambrosial air from the spruces surrounding the yard.

I didn't get a chance to eat the bagel until later in the day, when it was cold and hard: a knock on my front door turned out to be our big Sheriff Holm, bursting out of his olive uniform and smiling suspiciously at me as he offered his hand. He had a large, round Scandinavian head and a blunt nose. He didn't want a bagel, so I led him into the living room, where I offered him a straight-backed chair, a white oak Shaker knockoff I'd made myself, an extraordinarily uncomfortable thing that gave its occupant the feeling of enduring an inquisition, while ensuring the brevity of a visit. I knew instinctively that this would be the right approach, given the startling appearance of the law. The chair made twerps out of most people, but the sheriff looked like he owned it. It may even have added to his authority. He got right to the point.

"Do you know where your car is?"

"I don't. It was stolen."

"And you never got around to reporting it?"

"I was with an emergency-room doctor, tending to other matters. Has it been found?"

"It's in Torrington, Wyoming, full of bullet holes."

This was a good time to say nothing.

"They've got the guy," he added.

"What about the girl?"

"In the hospital. She's not gonna make it. They robbed the Sinclair station in town, rolled their car, and then got some help from you."

"Well, I wouldn't call it—"

"Really? Then why didn't you report it?"

"It was late."

"Pard, we answer the phone twenty-four-seven."

"I should have called. Of course, I should have. I should have picked up the phone and called."

"I could probably make a case here. I'm not going to, because I don't think it would fly. But it never needed to come to this. Maybe you should think about that. There wasn't nothing in the world wrong with that young woman. You ever see a pretty gal in a morgue? I don't recommend it."

He gave me time to absorb this, but at that moment my mind was elsewhere. "Who's that old cowboy walks around town in the middle of the night?"

It took the sheriff a moment to answer. "If he has a name, I wouldn't know it. Why do you ask?"

I still had my work to do. I was able to use a piece of broken mirror for the pond. I just couldn't make out how far back to go to find the part that wound up in Torrington. This was going to take a while.